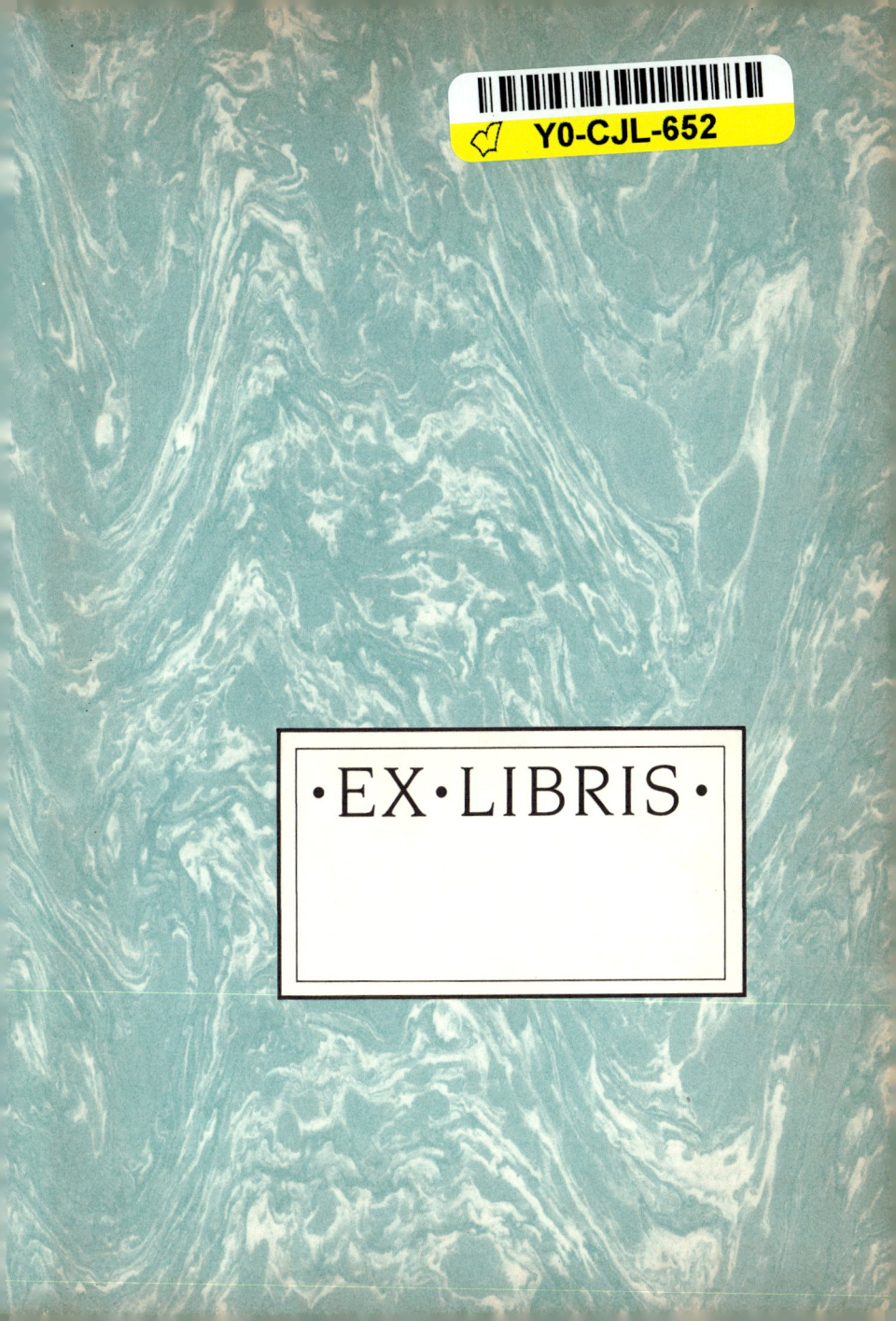

READER'S DIGEST

CONDENSED BOOKS

STRAWBERRIES
by Paul Blakey

READER'S DIGEST CONDENSED BOOKS

VOLUME 4 1992

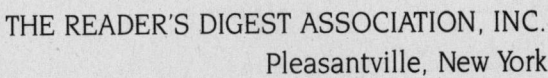

THE READER'S DIGEST ASSOCIATION, INC.
Pleasantville, New York

READER'S DIGEST CONDENSED BOOKS

Editor-in-Chief: Barbara J. Morgan
Executive Editor: Tanis H. Erdmann
Senior Managing Editor: Marjorie Palmer
Managing Editors: Jean E. Aptakin, Thomas Froncek,
Herbert H. Lieberman, Joseph P. McGrath, James J. Menick
Senior Staff Editors: Anne H. Atwater, Thomas C. Clemmons, Maureen A. Mackey,
Angela H. Plowden-Wardlaw, John R. Roberson, Ray Sipherd
Senior Editors: Dana Adkins, M. Tracy Brigden, Catherine T. Brown, Linn Carl
Senior Associate Editors: Christopher W. Davis, Catharine L. Edmonds,
Ainslie Gilligan
Associate Editors: Julie S. Beaman, James R. Gullickson,
Barbara M. Harrington, Paula Marchese
Senior Staff Copy Editors: Maxine Bartow, Jeane Garment, Jane F. Neighbors
Senior Copy Editors: Claire A. Bedolis, Rosalind H. Campbell, Marilyn J. Knowlton
Senior Associate Copy Editors: Jean S. Friedman, Jeanette Gingold, Daphne Hougham,
Tatiana Ivanow, Charles Pendergast, Miriam Schneir
Associate Copy Editors: Fay Ahuja, Barbara Booth, Alexandra C. Koppen,
Peter E. Murphy
Editorial Administrator: Donna R. Gataletto
Art Director: Angelo Perrone
Executive Art Editors: William Gregory, Soren Noring
Art Editor: George Calas, Jr.
Senior Associate Art Editor: Katherine Kelleher
Assistant Art Editor: Marcelline Lowery
Director, Book Rights: Virginia Rice

International Editions

Executive Editor: Gary Q. Arpin
Associate Editors: Bonnie Grande, Eva C. Jaunzems, Antonius L. Koster

Reader's Digest Condensed Books are published every two to three months at Pleasantville, N.Y.

The condensations in this volume have been created by The Reader's Digest Association, Inc., by special arrangement with the publishers, authors, or holders of copyrights.

With the exception of actual personages identified as such, the characters and incidents in the fictional selections in this volume are entirely the products of the authors' imaginations and have no relation to any person or event in real life.

The original editions of the books in this volume are published and copyrighted as follows:
Such Devoted Sisters, published at $22.00 by Viking Penguin, a division of Penguin Books USA Inc.
© 1992 by Eileen Goudge
Rules of Encounter, published at $21.95 by St. Martin's Press
© 1992 by William P. Kennedy
The Love Child, published at $20.00 by Summit Books, a division of Simon & Schuster, Inc.
© 1990 by Catherine Cookson
American Gothic: The Story of the Booth Tragedy, published at $23.00 by Simon and Schuster
© 1992 by Gene Smith

© 1992 by The Reader's Digest Association, Inc.
Copyright © 1992 by The Reader's Digest Association (Canada) Ltd.

FIRST EDITION: Volume 202

All rights reserved. Unauthorized reproduction, in any manner, is prohibited.
Library of Congress Catalog Card Number: 50-12721
Printed in the United States of America
Reader's Digest and the Pegasus logo are registered trademarks of The Reader's Digest Association, Inc.

CONTENTS

SUCH DEVOTED SISTERS   7
by Eileen Goudge
PUBLISHED BY VIKING PENGUIN
A DIVISION OF PENGUIN BOOKS USA INC.

RULES OF ENCOUNTER   183
by William P. Kennedy
PUBLISHED BY ST. MARTIN'S PRESS

THE LOVE CHILD   349
by Catherine Cookson
PUBLISHED BY SUMMIT BOOKS
A DIVISION OF SIMON & SCHUSTER

AMERICAN GOTHIC   477
The Story of the Booth Tragedy
by Gene Smith
PUBLISHED BY SIMON & SCHUSTER

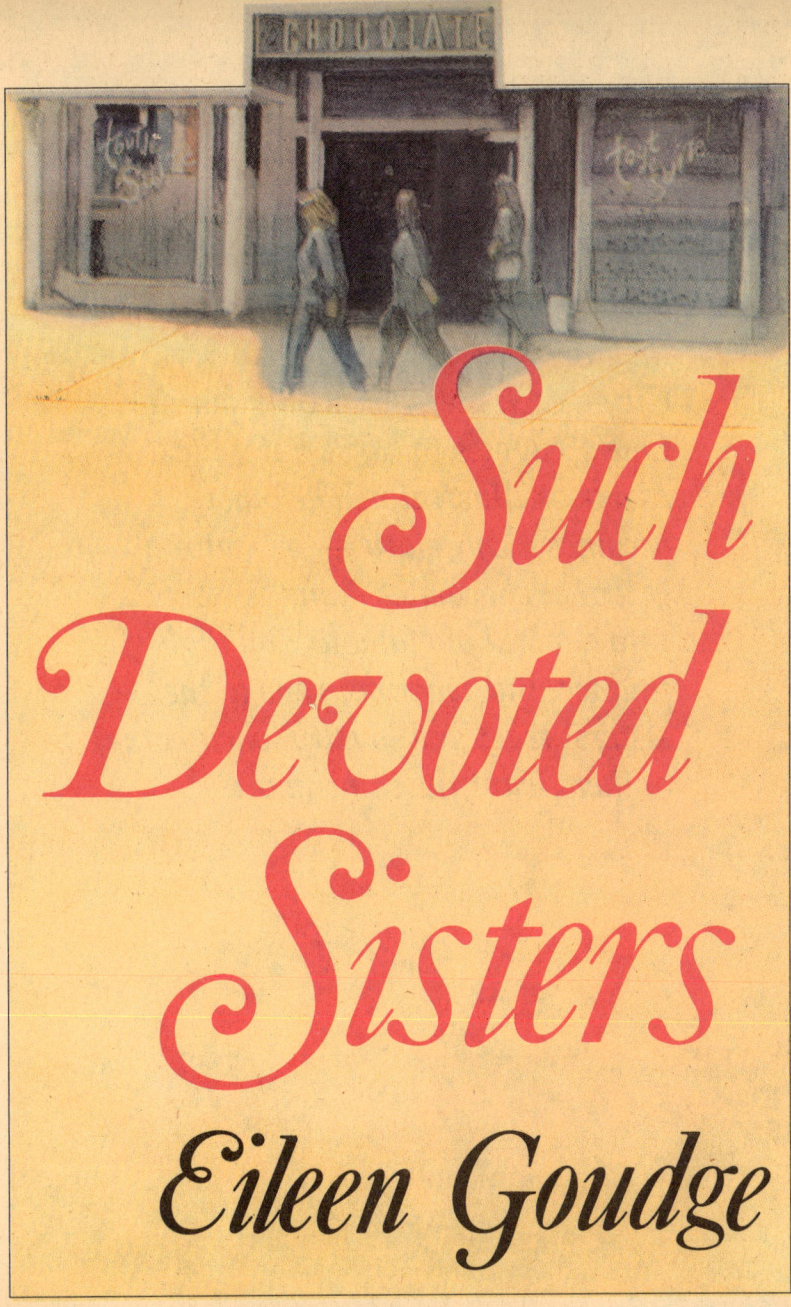

Such Devoted Sisters

Eileen Goudge

*T*rust and unfailing loyalty—that's what being sisters meant to Annie and Laurel. Runaways from a troubled home in California, they're on their own in New York City—each the other's only family. One struggles to carve out a life as a book illustrator. The other becomes a chocolatier—a creator of gourmet chocolates—and is swept into a world of glamour and high finance. But what happens to the sisters' trust and loyalty when both of them want the same man?

Prologue
California: 1954

Dolly Drake got off the bus at Sunset and Vine. In the heat-shimmery air the sidewalk seemed to heave as she stepped down onto it in an almost seesawing motion, as if she were standing on the deck of a ship at sea. Her stomach pitched and her head throbbed. Before her the great curved flank of the NBC building reflected the sun back at her in a blast of white light that struck her eyes like hot needles.

Must be coming down with something, she thought. A touch of flu . . . or maybe the curse.

But no, she wasn't sick, she realized with a pang. This was no flu bug. It was a whole lot worse. She felt sick in her soul.

Dolly thought of the letter in her purse. Looking down at the shiny patent leather bag looped over her arm, she saw the letter as clearly as if she'd had Superman's X-ray vision—the long white business envelope folded in half, then again for good measure.

Inside was a single mimeographed sheet, minutes of a meeting of the Common Man Society. The date at the top was June 16, 1944. Ten years ago.

So what? she thought. A fellow-traveler club that broke up years ago, with a bunch of members nobody ever heard of. Except for one. A faded but still legible scrawl on the bottom line. A name almost as familiar to millions of good Americans as their own. A name Senator Joe McCarthy, back in Washington, D.C., would surely want to pounce on. The bottom lines read "Respectfully submitted, Eveline Dearfield, Recording Secretary."

But that, of course, was long before Eveline got shortened to Eve, before she won an Oscar and married hotshot director Dewey Cobb. Before she stopped giving two hoots about her sister, Dolly.

Dolly sucked her breath in, a lungful of air that tasted like melting tar. She thought of the air-conditioned Cadillac that Eve rode around in these days—white as a virgin bride, with cherry-red seats and a roof that folded down. Dolly imagined what it would feel like to be in that Caddy now, gliding up Sunset Boulevard with her hair blowing in the warm breeze. People rubbernecking to gape in admiration and envy, and wonder to themselves, Who is she? Somebody famous, I bet.

A car horn blared, and the image was bumped rudely away. Then a group of would-be actresses—too young and blond and doe-eyed to be anything else—jostled Dolly as they walked past, gossiping in low tones. One of them wore a pair of silk stockings that were slightly mismatched—the result of careful scrimping, no doubt. Dolly smiled grimly and thought of the can of Campbell's chicken noodle that awaited her back at her Westwood bungalow. Mixed with two cans of water instead of one, along with a dollop of ketchup and a handful of saltines, a can of soup filled you up right fine. Well, almost. And maybe she'd even treat herself to a Hershey bar for dessert. Chocolate was the one thing that almost always lifted her spirits.

But right now the thought of food was making her stomach knot up. Give Eve the slap in the face she deserved? Could she? But how could she deliberately hurt—maybe ruin—her own little sister?

In her mind, traveling back through the dusty miles and years to Clemscott, Kentucky, Dolly could still hear Preacher Daggett thundering from the pulpit in his syrupy drawl, *"Put on the armor of God, that ye may stand against the devil."*

Yeah, right, Dolly thought. And who was standing up for me while little Evie was out snatching up every decent role I went after? And my guy, too. A town full of men, and she had to get her hooks into mine.

Tears started in the back of her throat. Hard tears that burned like acid. She gave the corner of each eye a swipe with the heel of her hand and sniffed deeply. Damned if she'd get caught bawling in public, showing up at Syd's with her eyes all red and puffy. If Mama-Jo had taught her one thing in this life, it was to keep your dirty linen in your own hamper.

Dolly crossed the street and headed north, up Vine. The hot air seemed to drag at her, as if she were plowing her way through something solid and viscous. She stepped up her pace; Syd got mad when she was late. Then she thought, To hell with Syd. That's what I pay him for. Except, when you got right down to it, an agent's ten percent of nothing was . . . well, nothing. Her last picture, *Dames at Large,* hadn't even gone into general release.

That's the ticket, all right. Dolly Drake winds up with zero, while little Evie has handprints in the sidewalk outside Grauman's.

And now Val, too.

Dolly reached the Century Plaza Hotel, its windows turned to mirrors by the sun. Briefly she saw herself reflected: a pretty woman in her late twenties—she'd be thirty next May—bottle-blond hair unraveling from the combs that held it up in back. A bit on the plump side, maybe, wearing a flowery pink rayon dress—her best.

She thought again of the envelope in her purse and felt her stomach turn. She'd received it in yesterday's mail, along with a note from Syd: "Call me." First time she'd ever heard from him through the mail. His whole life was on the phone. But this was different. Syd had a real axe of his own to grind. Six years ago Eve dumped him—and not only as her agent—a week before they were to be married. Syd had gone on a bender for two weeks, not seeing anyone, not even answering his phone, which for him was like cutting out his tongue. Since then, there had been a new, sour edge to him.

Dolly knew that the last thing Eve wanted was to overthrow the U.S. government. Probably some assistant producer had taken her to the meeting on a date and then asked her to take some notes. By the next day she must have forgotten all about it. Otherwise, wouldn't she have at least mentioned it to Dolly?

But now anybody who had been the slightest shade of pink—or who was just plain accused of it—was getting fired and blacklisted. No work anywhere in town. Like a silent death.

And if she went along with this, one of those poor blotted-out souls could be Eve.

Dolly felt a flash of hot bitterness. *Serve her right, wouldn't it just? Show her what it's like down on the dirty pavement with the rest of us. And then what would Val Carrera think of her?*

All night Dolly had wrestled over what to do, and now she knew why. She hadn't wanted to face the truth, but there it was. *Did Eve think twice before sticking a knife in my back?*

Dolly, her mouth set in a grim line, turned west onto Hollywood Boulevard and into the cool marble lobby of the office building on the corner. Well, she wouldn't definitely make up her mind until she talked it over with Syd. When she called him yesterday, he'd said he had something to tell her, something really big. But what could be bigger than this?

"IT'D be like . . . murder," Dolly said.

Seated on the low Scandinavian couch opposite Syd's kidney-shaped desk, she fingered the envelope she had taken from her purse, regarding it the way she would a nasty little dog that's quite capable of nipping you. Here, for some reason, it seemed more real . . . and more unthinkable . . . than it had on the way over.

Dolly stared at Syd. The kind of handsome Mama-Jo would've called slick as snake oil. Right now, with his feet propped on the desk, his brown eyes boring into her, Dolly felt as if she were staring down the twin barrels of Daddy's 12-gauge Winchester. Syd's eyes, set alongside a jutting Roman nose, seemed almost gleeful.

"Why me?" Dolly pressed. "Why send that thing to *me* when you could've been the big patriot and presented it personally to Senator McCarthy . . . if you hate Eve that bad?"

"You got it all wrong. This is business—*your* business—nothing personal on my end," he said evenly, betrayed only by a cold flicker of his eyes. "Now you're ready to talk, am I right? Are we having a conversation here?"

She leaned forward, trembling a little, hating him for knowing her heart the way a local boy knows the hidden back roads of his hometown. And for giving her a choice she never should've had.

"Okay, but don't you forget she's my *sister.*" Dolly thought of her niece, too—Eve's little Annie. Both of them her flesh and blood.

"First hear me out," he said, his tone reasonable, even soothing. "Then you make up your own mind." He waited until she'd settled back against the spongy sofa. "That's better. Dolly, sweetheart, you know what's wrong with you? You're nice. And in this business, nice is just another word for stupid. Nice and a nickel will buy you a phone call. What it *won't* get you is the lead in *Devil May Care.*"

There was a lapse before Dolly made the connection. Then it hit her like a double bourbon straight up. Maggie Dumont, the part every star in town was angling for. But Eve had it sewed up.

"Even if Eve got knocked out of the running, what makes you think the director would consider me?" she demanded.

"*Think,* Dolly, sweetie. *Devil* is Preminger's picture, and he'd turn handstands for Eve Dearfield. He's crazy about her. If he can't have Eve, what's the next best thing?"

Could that be true? Dolly wondered. No question, she and Eve did look alike. Only sixteen months apart, practically twins, except that Eve was beautiful, and she was . . . well, okay, pretty. Eve's hair was naturally blond, almost platinum. Dolly's, under its dye job, was just plain dishwater. And where Eve's eyes were a deep, startling indigo, hers were the washed-out blue of faded denim.

No, she thought. No way would Preminger cast a B-movie lookalike when he could have the real thing. But if Eve was out of the way . . .

She thought of Val, surprised by the keenness of the ache she felt. It had happened almost a year ago, and she hadn't known him more than a few weeks to begin with—certainly not long enough to go around moaning about a broken heart.

It was Eve who had hurt her, she realized. Not Val.

Syd hunched forward, palms flat against the desk top.

"Dolly, sweetie, you still don't get it, do you?" He spoke softly, but each word hit her like an icy drop. "What Eve has that you don't is fangs. She'd *kill* to get a part, any part. You, Dolly, you're too soft." He paused, waiting for her to absorb all this. "Show me how much you want this, baby. Show me you'd do *anything,* and you'll be halfway there. Then"—he smiled—"if something should happen to Eve, like she just happens to get blacklisted . . . Well, what do you think Preminger's gonna say when you walk into his office looking damn near enough like Eve to be her twin?"

Dolly only half heard him. Her mind suddenly was elsewhere. Clear as a Technicolor movie, she was seeing two bleary-eyed girls stepping off a Greyhound bus—Doris and Evie Burdock, come all the way to Hollywood from Clemscott, Kentucky—lugging a single battered suitcase between them, giggling, punch-drunk with exhaustion and high spirits. She could hear Eve's voice ringing across the years: *"It's just you and me from now on, Dorrie. We'll always have each other. . . . Nothing will ever come between us."*

Dolly squeezed her eyes shut, a pulse throbbing over one eye. When she opened them, she saw that Syd was eyeing her with something close to sympathy. She stood up, the envelope fluttering from her lap onto the carpet.

"I'll think about it," she said.

"You think too much. Anyway, it doesn't have to be the end of the world, you know," he urged, lazily unfolding his lanky frame from the swivel chair, clasping her hand in a moist handshake that made her itch to wipe her palm on her skirt. "This whole McCarthy scare'll probably blow over in a month or two. She might lose out on a few pictures, but knowing Eve, she'll be back on her feet before you can say, 'That's a wrap.' "

Not until she was outside and halfway to Sunset did Dolly realize she was still clutching the letter. She thought about tearing it up and tossing it in a trash can. But she didn't see one, so she shoved it back into her purse and kept walking.

"AUNT Dolly, how did that crack get there?" Annie sat on a high stool in the kitchen of Dolly's Westwood bungalow, swinging her little feet back and forth between its rust-speckled chrome legs.

Dolly, stirring a saucepan at the stove, looked over at her niece, then up at where Annie was pointing, at a plastered-over crack that bisected the ceiling.

"That? Why, honey, that's what you call history. This old place is a map of every earthquake to hit Los Angeles County since the walls of Jericho came tumbling down."

With her eyes glued to the ceiling, Annie wore a look of pinched concern on her face. "Is it gonna fall down on us?"

Dolly went over and hugged her with a little laugh. "Course it's not gonna fall down. It's stayed put this long."

Looking at Annie now, Dolly saw a grown-up in a child's body—a somber little lady with her mother's indigo eyes and her father's dark, straight hair. *Poor thing, she's had enough fall down on her head to know to duck. Her father's getting killed in that plane crash last year and Eve's taking off for Mexico to film* Bandido *before the flowers on Dewey's grave had hardly wilted.* Annie had been raised mostly by nannies—six, or was it seven? Dolly had lost count. The last one eloped just two days ago. Eve had phoned Dolly in a panic. Would she baby-sit tonight? Unless she needed something, Eve hardly ever called her anymore.

Dolly had been on the point of saying no, but then she thought of Annie alone in that big house in Bel Air with some strange baby-sitter, and she relented. She adored Annie, and it just clean broke her heart to think of the loneliness the kid had to put up with.

"When's Dearie coming back?" Annie wanted to know. That funny nickname—Dearie—never Mama or Mommy.

"She didn't say, hon."

"Where did she go?"

"A party, she said. A big star like your mama has to go to a lot of parties. It's like . . . well, sort of like part of the job."

"Is Val part of the job, too?" Annie stopped swinging her legs and stared at Dolly with enormous ink-blue eyes.

Dolly's heart caught in her throat. "Not exactly," she ventured.

"I don't like Val." Annie's face became very tight.

"Oh, sugar, Val doesn't mean no harm. He's just not your daddy," Dolly soothed, hoping to jolly her out of it. She sighed. "Come on now. Help me set the table. Soup's on."

Later, when they'd eaten and the dishes were washed, she tucked Annie into bed in the tiny bedroom and made up the sleep sofa in the living room for herself. Who knew when Eve would roll in—maybe not until morning.

Dolly changed into an old silk kimono and curled up in the sagging club chair by the half-open front window, hoping to catch a breeze as evening cooled into night. Suddenly she felt so heavy and tired. Minutes later she was asleep.

The slamming of a car door woke her. Swimming up through gritty layers of sleep, she squinted at the glowing face of the clock atop the battered footlocker that served as a coffee table. Five after six. Her neck felt cramped from being scrunched against the backrest, and her legs tingled as she stretched them.

Pushing aside the frayed curtain, she peered out the window. Eve had arrived. She was weaving her way up the pathway with the elaborate caution of someone who's drunk too much. In the milky predawn light her strapless, blue satin evening dress appeared almost liquid, and her platinum hair gleamed like polished silver. Reaching the front door of Dolly's bungalow, she swayed against the peeling doorframe, leaning a pale shoulder against it for support.

"You'll never guess. Never, never, never," she burbled excitedly.

Her breath smelled sweet and somewhat effervescent, like orchids and Champagne. Shadowed by the narrow porch overhang, her eyes were huge dark puddles. "I got married!"

"What?"

"It was Val's idea. At the Preminger party he just got the notion, and I said, 'Well, why not?' and we both jumped in the car."

Dolly just stood there, stunned, listening to the crazed ticking of a moth beating itself to death against the dim yellow porch light, her face burning in the cool night air as if she'd been slapped.

Eve wiggled her hand in front of Dolly, and Dolly saw that the finger that had once worn Dewey Cobb's antique gold band now sported a glittering pear-shaped diamond.

At the curb, the horn of Eve's white Cadillac honked impatiently. Then Val stuck his head out the driver's side and called, "Come on, baby. You gotta be at the studio in two hours."

Dolly thought of the first time she'd seen Val. She'd been making her way across the RKO lot to the soundstage where they were filming *Dames at Large*. Crossing a western street, she'd looked up just as a tall man in cowhide chaps leaped off the roof of a false-front saloon. While Dolly watched, her hands clutching her breast, the stuntman landed precisely in the center of a hay-filled cart.

Val Carrera was the most beautiful man she'd ever laid eyes on. When he made his way toward her and asked if she'd join him for a cup of coffee, she didn't hesitate for a second.

After coffee, and then later that day, after drinks and dinner, they'd gone back to his apartment in Burbank. And stayed there for an entire weekend. Dolly didn't know for sure if this was love, but it sure felt like *something*. Val must have thought so, too, because he was with her nearly every day for a month, and the whole time, he could never keep his hands off her.

Until he met Eve.

Dolly, watching her sister yawn and stretch languidly like a Siamese cat that's just finished off a bowl of cream, felt an odd weakness spread through her limbs. Speechless, trembling, she stared, unable to move. *Does she think I have no feelings? That her happiness counts more than mine?* Maybe that was it. Maybe Dolly was supposed to feel sorry for Eve and step aside gracefully because, poor kid, she'd lost Dewey . . . or maybe simply because she was Eve Dearfield—a star, *somebody*.

The memory of the night she'd walked in on them at Val's apartment came crashing back—Dolly screaming at Eve, telling her she was a rotten, selfish bitch; Eve weeping and saying how sorry she was. And somehow, despite her rage and hurt, Dolly had ended up forgiving and even consoling her sister.

Now it all flooded through her again—all the pain and bitterness and resentment. Eve hadn't really cared one bit about her feelings, not then and certainly not now.

"We drove straight through, Vegas and back." Eve flung her arms about Dolly's neck. "Be happy for me, Dorrie. Please be happy for me." When she pulled away, Dolly saw that her cheeks were wet and her eyes were shiny. "Is Annie awake? I can't wait to tell her!"

"It's six in the morning," Dolly replied dully.

"I'll get her." Eve darted past her and returned a minute later, holding the sleepy-eyed little girl by the hand.

Dolly watched them walk side by side down the path, amid the sprinklers' stuttering spray, a gleaming blue blade of a woman and a stalwart little girl dressed in a cotton nightie and clunky orthopedic shoes, clutching her clothes in a bundle under one arm. Dolly felt her heart rip open, letting in a searing-hot pain.

Then Eve half turned, switching on her brightest smile—the one she reserved mostly for reporters and fans.

"Oh, did I mention . . . Preminger's promised me Maggie in *Devil May Care*. But there's a small part he hasn't cast yet: Maggie's kid sister. I told him you'd be perfect for it. Tell Syd to give him a call."

Dolly felt her last thread of loyalty give way.

She waited until the Cadillac's taillights disappeared into the gloom; then, moving like a sleepwalker, she went into her tiny bedroom, still fragrant with Annie's sweet baby smell, and rummaged in her dresser until she found an envelope. She addressed and stamped it, and carried it back into the living room, where she retrieved the mimeographed sheet folded inside her purse.

Still in her kimono and slippers, clutching the sealed letter, Dolly walked to the mailbox on the corner and slipped it inside.

The envelope was addressed to Senator Joseph McCarthy, Capitol Hill, Washington, D.C.

It wasn't until the box clanged shut that Dolly came to her senses as suddenly as if she'd been slapped. She sagged against its cool metal side, all the blood in her body seeming to drain right down into the soles of her slippers.

"What have I done?" she cried in a strangled whisper. "What have I done?"

PART ONE: 1966
Chapter One

ANNIE lay in bed staring at the dragon on her wall.

It wasn't a real dragon, only the shadow of one. Each of the tall posts on her Chinese bed was carved in the shape of a dragon, its tail starting at the mattress and ending at the top in a great snarling head with a forked tongue. She remembered when her mother had sent her the bed, for her fifth birthday, all the way from Hong Kong, where Dearie had been filming *Slow Boat to China*. The moment Annie saw it, she loved it. Dragons weren't afraid of anyone or anything . . . and that's how she wanted to be.

But right now Annie didn't feel quite so brave. She felt small and scared—closer to seven than seventeen.

Lying very still, she listened. All she could hear was the rapid thumping of her heart, then the usual creaks of Bel Jardin settling into itself. Now it came to her—the sound that a moment ago she had hoped she was only imagining: the low growl of Val's Alfa Romeo as it sped up Chantilly Drive and rumbled up the crushed-shell driveway.

Earlier tonight, when she was getting ready for bed, she'd heard her stepfather go out and had felt light-headed with relief. She'd prayed he would stay out a long time, maybe all night. But now he was back. A cold fist of dread squeezed her stomach.

She sat up in bed holding her pillow scrunched against her chest, nibbling on a thumbnail that was already bitten down to the quick. She'd always felt so safe here in this room, and now somehow it was more like a cage—or a baby's barred playpen—a little girl's room full of things she'd long ago outgrown. Had Dearie stopped noticing she'd grown up, or was it just that when her mother drank, she didn't care?

Annie stared at the pale blue bookcase filled with all her favorite childhood books. Nancy Drew would've figured out what to do, she thought. If Val tried to mess with her, she'd climb into her roadster and roar off into the night.

Except Nancy Drew didn't have an eleven-year-old sister. A sister Annie had done everything for since she was in diapers, and whom Annie loved more than anything. The thought of leaving Laurel here alone with Val made her stomach ache even more.

To calm herself, she went over the plan she had been mapping out in her head. Next time Val went out on a date or a job interview, she would pack two suitcases—one for her and one for Laurel. Then the two of them would run away. But where? The only relative Annie had ever heard of—besides Uncle Rudy, who was Val's brother and, moreover, an even slimier creep—was Aunt Dolly, whom she hadn't seen or spoken to in ten or twelve years. Annie had a hazy memory of being at a sunny beach with a smiling lady with lemon-colored hair who was helping her dig a hole to China.

Aunt Dolly.

What had become of her? Long, long ago Annie remembered overhearing Dearie tell Val that her sister, Doris, had gotten herself a rich husband and moved to New York and good riddance. But was Aunt Dolly still in New York? Would she want to see her nieces? Probably not. For Dearie to have been so mad at her, there had to have been a good reason.

And even if they had a place to go, what about Val? Sure, he wouldn't chase after her if she took off—they'd never gotten along. But Laurel was his flesh and blood. Not that he'd ever paid her much attention. She was like a toy to him. Weeks went by when he hardly noticed her; then, suddenly, he'd scoop her onto his lap and tickle her until she cried, or feed her ice cream until she was sick. Still, he was her legal father. Annie's running away was one thing, but if she took Laurel, Annie knew Val would call it kidnapping.

Val might even try to have her arrested and thrown in jail. Annie felt her heart lurch in panic at the thought.

But what else could she do? In Spanish, Bel Jardin meant "beautiful garden," and she loved this great old house, with its Spanish-tiled roof and pale yellow stucco walls festooned in bougainvillea. It made her ache to think of leaving and not being able to start college next week, as she'd planned. She'd been accepted at Stanford but had turned it down in favor of U.C.L.A. so she could stay close to Laurel. But to live here with Val? She'd rather die.

She remembered last night—Val's following her upstairs and sitting on her bed, saying he wanted to talk—and hugged herself tighter, shivering. She had gotten the creeps just looking at him.

"Look," he'd launched right in, "I'm not gonna beat around the bush. You're not a kid anymore." His large hand shot out and closed over her wrist; then to her horror he drew her onto the bed beside him. "The thing is, we're broke."

Annie, shocked, had sat frozen. "You *spent* everything we had?"

His eyes had slid away from hers. "It wasn't like that. It didn't happen overnight. And it wasn't like we had money coming in. Your mother— She hadn't made a picture in twelve years. And when the school folded . . . You know how it is."

Val, who had a black belt, had started a karate school a couple of years before, but like everything he did—being a real estate broker and then a foreign car salesman—he'd screwed it up somehow.

"What's going to happen?" Annie had made herself ask. She hated feeling so powerless, having to depend on him for things. If only she was old enough to be in charge!

He'd shrugged. "Sell the house, I guess. Rudy says we should be able to get a pretty good price for it, but we owe a lot, too, so there won't be much left over."

Val's brother, Rudy, was a couple of years older than Val, short and ugly but a lot smarter—a hotshot divorce lawyer. Val wouldn't make a move without asking his brother's advice, but Dearie had never liked or trusted Rudy, and thank goodness she'd been savvy enough to let someone else handle the trust money she'd set aside for Annie and Laurel—twenty-five thousand each. The only bad thing was, Annie couldn't touch hers until her twenty-fifth birthday. Right now that seemed eons away.

"We can look for something smaller," Val had said. "Something closer to downtown . . . where you can catch a bus to work."

"I'll be in school." Annie was struggling to keep her voice even. "I thought I'd pick up a part-time job on campus."

"Yeah, well, here's the thing. Rudy can set you up with something in his law office. Full time. You can type, can't you?"

Suddenly she understood. Now that he'd run through all their money, he wanted *her* to take Dearie's place. She would go to work, forget about college, support all three of them. And he was so obvious about it! She wanted to hit him, smash her fists into his smug face. But she could only sit there, trembling, speechless.

Val, mistaking her helpless rage for sorrow, had put his arms around her, patting her clumsily. "I miss her, too," he murmured.

She tried to pull away, but he only squeezed tighter. Now the embrace became something more. He was stroking the small of her back, her hip. His rough cheek pressed against hers, his breath warm and quick against her ear.

She felt sick.

Steeling herself, Annie had given him a hard push and jumped to her feet. "I have to brush my teeth," she'd said. Then she rushed into the bathroom and locked the door. She ran a bath and stayed in it for an hour. When she got back to her room, Val had gone.

Today, all day, she had managed to avoid him. But now he was back, and if he felt like coming into her room again, there was no lock on the door to stop him.

Annie heard the front door slam downstairs, then the soft clacking of shoes against the tiled foyer. She could hear him climbing the stairs now, his footsteps heavy, measured, but muffled by the Oriental runner. Just beyond her door he slowed . . . then stopped. Her heart was pounding so hard, she was sure he would hear it.

Then after what seemed to her like an eternity, she heard him move on. Annie let her breath out in a dizzying rush. She felt flushed and weak, as if she had a fever. A swim, that's what she needed. And the pool would be perfect—cool and still.

Annie waited until she was absolutely certain Val had gone to bed. Then in her nightgown she tiptoed out into the hallway.

Reaching the half-open door to Laurel's room, Annie paused, then slipped inside. Looking at her sister asleep on her back, her small hands folded neatly across the blanket that covered her, Annie thought of the print her art teacher had shown in class last year. A famous painting of drowned Ophelia floating face up in the water, her long golden hair drifting like seaweed about her still, white face. Annie's heart caught in her throat, and before she could stop herself, she was listening for Laurel's breathing.

There it was, but so soft it could have been a breeze blowing through the open window. Annie relaxed a little. *Don't worry, Laurey. I'll take care of you.*

That time when Laurel had scarlet fever, when she was two, came back to her in a hot rush. That morning when she'd looked into her baby sister's crib and found Laurel gasping for air, her face purple, her tiny arms thrashing. Annie, only eight and scared out of her mind, had snatched Laurel up and had run through the house screaming for Dearie. She could feel Laurel's frail chest hitching desperately. Despite how little Laurel was, she was still too heavy for Annie and kept slithering from her grasp.

She had finally found Dearie passed out on the living-room sofa, an empty brandy bottle on the coffee table in front of her, exhausted from being up all night with Laurel. Annie, sobbing, more scared than she'd ever been, had hit her, pushed her, shouted in her ear, trying to make her wake up. But Dearie wouldn't budge. There was no one else; it was the maid's day off, and Val was gone. Annie, terrified, had thought, I'm just a kid. I can't do this. I can't save Laurey.

Then a voice inside her head commanded, Think.

She remembered a long time ago, when she herself had had a bad cough and stuffy chest, and Dearie had put her in a steamy bathtub, and how it had made her breathe easier.

Annie had lugged Laurel into Dearie's bathroom and cranked on the tub's hot-water tap. Then, sitting on the toilet with Laurel face down across her knees, she began to pound on her back, praying that whatever was choking her would somehow pop out.

Nothing so dramatic happened, but as steam billowed and stuck Laurel's hair to her scalp in wet clumps, her breath gradually returned and the awful purple color faded.

Then with a tremendous whoop Laurel began to cry. She was going to be all right. Annie's face felt wet—from the steam, she thought. Then she realized she was crying.

And she realized something else—that she was Laurel's real mother, that God had meant for her to look after and protect her sister always.

Annie now pushed her fingers through her hair, still a little shocked by its shortness. She'd hacked it off only last week with Dearie's sewing scissors. For some reason it had made her feel better, seeing all that dark hair clumped at her feet . . . as if she were shedding an old skin and making way for a new Annie—strong, shining, brave.

Downstairs, in the sun-room that opened onto the patio, the moon shone through the palmettos in their huge terra-cotta tubs by the French doors. Stepping outside, Annie could see the pool gleaming darkly, its glassy surface twinkling with sparks of orange light reflected by the electric tiki torches.

She peeled off her nightgown and dived in.

The cool water slicing along her naked body felt wonderful. She stayed under for half a length before she broke the surface, gulping in the night air, fragrant with the scent of honeysuckle and the faint smokiness of a brushfire burning way off in the canyons. She could hear the rustling of the hibiscus hedge surrounding the patio. She had to do something . . . and soon. Or she'd stay stuck with Val, cramped in a tiny house with no place to hide, and roped to a desk typing stupid letters for that troll Rudy.

She remembered, too, how Rudy always seemed to be staring at Laurel, his bulgy eyes fixed on her like a toad's on an iridescent-winged dragonfly. Seldom approaching her, but those eyes—always there, watching. A shiver coursed through Annie. What did Rudy want from Laurel? The same thing Annie suspected Val wanted from *her?*

No, that was too gross, too unthinkable. They just had to get out.

In her mind Annie heard her mother drawl, *"The good Lord is fine for praying, kiddo, but when the going gets rough, you'd best be off your knees and on your feet."*

Annie now felt angry. Oh, yeah? she thought. Then how come you killed yourself?

She pushed off against the slippery tiles with her feet and began furiously stroking her way across the pool. Gradually she felt her anger dissolve into sorrow. If only Dearie had talked to her before she took those pills. Now as Annie climbed out of the pool and pulled on her nightgown—why hadn't she thought to bring a towel?—it hit her like a slap that she really *was* on her own.

Shivering and dripping her way across the sun-room, Annie caught a sudden flicker of movement out of the corner of her eye. She froze, and looked up. Val was standing framed in the archway leading from the living room. For an instant she thought she might pass out. There was no sound other than the soft ticking of water as it dripped from her wet hair onto the tiled floor.

Moving with oiled grace, he glided across to where she stood. He was wearing a pair of navy satin pajamas. In the orange glow of the electric tiki torches filtering in through the wide French doors, his tanned face, striped with shadows, reminded her of a tiger's.

"You oughta put something on," he said. "You'll catch cold."

"I was just going in." She began walking quickly toward the archway. *God, let him leave me alone.* She felt his eyes on her and realized that with her wet nightgown clinging to her, she might as well be naked. She felt herself grow hot with embarrassment.

In the cavernous living room, Annie was crossing the rug in front of the fireplace when she felt Val's hand on her wet shoulder. She spun away, banging her knee against a massive carved chair.

Then she saw that he was only offering her his pajama top, which he'd slipped off when her back was turned. She felt flustered, not knowing how to react. Why didn't he just leave her alone?

She tried to step past, but he caught her roughly. Holding her pressed against him, he stroked the back of her head. "Give me a break, kid. It hasn't been easy for me, either." On his breath she caught an all-too-familiar whiff of booze.

Anger took hold of her, and she tore away, hissing, "It's all your fault! You never loved her! You only married her because she was famous and rich. And then when she . . . she couldn't work anymore, you treated her like she wasn't even there."

"She was a drunk," he snarled, "way before I met her. You know the saying: Once a drunk, always a drunk."

Over Val's shoulder, on the fireplace mantel, light winked off a shiny metal surface—Dearie's Oscar, the Best Actress Award she'd won for *Storm Alley*. Annie remembered how proud she'd felt staying up late to watch her mother on TV, seeing Dearie floating up onto the stage, hoisting the glowing statuette in triumph.

Tears pricked at Annie's eyes, but she bit them back. She wouldn't cry in front of Val. "If my mother drank, it was your fault."

"You little bitch." Val grabbed her, his fingers digging into her upper arms. "You never even gave me a chance. Spoiled brat with your nose in the air. You had it in for me since day one."

His eyes glittered in the darkness—black prisms reflecting a whole spectrum of ancient hurts.

Annie felt shaken. She'd never seen Val this mad. "I'm going up now," she said, shivering. "I'm really cold."

His lips stretching in a cold grin, Val leaned down for his pajama top and tossed it at her. "Put it on." It wasn't an offer.

Annie dropped the bundle of cloth as if it were a snake.

With a low moan Val fell on her.

At first she thought he was going to hit her. It *felt* as if he *had* hit her—a bruising blow to her mouth. Then she realized what it was. He was kissing her.

She tried to scream, to pull away, but he held her tight. *This isn't happening. God, please make this not be happening.*

"I wanted you to like me," he said in a little boy's petulant voice. "I tried, but you . . . you wouldn't let me."

Annie, terrified, struggled to free herself. "Please let me go." She thought of something else. "Laurey might wake up."

"Do you think *I* wanted it to end like this?" he went on as if he hadn't heard. "You don't know what it was like for me."

"Val," Annie pleaded, truly scared.

With one arm he held her tight, while with the other he began touching her. Annie felt as if she were dying.

Summoning all her strength, she somehow managed to rip herself free of him. Ducking past Val, she felt strangely light, her arms seeming to stretch on forever, until finally her fingers closed about something cold and hard—Dearie's Oscar. Blindly Annie swung the heavy statuette like a club. Out of the corner of her eye she saw Val feint to one side as she connected. The impact slammed through her arm like an electric jolt, and she felt as shocked as Val looked.

Blood streamed from a cut over his right eyebrow. He froze, his face the color of cottage cheese. "Oh," he said in soft surprise. He sank down abruptly on the wide leather sofa. A moment later he toppled onto his side and grew still. Frighteningly still.

I've killed him, Annie thought.

Terror was waiting for her somewhere in the back of her mind. But right now she felt numb. Staring down at Val's bloody, sprawled form, she thought calmly, sensibly, I won't pack much. A change of clothes, underwear, toothbrush. And Dearie's jewelry.

Packing was easy. It was waking Laurel that was the hard part. She slept like the dead. And when Annie finally got her up, Laurel wore a glassy look, as if she wasn't quite awake.

"I have to go away," Annie told her. "I won't be coming back. Do you want to come with me?"

The glassy expression was gone; Laurel's face crumpled in dismay. "Where are we going?"

Annie was encouraged by the "we."

She tried to think, but couldn't come up with an answer. "On a bus" was the best she could do. "You'd better hurry and get dressed before . . . before he wakes up."

Then because Laurel looked so worried and scared, Annie hugged her. "It's going to be all right," she said. "In fact, it'll be fun. A real adventure."

Laurel gave her a long look that seemed burdened with far more than any eleven-year-old should have to carry. "It's because of . . . of Val, isn't it?" she whispered. "Something he did?" Not Daddy or Dad; since she could talk, she'd called him Val.

Annie nodded, her throat suddenly tight.

"Annie," Laurel whispered sheepishly as they were leaving, "can I take Boo?" Boo was her old baby blanket, nubby and tattered from a thousand washings. She didn't like to admit she still slept with it, but Annie knew how much Boo meant.

"Course," she said.

At the front door Annie paused, remembering another keepsake: Dearie's Oscar. She was scared of going back in there, but couldn't bear the thought of leaving it behind.

"Wait here," she whispered.

Her heart slamming against her ribs, Annie slipped back into the living room and snatched up the Oscar from the rug where she'd dropped it, quickly averting her eyes from the still form on the couch. Reaching Laurel's side, she saw a horrified look on her sister's face. Annie looked down at the statuette and saw the blood smearing its bright surface.

Then, wordlessly, Laurel took it from Annie, using her precious Boo to wipe it clean. She handed it back to Annie, who quickly stuffed it into her bulging overnight bag. Looking into Laurel's trusting eyes, she found the strength to push open the door.

Minutes later as they made their way in darkness down the long, curving drive toward the wrought-iron gates at the bottom, Annie turned for one last look at Bel Jardin. Above the palms that lined the drive, she saw the first milky light of dawn touch the top of the tiled roof, and she turned away, quickening her step.

At that moment, clutching the heavy overnight bag, Annie's courage seemed to wither. Where on earth was she going? And what was she going to do when she got there? Then, strangely, she felt an invisible hand against the small of her back giving her a gentle push. Inside her head a sweet, throaty voice drawled, *"Once*

you've made up your mind to go someplace, don't waste all your time fiddling with your shoelaces."

Annie straightened suddenly, hitching the heavy suitcase a little higher so she could walk faster. She reached for Laurel's hand. "I hope you wore socks." She spoke briskly to her sister, who trudged listlessly alongside her, hugging a tattered baby blanket smeared with her father's blood, a pale golden-haired stalk of a girl dressed in pink. "You know how you get blisters when you don't wear socks. And we have a long way to go."

Chapter Two
New York City

LAUREL pushed the sausage to one side of her plate. Maybe if she hid it under her toast, Annie wouldn't notice. She felt too sick to eat another bite, but the last thing Laurel wanted was for Annie to start in again about her being too skinny.

Anyway, look who was talking! Annie looked awful with her cheekbones sticking out and those brown smudges under her eyes. Why hadn't she ordered something besides toast? She looked hungry enough to gobble up every stale doughnut in this diner.

But no, they had to save for when they found an apartment. But when would that be? A whole two weeks in New York, and they were still stuck in that smelly dark room at the Allerton.

In the beginning the nine hundred and seventy dollars they'd gotten for Dearie's jewelry had seemed like a king's treasure, but now it was almost all gone. Everything cost so much! Annie hadn't told her they were almost broke, but Laurel had seen the worried look on her sister's face last night when she carefully counted out this week's money for Mr. Mancusi at the front desk. She saw it now, too, in the way Annie nibbled her toast, trying to make it last. Laurel wished she could be strong like Annie.

If only I was older. Then I could look for a job, too, and Annie wouldn't have to do everything herself.

But who would ever hire an eleven-year-old kid, when Annie, who looked older than seventeen, was having a hard time?

Laurel watched Annie break open another plastic container of grape jelly and begin spreading it thickly on her last wedge of toast. She felt a surge of love for her sister. At least she had Annie.

What if she was alone? The thought made her stomach dip crazily.

Annie looked up and said, "I have a feeling this is our lucky day." She sounded so cheerful and determined that Laurel believed her. Then she remembered, Annie said the same thing *every* day.

Laurel pushed her milk glass across the Formica tabletop. "Here, you finish it."

Annie frowned and pushed it back. "You need it more than I do. Anyway, I'm full."

It was a lie. Annie meant well, but Laurel wanted to shout at her sister, plead with her to please, please stop being so nice. But all she said was, "Can I see the paper?"

One thing they had to buy every day was *The New York Times*. Sunday's fat edition, with today's date at the top, October 9, lay next to Annie's plate; she hadn't looked at it yet. Did this mean she was losing hope?

Some of the apartments they'd looked at were nice but way too expensive. Or they were so awful, in neighborhoods where the sidewalks were lined with overflowing garbage cans. In one, when the super switched on the light, a whole parade of cockroaches began scurrying over the kitchen counter.

Where Laurel really wanted to be at this moment was back home at Bel Jardin. She badly missed her room, with its sunny window seat crammed with stuffed animals. In a weird way she even missed her father.

She imagined Val asleep in the bed he'd once shared with Dearie. Then the image dissolved, and all she could see in her mind was blood. Val's blood. And the darkness that had followed her and Annie all the way to Sunset, where in the yellow glow of streetlamps, she'd seen the dried blood on Boo. She remembered dropping her old blanket in the first garbage can they came to, yet feeling as if somehow *she* was the one being left behind.

If only Annie would tell her what Val had done that night to get her mad enough to hit him. Imagining Val dead, lying on the sofa in a pool of blood, she felt gripped by an icy chill.

No, she told herself, Val *couldn't* be dead.

But if he were alive, he might be out looking for them. Annie had said they had to be careful not to get caught, or Val would take Laurel away. And maybe even get Annie arrested for kidnapping.

Annie in jail? Laurel couldn't bear the thought. Nor could she imagine being separated from her sister. So she had to be very careful and not tell anyone too much about herself.

Annie was now buried in the Help Wanted section.

"Listen to this," she said. " 'Gal Friday. Hat company seeks energetic young person for busy office.' I'd be perfect for it."

"But if they give you a typing test—"

Annie cut her off, smiling forcefully. "Last time, I was nervous. The next time, I'll do better. I know I will." She looked down at Laurel's plate, and Laurel saw a worried look on her face. "You didn't finish your breakfast. Are you feeling okay?"

"I ate as much as I could. Why don't you have the rest."

Annie looked up sharply, as if she thought Laurel might just be pretending not to want it. Then hunger won out. Grabbing her fork, she gobbled up the rest of the scrambled eggs and sausage. Then with her last piece of toast she scoured the plate clean. Watching her, Laurel felt the ache in her own stomach ease.

"Will that be all?" The waitress was standing above them. Not waiting for an answer, she slapped the bill down on the table.

Annie paid, then grabbed her purse and slid off her seat. "Come on. I'll bet there'll be something in the *Village Voice.* Let's go look."

On their way out, passing the quick-serve counter, Laurel caught sight of a folded newspaper left on one of the stools. Too small to be the *Times.* Laurel snatched it up and tucked it under her arm.

Outside, pausing on the sidewalk while Annie went into the candy store to look at the *Voice,* Laurel unfolded the paper and saw that it was the *Jewish Press.* Would there be apartments in here? She turned five or six pages, and then she saw APTS. UNFURN. The very first one seemed to jump out at her.

> Midwd. 1 bdrm. Top of 2-fmly hse w/grdn. Quiet neighborhood. $290. Shomer Shabbat. 252-1789.

Her heart bumped into her throat. But where was Midwood? At that price it had to be Brooklyn. It sounded perfect.

A funny name, she thought—Shomer Shabbat. But just about everyone in New York had strange names. Like the night clerk at the Allerton, Mr. Tang Bo.

There was a pay phone by the candy store's front door. She dug out a dime and dialed the number from the paper. After one ring it was picked up.

"So don't keep me waiting in suspense," a lady's voice chimed right in. "Refrigerators, I'll bet you he said, don't grow on trees."

Bewildered, Laurel stammered, "H-hello?"

There was a short silence; then the lady laughed—but a nice, jolly laugh. "You're not Faigie, are you? Who is this?"

Laurel felt like quickly hanging up, but the voice at the other end sounded so nice, she forced herself to speak.

"This is Laurel . . . uh . . . Davis." Or was it Davidson? She'd heard Annie tell so many lies she couldn't keep them straight anymore. "Your apartment," she blurted. "The one you advertised. . . . We, my sister and I, that is— It's not taken, is it?"

"How old are you, darling?"

"Twelve." She could get away with one extra year. "But my sister's twenty-one," she added quickly.

"She's got a job, then?"

"Oh, well, yeah . . . she does. In a hat company. In the office. See, we're from . . . uh . . . Arizona, and we really really need an apartment, especially one with a garden."

There was a long pause; then Mrs. Shabbat sighed and said, "To be one hundred percent honest, I don't know if you're the right tenants for me, but you sound like a nice girl. I suppose it wouldn't hurt for you to have a look. So you want to come over now?"

Laurel felt light with relief. "That would be great," she said, trying to hold her excitement in. How long would it take to go by subway to that part of Brooklyn? She took a wild guess. "How about in an hour? Will you be home then?"

"Where else? I'm in my ninth month, Laurel Davis. Only, God bless him, this baby is in no hurry to come out."

Laurel hadn't even met this Mrs. Shabbat, but she couldn't remember when she'd liked anyone so much right off the bat. Quickly, feeling hot with excitement, she got the address and directions, and rushed to find Annie.

Laurel had never felt so proud. She'd show Annie she was grown up, responsible. Everything was going to work out. She was sure of it.

LAUREL and Annie got off the subway at the Avenue J station. They hadn't walked more than two blocks when Laurel began to feel as if they didn't belong, as if they'd been whisked here by a cyclone, like Dorothy and Toto into the Land of Oz.

She couldn't help but gape at a group of boys huddled under a produce-market awning, jabbering in what sounded like a foreign language. They all wore black hats and oversized black suits, and on either side of each boy's head a long curl hung down.

Annie was peering at a street sign. "Are you sure we're in the right place?"

"East Fourteenth. That's what she told me."

They passed a bakery with a mouth-watering display of fruit tarts, and a delicatessen with salamis big as baseball bats.

"I think this is it," Annie said.

Laurel stopped and stared at where her sister was pointing: a two-story wooden house, with a little front porch and a tiny lawn surrounded by a neat hedge. She noticed a tricycle on the front walk, and up on the porch, a cozy jumble of chairs. It wasn't Bel Jardin, but it looked nice . . . and well, homey. A sign over the door read THE GRUBERMANS. Laurel's heart lifted. A real family lived here.

But wait. The name was supposed to be Shabbat, not Gruberman. Could this be the wrong house?

"Don't get your hopes up," Annie warned, but Laurel could see that she was excited herself. "They'll probably say I'm too young."

Even so, Laurel squeezed her eyes shut and prayed, Please, God, let Mrs. Shabbat take us.

Annie pulled her up the path and pressed the doorbell.

"Coming, I'm coming!" someone yelled to them from inside.

After a long minute the front door swung open. A woman stood before them. An apron was tied about her enormous belly, and a round face with crinkly brown eyes smiled at them. "Miss Davis?"

"Yes," Annie answered at once. "I'm Annie . . . and this is my sister, Laurel. She's the one who called you."

"And I'm Rivka Gruberman." She smiled at Laurel. "And you talk lovely on the phone, darling, but I've never seen such young girls as you two looking for an apartment. You understand, I can't have someone who's going to move right back to Mama."

"We don't have a mother," Annie answered quietly.

"Oh," said Rivka, nodding several times, then opening the door wider. "Well, you better look at it."

Rivka gave them a sharp glance as she ushered them into a dim vestibule smelling of cooked carrots, but said nothing more as huffing and puffing she led them up the narrow stairs.

The apartment was small: a tiny kitchen with yellow cabinets, a living room with a faded green carpet, and a bedroom not much bigger than Laurel's closet at Bel Jardin. But the place was clean, and all the walls had fresh light blue paint.

"It's a very nice apartment," Annie said firmly. "We'll take it."

Rivka eyed them carefully. "Before you make up your mind, you would like to see our *shul,* no?"

Something was wrong; Laurel could feel it.

Annie, her face reddening, echoed, "Your *shul?*"

Rivka gave them a long look and said gently, "Come, *shainenkes,* come downstairs with me. Manhattan's a long trip, and you could use some hot tea and maybe a piece of babka, yeah?"

Downstairs, the Grubermans' apartment was a madhouse. Children everywhere—older boys on the sofa, reading aloud to one another in that same foreign language Laurel'd heard on the street; two little ones with toy trucks, scooting about the cabbage-rose carpet; a baby in a playpen, banging a set of plastic keys against its bars.

"*Sha,* everyone, we've got company!" Rivka yelled as she sailed through, but no one paid any attention.

In the big, cheerful kitchen, a dark-haired, pink-cheeked girl about Annie's age was rolling out dough on the counter.

"My oldest," Rivka said, waving a hand in her direction. "My Sarah." The girl nodded shyly, and went back to her rolling pin.

This house, this woman reminded Laurel of the old woman who lived in a shoe, who had so many children she didn't know what to do. Except Mrs. Gruberman seemed so happy. And nice.

Laurel and Annie sat down at a long table. Looking around, Laurel noticed something odd. Everything was in twos: two sinks, two sets of cupboards, even two refrigerators.

"I see you looking at my refrigerators," Rivka observed. "It's because we're kosher, darling. Everything that's meat and everything that's milk we keep strictly separate."

Rivka bustled about the stove, putting the kettle on and lighting the fire under it. Then she turned to face them, hands folded over her fat belly. "So, what shall I do with the two of you? You don't even know what *Shomer Shabbat* means. Am I right?"

Laurel's heart sank.

"We're not Jewish," Annie confessed.

Rivka sighed, and then ruefully nodded. "Darlings, this I saw the second I laid eyes on you. I'm sorry. *Shomer Shabbat* means 'Sabbath observers only.'"

"We won't make one bit of noise on the Sabbath," Annie pleaded. "My sister and I, we don't have a TV, or even a radio."

Rivka shook her head while plunking mugs of steaming tea in front of them. "You seem like nice girls. Please, don't take it personal." She set out a plate of yeasty cake laden with raisins and nuts, which smelled as if it had just come out of the oven.

Laurel's mouth watered. Her eyes were watering, too. Feeling hungry and miserable, she helped herself to a big piece.

"I have money. I could pay you the deposit right this minute," Annie pressed, desperation in her voice. "Cash."

"Please," Rivka replied sorrowfully. "It's not the money."

"But . . ." Annie started to plead; then suddenly her mouth clamped shut. Laurel knew that look—it was Annie's stubborn look. "It's okay," she said briskly. "I understand."

Tears welled in Laurel's eyes. Why didn't Annie tell her that they'd looked everywhere and they were too exhausted to look anymore? Why couldn't she admit she was hungry? Laurel saw Annie eyeing the cake, but no, she was too proud to take any.

Then Laurel had an idea. "I could baby-sit for you," she said softly. "I wouldn't even charge for it."

Shaking her head pityingly, Rivka turned back to her stove, picking up where she must have left off when they'd arrived, flouring chicken drumsticks and dropping them into a hot skillet.

Annie stood up. "Thank you anyway, for showing us the place. Laurey, I think we'd better be go—"

She was interrupted by a wail from the other room. The older girl, Sarah, shot her mother a pleading look and said, "Please, Ma, I have to finish this before Rachel gets here to help me with my algebra."

"And I"—Rivka threw up her floury hands—"have four hands all of a sudden?"

Laurel, guided by instinct, rushed into the next room and scooped the crying baby from her playpen. While the boys on the sofa looked on in fascination she peeled off the baby's plastic pants. Then Laurel saw why she'd been crying—one of the diaper pins had popped open and was sticking her in the side.

She had just gotten the pin out when Rivka rushed in. She hoisted the baby onto her big belly and smiled at Laurel.

"So? You know about babies? You're just a baby yourself!"

"I know a lot about babies." Laurel lied.

"A pin was sticking Shainey!" cried a dark-haired boy. "The girl pulled it out."

Rivka covered the baby with kisses, then said, "By my husband, it's enough already I have the older girls to help out." She sighed. "But with Sarah and Chava and Leah in yeshiva all day and this new one coming any minute, I could use a little more help."

Laurel looked up into Rivka's kind face and saw an uncertainty that hadn't been there a few minutes ago. She felt a surge of hope. We'd be safe here, she thought. Safe from muggers and mean landlords and cockroaches. Safe from policemen and from Val.

"Stay," Rivka said softly. "Meet my husband, Ezra. He'll be home soon. Maybe he meets you, and then he'll change his mind."

Laurel let her breath out, feeling a rush of happy relief. And pride, too. Because she was the one who had made all this happen. She grinned at Annie, who grinned back.

Somehow Laurel felt sure it was going to be okay. For right now, at least. She didn't want to think about going to school in this weird neighborhood or whether or not Annie would find a job.

Later, if they could have the apartment, she'd ask Mrs. Gruberman about the bearded men with the round fur hats and the boys with long curls.

She could see she had lots and lots to learn.

Chapter Three

Dolly slammed down the phone.

She felt mad enough to spit. Those customs morons at JFK had been sitting on her shipment for four whole days. And the inspectors she'd spoken to were too lazy to find out why. Damn it! What the devil did they expect her to do with two thousand dollars' worth of highly perishable chocolates going soft in some customs shed?

But that's not what's really needling you, is it? You're just using this to let off steam.

Remembering that phone call from Ned Oliver a few weeks ago telling her that Evie's girls had run away from home, Dolly felt a stitch in her gut. Ned, her old friend, had secretly kept Dolly up to date on Annie and Laurel over the years.

Those poor girls! It had to be Val's fault somehow. But why blame Val? When you got right down to it, wasn't *she* the one to blame? If it hadn't been for her knifing Eve in the back, probably none of this would ever have happened.

Dolly began to get that familiar downward-spiraling feeling, and she quickly caught herself. She had to find her nieces somehow.

Itching with impatience, she grabbed the phone and dialed the private investigator she'd hired out in L.A.

"O'Brien," he answered.

"Dolly Drake here," she told him. "You turned up anything on my nieces yet?" The other times she'd called, he'd merely told her to be patient. Why should today be any different?

"Funny you should call. I've been trying to reach you, but your phone's been busy. Look, don't get too excited, but I think I know where they are. I talked to a Greyhound driver who recognized the photos. He says they were headed for New York City. But . . ."

New York? Here! Dolly's heart lurched.

"The chances of finding a couple of runaways in such a big city, I have to tell you, could be a million to one. You're best off sitting tight. They get desperate enough, they'll call home."

"No," she told O'Brien. "You keep looking." But as she hung up, she felt suddenly leaden. She could not count on O'Brien. One way or another, she would have to find them.

Get busy, she told herself, and maybe an idea will come to you.

In the tiny office above her shop, Dolly squeezed out from behind her desk and walked over to the refrigerated case containing her overstock. Fifty-eight degrees. Not enough to cause condensation, but exactly the right temperature to keep her precious chocolates from melting or from turning gray with bloom. Fine chocolates, she had learned, needed to be coddled, babied. But what good were all her precautions here when her next two weeks' inventory was going stale in some shed at the airport?

Dolly felt the beginning of a headache. Then she remembered something else, something good: Henri's plane was due in at JFK around five. She should've asked him to pack an extra suitcase full of chocolates. In his shop in Paris, the original La Maison de Girod—shortened here to Girod's—they were made fresh daily.

Then it occurred to her—two birds with one stone. Why not? She'd go straight to the top, to McIntyre himself. He was the import specialist. She could personally try to sweet-talk him into releasing her shipment and then afterwards meet Henri's plane.

Her spirits rose. Wouldn't Henri be surprised, and pleased? Usually she waited for him at her apartment, with Champagne on ice and wearing nothing but black silk-chiffon.

Dolly caught her reflection in the refrigerator's glass door. Her dress was a brilliant tomato red with a navy polka-dot panel over her bosom. In her ears she wore the ruby-and-diamond earrings Dale had given her for their fifth—and last—anniversary.

Dolly believed in bright colors. She loved things that glittered and twinkled—rhinestone buttons, shiny patent leather shoes, oversized jewelry. Dale had once joked that the inside of her closet looked like Carmen Miranda's turban. The way Dolly saw it, the world was already gray enough without adding to its misery.

Dolly straightened her upswept honey-blond hair and applied a fresh coat of Fever Red to her lips. Oh, she knew how the blue-rinse dowagers in her Park Avenue building gossiped about her. *"Loud, vulgar, cheap,"* she could almost hear them whispering. *"Her late husband was some oil wildcatter. She was waiting tables when he married her. Lavished a fortune on her . . . as if it did any good. She still looks right out of a five-and-dime."* Well, what did she care? Those antique snoots, with their dreary clothes and tasteful pearls, what could they offer her that was better than what she already had with Henri?

Henri.

Just thinking about him made her feel as if she were coming in from the cold. And it had been so long, almost three months. Oh, she couldn't wait.

But at the same time she felt uneasy. Tonight she was supposed to give him her answer. She had promised she would.

And if I say yes? If I agree to move to Paris? Dolly let herself imagine the two of them together—nights in Henri's arms, weekends roaming the galleries on the Left Bank.

But, damn it, Henri was still married. *"You can look at a mule ten different ways, but it's never gonna be a horse,"* Mama-Jo always used to say. And well, no matter how you sliced it, she'd only be what she was now—Henri's mistress.

And what about Girod's? Dolly loved knowing each time she unlocked the iron grate at 870 Madison that the shop was hers, that it couldn't fire her or simply fade away like one more dead-end screen test. She needed Girod's—the chitchat with the customers, the figuring and ordering, the satisfaction of selling, the fun of arranging windows. And of course, all those heavenly chocolates.

Dolly thought back to when she'd first decided to open a chocolate shop. One rainy spring day, some months after Dale had died, when the thought of spending the rest of her life alone had almost sent her reeling back to bed, she'd packed a suitcase, grabbed a battered French phrase book, and escaped to Paris.

On the Rue du Faubourg St.-Honoré, she'd happened upon La Maison de Girod. Within the hour, having sweet-talked her way into a tour of the chocolatier's basement kitchen and sampled flavors that tasted too delicious to have been created on this earth, she'd learned that Monsieur Henri Baptiste was indeed eager to franchise a Girod's outlet in New York. Dolly suddenly knew exactly what she wanted to do when she returned home.

And now, after five years, her little Madison Avenue shop felt more like home than her cavernous Park Avenue apartment. Did she love Henri enough to give it up?

Stop torturing yourself. . . . You can make up your mind when you see him.

Impatient now to get to the airport, Dolly dialed her apartment and told her driver, Felipe, to get over to Girod's as soon as he could, with a bottle of Champagne on ice.

Now she had to come up with some charming way to unbend the import specialist McIntyre—not a bribe, but some kind of *incentive*. He *had* to release that shipment.

Dolly plunged into the closet-size storeroom catty-corner to the office. She'd bring McIntyre some chocolates, she decided, something really special. Her gaze scanned the stacks of flat cardboard yet to be folded into boxes embossed with Girod's gold imprint. Above, lining the shelves, were the special containers, ones she'd collected herself: antique cookie tins and art deco canisters, gaily painted Mexican boxes, baskets studded with seashells.

Gloria De Witt, her assistant, called this room Dolly's magpie's nest. And now, rummaging through her treasures, Dolly wondered what in the world would impress a seen-it-all customs agent.

Then she spotted it. Perfect—a cookie jar in the shape of an apple. She would fill it with rum caramels and Champagne truffles, and play Eve to McIntyre's Adam. It had worked in the Good Book. Why not now?

With the cookie jar tucked under her arm Dolly made her way down the world's narrowest staircase. It had to have been built with a midget in mind, she thought. Definitely not for a size fourteen on five-inch spike heels. Downstairs, Gloria was folding boxes. She looked up at Dolly, her enormous brass earrings tinkling like wind chimes.

"You manage to kick some butts at customs?"

"Better." Dolly held up the apple jar and grinned wickedly. "I'm mounting a personal attack. Death by chocolate."

"Amen to that." Gloria laughed.

Dolly was just finishing filling the cookie jar when she spotted Felipe pulling up across the avenue. She grabbed a shopping bag and threw on her coat. Dashing out into the street with barely a glance in either direction, she reached Felipe—but not before a taxi missed hitting her by a hair.

"You don' watch out, you gonna get youself killed one a these days!" her feisty Guatemalan driver scolded her affectionately as she slid into the back seat. Dolly shrugged. Henri, too, was always after her for her reckless jaywalking.

As the Lincoln inched its way along the Long Island Expressway, Dolly's thoughts returned to Annie and Laurel. Did they have any money? A place to sleep? Enough to eat?

Lord, what it must have been like for them those last years—Eve's drinking more and more out of control, then the drying-out spells, when she'd be gone for months at a time.

Hollywood had buzzed over Eve's stone-faced refusal to give McCarthy one single name and Preminger's snagging Grace Kelly in her place. Her agent, Syd, had been way off about Dolly's prospects, but what she had cared about was making Eve understand how sorry she was.

Dolly had so wanted to help her sister. And there wasn't a day when she didn't regret having sent that damn letter. But every time she called, Eve's Spanish maid would say, "Missa Dearfield no home." Eve never returned one of her calls.

Twelve years. It had taken Eve that long to die. And now, because of what Dolly had done, Eve's girls were out there somewhere, probably scared to death.

Dolly covered her face with her hands and wept. She didn't deserve anything. She didn't deserve Henri. Nor had she deserved the man she'd married—huge-hearted Dale, who had picked her up when she was waiting tables at Ciro's, lavished her with affection, and died leaving her so wonderfully well provided for.

She closed her eyes and allowed herself to imagine being reunited with her nieces. Lord knew, she couldn't replace Eve, but she *could* be sort of like a mother to those girls, couldn't she? She'd longed for children of her own, but the tests had shown that Dale's sperm count was impossibly low. No babies ever . . .

But wouldn't this be almost as good in a way? If she could be a mother to her nieces, wouldn't it in some small way help make up for what she'd done to Eve?

The green approach signs for JFK could be seen up ahead now. Minutes later they were pulling up in front of cargo building 80, and Dolly was dashing in, shopping bag tucked up under her arm. Inside, the place looked even more dreary than it had outside: pea-soup walls, scuffed linoleum floor, furniture that looked as if it belonged in the Bates Motel, right out of *Psycho*.

She found McIntyre's office easily enough; his plastic name tag was in a slot by the door. Though they'd spoken to one another a number of times over the phone, they'd never actually met.

"Dolly Drake," she introduced herself after knocking softly at his open door, and at his sheepish wince, she grinned. "Guess you know why I'm here."

She slipped the apple-shaped cookie jar onto his desk.

McIntyre's smile faded. "Hey, come on. You know I can't take that. You don't want to get me in trouble, do you?" He was a middle-aged man with sallow skin and red hair shot with gray.

She suddenly felt ashamed. But she forced a brilliant smile, exclaiming, "Why, Mr. McIntyre, what a thought!"

"The plain fact is, Dolly"—he held up some papers—"approval on your shipment is being held up until the lab results come back. We do a random check every so often on the alcohol level, to make sure it doesn't exceed regulations."

Dolly felt her neck muscles knot with frustration. Hell's bells, *she* knew the law, and so did Henri. Why, there wasn't enough liquor in Girod's chocolates to inebriate a kitten!

What now? It was McIntyre's rubber stamp and his alone that

would release her shipment. Then it struck her: *Why couldn't they have the test right here and now?*

"Mr. McIntyre, I'm going to ask you to do yourself and me a small and perfectly legal favor. Try one. No one in the history of the United States ever lost their job for eating one chocolate bonbon." She lifted the lid and gently extracted one of the dark rum caramels. As the weary official was opening his mouth to protest, she popped the bonbon in. "Tell me what you think."

A look of annoyance creased his face. But he was chewing it, not spitting it into the ashtray. He kept on chewing, his eyes drifting shut. And now—praise the Lord!—he was smiling.

McIntyre swallowed and then reached for another. "No alcohol in these," he said, grinning. "But wow, they ought to be outlawed."

Dolly felt a rush of triumph that left her a little dizzy.

Five minutes later she was back in her Lincoln, heading out to Air France cargo to pick up her shipment.

After that, Henri.

"DOLLY?" Henri called softly in the darkness.

Dolly looked up from the television she'd been staring at. He stood at the entrance to the den—a stocky figure wrapped in a silk dressing gown, his thick pewter-colored hair mussed with sleep. A present from her, that robe—a little fancy for Henri, who was more the plain terry type. Still, he wore it to please her.

"I couldn't sleep," Dolly told him. She'd been worrying about Laurel and Annie.

But now she had to think what to do about Henri.

On the way from the airport Henri had told her that he had come across the most charming flat with a garden view, a stone's throw from Girod's. He had even left a deposit to hold it for a week.

What should I tell him? The thought of being with Henri shimmered in her head like a green oasis in a desert.

But the truth was that things had changed since she'd promised him she'd think about moving to Paris. She couldn't leave now, not until Annie and Laurel had been found. And even after that, there were still, let's face it, Henri's wife and children.

Henri sank down beside her on the deep sofa, tucking an arm about her. He kissed her shoulder, the ends of his mustache pleasantly scratchy. *Oh, was that nice!* After Dale she'd thought she would never again know that sweet tug a woman feels in her belly when her man kisses her.

She thought of the first time she'd laid eyes on Henri, in the kitchen of his shop, bent over a steaming copper caldron, holding a wooden spoon to his lips. Surrounded for the first time in her life by chocolate on all sides—sheets of chocolate, tray after tray of bite-size dollops of *ganache*—Dolly felt as if she'd died and gone to heaven.

Now, snuggled against her, Henri whispered, "Without you, the bed is cold. And I miss your snoring."

"Like hell I snore!"

Henri grinned. *"Exactement."*

"My grandpa used to say, *'You can dress a frog in silk drawers, but that don't stop him from croakin.'* " She elbowed him lightly in the ribs. "Hey, you ever been west of the Mississippi?"

"When I was very young, my parents took me to Yellowstone Park to see—how do you say?—Old Reliable."

She giggled. "Old Reliable? Sounds like the stuff Mama-Jo used to swallow before bedtime. You mean Old Faithful, don't you?"

He rolled his eyes and chuckled.

"You know what I love about you, *ma poupée?*" he said. "You make me laugh." He kissed her, and she felt an almost electric sensation shoot from her lips to her lower belly.

"No," she murmured, pulling away. "Henri, we need to talk."

His slate-colored eyes regarded her from beneath his bushy brows. "But of course," he said, nodding gravely.

It came straight to her then, the decision she'd been holding at arm's length all evening. What surprised her was the pain she felt, the sharpness of the ache gripping her chest.

Dolly took a breath. "I'm not moving to Paris," she told him. "Not now, anyway. It wouldn't be right, not with . . . with the way things are. Your wife . . ." She gulped. Henri started to speak, and she held up her hand to stop him. "Oh, I know you don't love Francine. And I know all your reasons for not divorcing her: your children, your religion, Francine's father. . . ."

Henri's face sagged. He seemed suddenly a decade older than forty-seven. "What you don't know," he finally said, "is how she despises me. If not for her father, she says, I would still be an assistant chef at Fouquet's. It is not true, of course, but until the old goat takes his retirement, I remain under his thumb."

Once, while in Paris on business, Dolly had met Henri's wife—a grim woman who looked as if she'd devoted her forty-odd years to mastering the art of smiling without moving her lips. No denying she was good-looking—or had been, at some point—with her blade-thin figure and chic clothes. But now, twenty years into their marriage, Francine was like some spindly chair in a museum on which one wouldn't dare sit.

Dolly felt resentment growing inside her. *How can he stay with Francine when it's me he loves? Why doesn't he just go ahead and divorce his wife, Papa Girod be damned?*

But Dolly knew it wasn't that simple. If Henri walked away from Francine, he'd have to leave Girod's. And Girod's was more than a business to him; it was his whole life. His son was pretty much grown, but he absolutely doted on eleven-year-old Gabrielle.

"It's not just your . . . situation," Dolly said. Quickly she told him about Annie and Laurel. "So you see, I *have* to stay here. I've got to find them. You see that, don't you?"

Henri frowned, but then he gained control of himself.

"Of course I do. And you will, *ma poupée*," he conceded sadly. Then after a moment he ventured, "But instead of looking everywhere for them, could you not perhaps bring them to you instead?"

"What do you mean?"

"Perhaps an advertisement in the newspaper?"

Dolly thought for a moment, growing excited. Yeah, it could just work. She hugged Henri, feeling a surge of hope. Tomorrow, first thing, she'd see about placing an ad.

"You're a genius. How am I ever gonna get along without you?" She felt a desperate urge to be wrapped up in him, engulfed by his body. "Come on. Let's go back to bed."

Moments later Dolly kissed him and forgot everything but how wonderful she felt. What could be sweeter than this? A man who loved her, who thought she was beautiful. Why, she could die this very minute, and she wouldn't feel she'd missed out.

"Looks pretty foxy," Gloria said.

"If it works." Dolly held up crossed fingers.

She had the *Times* open atop the display case and was staring at the half-page ad. A selection of chocolates was featured at the top, plus the usual copy about Girod's seventy-five years of international awards. And smack in the center, a cutout from an old glossy of Dolly from her Hollywood days—heavy lipstick, tight sweater, cone-shaped brassiere and all—the weirdest chocolate ad in history. But she was hoping—grasping at straws, really—that Annie might see it and recognize her. Her name below it read, big as you please, DOLLY DRAKE, PROPRIETOR.

The important thing now was to get to her nieces before anything happened to them. She shivered, tugging on the arms of the pink sweater draped over her shoulders. The radio had said it might snow this week. She imagined Annie and Laurel shivering on the sidewalk somewhere, and her heart twisted in her chest.

Two days later snow was coming down in earnest, and Dolly had almost given up hope of ever finding the two girls. She was checking over the day's receipts when the bell over the door tinkled. Looking up, she watched a tall, angular young woman hesitate a moment on the threshold, then take a deep breath as she entered the shop. She wore a thin coat, and loafers that looked soaked. Her dark shoulder-length hair wasn't covered, not even with a scarf.

Dolly was about to turn away, leave this one to Gloria, but something about the girl held her. That long neck and those high cheekbones, those startling indigo eyes. The girl looked straight at Dolly, and Dolly felt her heart tip sideways in her chest.

"Annie," she whispered, "honey, is that you?"

"Aunt Dolly?"

Then all at once it struck her: *She's really here.* Dolly started to cry. "Oh, sugar, I was afraid— Well, don't just stand there. Come here and let me give you a hug." She gathered Annie into her arms.

Annie remained stiff at first; then, tentatively, her hands came up and circled Dolly's back, and with a sigh she rested her head against Dolly's shoulder, like a weary traveler easing a heavy burden.

"I saw your picture in the paper." Annie drew away, a thin smile touching her lips.

A thousand questions came to Dolly all at once. But she asked only the most important one: "You okay, sugar?"

"Sure." Annie was glancing fearfully about the shop, as if she half expected someone to spring out and clap a pair of handcuffs on her.

"I don't bite," Gloria called out, moving out from behind the counter. "Hi, I'm Gloria. I guess you two have a whole lot of catching up to do, so why don't I close up and let you go at it."

Dolly led Annie up to her office and plugged in the space heater next to her desk for extra warmth.

"Now slip out of those wet shoes," she told her niece, "and I'll make you a cup of tea. You like chocolate?"

Annie nodded, looking around her. "Please . . . don't tell Val," she pleaded softly. Her clear eyes fixed upon Dolly with a scared, desperate look, but Dolly saw a glint of steel there, too.

She didn't want to make a promise she couldn't keep, but at the same time Dolly sensed that a wrong word now would send Annie bolting like a panicked deer. "Why don't you tell me all about it," she said, "and let me decide. Fair enough?"

Annie was silent for a long moment; then she said, "I guess so."

Dolly made tea on the hot plate and brought it to Annie in a thick ceramic mug. Annie held the mug against her knee, cupping her fingers about it, and began to talk.

Haltingly at first, then with gathering passion, she told Dolly about Eve, how she'd died. And then Val, acting so strange . . . and, finally, the night she and Laurel ran away.

"I couldn't stay," Annie said, leaning forward, her eyes bright and her cheeks a little flushed. "He would have . . . Well, I didn't stop to think it through all the way. I just grabbed Laurey and—"

"He's saying you kidnapped her."

The color drained from her niece's face. "It's not true! Laurey wanted to be with me! And I wouldn't have come to you. Not unless I was really desperate. I—I didn't think you'd want us."

Dolly felt the bare honesty of her words sock home.

"Did your—" She licked her lips. Her heart was doing a crazy riff against her rib cage. "Did your mama ever talk about me?"

"You had some kind of fight, didn't you? She never said what it was about."

Dolly felt her body sag with relief. *Thanks to heaven, she doesn't know the whole story.*

"Sometimes people say . . . or do . . . something hurtful that they're sorry for later. And the more you love that person who let you down, the worse it hurts." She sighed, the old pain surfacing.

Dolly looked into Annie's eyes—so much like Eve's it nearly broke her heart—and found herself saying briskly, "Val doesn't have to know. Now drink your tea, and let's see what we can do about straightening out this mess before it gets any worse."

Chapter Four

"Annie, *why* can't we spend Christmas with Aunt Dolly?" Laurel stopped in the middle of the sidewalk, looking up at her sister.

Annie felt a bead of annoyance form in her stomach. *How many times must I go over this with her? Why can't she just trust me?*

But she bit back the harsh words and reached for her sister's mittened hand. "Look, Laurey, we can't go to her apartment, because people would see us and it might get back to Val."

Laurel, dropping her gaze, said nothing. Annie wondered if she was wishing she were at Bel Jardin with Val instead of here. Her insides suddenly felt as chilled as her cold-reddened hands. Should she tell Laurel everything that had happened that night with Val—the real reason she'd had to run away?

No. It was too awful to talk about.

"But you're *working* for Aunt Dolly," Laurel reasoned. "And what's so safe about that?"

"At the shop nobody but Gloria knows she's my aunt," Annie explained. "But her apartment has doormen, nosy neighbors. If we started hanging out there, pretty soon everybody would know." She gave her sister a nudge. "Now come on, or you'll be late for school."

Laurel glared at Annie. "I don't care! I hate it here! It's cold and yucky . . . and . . . and"—her voice wobbled—"we'll be all alone on Christmas!"

"What about the Grubermans?"

"The Grubermans don't celebrate Christmas." Laurel's wide blue eyes glittered with unshed tears. "And we might as well be Jewish if we're not even going to have a tree."

Annie couldn't think of anything to say. She wanted a tree, too. Should she have taken the money Dolly offered? She thought back to that first day at Dolly's shop, her aunt's pressing several folded twenties into her hand and pleading with her to take them. But Annie just couldn't. If she accepted Dolly's charity, wouldn't she somehow be betraying Dearie? Once her mother had referred to her sister as a two-faced snake in the grass. Did that mean that Dolly, no matter how nice she acted, couldn't be trusted?

She'd settled instead for agreeing to work for her aunt, and accepted a small cash advance against her salary. But now it had been three weeks, and she still hadn't saved enough to buy half the things they needed. The list seemed endless: long underwear, warm clothes, heavy boots, dishes, sheets, towels.

She glanced over at Laurel, wearing a Salvation Army duffle coat that didn't quite reach her wrists. Laurel's bright hair spilled like sunshine from under the red knit cap squashed over her head, but her lips and the tip of her nose were tinged with blue.

"Are you warm enough?" Annie shivered inside her own coat, a man's gabardine that flapped at her ankles.

"I'm okay," Laurel said. "I've got a sweater on under this. Rivka gave me one of Chava's that didn't fit her anymore."

More likely Rivka had seen that Laurel needed a sweater and had hunted one up that would fit her. Rivka had practically adopted Annie and Laurel into her big, noisy family, and Annie couldn't help being grateful for the cast-off clothes and extra blankets, the fresh-baked kugel and loaves of challah she sent up to them.

"Guess what?" Laurel said. "After school today Rivka's gonna show me how to sew, and when I get good enough, I'll even make *you* something. . . ." Her voice trailed off, and she peeped up at Annie with a sheepish expression. "Annie, I'm sorry I got mad at you. But it *would* be nice to have a little tree."

"Yeah, it would." Annie forced herself to sound cheery, but inside she felt terrible. The fir trees they trucked into the city were so expensive. Ornaments, too. No, it was out of the question.

At Avenue K and Sixteenth Street, Annie caught sight of P.S. 99, a massive, grim-looking brick building surrounded by a high chain link fence. Annie remembered going to enroll Laurel. She'd been so nervous, saying that she was Laurel's guardian and that her school records had been lost in a fire. But the school secretary hadn't even seemed suspicious, just bored. Now Annie knew it was because a lot of the kids here were illegal, with parents from places like Haiti and Nicaragua who didn't even have green cards.

"Our class Christmas play is this Friday night," Laurel said when they'd reached the graffiti-sprayed doors. "I'm in charge of the scenery. It's going to be really neat."

"I can't wait to see it."

Laurel was so artistic. Annie remembered the wonderful cards she used to draw for Dearie—amazingly lifelike dogs, monkeys, squirrels. And she had such an eye for color, too. Like the other day, rescuing that old paisley shawl Rivka was throwing out, seeing how perfect it would be to dress up their own shabby couch.

"Do you think Dolly would come, too?"

"Why don't I ask her? I bet she'd like that." With forced brightness Annie added, "Look, Laurey, about Christmas . . . Why don't we invite Dolly over to *our* place? We'll get some holly and hang some mistletoe. And we'll sing all the carols."

"The Grubermans will hear us." Annie could see the tiniest smile was prying at the corners of Laurel's mouth.

"Let them," she said, feeling her spirits rise. "So what if everyone in Brooklyn hears us!"

A MINIATURE Christmas tree lit with tiny white lights and tied with gilt-wrapped bonbons twinkled in Girod's front window.

Annie was checking an order form against the merchandise.

1 doz. dark-chocolate hazelnut rums
1 doz. white-chocolate espressos
3 lbs. bitter-chocolate almond bark
4 doz. Champagne truffles

All there, cradled in molded Styrofoam trays, in a big brown-and-gold Girod's shopping bag on the counter in front of her.

She glanced at the invoice: Joe Daugherty. The address was a restaurant—Joe's Place—on Morton Street.

Just her luck. All the way down to the Village. And it was snowing like crazy out there. Oh, well, at least she'd be in a warm cab. And maybe, since it was almost four, Dolly would tell her to go on home after she'd delivered her package.

ANNIE didn't look down as she was getting out of the taxi, and by the time she did, it was too late. Her foot slid out from under her on the icy curb, and she landed on her bottom with a hard smack that sent her shopping bag of chocolates flying.

Picking herself up, she prayed that none of the chocolates were broken. She felt like enough of a klutz without having to go through a bunch of explanations and apologies.

Joe's Place turned out to be one of those aged Federal-style brick houses common to the Village, narrow as a chimney, with a few stairs leading up to a paneled door set with an oval of beveled glass.

Buzzed in through a wrought-iron gate, Annie immediately smelled baking bread as she entered the door beyond. Down a dimly lit hallway she could see into the kitchen. She heard voices, the clatter of pots, the hiss of steam.

Then a smashing sound, crockery crashing against a tiled floor. "Damn it!" a voice roared. "You idiot!"

Annie jumped.

The voice coming from the kitchen seemed to reverberate, as if directed exclusively at her. Annie shrank back as a figure appeared—a lanky man in his early twenties, his rangy height making even five-foot-nine Annie feel short. He wore a stained apron over blue jeans, and a faded chambray shirt with its sleeves rolled up over his elbows. His longish hair was pushed back from a sweaty forehead, and his eyes swam murkily behind steam-fogged eyeglasses.

"Yeah, what do you want?" he barked.

"I . . ." For an awful moment her mind went blank.

Before she could get the words out, he blurted, "Look, I'm really busy. One of the ovens just fritzed out on me, and two of my waiters are out sick, so whatever it is you want, spit it out."

Something in Annie snapped. "I don't *want* anything," she said haughtily, thrusting her shopping bag at him. "If you're Joe Daugherty, just sign the stupid invoice, and I'll get out of your way."

The condensed steam on his lenses began to evaporate, revealing eyes that looked gentle, wide, and brown. He looked chagrined.

"I'm sorry. Look, can we start over?" He turned a sheepish grin on her. "I *am* Joe Daugherty, and I've been having a day you wouldn't believe. I guess I just sort of came unglued."

Annie thought of the guy—some poor dishwasher, no doubt—that he'd yelled at back there. She wasn't buying his Mr. Nice Guy act.

"Right." Crisply she handed him the invoice. "Sign here." Then she remembered that the chocolates might be damaged. She swallowed hard and said, "Wait. I slipped and fell on the ice on my way over, and some of the chocolates might be . . . uh . . . broken."

Annie waited for the other shoe to drop, for this guy to explode again, but after a tense moment he surprised her by laughing. It was a low, easy laugh that made her want to smile in spite of herself.

"I guess this isn't your day, either," he observed mildly. "Sorry about your fall . . . and you can stop looking at me like I'm going to cut you up and serve you for dinner. I really *am* sorry I snapped at you. You may not believe this, but I'm actually a pretty mellow guy. I have a long fuse, but when I blow, I *really* blow."

"Great. But what about the poor guy in there you dumped on?"

Daugherty looked puzzled; then he began to chuckle, and in a minute was roaring with laughter. "*I* was the one who dropped those dishes. I was cursing myself out."

Annie didn't know what to say. Then she began to laugh, too.

"Why don't we step into my executive boardroom and assess what damage has been done," Joe suggested wryly. He led the way to a tiny, grungy office, where he gestured for Annie to sit. "You must be new with Dolly," he said. "You're . . ."

"Annie. I just started last week."

"Funny, I would've pegged you for the college type. Vassar or Sarah Lawrence, maybe."

"Well, you'd be wrong, then," Annie answered evenly. College, which she had once yearned for, couldn't have been further away.

"Hey, I'm one to talk. I deep-sixed law school to open this place. My old man is figuring this is temporary insanity. He's even saving a space for my nameplate on the door to his old office: Poth, Van Gelder, Daugherty, and Prodigal Son."

He took his glasses off and began polishing them, and Annie saw that his eyes weren't really brown: they were sort of a cross between green and brown—a shifting mossy hazel. He just missed being handsome—not ordinary handsome, but really knockout handsome, like a movie star.

Annie realized she was staring and jerked her gaze away as he signed the invoice with a flourish. "Stuff the chocolates," he said. "Even if a few of them are smashed, it's too ugly out there for you to make a second trip."

Seeing how hard he was trying to make up for how he'd acted before, Annie actually found herself smiling.

"You haven't been in New York very long, have you?" he asked.

"Why? Does it show?"

"Your smile—it's definitely west of the Mississippi."

"How do New Yorkers smile?"

"They don't."

She giggled. "Does it ever get any easier here?"

"Nope. Only it sort of grows on you after a while. You'll see."

Annie stood up. "I'd better go. I have to get home." At the door she stopped and looked back. "Uh . . . well, thanks."

She was making her way out down the hall when he called, "Wait!" He loped past her, and minutes later reappeared holding a large plastic carton. He presented it to Annie as if it held the crown jewels.

"To make up for acting like a jerk," he said. "Merry Christmas."

Annie heard a faint scratching sound and peeked inside. A big lobster scuttled feebly about in some seaweed. She was so startled she nearly dropped the container. She looked up at Joe, at his handsome face so full of good intentions. No, it wasn't a joke.

But what on earth was she going to do with a . . . a *lobster?* She didn't even have a pot to cook it in.

"Uh . . . thanks," she managed, reddening a little. "I'm sure it'll be . . . uh . . . delicious. Well, thanks."

"Don't mention it. And hey, drop by any time."

Trudging through the snow to the subway at West Fourth, Annie spotted a man selling Christmas trees out of the back of his truck. Her heart sank. If only she could afford one. And the irony of it was, this lobster, if she'd bought it in a store, would have cost a lot. With that money she might have been able to buy a small tree.

Then it hit her.

She walked over to the truck. The man—burly and bearded— was nailing a cross of two-by-fours to the trunk of a bushy fir.

"Can I do for you, miss?"

"I was just wondering— Would you be interested in trading one of your trees for . . . for . . ."

"Whatcha got there?" He tossed his hammer down.

Annie opened her box and held it up so he could see inside.

The man looked at her as if she'd just offered him a slice of green cheese from the moon. But after he'd poked the lobster to see if it was still kicking and after she had agreed to accept his skinniest, spindliest tree, she had a deal.

Annie thought of how pleased Laurel would be, and how they would decorate it with paper chains, popcorn, and tinfoil stars. Maybe it would turn out to be an okay Christmas after all.

EVEN in L.A., Val thought, December was a misery.

As he churned his way across the pool at Bel Jardin he tried not to feel how cold the water was or how his head was throbbing, or to think about the real estate broker and her snob clients who right now were tramping around inside his house, peering into closets and pointing out cracks in the plaster.

Instead, Val thought about Annie.

The rotten kid. She'd had no right to clobber him like that. Fifteen stitches.

He didn't care about finding her. But Laurel, that was different. If he could just get his daughter back, there ought to be some way of getting ahold of that trust money of hers.

Fifty laps. Val grabbed the ladder and hoisted himself out of the pool. He was breathing hard now, heart pounding.

"How can you swim in that muck?" A gravelly voice penetrated the red tide surging in his ears. "You oughta get it cleaned."

Val focused his bleary, chlorine-stung eyes on the stubby figure sprawled on a nearby chaise. As always, he felt a tiny prick of incredulity. No one in a million years would guess that Rudy was his brother. A full foot shorter, squat, balding, and ugly. In his Hawaiian shirt and Pepto-Bismol-pink shorts, legs pinkening under a coat of tanning oil, Rudy reminded him of a roast pig at a luau.

"With what?" Val flung himself into the nearest deck chair. "You think the old lady fixed it so I'd be left with anything? If I still had Laurel, things might be different, but—"

His words were cut off by Rudy's jumping up and strutting over to him. "Relax. In another week or two the girls'll run out of money, and you'll find them right on your doorstep, scratching to be let in."

"I don't know." Val fingered the scar over his eyebrow. It still felt tender, and under it was a hard ridge. "If they had somebody to go to, maybe they wouldn't be in such a big hurry."

"Like who?"

"Dolly, maybe. The way she was acting over the phone, I got a funny feeling she might know something she's not telling. If only I had the money, then I'd fly out there and see for myself." He thought about asking Rudy to spot him a few hundred, but then he remembered he was already in the hole to him for almost a grand.

Rudy's grin seemed to slip a notch, and a hard gleam stole into his beady black eyes. "What you need is a drink," he said. "How about I fix us a couple of Bloody Marys."

Later, as they sipped their drinks under the magnolia at the outdoor bar, Rudy said, "Tell you what. Day after tomorrow I'm flying out to New York to see a client and collect some depositions. Afterwards I could drop in on Dolly, check out her story."

Val sat up straighter. "Would you? Hey, that'd be great." Gruffly he added, "Thanks."

Rudy shrugged. "Hey, no sweat. What are brothers for?"

It never even occurred to Val that Rudy was doing this not for him, but for Laurel.

In his mind Rudy saw his niece standing in the doorway at Bel Jardin, hovering just beyond his reach—her sweet face and those big blue eyes. She was spooked by him, he knew. What kid wouldn't be? But now, if he could somehow track her down, things would be different. Never mind about Annie—with her fierce eyes and sharp gestures, she'd always made him want to keep his distance. Sweet Laurel was all he cared about. And if he found her, he'd figure out a way of keeping her to himself, away from Val and his moneygrubbing. He doesn't deserve Laurel, Rudy thought.

Rudy's heart twisted in his chest. What if Dolly *did* know something? She sure wouldn't come right out and tell him her secret. In her mind, no doubt, that'd be the same as telling Val.

Well, if she was lying, he'd see right through her. Yeah, he'd know. And then he'd have Dolly tailed, and sooner or later she'd lead him to Laurel.

He felt better. Two days later he'd be in a cab bouncing over the potholes on his way to Dolly's shop. Could Val be right? Did Dolly maybe know where Annie and Laurel were? He felt excited, hopeful, but his stomach was in knots.

LAUREL peered through the slit where the stage curtain met the wall. From where she stood at a darkened edge of the stage, she scanned row after row, but Annie and Aunt Dolly still hadn't arrived. Where could they be? It was almost six thirty, and the play was half over! Could something have happened to them?

"Group four," she heard Miss Rodriguez whisper. "Laurel, Jesús . . . you're on next. Line up when I give the signal."

Phutt! Phuuuuuut! Jesús had a hand tucked under one armpit and was pumping his elbow, making it sound as if he were farting.

Laurel felt like jabbing him with her papier-mâché scepter, but she didn't dare. Yesterday, when she won the spelling bee, he'd tried to trip her on her way back to her seat.

The teacher scowled in their direction.

Looking past the folding screen that separated her group from the stage, Laurel could see Andy McAllister, who was playing Scrooge, swaggering about the stage. She bit her lip. It'd be her turn to go on in just a minute.

Laurel was the Ghost of Christmas Present. She was wearing a red chenille robe that was so long it dragged on the ground, and a crown made out of plastic holly leaves. She had to speak sixteen whole lines, but if she was thinking about her sister and her aunt the whole time, how would she be able to remember them? And the set—she'd worked so hard on it! Annie would be so surprised when she saw what a great job she'd done.

But Annie wasn't here.

"Who was you lookin' for, Beanie?" a sly voice whispered in her ear. Jesús—ugh! The first day of school he'd named her String Bean, then shortened it to Beanie. "The *Prez*-i-dent, maybe?"

"N-nobody," Laurel stammered. She hated Jesús.

He pressed closer. "Your mother ain't coming neither, huh?" His voice dropped to a conspiratorial whisper. For once he sounded almost . . . well, *nice*.

"My mother's dead." Laurel was somehow shocked into admitting the truth.

"Yeah, so's mine. She always tellin' me that, so I'll leave her alone. She tired all the time."

"Why's that?"

"Workin'. Sal's Pizza in the daytime, and after that, she do the cleanin' up at Sunnyview—you know, where all them old people sit around like mummies. It's 'cause my father's an s.o.b." Jesús' dark eyes flashed with scorn. "And now he's gone."

Jesús stared at the floor, his thick black bangs fanning away from his forehead.

Laurel gazed at him. Suddenly she realized he wasn't faking. All that other stuff—the mean things he did—that was the act.

She touched his arm. "Hey, you okay?"

Jesús jerked his head up as if she'd stuck him with a pin. "I'm glad he's gone," he hissed. "I hate him."

"Sh." Miss Rodriguez frowned at them, raising a finger to her lips. She flapped a hand at Laurel. "You're on!"

Laurel could feel her face going rubbery, her eyes hot. Any

second now she would be crying. With everyone staring at her.

"Behold, the Ghost of Christmas Present," Dickie Dumbrowski trumpeted in his froggy bellow.

"Be-hold, Dickie Dumb," Jesús muttered as Laurel slipped past, shocking her into a giggle. The urge to cry faded.

Gliding onto the stage, Laurel felt almost grateful to Jesús.

RUDY's voice drifted up the stairs. Where Annie was crouched, in the narrow space between the desk and the wall in Dolly's office, she couldn't hear his words, only his flat growl, like grinding machinery. Any minute now, she'd hear him creaking up these stairs. He'd find her. And then Val would come and take Laurel away.

Thank God she'd been up here when he'd come in. She'd heard the bell over the front door tinkle, then his familiar, grating voice calling out, "Hello, Dolly!" A low chuckle. "Hey, isn't that a song? Bet you're surprised to see me, huh?"

In some ways Annie was more afraid of Rudy than she was of Val. Because Rudy was so much smarter, and Val always listened to him and went along with him. Like the time when Dearie's drinking got so bad, and Rudy convinced Val to commit her to Briarwood. When she got out, she was like a zombie; she'd sit for hours and hours, just gazing at nothing. Six weeks later Annie found her mother on her bathroom floor, cold as ice, an empty Darvon bottle on the sink above her. They buried her two days after that.

And the way Rudy looked at Laurel—it was so creepy. Not talking to her much or even trying to play up to her . . . just staring at her all the time, like a fat carp eyeing a minnow.

Rudy would be a lot harder to fool than Val. Could Dolly pull it off? She wished Gloria hadn't left early; she at least would have kept Annie posted on what was going on down there.

A new thought made Annie break out in goose bumps. What if Dolly told him *everything?* She seemed so good and kind, but Annie still remembered Dearie's saying her sister couldn't be trusted.

Please, God, not now, just when things are starting to go right.

She liked working at Girod's, a lot more than she'd thought she would. And Laurel finally seemed to be settling in at school. All week she'd talked about nothing but her Christmas play. If they didn't leave now, they might miss it. But she couldn't exactly waltz downstairs and remind Dolly of that.

What would Laurel think? She'd be so disappointed . . . and probably worried to death.

I've got to let her know I'm okay.

Rivka. Maybe she could call Rivka and ask her to rush over to the school and tell Laurel she'd be late. But then she remembered, No, it was Friday evening, *Shabbat.* It was forbidden for Rivka even to switch on a light. Annie wouldn't be able to get through to her. At sundown Rivka took her phone off the hook.

Annie made herself stand up slowly. Still shaky, she reached for the phone on the desk and tiptoed with it into the tiny bathroom, where Dolly always took it when Henri called from Paris—as if she and Gloria didn't already know about them.

There *was* someone she could call besides Rivka.

She remembered Joe Daugherty's warm smile when he'd stopped in yesterday to ask her to lunch. Was he just being nice? Maybe, but at the little deli where they'd stuffed themselves on pastrami on rye, and talked and laughed for more than an hour, she'd begun to think that she'd made a friend.

Annie dialed the number quickly, before she could change her mind.

At the other end the phone began ringing over and over.

Then Joe's voice came on, sounding out of breath. " 'Lo. Joe's Place." He sounded rushed.

"This is Annie. Annie Cobb," she gasped. "Joe, I know this is going to sound funny, but—but I need your help."

She took a breath and blurted out enough of the story for him to understand why she felt so desperate. It gave her an awful upsy-daisy feeling, opening herself to him.

There was a long silence, and Annie was suddenly scared he was going to tell her he was too busy. Then he said crisply into the phone, "You're in luck. My whole crew showed up tonight, and we've got our preparation nailed down. I can be at your sister's school in half an hour. I'll take her back to your apartment and wait with her until you get there."

He got directions from her, then hung up.

Annie started to sob, pulling her sweater up over her face so Rudy wouldn't hear. Okay, they weren't really safe yet, but just knowing Joe was willing to help made her feel she'd come to the end of a long road.

LAUREL TOOK HER BOW WITH THE others, ducking her head low so that her long hair fell in front of her face. That way, nobody could see she was crying. She just *knew* Annie wasn't out there.

She crept away, stumbling down the steps that led to the auditorium floor, and was slinking out into the corridor when suddenly a large hand gripped her shoulder.

Laurel turned, looking up at a tall man in faded jeans and glasses. She could see that his eyes were smiling.

"Laurel?" he asked.

She nodded, wary.

He smiled. "I'm Joe. Annie told me to look for the prettiest girl on the stage. She sent me over here to tell you she's okay, and Dolly, too. She'll explain everything when she gets home."

Something clicked in her head: *Joe . . . the lobster man?* It had to be him—those glasses and his wavy blond-brown hair. He was just the way Annie had described him. The cold spot in her stomach eased. "Annie's really okay?" she asked. "And Aunt Dolly?"

"Sure they are. Annie said they just got . . . held up. Why don't I take you back, and we'll wait for her. How does that sound?"

"Okay." Laurel nodded. "Then you can see our Christmas tree. The one you gave us."

"Tree? What tree?"

"The one Annie traded the lobster for."

Joe stared at her for a moment, then started to laugh. "She did that?" He shook his head. "Your sister is really something." He squatted down and placed his hands on her shoulders. "She told me about . . . well, your leaving home and coming here. I think both of you are pretty brave."

Laurel felt cold again. "Are you going to tell?" she whispered.

"No," he said, his eyes steady and serious, "I'm not going to tell." And she believed him.

Now he was rocking back on his heels and rising. He held out his hand, and Laurel took it without hesitating.

She thought about Santa Claus, a fat elf in a red suit, who she used to think was a real person. Now it occurred to her that if Santa were real, he might not look like that. He might be a tall man, and young—not much older than Annie—wearing faded jeans and a blue polo shirt, with glasses that slipped down his nose and eyes that crinkled up at the corners when he smiled.

Chapter Five

It'd been more than two weeks since Nan Weatherby's appearance at Joe's Place; if the review was going to appear at all, Joe knew it had to be in this week's issue of *Metropolitan*, due out today. But Joe had been told by Mr. Shamik at the newsstand that he wouldn't be getting his *Metropolitan* delivery until sometime after four. Hours away! How could he wait that long?

Well, he'd just have to, that's all. And maybe once he read it, he'd wish he hadn't.

No one was supposed to recognize *Metropolitan* magazine's arbiter of the food scene, but Joe knew who she was. Three stars from Nan Weatherby, or even two, would bring him all the bookings he could handle. He began to feel excited, but only for a minute. Nan Weatherby, he remembered with a pang, gave mostly scathing reviews.

His father's voice, dry and measured, droned in his head: *"I can't stop you, Joseph. Your grandmother left that money in your name, and it's yours to do with as you wish. But let me say one thing: You'll fail. Inside a year you'll be out of business. You'll fail us."*

Joe looked around the kitchen. He remembered Dad's seeing it for the first time and declaring, *"What this place needs is a wrecking ball."*

You're wrong, Dad, he thought. I'm not going to fail. But if I do, it's on my head. I'll never come begging to you.

Joe headed up to the dining room. He'd hired Laurel to letter menus for him, and he found her at a booth in back, exactly where he'd left her hours ago. A stack of completed menus was piled at one elbow. At a glance Joe saw that she'd done something extraordinary. He'd only intended for her to neatly write in the appetizers, entrées, desserts, and their prices. But this . . .

Picking up a finished menu from the pile, he saw that every corner and blank space was filled with delicate, exquisite ink drawings: morning-glory vines twisting around the borders, a bird's nest with tiny speckled eggs, a crested spoon with a top-hatted mouse sipping from it. Joe felt a tremor of delight travel through him.

Leafing through one menu after another, he was so awed that he all but forgot about the *Metropolitan* review. Laurel had done this? She was just a *kid*. These looked like the work of a Beatrix Potter.

Did she have any idea how talented she was?

Her pictures made him think back to Christmas. After Mom and Dad's annual holiday get-together, Joe had headed for Brooklyn, planning to surprise Annie and Laurel. But the surprise was on him. Walking into that shabby living room, he'd felt so good, instantly enveloped in warmth and Christmas spirit. Dolly had gotten there ahead of him, armed with a mountain of presents. But the way Laurel had looked at him when he handed her the shopping bag of gifts he'd brought for her and Annie—it was as if he'd presented her the moon on a silver platter.

Now, gazing down at her as she sat motionless except for the scratching of her fountain pen, Joe was struck by her loveliness. "Laurey," he called softly, Annie's nickname for her. She looked up at him and blinked. Joe held up a menu. "These are really something. I mean it. Who taught you how to do this?"

Laurel blushed, but he could see how pleased she was. "I learned how myself," she said. "Mostly I just draw what's in my head."

"That's quite an imagination you have."

Her color deepened. "Well, drawing isn't the only thing I can do. I'm learning how to sew. I made this." Proudly she smoothed the front of the plaid shift she was wearing.

He whistled. "I'm impressed. Your sister show you how?"

"Annie?" Laurel laughed and rolled her eyes. "She says she doesn't have the patience."

Joe thought of how restless Annie always seemed—even sitting, she couldn't quite keep still. And those alley-cat eyes of hers . . .

"Somehow that doesn't surprise me." He smiled. "But *you* . . ." He tapped the stack of finished menus. "These should be in a book or hanging on someone's wall. They're too good for this."

Laurel looked down. "Thank you for saying so. It's very nice of you," she said primly, but her smile was radiant. "But it's just for fun, really. When Miss Rodriguez catches me during class, she thinks I'm not paying attention. But you know what? I *think* better when I'm drawing. Know what I mean, Joe?"

"Sure I do. I feel that way when I'm making an omelette."

"Huh?"

"Come on down to the kitchen with me, and I'll show you."

Downstairs, Joe showed her how to crack eggs one-handed, and Laurel expertly whisked the eggs.

Seeing the glow on her face, he could almost—*almost*—forget that his career as a restaurateur might soon be demolished.

The buzzing of the service door cut through the kitchen noise.

Joe went to answer the door, and a tall figure in a dripping coat rushed in. Annie. "Joe, you'll never believe it! It's incredible! Oh, I'm all out of breath. It's pouring cats and dogs. And I ran six blocks without stopping."

Annie's face was flushed as she tore at the buttons of her shabby, sopping coat. Underneath he spotted a copy of *Metropolitan* magazine rolled up, and he felt his heart lurch.

"Three stars!" she cried, throwing her arms around him. "Oh, Joe, I'm so happy for you! Isn't it wonderful?" She drew back, flipping open the magazine. "And just listen to this: 'As soon as you walk through the door, you feel as if you're in a cozy country inn, with deliciously hearty food to match. The grilled salmon and spicy venison stew were worthy examples of regional cuisines elevated to the level of haute. . . .'"

Joe couldn't speak or move. Then in a dizzying rush it came to him: the rent, the payroll, and his overdue wine bills. He'd be able to pay them all and one day, maybe, take another floor.

A sound like wildly chiming bells rang in Joe's head.

"Joe!" Annie was pulling at his arm to get his attention. "Your phone. It's ringing!"

Joe rushed into his office and snatched up the receiver. Probably his first reservation from the review.

"Joseph, is that you?" No one but his mother called him Joseph. He felt himself tense.

"Darling!" She rushed ahead without waiting for him to speak. "Dad and I just saw it. It's marvelous, isn't it? Hugs and kisses and all that. And can you guess who just called me? Frank Shellburne. You know Frank, always looking for a tax dodge. Well, when he read that review, he wanted to know immediately if you'd consider selling out. I told him I'd have a word with you, and maybe you two could set up a meeting. Joseph . . . are you there?"

"I'm here, Mother." But his excitement was gone. "I'm here," he repeated dully.

"Promise you'll at least consider it," she said. "Daddy says it's not too late to squeeze you in next semester at Yale—"

"Mother, I have to go," Joe cut her off. "Look, do you want me to put you and Dad down for one night this week? If you ate here once, you might be surprised. Hell, you might even like it."

"Joseph, there's no need to swear. If your father could hear you . . . And don't pretend you don't go out of your way to needle him. I should think you would want to keep in mind Dad's heart condition. You know, you can be very selfish at times."

"I know," he said softly. "Mother, I have to go. Good-bye."

Slowly, carefully, he lowered the receiver. Standing in his tiny, cluttered office, he looked out the iron-barred window. He felt something brush up against him and jumped a little, startled. It was Laurel. She slipped her hand into his and gazed up at him as if she knew exactly how he was feeling. Was he that transparent?

Joe felt touched. He could hear Annie in the kitchen, her strong voice ringing out, and he wanted to plunge into her bracing presence, as if into a cool shower.

"EIGHT dozen . . . nine . . . ten . . ." Annie stopped counting and looked up from the trays of chocolates. "Dolly, how are we ever going to have these ready in time?"

She picked up a bonbon—chocolate specially ordered for David Levy's bar mitzvah, each one meant to go inside its own little silver foil–covered box. Except the printer had screwed up. He'd sent boxes with FOREVER, JAN AND JEFF, instead of MAZEL TOV, DAVID! And the bar mitzvah was tomorrow!

"We'll have to find *something* to put them in," Dolly said. "Oh, dear, how could this have happened?" She fiddled with her fuchsia scarf. In the two months she'd been working at Girod's, this was the first time Annie had seen her aunt looking so rattled. "I promised the Levys something really special."

"I have an idea," Annie said, feeling herself grow excited as she spoke. "We could wrap these in foil and put them inside three or four piñatas. I'll bet Laurey could make them."

As soon as the words were out, Annie wondered if she should have given her idea more thought. Mexican piñatas at a bar mitzvah?

"Piñatas," Dolly repeated, as if musing aloud. She began to chuckle, and then her chuckling rose into a full-bodied laugh. "I love it! It's brilliant! But I'd better call Mrs. Levy first." Dolly raced up to her office, where she kept her Rolodex.

When she returned, Dolly was bubbling over. "She was a little skeptical at first, but then she started to see how cute piñatas would be. How did you ever think of such a thing?"

Annie leveled her gaze at Dolly. "When I was little, Dearie gave me a birthday party with piñatas." She swallowed hard. "Dolly," she blurted out, "what happened between you and my mother?"

Dolly's sigh was more than a sigh—it sounded like the air being slowly let out of a tire or a balloon.

"Lord . . . it was all so long ago." She tried to smile. "It started with Val, I guess. Though, looking back, I believe your mama did me a big favor, marrying him out from under me."

"Val?" Shock rippled through Annie. "You and *Val?*"

"Oh, well . . ." Dolly's hand fluttered to rest on her full bosom, and this time she managed a weak smile. "Like I said, it was all such a long time ago. I don't honestly remember *what all* I felt for him." She straightened, pulling herself together with what appeared to be a great effort. "Now, what about those piñatas? Why don't you call your sister and see if she's up to the job."

Annie had the feeling there was more to Dolly's falling-out with her mother than just Val, but she didn't press her. Did she want to risk hearing something that might make her dislike her aunt? Annie called Laurel from the storeroom phone and asked if she'd be willing to make the piñatas. Laurel said she'd be thrilled to do it. She gave Annie a list of materials to pick up on her way home.

Annie grabbed her coat and was heading for the door when she stopped and turned back to give Dolly a quick hug. Looking up, she saw there were tears in Dolly's eyes.

"Thanks," Annie mumbled.

"What for?" Dolly seemed genuinely not to know.

"For . . ." She was about to say, For being there, for giving me this job, for being so nice to Laurey and me, but all she said was, "For everything."

SOMEONE was following her.

Annie had first noticed him as she was leaving the shop, a thickset man in a rumpled khaki raincoat. And now he'd been following her for blocks. Why? What could he want? He had to be connected to Val or Rudy. A private detective, maybe. Or else why would he be following her?

Annie felt a pocket of cold form about her heart.

You're being ridiculous, she told herself. Dozens of people, thronging the sidewalk, headed this way for the subway. Why should she imagine this man was after her?

Annie saw a variety store up ahead and ducked into it. Roaming the aisles, taking her time, she collected some of the items on Laurel's list: balloons, crepe paper, poster paints.

As she stood in line at the check-out counter Annie tried to forget about the man in the khaki raincoat. She had probably imagined the whole thing.

And she believed it, too.

Almost.

SITTING in a darkened East Village revival theater, Dolly felt her stomach knot with tension. She peered at her watch. It was getting close to midnight, the movie almost over.

Was he sitting somewhere nearby, she wondered, or up in one of the front rows? She had failed to spot him when she came in, but he'd probably slipped in after the movie started.

Meet him afterwards in the lobby, he'd said. Weird, his wanting to meet her here. What was he on—some kind of nostalgia kick?

The theater wasn't crowded. Dolly, not wanting to be recognized as the now aging star of the picture up on the screen, had chosen a seat in the back row. Right now she was watching a tightly corseted ten-foot image of herself sob, "How did I get myself *into* this?"

She was laughing, and it felt good. Why, she had about as much in common with that woman up on the screen as a green tomato had with a grackle. Sure, her acting might be a joke, but she'd come a long way since then.

Now the credits were rolling, the lights coming on. People were shuffling to their feet, filing toward the exit.

Dolly didn't budge. She was afraid, worried stiff about the man who supposedly was waiting to meet her in the lobby.

Rudy Carrera.

What could he want this time? She shivered at the memory of his call last night. There had been something in his voice. . . . No, not *something*, but something *missing*. He hadn't seemed desperately curious or terribly eager. It was as if he already knew.

Dolly felt her heart start pounding with dread.

It *had* to be money. Why else would he have called her? Because if he already knew how to get to Annie and Laurel, then what did he need her for?

Now, slowly rising to her feet, Dolly saw that she wasn't alone. A man hunched way down in the first row was getting up, too, making his way up the aisle. There was something about his troll-like body, that strutting cock-of-the-walk gait, that made her feel cold all over.

"Rudy." She almost choked saying it.

He stopped. "Hey, Dolly, nice seein' you again." He was eyeing her calmly, with amusement. "You know, I never saw *Dames in Chains* when it first came out."

"Not many people did."

"Too bad. You were terrific in it."

"Cut the crap," she hissed. "What is it you want?"

Rudy glanced around. "Let's get out of here," he said. "You know a place where we can talk?"

Up the avenue at an all-night deli, Rudy ordered two coffees and a pastrami on rye. Waiting for his sandwich, he lit a cigarette, leaned back, and squinted at her through the drifting smoke.

"I found them," he said.

Dolly felt as if she'd stuck her finger in a light socket. "What are you talking about?" she hedged.

"Look, I had an investigator friend follow Annie home the other day." Rudy patted his breast pocket. "I have the address right here."

"What do you want?" Dolly snapped.

Before he could respond, the waitress arrived with their coffee and an obscenely thick pastrami sandwich. He bit into it with relish, tearing off a huge chunk and chewing for what seemed like an hour. Finally he swallowed and dragged a paper napkin across his mouth.

He stared at her, his piggy eyes boring into her. "What do I want from you? Just a little cooperation." He tipped his chin back, eyes narrowing in concentration. "Set up a meeting with Laurel. I don't want to frighten her by popping up outa the blue."

Dolly was breathing too quickly. He was really scaring her now. It took a minute before she could say, "Why should I?"

"Because you want what's best for her, that's why." He was staring at her in a way that made her itch all over. "Because I'd guess you feel guilty as hell about what you did to Eve, and you want to make it up to her kids. Am I right?"

Dolly felt as if he'd somehow stripped off all her clothes, as if she were stark naked. She wanted to get out of there fast, leave this creep, and never see him again. But she forced herself to sit perfectly still. This was for Annie and Laurel, not for herself.

"What about Val?" she asked. "How come he's not here?"

"Val doesn't know about this, and I intend to keep it that way."

A shiver rippled up Dolly's spine. "Listen, buster, you better not have any perverted . . ."

"Hey, hey there." From the pouches of flesh on either side of his squashed-looking nose, his small eyes peered reproachfully. "You think I'm one of *those* creeps, get it out of your head. I just want to see the kid. Talk to her, get to know her a little. She's my niece, too, you know. I want what you want."

"Why now? I don't get it. And I sure don't see why *I* should help you."

Rudy's face darkened; then he pulled himself up and grinned. "Maybe because of the deal I have in mind. Your silence for mine. Even-steven."

"Wh-what?" she stammered.

"When I *do* talk to Laurel, you wouldn't want it to leak out just *who* it was that handed her mother in to Senator McCarthy, now would you? And in exchange I'll trust you not to say a word to Annie of our little . . . arrangement."

Dolly felt as if every drop of blood had been drained from her body. "You bastard. You're doing this to get back at Val. That's it, isn't it?"

"No, you've got it wrong. It's not that at all." He leaned forward slightly, color rising in his pasty cheeks. "I don't want to get *back* at Val. I just want something of his."

"What about Annie? How do you plan on keeping this from her?"

"Leave that to me."

Dolly knew then that she had lost. And that once again she would be dragged into deceit and betrayal. She'd have to lie to Annie, set up Rudy's meeting with Laurel behind Annie's back. Because if Annie ever found out, she'd grab Laurel and run away all over again. Dolly wanted to weep.

With Henri in Paris with no hope of his ever getting a divorce, she couldn't bear the thought of being without her nieces as well.

I betrayed my sister, Dolly thought, her heart feeling as if it were being ripped apart, and now I'll be betraying my sister's child.

"Why does it have to be a secret?"

Laurel peered at Uncle Rudy in the watery gloom. The aquarium at Coney Island seemed like a funny place for her to be meeting him. Aunt Dolly had said it wouldn't be any different from going to the park with her. But on the way over here in her chauffeured Lincoln, her aunt had explained that Uncle Rudy wasn't going to hurt her or tell on her—he just wanted to see her and make sure she was okay. But if that was all, then why had Dolly's face looked all puffy and red, as if she'd been crying? And why was Uncle Rudy now making her promise to keep this a secret, even from Annie?

Uncle Rudy had been nice, leading her through the shimmery-green walkways and pointing out the different kinds of fish. He hadn't tried to hug her or even hold her hand—she would've *hated* that. And he hadn't said one word about her and Annie running away . . . until now.

"Trust me," he told her. "It's better this way."

"But if Aunt Dolly knows, then shouldn't Annie know, too?" she asked. "If I told her . . . If I explained that you—"

"Look," he cut her off, "you're a big girl, so I'm gonna be straight with you." He leaned close. "Val . . . your dad . . . that night you ran away— By the time I got him to the hospital, he was out of it. The doctors did everything they could for him, but he . . ." Now Rudy was looking away. "He didn't make it."

Dead? My father dead? Laurel felt suddenly hot and dizzy. Then she remembered, Aunt Dolly had said she'd spoken with Val on the phone. So how could he be dead?

"It's not true!" she cried. "He *isn't* dead! Aunt Dolly would've told me."

"Your Aunt Dolly, she's looking out for you and your sister . . . just like I am. She knows what'd happen if this got out. If the police knew it was Annie that . . ." His voice trailed off.

Laurel shuddered, remembering the blood on Dearie's Oscar and on her blanket. "Annie didn't mean to. I know she didn't!" She was almost sobbing now.

"Sure, *I* know that." Now he was clumsily patting her shoulder. "That's just what I told the police—that it was an accident, that he must've fallen and hit his head on a table or something."

"You didn't tell them about . . ."

"Annie? Of course not. That's what I'm trying to tell you. I'm on your side. From now on, whenever I'm in New York, I'll visit you, and if you ever need anything, all you have to do is just pick up the phone and call me. Collect. But it's gotta be our little secret."

Laurel gulped back her tears. "But why can't Annie know?"

"You want her to know she's a murderer?" His voice was a gravelly whisper. "A thing like that, it could really eat away at a person . . . and maybe wind up pushing them right over the edge."

Like Dearie . . .

Laurel could feel tears running down her cheeks. A manatee swimming close to the glass seemed to be staring out at her, its eyes big and sad and eerily human.

"I won't tell," she said, her voice a ragged whisper.

She didn't feel so dizzy anymore, and the watery dimness of the walkway had settled enough, so she could finally breathe. She actually began to feel a tiny bit pleased with herself.

Even if Annie didn't know, Laurel told herself, *she* would. She'd know that she was doing something important, that she wasn't just some dopey little kid dragging her sister down.

She'd know that in a kind of a way she was taking care of Annie, just like Annie had always taken care of her.

PART TWO: 1972
Chapter Six

ANNIE, curled in the deep, swaybacked mission oak chair in Joe's living room, watched Laurel unwrap the birthday gift she'd given her—a beautiful lacquer box containing watercolor paints and a set of delicate brushes.

"It's Japanese," Annie told her. She remembered the hole-in-the-wall Oriental art store down on Barrow Street where she'd found it, and the elderly Chinese man who had waited on her. When she'd told him it was for her sister, who was turning eighteen, he'd given her a sheaf of handmade rice paper to go with it.

"Oh!" Laurel gasped, staring down at the box, tracing with her fingertip the mother-of-pearl rose on its lid. "It's . . . Oh, Annie, I love it."

She was sitting cross-legged on the Navajo rug near the couch where Joe sat, her shoulder almost grazing his knee. Now she was twisting around, holding the box up for him to see, as if this gift

Such Devoted Sisters

from Annie were something she was offering to *him* instead. "Joe, look, isn't it beautiful?"

"Beautiful," Joe agreed. And then Annie saw that he was looking not at the box, but at Laurel.

Barefoot, in her faded jeans and embroidered Mexican peasant blouse, her bright hair shining about her shoulders, Laurel looked so radiant, unaffectedly lovely, that Annie felt a stab of envy.

"I love it!" Laurel turned and beamed at Annie. "You always pick the perfect thing, and it's something I can really use."

"That's what sisters are for," Dolly piped. "It's up to aunts to give you *useless* things you'd never in a million years buy for yourself. Here." She thrust a small robin's-egg-blue box at Laurel—from Tiffany's, Annie could see at a glance. "Happy eighteenth."

Annie smiled, thinking of the little blue boxes like that one stacked inside her dresser drawer, six of them—one for every birthday since she'd come to New York. She watched Laurel open the box. Inside was a gold heart locket with a tiny diamond in its center.

"You're absolutely right." She laughed. "I never would have bought it. I couldn't have afforded it. But I love it. And I love *you* for thinking of it."

"My Sarah, she has such a locket," Rivka said, "with a picture of her husband." From her seat beside Joe on the sofa, she cast a meaningful glance at Laurel. If Laurel were Rivka's daughter, Annie thought, she wouldn't be going back upstate to finish her second semester at Syracuse University. She'd be getting married, too. Annie, at twenty-four, was an old maid already.

As if she'd read Annie's thoughts, Rivka sighed and said, "I still can't get used to it, you girls living in Manhattan. I should have to ride the subway an hour to see my two California *shainenkes?*" For the past five years Annie and Laurel had been renting an apartment in this building—a tiny one-bedroom, two flights up from Joe's.

"Next time, we'll come to you," Annie promised.

"And next time I come to Manhattan," Rivka teased, shaking her finger at Annie, "it will be to dance at your wedding."

Annie, blushing, fought the urge to glance over at Joe.

Rivka rose from the sofa. "Now, who wants cake?" She had made it herself—kosher, of course—carrying it all the way here in a hatbox on the D train from Avenue J.

"Do I get to blow out the candles first?" Laurel asked.

"Not until you open my present," Joe said. He got up and went into his bedroom, reappearing a moment later holding a small, square package clumsily wrapped in tissue paper.

Laurel unwrapped it slowly, revealing a hand-painted wooden box. Inside was a braided silver band.

"The Indians of Mexico make them," Joe explained. "They're called friendship rings."

Laurel was silent as she stared at it, seemingly mesmerized by the light flashing across its surface. Her head was down and her hair was curtaining her face, so Annie couldn't see her expression. Then Laurel looked up, a quick glance before looking down again, and Annie saw why she wasn't jumping up to hug Joe—her eyes were bright with tears, and her cheeks stained a deep red.

Then it hit her: *She's in love with him.*

After what seemed like an eternity, Laurel got up awkwardly and kissed Joe, not on the cheek, but on the mouth, deliberately lingering a split second longer than was merely polite.

"Thank you, Joe," she murmured.

Joe looked pleased, Annie saw, but also a bit embarrassed.

Images flashed through her head: Laurel, a skinny twelve-year-old, running along the sidewalk to catch up with Joe. Laurel in the kitchen at Joe's Place, kneading bread dough alongside him. Laurel, nestled up against Joe, watching *Invasion of the Body Snatchers* on TV, burying her face in his shoulder during the scary parts.

She's in love with him. The thought repeated itself in Annie's mind over and over. She'd always known it, hadn't she? The difference now was that Laurel was no longer a knock-kneed kid.

But that wasn't what was making Annie's heart bump up into her throat, she realized. It had suddenly occurred to her that Joe might be falling in love with Laurel.

Why not?

At eighteen, Laurel seemed older than most girls her age. Still a little dreamy at times, but so poised, gracious, and adept at doing things, like her artwork and sewing her own clothes. My little wife, Rivka used to call her. And so what if Joe was thirty-one? Lots of guys went for younger women. And lately Joe had been talking more about finding a wife and settling down. What would be so—

Stop it, she told herself. You're being ridiculous. Sure, Joe loves Laurel, but he loves her the way he'd love a little sister.

The way he loves me.

Annie felt a sharp pain in her chest. *Did* Joe look at her that way, as just a good friend—a sister, sort of?

She had first realized she was in love with Joe a few months ago, but she hadn't had the guts to tell him, not yet. Maybe in a few days, after Laurel went back to school.

"Happy birthday to you! Happy birthday to you!" Dolly's robust contralto broke into her thoughts. And now Joe was joining in. And Rivka, too, in a wavery soprano. *"Happy birthday, dear Laurey. Happy birthday to yoooouuuu!"*

Annie watched Laurel take a deep breath and, with her eyes fixed on Joe, blow out the candles on the cake.

I don't need a crystal ball to know what she's wishing. Annie felt guilty for wishing the same thing for herself, but, damn it, why should Laurel have any more of a right to Joe than she did? At Syracuse there had to be dozens of guys chasing after Laurel. In no time at all she'd be mooning over one of them, and Joe would go back to being no more than a big brother.

While Rivka was cutting the rich coconut cake and Laurel was passing out slices, Annie went over and sat down next to Joe. "How did it go last night?" she asked. "You know, with your party?"

Joe's Place had just branched into catering, and she knew they hadn't yet ironed out all the kinks. The restaurant, though, was almost running itself now and was fully booked almost every night. In the past six years it had become a Village institution.

"Not bad," he told her. "Except the lady's oven fritzed out, and we had to sweet-talk the next-door neighbor into letting us use hers. Other than having this ditsy neighbor crash my client's black-tie party in her sweatpants, it went okay. You still so dead set on opening your own shop?" His eyes, behind his round steel-rimmed glasses, were mildly challenging.

"I'd like to . . . if I ever get it together. You know, little details like knowing how to make chocolates and having enough money." She shrugged, keeping her voice light, as for one tantalizing moment she allowed herself to think about an apprenticeship in Paris. What better way to learn how to make her own chocolates than under Henri's Monsieur Pompeau, who had been turning out mouth-watering confections for Girod's for over fifty years? But she didn't want Joe or anyone else to know how desperately she wanted this. What if Henri didn't come through with the apprenticeship? And what if the money from Dearie's trust that she'd been counting on to start her business had somehow vanished, stolen by Val, whose silence all these years worried her almost as much as his lechery once had?

"I'm not worried about you," Joe said. "Anything you really want, you'll find a way of getting it."

Looking into Joe's flashing green-brown eyes, she longed to wrap her arms around him and see if his heart was racing the way hers was right now. *Oh, Joe, if you knew what I was wishing for now, would you still be so sure I'd get it?*

"What are you guys whispering about?" Annie looked up and saw Laurel standing over them, a plate of cake in each hand. She was smiling, but her eyes had narrowed the tiniest bit.

"You, of course," Joe teased. "I was wondering—now that you're eighteen and all—if you're finally going to introduce us to your mystery boyfriend."

"I don't know what you're talking about!" Laurel was trying to laugh, but the color in her cheeks was giving her away.

It was nothing new, this secretiveness of hers, but Annie wondered now, as she had a hundred times before, *What is she hiding?* All those evenings, getting home from work to find Laurel not home. She'd always say that she'd been doing homework at a friend's house or had stayed late at the library, but she'd cut her eyes away when she said it, and her cheeks would color.

"Then how come you're blushing?" Joe ribbed her, his eyes twinkling.

"I'm not!" Laurel's hands flew to her reddening cheeks, but her smile looked strained.

Joe, probably sensing he'd gone too far, tried to smooth things over. "Okay, okay. Forget I said anything." He wiggled his eyebrows, adding in a low, mock-seductive voice, "Maybe I'm just jealous. Maybe I want you all for myself."

Annie felt herself grow hot. Why was she getting so upset? Joe was just kidding around, same as he'd been doing with Laurel forever. Why should now be any different?

You know, even if Joe refuses to see it.

Enough. She had to tell him how she felt, before Laurel ended up getting hurt.

Now Dolly was standing up, reaching for her purse. "I'd like to make a little announcement," she said, looking straight at Annie, smiling, her face pink with anticipation. "I know this is Laurey's big day, but honey, I have something for you, too." She pulled out an envelope and handed it to Annie. "Go on," she urged, "open it."

Inside the envelope was an airline ticket—to Paris. She stared at it, numb with shock.

"I talked to Henri," Dolly gushed. "It's all arranged. One week from today you'll be working under Monsieur Pompeau."

"It's . . . so soon," Annie managed to get past her frozen lips.

"Sorry I couldn't give you more notice, but the other apprentice starts then, and Pompeau wants you both at the same time."

Now the numbness was beginning to fade, and feeling crept back in. She felt a burst of sudden joy—Paris! She was finally going to be a *real* chocolatier, not just an assistant manager in a shop.

Then her joy wilted. Three and a half months without Joe. Now it didn't matter if she told him how she felt. Either way, they'd be apart. And Laurel . . . Well, Syracuse was a lot closer than Paris. Maybe with Annie out of the way, Joe and Laurel would—

"Well, *say* something, for heaven's sake!" Dolly threw up her arms. "If I have to lose the best manager I've ever had, the least you can do is be happy about it."

"I . . . I don't know what to say." Annie stood up and hugged her aunt. "I don't know how to thank you."

And Annie *did* feel grateful, but at the same time she couldn't help thinking that Dolly had picked absolutely the worst moment to play fairy godmother.

AT THE Air France check-in desk, Annie heard her flight being announced. She turned to Joe. "I'd better go." She bent down to grab her carry-on bag, but Joe got to it first, hefting it easily.

"I'll walk you to the gate," he said.

"You don't have to."

She felt so awkward standing there with Joe in the middle of the international-departures corridor, the two of them acting more like strangers on a blind date than best friends. She felt a sudden urge to grab him and shout, I love you, damn it! Why can't you see that?

But of course, she wouldn't. Instead, she just trudged alongside Joe, sneaking sidelong glances at him. Why didn't *he* say something, *anything*, to let her know how he felt, if he was going to miss her?

He didn't speak until they reached her gate. Putting her suitcase down, he reached up to touch her cheek, his fingers cool and light. "I'm not going to promise to write. I'm lousy with letters."

"Well, I'll probably be too busy to write back, anyway." She looked down so he wouldn't see her disappointment.

"Annie"—he hooked a finger under her chin, tilting her head back—"that doesn't mean I'm not going to miss you." His crooked smile was fading now, his eyes serious.

"Joe, I . . ." She felt a high, throbbing ache in her throat.

Over the PA system the final boarding call was being announced. The lounge, she saw, was nearly empty now.

"I'd better go," she finished weakly.

She was about to turn when he caught her in his arms and pulled her close. He kissed her full on the mouth, a deep kiss that pierced her heart. *Dear God, is this really happening?*

A happy, stunned heat flooded through her, making her feel heavy and light-headed. Pulling back and looking into Joe's eyes, she sensed that under that calm surface he felt as shaken as she did.

Say it, she willed. Say you love me. You want me.

But all he said was, "So long, kiddo."

Annie, moving away from him, toward the ramp to the plane, half hated him for that—for kissing her, for letting her go off to Paris, where she knew she would dream about that kiss for weeks and weeks, not knowing exactly what it meant.

LAUREL stared at the naked man lying in front of her.

Dark hair down to his shoulders, a bandanna knotted about his forehead, his lean muscled torso just a shade lighter than the burnt-sienna pastel crayon she was using to sketch him with.

He looked about her age. There was something about him—an edge . . . a tautness. She sketched furiously, using bold, sweeping strokes. There. She was getting it now.

Laurel found herself thinking of Joe, imagining it was Joe she was drawing. In less than an hour she'd be on a bus heading home. And with Annie in Paris, Laurel, for the first time, would have the apartment—and Joe—all to herself. She prayed that tonight, when she got there, he'd be home.

Would things be different between them now? Could he begin to see her in a new light?

Thinking of Joe, Laurel felt herself blushing, and when she looked back at the model, she saw that he was staring at her with his tea-colored eyes. Stretched languidly on his side on a bench in the center of the classroom, he looked familiar. Was he a student? He wasn't in any of her classes, but she might have seen him on campus.

After class, as she was putting away her pencils and pastel crayons in her box, the boy sauntered over.

"Not bad." Flicking his hair off his shoulders, he stared at the sketch she'd done of him.

"Thanks." Laurel was relieved to see he'd put on some clothes—patched jeans and a dark blue T-shirt. Even so, having him so close, chatting with her after she'd been staring for forty-five minutes at his . . . well, *all* of him—it made her feel weird.

"You're trying to remember where you know me from, but you haven't figured it out yet, have you, Beanie?"

Laurel started and looked up. It hit her then: *The little boy in Miss Rodriguez's who'd made her life so miserable.* "Jesús," she cried, "no wonder I didn't recognize you. Last time I saw you, you were about five feet tall, and—"

"And I was wearing clothes." He grinned, as if he knew his frank, carefree nakedness had made her uncomfortable.

Laurel could feel the heat in her face seeping up into her hairline. Was it that obvious? Could guys tell just by looking at her that she was inexperienced . . . a virgin? Was that why Joe treated her like a kid?

"It's Jess now, not Jesús," he answered. "Jess Gordon."

"I heard you'd gone to a foster home after your mother died."

"You heard right. My foster parents, the Gordons, wound up adopting me. Beats me how come—I was murder in those days." He laughed an easy, rich laugh. "But *you* weren't scared of me."

She shrugged, and glanced at her watch. Ten to four—she'd better get moving if she was going to get down to the Greyhound terminal in time to catch the next bus to Manhattan. But Jess, with his mocking smile, was holding her somehow. "I guess I had bigger things to worry about back then," she told him.

She thought of Uncle Rudy. . . . Uncle Rudy, who had become her "mystery boyfriend."

All through that first year, then junior high, and Music and Art High School, Rudy would just show up there three or four times a year and take her for a ride in a limousine. Sometimes she'd catch him looking at her so hard it made her feel creepy inside. But he never touched her—not a hug, not even to hold her hand.

"Listen," Jess was saying, "me and some others, we're organizing this antiwar rally for next week. You interested?"

"Maybe."

She was against the war, sure, but all she really cared about right now was getting home to Joe. "I could help you out with posters. But I'm in kind of a hurry right now." Laurel saw that Jess was staring at her, his dark eyes hooded. He had an edge that made her blood pump faster. She shuddered, feeling suddenly scared.

Of Jess?

Maybe it wasn't Jess who scared her; maybe it was Joe—the thought of what he might do or say when she . . . when she . . .

But *could* she? Could she really make it happen? Could she make Joe love her *that* way?

Now Jess was shrugging. "No problem, Beanie," he said, tipping her a sly wink, as if he could read her thoughts. "I'll give you a call."

JOE stared at her. "Laurey, what are you doing here?"

She was wearing some kind of Indian smock made of crinkly raspberry-colored cotton. Tiny round mirrors were sewn into the bodice, and they glittered in the light.

"Joe!" She hugged him and kissed his cheek so lightly, so quickly, his senses barely had time to record it. "Surprised?"

"Let's just say I wasn't expecting you."

"Does that mean you aren't going to invite me in?"

"Actually, I was just on my way out." Seeing her look of disappointment, he explained, "My mother. I promised her I'd catch this opening down in SoHo. You want to come along?"

"I'd love to." He saw her eyes light up and felt a short, sharp tug inside his chest.

He knew that look; he had, in fact, been avoiding it for a very long time. He'd pretended it wasn't what he thought it was. And now she was here, and, truthfully, was it such a surprise? Hadn't he known deep down that she *would* come—that he'd have to face this sooner rather than later?

But what was he supposed to do? What could he say that wouldn't break her heart, make her hate him?

"I thought you and your parents weren't getting along," Laurel said as they were strolling toward Seventh Avenue to catch a cab downtown. She tucked her arm into his.

"Well, we're not talking *Make Room for Daddy* here," he countered. "But yeah, I guess things are loosening up a little. Get this— last week my mother and the great Marcus Daugherty finally deigned to eat in my restaurant. I'm thinking of having a brass plaque inscribed and put over the table where they sat."

"Don't make fun, Joe. I think it's nice that they came."

"So do I, actually." He *was* glad . . . or maybe just relieved. This tug-of-war between him and his parents had been going on so long, he didn't feel the least bit smug about the fact that he'd won.

As they reached the corner, Joe watched the neighborhood greengrocer unpacking a box of oranges onto his sidewalk display.

Remembering that Laurel might be hungry, Joe asked, "Have you eaten? There may be some wine at this art show, but not much in the way of edibles."

"It's okay," she said. "I had a sandwich on the bus."

"Come on. That long ride—you've got to be starved." Leaving her on the sidewalk, he ducked into the market and grabbed a handful of the tiny, tart kumquats he knew she loved. On impulse he snatched a yellow rose from a bucket by the register. Returning to Laurel and handing her the fruit and the rose, he saw her eyes widen in delight.

Watching her bite into a kumquat, her mouth puckering at its tartness, he thought, Boy, she's beautiful. Those blue eyes, with their thick dark lashes. And those lips . . .

He realized he wanted to kiss her. Very much.

I must be losing my mind. What about Annie?

Annie. He loved her, he missed her, and, damn it, yes, he wanted her. For months, years even, he'd put off telling her how he felt. It was too soon. He wasn't ready to get serious. But gradually, when the prospect of a wife and kids no longer seemed part of some nebulous future, he began looking at Annie with new eyes. Did she love him? Maybe. But was she really ready for a husband, house, kids? No. She was on fire, needing to *prove* herself somehow. Wait, he'd told himself. Wait until she wants this as much as you do.

But why, if he loved Annie, was it Laurel he felt drawn to now? What was it about her that made him want to hold her, lie down beside her, sink into her as he would into cool, still water?

Get a grip on yourself. This isn't a movie, he told himself. This is real. Somebody could get hurt. Hurt real bad.

But it wasn't until a few hours later, back from the opening, that Joe realized that one of the people who might get hurt could be him.

He'd intended to wind up the evening with a quick good-night peck, but as he was letting himself into his apartment Laurel clung to him and whispered, "Let me stay with you tonight, Joe." Her voice was quiet, controlled, but he could hear the slight tremor in it. He knew her so well; he knew it was when she was scared that she acted the most nonchalant. In that way she and Annie truly were sisters.

Joe felt as if he'd been sucker-punched. Had he heard right?

"Laurey, I . . ." His voice choked up on him. He cleared his throat and took her hand. "Look, I have a feeling that no matter what I say, it's not going to come out right, and I . . ."

I'm in love with your sister. Is that what he meant to say?

But was it even true? How could he be in love with Annie if he felt this attracted to Laurel?

"I don't want to hurt you," he finished, feeling weak, cowardly. Hearing footsteps below, he gently pulled her inside and shut the door. It was dark, but he didn't reach for the light switch.

"You don't love me," she said. "Oh, I know. You love me, but you're not *in* love with me. Is that it?"

She laughed shakily; then with a fierceness she said, "Joe, this isn't some crush. I love you. I always have."

Before he could stop her, or stop himself, she was slipping her arms around his neck, drawing him to her. He felt her flesh against his, cool and silken, and her lips soft and sweet. He wanted to tear himself away, stop her from pulling him in the wrong direction, but her mouth . . . her sweet mouth . . .

She's just a baby, he told himself. He had to stop this before he took a path that would lead him forever away from Annie.

Joe drew away, trembling. "Laurey, this isn't . . . us. It's just, well, things are a little up in the air right now."

"Annie, you mean." Her voice was shaking; he could hear the tears close to the surface. "You think this has to do with Annie being gone. That I'm somehow . . . that I'm just *overreacting.*"

"No. This has nothing to do with Annie." He could tell from the way she was looking at him that she didn't believe him.

"Okay, then." She pulled in a deep breath and reached for the door knob, twisting it sharply. "Okay." Forcing a smile that appeared almost ghastly, she said, "Well, good night."

She opened the door and walked out, her shoes clicking against the stairs with hard, rapid strokes, and Joe, watching her go, ached. He ached to wrap himself around her, make love to her. But if he did that, wouldn't he be hurting her even more?

Chapter Seven
Paris

ANNIE watched as tiny white-maned Monsieur Pompeau peered into the pot of melted chocolate—or *couverture*—she had been stirring.

She held her breath, her heart racing. After two weeks she still had trouble melting chocolate without scorching the bottom or causing the cocoa butter to separate. Gauging the temperature—that was the tricky part.

So far the chocolate looked okay—dark brown and satiny. Still, she felt herself tense as Pompeau dipped a spoon into the pot and raised it to his lips. This afternoon he would tell Henri Baptiste whether she had any promise as a chocolatier. And if the report was bad, Henri would feel he had to dismiss her. Apprenticeships at Girod's were precious, the waiting list endless.

Pompeau's wizened face puckered as he ceremoniously tasted the *couverture*. "*Non, non, c'est gâtée!*" he pronounced sadly. "The bouquet, he has gone away."

Annie felt numb. All around her, figures in starched whites were bustling about the large kitchen. Light sparkled off the copper caldrons, the marble counters, the refrigerator doors.

"You permitted it to make the vapor, you see that? And now he has become like mud. *Regardez cela!*"

Annie peered into the oversized double boiler on the cooktop in front of her. Instantly she saw he was right. The lake of silky dark brown chocolate had begun separating into grainy lumps.

"I'm sorry," she said, struggling against the urge to cry. "I thought I was doing it the way you—"

Pompeau cut her off with a wave of his hand.

"*Non, non!* The words I tell to you, they are only words. The *chocolat,* you must know *here* when it is right." He tapped his breast.

"Let me start over. I'll get it right this time. I—"

Again he cut her off, this time with a flap of his white apron, shooing her away as if she were a stray alley cat that had wandered in.

At the other end of the long cooktop Emmett caught Annie's eye and gave her an encouraging thumbs-up. Thank God for Emmett. Always there with a wink or a smile.

Signaling to her, he lifted a coffeepot from the counter and poured *filtre* into two thick white china cups. Coffee break. At nine thirty Pompeau allowed them a luxurious ten minutes. But could it be that late already? She'd started work at six a.m., and it seemed as if hardly an hour had passed. They'd have to move fast, before the nougat syrup bubbling on the stove peaked.

Annie followed Emmett into a small storage area. He walked with a jaunty stride, broken by a slight limp. He wore a red Henley jersey stretched across a chest as thick and solid as a hickory stump, faded jeans, and snub-nosed cowboy boots that clacked on the tile floor. If he hadn't told her about his crippled foot, she might never have guessed it was more than a slightly twisted ankle. Ask him about it, though, and he'd give her that big smile, wide as Texas, and drawl, "Only handicap I got is these here freckles. Must've stood in front of a screen door too long with the sun shining through."

Annie liked Emmett's freckles. She liked everything about Emmett, from his coppery hair to his faint Texas twang, which he exaggerated when he was kidding around. He'd grown up in Texas, but since leaving home, he'd been all over, working on a beef ranch in El Paso, as an oil-field roustabout in Oklahoma, and in Louisiana as a shrimper, a boat builder, and a cook aboard a merchant ship. He seemed to have lived enough to be fifty instead of only twenty-nine.

They settled into a pair of rickety folding chairs set near a narrow table, and Emmett hiked his leg onto one of the extra chairs.

"You look like a mile of bad road," he told her. "Take a load off, Cobb. Old Pompeau's not so mean. I'll bet he drinks hot milk before bed and sleeps with a night-light. A regular old pussycat."

"An old concentration camp guard is more like it."

Emmett laughed. "Pompeau, he's not the problem. It's *you.* My guess is, whatever's eating you, he's twice as tall and ten times better-looking. Boyfriend back home, right?"

"Are you always this nosy?"

"Fraid so." He grinned.

"Well then, I guess you won't mind if I get a little nosy with you."

"Fire away."

"You never told me how you ended up here. I mean—chocolate?"

He shrugged. "Not much to it. I was working as an assistant pastry chef at Commander's Palace. You heard of it?"

"New Orleans. It's famous, isn't it?" She remembered Joe's mentioning it.

"You could say that. Anyway, turns out Paul Prudhomme, chef at the restaurant, and Henri Baptiste are old friends. Old Paul puts in a word, and next thing I know, they got me munching croissants."

Annie laughed. She found herself staring at him. Somehow she'd always thought of freckles as a flaw, but on Emmett they . . . well, they suited him. Made him even more rugged-looking. With his blue denim eyes and square features she could imagine him leaning against a split-rail fence, the mud-caked heel of one cowboy boot hooked over the bottom rail.

"I still don't quite get it," she said. "Why this? Why here?"

Emmett shrugged, and smiled. "Like you, I was figuring on having my own business one of these days."

"You sound like maybe you're having second thoughts."

"Could be. I'm beginning to think this is gonna be just one more dead end for me."

"Why don't you leave, then?"

"It suits me fine . . . for now."

"And after that?"

He brought his boot heel clopping to the floor and leaned so close she could feel his warm breath. Holding her gaze, he spoke with an intensity that startled her. "Land. Property. Buildings. My old man, he owned zip and was proud of it. Soon as he and Mom got settled in somewhere, it'd be time to move on." His eyes took on a feverish light. "When I do settle down, I mean to sink my roots so deep they'll be pulling them up in China."

"But owning things—that's not a living, not something you *do* every day," Annie persisted. At the same time she thought of Bel Jardin and felt a longing for her childhood home that brought a hot ache to her belly, as if she'd gulped her coffee too quickly.

"Owning," Emmett echoed. "Way I look at it, more you own, the more it'll keep your livelihood from owning you."

Annie understood. Security. That was something she'd never known, not even as a child. She realized Emmett had fallen silent and was staring at her.

"So, what about you? What are you doing here?"

Before she could say anything, they were interrupted by Pompeau's shrill voice crying, "Nougat! Nougat!"

Annie and Emmett rushed in just as Pompeau was pouring the kettle of hot caramel and nuts onto a long marble slab.

"*Allons!*" shouted Pompeau, signaling for the men to hurry.

Emmett rushed to the table, along with the two full-time helpers—Thierry and Maurice. The men descended on the pond of hot nougat with metal paddles, beating at it determinedly to flatten it before it cooled and became too brittle to work with. Then Annie watched Emmett begin cutting the warm, flattened nougat into even squares with the "guitar"—a tool with metal strings that looked like an oversized egg slicer.

Suddenly she became aware that Pompeau was staring at her, his small blue eyes hard as bullets. The despair she'd felt earlier came rushing back, but then something inside her stiffened. "Show me," she said in a firm voice. "Please. One more time. I want to learn."

Pompeau, she was half surprised to see, merely shrugged. "*C'est facile*," he said mildly. "Come, again I will demonstrate for you."

She followed him over to the cooktop. While Pompeau worked, dropping brick-size chunks of chocolate into the big double boiler, he explained how it was required that the chocolate be heated gently, as gently as you would bathe an infant. Now came the hot cream that would turn the melted chocolate into *ganache*—the truffle's soft center. He poured the cream into a separate pan and heated it. When it was almost hot enough to boil, he strained it through a wire colander into the melted chocolate.

After gently stirring the *ganache* until it was smooth and mocha-colored, the old man carried it over to some horizontal wooden doors, covered in silicone-treated paper, that were resting on metal shelving at one end of the kitchen.

"Monsieur Henri, this is his discovery." Pompeau beamed. "Clever, *non?* We could not find the trays large enough, so we find the old doors rescued from the demolished buildings."

Pompeau was now pouring the *ganache* in a dark, silky river onto the uppermost door. With a broad spatula he smoothed it, coaxing it outward to meet the edges of the paper. Then he stepped back. "*Voilà.* You see? No grains, no lumps. *Parfait.* It will cool, and then we shall do the enrobing."

On the other doors different flavors of *ganache* stood cooling; they would form the centers of Girod's world-famous truffles—bittersweet chocolate with soft mocha-Champagne centers, a puree of fresh raspberries in a smooth milk chocolate *ganache,* white chocolate and fresh-grated coconut dusted with ground pistachios from Sicily. Her own favorite was bittersweet and crème fraîche flavored with an infusion of smoky Lapsang Souchong tea.

An idea came to Annie, a way she might be able to redeem herself. *What if I created a whole new flavor? And did it so perfectly that even Pompeau and Henri would be impressed?*

It might work. It might also backfire. But hey, she'd taken a lot bigger chances than this, hadn't she?

Annie concentrated hard. Then she remembered the little bistro where she and Emmett had eaten the other night. After their cassoulet the waiter had brought a basket of pears—the best she'd ever tasted.

Chocolate and pears, would they go together? Maybe. But what if instead of fresh pears, she combined the chocolate with Poire William? She'd seen a bottle of the liqueur once, with a whole pear inside. The pear was grown that way, she'd learned, with the bottle positioned over the branch while the fruit was still a tiny green nub.

Of course, she'd have to ask Pompeau. But how? *Doesn't matter. Just do it now, or you never will.* Her throat seemed to tighten; then somehow she was telling him. She was sure he'd turn her down, or worse, laugh at her. But after a long moment he nodded.

"*Bien,*" he said. "To create a new flavor, it is more difficult than you imagine. But this way, perhaps, you will understand."

Yes, that I won't ever be any good at this. He's hoping I'll fail. Annie pulled her apron ties even tighter, knotting them so that they cut into her waist, making her stand up straighter. Then despite the panic in her cinched-in stomach, she went into the storeroom to get the chocolate she would need.

EMMETT, hoisting a tub of warm *couverture* from its seat on the tempering machine, winced slightly. His bad leg hurt him, though he'd never let on.

Then as always when his leg ached, he was remembering Atlanta, all those black people marching for what they wanted. Just happening by, Emmett had seen a black kid, no more than twelve or thirteen, pinned to the pavement by a slab-armed man twice his size who was beating him with the butt end of a shotgun.

Emmett remembered roaring as he dived at the man. The next thing he knew he was lying in a hospital bed, his mother's face hovering over him like an Arctic moon.

"Bullet sheared off half your anklebone. And three toes. Some muscles, too. . . . But don't worry. The doctors say you'll walk again." Spoken like it was nothing worse than a sprained ankle.

Emmett was jerked from his reverie by a hand on his arm, firm but gentle. He turned and saw Annie. Thin face, saved from mere prettiness by strong bones. Huge eyes the color of blue ink. No makeup, but then she didn't need any. Skinny as a rail.

"Let me give you a hand with that," she said, reaching for a handle of the heavy tub he was hefting.

He smiled. "Thanks, but I can manage. Just don't offer me your foot. I might take you up on it."

"Not funny." But a corner of her wide mouth curved down in a small don't-make-me-laugh smile.

She didn't move away. She was standing so close, he could smell her perfume—something musky and Oriental—overriding even the pervasive aroma of chocolate. There was a smear of chocolate on one cheek. He thought about licking it off.

Emmett felt panicky. What had come over him? He wasn't some teenager. He'd had plenty of women.

Suddenly he knew that if he took so much as a step in her direction, he could fall in love with Annie.

And, with Annie, he suspected that if he fell, it would be a long, hard fall.

ANNIE stared at the small chilled metal box she was holding. Inside was a single truffle, its glossy black coating of *couverture* dusted with toasted bitter almonds crushed to a fine powder.

Was it any good? Over the week, Annie had made fourteen batches of her pear *ganache,* and everyone around here who'd tasted her Poire William truffle had said they loved it. But Henri would be the judge—the only one who counted.

Annie mounted the narrow staircase leading up from the kitchen to the shop, which faced out onto the fashionable Rue du Faubourg St.-Honoré. Her hands shook a bit, but she forced herself to ascend briskly, one foot after the next.

What if he doesn't like it? What if it really is nothing special? Even so, she mustn't let it destroy her. She *mustn't*.

At the top of the stairs she passed through a narrow door and into the shop itself. She paused on the threshold, a bit dazzled. Girod's was like no other chocolate shop. It looked more like a reproduced nineteenth-century room in a museum: an Oriental carpet; muted gold-flecked wallpaper above walnut wainscoting; on one wall, glass shelves on which artisans' works were displayed.

What Annie loved best of all were the chocolates themselves—on all sides, displayed on silver trays like precious jewels, and in fluted crystal dishes. But right now Annie knew it was Henri to whom she needed to devote all her attention. He caught sight of her and grinned, his mustache twitching up at the corners, his broad face creasing. "Ah, how does it go, Annie!" he called. Then, looking beyond her, he added, "And Bernard, how is it that you do us the honor of climbing the stairs in the middle of the day?"

Annie realized with a jolt that Pompeau had followed her. Of course, the old fussbudget couldn't resist seeing her make a fool of herself. Her cheeks burned, but she wouldn't give him the satisfaction of seeing how nervous she was.

Behind her she heard Pompeau give a low, raspy chuckle. "I may be of a certain age, but in a few weeks, when I take the baths at Baden-Baden, I will be made young again. And you?"

Henri sighed, and something dark, like a cloud shutting out the sun, flitted across his face.

He misses Dolly, she realized. She knew because she'd so often seen the same sad expression of longing on Dolly's face. They only saw each other every other month, and the letters and phone calls in between were clearly not enough to bridge the gap.

But if Henri was sad, he seemed determined not to let it show. As Pompeau stepped past Annie, Henri strode over and clapped the old man's stooped shoulder. Then he kissed Annie on both cheeks, greeting her as if he had not seen her in years. "Annie, Monsieur Pompeau here—he has not terrorized you, I hope, into losing your voice, hmm?" His gray eyes shone with kindness and good humor.

"Monsieur Henri, I don't wish to impose on your time," Pompeau began, "but Mademoiselle Cobb—"

"It's a new flavor we came up with," Annie abruptly interrupted. "We'd like your opinion." If Henri hated it, she'd take the blame, but until then, she didn't want him to be prejudiced by her inexperience.

She handed him the box, her heart pounding. Henri peered at the lone truffle for a long time, examining it the way a doctor might study a wart. Then as Annie watched, her every nerve strung taut, he popped the truffle into his mouth and chewed thoughtfully.

Just as she thought she couldn't bear the suspense a moment longer, Henri smiled.

"*Formidable!*" he pronounced. "It has a marvelous texture, and the taste . . . sublime. Bernard, I compliment you. This is an achievement. And will do well with our customers, I am certain."

He thought the old man had done it! She felt sick. What should she do now?

"I . . . you see . . . it was . . ." She watched Pompeau flush a brick red and begin to sputter.

Then something occurred to Annie. Maybe letting him take the credit could help her even more than if she took it for herself.

"Monsieur Pompeau has a gift like no one else," she put in quickly. "It's such a privilege for me to work with him."

Had she gone too far? Then she saw how the old man was puffing up with pride. The glance he shot in her direction was one of pure delight. Good, she'd made the right choice. It was to Pompeau that she had to answer each day, not Henri. And if Pompeau decided to like her, to take her under his wing, she could really *learn* from him.

Annie felt a surge of happiness that seemed to fill her with bright light. She was magic. Nothing could stop her.

"You're not enjoying this," Emmett whispered.

Annie felt a stab of guilt. Their big evening out—a chamber music concert at the Sainte-Chapelle—and she was ruining it for Emmett. Under the spotlight, the cellist was playing Mozart, the music resounding in this soaring space with a clarity she'd never before heard. But she couldn't concentrate, couldn't keep her mind off Joe.

Two months, Annie thought, and not a phone call. Even now with Emmett she felt a loneliness so deep it ached in the pit of her stomach. It had to be partly this place, too, this heavenly music—too much loveliness could break your heart. Especially feeling as miserable as she did.

"It shows?" she whispered to Emmett.

"We don't have to stay."

"But . . ."

Before she could remind him how much he'd spent for the tickets, she felt him tugging her to her feet. Together they slipped down the narrow aisle alongside their row of chairs. Outside, in the stone courtyard abutting the entrance, Annie turned to him and said, "Em, there's absolutely no reason for you to miss the concert because of me. I can make it home on my own."

"Listen, Cobb, I've got an even better idea." He hooked an arm about her shoulders. "I know a café not far from here. When you're feeling low, a Pernod and a shoulder to cry on beats Mozart any day."

"Stop being so nice! You're making me feel even more guilty."

"In that case, I'll let you pay for the drinks."

"Okay." She laughed. "It's a deal."

As they strolled in the mild summer evening Annie glanced at Emmett. He was wearing gray slacks, and a tan blazer over a white button-down shirt. She couldn't help thinking how handsome he looked; he could have passed for a young lawyer or stockbroker—except for his boots. Annie had never seen him without those old cowboy boots—tanned leather rubbed smooth as driftwood.

She felt a surge of gratitude toward him, for being a friend and at the same time not putting even the slightest romantic pressure on her. After all their weeks of working together so closely, he'd never even kissed her good night. Crossing the Seine at Pont St.-Michel, Annie wondered what it would be like if Emmett kissed her. She felt suddenly, acutely conscious of the warm weight of his arm draped about her shoulders.

The crowded sidewalk café was only a pleasant walk from the bridge. Annie and Emmett waited a few minutes until they spotted a couple leaving and then quickly slid into their seats. "You want to talk about it?" Emmett asked after they'd ordered.

"No," she said. "There's really nothing to tell."

"Let me guess—tall, dark, and handsome?"

Annie felt her face flush. She looked at Emmett and saw that he was wearing a languid smile, his blue eyes flicking over her as if trying to read her. But she sensed the empathy behind that smile.

"There's no reason for him to get sentimental just because I'm here and he's there," she blurted in a firm voice, more to convince herself than Emmett. "I mean, we're just good friends. Why should he suddenly start writing me love letters when he's not in love with me?"

"But you're in love with him." Emmett's gaze fixed on her, mildly challenging.

"No! I mean . . . well, maybe. Oh, Emmett, I don't know anymore. How long can you stay in love with someone who doesn't feel the same as you?"

His eyes narrowed, as if he were gazing into bright sunlight. "A long time, I reckon."

Annie knew he wasn't just talking about her, but before she could probe further, a waiter appeared with their drinks.

Soon, feeling light-headed from the Pernod, Annie said, "I lied before, when I told you I wasn't sure if I loved Joe. I do. Why is that so hard to admit?"

"Because you're afraid of making a fool of yourself," he said. "You're not alone, Cobb. Most folks'd rather be hit by a bus than be made a fool of. Specially in love."

"If only I *knew* how he felt, then . . ." She shrugged.

"You sure it's *him* holding back? Or could it be that it's you?" He tipped his head to one side, eyeing her with some amusement.

Annie, feeling his words hit home, stared into her empty glass. She realized with a ripple of unease that she was a bit drunk.

"I think I'd better be getting back," she said. "I don't know about you, but getting up at five every morning means that by ten o'clock at night I'm ready to turn into a pumpkin."

He laughed. "Now that you mention it . . . yeah, you are looking a little orange around the gills."

Minutes later, recrossing the river, it struck Annie that in just a few weeks she'd be back in New York. And Emmett . . . well, who knew where he'd be? Maybe they would never see each other after that. She felt a pang, and as they stopped to watch a barge decked in fairy lights glide under the bridge, she impulsively leaned over and kissed him lightly on the lips.

Then, unexpectedly, Emmett was kissing her back, holding her so tight she couldn't have gotten away if she'd wanted to—which somehow she didn't.

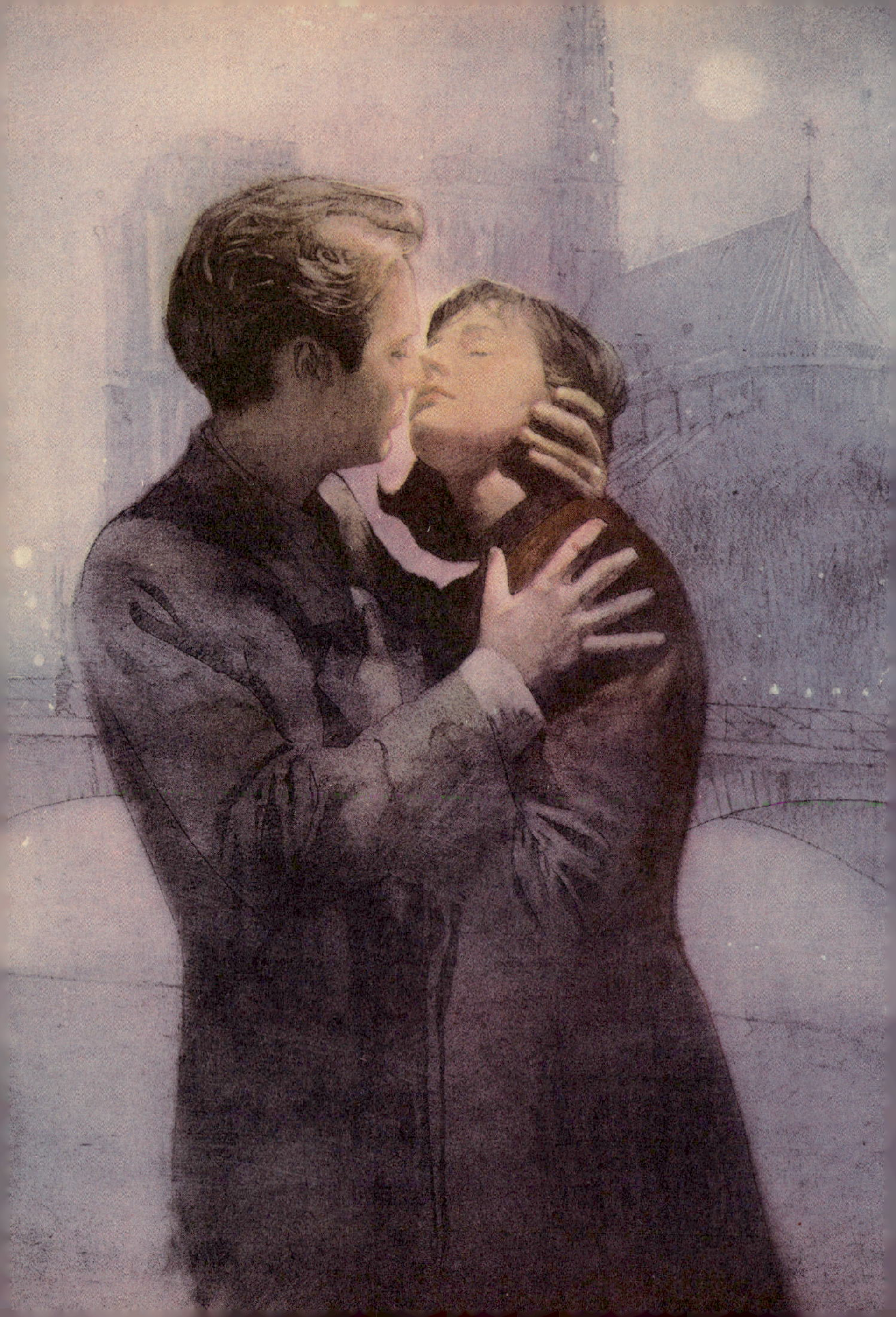

Annie felt a sharp tug low in her belly. The blood seemed to drain from her head; sparks of light danced on the insides of her eyelids. She felt heat rising in her, collecting in the hollow space where moments before her stomach had been. How could this feel so good when it was Joe she wanted, not Emmett?

Emmett, drawing away, seemed to stagger a bit, and she wondered if maybe he was a little tipsy as well. And whether if they'd been perfectly sober, this would have happened at all.

"Well," he muttered, rubbing his jaw, "where do we go from here?"

"Not my place." She gave a short, breathless laugh. "Madame Begbeder would throw us out."

"That kind of whittles it down, doesn't it?" He stepped back and grabbed her hand, squeezing it hard.

Before she could think it over, they were in a taxi, rocketing along a boulevard on the way to the Place Victor-Hugo, where Emmett was subletting. Annie felt both exhilarated and oddly resigned, as if she'd climbed aboard a roller coaster and now had to see it through to the very end.

Then they were inside the narrow, high-ceilinged salon where Emmett lived. The woman who owned the place would have smiled, Annie thought, to see Emmett, broad and rugged, clumping in his cowboy boots amid the plump satin-covered sofas and spindly Empire chairs.

I should turn around right now, this very instant, Annie thought, but she felt drawn to him. She didn't love Emmett . . . but, damn it, she *wanted* him.

Emmett, who seemed to sense her confusion, came to her and, with his arms loosely about her shoulders, kissed her forehead.

Annie felt embarrassed. "Emmett, I shouldn't have come. This is crazy. I don't love you. And you don't love me."

"And you . . . you're not the kind of girl who'd go to bed with a man just for the fun of it, right?" He was mocking her now.

"Not if I wanted us to stay friends afterwards."

"Is it *us* you're worried about, or this fellow back home?"

"No." She lied. "It has nothing to do with Joe."

He shrugged, and stepped back with an easy chuckle. "Hey, Cobb, you could walk right out of here this minute, and I promise you, there won't be a speck of hard feeling. On the other hand," he added soberly, "if you stay, I can promise you something a lot better."

When he kissed her this time, Annie felt it flash through her like summer lightning. In the heat that followed, she thought, Joe . . . I don't need him. And she felt a small, mean triumph.

Then Emmett was leading her into the bedroom. A massive headboard dominated the tiny space. As if in a dream, Annie lay down on the bed and let Emmett undress her. His callused fingers were rough but surprisingly tender and adept. He kissed her lips, her temple, her throat, causing her to shiver and her heart to race.

Now, watching Emmett sit down on the bed and begin prying off his boots, she wondered how seeing his crippled foot would make her feel.

When she did—its purple, puckered flesh and oddly bent shape—she felt a welling of tenderness. She touched it lightly. "Does it hurt?"

"Only when I'm walking in places I shouldn't," he said with a wry, cockeyed smile.

"Like now?"

He shrugged.

"Emmett, I'm scared."

"It's okay. I'm a little scared, too."

But he didn't seem so. Instead, he seemed utterly unselfconscious, as if this were an everyday thing, their being together like this. And then for Annie it became natural, too.

Chapter Eight

ANNIE looked around Dolly's living room, filled with party guests. Nothing much had changed in the months she'd been away. The white leather sofa faced the fireplace just as it always had. Behind it, the wet bar with its buttoned-down leather base—a relic of the early '60s. She could imagine Rock Hudson in a tuxedo leaning an elbow against the lacquered surface, sipping a martini.

But something has changed. I have.

Watching Dolly, elegant in a low-cut, ruby velvet caftan, darting among her guests, Annie felt as if part of her belonged and part had become a stranger.

She looked about, searching for the one face that would make her feel as if she had truly come home.

Joe.

Where was he? Yesterday she'd been too exhausted to see anyone until she'd had some sleep. Then late this afternoon she was jolted out of a dream by Dolly's telephoning to say that her driver would be picking her up in one hour and she was to put on her sexiest dress. Her aunt, it seemed, was making her a little homecoming party.

Annie caught a glimmery reflection of herself in the huge window. Had she overdone it with this dress? What would Joe think? It was chic, *très parisienne*—this black crepe sheath that skimmed her thighs well above the knee, adorned only by a loop of opera-length faux pearls knotted just below her plunging neckline. She'd worn this on her last night in Paris with Emmett. Remembering the obscenely expensive dinner he had insisted on, the Grand Cru wine they'd drunk too much of, and afterwards going back to Emmett's apartment, Annie, suddenly aware that her face was on fire, quickly slammed her mind shut against the memory.

Emmett. Would she ever see him again? He'd talked about coming to New York, but he didn't say when. And what difference would it make if he did come? Whatever they'd had in Paris wouldn't, *couldn't,* be a part of her life here in New York. Still, at the thought that she might not see him, Annie felt a pang of regret.

Threading her way through a cluster of people at the bar, Annie accepted the dripping glass of Champagne the barman thrust at her. Then she spotted Laurel at the far end of the bar. She looked gloomy, and Annie felt a dart of unease. At the JFK arrivals terminal, her sister had seemed so happy to see her, but in the car driving back, she'd sort of clammed up.

Something's wrong with Laurey. Annie had noticed it right away, but until now, it hadn't fully sunk in.

Annie hiked herself onto the barstool beside her sister. "What's up, Doc? You look a little down. I guess this isn't your kind of party. No Grateful Dead . . . no black lights . . . no body paints."

Laurel shrugged, smiling. "I guess I'm in the wrong place, then."

"It's not my scene, either," Annie confided.

"Hey, you're the guest of honor."

"Listen, I'm sure Dolly meant well. She usually does. But . . ."

"But," Laurel echoed.

"Remember the white stretch limousine she rented for your junior prom?"

Laurel winced. "*Red* seats. I almost died of embarrassment. And a *bar.* On the way to the restaurant Rick Warner just sat there staring out the window. It was *awful.* If Joe hadn't . . ."

"Yeah, I remember." Annie finished with a laugh. "He showed up just in time to rescue you with his beat-up old Ford." She'd heard this story many times—Laurel's coming out of the restaurant and finding Joe, who, with a conspiratorial grin, had tossed Rick his car keys and then climbed into the limo idling at the curb. "Hey, have you seen much of Joe this summer?" She tried to sound casual, but it came out false, pitched too high.

She wasn't prepared, either, for Laurel's reaction. Her sister flushed, and her eyes slid away.

Panic crept into Annie's heart. How stupid of her to have thought that what Laurel felt for Joe was just some silly girlish crush.

"Joe?" Laurel muttered. "Not much. My job kept me pretty busy." She managed a tiny smile. "Though no one ever told me that interning in the creative department of an ad agency means mostly sharpening pencils and fetching coffee."

"I guess Joe must be busy with the restaurant, too."

"I guess so."

Annie waited for her to elaborate, but Laurel seemed far away somewhere, off in her own world.

Out of the corner of her eye Annie caught sight of a familiar face—Gloria De Witt, Dolly's old assistant. She was waving enthusiastically to Annie from across the room.

"I see someone I want to say hello to," she told Laurel. "Talk to you later." She slipped off her stool and made her way over to Gloria, who slung an arm casually about Annie's shoulders.

"How does it feel to be back? You leave your heart in Paris?"

"No, I was too busy being a slave for that kind of thing," she told Gloria. Well, it was partly true. She *had* felt like a slave to Pompeau.

"Hey," Gloria said, looking at something beyond Annie's shoulder, "will you look at who the cat just dragged in?"

Annie's heart gave a little slip-sliding thump, and she turned so suddenly she nearly spilled her Champagne. "Joe," she said with a tiny gasp, but he was too far away to have heard.

He was just stepping into the living room, the lenses of his round wire-rimmed glasses flecked with September rain—rain that had also brought out the curl in his streaky brown hair.

Then his gaze caught hers, and suddenly he was close enough to touch. But she didn't embrace him. She just stood there, an unbearable awkwardness clamped over her like a bell jar.

He doesn't want me. He never did.

She found herself saying the first stupid thing that popped into her head. "I didn't know if you were coming or not."

"I got held up," he said. "Traffic jam. I ditched the cab and walked." He forked a hand through his damp curls, making them spring up in wild corkscrews. "So how does it feel to be back?"

"Good," she told him. "Still a little tired."

"You look wonderful. Fantastic. I mean it."

"Can I get you some Champagne?" She could feel herself running out of small talk. Her voice had a funny, overbright ring.

"What happens if I say no?" Joe seemed to have picked up on her nervousness and was trying to put her at ease.

She smiled. "As soon as Dolly notices you don't have a glass in your hand, the waters of Babylon will flow."

"In that case," he said, seizing her hand, "we'd better get out of here." He tugged her toward the dining room.

The prettily garnished platters of shrimp toast, crab cakes, and stuffed mushrooms that two tuxedoed waiters were passing about the living room had grown sparse. Waiters in crisp white shirts were laying out platters of food for the buffet supper. Annie saw one of them look at Joe and touch his forehead in a jokey little salute.

"I see you got the Belons," Joe addressed him, pointing at a tray of half-shelled oysters on a bed of chipped ice. "Good. I wasn't sure they'd get delivered in time."

"Close call," the youth replied with a shrug.

"*You're* catering this?" Annie whispered. "Dolly didn't tell me."

"She wanted it to be part of the surprise."

"It's wonderful . . . what I've tasted so far, that is."

"The catering is really taking off. Only problem is, the kitchen's too small to handle the extra volume, so I'm expanding."

"Won't that cost a mint? You don't even own the building." Falling back into their familiar habit of talking shop was like slipping into an old pair of loafers. She felt herself relaxing.

"I was getting to that part."

"Joe, you didn't! You actually *own* it?"

"Well, mostly it's the bank that owns it, but the deed's in my name. I was pretty lucky. My landlord was in a hurry to unload it. I would've written to tell you, but I only closed last week." He took off his glasses, wiping them with his handkerchief. "What about you? When are you going to strike out on your own?"

"As soon as I can get the bank to release my trust."

She'd had two letters from Wells Fargo out in Los Angeles, and it was still there—twenty-five thousand plus the interest that had been piling up over the years. And since she was only months away from turning twenty-five, her trustee had agreed to release the money early.

Joe cast a glance at Dolly, who was flitting through on her way to the kitchen. "You wouldn't be moving in on anyone's territory?"

"Dolly's given me her blessing. She says the competition will keep her on her toes."

"Well, of course, you have *my* blessing. Though I doubt you'll need it. You could take on the national debt and come out ahead."

Annie felt a flicker of annoyance. What was that supposed to mean—that she was some superwoman? Because she was determined and capable, she couldn't ever feel weak or scared?

Tears filled her eyes.

Then, suddenly, Joe was pulling her off to one side, through the swinging door into a narrow closet that once upon a time had been a butler's pantry. In the close darkness she felt overwhelmed by Joe's nearness and the heat of his body so close to hers.

He touched her cheek and said softly, "This isn't how I imagined it would be. I guess you can look forward to something so much that when you finally get it, you're too paralyzed to make a move."

"Oh, Joe." She could feel tears pressing like hot nickels against the back of her eyes. "Don't say you missed me, or I'll cry. Buckets. You'll think you never came in out of the rain."

She grabbed a handful of his shirt and whispered with desperate urgency, "No, say it. If you don't say it, I'll cry when I get home. I'll even say it first. Joe, I missed you. I missed you so much I thought it'd eat a hole right through me."

He gripped her upper arms tightly, but he didn't kiss her. She saw there were tears in his eyes, too. "Listen, if I'd told you how much I was missing *you*, it would've come out sounding like I'd cribbed it from *Now, Voyager*." He added softly, "I wanted to see you first, find out if you . . ."

She began to laugh, leaning against the wall behind her, weak with relief. "And all that time I was thinking—"

"What?"

"It's just . . . Oh, it seems so silly now, but I thought . . . well, that maybe you'd met someone while I was away."

His eyes cut away from hers. "There's no one, Annie."

Was he telling the truth? There had been something in his voice just now . . . and in his eyes.

She felt a stab of jealousy, but told herself quickly, Okay, so what if he went out with someone? Who am I to judge, after Emmett?

"I love you, Joe." There. It was out. She'd said it.

Joe's grip loosened, and his hands slid down her arms, finally capturing her wrists, gently . . . so gently. She felt as if her heart might burst. He brought her hands up and held her palms to his cheeks. His face felt very warm—no, *hot*—as if he, too, were burning up.

She had fantasized about this moment for so long that even now it didn't seem quite real—as if she were in some kind of dream.

"I thought a lot about how it would be when you got home," he said in a low, thick voice. "I thought about this." He brought her palm to his mouth and kissed it, and Annie thought, Yes, it is possible to die from too much happiness all at once.

She wouldn't let herself think about Laurel, about how hurt her sister would be. Later. There would be time to deal with all that later. Here, now, she wanted this moment all to herself.

"ANNIE?"

Annie was scrubbing the last of the cold cream from her face when Laurel came into the tiny bathroom and perched on the edge of the tub. Sitting there, wearing a man's T-shirt that came down almost to her knees, Laurel looked even droopier than she had coming home from the party an hour ago.

"Hmm?" Annie answered, turning back to the wide pedestal sink where she stood. In the mirror she could see Laurel's reflection, her face a pale oval set above a pair of thin, sagging shoulders. The skin under her eyes looked bruised somehow.

"I'm pregnant." Laurel's soft voice dropped into the stillness like an explosion.

Annie felt a shock travel through her, like touching an exposed wire. "Oh, Laurey." She turned to face her sister, feeling a chill that seemed to rise out of her bones.

"You look worse than I do." Laurel managed a tiny smile.

"Maybe you'd better sit down."

"I think maybe you're right."

In the tiny bedroom, Annie sat down on the bed facing Laurel, who was curled up in a flowered easy chair by the window.

"How many weeks?" she asked, determined to be sensible.

"Three *months*. Too far along for an abortion, if that's what you mean."

"Oh, Laurey, I wasn't— Why didn't you tell me?"

"I only saw a doctor a couple of days ago. I know that sounds really stupid, but you know how irregular I've always been. I just kept thinking I'd missed a couple of periods."

"Okay." Annie took a deep breath. "Do you want to tell me how it happened?"

Laurel gave a short, mirthless laugh. "The usual way, I guess."

"You know what I mean."

"You want me to go back to the very beginning? Okay, how about we start with, 'Once upon a time there was a girl named Laurel who loved someone so much she thought she could make him love her back by—' " Laurel broke off, and tears welled in her huge eyes.

She saw the puzzled look on Annie's white face and longed to cry out, I only wanted Joe to love me. And maybe deep down I thought that somehow, by sleeping with Jess, I could make Joe see that I was mature enough for him.

But for some reason she didn't quite understand, Laurel found herself holding back.

Annie longed to go to her sister, to comfort her. But there was something steely in Laurel's expression that warned Annie to keep her distance.

"Does he know?" she asked gently. "Have you told him?"

"You mean, did I make a complete fool of myself?" She sounded angry. "Anyway, it's got nothing to do with him."

"What do you *mean?* Believe me, whoever he is and whatever you think of him, he's in this with you fifty-fifty."

Laurel shot her a hard look that cut Annie to the bone. "You don't know anything about it," she said. It's not Joe, she wanted to say, but again Laurel held back.

"Well, of course I don't. You're not *telling* me anything. If you love this guy so much, why can't you tell him?"

Laurel just shook her head, staring down at the carpet.

Annie felt both hurt and exasperated. "Stop acting as if I'm out to get you, Laurey. I just want to *help* you."

"Well then, maybe *you* should talk to him." Laurel's eyes flashed.

"*Who?*"

Even before Laurel answered, Annie sensed she was about to hear something she didn't want to. In the space that stretched between her sister and her, Annie felt an invisible tunnel form, a tunnel down which Laurel's voice seemed to whistle toward her like the coldest of winds.

"Joe," she heard her sister say.

LAUREL couldn't face Annie. She stared down at the carpet, faded in spots, so that it looked sadly frayed. In her mind she could still see vividly Annie's shocked, horrified expression. But it wasn't shame that made her look away from her sister; it was something worse. She had a terrible mean urge to smile.

That was what was making her feel ashamed. What rotten part of her soul could it have come from? How could she *want* Annie to suffer? How could she have led Annie to believe that it was Joe who'd gotten her pregnant? *I saw them at Dolly's party. He loves her. It's Annie he wants. Annie, Annie, Annie.*

"Joe?" she heard her sister repeat, exhaling sharply, as if the air had been forced out by a hard punch to her stomach. "*Joe?*"

Laurel kept her eyes fixed on the carpet's balding swirls.

Should I tell her the truth?

She felt rocked by a sudden swell of shame and love. How could she hurt Annie? She loved her sister. If it weren't for Annie . . . No, she had to tell Annie about Jess.

Laurel let the memory come. She recalled exactly how it had happened. She had wanted Joe, not Jess. But Joe, she remembered, didn't want *her*. He'd sent her away that night after they'd kissed. And hadn't he told her that they couldn't ever be anything more than friends? Friends! She felt the hurt all over again, hurt that made her hollow inside, a great burning shell. Going to bed with Jess, she realized now, had just made it worse. It had been another way of hanging on to Joe, of driving the knife in a little deeper.

Now facing Annie's shocked gaze, Laurel realized something odd—the possibility of getting pregnant had never entered her mind. Not at the time. Unless deep down she had secretly *wanted* something like this to happen, something cataclysmic and final.

She hadn't told Jess, and she didn't intend to. He hadn't written or called all summer. So somehow she'd begun thinking of it as Joe's baby . . . conceived out of her love for him.

Still, she would have to tell Annie how it had really happened.

"Does he . . ." Annie swallowed with what appeared to be an effort. "Does Joe know? Have you told him?"

"No."

"Why not?"

The words were on the tip of her tongue: Because it's not his baby. She wanted to say them, but again something stopped her.

"I haven't told *anyone*," she said, horrified and amazed at her smooth cunning. Stop this! she snapped at herself. It's wrong! It'll break Annie's heart!

The way yours is broken, you mean?

Then Laurel was remembering watching them at Dolly's party, remembering how she'd felt. And how she had felt year after year, always following in Annie's footsteps. And now this—the only thing that she had ever *really* wanted—Annie had taken from her. All her longing and resentment came boiling to the surface.

"I can't think about it right now," she controlled herself enough to say. "I don't feel too good." And as she spoke, Laurel realized how exhausted she was. She felt so tired she could hardly stand.

I'll tell her tomorrow, Laurel thought.

ANNIE, gripping the banister for support, slowly descended the stairs to Joe's floor. She felt weak and frail, as if in the last half hour she'd become an old woman.

Joe's baby. No. Not Joe. Not possible. Only minutes ago she would have sworn to it, bet her life on it. But now . . .

She pictured Laurel, white as a sheet, looking both scared and defiant—almost as if she was protecting him. Why would she lie? Why would she have made up something as horrible as this?

Annie's knees buckled, and she sagged against the banister, covering her face as a sob broke loose. How could he have done this to her? To Laurel? *How?*

Anger rose in her, engulfing her. She reached the door to Joe's apartment, then rang the bell.

Joe appeared, so quietly she was only barely aware of the door swinging open. He was barefoot, holding a coffee mug.

"Annie!" He broke into a grin, which faded just as quickly. "Annie, what's wrong? Are you all right?"

She nodded, but somehow she couldn't speak.

"Is it Laurey? She looked really out of it at the party, like she was coming down with something."

It was as if he'd grabbed her, shaken her, sprung her voice free so that the words tumbled out.

"She came down with something all right." Annie shot him a cold look. "She's pregnant."

"Pregnant?"

Annie shouldered past him into the living room. She heard the door click shut, and glancing back, she saw Joe standing there.

Then in three long strides he was beside her, reaching out. Annie jerked away.

"Don't," she said.

Joe looked startled. Even more than that, shocked. As if she'd pulled off a mask and underneath was a face different from the one he'd always known. A stranger's face.

"Annie, for Pete's sake, what is going on?" He managed to grab hold of her elbow, and she could feel his fingers squeezing. "Listen, you don't think I *knew*, do you? Is that why you're mad?"

"Stop it," she hissed. She couldn't believe he was doing this, lying to her, pretending not to know anything.

"Stop what? What are you talking about?"

"How can you just . . . stand there . . . acting as if . . . as if you didn't know?"

She saw color flare along the side of his neck and his eyes grow shiny, the look he got once in a blue moon when he was about to lose his temper. But then with visible effort he dropped her arm and brought himself under control, stepping back.

"Okay, I can see you're not in any kind of mood to talk about this rationally, but do you mind telling me what you're so angry about?"

"Laurey told me. About you and . . . and everything."

There. That guilty flicker. In his eyes, just now. Unmistakable.

"What's 'everything'? What was there to tell?" His face seemed

99

to close, become unreadable. "I figured that as soon as some good-looking, artistic-type guy took her by the hand, she'd fall in love and forget she'd ever felt that way about me."

"Joe." A huge pressure was building inside Annie's head, making it feel as if her skull might split open. She felt as if she were screaming, but her voice was almost normal. "Joe, I can't believe you're doing this . . . trying to pretend it wasn't you. I *know*, damn it."

"You think I—" He stopped, cocking his head a little to one side, looking at her with stunned disbelief.

"I don't think. I *know*, Joe. How *could* you?" She was sobbing now, her whole body seeming to fold in on itself. "I trusted you! Laurey trusted you! How could you do this to us!"

"I didn't—"

"Stop it! Stop lying!"

"Damn it, will you just *listen?*"

Out of nowhere Joe's fist came looping at her, a rush of air kissing her cheek; then his hand was smashing the wall inches from her head. There was a crumpling sound, followed by small chips that struck the side of her face in a stinging hail.

Annie was too stunned to move. *That blow was meant for me. He wanted to hit me. How had all the sweetness of just a few hours ago come to this?*

Two stairs. Three . . . five . . . seven . . . eight. She counted them as she climbed them. Now she was on her landing, fumbling with her key. When she snapped on the light, Laurel, asleep on the sofa bed in the living room, jerked upright, swollen-eyed.

"Annie," she cried, "what happened? Where have you been?"

Annie collapsed in the chair by the sofa.

"Joe . . . I told him." Her voice came in quick, gasping sobs. "But he . . . he said . . ." She stopped, remembering that look of wounded perplexity she'd seen on his face.

And then she knew this had to be a nightmare because she heard Laurel cry, "Oh, Annie! I didn't mean to make you think it was Joe. Not really. It just came out that way. Joe . . . he never . . ."

Annie couldn't believe what she was hearing. She looked up, trying to focus her stinging eyes on her sister. "Are you saying Joe is *not* the father of your baby? That you and he *aren't* lovers?"

"It was someone from school," Laurel said. "Jess Gordon. I knew him in Brooklyn. It was just . . . Well, I'm not in love with him."

"But you *are* in love with Joe."

Laurel held her gaze. "Yes." No apology. No excuse.

"Why did you lie, then? Why did you tell me . . ." She started to choke and clamped her lips shut before a sob could escape.

I didn't even give him a chance to explain. I didn't believe him. Will he ever forgive me? Will he?

In a clear voice that held no regret Laurel replied, "I didn't tell you he was the father, Annie. That's just what you *heard*."

Anger flared in her—sharp, galvanizing. "Damn it, Laurey, don't you put this on me! Don't you dare! You said the words. You wanted me to believe it was Joe!"

"I didn't mean to. But when I realized that you'd misunderstood, well . . ." Now Laurel's voice caught, and her eyes narrowed. "You love him, don't you? You want him for yourself. It's not *me* you're upset about, the fact that I'm pregnant. It's just Joe. Isn't that right? Well, *isn't* it?" Her voice rose to an alarming shrillness.

Annie, before she could stop herself, was lunging forward, grabbing Laurel's thin shoulders and shaking her. "How could you? Damn it, how could you? Haven't I always watched out for you, done everything for you? How could you do this to me? How?"

Framed by the absolute whiteness of her face, Laurel's large, clear eyes seemed to cut right through Annie's. "You never asked," she said with a bitterness that seemed utterly unlike the Laurel she had always known. "You just assumed that wherever you went, I'd follow. But Annie, you never asked. You've always done just exactly what *you* wanted. Maybe for once I'd like to be first."

Annie stepped back, stunned by the force of the sudden hate she felt. How could she hate her own sister so? Right now she had to keep her arms locked at her sides to keep from striking her.

"Do what you want, then," she snapped. "Just don't expect me to be there when you *do* need me."

Chapter Nine

ANNIE stared at the empty coffee shop with the FOR LEASE sign in its boarded-up window. Ninth Avenue between Fourteenth and Fifteenth—definitely not a great neighborhood. Could this be the right place? Shivering as gusts of wind whipped around her,

Annie glanced at the address Emmett had given her. This was it, all right. But what a dump! She noted the empty half-pint bottles littered in front of the door, and her heart sank even further.

Annie glanced at her watch. Quarter to twelve. Emmett would be here any minute. All of a sudden she couldn't wait to see him. She marveled at how lucky it was that at what had to be the lowest point in her life, Emmett Cameron had shown up. She remembered his calling a couple of weeks after that awful night with Joe. He was in New York and had gotten a job in a real estate firm. Could she meet him for dinner that night at the Chelsea Hotel?

Seeing him waiting for her, beer in hand, at El Quijote's massive old-fashioned bar, wearing that cowboy grin, she'd felt something in her let go. And then Emmett was walking over, hugging her, so solid. She'd felt safe, grounded, and at the same time oddly charged, every circuit in her body suddenly alive and crackling.

Since then she'd seen him a lot. And Emmett, thank goodness, was putting no pressure on her. That was a relief because these days all she had in her to give him was some companionship. It was Joe she still wanted, needed . . . and yes, missed. An ocean even wider than the Atlantic separated them now—an expanse of icy politeness she found herself drowning in each time she passed him on the stairs or mumbled hello to him at the mailboxes.

She'd twice tried to apologize in the past four months, but she knew her being sorry just wasn't good enough. She sensed she had broken something precious, something that could never be made solid again.

"Hey there, early bird."

Annie turned to find Emmett walking toward her, his red hair flecked with snow. She felt warmed just seeing him. He fished a ring of keys from his pocket and unlocked the metal accordion gate, then the front door.

"Don't look so gloomy, Cobb," Emmett told her when they were inside. "It's second class, but it's not the South Bronx."

Annie eyed the empty circular holes in front of the counter, where stools had been ripped out. Cigarette butts and cellophane wrappings littered the worn-down, warped vinyl tiles. "It's not exactly what I had in mind," she began gently.

"Look, it's a rathole. But a good cleaning crew and a few coats of paint, and you'd be halfway there."

That might be true, she thought, but even with this place fixed up, it was a far cry from Madison Avenue. On the other hand, she reminded herself, she couldn't afford Madison Avenue.

And there was Emmett, looking so confident, as if one slap of a paintbrush would do it all. She could see how he might have talked that syndicate of doctors into buying the loft building his boss hadn't been able to sell. Already Emmett's commissions had to be substantial. Soon, she bet, he'd be buying property on his own.

No more funky clothes, either. He was wearing a rich-looking camel-hair coat over a finely tailored gray worsted suit. The only memento of the old Emmett was his cowboy boots—tanned and creased with age, but saddle-soaped and newly heeled.

Annie ran a finger along the grimy counter. "Oh, Em, I don't know. . . ." She looked around again. "Well, I'll definitely think about it. And I'll want to look at it again with a contractor."

"While you're thinking about it, how about grabbing a bite with me? I know a great deli just a few blocks from here."

Annie was tempted. But she'd planned on dropping by Joe's restaurant to see the new addition, which had to be nearly finished by now. An excuse—really, she just wanted to see him. And at the restaurant he couldn't duck away or ignore her.

Still, she couldn't help feeling torn. She liked Emmett enormously. In a way she even loved him. Or at least she thought she *could* have loved him . . . if it hadn't been for Joe.

"Thanks, Em, but I've got another appointment." She cut her gaze away from his, suddenly unable to look him in the eye. "I'm supposed to meet this confectioner who's selling his equipment. I may be able to get a good deal on some of the stuff I need."

Emmett shrugged. Outside, as he was locking up, he asked, "By the way, how's your sister? Isn't she about due?"

"Not until the end of next month." Annie didn't want to talk about Laurel or the baby. Just talking about her sister, she could feel the tiny spur of anger buried in her heart begin to chafe and burn.

"Is she still thinking of—" Emmett stopped himself, seeming to hesitate about bringing up a sore subject.

"Giving the baby up for adoption? She's talked about it, but she hasn't made up her mind." Annie didn't realize how tightly clenched her hands were until she felt her nails—the chewed-down remains of them, anyway—digging into her palms.

Such Devoted Sisters

"Hey, Cobb, relax, will ya?" She became aware of Emmett touching her arm. "No need for you to be taking on the whole world's problems. Right now, shouldn't you just concentrate on getting this business of yours going?" He smiled. "If you're busy for lunch, how about dinner? My place?"

She shook her head. "I'd like to, but I'm going to a *Bris*."

"A *what?*"

"My friend Rivka's daughter Sarah just had a baby. Her third. A boy. A *mohel* does a circumcision, and there's a little party afterwards. You want to come?"

Emmett arched a brow. "Not me. The whole idea of somebody's snipping away at the family jewels makes me a little nervous."

"I always close my eyes."

"Yeah, well, you can afford to."

Annie thought about Laurel's baby. Boy or a girl? She might never even *see* it, she realized. And that would probably be best, though she didn't know how Laurel was going to live with herself.

Lately a lot of things about Laurel had been bothering her. Like her asking Joe to be her Lamaze coach. With Joe there, Laurel said, she fit in with the other couples. *Married* couples.

And Joe, damn it, had agreed. But who was Annie to say it wasn't right? What claim did she have on Joe anymore?

Annie looked at her watch. "I'd better get going, or I'll be late." She felt guilty about lying to Emmett.

Out on the sidewalk, Annie watched Emmett amble to the curb to hail a cab. When it pulled over, he held the door for her.

"Good luck," he said.

"Thanks," she said, thinking of Joe. "I'll need it."

THE framing for the walls looked complete. In some places they were already sheetrocked. The sharp, sweet smell of sawdust filled Annie's nostrils, bringing her a glad, hopeful feeling.

"I can't believe it," she said, turning to Joe. "Last time I was here, this area was just a weed patch."

He took her elbow lightly and steered her around a big coil of conduit. "We should be ready for plaster and paint in a week or so."

Annie nodded. She couldn't take her eyes off Joe. She felt as if she hadn't seen him in years. He looked the same. So what was different? And then she got it: *He's keeping his distance.* He stood close to the wall, one hand braced against an exposed stud, leaning away from her, his brown hair flecked with sawdust. Whose permission did she need to cross the three steps that stretched between her and Joe? But Annie could not bring herself to make the move.

Then he caught her gaze and said cheerily, "Listen, it's pretty noisy out here. Let's go inside where we can hear ourselves think. You feel like a cup of coffee?"

In the kitchen, Joe poured coffee into two mugs and carried them upstairs to a booth in the deserted dining room. "Everything okay with Laurey?" he asked cautiously, sipping at his coffee.

I didn't come here to talk about Laurel, she felt like shouting.

"Laurey's fine," Annie said. "Joe, I . . ." She set out to say how much she'd missed him, but the words wouldn't come.

"How's the search for shop space going? Have you found anything yet?" he asked quickly—a little too quickly.

"I think I may have," she replied. "But I haven't made up my mind yet. It's a little grungy."

"You should've seen this building before I took over," he told her. "It looked like the morning after a Hell's Angels' bash."

What Annie was seeing in her mind, though, was a hole punched in a living-room wall. A hole the exact size of Joe's fist, with bits of plaster clinging to its ragged edges and hairline cracks radiating out into the wall around it like tiny thunderbolts.

And then she became aware that Joe was leaning forward, frowning slightly. "Annie, are you all right?"

"Yeah, sure—" She caught herself. "No, I'm not okay, Joe. I don't think I've been okay since September. You don't know how many times I've wanted— Well, I *did* try to talk to you about it, to explain, but maybe it was too soon. Maybe . . ."

A strange expression crossed Joe's face.

"Look," he said, "if it means anything, I . . . I shouldn't have blown up the way I did."

"How could you *not* have?" she cried. "How could you . . . after the way I acted, the things I said?"

"You only said what you thought was true." He shrugged. "I forgave you a long time ago. But forgiving isn't the same as forgetting, Annie." His mouth curved down in a slow, sad smile. "Please, don't misunderstand me. I think maybe it happened for the best."

"The best?" she croaked. "How can you say that? Joe, I *need* you."

"You don't need me, Annie. You don't need anyone. Not really." He gave her a look of infinite sadness. "Annie, it wouldn't have worked, you and me."

She felt like a brittle eggshell about to crack. Tears flooded her eyes. She wanted to tell him, *insist* that he was wrong . . . dead wrong. But the look in his eyes said it was too late.

"I love you, Joe," she told him instead. "More than you know."

His face seemed to contort with pain; then he straightened himself and shook his head. "No, you *think* you do. But don't you see . . . love and trust, they come together in the same package. And if you try to separate them, the whole thing comes apart."

It hurt, but at the same time she thought, He's right. That was the awful part. Except for one thing. If she had never loved him, then why did she feel as if she were being stabbed in the heart?

"I think we've both said enough for now," she told him. "I'd better be going." She slid off the bench and rose to her feet.

Joe didn't try to stop her.

"Tell Laurey I'll pick her up at seven tomorrow," he said.

Right. Their Lamaze class. She felt a swift, unexpected thrust of resentment. Then it struck her: *Suppose Joe is falling in love with Laurel? She's beautiful, talented, lovable. Why shouldn't he?*

Because if she were to lose Joe to Laurel, that would mean losing Laurel as well—the only two people she really loved. And how could she keep going after that?

ANNIE watched the *mohel* squeeze the clamplike device over the baby's tiny penis, severing its foreskin with a single neat snip. Out of the corner of her eye she saw Sarah hide her face against her husband's shoulder. Annie knew how Sarah had to be feeling . . . wishing she could take away her son's pain and make it hers.

"See how brave he is! Hardly a peep," Rivka whispered to Annie. Her round face was beaming. "Forgive me if I'm kvelling, but from this boy we'll take great pleasure. He'll make us proud. I can feel it."

Then with a big intake of breath, baby Yusseleh began to shriek. Annie watched as the *mohel* calmly wrapped a bit of gauze about the newly circumsized penis and deftly pinned on a clean diaper. He handed the baby to his nervous-looking grandfather Ezra and began intoning the blessing.

Every eye in the group seemed to be on the little star of the show, but Annie was noticing Laurel, standing off to one side. She looked haggard, morose. Was she thinking that she might never hold her own baby the way Sarah would cuddle little Yusseleh?

In spite of herself, Annie wanted to go to her sister. How awful she must feel!

Then a wave of bitterness welled up in her. Why, she asked herself for the thousandth time, had Laurel wanted to hurt her by pretending her baby was Joe's?

Why?

But now Dolly was sidling over to Laurel, hooking an arm about her thin shoulders. Annie watched as the two of them went off down the dim hall leading to the bedrooms. She hesitated, then threaded her way across the crowded room and followed them.

She found them in Shainey's room, perched on the edge of the bed. In one corner stood a crib that Rivka kept for her grandchildren. Annie paused in the doorway, feeling awkward, as if she might be intruding. But how could that be? Didn't she know Laurel best?

Dolly looked up at her with a bright welcoming smile. Laurel didn't even glance up.

"Why, it's enough to make *anybody* upset." Dolly plunged into the awkward silence. "That poor little thing lying there on that table, getting snipped at like a leg of lamb."

"That's not it." Laurel's head snapped up. "That's not it at all."

"Why don't you tell me, then?" Dolly asked gently.

"It's *my* baby." Laurel locked her hands over her stomach. "I don't want to give it up, but I'm afraid to keep it. I don't feel ready to be a mother." Her voice caught. "I don't know what to do."

Annie opened her mouth to speak, but no words came out. She felt so torn, both irritated with Laurel and sorry for her. For months she'd been trying to talk to Laurel about the baby.

"Oh, you poor thing." Now Dolly was fluffing up like a mother hen while Annie watched. And then her annoyance with her aunt faded. There were *tears* in Dolly's eyes. "I've been so worried about you. About this . . . this awful choice you're having to make."

"What do *you* think I should do?" Laurel asked.

Dolly chewed her lip. "The mess I've made of my life, I wouldn't dare tell another living soul what he or she ought to do. All I know is what I would do if I were in your shoes . . . how I'd feel if I were somehow blessed with the miracle of a baby."

"You think I should keep it?"

Dolly blinked away the brightness in her eyes. "Oh, sugar, if you *did*—and I'm not saying you *should*—it would be the most loved little baby in the whole universe. Between you and me and Annie . . . why, I can't think of a blessed thing it'd be wanting for."

Annie felt a sob rising in her. Somehow, with all her bumbling, Dolly had found exactly the right thing to say.

"Dolly's right," she told her sister, managing to keep her voice clear and steady. Now she found herself walking over, sinking down beside Laurel. "We'll manage somehow. Haven't we always?"

Laurel shot her an odd, flat look. "You have. *You* always manage somehow, Annie." Her voice held a note of accusation, but only a faint one. Mostly she sounded sad. She stood up. "Excuse me, but I have to use the bathroom."

When she was gone, Annie felt defeated somehow. Weren't she and Laurel supposed to be on the same side?

Annie became aware of Dolly touching her arm, and she turned to face her. "Why didn't you ever have kids?" she asked, suddenly curious. "I mean, you and your husband."

"We tried. But Dale . . . I guess there must've been a cog loose somewhere. And later with Henri—" She broke off with a shrug.

"You miss him, don't you?" Annie said softly.

Dolly shrugged again, but Annie saw her lips tremble. "Oh, well, us Burdock gals, we don't give up so easy."

"Guess I'm pretty stubborn, too," Annie said with a laugh.

"It must be hard for you," Dolly said. "Taking the back seat this time when you're used to being up there at the wheel."

"Something like that."

Dolly surprised her by clutching her hard, squeezing so tightly Annie could hardly breathe.

"I made a mistake once," Dolly said in a fierce, hoarse whisper. "And I'll never forget the lesson it taught me. You and your sister—don't let anything . . . or anyone . . . ever come between you, or you'll regret it for the rest of your life."

RUDY stared at the bright mobile dangling over the empty crib. It was the most elaborate one in the store—an array of small gingham teddy bears, each one holding a tiny fishing pole with a nylon string attached to it, from which another teddy bear dangled.

Beside him Laurel said softly, "I like to come here sometimes in the afternoon, when I'm too tired to do any more drawing. It makes me feel . . . I don't know, connected somehow. Like I'm really having this baby. Like I'm really going to be a mother."

Rudy felt his heart catch. With her stalwart expression not quite hidden, Laurel reminded him suddenly of her mother—how Eve had looked when she was pregnant with Laurel.

As he thought about what he had to talk her into, Rudy's heart began to pound. He'd have to be careful how he put it to her. Because if she knew he wanted the kid for himself, she'd never buy it.

He felt a sharp longing, like a stitch in his side. A child. His own kid. Somebody who'd look at him and see not a fat little pygmy, but just good old Dad.

"You like to come here just to look or what?" he asked, praying she wouldn't say she had already bought a bunch of this stuff and had it back at her apartment sitting there ready for the baby.

"Just looking. I mean, what's the point of buying stuff if—" She stopped, sucking her breath in sharply. In a low voice she added, "I've been thinking . . . What if I kept it? The baby, I mean. Oh, I know it'd probably be horribly selfish of me. I mean, a baby should have a mother *and* a father, but well . . . I can't help wanting it, can I?" Her blue eyes shimmered, and she caught her lower lip in her teeth, as if to keep her tears from spilling over.

Rudy leaned close. Here was his opening, his chance. "Listen," he said, "I might be able to help. I have someone who would be interested—*real* interested."

"You mean . . . in adopting?" Laurel's voice dropped to a whisper. Her eyes looked back at him, huge, scared-looking.

"Yeah, that's right."

"A family?"

Rudy felt himself beginning to sweat.

Tell her it's you. Explain how you'd be the best dad any kid could have, that he . . . or she . . . would lack for nothing in this world.

"Well, see . . ."

"Because it'd have to be," she said. "Otherwise, I wouldn't even consider it. I mean, if my baby wasn't going to be part of a family— a real *family*—what would be the point?"

Rudy took a deep breath. "They don't have any kids, so they're not a family *that* way . . . but the sweetest couple you'd ever want to meet," he began. "Husband's a real estate developer; wife raises dogs. Puppies running around everywhere. They've been trying for years and years to have a kid, but the doctors tell them it doesn't look too good. Nice people. They'd be terrific parents."

"Did you tell them about me?" She looked stricken.

"Hell, no. I wouldn't do that. Not without talking to you first."

He could tell Laurel was struggling. "I don't know. . . ." Her gaze drifted off in the direction of the teddy-bear mobile. She pushed at it gently, making the little bears dance. She was trying very hard, he could see, not to cry.

Now, he told himself. He had to really pitch it before she backed away. "You'd be doing it for the baby, not for that couple," he told Laurel. "And for yourself. You're young. Why go and mess up your life now? Think about it, Laurel. I mean, *seriously.*"

"I *am*." Whipping around to face him, she said sharply, "I think about it every day. And do you want to hear something really crazy? For the first time I'm glad my father is dead. I'm sure it would've hurt him to know I was somewhere out there where he couldn't reach me."

Rudy felt a prickling under his wool scarf. He wanted to tell Laurel that there was no need for her to mourn Val, but how could he without admitting that he'd lied to her all those years?

"You wouldn't be giving it away," he told her instead. "Not like that, not like giving away something you didn't want. You'd be giving him something good, a chance at a normal life."

Now Laurel's eyes were narrowing suspiciously. "Why are you doing this? Why do you care so much?"

Easy, he told himself. Don't push or you'll blow this.

Rudy shrugged. "Hey, if it's a crime to care about somebody," he said lightly, "then call me guilty."

She touched his arm. "Uncle Rudy, I didn't mean . . ."

"I know." He smiled. "It must be tough, what you're going through." He watched her chew her lip, and felt a flicker of hope.

"Can I think about it?" she asked.

"Sure," Rudy told her. "This couple, they'll stay right where they are until you decide."

"Okay," Laurel said, "let's get out of here."

Outside, on Seventh Avenue, Rudy squinted against the sun burning its way through a milky haze. "Buy you a cup of coffee?" he asked.

"Thanks, but I'd better be getting back," she told him. "Did I tell you about those drawings my art teacher sent to a publisher friend of hers? Well, this publisher wants me to illustrate a children's book. I have to get home and start working on some sketches."

"Hey, that's terrific. I mean it." Rudy was happy for her, but he suspected her real reason for being in such a rush to get home just now was so she could be alone. "I'll give you a call sometime tomorrow," he told her. "Think about what I said."

"I will," she told him. She was looking directly at him, her eyes full of pain, and he knew she was telling the truth . . . that she would think about it. And think hard. He'd made it this far at least.

Chapter Ten

ANNIE watched Emmett stamp on the doormat as he came in, small rivulets of water cascading off his boots. She waved to him from behind the display case where she was waiting on a customer.

"I'll have one of those. Just one." The plump woman in a raccoon coat pointed a gloved finger at a tray of dark, lumpy chocolates. Not dainty like Girod's—these were the size of golf balls. A mistake Annie had made with her very first batch, which strangely, wonderfully, had turned out to be a success. The woman gave a nervous laugh. "I'm supposed to be dieting."

Annie glanced up and saw Emmett now leaning against the old marble-top shaving stand on which sat the cash register. He caught Annie's eye and winked. She quickly looked away, busying herself with wrapping the single bourbon truffle in flimsy crimson tissue and placing it in a small crimson bag embossed in gold script with the name she'd given her shop: TOUT DE SUITE.

She handed it to the woman, who was smiling delightedly. Annie felt both irritated with Emmett and happy to see him. She'd agreed to meet him for dinner, but at Paolo's, not here. It was only a quarter to six, and she wouldn't even be closing for another fifteen minutes. And after that, she'd still have to tally the day's receipts, take inventory, and check to see if her assistant Doug had really fixed the tempering machine. So why was Emmett giving her that impish smile—as if she didn't already know!

Warmth crept into Annie's cheeks as she remembered Emmett,

earlier this week, inviting her to go away with him for the weekend. She'd told him no, but he'd merely shrugged, as if he felt confident it was only a matter of time before she would cave in. After all, what was holding her back?

Annie couldn't have explained it to him. She wasn't even sure she understood it herself. When she was with Emmett, she felt this urge—a compulsion almost—to touch him, to feel the span of his broad hand covering hers, to stroke the underside of his jaw. But it wasn't love, what she felt for Emmett. It couldn't be, because how then could she still feel so strongly about Joe?

If it weren't for Emmett, she knew she'd never do anything in the evenings but drag herself home and crawl into bed. After getting up at five each morning to pick out fresh fruit at the wholesale market, then coming here, setting up in the kitchen, constantly checking that her two assistants, Doug and Louise, didn't burn anything or fall asleep stirring the huge pots of *ganache,* then racing through the rest of the day, waiting on retail customers or hailing cabs to get to a meeting, Annie was usually ready to drop. Yet Emmett's popping in was like a cool breeze on a hot day. It revived her somehow.

"You're early," she told him when the plump woman left.

"I was showing a loft in Tribeca, and I thought I'd drop in, see if you needed a hand with that tempering melter."

"Doug supposedly fixed it before he left."

"Mind if I take a look?"

"In those clothes?" As he was shrugging off his overcoat she took in his muted cashmere blazer and silk tie. "You know you're going to get chocolate all over you."

But Emmett's blazer was already off, and he was rolling up his sleeves. "Good. I'll taste irresistible, then. Make it twice as hard for you to say no to this weekend." He winked at her again, then came around to her side and hooked an arm about her shoulders. "And even if you do, I may shanghai you. For your own good. Before you work yourself to death."

Annie drew away. "Em . . ." she started to say.

He held a finger to her lips. "Later. We'll talk about it over dinner." He stepped back with a smile as slow and sure as a sunrise. "Now you close up the joint while I go check on that melter."

Grabbing her clipboard with order forms for bulk supplies from the shelf, Annie was seized by a sudden exhilaration. Tout de Suite had happened so fast—was *still* happening so fast—that even when she slept, she dreamed she was working.

She remembered her revulsion the first time she'd seen the place. Now, seeing the walls with their gay, strawberry-trellis paper and the floorboards painted country white and covered with colorful hooked rugs, she felt a rush of satisfaction. Across the front display window she'd hung white eyelet-lace curtains and fixed antique gaslight sconces to the walls. Along the top of the display case she'd placed white wicker baskets filled with slivers of almond bark for customers to nibble on while they waited.

Annie remembered how she'd feared that no one who could afford to buy fancy chocolates would ever venture into this grungy neighborhood, even if the word ever got out about how good her stuff was. And on the three wholesale accounts she'd managed to land, the profit margin was so low at first that she thought she'd never keep afloat. But since opening up six weeks ago, her retail trade had grown steadily. Hard to believe that now people were sending their drivers from as far away as Sutton Place.

Annie, suddenly too tired to stand, sank down onto the old piano stool that stood between the wall and a secondhand sewing stand crowded with jars of candied grapefruit and orange peels dipped in chocolate. From the kitchen came the dreadful broken-sounding clattering of the melter starting up. Obviously, Doug hadn't fixed it properly. But would Emmett have better luck? Maybe she'd need a new one—not that she had money to buy it.

She sighed. *I miss Joe.* The thought gripped her with sudden force, leaving her weak and breathless.

Since that day at the restaurant they'd hardly spoken. He was busy with Joe's Place and she with Tout de Suite. They smiled and nodded to one another in the hallway. Once in a while he'd chat for a moment about Laurel, who was due any time now.

These days Joe saw more of Laurel than she did. One night a week he took her to her Lamaze class, and on other nights, when he wasn't too tired, he'd phone and she'd go down and practice her breathing exercises at his apartment.

Laurel had grown secretive. She hardly talked to Annie about anything other than the book she was illustrating or Tout de Suite. Never about Joe. It was almost as if the two of them had formed some kind of . . . well, an unspoken pact.

Six months ago Annie could not have imagined she'd ever be jealous of her sister, but weirdly, she was.

So what right have I to be jealous of Laurel? Especially now. At least I have Tout de Suite, but what does she have, really? A make-believe husband, a baby she's about to lose?

Annie could hear the melter's clattering smooth to a steady hum. Relief swept through her. Well, at least she wouldn't have *that* to worry about, not for the time being. Emmett had once again pulled a rabbit out of his hat.

PAOLO'S, on Mulberry Street, was a Little Italy institution, every inch of wall space covered with autographed eight-by-ten glossies of celebrities who'd dined there. At a table against the rear wall Annie spotted a swarthy barrel-chested man in a double-breasted suit wolfing down a big bowl of spaghetti, while a couple of younger men, clearly his thuggish bodyguards, occupied a smaller table near the entrance, their eyes roaming the packed dining area.

"Are they for real?" she whispered jokingly to Emmett.

He leaned across the table and whispered, "That's Cesare Tagliosi. He's right up there in the Bonnano family. I met him through this warehouse deal my boss and I are putting together. Tagliosi and Ed Bight—the guy who's selling the warehouses—are business partners. But my guess is it's the kind of business where Tagliosi does the talking and Ed listens . . . if you get my drift."

"You mean, it really happens that way, like in the movies?" Annie asked. "I think I'd die." She caught herself and frowned. "No, I wouldn't. I'd tell him where he could shove it."

Emmett shook his head, smiling. "Sure, and the next day they'd be fishing you out of the East River. Face it, Annie, there are some things you just *can't* fight."

"I haven't come across one yet." She thought of Joe.

"Yes, you have." Emmett paused, watching as their waiter poured the wine he'd ordered. Then he looked at Annie and said, "Me. You can't fight me."

The easy smile had dropped from his face, and Annie could see now how much she meant to him. How could she have missed it before? Wasn't this exactly how she felt about Joe?

"Look, Em, I'm sorry if . . ." His hand closed over hers firmly, shutting off her words.

"No," he said, "no more excuses. Look, I'm not stupid . . . and I'm not so crazy about you I can't see straight." A corner of his mouth curled up slightly. "Not yet, anyway. I'll say it just this once, Cobb . . . and if you don't want to hear it, I won't say it again." He picked up his wineglass, gripping it so tightly Annie had a sudden vision of it shattering. "*Yes,* I'm in love with you. I *know* you're not in love with me. But if you think there's a chance you *might* be someday, even a *slim* chance, then, damn it, take it."

"Emmett, what are you asking?" Annie forced herself to meet his steady gaze. "What exactly do you want me to say?"

"Say you'll go away for the weekend with me. Just that. I'm not asking for the moon, Annie Cobb."

"Just the sun and the stars," she replied lightly, suddenly too exhausted to argue.

He smiled faintly. "Yep. That's about the size of it."

Annie stared at his sturdy hands, at his knuckles big as knotholes in fence posts. She thought, So why is it so terrible to want him even though you don't love him? It's been so long . . . and what am I saving myself for anyway? Not Joe, that's for sure.

Thinking of Joe, she felt her heart bump. She looked down, feeling Emmett's gaze on her.

"Don't lead me on, Cobb," he said mildly. "If you don't want to, now or ever, just say so."

"Em, I'm afraid," she told him, leaning forward on her elbows. "And a little confused. I don't know what to tell you."

"How about the truth?" he said. His blue eyes peered at her, bright and sharp, over the rim of his glass.

"Okay," she told him, "the truth is, I have orders to fill by Monday, so I really can't get away. But I—" Even before the words were out, she wondered, Am I making a mistake? "I wouldn't mind having you ask me another time."

"Maybe I'll do that," he replied without a trace of rancor.

Their pasta arrived—steaming noodles piled with tomato, mushrooms, peppers, olives, all in a fragrant red sauce. After he'd eaten half of what was on his plate, Emmett was once again his old cocky self. "Hey, Cesare," he called over to the big man in the rubout suit, "how was your pasta? Good, eh?"

The man frowned at him; then recognition dawned, and he gave Emmett the barest of nods, wiping his greasy chin. If he thought

Emmett was being flippant with him, he gave no indication of it.

Annie ducked her head, hiding her face in her napkin to muffle her laughter. She felt shocked by Emmett's boldness. But then why should it surprise her? Since she'd known him, when had Emmett Cameron ever been afraid of anything or anybody?

LAUREL was soaking in the bathtub when she felt a tightness in her belly again.

It didn't hurt much—she couldn't call it a pain. Definitely not a *labor* pain. Actually, she'd been having feelings like this all morning, but she was pretty sure they were no big deal.

She remembered her Lamaze teacher saying that false labor—contractions that didn't hurt much and came at irregular intervals—was common. Earlier she'd timed a few of these, and they were jumping all over the place: ten minutes, then six, then ten again. She was tense—that was it. She decided a bath would relax her.

But to be on the safe side, maybe she should call Dr. Epstein.

Laurel started to pull herself up, and the tightness eased. She let herself sink back into the water's warmth. Why bother the doctor when it's probably still a long way off. Don't think about it, she told herself. It was as if an alarm had jangled in her brain, warning her to keep all thoughts of the baby out of her head. *They'll take it away. . . . I won't even get to hold it.*

Her head tipped back; tears slipped sideways down her temples, pooling in her ears. My choice, she reminded herself. No one was forcing her to give up her baby. Rudy had merely persuaded her that it was for the best. She remembered his phoning her the day after they'd met in the baby store. How relieved he'd sounded. Over and over he'd assured her she was doing the best thing. But now she wasn't so sure.

Again she found herself thinking, If only this were Joe's baby . . .

Maybe he did love her after all . . . just a little. And maybe he'd love her a lot more if it weren't for Annie. Tears filled her eyes, and she pressed her hands to her belly, fingers spread like starfish.

For one sweet interlude she imagined how it would be if she changed her mind and kept the baby. She'd buy that homemade-looking oak cradle she'd spotted in the window of the Salvation Army store on Eighth Avenue and put it right by her bed. Whenever he cried, she'd pick him up. And when he was older, she'd point out the evening star—the way Annie had once pointed it out to her—so every night he could wish on it.

Laurel yanked out the tub stopper. Then she heaved herself to her feet and stepped out onto the fluffy pink rug. Reaching for a towel, she felt that tight sensation across her middle again. She stood still, gripping the towel rack until the pain passed. A cup of tea was what she needed. Then she'd finish the last drawing for that book.

Laurel toweled off and slipped into her old chenille robe. With a steaming mug of chamomile she curled up on the big red hassock by the window with her sketch pad. In the drawing she was working on, a bear was rearing up on his hind paws in fury, having just found out that his bride had unwittingly betrayed him. She'd gotten the bear's enraged expression just right. But the bride seemed all wrong. Wouldn't she have jumped to her feet to beg his forgiveness and declare her love? This bride was . . . oh, face it, a *wimp*.

Suddenly it came to Laurel how the bride should be. She grabbed an eraser and with a few swipes rubbed out an arm, a leg, half a face. Then she began to sketch. Her pencil flew, her mind filled with visions of a frightened but determined woman . . . determined to get her prince back.

She lost all track of time and was only dimly aware of the contractions rolling through her like mild ocean waves.

But then a hard contraction, harder than any of the others, gripped Laurel so fiercely that she dropped her pencil. Shuddering from the pain, she hunched forward, clutching her belly. Damn, it hurt. This one really *hurt*.

She'd better call Dr. Epstein. No more fooling around.

She waited for the contraction to pass. It felt like an excruciating eternity. But when she tried to stand up, her legs collapsed underneath her like warm butter. They'd gone numb, she realized. She began to feel panicky. Now something was happening. *Definitely*.

The circulation in her legs gradually came back, but Laurel was still too shaky to stand up. She managed to get onto her knees and began crawling toward the phone. She could feel another contraction coming on, this one more racking than the last.

She pulled herself up, clutching the phone receiver in one hand. As she began to dial, the contraction seized her. She crumpled in agony, and the phone pitched to the floor with a crazed jingling.

"Oh!" she cried, clutching herself.

Something had to be wrong, she thought. It was not supposed to hurt this much, not this soon. Knives. It felt like knives.

The pain finally ebbed, but by then Laurel was no longer thinking about calling Dr. Epstein. Or Annie. There was one person, only one, she wanted now. *Needed.* She dialed the number and waited in sweaty panic while the phone rang and rang and rang.

"Joe's Place," announced a harried-sounding voice, *his* voice.

She forced herself to take a slow, even breath. "Joe? It's me, Laurey. Listen, I think I'm just about to have this baby."

THE front door was unlocked and slightly ajar. With a swift backhand stroke Joe knocked it wide open. "Laurey!"

No answer. His heart dropped. "Laurey!" he called again.

"Joe?" From the bedroom came her faint reply.

Laurel lay on her side on the bed. Her long hair hung in damp tatters over the edge of the mattress. Her face was very white.

Joe crouched at her side. He felt his heart lumbering in his chest. "Laurey, I'm here. It's going to be okay." He struggled to clear away the fear that cobwebbed his mind. "How far apart are the pains?"

Laurel shook her head, forcing her words through gritted teeth. "All . . . together."

No intervals at all between the contractions. That meant she was in the final stage of her labor. Why hadn't she called him sooner?

Joe felt a low swell of resentment. Why did she have to call him at *all?* How had he gotten into this? Why, when she asked him to be her Lamaze coach, hadn't he turned her down? At the very least, couldn't he have had the guts to admit that the main reason he'd ever agreed to it was to hurt Annie?

All right, he had been concerned about Laurel. He still was. But mostly he was so angry at himself he could barely concentrate.

Laurel gripped his forearm with all her might. "Joe . . . I'm scared," she gasped.

Me, too, kiddo.

"What did the doctor say?" he asked.

"I . . . I haven't talked to him. After I called you, I had to . . . to lie down. It hurts so much!" She hugged herself tighter, her face crumpling into an agonized grimace.

"Where's his number?"

"In the . . . the little blue book . . . under the phone."

"I'll be right back. Hang on, Laurey."

He found the blue address book and dialed Dr. Epstein's number. The doctor told him what he already knew: get Laurel to St. Vincent's, pronto. Epstein said he'd phone for an ambulance—it shouldn't be more than five minutes.

Next Joe tried the number at Annie's shop. A girl who sounded very young informed him that Annie was out. He left a message saying that he was on his way to the hospital with Laurel, and the girl breathlessly promised to do her best to find Annie.

Waiting for the ambulance to arrive, Joe returned to the bedroom and found Laurel on her back, clutching a knee in each hand.

"The ambulance'll be here any minute," he told her. "And Dr. Epstein will be waiting for you at the hospital."

"I . . . don't think . . . I can . . . Oh, damn."

Joe strained to remember the breathing exercises they'd practiced in Lamaze. Fine coach he was turning out to be.

"Pant," he urged. "Shallow breaths. That's it."

Laurel kept up the panting for another minute or so, then fell back. "No!" she screamed. "I can't do this. . . . Please don't make me do this!"

Instinctively Joe gathered her into his arms.

"You *can*," he told Laurel. "You can do it."

"Joe." He was close enough to feel her lips move under his. "I never . . . stopped loving you. Please . . . I'm sorry. I . . . I didn't mean to lie to Annie. It's just that I wanted it to be yours . . . *our* baby. Do you hate me?"

"No, Laurey, I could never hate you." He stroked her hair, which felt damp and hot. What *did* he feel?

He didn't know, couldn't sort out all the emotions Laurel summoned up in him. *In* love with her? No. But what he did feel was certainly more than brotherly affection.

"I didn't love him," she panted. "Jess. He . . . he was just somebody." She gasped, and her mouth dragged down in a horrible grimace. "It's coming, Joe! I can feel it!"

"The ambulance . . ." he started to say, as if this birth were something she could put on hold. But it was going to happen, he realized, whether the ambulance was here or not.

Laurel screamed. Blood had rushed up into her face, turning it a dark crimson. He realized that now she had to be pushing.

"It's okay," he heard a calm stranger speak. "Push if you have to."

Between Laurel's hiked knees he spied a dark, wet circle—the baby's head. Joe grew dizzy, as if a part of him were standing at a distance from all this, high up, watching himself. The dark circle widened. He could hear Laurel grunting as she pushed again . . . then again. He saw his arms stretch out, hands cupped to receive the infant's head. But something was wrong. The baby seemed stuck.

Then he dimly remembered something in a film they'd seen in Lamaze class about the baby needing at this point to be rotated a bit. Carefully, as carefully as if this child were a butterfly cupped in his palms, he turned the baby until he felt its shoulders loosen and finally slide free. Now came a long torso, a pair of rumpled red legs. Joe let his breath out with a whistling rush.

With one hand supporting the infant's head, Joe shouted, "It's a boy!"

The baby gave a choked, startled cry, then began to wail, thrashing his arms and legs. Feeling the infant's tiny wet body squirm in his hands, Joe was so thrilled that he started to laugh. Then, seemingly for no reason, he began to cry. He saw that Laurel, too, was laughing, and had tears streaming down her face.

Joe looked at the baby boy in his arms, tied to Laurel by its ropy cord, and for the first time in all his thirty-two years, he felt connected to something larger than himself. To God? The mysteries of the universe? No, smaller than that—a heartbeat, a new life, a measure of grace.

The baby had stopped crying. A pair of indigo eyes stared fixedly into his, and a tiny mottled hand locked about his finger. Joe felt a rush of unexpected joy that nearly knocked him over.

Before he was even aware he'd thought of it, Joe found himself saying, "Adam. His name is Adam."

VAL stood in the lobby of St. Vincent's Hospital and asked the lady behind the reception desk which room Laurel Carrera was in.

While she riffled through her alphabetized index cards he glanced around. What was he even doing here? His little girl, all grown up, a mother herself now, and he was probably the last person she'd want to see. Hadn't she made it clear how she felt about him all those years ago, when she took off without so much as a kiss-my-foot? If he hadn't seen that article in the Los Angeles

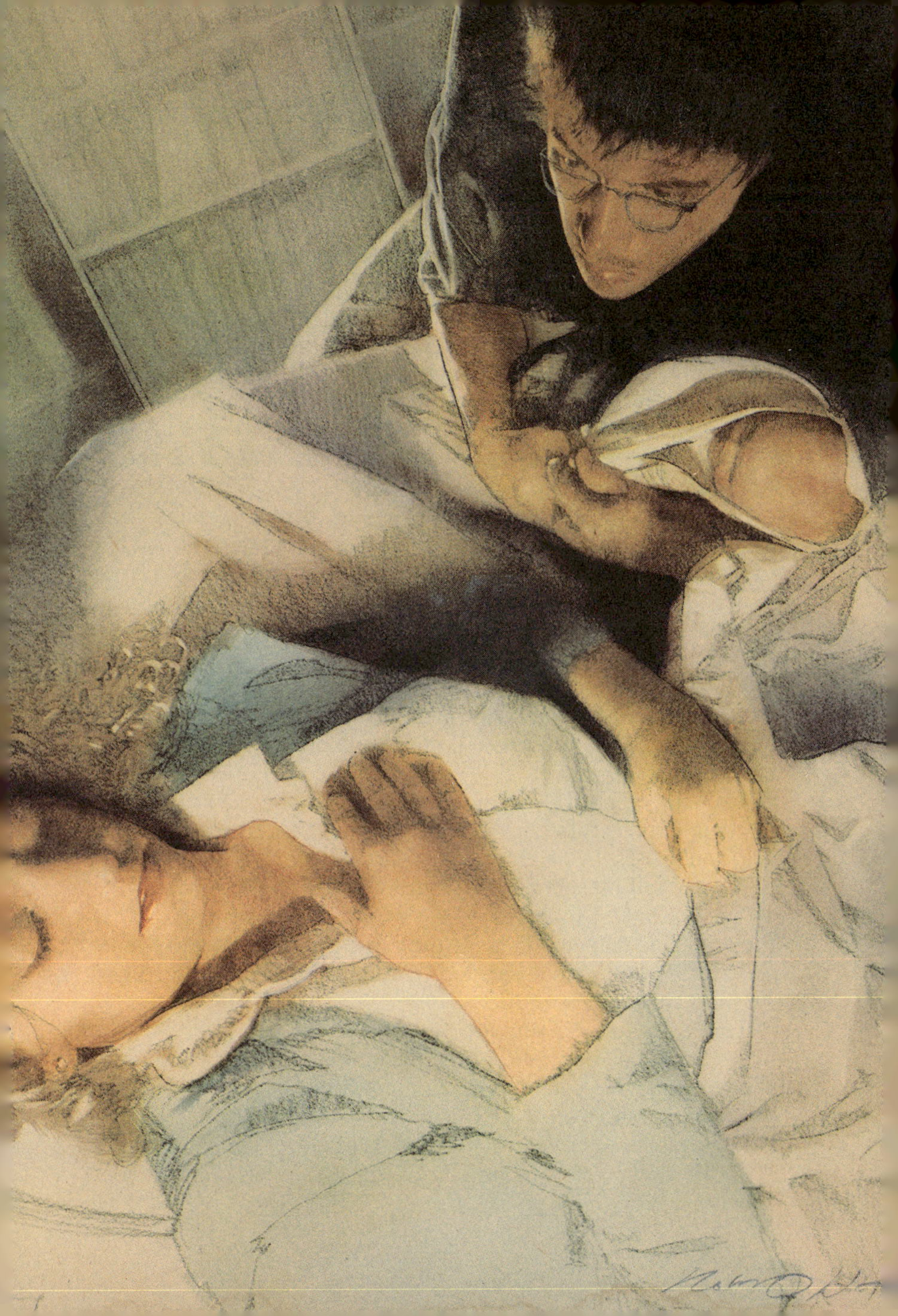

Times Magazine on Annie's chocolate shop, he wouldn't have known either of them was still alive.

No Laurel Carrera listed, Big Mama behind the desk told him. "Sorry, mister."

But he'd come all this way, blowing his last hundred on a low-fare red-eye to New York. He *couldn't* just walk away.

"What about Laurel *Cobb?*" A long shot, but worth a try.

Big Mama thumbed her card index and then looked up at him quizzically. "Third floor. Room three twenty-two."

Val tried to swallow, but his mouth felt dry as an old sock. It was close to noon, but he'd been up all night—five hours from Los Angeles International, and the whole time, he hadn't shut his eyes once. Thinking about Laurel. Wondering what she'd look like, if she'd be glad to see him.

The door to room 322 was propped open. There were two beds inside, but one was empty. In the other a slender woman sat propped up with pillows, her long blond hair tied back in a loose ponytail. She was staring out the window and didn't see him, so he had time for a good long look at her.

Laurel? That beautiful young woman, his little girl?

"Laurel? Baby?" He took a step inside.

She turned and stared at him, her eyes huge and uncomprehending. Then recognition dawned, and the blood drained from her face.

"Val," she croaked, "is it you?" She clapped both hands over her mouth and spoke through white fingers that dragged at her cheeks. "But you're . . . I thought you were *dead.*"

Now Val felt himself reel. "Dead? Where did you hear that?"

"Uncle Rudy t-told me that you'd d-died that night. That Annie—" She gulped. "H-he m-made me p-promise not to t-tell."

Rudy? *Rudy* had told her that? But why? Val felt as if he'd had the wind knocked out of him.

"How . . . how did you find me?"

"I read about your sister in the paper." He kept his voice even, while his thoughts continued to tumble. It hadn't occurred to him when he was reading that article, but from the very beginning Rudy had to have known where Laurel and Annie were living.

"*Annie* told you I was here?" Laurel's voice was hollow with disbelief.

"Not exactly. I . . . uh . . . followed her home from her store. Your super's wife told me where to find you."

Was she glad to see him? He couldn't tell.

"You're looking good," he told her. "I hear you had a kid."

"That's right. A boy." Her eyes welled with tears. Had he said something wrong?

Val grinned. "Hey, that makes me a grandfather." He paused, his grin fading. "It's been so long. I thought you'd forgotten about me."

"I would've written, but . . ." Her voice trailed off.

"Hey," Val said, "how about giving your old man a hug?"

Val sat on the edge of the bed and pulled her into his arms. She seemed to resist a bit, but then he felt her sag against him, the tension going out of her. He wondered if it was too late to try being a father to her. And for a fleeting instant it crossed his mind that maybe it wasn't too late to get his hands on some of that trust money.

Laurel drew back. "Uncle Rudy is handling the adoption," she said, sniffing. "He . . . he found the couple." She paused to take a deep breath. "That's why they put me here instead of in the maternity wing. I'm not supposed to be around the other mothers."

It all tumbled into place. The baby . . . the one Rudy had said he was adopting. Val had thought it was pretty weird anyone's letting a middle-aged loner like Rudy adopt her kid, but he'd figured that Rudy had to have all kinds of connections. But all the time it was Laurel's kid he'd been yakking about. *His* grandchild.

Val squeezed his eyes shut. *All this time Rudy knew where Laurel was, and he kept it from me.* Rage rose in him, and his hands closed about the bed's metal side rail, hard enough to cut off his circulation. He imagined it was Rudy's neck he was squeezing, and he could almost hear the separate crunch of each vertebra.

Then he realized something important: *Laurel didn't know Rudy was planning on keeping her baby for himself.*

When he finally spoke, Val was amazed at the steadiness of his voice. "Let me tell you a few things about good old Uncle Rudy."

"Bring me my baby."

Laurel felt as if she were shouting, but the nurse didn't even look up from the thermometer she was squinting at. "Well now, I don't think that's such a good idea," she said.

Laurel's eyes felt swollen and scratchy. And now this nurse had come bustling in to take her blood pressure and temperature, not even asking if she minded.

But worse than this nurse was the awful *emptiness* inside her.

Uncle Rudy. How could he have done something like this to her? Not just trying to take Adam for himself, but before that, making her believe her father was dead.

She recalled her shock at seeing Val walk in. She hadn't known what to feel. For so many years she'd thought of him as dead. They'd sat and talked for close to an hour, and every so often she'd found herself staring at him, noticing how much older he looked. He was still a sharp dresser, with his expensive silk jacket and Gucci loafers, but the jacket had to have been at least ten years old, and the cuffs were beginning to fray. And he hadn't once mentioned a job or what kind of house or apartment he was living in.

What he *had* talked about, besides Uncle Rudy, was the night she and Annie ran away. He'd told her how upset Annie had been about Dearie, and how when he tried to calm her down, she'd gotten furious at him, hysterical almost. Tears had welled up in his eyes. All he'd wanted, he'd said, was for them to be a family.

Now, thinking it over, Laurel realized that apart from being glad to see him and glad that he was alive, she felt sorry for Val. Even so, she was sure that there had to be another side to his story.

Look at all Annie has done for you. If you want the real story about that night, ask Annie.

But what did any of that matter now? All she knew, all she cared about was that her baby had been taken from her.

Laurel began to get a tight feeling in her chest. She was pretty sure she hadn't signed any papers or anything, so maybe it wasn't too late. But she had to see Adam again first. Until she actually held him in her arms, she didn't want to make up her mind. Laurel hadn't seen Adam since a nurse whisked him upstairs to the nursery two whole days ago. Now her milk was coming in. But that was a small hurt compared to the ferocious, aching need she felt. She could no longer bear it. She *had* to see Adam, to hold him.

"I don't care what you think," she told the nurse. "I want to see my baby. Get him for me, or I'll go get him myself."

The nurse frowned. "Well, honestly, I don't . . ."

Laurel swung her legs out of bed. She was trembling. Dr. Epstein had warned her against getting up. But right now she didn't care. The baby, her baby—the only thing she cared about was him.

"Get out of my way," Laurel commanded.

"Why don't you wait here while I see what I can do." The nurse bustled out.

Laurel waited a minute; then she followed the nurse out into the corridor. Bright fluorescents stabbed at her eyes, and the floor tipped to one side like a banking airplane. There was something wrong with her balance. She had to walk with one palm scooting along the wall to keep from falling into it.

She reached an elevator door and felt a burst of elation. Just another minute or two, and she'd be there. The door slid open, and a harried-looking man in a white doctor's coat stepped out. "Excuse me"—she snatched at his starchy sleeve—"which floor are the babies on?"

He gave her a curious look but appeared to be in too much of a hurry to give her bedraggled appearance any thought. "Eight," he said, jabbing a finger upward as he brushed past her.

Seconds later she was stumbling into a bustling corridor, with residents, nurses, and orderlies scurrying past. Taking slow sliding steps, she forced herself to keep moving. She saw something up ahead—a long pane of glass set into the wall, almost like a brightly lit shopwindow. That had to be the nursery. She made herself go faster despite the pain.

And then she was peering through the glass at rows and rows of spotless white bassinets, in each one a tiny, precious baby. One of those was hers. Her baby. Her son.

She tried the door marked STAFF ONLY and found it unlocked. She pulled it open and walked in. There appeared to be only one nurse on duty, a tall black woman. She looked up from diapering a red-faced infant on the changing table against the far wall.

"This area is restricted to hospital personnel," she informed Laurel in a clipped West Indian accent. "I'm afraid I am going to have to ask you to leave."

Laurel squared her shoulders and said, "I've come for my baby. Cobb . . . Adam Cobb."

"The babies are not scheduled for feeding for another hour," the nurse snapped. "Please return to your room, Mrs.—"

"*Miss* Cobb," Laurel interrupted, sticking her chin out. "And I'm not going anywhere until you let me have him."

The nurse's brown eyes sparked. "We have *rules* around here, young lady. We cannot have just anyone marching in here—"

"I'm not just anyone. I'm his mother." Saying it aloud caused something to crumple inside her chest. Her eyes filled with tears. "I'm his mother," she repeated. "Please, I only want to hold him."

The nurse stared hard at her, then relented. "All right. But you will have to stay here. I cannot let you take him back to your room."

"I don't care about that," Laurel told her, nearly swooning with relief. "Can I sit down?"

The nurse pointed to a rocking chair in the corner. Laurel sank into it gratefully, closing her eyes for a moment. When she opened them, she saw a pair of slender black arms extending a fleecy white bundle. Tightly wrapped in folds of flannel, a squashed red face peered from an opening at the top. Her heart turned over.

"Oh," she breathed. She held her arms out. Where she had felt unsteady before, her muscles now seemed springy with new strength. With the warm weight of her child something dropped into place inside her. Tears slid from her chin and splashed against the blanket. "Adam," she whispered.

She tried to imagine handing him over to some stranger and then walking away, going back to school, forgetting about him. But she couldn't see herself doing those things. She had thought that not having Joe's love was bad, but this would be much worse. It would kill her.

Adam had turned his downy head into her chest and was rooting against the front of her gown. Laurel opened it and felt his mouth instantly fasten onto her nipple and begin to suck. She sat back and closed her eyes, feeling a strong pull as the milk flowed into him.

She began to understand it . . . this mother-love. If she could paint it, she would need a canvas bigger than the Milky Way. And Adam would be right in the middle of it, like the first star of the evening, the one you wish on.

Chapter Eleven

EVEN before she could hear a voice on the phone, Dolly, listening to the crackling of the transatlantic line, felt her heart leap. "Henri," she cried, "that you?"

It had been so long . . . weeks since he'd last called; months since she'd seen him . . . months that seemed like a hundred years.

"*Ma poupée,* did I wake you?" came his voice, faint and crinkly with static. All at once it seemed as if no time at all had passed.

"Not a chance," she told him, though a glance at the faintly glowing malachite face of the clock on the mantel told her it was half past one in the morning. "I couldn't sleep to save my life. Must be something I ate." Only the second part was a lie.

Actually, she was sitting here in the dark, looking out her big window at the million fairylike lights of Tavern on the Green, far away across Central Park, and sipping a Cognac that she knew would probably make her feel worse later on. How appropriate that Henri should call just when she was thinking of how much she missed him, loved him, but still dancing around the thing that was really eating at her: that after eight years Henri wasn't any closer to getting a divorce than he had been in the beginning.

I have to tell him. No more. I can't do this anymore—sneaking around behind his wife's back, seeing him only five or six weeks out of the year. I love him too much.

"As a matter of fact, I'm having myself a pity party," she told him.

"*Pardon?*"

"A pity party. You sit around feeling real sorry for yourself, preferably when there's nobody round to slap you on the back and say, 'Hey, lady, snap out of it.' "

"I wish I were there," he said, sounding amused.

"Then it wouldn't be a pity party. It'd be a . . . Well, I'm too much of a lady to say what it'd be."

She prayed it was good news he was calling with; for one week, she'd had just about all the upheaval she could take.

The baby—Laurel's deciding to keep him—was a blessing, but it sure had knocked her for a loop. And Val Carrera's turning up after all these years, pouncing on Laurel when she was at her lowest, probably looking for ways to rake up trouble—why, it gave her chills just thinking about it.

Henri was chuckling. "*C'est ça.* But I did not call you at seven thirty in the morning—for you, I know, it is the middle of the night—just to say hello," he told her. "*Alors,* where to begin?"

"Why not skip over the beginning," she told him, feeling herself begin to tense. "I know it by heart."

"Well then—how do you say it?—the happy finishings."

Inside her chest Dolly's heart did a crazy bump-and-grind.

"Henri, what exactly are you trying to tell me?"

There was a pause, and she could hear his unsteady breathing. Finally he said, "Dolly, come to Paris."

"Henri, we have been through this again and—"

"*Non, non,* this time, it is different. Francine and I, we have now separated."

Dolly nearly dropped the receiver. "What did you say?"

"Francine, she has shown me the door," he said softly, but with a small note of triumph. "It appears my wife has taken a lover." He sounded gleeful; then his voice grew serious. "I must be honest with you, though. There will be no divorce. Francine will not accept that."

Henri's voice seemed to be fading, and then Dolly realized it was her pulse pounding in her ears that was making it hard to hear. "Henri, what exactly are you proposing?"

"That you and I . . . that we live together. It is the modern way, *non?* After that . . ." His voice trailed off. He didn't have to say what they both knew: that he would marry her in a minute if he could.

"What about your father-in-law? Does he know?"

"Yes. We now have a new agreement. I am to receive his controlling interest upon his death. Of course, I am obligated to continue supporting Francine. But it is all completed with witnesses, signatures, and the notary. This is for me a great contract, a deliverance."

"Oh, Henri!" Tears of happiness filled her eyes.

"*Chérie,*" Henri continued soberly, "you have not answered my question."

Dolly's head was spinning. She didn't know *what* to think. The chance to be with him all the time, to live with him!

But she would have to move to Paris.

Paris was beautiful, and she loved it, but New York was her *home.* How could she leave—especially now? Laurel was going to need all kinds of help. And how, if she were three thousand miles away, could she be a proper granny to that precious little baby?

As much as she longed for Henri, she also longed for a real family; this baby would bond her to Annie and Laurel in a way that nothing else had. And her business? It had become more than just a means of making money—it was a cozy place where she and the people who came there felt at home.

"Henri, I've got to sleep on this," she said firmly. "Now don't go thinking I'm too chicken to say what's on my mind. The fact is, I don't know *what's* on my mind. Can you wait until tomorrow?"

He sighed. "Do I have a choice?"

"Nope."

"In that case, sleep well, *chérie,* and I love you."

As Dolly hung up, she thought there was about as much chance of her sleeping well now as there was of her walking on the moon.

ANNIE was gazing through the viewing window of the hospital nursery when she turned to find her aunt, brilliant in an emerald-green bouclé wool suit, dabbing at her eyes with a handkerchief. A gold bracelet jingled at her wrist, and on it Annie recognized the charm she and Laurel had given Dolly last Christmas: a tiny gold candy box in the shape of a heart.

"I think he looks like Dearie," Annie said, turning her attention back to the nursery. "Look at his chin, the way it's rounded." All the other babies were asleep, but Adam was wide awake. He waved his fists, and a tiny pink foot kicked loose from his blanket.

She felt Dolly stiffen beside her, then give a small sigh. "Why, maybe so. . . . I guess it's tough to tell at this age, isn't it?"

"I wish Dearie were here. I wish she could see her grandson."

Her own sudden longing for her mother came unexpectedly. It had been a long time since she felt even a distant ache at the thought of her.

Then Annie's thoughts turned to Joe, and she felt her tight grip on her emotions slip a little. Maybe, just maybe, it's still not too late for me and Joe, she thought. Everything would be different from now on. With Adam to mother, Laurel wouldn't have time to hang around Joe so much. She had even talked about moving out, finding her own place. At first Annie had been against it, but now she was starting to think it might not be such a bad thing. It was as if Joe were her center, her core; without him she'd fly off in a million directions.

And what about Emmett? Where did he fit in? That night after dinner at Paolo's they had gone back to his apartment. How could anything that good be just a fling? She knew she didn't love Emmett the way she loved Joe, but what she *did* feel was certainly more than mere fondness.

"Carnations," Dolly was saying. "I remember when you were born, your father filled Evie's room with pink carnations."

Annie smiled. "I think it's feeding time," she said, watching a nurse bend over Adam's bassinet and lift him out.

Dolly turned to Annie, her blue eyes bright and a high flush making her rouged cheeks even pinker. "Do you think they'd let me hold him? Just for a minute. I wouldn't get in the way."

"Why don't you tell the nurse you're his grandmother? You practically are, anyway."

Dolly looked as if she were going to kiss her, and Annie instinctively found herself sidling away.

"I'll go see if Laurey's ready," she told Dolly. "Give Adam a kiss."

Annie was on her way back to the nursery when she saw one of the elevator doors slide open and a tall, spectacled man step out, his head bent low, as if he were used to ducking through doorways. She felt her heart leap.

"Joe," she called softly.

"Hey, Annie. How's Laurey?" he asked.

"Fine. We're taking her home. Joe, I . . ." She swallowed hard and felt her throat clench. "I guess I ought to thank you. For getting Laurey safely through this. I'm glad you were there."

He shrugged as if it were no big deal. "Any kid in that big a rush to get born doesn't need much of a hand."

"He doesn't look a thing like Laurey."

"The eyes," he said, solemnly touching the corner of his own eye with his index finger, "they remind me of yours."

Annie felt herself grow warm. Did he know what he was doing to her? Why, if he was going to keep his distance, did he have to remind her of what they'd come so close to sharing?

But all she could do was smile. "His father is Puerto Rican. Laurey actually knew him back in Brooklyn, it turns out. Then they met up again at Syracuse. Quite a coincidence, huh?"

Joe flushed, and as he looked away, she thought she saw something in his eyes—a flash of emotion that came and went so quickly she wasn't sure whether she'd imagined it or not.

Jealous? Could he be jealous that he's not the father?

A strained silence settled between them. Finally he gestured toward the dreary-looking lounge. "Can I buy you a cup of coffee?"

Annie thought a cup of coffee right now could well burn a hole right through her stomach. Nevertheless, she found herself nodding. "Just a quick one. I promised Laurey I'd be right back."

The visitors' lounge was empty. Joe led her over to a pair of molded plastic chairs, where they sat side by side, hands folded about the steaming Styrofoam cups. Annie felt like a statue carved out of ice, yet her heart was racing.

"How's it going?" he asked. "The business, I mean."

"Too good," she told him. "I hired a new girl to help Louise in the kitchen. If it keeps up like this, I'll have to put on a swing shift. We can barely keep up with all the orders." She set her cup down. "How are things at the restaurant? I mean, with the new addition and all."

"Bursting at the seams already." He smiled. "Thanks in part to my parents. Would you believe they eat dinner there at least once a week? Miracles never cease, huh?"

She found herself smiling, in spite of her tenseness. "I'm glad."

"Annie." She felt Joe's eyes on her, but she didn't look at him. She didn't know why, but she sensed he was going to say something she didn't want to hear.

"There's something you should know," he went on in a quiet, almost hushed voice. "I'm glad I ran into you, but I just want you to know I would have called you anyway. I haven't said anything to Laurey. I wanted to talk to you first."

She tugged her gaze upward, forcing herself to meet his eyes. And what she saw in them was terrible. Pity. He was *sorry* for her.

"What is it, Joe?" she demanded. "For pity's sake, what is it?"

"I'm going to ask Laurey to marry me."

Her mind seemed to separate from the rest of her and float above her body. "What?" she heard herself say, but the word seemed not to be connected to her.

"Annie . . ." He tried to take her hand, but she whipped back so violently she banged her elbow against the back of her chair.

"I don't want to hear it," she said. "Please, don't make me listen to this."

Slowly he removed his glasses and rubbed the bridge of his nose. His eyes were bloodshot, as if he hadn't slept in days.

"Are you in love with her?" she forced herself to ask. "Is that what this is all about?"

He paused.

She felt a piece of her injured heart rejoice. How much could he love her if he had to stop and think about it?

"You could say that," he responded, seeming to choose his words carefully. "I don't want to hurt you or insult you. But let me say that there really *are* more than one or two kinds of loving, and there's a whole lot of gray shading in between."

"I hope you're not planning to put it to Laurey that way," she said bitterly. "You're not doing her any favors, you know."

"It's more complicated than that, don't you see? Damn it, I wish it weren't! I wish I could say I was just being Joe Samaritan, and then let you talk me out of it."

"Do you *want* me to talk you out of it?" She stared at him.

He didn't answer. "I don't know," he said. "What I *do* know is that what I feel for you hasn't changed."

Annie struggled against the tears swelling at the back of her throat. She should tell him how she felt, she thought. She should beg him not to do this thing. But something was holding her back. Pride? She didn't know. All she knew at this moment was that she hated the man sitting beside her, hated him and loved him with all her heart and soul. She'd felt this way once before—the dreary afternoon she stood in the cemetery watching Dearie's coffin being lowered into the ground. Except that this time it was worse. The person who had died was herself.

"Go," she told him, her voice flat. "Go to Laurey."

LATER that day Dolly dialed Henri's number and waited patiently while the line beeped and buzzed its way to Paris. She was in her office, upstairs at Girod's, where she felt more in control, more in charge of herself than at home. Even so, she felt sick at the thought of what lay ahead.

"Henri?"

"Ah! *Chérie,* you must have been reading into my thoughts. I could not wait any longer. I was just now going to call you."

The sound of his voice caused her to grow light-headed, as if she'd drunk Champagne. How, in the few hours since they'd spoken, could she have forgotten the effect his voice had on her?

Dolly faltered. But then she remembered how that little baby had felt in her arms. She could feel the warm imprint of his body against her bosom still, the firm pressure of his tiny fist wrapped about her finger. Adam was just a part of it, she knew . . . but he seemed to embody it all, everything she stood to lose.

"Henri, I can't. I just can't do it," she told him, a great aching hollow opening inside her. Tears streamed down her cheeks faster than she could mop them up with her handkerchief. "I'm a great-aunt now. Laurel's had a darling baby. His name's Adam, and he's just beautiful. And Laurel needs me, and the baby does, too. And I guess I need him."

For the longest time, except for the rustling of long-distance static, the line was silent.

Finally Henri said, "Just now I was remembering our last time together . . . how we never said good-bye, not the words. Perhaps we knew one day there would come a time for speaking them."

She smiled through her tears, surprised at the keenness of the hurt she felt. Her heart had been broken so many times, she'd have thought there'd be nothing left of it.

"I love you," she told him. "Oh, Henri, what do I say now?"

There was a long silence in which Henri seemed to be losing his struggle. At last he spoke, but his voice had the choked, tinny sound of a man close to tears.

"Just say *au revoir*. After all these years who can tell what tomorrow will bring us?"

Dolly knew it was time to hang up, but she clung to the receiver. If she let go, she felt she'd be severing some vital artery that could never be made whole again. But even as she held on, she could feel it all unraveling, everything they'd shared.

"*Au revoir*," Dolly spoke softly into the receiver. A tear dripped from her chin onto the coiled phone cord.

"*Au revoir, ma poupée.*"

Dolly placed the receiver gently, gently in its cradle.

PART THREE: 1980
Chapter Twelve

THE maître d' led Annie to a window table in the Grill Room. Slipping into her seat, she breathed a sigh of relief that she'd gotten there ahead of Felder. The Four Seasons was too grand a place to dash into with your hem flapping, which she knew was how she arrived at most places these days. So although she didn't usually care much about being seen in the right places or about what she looked like, today it might make a difference—because today, somehow, she had to get this man to save her.

She probably ought to have brought a lawyer with her, or one of Emmett's Wall Street buddies. What did she know about making major financial deals? If she hadn't been such an overconfident idiot in that department, she wouldn't even be here now.

"Shall I bring you something from the bar while you're waiting?" the maître d' inquired.

"Perrier," she told him. It would help settle her stomach.

She glanced at her gold watch, a present from Emmett a month ago, on her thirty-second birthday. Felder would be arriving at any moment; should she have waited before ordering her drink?

Watching her waiter thread his way among the well-spaced tables, Annie grew disgusted with herself. If she couldn't do a simple little thing like ordering a drink without worrying, how on earth could she expect Felder to make a million-dollar deal with her?

"Miss Cobb?"

Annie looked up at the stocky middle-aged man with bristling gray hair who stood over her. Felder? But he didn't look at all the way she'd imagined. Except for the beautifully fitted muted-plaid suit he was wearing, the man standing before her might have been a plumber or a butcher or a housepainter—not someone who'd parlayed his way up to ownership of a hugely successful chain of discount department stores.

"Annie. Please, call me Annie."

She started to get up, smiling brightly, but he didn't smile back. Already she felt she was blowing it.

How she *needed* this to work. On top of the absurd rents she was already paying on her shops on Madison Avenue and now in Southampton, she'd known she was sticking her neck out by leasing at Glen Harbor's new, elegant Paradise Mall. To date, less than half of the mall's pricey pickled-oak-paneled stores had been leased. Her ground-level shop was *bleeding* money.

And that was just the tip of the iceberg. With the new plant in Tribeca she had to admit she'd overreached herself. Financially, she was perched atop a precarious sandcastle that could be about to cave in. If she couldn't restructure her finances, and do it fast, Tout de Suite might be going down the tubes *tout de suite.*

She'd read in *The Wall Street Journal* that Felder's was planning to revamp some of its departments into small, intimate boutiques—including a gourmet-food section—and she'd sent samples and literature that very same day. Then, just a week later, Hyman Felder himself had called and invited her to lunch.

He eased his bulk into the chair opposite her. A waiter materialized with her Perrier, and Felder ordered a Dewar's with soda.

"You're younger than I expected," he began. "You mind my asking how old you are?"

"I'm thirty-two," she told him, adding with a laugh, "But it's not the age itself I mind. What bothers me is not knowing how I got there from twenty-five in what feels like about two weeks."

He chuckled. "Please, I got *daughters* older than you. I was around when they built the Brooklyn Battery Tunnel." He fished a mini ice cube from his newly arrived drink and popped it into his mouth. "But one thing you learn after a lotta years in business is what's successful today usually ain't successful tomorrow. I opened my first store after the war, when discount was the name of the game. Now everything is designer. It's a whole different ball game."

"Did you like the samples I sent you?" she asked.

"Wish I could say I did. Truth is, I can't touch the stuff." He pressed a hand to his bulging midsection. "Some fancy doctors tell me that if I don't take some of this off, I'm gonna make Mrs. Felder a very rich widow in the near future."

"But—"

He held up a hand. "Hey, what I like is that you called. And the same day it all hit the press. But you see, for Felder's Pantry I was thinking, well, smelly French cheeses, high-end Colombian coffee beans, that kind of thing. Candies, too, but they'd have to be in boxes, like in the supermarket, only better quality."

"It's a wonderful idea, but what I had in mind for you is a whole separate boutique," she told him, swallowing hard. "Sort of a . . . a miniature version of Tout de Suite."

She leaned forward, locking her gaze on him. "You're a very smart man, and you're right—these days people want quality, and they're willing to pay more for it. Last year Tout de Suite grossed three million. This year it looks like we'll be up forty percent."

"With half a million plus in unsecured debt, a sixty percent jump in your payroll, mortgage payments on your new plant, and a lease commitment in that new ghost town of a mall in Glen Harbor. But hey, it could be worse." The jovial Felder of a minute ago was now transformed into the flint-eyed Felder of legend.

He held up his hand like a traffic cop. "But you shouldn't get the wrong idea. I'm not knocking you. You think I built Felder's with a triple-A bank account and solid-gold bricks?"

"Then what sort of arrangement did *you* think we might make?"

"Look, we just met. We gotta feel our way."

"You do understand that I don't feel I'm asking for any favors. Tout de Suite's chocolates are the best."

"I like your chutzpah. 'The best.' Sounds great, but says who? You? How do *I* know you're the best?" He stared at her, challenging her with an expression halfway between a smile and a shrug.

Her mind was racing. *Come on, Annie. You've been in tight spots before.* An idea came to her. *Gourmand* magazine's annual chocolate fair at The Plaza was a week from Saturday. Chocolatiers were coming from the world over, the biggest names—Godiva, Kron's, Perugina—and all the tiny great ones like Girod's. As always, there'd be a banquet, dancing, speeches, prizes. Going up against those heavy hitters would be a bit like David versus Goliath, but for a fairly new operation like hers to win the general excellence award would mean manna from heaven: great free advertising, a tremendous boost in retail, and lots of new contracts with hotels and gourmet outlets.

"I'm competing in the *Gourmand* chocolate fair a week from Saturday. In my business that's the equivalent of the Academy Awards," she told Felder. "If I take one of the prizes, will that be enough to convince you?"

"First prize?"

"You're really pushing me."

"*You* said you were the best."

Annie swallowed hard against the knot in her throat and said, "All right. First prize. But what then?"

He laughed, shaking his head as he picked up his menu. "You bring home the trophy, and we'll talk turkey."

LESS than an hour after her lunch with Hyman Felder, Annie stood in the small test kitchen in Tout de Suite's Washington Street factory peering over Louise's shoulder while she put the finishing touches on a cinnamon-truffle cake—four layers of rum-soaked chocolate *génoise* filled with cinnamon-chocolate *ganache* and praline buttercream, the whole thing frosted with *ganache,* then coated with a bittersweet glaze and ringed with toasted hazelnuts. "Mmm, looks perfect," she told Louise. "Maybe a few more hazelnuts?"

"Come on. You said it was perfect." Louise stopped frosting her cake and looked at Annie.

"Well . . . *practically* perfect."

Louise laughed. "That line probably ought to go on your tombstone: Here Lies Annie Cobb, Practically Perfect." She licked a dab of frosting from the back of her thumb. "Oh, Joe called. He said just call him back when you get a free moment."

"You mean sometime in 1993?"

Annie laughed at her own joke, but inside she felt a tug. Six years, and yet when she heard his name—or worse, when she saw him—a sudden lick of heat, followed by light-headed panic. Sure, everything was fine these days. Good friends, just as they'd always been, nothing more. Now and then Joe stopped by for coffee. Mostly, though, she saw him on family occasions.

But still, whenever he greeted her with a hug or touched her hand to make a point, something inside her stirred. Did Joe feel it, too? If so, he kept it hidden. They kept it light and jokey, especially in front of Laurel. Sometimes the whole thing *seemed* real. But Annie knew it wasn't; it was an act, as elaborate as Kabuki theater.

If only . . .

Annie resolutely shut her mind against the thought that seemed always to be crouching there. She could not, *would* not, let herself imagine what her life would be like now if *she* had been the one to marry Joe. He was her sister's husband—end of story.

I should call Emmett instead, she thought. Remind him to pick up his new suit so he'll have it for tonight. The party they were going to was to celebrate the publication of Tansy Boone's newest dessert cookbook, which included several of Tout de Suite's recipes. Tansy had persuaded Stanley Zabar, an old friend, to let her hold the party in his store, and Annie had offered to supply the desserts.

Lost in her work, she didn't hear the footsteps behind her.

"Annie?"

She turned, startled. "Joe!"

"Sorry, I didn't mean to sneak up on you." Smiling that slipsliding smile of his, he put out a hand, palm up, in a conciliatory gesture. "Have a minute? You feel like taking a walk?"

Annie had about nine hundred things to do, but she found herself nodding. "Sure, why not?"

Such Devoted Sisters

Once she got outside, she was glad she'd said yes. Fall was here, really here, and until now she'd hardly noticed. Leaves from the catalpa tree outside her building littered the sidewalk, and the sky was the crisp menthol blue of after-shave.

They walked side by side down Washington Street without talking. Joe was so quiet that Annie began to worry. Finally he turned to her and said, "It's my father. He's getting worse."

"Joe, I'm sorry." Marcus *had* gone downhill since Joe's mother died last May; Annie had seen that much herself. He was having weird mood swings and memory lapses. The doctors called it Alzheimer's.

"Even with half his mind gone, he's impossible." Joe sounded angry, but she could see the lines of weariness in his face . . . and yes, the caring. "I've had three nurses quit on me in the last month and a half." He gave a short, incredulous laugh.

"What are you going to do?"

"Well"—he took a deep breath—"last week I made an appointment with that counselor I told you about. She assesses people—families, really—in this kind of situation. She visited Dad the other day, and then she came to see me today at the restaurant."

"And?"

"She's recommending that he be placed in a home." He turned to Annie, a sad smile surfacing on his face. "The other night when I was tucking Adam in, he looked up at me and said, 'You know, Dad, sometimes second grade stinks.' " Joe laughed, this time with genuine amusement. "That about sums it up, don't you think?"

I sure do, Annie thought, but she wasn't thinking of old age. Just of how unfair it was that you could love two people as much as she loved Joe and Laurel, and know that one love must cancel the other. Unfair to Emmett, too. They'd been together so long—sometimes it felt like they were already married—but she hadn't ever been able to take that final step. Maybe she never would. Not until she truly believed that Joe wouldn't care or that she wouldn't.

It's been six years, so isn't it about time you accepted reality?

"I haven't told Laurey. It'll really upset her. From the start she and Dad really got along. She's crazy about him." He looked down, but not fast enough. Annie had seen something in his eyes . . . something dark and unsettling.

"Joe, is . . . is everything okay between you and Laurey?"

He paused a beat too long. "Sure. Why do you ask?"

"I don't know. Forget it. It's none of my business anyway."

He smiled. "Well, well, you *have* changed."

Annie, relieved by his change in tone, quipped, "Only during business hours. Evenings I turn back into a yenta. Rivka says I'm so good at it I could give lessons." She paused. "Joe, about your father—if there's anything I can do . . ."

He shrugged. "Thanks. I'm okay. Just needed to unload on someone, I guess. You know, sometimes I think it'd be easier on all of us if the old man would just die." He stopped, looking rueful. "I've never admitted that to anyone."

"It's okay," she told him. "I'm not shocked. In fact, I think your father would prefer it that way, too."

He touched her arm and said softly, "Thanks."

Joe took her hand, and they walked back that way, as if they had been doing it all their lives. For the first time in years she felt relaxed with him, and oddly content. But still, something dark stirred inside her. An expression of Dearie's nibbled at her mind: *"Let sleeping dogs lie."* But how were you supposed to do that once they woke up?

IN ZABAR'S mezzanine, under a ceiling hung with bright enamel kettles and triple-tiered wire baskets filled with tea towels and pot holders, Annie worked the room, kissing a cheek here, shaking a hand there, stopping to chat with those she knew.

By nine, waiters dressed in crisp chef's whites were setting out coffee and trays laden with Annie's desserts. And lots of people seemed to be snatching them up.

But something wasn't right. Suddenly she didn't feel "on." As the raves for her tiny white-chocolate dessert cups filled with brandied mousse came at her, she wasn't getting her usual surge of triumph. All she was getting was a headache.

She was making her way over to the dessert table when Emmett came over and slipped his arm through hers. "You've got that look," he said affectionately, smoothing back her short dark hair.

"What look is that?"

His blue eyes sparkled. "Like General MacArthur storming Corregidor. Relax, Cobb, it's just a party. You don't have to conquer everyone here with your charm."

Annie stared at him and felt a mixture of affection and exasperation rising in her. He could be such a pain sometimes, but she never grew tired of him. Right now, in his new suit—a soft, charcoal gray with faint burgundy stripes—he looked quite distinguished, as befitted a new partner of a major real estate firm.

"I wouldn't *be* here if it wasn't good for the business," she told him. "Just now, when I was talking to Ed Sanderson, he said he'd like to do a whole spread on me for *Chocolatier* magazine."

"I'll bet he would." Emmett winked lasciviously.

"Em, if you don't stop making fun of me, I'll—"

He caught her upper arm, drawing her close. "You'll what? Kick me out of bed?"

"Just the opposite. I'll keep you there until you beg for mercy."

He rubbed his lips lightly against her temple and whispered, "What do you say we head off to my place so we can get started?"

Annie felt herself grow warm. Damn him, why did he *do* this to her—tempt her when she least wanted to be? Tonight she'd wanted to sort out her thoughts, replay her conversation with Joe. She shook her head. "In a little while. There're a few people I want to talk to that I haven't gotten to yet."

A dark expression flitted across Emmett's square, seasoned face, but he merely released her and gave a light shrug. Annie felt a dart of worry. She was putting him off, and he knew it. I don't want to lose him, she thought. Yet how could she tell him that she loved him, *adored* him . . . but not enough to marry him?

"Em, I'm sorry."

"No big deal." He glanced at her, a sharp, assessing gaze. "But look, I'm beat. Mind if I cut out on my own?"

"Only if you promise to have dinner with me tomorrow night."

He winked. "You got yourself a deal."

Watching his broad back as he wound his way toward the stairs, Annie felt her gloom deepen. How long, she wondered, how long before he walked away for good?

Suddenly she felt tired. She wanted to run after him, tell him she'd changed her mind, but her feet seemed bolted to the floor. She found herself thinking of all the movies she'd seen with people running alongside trains they had no hope of catching, the teary-eyed love object peering anxiously, fruitlessly, from the window. Though she hadn't moved an inch, Annie felt short of breath, and there was a throbbing in her temples, as if she, too, had been running to catch a train she'd already missed.

Chapter Thirteen

Laurel caught the softball and tossed it back to Adam. She watched him jump for it, arms straining skyward, his Big Bird T-shirt pulling away from his grass-stained jeans. The ball grazed the top of his glove, landing with a thump against the back of the house and scattering small flakes of paint, like confetti, over the grass below.

The place could use a new paint job, Laurel thought. It seemed just months ago that she and Joe had had the whole exterior primed and painted. But that hadn't been since they first moved in. Adam was just starting to crawl then. Six years . . . Could it really be six years? Her gaze scanned upward, taking in the two-story Cape Cod with its charming blue shutters and big, screened sun porch. For almost a year she and Joe had knocked themselves out fixing it up. But it had been worth all the sweat and hassle. Bayside was only a half-hour train ride to the city, and yet they had flowers, a vegetable garden, and this good-sized grassy backyard for Adam to play in.

"Mo-o-o-ommm."

Laurel saw him standing by the line of tall hydrangeas dividing their yard from the Hessels'.

"Watch out, Mom. This'll burn a hole right through your glove!"

"But I'm not wearing a—"

Laurel was so struck by the look of manlike determination on his small amber-skinned face that the words died on her lips. The ball flew upward and seemed to hang in the air before crashing down through the branches of the old apple tree under which she stood. Bending to retrieve it, Laurel thought how much like his real father Adam looked just a second ago, his dark eyes glittering. She remembered the airmail letter she'd gotten from Jess the year Adam turned three. He'd joined the Peace Corps and was living in Mexico. Then he'd met a local girl, and they were going to be married.

The memory of her own hasty marriage at city hall came flooding back. No white dress or veil, no bouquet, no rice even. But she'd been so over the moon she hadn't cared one bit. She had everything she wanted standing right next to her.

But Joe, had he felt such happiness? Kneeling on the grass, Laurel froze, her fingers clenched about the ball.

Don't cry. You mustn't. Not in front of Adam. But the tears were already starting, and with them came the image her mind had been replaying over and over since yesterday: Joe and that woman at the restaurant. She'd dropped off the finished drawings for *Sally, the Silly Goose* at the publisher and then stopped by the restaurant to surprise Joe. Coming up into the dining room, she'd spotted him with his back to her, in a booth with a pretty auburn-haired woman whom Laurel didn't recognize. They were both bent forward, so absorbed in each other that neither one noticed her standing there. The woman was holding Joe's hand tightly between both of hers. Joe's face was hidden, so Laurel couldn't see his expression, but she could tell he was upset. An apology? A lover's quarrel? A farewell?

And now, all over again, she was feeling the horror she'd felt then. All day today she'd been trying hard not to imagine the two of them telling each other little jokes, kissing, making love. What if there was some innocent explanation for what she'd seen?

Okay, maybe there was. But it wasn't just the woman in the restaurant. Lately Joe had seemed so distant and preoccupied. He hadn't made love to her in weeks. And this distance wasn't something that had just cropped up in the last month or so.

You knew. Even when he said the words, you knew when he married you that he didn't love you, not passionately, totally, the way you love him . . . and you took him anyway. So if he's having an affair, why should it be such a shock? At least it's not An—

"Did you see that? Wow-ee, Mom. Did you see how high it gotted? Right up to *space* prac'ly!"

Adam's voice yanked her back to him. Raking her knuckles across her wet eyes, she stood and went over to her son.

"If I were a talent scout," she said, hugging him, "I'd sign you up for the Yankees . . . or maybe NASA. The way you snagged that ball, I'll bet you'd be good with rockets, too."

Adam pulled away from her, saying, "Kids can't be scientises."

Her heart caught. *His world is so orderly. Color inside the lines, and you can't go wrong.*

Laurel wished life *were* that easy. Joe's love—all the years she'd struggled to win it, she'd been so sure it was only a matter of time. Now she wasn't so certain.

"Mommy?"

Now Adam was running in crazed circles about the lawn, flapping his arms.

"Brrrrrrrrrrr . . . I'm a rocket! Watch me go!"

"Where are you going?" she asked him.

"Mars!"

"Oh, that's too bad. I live on Jupiter. I was hoping you could drop me off on your way back."

Adam giggled. "Mommy, you're silly."

"Look who's talking."

"What if you *really* lived on Joopder? Who would tuck me in?"

"Daddy, of course." A tight, hot band formed about her heart.

"Annie, too!"

"Oh, I don't know. Your aunt Annie is pretty busy."

"But not too busy for *me*."

"Of course not." Annie, though frantic with her chocolate business, always managed to find time for Adam.

"She's coming today, isn't she? Isn't she?" Adam demanded.

"Later," Laurel told him. "After your nap."

"Ahhhhh . . . only babies take naps." He rose, adding slyly, "I bet Annie wouldn't make me take a nap."

"Well, Annie isn't here, so you'll have to do what your mean old mommy says." Laurel steered him in the direction of the house.

When she had him settled in his room, she went downstairs, made herself a cup of tea, and carried it into her studio. It had a window that gave her wonderful morning sun to paint by, and in the afternoon she sewed on the old Singer in the corner. Right now she was working on Annie's dress for the chocolate fair. Her sister had spotted this particular dress in an Italian *Vogue* and had fallen in love with it. And naturally, bigmouthed Laurel had to offer to make it for her.

She slid onto the stool that faced her drawing board. There were several ideas for the next drawing in the story she was working on, and she wanted to sketch them while they were still fresh in her mind. She tore a fresh sheet from her sketch pad, looked at it, but then her mind went blank. A wave of tiredness swept over her. Like all the times she'd been pregnant: drowsy, drugged almost.

Laurel felt her chest squeeze tight. Those babies—three of them—no bigger than the heads of pins, but losing each one had been terrible, almost as terrible as if she had lost Adam.

Joe's babies, his sons and daughters.

If she'd carried even one of them to term, would things be different now between her and Joe?

Inside, Laurel felt herself spiraling downward, and she took a deep breath, steadying herself. Why had she volunteered to make that dress for Annie? Why was she always trying so hard to please her sister? Sometimes it felt as if . . . well, as if she were struggling to make amends for some terrible injustice she'd inflicted on Annie.

And it wasn't Annie who was making her feel this way, either. Annie was terrific. And so great with Adam. It was just that she could be so *overwhelming* at times. Like a tornado—blowing in through the front door, high heels clacking, gold earrings flashing. After Annie's visits things seemed duller somehow. This house, with its bright quilts and woven wall hangings and stripped-pine furniture, seemed to lose its color.

Did Joe feel that, too? He must . . . and sometimes it drove Laurel crazy with jealousy. At times, seeing how happy and . . . well, *charged* he was around Annie, Laurel would feel as if she were fading right into the walls. She had to remind herself that she, too, was an interesting person. Besides taking care of Adam and this house, two of the books she'd illustrated had been nominated for the Caldecott Medal, the prestigious children's book award. Her show at that gallery on Spring Street had gotten two respectful notices and one glowing one, and she'd even sold six paintings. So why on earth should she feel second-rate?

An image of Joe and the pretty auburn-haired woman stole into Laurel's mind, and a knifing pain surged low in her belly.

Annie. What would she do if she were in my place?

Oh, why did it always have to come back to Annie? This was *her* life. She didn't need Annie or her butting in. *Remember how she hit the ceiling when you told her about Val's coming to visit?*

Laurel now imagined how outraged Annie would be if she knew about the money she'd been sending her father. It had started years ago—Val's phoning and explaining sheepishly about this bind he was in, just temporary, but could he "borrow" enough to tide him over? Somehow, though, the loans were never repaid. Laurel didn't really mind. She felt sorry for Val.

Oddly, it was Rudy she missed, though she hadn't answered any of the dozens of letters he'd sent. She knew she ought to really hate him for what he'd done, but she sensed that his lying to her wasn't born of malice. And if it hadn't been for Uncle Rudy, she might have actually given Adam up for adoption.

Thinking of Adam, Laurel badly needed to talk to someone. Should she tell Annie about this thing with Joe? If she didn't talk to somebody, she felt as if it would burn a hole right through her.
Maybe somehow she'll be able to help.

Thinking of how good it would feel just to unburden herself, Laurel straightened up and with pieces of masking tape began fixing a clean sheet of thick drawing paper to the table's tilted surface. With a charcoal pencil she roughed out a sketch of a unicorn. Not an ordinary unicorn—this one had wings, iridescent wings, like rainbows—and it was flying, soaring among the stars.

"A LITTLE higher, I think," Annie told her. "Just above the ankle."

Laurel, on her knees on the living room's braided rug, removed the pins clamped between her lips and gazed up at her sister, glorious in the gown that until a few minutes ago had been just a hank of fabric sagging from its hanger. On Annie it rippled, it glowed, it *danced*—rubbed velvet, the pinkish gold of hammered copper, supple as silk, with a subtle drape that softened her angular shoulders and emphasized her small breasts. Laurel thought it looked spectacular. She stuck a few more pins in and stood up. "There. Go take a look. Try the mirror in the bedroom, only promise not to look at anything else. The room's a mess. I haven't even made the bed."

The whole house, in fact, was a mess. Laurel looked about her, at the cushions scattered with crumbled saltines, at the sticky ring a juice glass had left on the drop-leaf table.

Then Laurel realized that Annie had made no move to leave, and was staring at her with her I-know-something-is-wrong look.

"I don't give a damn about the bed," she said sternly. "It's *you* I'm worried about. Laurey, you look like hell. What's wrong?"

Laurel felt as if there were sandbags tied to her arms and legs. She was so tired. "Nothing," she said. "I took a nap before you came. That's why the bed isn't made."

Annie peered at her with new sharpness. "You're not sick . . . or anything?"

"You mean, am I pregnant?" Laurel snapped. She thought of Joe's not touching her night after night. "If you want to know the truth, it'd be a miracle."

For a moment Annie stood silent. She looked shocked.

145

Then she said, "Is something going on between you and Joe?"

"Nothing a good faith healer couldn't fix." Laurel gave a short, dry laugh.

"Is it something he did?"

Laurel felt as if she was slowly losing her grip. It would be so easy just to let go, to let Annie comfort her. But no, better not.

"I'm glad you like the dress," she said brightly. "Velvet is harder than silk to work with. I don't know how many times I had to rip out that left seam and do it over." But then her control broke, and a sob slipped out. "Oh, Annie, he's having an affair."

She told Annie about the woman at the restaurant, about how awful it had been . . . and how she'd wanted to die. Even now, just talking about it, she felt some little piece of her shrivel up. Tears were rolling down her cheeks.

Stop it, she commanded herself. But she couldn't.

And then Annie started to laugh. She was *laughing*.

Laurel's face stung as if she'd been slapped.

Annie came over and grabbed Laurel's hand. "Laurey, you've got it all *wrong*. Joe isn't having an affair. That woman you saw is a counselor. Joe told me the whole story—about his father's not being able to manage anymore with just a nurse . . . about this counselor's recommending a nursing home. You can imagine how upset Joe must have been. She had to have been *comforting* him, don't you see?"

Oh, yes . . . Laurel saw. Everything, clear as day.

Joe had made this momentous decision about his father, and he hadn't once mentioned it to her. And it was Annie he'd confided in. Not her, his wife, but Annie.

Now it was Annie who looked ill, the color draining from her face. "Laurey, what's wrong? What *is* it?" Annie sounded frantic.

Laurel stared at her sister, feeling an avalanche of love, grief, sorrow, and resentment. "You," she said, the rushing in her ears so great she had to shout to be heard over it. "*You're* what's wrong."

Annie jerked, a hand flying to her mouth. "What?"

Laurel glared at Annie. "How can you pretend when we both know it's *you* he wants? And you want him, too. Isn't that why you've been stringing Emmett along all these years? Stop being so damn noble and *admit it*." She felt herself unraveling. "Admit you want him for yourself!"

A thundering silence filled the room.

"Mommy?"

Laurel jumped as if she'd been struck. She looked over at Adam, standing frozen at the bottom of the stairs. The front of his shirt was streaked with paint, and he held a paintbrush in one fist. His eyes were huge and scared. How much had he heard?

She wanted to run to him, but she couldn't seem to move. Annie swooped across the room and took Adam by the hand.

"My goodness, look at you! More paint must've gotten on that shirt than on the paper. Do you want to show me what you've done?" She was upset, too, her voice ragged, but she was hiding it well. She was protecting Adam, just as she'd once protected little Laurey.

With a quick, sharp glance over her shoulder at her sister, Annie steered Adam up the stairs. Laurel stared after them for a moment, then sank down on the sofa, determined not to cry.

JOE swung his Volvo into the driveway, crunching over a blanket of fallen leaves. The house was dark except for a light in the upstairs hall. Nearly midnight. Laurel and Adam were probably fast asleep by now. And that's where he longed to be. What a night. With orders stacking up and everyone working double time, the dishwasher had to go on the fritz, flooding the kitchen floor.

But none of the restaurant headaches compared with what he had tomorrow—a two-o'clock meeting with the director of the St. Francis Center. And then he'd have to do what he'd been putting off for days: break the rotten news about Dad to Laurel. She'd probably insist they take the old man in, and he'd end up sounding like a grade-A louse for saying no. Damn, what a mess.

But as he got out of the car and started along the concrete path by the side of the house, Joe began to feel calmer. He could feel the night air against his cheeks, and he could see his breath puffing out in wispy plumes. He found his way easily in the dark to the side door that opened into the kitchen. But at the back of his mind he sensed something was out of place. Then it hit him: *The light wasn't on.* When she knew he'd be getting home late, Laurel always left the light on over the little wooden porch where he was now standing.

Had something happened to her? As he turned his key in the lock and stepped inside, he felt a vague unease. He cut through the kitchen, which he could see hadn't been cleaned up. Dishes piled up on the counter, toast scraps and crumpled napkins scattered over the pine table in the breakfast nook—that wasn't like Laurel.

He made his way through the dining room, with its round oak table and carved breakfront filled not with fine bone china, but with Mexican pottery in bright, primary colors and Laurel's precious knickknacks—lopsided clay animals Adam had made, an intricately painted Russian box, a pair of pewter candlesticks, a small basket heaped with bright marbles.

Laurel's house, he thought. He lived here, but it was really hers, her creation. It struck him that he'd never fully appreciated how restful it was. When he arrived home each night all wound up, just walking in, he felt soothed.

Now he was climbing the stairs, quietly and quickly taking them two at a time. Reaching the second floor, he popped his head through the open door to Adam's room. Adam lay curled on his side, fast asleep, most of the covers kicked off. Joe felt his tension ease a bit. *You see? If anything had happened to Laurel, would Adam be here sleeping so peacefully?*

He tiptoed over and kissed his son's damp, toothpaste-smelling cheek, and was gripped by longing, as if he were somehow hoarding moments with his son and his wife, storing them up against the day when they'd be gone and he'd be left only with memories.

Joe felt the stitch in his gut tighten once more. How had it come to this? With Laurel he'd tried so damn *hard* to keep things together. But it was like running in sand. He always seemed to be going too slowly. Could he be trying *too* hard?

True, he hadn't been *in* love with Laurel when he married her. Bewitched, bothered, and bewildered, yes, but not the deep love he felt for her now, that had needed time to grow.

Still, deep down she had to have suspected that he loved Annie, too. Wasn't that the root of their problem now? Wasn't that why he couldn't touch her in bed anymore without feeling guilty?

But he didn't want to lose her.

When he looked at her, what he saw was a beautiful, smart, talented woman, a ferociously devoted wife and mother.

Joe gently pulled the covers over Adam and slipped out. His and Laurel's bedroom was next to Adam's, but when he peeked in, it was dark. The bed was empty.

Heading downstairs to Laurel's studio, he saw a sliver of light under its closed door. Standing outside, he knocked softly. "Laurey?"

No answer.

He eased open the door and saw her perched on the stool before her drawing table. In the white cone of light cast by the lamp clamped to the side of the table, her hand, madly sketching, seemed to glow with a light of its own.

"Laurey?" he called again, stepping inside.

Her head jerked up, and she swiveled to face him. She was wearing a loose silk robe, and its shimmering folds hung on her. It struck him how thin she'd gotten, seemingly overnight. She looked ill. Joe felt his heart turn over. What was going on?

"Hi. Sorry if I scared you," he said. "Deadline?"

She nodded. "They need it by Monday." Her voice sounded flat, toneless. "It's not working, though. It's the unicorn. He's not . . ." She swallowed.

Joe stepped closer, peering over her shoulder. The nearly finished drawing of a winged unicorn seemed to leap out at him, all fluid lines and supple movement. Extraordinary. She was so talented.

"What I wanted." She frowned, and stared down at the floor. "He's just a horse with wings and a horn."

"Is there a difference?"

She looked up at him, as if surprised that he couldn't see what to her was so clear. "He has to be . . . magical." Now there were tears in her eyes. "Don't you *see?* When I draw, no matter how fantastic the thing is, I believe in it. That's what makes it work."

"And you don't believe in unicorns? Or is it just this unicorn?" He smiled, hoping intensely to lighten her mood.

She stared at him, an expression of terrible sadness passing over her delicate face. Joe felt suddenly as though he were skidding, skidding all out of control, into the lonely future he'd feared.

"I can't seem to believe in either." A shudder passed through her, and she hugged herself, pressing her knees together tightly. Softly she said, "Joe, I want us to . . . to be apart for a while. Please don't argue. I don't think I could stand even talking about it right now." She took a deep, gasping breath.

Joe stared at her, not believing what he was hearing, yet at the same time feeling curiously relieved—as if he'd known this was going to happen and had been waiting for it. "Laurey, what is it?" He took a step toward her, but she held out her hand to stop him.

"Look," she told him, "it wouldn't do any good to start throwing around accusations. When Annie told me about your father, I felt so . . . so . . . Well, but then I realized it wasn't anything new—my feeling left out. What's new is that I . . . I don't believe in us anymore. All the things I hoped for . . . they just aren't going to happen, are they?"

A great drowning sorrow flooded through Joe. With every fiber of his being he wished that he could convey somehow to Laurel how desperately he loved her, needed her.

"I'm sorry I didn't tell you about Dad. I was going to—" He broke off. "But that's not really what this is about, is it?"

"No."

The look on her face told him what she was thinking, and before Joe could stop himself, he was saying it: "Annie?"

Laurel looked straight at him. "Yes."

"Laurey, I—"

"Joe, will you just *go*." Her look was hot and furious.

He didn't want to go away. If he insisted on hashing it out right here and now, Laurel, he knew, would probably give in. Things would be smoothed over—for a few days, anyway.

But in the end nothing would change. Maybe in some way she was being wise. And didn't he owe her this, honoring her wish? And who knew . . . maybe doing this would somehow help them.

But if this was the right thing, why did it have to *hurt* so damn much?

"I'll pack a few things," he said, his words thudding in his ears.

"Will you be staying at the apartment?" She cast him a forlorn glance, then quickly added, "Adam will want to know."

"Yeah, sure." Apartment? For a second he had to think. Then he remembered the old place on Twenty-first Street. He'd hung on to it because his rent was so cheap, and he could crash there when he was too bushed to drive home. But to live there again?

"What should I tell Adam?" Laurel was asking.

Joe hesitated. It occurred to him that much more than Adam's security might be at stake. Maybe his and Laurel's whole future. He did not want to lose all that. Not even one bit of it.

Joe did then what he'd wanted to do the minute he saw her. He crossed the room, catching her in a hard embrace.

"Tell him I'll be back," he murmured, then quickly let go.

Chapter Fourteen

EMMETT, standing in a large workstation near the second-floor entrance of the Tout de Suite factory, breathed in the rich, dense aroma of chocolate. Funny thing, he thought, how a certain smell could trigger a memory. Years from now, when he smelled chocolate, would he remember Annie at one in the morning tumbling into his bed after a long night at the factory, the scent of chocolate on her skin, her hair, her lips? Or would it make him think of this night . . . of having to tell her good-bye?

Don't, he told himself sharply. You haven't left yet. You haven't given her a chance to change your mind. He'd tell her about the offer he'd gotten—sales manager at Fountain Valley, ninety million dollars' worth of luxury houses just outside of La Jolla. He'd tell her the time had come for her to fish or cut bait. He needed her once and for all—to become his wife. Or he'd best forget about her and move on.

He watched her now, working alongside Doug and Louise, her hair damp and spiky, her hands and the front of her apron covered with chocolate. They were dipping plastic leaves into melted *couverture* for the tree—made entirely from chocolate—that would be the centerpiece of Tout de Suite's display at tomorrow's *Gourmand* chocolate fair. When the *couverture* on the leaf was dry, it could be peeled off and, using a warm chocolate paste, "glued" to a branch of the tree. Four feet high, its trunk and branches carved from solid chocolate, it was more than ambitious—it was a masterpiece.

"I've never heard of anyone being able to make a whole tree from scratch . . . except maybe God," Emmett joked.

"Yeah." Annie sighed. "Except God created the whole world in six days. If I stopped to think about how long I've been getting this display together, I'd probably pass out."

"Maybe it's time you *did* pass out," Doug volunteered. "We started at six thirty this morning, and it's now midnight."

"Thanks so much, Douglas." Annie shot a withering glance in his direction, a smile nonetheless tugging at her lips. "How would I ever keep track without you?"

"Anything I can do to help?" Emmett asked.

"Yeah." Louise shot a worried glance at Annie. "Get her out of here. Please. Just for an hour. She's been here longer than any of us, and won't take even a five-minute coffee break."

"Fat chance!" Annie yelled as she was carrying a tray of finished leaves over to Doug. Then her foot caught on something, and she staggered, the tray nearly sliding from her grasp.

Doug caught the tray, and Annie, with a loud exhalation of breath, rocked back on her heels. Placing her hands on her hips, she glared at Louise. "If I don't get this display finished by tomorrow and looking good enough to win first prize, I might as well just retire. Because unless I make that deal with Felder, there may not *be* any excuse left for busting my buns."

In her jeans and chocolate-smeared apron, her forehead shiny with sweat, she looked ready to collapse.

"There really isn't that much more to do," Doug told her. "Lou and I, we can handle the rest on our own. Trust us."

"I don't know. . . ." Annie was weakening, but she still resisted.

"Either you go, or we go on strike," Louise threatened.

"You wouldn't!" Annie gasped.

"Try me," Louise replied, plainly in earnest.

Then Emmett, surprising himself almost as much as her, grabbed Annie around the waist and hoisted her over his shoulder.

"Sorry, Miss Kitty, but it's for your own good," he drawled. Glancing back over his shoulder, he saw Louise gaping at them.

"Em, stop it. Put me down! I won't be carried out of here like a sack of potatoes! I have to . . ." Annie stopped struggling and started to giggle as Emmett reached the door. With a grunt he set her down, using his body to hold her against the door. "Can I trust you? Or do I have to tie you up?"

"Em, you're crazy." She clapped her hand over her mouth to stop herself from laughing.

"Crazy about you." He pulled her hand away and kissed her mouth, feeling her resist, then grow still and soft. He felt the ache in his belly deepen. How could he walk away from her?

She drew back. "Okay, okay, you win." She sighed, and let her head rest against his shoulder. "But promise me one thing."

"Anything."

"That you'll stop talking like Matt Dillon. It's starting to make me nervous."

"Why's that?"

" 'Cause at the end of every *Gunsmoke* episode, there was always a showdown."

Was she worrying about tomorrow's fair, or was she maybe sensing that the time had come for a showdown with him?

Minutes later they were strolling up Washington Street toward an all-night pizzeria on West Houston. Hell, Emmett thought, maybe I should get this thing off my chest here and now.

I'm thirty-six, Annie, and sick of waiting. Tired of being on hold. I make a nice living selling apartments and houses, and I still don't own one of my own. Like a drifter with more dreams than brains, I've been waiting for when we could buy one together.

Now, looking at Annie beside him, he knew her affection—her love, if you could call it that—was what kept him going, in spite of what she felt about Joe Daugherty. For half her life she'd been in love with the guy. How could he compete with an obsession?

Emmett touched her elbow. "You nervous about tomorrow?"

"Better now." She smiled at him. "I'm sorry, Em. I know I haven't been around much lately. There's just been so much going on." She let out a breath that left a faint wisp of smoke in the chilly air. "Anyway, you haven't exactly been lounging around these past few weeks. Did you close on that building on Mercer?"

"Not yet, but it's going to go. Just tonight, as a matter of fact, I had dinner with the guy who's organizing the limited partnership."

Annie, caught in the midst of yawning, shot Emmett an apologetic look. "Sorry. I didn't get much sleep last night."

"Working?"

"No. I was on the phone with my aunt. We're really worried about my sister."

"Laurel? She sick?"

Annie shook her head and looked away. "Not exactly. But Dolly says she's really broken up. Joe . . . well, he's moved out . . . back to his old apartment. Laurey asked him to."

Emmett slowed his steps. "You think they'll work it out?"

"I don't know."

Did she mean she hadn't a clue . . . or was she hoping they *wouldn't* get back together? Thinking of Joe and Annie having a clear shot at what he, Emmett, had wanted for so long made his stomach wrench. Suddenly he felt worn down.

"Annie, there's something . . ."

But before he could get the words out, Emmett saw that they were nearing Arturo's, with its garish sign advertising pizza and calzone.

"What?" She half turned toward him with an expectant smile. No, he thought. Better wait. Right now she needed to relax.

"It'll keep," he told her. "I'll tell you later."

After the fair, he thought, when she wasn't feeling so pressured. He'd explain how New York was making him feel hemmed in, and that unless she gave him the reason to do so, he couldn't see himself sticking around. Because this time, after he asked her to marry him and she said no again, he knew he'd need to be miles and miles away from her. Or how else would he keep from turning right back around and making a damn fool of himself all over again?

ANNIE came to a halt in front of the building where she and Laurel had once lived. She'd been walking, lost in thought, and had no idea how she'd ended up there. The sidewalk was deserted; it had to be three or four in the morning.

She remembered going to Arturo's, wolfing down two slices of pizza, then Emmett's forcing her into a cab, ordering her to go home and get some sleep. Exhausted, she'd let the cabbie take her to her homey but messy apartment. There, too tired even to switch on any lights, she must have fallen onto her bed, clothes and all. Vaguely she recalled waking up a couple of hours later, her heart pounding, feeling trapped. Dying to get out . . . get some fresh air.

Then, as if in a fog, not really seeing where she was going, walking . . . walking . . . walking.

It occurred to Annie that in some deep part of her she must have known all along that this was where she'd been heading.

To Joe.

She saw the lights blazing on the second floor, and somehow she wasn't surprised.

She had to see him, had to find out if Laurel was right . . . if *she* had something to do with Joe and Laurel's splitting apart. What if it was true? Did she *want* it to be true? Now she was mounting the building's stone step, pushing open the heavy glass door to the narrow lobby. Her hand went almost automatically to the bell for Joe's apartment, and she jammed her thumb against it.

The intercom crackled; a distorted voice echoed in the stillness. Joe. He sounded as if he'd been expecting her . . . or somebody.

Annie climbed the stairs. This is crazy, she thought. I shouldn't be here. I'll probably only make things worse for Laurel.

Nearing the top of the stairs, she saw Joe waiting on the landing in front of his open door, the light at his back. She kissed his cheek and walked passed him, through the door, and into the bright living room. Turning, she saw him standing in front of her, looking mildly baffled.

"Annie, what are you doing here?"

"Would you believe I happened to be in the neighborhood?"

He rubbed his face with his hand. "At four in the morning?"

"I couldn't sleep."

"Yeah . . . me, too." He blinked, shaking his head as if to clear it. "Coffee? I made enough to keep the whole city wired."

"No, thanks." She looked around. It had been years since she was here, but it was exactly the way she remembered it. "It's strange," she said, "being here again. Seeing you in this place. It's like you never moved out."

"It doesn't feel that way. Somehow it just doesn't fit. It feels like I'm trying to cram myself into something I've outgrown."

Annie touched his forearm. "Joe, what's going on with you and Laurey? The other day when I was out there, she seemed pretty upset. But I never thought—"

"What did she say?"

"She seemed to think . . . well, that maybe you were having an affair. She'd seen you with that woman at the restaurant—that counselor. But when I told her she had it all wrong, she . . . she got really angry. Said a lot of crazy things. About me . . . and you."

"Maybe they're not so crazy. Maybe *we're* the ones who are."

He was looking at their reflections in the darkened window, wearing an odd, distant expression.

Suddenly Annie felt weak, as if she couldn't trust her legs to support her. She sank onto the hard leather sofa, her heart leaping inside her. "Joe, you and Laurey aren't thinking of . . ."

"Divorce?" He stared at her, his eyes bleak. "Hell, no, not that. Laurey just wants some time alone. To think. See where we're headed." His mouth twisted in a bitter smile. "Euphemisms. What she's really saying is, You let me down, you s.o.b."

Maybe you did. But I'm partly to blame, too.

Outwardly Annie had let go of Joe, but not in her heart. There she held fast to her love, secretly tending it, using it to keep Emmett at arm's length . . . and maybe using it, too, to punish Laurel for taking Joe away from her.

Such Devoted Sisters

But if that was true, she hadn't meant to.

"Laurel's just hurt. She'll get over it," Annie said.

"No, it's more than that." Joe sank onto the sofa beside her, his forearms resting on his knees. "She's . . . different. I married a kid. Now that kid is grown up. She loves me, but she doesn't really *need* me anymore, not the way she used to. And that's okay. But, you see, the thing is . . . *I need her*." His voice choked on the last words.

"Then *why*? Why all this?"

"Because she knows how I feel about you."

Annie felt cold deep in her bones.

"We haven't done anything wrong," she said.

Joe let his breath out with a whistling noise. "Sometimes I think *everything* we've done was wrong. All our pretending."

She wanted to cover her ears, shut out his voice. "No!" she cried. "I wanted . . . *honestly* wanted you and Laurey to be happy."

Joe looked up at her, the pain in his eyes unbearable. "Sometimes I think," he began slowly, "that if we'd only made love, you and I—just once—then I wouldn't have felt so . . . cheated."

Silence seemed to be swallowing them. There was only the throaty murmuring of a pigeon outside the window.

"Do you want to make love with me now?" The question slipped out of her before she realized she was saying it. She sat back, shocked, breathless, her heart galloping.

Yet she also felt strangely calm. She'd traveled forever to get here, and maybe now the journey would be over. Wasn't this what she'd come here for? To quench a desire so old it had become part of her, her bones, her flesh?

Joe stared at her, his eyes holding her with the tenderness of an embrace. Then he stood up and walked into his bedroom.

Annie, as if in a trance, followed him.

The room was dark except for the glow from the yard, giving everything an oddly stark look. Joe said nothing while she undressed, his eyes fixed on her, unreadable. Then he pulled off his sweater and stood before her, his long torso stippled by the shadow of an ailanthus tree.

An image of Laurel edged its way into her mind, but she blocked it out. This belongs to me, she told herself fiercely. To us.

They stood before one another, not touching. Yet Annie felt as if she were gripped in an electrical field, the air around her charged with static. There was a high humming inside her head. She felt scared, weak, and trembly, barely able to stand. But if a speeding train had been thundering right at her, Annie could not have moved.

Joe began to touch her. Her hair, her face, his fingertips brushing lightly over eyelids, nose, lips, ears. It was as if he were mapping her out, memorizing her. They were joined at so many points, it was strange to realize how much there was still to discover. A universe.

"Oh . . . Joe."

Finally he kissed her. No, not just a kiss. It was more . . . so much more. Bright heat filled her. The room swayed, tilted. Now she was lying on the bed. He was beautiful.

She began to cry silently, tears running from the corners of her eyes. She wanted him—oh, she wanted him—but she didn't want this to end, either. She longed for this to go on forever.

LYING there afterwards, Annie thought, Is it possible to let go and still go on living?

Yet even if she did let go of him, she felt as if a circle inside her had finally closed. She felt strangely at peace.

The world began to trickle in. Muted voices drifting up from below. Outside, the rattle of a garbage can.

Morning.

She turned to Joe, who lay curled by her side, one long leg hooked over hers, an arm looped about her middle.

"I love you." The words came easily, like a line she'd rehearsed countless times inside her head.

Joe brushed a tendril of hair from her cheek.

"It was easier than it ought to have been," Annie said.

"Don't say that." He placed a finger against her lips. "I can't feel guilty. Maybe I should, but it seems like in trying to be honorable and upright, we've both done more harm than good."

"Joe, do you think if we had . . ." She tried to sit up, but Joe held her gently pinned.

"Annie, I don't know what's going to happen tomorrow or the next day or next year. But I know one thing—I love you."

The image of Laurel flickered, then died. Tomorrow she would face it. The guilt, too. Couldn't this one moment be hers?

"Again, Joe," she whispered. "Make love to me again."

But she could feel it—the moment falling away even as she clutched it to her, as if she were drinking from a cup with a hole in the bottom, trying desperately to quench her thirst before all the water trickled away.

Chapter Fifteen

Dolly swept into the reception area outside the ballroom and was enveloped at once in a haze of cigarette smoke. So many people! The narrow, high-ceilinged room was jammed—tuxedoed men, gowned women in fluttery silk and glittering sequins. Looking around, Dolly found herself remembering other years, other chocolate fairs, when she and Henri had held hands under the dinner table, almost counting the minutes until they could go back to her apartment and snuggle up.

She felt an ache in her chest and brought her hand to her bosom above the scooped neck of her emerald satin gown. Henri. Damn it, where was he? He *had* said he'd be here, hadn't he? But the message on her answering machine had been so garbled, so much background noise. He'd been calling from Charles de Gaulle Airport, and he'd said he'd be in New York for the fair. And—at this point her heart had taken a plunge into ice water—he'd said he needed to speak with her about something very important.

Funeral—was that a word she'd really heard in all that static? Could old Girod have died? And if he had, did that mean Henri was finally free? She *had* to find Henri. She had to *know*. Maybe he was in the ballroom checking on Girod's display.

But when she entered, the ballroom was devoid of people except for hotel staff putting finishing touches on the tables and *Gourmand* judges scribbling notes about the displays. Later the judges would sample and evaluate the edible entries.

At one end of the main ballroom there was a stage framed in great swags of rose-colored velvet; in front of it, the chocolate displays sat on long white-clothed tables. Each display was set slightly apart, and on a small gold card was the name of the chocolatier it represented. She saw a chess set—its board and carved pieces made entirely of dark and white chocolate. Next to it, a chocolate replica of a Spanish galleon, complete with a life-size ship's log, spyglass, and bag of gold-foil-wrapped "doubloons." And in the center of the big table—a fairy castle made out of chocolate puff pastry, surrounded by a moat of whipped cream.

Then she saw the tree.

It was the centerpiece of Tout de Suite's display, ringed by exquisite-looking cakes on rustic wooden plates, and truffles spilling from baskets made of chocolate twigs. A "picnic"—how clever of Annie! Walking over for a closer look, Dolly saw that the trunk and branches of the tree were molded from the darkest bittersweet, studded with crushed nuts and feathered with a sharp knife to give it the look of rough bark. And suspended from its branches were dozens of small, mouth-watering marzipan pears.

A triumph—and Annie, her own Annie, had made it. Dolly felt pride welling up in her. First prize. Annie had said she had to win, and Dolly now felt sure she'd get it.

Her mind turned back to Henri as she inspected Girod's display—an array of small tortes, bonbons, and truffles, set at varying heights, like a garden in bloom. She saw that in the middle of their display an area the size of a serving platter had been cleared—as if at the last minute Pompeau had decided to make room for an addition. But if he'd wanted to include something else, wouldn't he have done so? Unless . . .

Dolly buttonholed a judge she knew. "Do you know Monsieur Baptiste from Girod's? Have you seen him?"

"Henri? Sure. He's in the kitchen working on something."

He's here. Dolly's heart was thumping, and all of a sudden the room turned warm. "Thanks," she said. She was about to hurry off toward the kitchen when she spotted Annie.

Her niece, wearing a full-length velvet dress the color of hammered copper, was deep in conversation with an older man—stocky, florid-faced, gray crew cut. Hyman Felder. Dolly could see the tension knotting Annie's shoulders. Winning first prize meant so much to her. Dolly knew that Tout de Suite needed it merely to stay afloat. *Please, let her win.*

Dolly was angling her way over to Annie when a tuxedoed man up on stage spoke into the microphone. "Please . . . everyone find your seats. Dinner is being served."

Dolly felt a rush of dismay. Now she'd have to wait and just hope that Henri was going to be at her table. She gritted her teeth in frustration. *Henri, where the devil are you?*

Such Devoted Sisters

"YOU'VE GOT GUTS," FELDER SAID. "Taking a chance on something so risky. A chocolate tree?" He shook his head admiringly.

"Taking chances is what it's all about, right?" Annie sipped her Champagne while trying to look relaxed. But, suddenly, Annie felt she didn't want to smile anymore, talk anymore, be here in this crowd. Images of last night with Joe flitted through her head like grainy frames from a worn-out movie print. As if it had happened years and years ago. Not the beginning of a love affair. More like something remote, from another era.

Was that what it had been . . . a good-bye?

She felt a sweet sorrow rinse through her.

They probably had both known it was the end. Now, no matter what happened with Laurel, she and Joe would never be more than what they'd always been—friends who had loved one another; lovers who had loved others better. She felt sad but somehow complete.

Across the crowded esplanade she caught sight of Emmett and felt a wobbling sensation inside her chest. She ought to be with him right now, working things out with him, not Felder.

He hadn't approached her in the reception area. But now he began working his way over. He wasn't smiling.

"Would you excuse me a moment?" she said, giving Felder her brightest smile. "I see someone I must talk to."

Felder bobbed his head, dismissing her with a genial wave. "Sure, sure. You go ahead."

When she turned, she was treated to a closeup view of Emmett in a dark blue tuxedo. "Annie," he said, "may I talk to you—alone?"

She nodded, her heart plunging with a sharp downward twist. *Something is wrong. Very wrong.*

Now Emmett was guiding her swiftly into the reception area, where only a few stragglers lingered. As he turned to face her his blue eyes were cool and flat. Why was he looking at her that way?

He knows, she thought.

There was so much she wanted to tell him, things that should have been said years ago. But oh, that look . . .

"Annie—"

"Em, I know what you're going to say," she broke in, her heart banging against her rib cage. "Please, don't say it. Not yet. We'll talk later, when we get home . . . when all this is over."

"It *is* over. This. Us. I've had enough." She heard no anger in his voice, only sorrow and regret. "Look, I'm not blaming you. I knew what I was getting into, and like a dumb rodeo cowboy, I figured the guy who stays on the bronco's back longest is the one who wins. In life, though, I guess nothing's that simple."

She watched his lips move and wanted him as eagerly and hungrily now as she had wanted Joe the night before.

"I love you," she told him, and for the first time she knew that she meant it.

His blue eyes, flickering like neon, cut into her. "I was worried about you last night after I left you. So this morning I stopped by to check up on you. Five o'clock, and you weren't home. . . . And then I remembered about Joe." His big hands, she saw, were clenching and unclenching at his sides. He shook his head. "I realized something last night. I always thought of love as something infinite, like the stars or God. But it's not. You can run out of love just like a car running out of gas. I'm tired, Annie. I've got nothing left."

Annie felt stunned. Tears rose in her eyes and began spilling down her cheeks. She had to make him understand. She had to make him *know* how much she wanted him . . . now . . . and tomorrow . . . and forever.

"Em . . ." Her voice cracked and then faded. She wanted to beg him, but she was stuck with her stiff spine just as Emmett was with his crippled foot. Something held her back.

"Anyway," he went on, "I wanted to let you know I'm not sticking around for the banquet. I really just came to say good-bye."

"Dressed in a tux?" She managed a wobbly smile.

One corner of his mouth tipped up in a smile. "Couldn't ride off into the sunset looking like a deadbeat, could I?"

Ride off? "Are you going somewhere?"

He shrugged. "I'm pulling up stakes here. Moving out west." He grinned. "There I go sounding like Matt Dillon again."

"Matt Dillon didn't make a living selling real estate." She sniffed hard and pushed her tears away with the heel of her hand, angry at herself, angry at him. It was wrong. He had no right leaving her. "I don't want you to go. You know that, don't you?"

Emmett looked at her a long time, and as a shadow passed over his face she thought he might change his mind. Then he kissed her lightly and said, "There's a difference between not wanting someone to go and wanting them to stay."

For a long moment he lingered, and his gaze held hers. Then he touched her cheek briefly, sadly, and turned.

Watching him walk away—a big rusty-haired man with one crippled foot and one good one, and more heart than she'd ever deserved—she felt like crumpling onto the carpet under the gilded ceiling and crying until she had no more tears.

But no, she couldn't. Not now. Later, when she was alone.

Feeling cold and numb, she turned and started back toward the ballroom. Though she yearned to chase after Emmett, she knew that if she didn't stay here and win Felder over, she might lose not only Emmett but her business as well.

She'd have nothing.

Blinking away her tears, she swept in through the doors, holding her head up like a queen proceeding to her coronation.

"*Damn!*" Henri swore as the sheet of chocolate he was cutting in The Plaza kitchen broke in two.

His hands were shaky, but he forced himself to work slowly. The thing had to be perfect, flawless . . . a way of showing her how much he still loved her. Just a few more pieces, and it would be finished—the lake in the Bois de Boulogne, where all those years ago, on their first outing in Paris, he'd taken Dolly.

The lake itself he'd fashioned from a thin oval of chocolate brushed with white chocolate to give it the look of a rippled surface. Around the edges of the lake, slender dagger-shaped wedges formed tall reeds, some dusted with cocoa to give it a textured look. There were lily pads made of milk chocolate, blooming with white-chocolate flowers, their petals thin as eggshells. And in the center a chocolate rowboat with two figurines in it—a man and a woman.

Would she recognize it? Would she remember? Even if she did, she might not want him anymore.

So many years wasted.

As Henri worked, his thoughts traveled back to events that were still fresh in his mind: his father-in-law's death and the reading of the will. The old man had kept his promise. Thirty-five percent, in addition to the twenty he already owned, gave Henri an uncontested controlling interest. But then there had been a catch. If for any reason Henri and Francine divorced, the interest would revert in its entirety to Francine.

Henri had felt as if a brick had crashed down on his head. Had he heard correctly? He had forced himself to look at Francine, saw her smug self-satisfied expression, and knew then that it was true. They had planned it, the two of them—fashioned the chain link by link—to shackle him to Francine for the rest of his life.

Non. If Dolly would have him, they would begin again. Here. Together. He had some money put aside, and there were his shares of Girod's, for which Francine—if she wished to keep them in the family—would have no choice but to pay a good price.

Girod's. The thought of never again stepping into his beautiful, beloved shop was almost unthinkable. But he could do it.

So yes, this replica of a lake was more than just pieces of chocolate cut out and glued together. It represented all he knew, the skill his hands possessed. And what better way of expressing his feelings to Dolly? His heart had gone into every lily, every reed.

After applying the last of the leaves and spraying the entire model with confectioners' glaze, Henri tore off his apron and stood back to admire his creation. Yes, she would recognize it.

Henri checked his watch. *Mon Dieu,* already half past eight! Carefully, carefully Henri lifted his masterpiece, which sat on an acrylic board like some magical storybook island. His throat thick with longing, he balanced his great gift to her with one hand while he pushed open the kitchen's padded door with the other.

A WAITER raced past Annie with a little rush of warm air. Up on the velvet-curtained stage at one end of the ballroom, a portly man in a tuxedo was making an announcement. Now that dinner had been served, he said, the prizes would be announced, and then dessert.

Annie, seated between Felder and Dolly at a table near the stage, knotted her fists in her lap, where no one could see them, and watched the president of the Confectioners' Association approach the microphone. "I'm delighted to announce the judges' number one choice in the category of general excellence—"

She held her breath. *Please, please . . . I need this so much.*

"Le Chocolatier Manon."

Annie felt a rush of heat to her cheeks, as if she'd been slapped.

Applause filled the room, nearly drowning the next words, "And in second place, let's give a nice hand to Tout de Suite."

Dolly saw the look on Annie's face, and her heart sank. As Annie rose to her feet Dolly's eyes filled with tears. The room blurred, and Annie seemed to take on a starry corona, red sparks glinting in her hair, the folds of her dress spilling pockets of light as she moved forward, chin high, to claim her prize.

Then, across the room, seated at the table nearest the stage, Dolly spotted Henri. He'd come. He was here! Their eyes met. Henri didn't smile or wave. He just stared, and though he hadn't moved a muscle, she felt as if he were rushing toward her. Then she saw he was pointing at the Girod display table right near her. Why? She half rose to get a better look, and oh, blessed Lord . . . reeds, lilies, a lake, a boat . . . Why, it had to be . . .

The Bois de Boulogne. That first day they'd spent rowing. Dolly felt an exquisite warmth spread through her.

He still loves me.

Then she turned and saw that Felder had gotten up and was heading toward the exit. Annie would be devastated!

Dolly, torn between Henri and her niece, hesitated only a moment before leaping from her chair and following Felder into the lobby. She caught sight of him as he was disappearing down the wide marble staircase that led to the main floor below.

Anxious now, Dolly dashed after him. She was nearly out of breath by the time she reached the ornate lobby with its cascading chandelier. Not waiting for the doorman, she pushed open the heavy glass door and ducked outside. Once again she caught sight of Felder. He was crossing the street toward a stretch limousine. With scarcely a glance in either direction Dolly ran after him.

"Mr. Felder!"

Too late, she heard the squeal of brakes. Something was slamming into her; she felt herself crumpling, the sky tipping over onto her head. Disjointedly she thought, How silly of me.

Jaywalking. How many times had Henri warned her?

Now a bright white light was seeping into her head, blocking out her pain, making even the rumble and screech of traffic fade. And oddly, Dolly wasn't scared anymore. She felt as if this was where she'd been heading all along . . . ever since the moment she'd let that hateful letter slip from her fingers into that mailbox.

A chill sank into her bones. She felt herself slipping . . . slipping away. Her gaze was drawn upward by a peculiar light—the sun glinting on a wave as it combed toward shore.

The wave broke. A young girl's delighted laughter rang in her ears. She could smell salt air, hear sea gulls.

Dolly saw her sister running along the beach at Santa Monica.

Look, Dor, we made it! Cali-for-ni-yay. We're here! Can you believe it? All that other stuff—it's all in the past. Clemscott's just a bad dream. From here on, I'm somebody. I'm a . . .

"Star," Dolly whispered, and felt herself sink down, the warm sand closing over her head.

Lilies?

An enormous bouquet of them, stiff and white as candles, swam into her view. In the light seeping through the shuttered blinds they seemed to glow. But lilies were for funerals. . . .

Dolly tried to press her eyes open wider, but it felt as if sandbags were sitting on her eyelids. "I'm not . . ." She started to say she wasn't dead, not yet, that the lilies didn't belong here, but the only sound she could make was a gargled croak.

Out of one slitted eye she saw Henri's shadowy form unfold itself from a darkened corner. Then arms were encircling her, lips pressing against her cheek, her forehead. She could feel him—his warmth, his solidness, the prickling of his mustache.

"Henri?" She tried to lift her arms—one of them appeared to be hooked up to an IV—to embrace him, but the effort sent a rocket of pain exploding through her rib cage.

"*Non* . . ." She could feel Henri lightly pressing her shoulders. "You must not move. It is better if you remain still."

"Where . . ." She opened her eyes, and he came into focus.

"Lenox Hill. It is a good hospital, they tell me."

"How long have I been here?"

"Since yesterday night."

"You mean, all this time I've been out like a light?"

"You do not remember last night, your niece's being here?"

"Annie?"

"Yes. And Laurel, too. She telephoned last night two times and came to see you this morning. You opened your eyes, but we could not know if you saw her. We had so much fear . . . but now the doctors, they have reassured us. Four broken ribs and a bad concussion, very bad, but you are strong. You will get better."

Dolly clutched Henri's hand. "Lilies," she slurred, knowing it had to be the sedatives that were making her feel this woozy. "They've got no color. I can't abide lilies."

"*Oui, ma poupée.* Mr. Felder does not know you as I do. When we are married, you shall have roses—bright red and yellow ones—and you shall wear red. . . ." His voice caught. "A red dress, like the one you were wearing that first day you came into my shop."

What was he saying? Was he really asking her to marry him?

"Henri, are you . . ."

"No, please . . . let me say it. I know I have waited much too long for this, and you may no longer wish to hear it. But yes, I wish you to become my wife. I have quit Girod's, and that means you must quit also. Do you think we could ever start again from the beginning?"

Dolly was now struggling against the tide of wooziness, struggling to tell Henri what she'd been waiting six years to say. How no other man had ever measured up to him. How it didn't matter that they'd have to start over from scratch; she'd love every minute of it. And yes, she wanted him . . . in her apartment, in her bed, his toothbrush next to hers, his robe hanging on the back of the bathroom door.

Her heart was thumping like crazy, each thump bringing with it a wallop of pain, but that didn't matter. What mattered now was getting it straight, getting the words out.

But all Dolly could say was, "Try me."

THREE days later Dolly was sitting up in bed—sipping a ginger ale and wondering if her being so impatient to get out of this place meant she was getting better—when Annie walked in.

"Hi," her niece greeted her, depositing several glossy magazines on the table beside Dolly's bed before dropping a kiss onto her forehead. "You look as if you're feeling better."

"Heaps," Dolly told her. Annie had visited her every day, always bringing her some little thing to brighten her up—a bouquet of chrysanthemums, a basket of raspberries. If there was a silver lining to this ordeal, it was spending these precious hours with her niece.

But still, something inside Dolly twisted and turned. The time had come to put an end to this eternal gnawing inside her, this guilt—to tell Annie the truth about what had come between her and Eve.

For now, though, Dolly sidled onto a safer topic. "How did your talk with Felder go?" she asked.

Annie brightened. "He says he's still interested in making a deal with me . . . that if my aunt thinks highly enough of me to go dashing out in front of a taxi for me, I must be something pretty special." She grinned. "But you know what I think?"

"What's that?"

"That you're the special one." Her eyes turned suddenly bright. "I don't know if I should be thanking you for almost getting yourself killed for me, but would it help just to tell you I love you?"

Dolly felt a jolt. Not in all the years she'd known her, had Dolly ever heard Annie say those words to her. Her eyes filled with tears. "Oh, sugar, it does me a world of good, your saying that. But . . ."

Now was the time. Before the moment slipped past. The truth about dear, self-sacrificing Aunt Dolly.

"Annie," she began, capturing her niece's moist hand and tugging her gently down onto the bed beside her, "there's something that's been on my mind for a long time. If I don't get it off my chest now, I don't know when I'll ever again get up the nerve."

"It's about Dearie, isn't it?"

Dolly nodded, her throat suddenly thick.

"Your mama was a good person," she began. "And I did a terrible thing that ruined her career and broke her heart. I just want you to know—"

"You don't have to say it," Annie broke in, squeezing Dolly's hand. "For a long, long time I wondered what had happened between you and Dearie. And now"—she paused—"I know that whatever it was, nothing can change how I feel about you. And whatever it was that made you think you're responsible for the way things turned out . . . Well, she made her own choices, too. I loved her. She was my mother. But she wasn't perfect."

Dolly felt relief, like a vast ocean wave, sweep through her.

"I loved her, too," she said. Oh, how good it felt to be able to say those words aloud without feeling like the worst sort of hypocrite!

"I know," Annie said. "Why else would I be here?"

Chapter Sixteen

LAUREL eyed the flowers Dolly was clutching as she made her way up the aisle of the sedate church. No traditional bridal bouquet for her aunt, just a single spray of orchids—deep purple striped with yellow. Her dress, too—not white lace, but a red silk suit. A huge cartwheel hat was tilted at a jaunty angle atop her platinum hair, giving her the look of a '40s movie siren. Dolly's gaze was fixed on the altar where Henri, in a pearl-gray cutaway and vest, stood waiting.

Sitting on her hard pew right up in front, Laurel felt her throat tighten. She was happy for Dolly. No one deserved this happiness more. But Dolly was not the reason she was choked up right now.

She glanced over at Joe, seated across the aisle. Beside her, Adam squirmed and whispered, "Why can't Daddy sit with *us?*"

"Because," she whispered back.

This was hardly the time to go over it again with Adam.

Eleven and a half months, and I still break out in goose bumps whenever I see you. I'll catch myself setting an extra place for you at the table . . . or I'll be calling Annie or Dolly and realize I've dialed your number by mistake.

Can I go on like this? Can I keep on living without you?

Well, you have, for almost a whole year, she told herself.

She'd gotten through those first weeks of misery by imagining her life as a painting she was gessoing over, preparing a blank white canvas on which she would paint something new, something better.

And she'd managed to pull it off, hadn't she? More commissions than she could handle. And now a book she'd both written and illustrated on the *Publishers Weekly* young reader's best-seller list.

But if she'd grown so strong, how was it that all her carefully cultivated independence crumbled the second she laid eyes on Joe?

Laurel, swallowing hard, focused on Annie, seated on her left, next to Adam. *Please, God, give me some of Annie's strength.*

But Annie, she saw, was weeping. Was she thinking about Emmett, missing him . . . or was it Joe?

Laurel tried to concentrate on what the bald-headed, hawk-nosed minister was saying, but she found herself thinking of Uncle Rudy, remembering that L.A. lawyer phoning three months ago. "Your uncle has died," he'd said. Cancer. How sad she'd felt, then how shocked. He'd left her and Adam a fortune—a house in Malibu, not to mention checks every month from partnerships in shopping malls and office buildings. He'd given her financial security. Now she would never need Joe's money, or any man's.

But this isn't about money, is it?

Laurel looked around, recognizing a number of the guests: col-

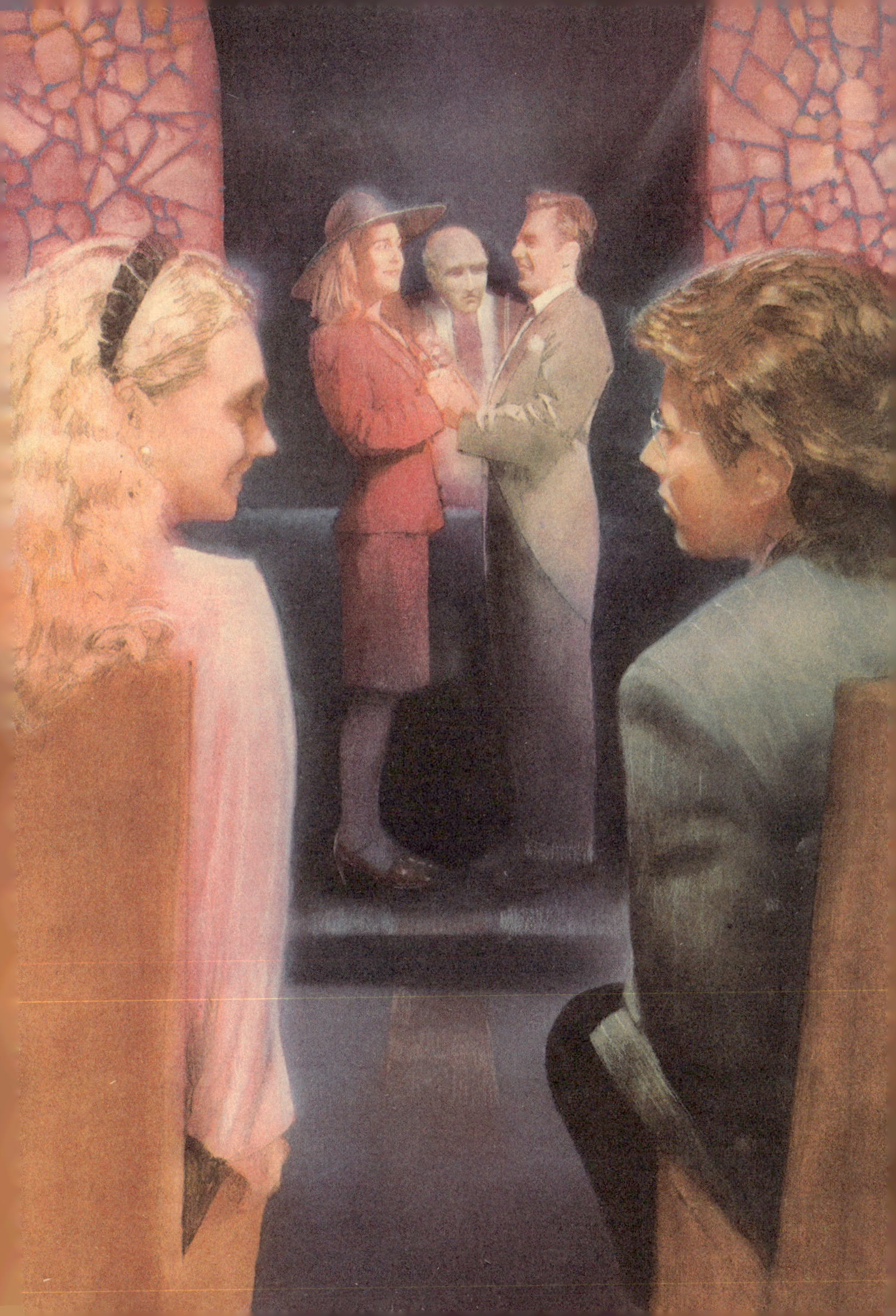

leagues from the Confectioners' Association; Dolly's housekeeper; her driver, Felipe; Gloria De Witt, who'd once managed Dolly's shop. And Rivka, wearing a modest blue sweater dress, had come, too. Religious Jews, Laurel knew, weren't supposed to enter churches, but for Dolly, Rivka had made an exception.

Laurel had promised herself while Dolly and Henri were exchanging their vows that she would not look at Joe. But now, like an alcoholic too weak to resist, she sneaked a sidelong glance.

Joe's gaze also wasn't on the altar—he was looking straight at her. Laurel felt guilty, as if she'd been caught cheating on an exam. She could feel blood rushing up into her face.

And he wasn't just looking; it was the *way* he was looking at her: puzzled, as if she were a stranger he thought he might have met and was trying to place.

Excuse me, madam, but you look awfully familiar. Are you sure we weren't married at one time?

Laurel, feeling a giggle about to erupt, had to clamp the tip of her tongue between her teeth. No matter how bad things got, she had Adam . . . and Annie, too. No matter how mad at Annie she sometimes got, they were joined forever. Sisters.

Even so, thinking ahead to when Joe would be free to marry someone else, Laurel felt gripped by a queasy weakness. That had to be why she'd put off discussing their getting divorced. Was it because she was afraid he'd marry Annie?

No, he couldn't. She'd give anything for another chance with Joe. But Joe had to want it, too. She couldn't make him want her. She'd already tried that, and look where it had gotten her.

Arriving at Dolly's apartment, a bit late after being stuck behind a double-parked delivery truck, Laurel found the wedding reception in full swing. She deposited Adam with Henri's eight-year-old twin grandsons and watched him immediately drag them off to the guest bedroom, where Dolly kept a box of toys. Then she walked over to the bar and poured herself a drink.

"Laurey."

At the sound of his familiar voice she turned too quickly, vodka splashing over the rim of her glass. She looked up into a pair of round steel-rimmed glasses, at reflected images of herself flickering in his lenses.

"We need to talk," Joe said in a low voice. "The terrace. We'll have some privacy out there. I'll get your coat."

Laurel didn't argue. Just nodded, and waited quietly.

He's going to tell me he's seen a lawyer, that it's time we got divorced. Oh, he's right, of course . . . but can I bear it?

Outside, she didn't bother to button her coat. The October wind was whipping at her hem, but she wasn't cold.

Don't wait for him to say it. Get this over with while you still have a shred of dignity left.

"I think I know what this is all about, Joe, and I don't want it to be any harder than it already is. You know, the way couples end up fighting over dumb things like who gets the martini pitcher."

Joe smiled. "We don't have a martini pitcher," he pointed out.

"Well, you know what I mean."

"Yeah, I think I do."

"I mean, things aren't the issue here, are they? Oh, I suppose we'll have to do some . . . sorting out. You know, like with Adam." She took a deep breath. "It's just as well, I guess, I never had those other babies."

"Don't say that." Joe grabbed her by the shoulders. "Don't ever say that." He sounded angry.

"Why not?" She glared at him, her hurt welling to the surface. "It's true, isn't it? Another child would've been one more thing standing between you and . . . and what you really want."

"What makes you so sure you know what I want?"

"How can I know when you never tell me anything! Damn it, Joe, you should have told me. About your father. About Annie. Everything. You should have told me in the very beginning that you were only marrying me because of Adam!"

"That isn't true."

"Of course it's true. I knew it then, deep down, and I wanted you badly enough to marry you anyway."

His eyes filled with tenderness. "Laurey . . ."

Say it, she pleaded silently. Please just say it and get it over with.

"I love you."

She pulled away, trembling. "That's not fair!" Tears were running down her cheeks. "Joe, please stop this. Just *stop*."

Laurel, feeling desperate, walked away from him, going all the way around the terrace to the Park Avenue side. Blindly, savagely, she wrenched the gold wedding band from her finger and flung it over the wrought-iron railing. She watched it arc toward the street, twelve stories below. She imagined it simply dissolving into the air—a sorcerer's spell, which she had now broken forever.

Looking back at Joe, she saw that the blood had drained from his face. Suddenly he bolted across the terrace, flung open the sliding glass door, and disappeared inside the apartment.

Where had he gone? What did it mean?

Then in a dizzying rush it struck her: *Her ring. He had gone after it. Like Jason charging after the Golden Fleece.*

She leaned over the wrought-iron railing, peering down. Vehicles the size of Adam's toy cars were streaming in opposite directions along Park Avenue. Then she spotted him—a tiny figure darting out from under the apartment building's green-and-white canopy. At the curb he appeared to be hesitating; then he was plunging headlong into the ongoing traffic. Laurel, her blood drumming in her ears, watched him stride before the oncoming cars, arms extended like a cop's, bringing some to shrieking halts, while others swerved and fishtailed around him. A cacophony of angry horns blasted her ears.

Joe, like a man obsessed, ignoring them all, hunkered down—right there in the middle of the chaotic avenue.

"Joe, come back! Come back here!" She knew he couldn't hear her, but she couldn't stop herself from screaming.

With the traffic now surging around him, she lost sight of him. At last she spotted him. He was standing in the middle of Park Avenue on the dividing strip, legs apart, holding what had to be her ring up to the sky, as if it were an Olympic gold medal.

"Joe . . . you idiot," she choked.

Minutes later he returned to her side, his eyes bright with triumph. "Laurey," he panted, "I can't change what happened back when we got married. All I know is how I feel now. I love you. I can't fall asleep at night without you next to me. I can't get through a single hour without missing you. Laurel Daugherty, will you marry me?"

She stared at him, too stunned, too overflowing with happiness to know quite what he meant or what she should say. "Are you sure it's me you want . . . not Annie?"

"You, my sweet Laurey." He touched her cheek. "Only you."

Joe snatched up her left hand and eased the ring back onto her finger. Then he was kissing her hand, holding it to his lips.

"Say I do," he murmured, pulling her into his arms. "Quick, before I do something really nuts, like throwing myself over this balcony."

Laurel pulled in a deep breath of frosty air. "I do!" she cried, loud enough for all of Park Avenue to hear.

BACK inside, while Joe went off to look for Adam, Dolly came over and slipped an arm about Laurel's shoulders. "Anyone with eyes can see I don't have the market cornered on happiness today," she said, smiling.

"Joe and I . . ."

"You don't have to say it. It's written all over your face. Oh, sugar, you've just given me the best wedding present I can think of." Dolly hugged Laurel, then gave her a little shove. "Now go on, get out of here. Get on home, where you can celebrate properly." She winked and gave Laurel another little push. "And don't worry about Adam. I'll have Felipe take him home later on . . . after you and Joe have had a chance to get reacquainted."

Laurel kissed her aunt and said good-bye to Henri, but she didn't see Annie. Probably she was in the dining room checking on the triple-layer white-chocolate cake she'd made for the occasion. Laurel felt the tiniest bit relieved. She didn't really feel like talking to Annie right now. Joe had gone to get his Volvo, parked a few blocks away, and would meet her in Bayside. She could hardly wait to get home.

Outside, walking briskly east toward her own car, Laurel became aware of the staccato tapping of heels behind her.

She turned and saw Annie hurrying toward her. Laurel waited. Seeing her sister, as always, brought forth a grab bag of feelings: love, resentment, guilt. What now? she wondered.

"Dolly told me," Annie panted when she'd caught up, "about you and Joe. I wanted to tell you how happy I am for you." Laurel searched her face, but Annie's expression was sincere.

"Thanks," Laurel told her, feeling suddenly awkward, not knowing what else to say except, "You're not leaving, too, are you?"

"No. I'm going back now to help serve the cake."

"I saw it. It's beautiful. It looks like the ceiling of a Victorian parlor . . . all those rosettes and swags and curlicues."

"That's where I got the idea, actually. From a mansion in Newport." Annie laughed. "I showed Hy Felder a picture of a cake just like Dolly's, and he ordered one for his daughter's wedding."

"How's it going with Felder's?"

"Looks like it'll be another few months before the grand opening, but I'm gearing up to go into production."

"The rate you're going, you'll need a factory the size of Brooklyn before too long." Laurel glanced at Annie. "By the way, have you heard anything from Emmett?"

Annie looked away, but not before Laurel had seen the hurt in her eyes. "Not a thing. You know what they say, A clean break heals the quickest." Then she added lightly, "I guess I'm just not cut out for marriage. Or maybe I'll end up like Dolly, marching down the aisle when all my friends are having grandchildren."

"What about kids?" Laurel asked.

Annie was silent for several long minutes. "I was just remembering," she said at last, softly, "those first weeks in New York, when you used to cry all the time. I felt like I'd done this terrible thing that you'd hate me for."

"I didn't hate you," Laurel said. "I just felt so uprooted. Like Dorothy in *The Wizard of Oz*. And all the time I was scared."

"Say it, why don't you?" Annie gave Laurel a sharp, wounded look. "You blame me for taking you away."

A deep calm flowed through Laurel. "No, Annie, I don't blame you. You did what you had to do. And I followed. . . . What choice did I have? Without you there, it would have been awful."

"We're sisters," Annie stated matter-of-factly. "Sisters look out for each other."

"But don't you see? It was always you looking out for me. Never the other way around." She touched Annie's arm. "I'm sorry about the way things have been. It's just that with Joe gone . . ." She let her voice trail off, not sure what, exactly, she wanted to say.

"I know." Annie's eyes, shining with emotion, met Laurel's, and Laurel felt as if they'd just made an unspoken pact.

"Well, I guess I'd better get going," Laurel said. "Joe'll be wondering what's kept me."

"Joe? Oh, yeah . . . sure. Well . . ."

Laurel watched her sister start to step back, looking suddenly awkward and slightly forlorn. Not watching where she was going, she caught the side of her heel in a deeply indented crack in the sidewalk. Thrown off balance, she lurched forward.

Laurel started to catch her, but her stance was somehow wrong, and she went sprawling onto the sidewalk with Annie on top of her.

After the first shocked moment, Laurel was able to sit up, pushing Annie up with her. As they sat there Laurel felt overcome, realizing how much she loved her sister. How much she still needed her in all sorts of little ways.

Suddenly she found herself giggling.

Annie, laughing a little, too, and wiping her eyes on her sleeve, said, "Don't look now, but there's a woman over there who thinks one of us is getting mugged."

Pulling herself up, Laurel helped Annie to her feet.

To the woman staring at them openmouthed, Laurel called, "It's okay. We're sisters!"

Epilogue
California: 1983

ANNIE handed her car keys to the parking valet and started up the canopied walkway leading into the Beverly Hills Hotel. Driving in from Los Angeles International Airport, she'd felt tense. But here in this lovely shade, tubs of pink azaleas and ruby rhododendrons flanking her on both sides, she felt herself begin to unwind. She glanced at her watch. Twelve forty—she had hours until her meeting. Time for a short nap, and maybe afterwards a swim.

Then she thought of *who* she was meeting and why, and she felt her stomach tighten.

Emmett.

More than a year and a half since she'd seen him, and in all that time not even a postcard. Then last week the shock of his voice over the phone drawling, "Hey there," as if it had been merely days, not ages, since they'd last spoken. He had his own real estate agency now, he told her, in Westwood. He was "doin' okay," which, given Emmett's laid-back way of putting things, could have meant anything from a hole-in-the-wall with an answering machine to some swank address with a dozen employees. But he hadn't just called to shoot the bull. He had something he thought she might be interested in.

Bel Jardin. It was on the market, and he had an exclusive listing.

Annie, so close now to her childhood home, felt her heart begin to race. That she might once again actually live in Bel Jardin seemed like a fairy tale too good to be true.

Suppose it's way more than I can afford. What's the point of flying out here just to take a stroll down memory lane?

Face it. Bel Jardin was not the only reason she'd come.

She imagined Emmett's sharp blue eyes crinkling in amusement. Could he possibly know that after he'd called, she had to soak in a hot bath—in the heat of July—to stop her shivering?

No, no way. By now he was probably married. He hadn't mentioned a wife, but then why should he? It was just a business call.

"May I help you, ma'am?"

Someone was speaking to her, Annie realized, a white-jacketed young man behind the desk.

"A reservation for Annie Cobb," she told him.

"Do you have any luggage?" he asked after she'd signed in.

"Just this." Annie hefted her single suitcase, and the bellhop, who looked like a former Olympic athlete, deftly took it from her and led her across the wide lobby.

Upstairs in her room, Annie kicked off her pumps and sank down on the bed. Despite the air-conditioning, her silk-and-linen suit felt as uncomfortable as thick wool. Well, if she moved out here, she'd have to buy a whole new wardrobe.

She'd been toying with the idea of keeping her apartment in New York and living in L.A. part of the year. The opening of Tout de Suite on Rodeo Drive next month would keep her hopping out here for a while anyway. And now, with Dolly and Henri supervising the manufacturing, the stores, and Felder's boutiques, she could scout out some other West Coast locations as well.

But Annie couldn't help feeling that coming out here would somehow be running away. But not from Tout de Suite—the business was now even more successful than she could ever have dreamed. And not from Laurel—she felt closer to her sister than she ever had. And Laurel, in her sixth month—already big as a house, radiant, bubbling over—didn't need her next door.

Might the running be not away, but *toward* something—the happiness that was always just beyond her reach? How many times had Rivka told her she ought to be married. Thirty-four. In Rivka's world she was an old maid.

But the men since Emmett—tied to their mothers, their therapists, their jobs. Most of them were nice, fun for an evening or a weekend. But for a lifetime?

Why, when she had him, hadn't she valued Emmett more? Why hadn't she begged him to stay, to give her another chance?

ANNIE, seated at a redwood patio table on the deck of the Crow's Nest in Santa Monica, overlooking the Pacific, sipped her white zinfandel and waited for Emmett. The tables around her, she noticed, were filled mostly with people even younger than she. Hip Californians. Annie felt overdressed, out of place. Would Emmett take one look at her and notice how she didn't belong?

A shadow fell across her, and she looked up, shading her eyes. Then he was bending down—warm, dry lips brushing her cheek.

"Hey there, good-looking." He dropped into the redwood chair opposite hers. "You beat me to it. I was gonna have vintage Champagne on ice when you got here."

She was feeling all wrong, her heartbeat picking up, her breath growing suddenly, alarmingly short. She folded her hands about the stem of her wineglass. "Hi, Em. It's good to see you."

"You're looking prettier than ever. Success agrees with you, I see. Congratulations. I hear you're opening up a store out here."

"Is that why you thought I'd be interested in Bel Jardin?"

"Naw. I'd have called if I'd heard you were moving to Borneo. I know how much that old place meant to you."

"Who said anything about moving?" She heard the defensive edge in her voice and immediately wanted to kick herself. Was she trying to convince Emmett or herself?

"Let's just say that for whatever reason, I figured you'd be interested." Emmett now was squinting out at the Santa Monica pier, and she noticed little sun lines radiating from the corner of his eyes. But otherwise, the same old Emmett. He hadn't gone native, thank heaven. She looked down and saw those same old cowboy boots of his. More weather-beaten, maybe, but obviously cared for. Seeing them, Annie felt an absurd happiness steal through her.

"I ought to be congratulating you, too." She had to change the subject. "I called your office to confirm our appointment. A very nice lady told me you were out, but would I like to speak to one of the other salespeople. Hey, Em, how many do you have?"

"Just two," he said. "But yeah, I'm doing okay. I like it out here."

And you . . . How are you? she longed to ask. In love?

But all she said was, "Well, I'm not surprised." A waiter, she saw, was approaching.

Emmett pointed at her glass. "You want another wine?"

"No, thanks. I'd probably fall asleep on you."

"Well then"—he pulled himself to his feet—"let's roll."

"Okay." She watched a volleyball shoot into the air and over the deck railing, Emmett catching it easily and tossing it back, as if he were one of the players.

Right now, if he'd asked her to, Annie would've gone with him to the moon.

"You still haven't told me a thing." They were in Annie's rented Ford, and she was turning off Sunset Boulevard onto a narrower tree-lined road leading up into Bel Air. She could feel her stomach fluttering. "I mean, if they're asking the moon, I have no business even looking at it."

"It won't cost you a thing," Emmett said.

Annie nearly slammed on her brakes. "What?"

"Just what I said."

"Em, if this is some kind of joke . . ."

"It's no joke. Annie, I didn't want to say anything before . . . but Bel Jardin's been sold."

Now she *was* slamming on the brakes, hard enough to fishtail off the road onto the shoulder.

"I'm sorry, Annie." She felt his hand on her arm and jerked away. "It just came up this morning. Listen, if it makes you feel any better, you were probably right about not being able to afford it. It went for over three million."

She turned to Emmett, sitting there calmly beside her, as if this was just some minor inconvenience. "Would you mind telling me what we're doing here? I mean, if Bel Jardin's been sold, what's the point of me looking at it?"

"You're here, aren't you? What's the harm?" He grinned. "I nearly forgot that temper of yours. Hell, Cobb, once you got a notion into your head, you always did like to hang on to it."

"As if I'd have gotten anywhere in this world if I hadn't!" Annie, oddly, was starting to feel better.

"Who says," he asked gently, "there's anything wrong with the way you are?"

"*I* do! Maybe I just should've been happy with what I had. Maybe I was a damn idiot not to see what was right in front of me the whole time." A pressure was building behind her eyes.

"Are we still talking about Bel Jardin here?" He spoke quietly, yet his voice seemed to echo inside her head.

"No," she said sharply, "we're not." With a wrench of the steering wheel she turned the car back onto the road, knowing that if she didn't get going, get *moving*, she'd probably do something dumb, like telling Emmett she was in love with him.

Then she was winding her way up Chantilly Drive, and there, gliding out from behind a tall oleander hedge, was Bel Jardin. The house, at the end of the long crushed-shell drive lined with steeple-high palms, glowed in the setting sun.

Oh, how good to see it! Annie could feel her annoyance at Emmett fading, and she was gripped by an excitement. Pulling to a stop at the end of the drive, she got out and sucked in a deep breath. Lemon blossoms and jasmine. And look how the bougainvillea had climbed up around the porch. She stared at the heavy, carved door and felt her heart turn over in her chest.

Home. She was home.

Annie turned to Emmett. "Are they home?"

"No. But I have the keys. Want to go in?"

"Oh, Em, I don't know. Maybe I'd be cheating myself. Seeing it the way it is instead of the way I remember it."

"Why don't you describe it to me while we take a look around? Who knows, maybe the new owner would like a few suggestions."

"Why should he?"

"I don't know. Why don't you ask him?" Emmett draped his arm around her shoulders. "He's standing right here."

Annie stepped away, her knees buckling a little.

"You?" she gasped. "*You* bought Bel Jardin. But why?"

Emmett's blue eyes seemed to blaze with an almost unnatural brightness.

"Because for almost two years I've been trying to get your own sweet, stubborn self out from under my skin, Annie Cobb, and I haven't had a helluva lot of luck. When this listing fell into my lap, I sort of figured it was fate. And then after I talked with Laurey—"

"You called Laurey? What did she say?"

"That you'd once told her that not marrying me was the biggest mistake you ever made. So I figured, well, maybe you'd be interested in sharing Bel Jardin with a reformed drifter like me."

"That's about the nicest thing you've ever said to me." Tears filled her eyes, and her vision blurred. Her relief and joy were so vast she could not have put them into words. "Now, will you shut up and kiss me."

He did. A kiss that made her remember everything good she had ever longed for in her entire life. A sweet, golden warmth filled her. Rapture. There could be no other way to describe this feeling . . . this dazed lightness, this heart-struck bliss.

In her mind she heard Dearie say, *"Grab it, kiddo. . . . A second chance like this one may never come your way again."*

"Let's go inside," Annie said, pulling back and taking Emmett's hand. "And I'll show you where we'll put my mother's Oscar."

ABOUT THE AUTHOR

Walking into Eileen Goudge's Manhattan town house makes the noise and bustle of the city seem far away indeed. Tapestried walls and carved Victorian antiques create a sense of elegance and history. And seated in the midst of it all, Eileen Goudge looks as if she's been here all her life.

Actually, that couldn't be further from the truth. This prolific author started out, at twenty, as a divorced mother living on welfare in California, where she grew up. "It was the worst year of my life," she recalls. "There is a shame that comes with poverty. It's humbling in a devastating way."

A second marriage rescued her from welfare, but only barely. However, it was during this time that the author began to write—first magazine articles, then young adult fiction. (She was one of the original writers for the much praised Sweet Valley High series.) This newfound success gave her the self-confidence to end a marriage that had turned unbearable. She took her two children and, like Annie and Laurel, moved to New York. There she continued to turn out her teen books—one every six weeks—until she finally achieved some financial security.

Eileen Goudge

Eileen Goudge is now married to literary agent Al Zuckerman, and between them they have five children. In spite of the demands on her time, Goudge is able to devote herself to the writing she likes best: adult fiction. In 1989 she published *Garden of Lies,* an enormous best seller.

For *Such Devoted Sisters,* Goudge drew largely from her own life experiences. Her love of cooking desserts inspired the chocolate angle, and with four sisters, she found herself very familiar with sibling rivalry.

Though her early struggles are now past, she still remembers them clearly. "I really am blessed," she says. "Whenever I see people on the street, I always give them something. I have to think how close I came to ending up almost the same."

PHOTO: MARC RABOY

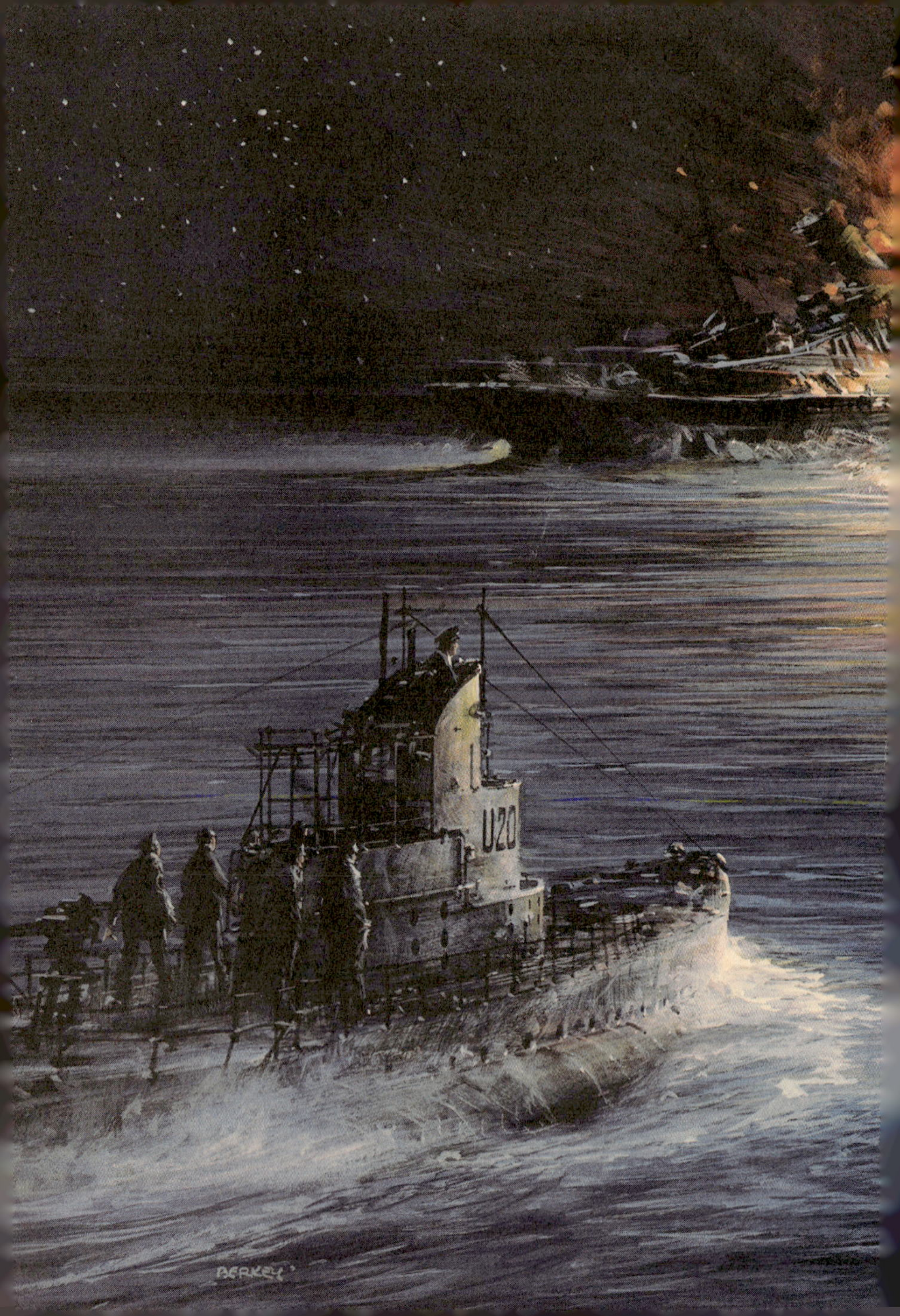
U20
BERKEY

RULES OF ENCOUNTER

WILLIAM P. KENNEDY

The time: the dark dawn of World War I. German U-boats are sabotaging Britain's North Atlantic shipping lanes. To Winston Churchill, young First Lord of the Admiralty, it's clear that England must bring a reluctant America into the war. His desperate plan: provoke an incident so heinous, so outrageous that the Americans must respond. But there are rules against the sort of encounter Churchill envisions, rules that must now be broken.

Fall 1914
CHAPTER 1

London. "The United States is a peace-loving nation, committed to peace throughout the world. President Woodrow Wilson is pledged to keep our country neutral in this terrible world war, a friend to every nation involved on every side. And it is as a friend of England that I present his proposals for an honorable peace."

Colonel Edward House was Woodrow Wilson's personal friend and confidant, his handpicked emissary to the warring nations of Europe. He had come to London with Wilson's idealistic plan to bring the war out of the trenches and to the more civilized setting of the conference table, and was in the process of presenting it to the leaders of His Majesty's government.

No one was really listening. What England needed to end its war with Germany was not a peacemaker, but an ally.

Germany had struck into France with incredible swiftness. England's army crossed the Channel to aid its French ally, but the British were driven back by the German onslaught. Then when it seemed defeat was inevitable, the ragtag Russian army attacked Prussia. One of the German armies was sent to deal with the Russians, which turned the German advantage into a stalemate, and the war dug into a line of trenches across northern France.

The standoff wouldn't last forever. Once the Russians were defeated, the Germans would return. The only hope of victory that British generals and admirals had was that their own lines could be strengthened before the Russians collapsed. And their only source of new strength was the United States. They needed America in the war, on their side. Not at the head of a conference table.

"And therefore the President proposes freedom of the seas, guaranteeing to the ships of all nations access to the ports of any nation," Colonel House droned on.

Absurd, the British leaders thought. Their most effective weapon was their naval blockade across the North Sea, cutting off all maritime commerce with Germany. They had no intention of letting any ship get within a hundred miles of a German port.

There was polite applause as House finished his presentation. He poured a glass of water from a pitcher on his lectern and sipped it as he waited for questions.

"Colonel House." The questioner was a cherubic-faced young man of barely forty. He wore the gray morning attire that was the uniform of civilian government officials.

"Yes, Mr. . . ."

"Winston Churchill," the young man said. And then with a mischievous grin, "I believe I'm First Lord of the Admiralty."

"Yes, of course," House pretended.

"While we are most respectful of your President's commitment to neutrality," Churchill said, "I wonder if there is anything that might persuade him to take a more active role in the war?"

"More active?" The President had offered to serve as the architect of a lasting peace. What could be more active than that?

"To declare war on Germany," Churchill said, clarifying any ambiguities.

The colonel stiffened. "Mr. Churchill, there is nothing that will bring the United States into this war."

"Nothing?" Churchill pressed, blinking in astonishment.

"Well," House reconsidered, "if the Germans were to attack American citizens, then certainly we would be forced to fight. But of course, that would be highly unlikely."

"Highly unlikely," Churchill agreed, settling back into his chair.

He was buoyant as he walked from the meeting.

General John French, commander of the British armies in France, caught up with him. "Not much hope from that quarter."

"Oh, I think we can count on the Americans."

French was stunned. "I thought he made it quite clear that there would be no help from across the Atlantic."

"Unless the Germans attack American citizens," Churchill reminded the general. "What we have to do is assemble some Americans and then persuade the Germans to attack them."

"You can't be serious," French said. "How would you ever get Americans in front of a German gun?"

"I was thinking of a ship," the First Lord of the Admiralty answered.

The North Sea. Daylight. A pale knife-edge cut through the mist, separating the night from the distant outline of the Dutch coast. The west wind seemed suddenly to die, and from the east came the first squawking of the gulls. Standing on the wing of *Aboukir*'s bridge, Commander William Day could suddenly make out the bow of his own ship and the white foam that washed out of its way.

"Sunrise, Quartermaster," Day called as the small leaden arc of the sun appeared. The North Sea was colorless in the fall, and in the rain even the tint of the sun was difficult to discern.

"Sunrise at 0614 hours," the quartermaster chanted as he made the appropriate entry in the log. He leaned out of the wheelhouse and looked up at the signal bridge. "Morning colors," he ordered, and in response the Union Jack slid up the signal mast.

They were steaming north by northeast, parallel to the coastline, in a broad triangle. *Hogue* was closest to the beach, and *Cressy* was up front in the van. Day was just able to make them out.

"Number One." Captain Drummond always addressed his officers by their billet titles. He came and stood beside Day.

"Good morning, Captain."

"Nothing much good about it," Drummond mumbled, sniffing at the heavy air. "Where's the barometer?"

"Holding at twenty-eight and a half," Day answered.

"Looks like we're in for another day of this muck." The captain rose up on his toes, pressed his hands into the small of his back, and leaned backward. A chain of cracks sounded from his spine. "The dampness gets into everything."

As the two men stood side by side, they seemed to be from different planets. At the age of thirty, Day towered over his commanding officer. He was over six feet, with broad shoulders and powerful arms inherited from his longshoreman father. Drummond was a short, slight man, whose physique suggested scholarship more than hard work. Day had a dark complexion, with angular features and deep-set, brooding eyes. Drummond's thin white hair blended easily into a soft, pink face.

"Any orders from the flag?" Drummond was asking whether the squadron commander, who had his flag aboard *Cressy*, had sent any signals.

"Turn to two eight five at 0700," Day answered.

"Why in hell are we steaming in circles off the Dutch coast?" Drummond cursed. "If the German fleet comes out, they won't be heading in our direction. They'll go north." He looked into the wheelhouse and focused on the chronometer. "I'll take my breakfast before the maneuvering starts, Number One."

"Aye, sir."

Day looked toward the coastline. He could now make out the superstructures of *Hogue* and *Cressy*—the masts streaming their wireless antennas—and the four stacks that rose above each hull. They were ancient ships, but they were the only ones available for patrolling the northern approaches to the English Channel. All the British dreadnoughts were needed for patrols north of the Orkneys to keep the German fleet from breaking out into the Atlantic. *Heaven help us*, Day thought, *if the German High Seas Fleet ever does come out. Cressy*-class cruisers had only nine-inch guns as their main battery. The new German cruisers, with their fifteen-inch guns, could drop shells on *Cressy, Hogue*, and *Aboukir* for half an hour before the English ships could even bring them into range.

Day checked the chronometer: 0625. In thirty-five minutes the signal flags on *Cressy* would drop, ordering the squadron to turn to the west. He stepped into the wheelhouse and pulled the cap from one of the voice tubes. "Engine room, this is the bridge."

"Engine room, aye." The voice came from deep within the ship.

"We're going to be maneuvering in a few minutes," Day said. "You might want to bring up your steam now."

"Aye, aye, sir," the hollow voice responded.

Day raised his binoculars and scanned the horizon. To the east, there was a faint trace of light, broken by the flat landfall of Holland. To the north and west, still nothing but murky darkness.

Suddenly the ship lurched, as if struck by a giant hammer, its steel side crashing like a cymbal. Day toppled and slid across the deck until he smashed against the wheelhouse. He looked up to see a wall of black water rise high above the port wing, followed by a cloud of hissing steam. Instantly fire alarms began clanging deep within the hull.

"A torpedo!" screamed the helmsman, who had been slammed to the deck by the violent twisting of the ship's wheel.

"Hold her on course," Day yelled as he struggled back onto his feet. He ran into the wheelhouse and uncapped the voice tube. "Engine room, this is the bridge."

A voice shouted back above the howl of escaping steam. "We're taking water into the boiler rooms. We've got a hole clean through the portside bunker. And we've got busted steam lines."

Day was suddenly aware that the deck was tilting to port. "Open the starboard sea cocks," he screamed back down the voice tube. "Flood the starboard coal bunkers."

"We're already taking on more water than we can handle."

"Flood them. Now!"

There was a pause, and then, "Aye, aye, sir."

The explosion, Day realized, had blown a hole through the port bunker to the sea. Now seawater was filling the half-empty bunker. The imbalance would roll the ship over in a matter of minutes. He had to open the starboard bunker to keep *Aboukir* upright.

He charged out of the wheelhouse and up the ladder to the signal bridge. "Signal to *Cressy*," he screamed above the deafening alarm bells. " 'Struck by mine or torpedo. Losing speed, and listing.' "

"Aye, aye, sir," the signalman acknowledged as he tore the weather cover off the carbon-arc signal lamp.

"Number One!" Captain Drummond had staggered out onto the wing. "What happened? Do we have damage reports?"

"A torpedo," Day snapped. "Our port coal bunkers are open to the sea. I've ordered the starboard bunkers flooded. I'm going to tell the black gang to vent steam."

Drummond nodded. Once one bunker was open, *Aboukir* was doomed. All they could do was prolong the death agony until the crew could make it safely over the side.

"Message from flag!" the signalman screamed. " '*Cressy* . . . coming . . . alongside . . . to . . . render . . . assistance,' " he mouthed as he read the flashing light on *Cressy*'s bridge. " '*Hogue* . . . will . . . provide . . . protective . . . screen.' "

Drummond and Day watched as *Cressy* leaned into a tight turn, swinging her bow at the stricken *Aboukir*.

189

Rules of Encounter

Forty feet below, the engineers waded waist-deep in inky black water as they went from valve to valve, venting away the ship's steam. In the boiler rooms, the stokers were raking out the fires.

"Bridge, this is the engine room," the chief engineer shouted through the voice tube. "We've got all the sea cocks open. It's no good. The starboard bilge must be out of the water."

"Get all your men topside," Day said.

They only had a few seconds left. Within the ship everything loose was falling toward the port side. Heavy machines would soon begin to tear free. Any moment the ship would roll over and die.

Captain Drummond was looking straight down from the port wing, waiting for the rush of water along the side of the ship to slow. He wanted the ship dead in the water before he ordered the boats lowered and his crew over the rail. But even as she moved forward, the ship was twisting over onto her side. He made his decision.

"Abandon ship!"

"Cut the lifeboats free," Day screamed. He couldn't lower them. The boats on the port side were hanging ten feet away from the ship. No one could reach them. Those on the starboard side were hanging in over the deck.

Crewmen formed fire lines, passing life jackets out from their lockers. As quickly as the men were able to fasten on jackets, they jumped over the port rail into the sea.

"You, too, Number One," Drummond said.

"We'll go together," Day said.

Drummond shook his head. "I'll stay until *Cressy* comes."

"You don't have time," Day began, but his words were lost in a screech of tearing metal. The number one stack broke and fell like a tree, crashing down on the seamen struggling in the water.

Day wrapped his arms around Captain Drummond and wrestled him over the lifeline. As *Aboukir* continued to roll, the rising sea lifted them off the bridge and floated them clear. The ship paused on its side for only an instant before its decks and superstructure fell under. She turned completely over, the whalelike curve of steel broken only by the propellers, which slowly rose into the air.

For a half mile behind the sinking ship, its crew was stretched out in a line of bobbing heads. Choking men struggled toward the overturned boats. Others screamed out in pain. Some were still and silent, blank faces kept afloat by the life jackets.

Commander Day held Captain Drummond in his arm as he kicked out toward the floating flag cases from the signal bridge. The older man struggled for a handhold, and then Day vaulted him onto one of the cases. Drummond reached back to help haul Day on top, but the commander was already swimming back toward a signalman who was thrashing in the water.

The signalman pounced on Day as soon as he was near, and for a moment they struggled before Day got an arm around the boy's neck, turned him over onto his back, and started kicking back toward the floating flag cases. It was then that he saw *Cressy* as she appeared around the capsized hull of *Aboukir*.

The flagship had slowed toward the line of men who were screaming and waving frantically to be rescued. Aboard *Cressy*, crewmen lined the rail, lowering nets and ropes over the side. Then well behind *Cressy*, Day saw *Hogue*. She was moving at full speed, belching clouds of thick smoke as she searched for a submarine that might be lurking beneath the water.

Drummond reached down and caught the signalman by his shirt collar. Day got his shoulder under the boy, and together they were able to lift him up next to the captain. "Get aboard," Drummond called to Day. The commander was reaching up when the sky suddenly flashed with light, and the air vibrated in a thunderclap.

"Good God," the captain prayed. In the distance *Hogue* shuddered beneath a billowing cloud of smoke. She seemed to skid sideways, kicking up a wave of white water as she stopped dead. Then there was a second flash, this one near her stern. The old ship began to roll to starboard, her decks and then her gun mounts disappearing into the sea. Her crew fell like raindrops into the water.

Aboard *Cressy*, the crew scampered away from the railing, abandoning the nets and lines. The flagship moved away from the drowning men, rushing off toward the sinking *Hogue*.

Cressy had no choice but to attack. If she stopped to rescue *Aboukir*'s crew, she would be an easy target. The submarine had to be somewhere beyond *Hogue*. As soon as she had gathered enough speed, *Cressy* began zigzagging. In the water around *Hogue*, sailors waved deliriously at what they thought was approaching rescue. Their calls turned to screams of horror as *Cressy* charged through their midst, her wake tossing them aside like bobbing corks.

Drummond and Day watched *Cressy* race a thousand yards

north, then turn back toward the rising steam of *Aboukir*. Screams came from the water around them. *Aboukir*'s crewmen had seen *Cressy* steam over *Hogue*'s survivors in her frantic chase toward her invisible tormentor. Now she was coming straight toward them.

And then she exploded. The blast threw a waterspout up along her starboard side, and a cloud of coal dust belched from her shattered hull. Immediately she began to lean to starboard. Her coal bunker, like those of her sister ships, was flooding quickly, its weight dragging the ship into a roll from which there was no hope of recovery. *Cressy*'s whistle sounded her death groan. Then she began to settle into her own black stain, joining *Hogue* and *Aboukir*, which had already vanished.

Now there were a thousand men thrashing in the water, struggling toward bobbing pieces of debris. Cries echoed across the flat surface of the still water.

Day identified one of the voices, slid down from the flag box, and struck out toward the helmsman, who was pleading for help. As he was pushing the man up next to Captain Drummond, he heard another voice nearby. A pale face bobbed up a few yards away, and Day was able to reach out, seize the man's life jacket, and drag him alongside. In just a few minutes he gathered six of *Aboukir*'s crew—three on top of the floating flag locker, three with him in the water.

Then through the pained wail that blended hundreds of voices, he heard a new sound—the dull throbbing of an engine.

"The murdering bastard." It was Captain Drummond, sitting on top of the flag locker, who saw it first. Day turned and saw the ghostly shape of a submarine cutting through the mist. The droning noise grew louder, and the details of her structure began to take shape. He could see the top of her bow as it sent up a misty spray. And then he saw a man standing atop the conning tower, looking around in disbelief at the destruction he had caused.

The submarine came closer, and as it moved, the air around it became deathly still. Voices stopped in the throats of the men in the water as they came face to face with the image of death, moving like a shark through their midst.

"Bastard," Drummond suddenly screamed.

The submarine captain raised his hands in a gesture of helplessness. As the U-boat drifted past he stretched out his arms, embracing the tiny size of his craft. How, he seemed to be asking, can this little boat rescue so many? The beat of the engines suddenly quickened, and the ghostly craft disappeared into the low-lying mist.

Day tightened his grip on the edge of the locker. He was exhausted, and the weight of his clothes dragged him lower in the water. He could taste the sulfur in the coal slick floating under his chin.

London. Alfred Booth raised the glass of port to his lips, pausing for a moment so that he could savor the sweet bouquet. His cousin George looked on apprehensively from across the table.

"Very nice," Alfred pronounced. He sipped, then closed his eyes to block out all distractions. "Very nice, indeed."

"I'm so glad you like it," George said. He signaled the waiter, who approached with a wooden chest of cigars.

Alfred reached for a cigar, but his eyes looked over the top of the box and fixed suspiciously on his cousin. Though they each ran half of the family business, they didn't generally socialize together. As chairman of the Cunard line, Alfred was involved with the shipping barons of the great port of Liverpool, while George, as the family's financial genius, spent most of his time in London. It had been over a year since George had last invited Alfred to dinner at his club, and his solicitude was alarming to his cousin.

George cleared his throat. "I suppose you've guessed that there is something I need to discuss with you."

"I thought there might be," Alfred said, lighting his cigar.

"Well, in truth, it's not just me. One of my associates is going to be joining us." George glanced at his watch. "Any minute, in fact."

"Who?" Alfred demanded, his eyes narrowing.

"Winston." George watched Alfred's jaw tighten. "Please. I wouldn't have done this if it wasn't absolutely necessary."

Alfred pulled back from the table. "This is outrageous," he fumed. "You know my opinion of that . . . upstart."

"It's about the war effort," George tried.

"It's about *Lusitania*," Alfred fired back.

"Well, yes. As a matter of fact, it is."

"Then the First Lord of the Admiralty can make an appointment during business hours," Alfred said, jumping to his feet.

"Sit down, Alfred," George Booth ordered. *"Sit down."*

Alfred's jaw slackened, as if he had been slapped. No one spoke to him in that tone of voice. He settled slowly back into his chair.

"I'm sorry," George said, "but the truth is, I arranged this meeting for your sake, not for his. Churchill doesn't have to ask for your cooperation. He has the authority to order it."

Alfred Booth nodded slowly. "I know that," he admitted. "If the Admiralty wants *Lusitania*, it has the right to take her. Probably best if it did. Cunard can't afford to keep her in operation. Maybe it's time she did her tour as a cruiser."

Lusitania had never turned a profit. The great liner had been built to Admiralty specifications that called for twice the engine power of her transatlantic competitors. Her advanced turbines gave her more speed than any vessel afloat, but the twenty-five giant boilers that fed them steam consumed more coal in a one-way passage than most liners used in the round-trip.

The moment her keel had been laid, she was intended to be converted into a naval cruiser in the event of war. Mounting rings for eight long-range naval guns were already built into her decks. Valuable cargo space was given over to ammunition magazines and to elevators to hoist six-inch shells up to her gun mounts.

George Booth shook his head. "Winston wants to keep her in regular passenger service," he answered.

Alfred's blank expression showed that he didn't understand.

George leaned over the table confidentially. "It all has to do with the supply of war materials. We're firing more shells in France each day than we can make in England in a week. And there's guncotton. We have all the mines we need to lock the German navy into the North Sea. But we have no explosive guncotton to put into the mines. Our only chance is to buy what we need in America. So I've set up a purchasing commission there, and we've hired the Morgan Bank to finance our purchases. We can buy just about anything we need. But our biggest problem is getting the supplies across. That's what Winston wants to talk to you about."

As if on cue, Winston Churchill strode into the dining room, his short, round physique impeccably turned out in white tie and tails. He paused to order a bottle of Champagne from the maître d' and to select a cigar, then walked up to the table. "George."

George Booth rose and gestured Churchill into a chair.

"Alfred," Churchill said as he held the cigar up to the light that the waiter struck. "How good"—he puffed a few times—"to see you." One more puff, and then a brisk exhale of smoke.

"A pleasure," Alfred managed as Churchill turned away to examine the bottle of Champagne the wine steward held.

"That will do nicely," Churchill told the steward. "George, shall I put this on your bill?" George nodded. Alfred winced.

"Alfred," he began, "has your cousin explained our problem?"

"About transporting war materials? Yes, he has. But I was still a bit confused as to Cunard's role. It would seem you would need freighters rather than passenger ships."

"For special cargoes we need fast passenger ships," Churchill said. "You're familiar with the maritime rules of encounter?"

"Of course," Alfred responded.

These rules of encounter were recognized by all nations. In time of war, warships were entitled to sink commercial vessels, but only after providing for the safety of all civilians aboard. They were also entitled to stop them, board them, and search for contraband. If they found nothing, the commercial vessel was entitled to pass. But if they found war materials or military personnel, they were entitled to seize the vessel as a war prize. Or they could simply sink her after placing civilians into lifeboats.

"We plan to use passenger ships to carry munitions from America," Churchill explained as he sipped his Champagne. "Submarines can't simply fire torpedoes at passenger ships. According to the rules, they have to surface and order them to stop. And they can't very well board and search *Lusitania,* because there's no way they can catch her. And even if they did, they couldn't sink her. How could they provide for the safety of two thousand passengers?"

"Submarines?" Alfred asked. "I thought you were concerned about the German fleet."

"The German fleet isn't the problem," Winston said, hunching over his cigar. "If it comes out, we'll sink it. It's the U-boats. Last week we lost an entire squadron of cruisers in half an hour, all sunk by a single submarine twelve miles off the Dutch coast."

Alfred was stunned. "I hadn't heard."

"We're not talking about it," Churchill said. "No point in stirring up a panic. The fact is, all the ships in the King's navy can't keep the sea-lanes open." He set an ashtray in the center of the table. "Here's England." He put his Champagne glass beside it. "Here's Ireland. Every pound of war materials that George buys in America has to come through here to get to England." He moved the tip of his cigar around the bottom of the glass and into the space between the glass and the ashtray. "Across the southern coast of Ireland and up through Saint George's Channel. Put half a dozen submarines in the area, and you can shut down England."

Alfred looked up, and instead of the smug little man who had ingratiated himself in high places, he saw a statesman who was plainly frightened. "They could do it to us," Alfred mumbled.

Winston nodded. "This war won't be won or lost in France." He pushed the wet end of his cigar down on the tablecloth. "It will be fought right here, off the Irish coast."

"But if *Lusitania* carries munitions, then she gives up her rights under the rules of encounter," Alfred Booth said.

"The munitions will never appear on her cargo manifest," Churchill answered.

"But if the Germans even suspect—"

"The ship will be carrying civilian passengers, many of them Americans. Even if the Germans suspect she's carrying munitions, I don't think they'll want to invite the Americans into the war."

"But where will she carry the ammunition?" Alfred questioned.

"You're going to pull her out of service for a brief overhaul," Churchill answered. "Basically, we're tearing out everything below the main deck and forward of the number one boiler room. The entire bow of the ship will become a magazine."

Alfred Booth looked at Churchill's cherubic jowls. "You're asking me to be a contrabandist," he said.

"We're asking you to be a patriot," Churchill answered.

Alfred sat in stunned silence. A munitions ship disguised as an ocean liner, with innocent passengers unaware that their lives were being offered to protect the deadly cargo. It was unthinkable. Absolutely immoral. Then he looked at the ashtray that represented England and the cigar stain that marked his country's lifeline. "Yes, yes, of course," he finally managed. "It all makes perfect sense."

CHAPTER 2

New York. Strings. Definitely strings. There was no doubt about it. He had made the right choice.

Even from the terrace of his estate on the North Shore of Long Island, Sir Peter Beecham felt a tingle of excitement as he listened to the musicians tuning their violins in the ballroom. He had toyed with the idea of something trendy. Maybe a shirtsleeved trio playing ragtime. After all, the party was for Jennifer, and the music was for her and her friends. But he had reminded himself that no matter what the occasion, the party was always for the Americans. And in the company of Europeans, Americans pretended to prefer strings.

He couldn't explain Americans. They were the most independent, decently democratic people in the world, but he had closed dozens of deals simply by hinting at the opportunity for them to meet an English princess.

No doubt about it. Strings were definitely the right choice. Sir Peter looked out onto a hillside that rolled from his manor house down into Long Island Sound. It was fall, and the countryside was ablaze with color, the trees in tones of orange and yellow. If he looked west, he could see the fledgling skyline of New York City. He had made his fortune helping to build the industries of America, where the new world was pushing the old aside. Now he was calling on those industries to come to the rescue of England.

The invitations to Jennifer's coming out had been written from a list of America's power brokers. Among others, there were the chairmen of two steel companies, both considering contracts for two million shell casings. There was the president of the nation's largest chemical concern, a manufacturer of nitrate explosives. There were two shipping magnates. All these men were free to sell equally to the Germans or the English, and they would manufacture victory for the highest bidder.

To stay ahead in the bidding, Sir Peter needed vast supplies of credit. So J. P. Morgan had been invited, along with two of his top lieutenants. Morgan had refused—he detested social events—but his lieutenants had accepted.

And then there was government. Authorities had to be persuaded to look the other way as contraband was being loaded, and to scratch their signatures on cargo manifests that they knew were false. Dudley Malone, customs collector for the Port of New York, had therefore received an invitation. And Germany could certainly be expected to file protests with the Department of State over America's outrageous breach of its obligations as a neutral power. Which explained why Robert Lansing, counsel to the State Department, was listed as a guest of honor.

Rules of Encounter

The invitations were not entirely cynical. In the ten-year course of Sir Peter's business dealings in North America, he had befriended at least half of these men. And when George Booth had asked him to head up the British purchasing agency in the United States, Beecham had gone out of his way to make the acquaintance of all the others.

Beecham's guests began arriving. His wife, Anne, stood beside him as he welcomed each couple. She was a marvelous asset—dignified, more vivacious than her fifty years would suggest, and with beauty that made a mockery of youth. She not only put a name with every face but made even the most formal relationship seem like a lifelong friendship.

Robert Lansing arrived with his wife, the daughter of a former Secretary of State. He was a tall man, with his full head of gray hair nicely styled, his mustache carefully contoured. His eyes twinkled as he smiled an elaborate greeting to Anne.

"Strings," he noticed. "I love an evening of strings."

The guests broke into small groups—the manufacturers in the center of the room, the financial men near the orchestra, and the steamship owners by the French doors that looked out over the sound. Jennifer's young guests, who seemed to laugh more than talk, stayed close to the bar. Waiters circulated with trays of Champagne and hors d'oeuvres.

And then came Jennifer's moment. The orchestra played a spirited fanfare, and all heads turned in anticipation toward the staircase, where Jennifer suddenly turned into view. She was tall and thin, the perfect figure for the narrow floor-length underskirt and blousy tunic that had been the spring revolution in Paris. Her deep complexion complemented the almond white of the brocade. She wore her dark hair up, showing a long neck and soft shoulders.

Sir Peter crossed to the bottom of the stairs and extended his hand. Jennifer descended the steps. When he turned, with his daughter on his arm, there were tears of joy in his eyes. He led her into the ballroom, where his guests exploded in applause.

Jennifer was his life, a fact that his wife understood better than he did. Peter thought of himself as a thick-skinned businessman, but Anne knew him to be an apprehensive father who caved in to his daughter's every wish.

Sir Peter introduced her to each of his guests. It was a rite of passage—the moment when he admitted publicly that his little girl had become a woman. Anne relished the moment. The two people she loved the most seemed so happy.

The conductor turned to his musicians and whispered the name of a waltz. Peter led his daughter to the center of the ballroom and circled the floor to smiles and applause. Then Jennifer asked the others to join them, and the ballroom came to life.

Peter handed his daughter to one of the young men and did a turn around the floor with Anne. "Can you give me a few minutes before we serve?" he asked. She nodded without losing her smile.

He carried two whiskeys to the library, where he had a rendezvous with Robert Lansing.

"You're a very lucky man, Sir Peter." Lansing tipped his glass in a toast. "Your daughter is lovely."

"Thank you, Robert." Peter gestured toward one of the leather chairs, and Lansing's expression grew grave as he sat.

"Ambassador von Bernstorff was in this morning," Lansing began. "He brought Franz von Papen with him."

Beecham nodded. The German ambassador and his military attaché were overdue. The true nature of the cargoes Sir Peter was loading aboard neutral vessels and passenger ships would never be officially acknowledged. But in the course of arranging passage and loading and unloading cargoes under the noses of port commissioners, it was impossible to keep his activities secret.

"They're warning us of their right to sink any ship carrying war materials," Lansing continued. "Von Papen said Germany could assume no responsibility for American citizens who travel on passenger ships carrying contraband." He shook his head in despair.

"Outrageous," Sir Peter sympathized. "I know of no government more diligent in checking cargo manifests than your own."

"That's exactly what I told them," Lansing agreed. But there had been no candor. He knew perfectly well that the British were loading cargoes after they had filed official manifests. American law allowed for supplementary manifests, covering last-minute cargoes, which were handed to the pilot as their ships departed. Port commissioners and customs inspectors had no way of verifying whether the supplementary manifests were true.

"Robert, I assure you that we are abiding by the laws of your country. Oh, mistakes are made. But to suggest that there is contraband on passenger ships . . ." Peter lifted his hands in a gesture of helplessness. "Ridiculous."

Lansing rose and paced toward the fireplace. "The problem is that this is just the thing Bryan would love to believe." William Jennings Bryan, the Secretary of State, distrusted the British. He was anxious to assure that the administration's neutrality policy wasn't tipped in favor of Britain.

"Robert, I'm well aware how difficult this is for you. All of us respect your loyalty to your government's policy."

"It's just a matter of time. Americans are clearly behind the Allies. President Wilson has to begin to see the national will."

"Or his successor. There are a number of very powerful people in England who are hoping you might aspire to the job, Robert."

"The presidency?" Lansing tried to look shocked at the suggestion. "That's not even remotely possible," he protested.

"My purchasing committee is dealing with the biggest men in this country," Beecham countered. "These men are not neutral. They want to help the British cause. When they look to Washington, you're the only man they can agree with."

"But still—" Lansing started.

Peter held up a hand. "I'm wrong to even raise the issue. Suffice it for me to say that many of us hope to see a change in American policy by the next election. A change much along the lines of your own thinking." He rose to escort his guest back to the party.

Beecham knew perfectly well that Lansing thought of little else but the presidency. Sir Peter's hint of support from powerful friends was really a promise—if Lansing helped them get rich selling war materials to England, they would have enough money to buy him the White House.

The music grew louder as they walked toward the ballroom. "Ah, Cinderella has found her Prince Charming," Lansing said.

Jennifer was in the center of the room, swaying in the arms of a tall naval officer in full-dress uniform.

"My new aide," Peter said. "He's officially attached to our commercial delegation, but he'll be working with me."

"He seems captivated by your daughter."

"Nonsense," Sir Peter protested. "He's much older than Jennifer. Let me introduce him to you. A most interesting chap. One of the survivors of *Aboukir*."

He got them together as soon as the music stopped. "Counselor Lansing, may I present Commander William Day."

"An honor," Day said as he offered his hand.

"My honor," Lansing insisted. "I heard about your ship. Three of them, if I remember. A terrible tragedy."

Day nodded. "They were very old ships," he said. "The tragedy is that they were sailed by very young men."

Sir Peter had been careful in arranging the seating for dinner. Dudley Malone, the collector of customs, was to be parked between a young lady who never stopped giggling and Commander Day. Since Day would be loading contraband right under Dudley's nose, Sir Peter wanted them to get acquainted. Given the childish noises that would come from the young lady's side, Malone would certainly turn all his attention to the commander. Jennifer was to be at the center of the table, flanked by two young men.

Jennifer destroyed his plan. She brought William Day to a place beside her, sending one of the young men across the table to Day's place. That trapped Dudley Malone between the giggling girl and a young man who was determined to amuse her. Throughout dinner they leaned forward and talked under Malone's chin.

Sir Peter should have been furious with his daughter for her outrageous breach of etiquette. Instead he was thrilled he had provided a uniformed prince for her entertainment. She had claimed for herself the most interesting man of the evening.

The ladies withdrew at the end of the meal, and the servants brought brandy and cigars. Everyone was anxious to hear from the young British naval officer. To Americans the war was a championship fight, and now, in its early months, the fighters had only just climbed into the ring. The bell would sound when the German High Seas Fleet came out into the North Atlantic to challenge the English first line. The question that all of them waited for William Day to answer was which one was going to win.

He laughed at the question and shook his head slowly. "I don't think my opinion is worth very much. My total combat experience was the two or three minutes it took my ship to turn over."

"But is the Admiralty confident?" a banker pressed.

"Confident? Yes. If the High Seas Fleet comes out, there's a good deal of confidence that our navy will be up to the test."

"If?" one of the shipping barons asked. "They have to come out."

"I'm not sure," Day responded. "I think this may be a war of supply. And they can win that with their submarines. If the Germans starve us out, they don't need their High Seas Fleet."

"But can't the Royal Navy deal with a few submarines?" asked one of J. P. Morgan's bankers. "If it can't, why would anyone finance cargo vessels sailing into English waters?"

"Surely you're being too pessimistic," Sir Peter said, realizing that his suppliers might begin to think of England as a lost cause. "There has to be something we can do."

"The answer may be a large number of small ships rather than a small number of large ships," Day answered. "Submarines can only stay down for a few hours. They have to come up to replenish their air supply and charge their batteries. If we could blanket the shipping lanes, submarines wouldn't be able to operate there."

"Is that Admiralty policy?" an electrical manufacturer asked.

"No," Day admitted immediately. "It's just my own thought. I've had a lot of time to think about submarines lately."

There was an appreciative chuckle as the butler made the rounds with more brandy.

The North Sea. Was it smoke? Lieutenant Feldkirchner couldn't be sure. The way the boat was rolling, he couldn't steady his binoculars. And with the height of the seas, he was able to get only occasional glimpses of the horizon.

The timing was right. Submarine Flotilla Commander Bauer's sources had confirmed *Glitra*'s sailing from Oslo at noon the previous day, headed around the Orkneys, past the Hebrides, and down the North Channel, to Liverpool. Feldkirchner rechecked his watch: 0730. It had to be the freighter *Glitra*, right on schedule.

U-17 had left its home port, Emden, three days earlier, heading past the Frisian Islands and breaking out into the North Sea. She then ran due north to her patrol box, a hundred-and-twenty-mile square from the southern tip of Norway, across the Skagerrak, and down the west coast of Jutland. Bauer scattered his submarines into patrol areas surrounding England. Then he waited for information. He had informers in nearly every European and American port.

Feldkirchner stood on the conning tower, nine feet above the sea. The narrow hull rolled continuously, slamming to a stop each time the bow plunged into a wave, then shooting forward the instant the bow broke free. He was constantly ducking beneath walls of water and then struggling for balance to keep from being battered against the iron rails.

Belowdecks, the battering was even worse. The U-17's hull was only a hundred and twenty feet long and less than ten feet across. Packed into that small tube were two diesels, coupled to a motor-generator set. There were banks of lead-acid batteries, hundreds of yards of copper cable, water pumps, water tanks, and fuel tanks. To turn the boat into a weapon, there were five eighteen-foot torpedoes. There were compressed-air firing tubes and a firing computer, an ingenious arrangement of cams and gears that could take the speed and relative course of a ship and calculate the exact moment of fire. There were ammunition magazines and shell hoists.

And then there were the men, squeezed into the small, awkward spaces that were left over. To escape their hellish world of damp mildew, choking air, and glaring electric lights, they climbed out onto the decks whenever the boat was running on the surface. But with the heavy weather the decks were too dangerous.

The bow plunged, and Feldkirchner ducked behind the conning-tower shield. The ocean roared over his head, spilling torrents down on top of him. For an instant the boat seemed to be stuck motionless in the sea. Then the bow broke through on a wave, and there ahead of him was the freighter, plowing across his bow. Feldkirchner raised his range finder and took a reading on his target, still several miles away. He opened the hatch at his feet and dropped down the ladder, pulling the hatch closed over his head.

"Dive," he ordered his executive officer. He stepped to a plotting board to calculate his course to the intercept point, where he would break surface beside *Glitra* and put a shot across her bow.

At the executive officer's command, a series of orders passed through the boat. Engineers uncoupled the motor generators from the engines. The chattering diesels suddenly stilled, replaced by the whine of the motors, which now used battery power to drive the propellers. Seawater flooded the ballast tanks, and the boat slowly began to sink.

Suddenly there was silence. The boat fell from the wild, pitching surface to the dead stillness below.

"Turn to one one zero," Lieutenant Feldkirchner ordered.

"One one zero," the helmsman echoed as he swung the wheel.

"All ahead flank," the commanding officer intoned.

"All ahead flank." The chief of the watch rang the command on the engine telegraph, and the engine room responded.

"Rig for surface attack." The gun crew began loading three-inch shells into the ammunition hoist. A machine gun, already armed with a cartridge belt, was brought to the conning tower.

"How long?" the executive officer asked Feldkirchner.

"Eighteen minutes. Check her again in ten minutes."

They stood quietly. The preparations were completed. The gun crew hunched at the foot of the ladder to the after hatch, and the boarding party, their hands on the frame of a collapsible boat, waited beneath the forward hatch. The gunner was already at the top of the conning-tower ladder, his weapon cradled in his arms.

"Time." It was the executive officer, reminding Feldkirchner that the ten minutes had elapsed. Feldkirchner nodded, and turned to the periscope as his second-in-command pulled down on the counterweight cable. The polished steel tube rose inside its track.

For a moment all Feldkirchner could see was a moving hill of water. Then as the spray cleared, he saw the freighter bearing toward him, its bow pitching as it fought through the white-capped crests.

He called out the bow angle and fixed the image within the brackets of the range finder. Then he pushed the scope down. "Right on course," he announced. "Looks about one mile."

"About five minutes," the executive officer commented.

They waited again, hearing their own nervous breathing above the hum of the electric motors, and then there was a new sound, like distant thunder. It was *Glitra*'s screw as it cut through the sea.

Feldkirchner pointed at the periscope. "Let's take another look." Once again he eased the scope up. *Glitra* appeared off his port quarter no more than one hundred yards astern.

"Right to one six zero," he ordered, pushing the periscope down.

They listened carefully for any change in the sound of the propeller. If *Glitra* had spotted the periscope, then the freighter would probably make a sudden turn. But there was no change. The throbbing continued, growing louder.

"Surface," Feldkirchner ordered, starting up the ladder.

The bow planes were tilted upward. Compressed air was fired into the ballast tanks, making the boat slightly buoyant. The bow and conning tower exploded out of the sea at the same instant.

The gunner threw open the hatch and charged upward through the torrent of water that poured down into the tower. Feldkirchner followed behind him. He saw *Glitra,* running on a parallel course, no more than fifty yards off his port quarter. "Switch to the engines," he shouted through the hatch as he slammed it closed.

The instant the decks cleared the surface, hatches opened fore and aft of the conning tower. The gun crew sprang from the after hatch, each man connecting a safety line from his belt to a track in the deck. The boarding party climbed through the forward hatch, dragging the collapsible boat up behind them.

Feldkirchner watched his gunner bolt the machine gun into its stanchion. Then he looked at *Glitra.* These were his most vulnerable moments. His guns weren't armed. He was switching from the electric motors to the diesels. His crew was standing in plain sight. A gunner aboard the freighter could rake his boat with machine-gun fire, dropping his men like ducks in a shooting gallery. Or the freighter might cut his boat in half with her bow.

But there was no activity at all aboard *Glitra* as she pounded through the sea. No one on the ship had yet seen the submarine.

The gunner's mate at the deck gun held up his hand. Feldkirchner raised his own arm and then let it drop. A second later the deck gun fired with a sharp crack, and a column of water exploded into the air and broke across the freighter's foredeck.

Suddenly there was a face on the bridge, wide-eyed under a seaman's cap. The man looked in disbelief at the submarine, then disappeared toward the wheelhouse. An instant later another man, this one wearing an officer's cap, appeared on the bridge.

"Heave to," Feldkirchner screamed in English through his megaphone. "Prepare to be boarded."

The officer peered down incredulously. The boat was only a third as long as his ship and seemed barely afloat. He hesitated.

"Take the cargo rigging," Feldkirchner told his gunner. The machine gun chattered, and a stream of tracers reached out across the sea. Ropes frayed, and wooden blocks shattered. One of the cargo booms crashed down on the freighter's foredeck.

"Heave to," Feldkirchner screamed again.

The man disappeared into the wheelhouse. *Glitra* was still making good speed, but U-17 had begun building momentum as soon as she had switched to the diesels. Now the submarine was matching the steamer's speed, the two craft moving side by side.

A new figure appeared on *Glitra*'s wing, again in officer's cap, but shorter and older-looking than the watch officer. As soon as he saw the submarine, his hands flew into the air.

"Prepare for boarding," the lieutenant ordered. "Put a ladder over the side. My executive officer will come aboard."

Glitra's captain nodded vigorously. The freighter was already slowing, and the submarine had to slow its engines to stay abreast. Then when *Glitra* was nearly stopped, U-17's executive officer, who had climbed up onto the U-boat's foredeck, ordered the collapsible boat into the water. He followed two seamen aboard, and the small craft bobbed toward the ladder that was lowering along the steamer's side. The executive officer jumped onto the ladder and scrambled up and over the ship's rail.

"First Officer Otto Marx." The executive officer saluted when he reached the bridge.

"Captain Morrissey," the old man answered. He couldn't bring himself to salute the bearded young man.

"May I see your cargo manifest?" Marx asked politely. Morrissey led him through the wheelhouse to the chart room, where he opened the ship's safe and found the cargo manifest.

Marx shook his head at the first entry. "Stainless steel bars," he said with genuine sadness. The rest of the items included ball bearings, electrical wire, and optical lenses. "Half of these items are war materials," he continued. "Captain, I must claim my right to destroy this cargo. We will allow you ten minutes to put your crew in the ship's boat and stand clear. We intend to sink your ship."

"We won't be safe in a small boat in these seas."

"Safer than you'll be staying on board," the German said, then saluted and walked back through the wheelhouse.

Morrissey followed him down the ladder from the bridge to the main deck and watched as he climbed over the rail.

The small collapsible boat pushed off from *Glitra*, the two seamen struggling to get some rhythm into their oars. The sea was tossing in swells, making it difficult to keep the boat on a steady heading. Just as it reached U-17, a wave caught it, lifted it up, and tossed it over the top of the deck. Then the boat slid down the back of the wave and smashed against the conning tower, where Feldkirchner was standing. He grabbed the boat's bowline and took one turn around a cleat, hauling the small boat against U-17's deck.

Meanwhile, *Glitra*'s crew had swung out the ship's boat and were lowering it over the side. Her captain jumped aboard as the lifeboat dropped below the deck.

"Stand clear," Feldkirchner called through his megaphone as soon as the lifeboat was in the water. The crew pushed away from the hull and began rowing frantically past her stern.

The lieutenant turned to his gun captain. "Below the waterline, directly beneath the funnel. Commence firing," he ordered.

The gun crew aimed the rifle carefully, but the rolling of the deck made it impossible to fix their elevation precisely. The first round tore through the hull plating three feet above the surface of the sea and exploded inside. The second round hit short and exploded in a geyser along the ship's side. The third shot blew a hole right at the waterline. The next shot hit just below the surface, splitting one of the riveted seams. *Glitra* immediately took on a list.

"That should do it," Feldkirchner called to his gun captain. "Get your men below." He was interrupted by a metallic blast within *Glitra*'s hull. Cold seawater had reached one of her boilers, which had exploded. Bulkheads collapsed, allowing water to rush forward. Within a few minutes her stern lifted out of the sea, its enormous weight putting an unimagined strain on the ship's keel. With a sickening screech of metal the ship tore in half.

"All ahead two thirds," Feldkirchner called down to the control room. "Come to course one seven five." He looked up as the last edge of *Glitra*'s transom disappeared under a swell. Then he saw the lone lifeboat, its crew thrashing their oars about in heavy seas.

"Come topside, Otto," Feldkirchner shouted down to the control room below. Marx climbed up to join him.

"They're not going to make it." The commanding officer nodded toward the lifeboat. "We better give them a tow ashore."

Marx laughed. "First we put them in the water. Now we're getting them out. Does this make any sense to you?"

"Why should it?" Feldkirchner said, shaking his head. "These are English rules we're playing by." He maneuvered U-17 close to the lifeboat. At first the English crew sat hunched over their oars, fearing a mass coup de grace from the machine gunner, who still held his position on the conning tower. But when they saw the German sailor uncoiling a heaving line on the submarine's afterdeck, they scrambled for the line and secured it to a bow cleat. Feldkirchner then made for the Norwegian coast, with his enemies in tow.

Insane, he thought as he looked back at the small boat bobbing in his wake. The international cruiser rules insisted that he act like an armed cruiser, firing a shot across the bow of his prey and ordering the ship to heave to for searching. But his submarine didn't fit the traditional cruiser rules. Lurking beneath the waves, he was more than a match for any ship afloat. But when he surfaced, he became a weakling.

The Norwegian coast loomed up ahead. Feldkirchner could see the waves breaking on a rocky shore. He ran parallel to the coast until he sighted a break in the rocks. Then he ordered his boatswain out on the afterdeck to haul the lifeboat alongside.

"This is as far as we can take you, Captain," Feldkirchner shouted.

Captain Morrissey saluted. "Thank you, Captain," he said. "I'll make a full report on your proper conduct."

Feldkirchner returned the salute and watched as the men rowed toward the beach. A full report, he thought. That should have the English admirals holding their sides in laughter.

CHAPTER 3

New York. News of *Glitra*'s sinking hit the Manhattan shipping offices like a torpedo. Suddenly it was dangerous to carry war materials to the British Isles. Foreign steamship companies that days before had been courting Sir Peter Beecham's cargoes suddenly wanted no part of the nitrates, the shell casings, and the generators that he was buying from American manufacturers.

Insurance rates for ships bound for England were suddenly doubled. And if the ships were carrying anything that might be used to bludgeon a German, the rates were doubled again. Beecham was suddenly spending more to get his war materials across the ocean than he was to buy them.

"One ship!" he protested to Commander William Day. "A few rounds into the side of a rusting steamer, and the Huns are able to bankrupt England right out of the war."

"It may get worse," Day cautioned, "once the Germans give up the cruiser rules and start fighting by the submarine rules. They'll declare the Western Approaches a war zone, just as we've declared the North Sea a war zone. They'll sink anything that comes across their bow."

"Innocent passengers? Without warning? Preposterous," Beecham insisted.

"Naming it a war zone is all the warning they need."

Sir Peter saw war as a duel between gentlemen. There were strict procedures, dictated by good breeding. Day saw war as mindless brutality, a jungle game of kill or be killed. English mines didn't pause to allow innocent passengers to take to the lifeboats on ships traveling to Germany. Why should the submarine commander go through the niceties of the rules of encounter before firing?

Beecham spent every hour trying to find neutral ships to supplement the fleet of English steamers he had commandeered, and William Day was his constant companion. He used Day almost as a patriotic poster, shamelessly displaying him in front of shippers and insurers to wring out concessions.

"We're not really discussing tonnage, you know. We're discussing the lives of fine young men. Like Commander Day here, one of the few survivors of the *Aboukir* outrage. What we're talking about is giving these brave men a chance to fight back."

The steely eyes would soften as they looked up from the contract. "I understand the submarine rammed the lifeboats and ran over the men in the water. It must have been terrible."

Before Day could explain what actually had happened, Beecham would turn back to the contract. The agent, who could have demanded three times the going rate, would settle for twice.

Day's experience and his uniform were particularly important in dealing with Dudley Malone, the New York customs inspector. Malone was far too shrewd to be fooled by repackaging and relabeling cargoes. But even though he lived in a world defined by clerical forms and rubber stamps, his imagination traveled out over the dangerous seas. He had admired Commander Day when he first met him at Jennifer's party. The officer in the gold-trimmed uniform had become his alter ego. As he plied Day for information on warships and their tactics to feed his heroic fantasies, he signed and stamped forms that he couldn't bother reading.

Secretly Day wished that Malone would challenge his last-minute cargoes and supplementary cargo manifests. Would passengers sail aboard ocean liners if they understood the explosive force that was resting against their keels? He protested to Sir Peter about orders to load rifle cartridges on *Lusitania*. "Do you know what would happen to the passengers if a German submarine put a torpedo into that cargo?"

"They wouldn't dare fire on a passenger ship," Beecham countered. "That's why the passengers are perfectly safe, and the cargo."

If the young commander was essential to Sir Peter's workday, he was almost as important to Beecham's evenings. Jennifer had followed her prince from Long Island to Manhattan. She had moved into the family town house on Washington Square, leaving her mother's watchful eye for her father's more casual supervision.

During her first days in New York, Sir Peter would find her waiting up for him when he came home late, ready to serve him tea and his favorite biscuits. He would listen eagerly as she recounted all the things she had done during the day. Jennifer could take an hour describing dinner with Commander Day at Delmonico's.

"Every eye was on him," she rejoiced. "In his uniform he was quite the most handsome man in the room."

"I'm sure they were looking at you," Beecham teased.

"No. It was the women who stared. The lady at the next table almost fell off her chair, sniffing at his cologne. Just to drive her mad, I reached across the table and took his hand."

"You didn't," he protested. "Not in public?"

She laughed mischievously. "I most certainly did. You should have seen her expression. She stiffened like an old schoolmarm."

"Positively scandalous," Beecham censured. But he was smiling as he climbed the stairs to his bedroom. Such spirit! Such daring!

Weeks later it was he who was sitting up by the teapot waiting for Jennifer to come home. Commander Day would see her to the door, stepping in just long enough to pay his respects to Beecham.

Jennifer would explode the minute the door closed behind Day. "Oh, Father, William was simply wonderful."

"William, is it?" as he poured the tea.

"Well, you can't keep calling someone Commander while you're dancing."

"You were dancing? Where?"

"At the Winter Garden. There was a wonderful orchestra."

Beecham was happy to see Jennifer so happy. And grateful to Day for being so understanding of his daughter. With his aide watching her, Peter didn't feel guilty for leaving Jennifer so much on her own.

Anne began hearing about Jennifer's escapades from friends in the city. "I saw Jennifer just the other evening," one woman told her. "She looked so lovely in her bare-shouldered dress."

"How she's grown," another harpy cooed. "I couldn't believe it was Jennifer dancing with that wineglass in her hand."

"Anne, is it serious?" a friend begged. "Between Jennifer and that handsome naval officer? They're seen everywhere together."

Anne went to the telephone, rang the operator, and asked to be connected to New York. "I want to know about Jennifer," she told her husband. "Have you been keeping a close watch over her?"

"Of course. She's having a fine time here in the city."

"Too fine a time from what I hear," Anne fired back. "One friend tells me she's appearing in public half naked. Another says she's drinking. And she's too young to be keeping serious company with anyone, much less a sailor who's years older than she."

Sir Peter sighed. "Commander Day is simply looking after her for me. He has no interest in her. How could he? He's a commoner."

Anne groaned at her husband's density. "He's tall, handsome, and a war hero. Your daughter is an impressionable child who likes to rush into things. And the next thing she's scheduled to rush into could leave her with a warm bun in the oven."

Sir Peter gasped. "That is the most outrageous thought," he said. "Commander Day wouldn't think of . . . of . . ." He wanted to slam the telephone down.

For the rest of the day he eyed William Day suspiciously. Not that he thought for a moment that there could be anything serious between him and Jennifer. But she was only eighteen. There was no reason for her to charge so enthusiastically into adulthood. It was probably a good idea for her to spend more time with her mother. He would explain that he and Commander Day would be quite busy over the next few weeks. Then he would help her pack, and see her personally to the train in the morning.

London. To Winston Churchill it seemed so obvious. He had explained it in broad terms, and Captain Hall, head of naval intelligence, had filled in the details. Why couldn't the First Sea Lord, Admiral John Fisher, grasp the concept?

"It's illegal! A blatant violation of international law." Fisher's voice was tired and gravelly. The old man who sat hunched in a wing chair no longer had the vitality that had carried him to the very pinnacle of the Royal Navy. Nor did he particularly care for Churchill and Hall. He knew that the two younger men would do exactly as they wished, whether he agreed with them or not.

Churchill sat behind his desk at the Admiralty offices in Whitehall, his pink complexion darkening to red with mounting anger. Reginald Hall sat on a chair drawn up beside the desk, so that he and Churchill were facing Fisher as a team.

Churchill didn't need Fisher's advice, but he did need his support. When he went to brief the Prime Minister on his strategy for dealing with the submarine menace, he needed to be able to say that Fisher approved. He tried again. "The submarine is writing its own laws on naval warfare, Admiral. You yourself have said a submarine commander would be insane to adhere to the rules of encounter."

Fisher's puffy eyes widened. "But I never said that would give us the right to fly foreign flags on our merchant ships."

Churchill glanced in despair at Captain Hall. "Sir," Hall explained, "we know from our radio intercepts that the Germans are taking great pains to avoid involving neutral countries. They have set up extensive spy networks to track British ships with military cargoes and to avoid neutral ships. By flying our own flag on our merchant ships, we simply make their job easier for them."

"Then fly no flag at all," Fisher growled.

Hall looked at Churchill. The Admiral was worrying about flags and their proper use according to the rules of chivalry and about what history would say if he hid his ships under foreign colors. He couldn't understand that modern warfare was a struggle for survival and that the real issue here was the very existence of the British Empire.

"That simply won't do, Admiral," Churchill said. "The absence of a flag will be just as much a giveaway as the presence of a British flag. What we have to do is fly the flags of neutral nations."

"Then the Germans will have to attack everyone," Fisher argued. "Neutrals and British ships alike."

"Exactly," Churchill nearly shouted, thrilled that Fisher had finally gotten the point. "Or avoid attacking anyone. If they can't tell what is a British ship, they will have to treat them all alike."

"Then they'll simply stop each ship, board it, and demand its papers," Fisher argued. "That will tell them which ships are British."

Churchill's eyes closed in despair. Hall came to the rescue. "That's why we need the second part of the plan, sir. British merchantmen will be forbidden to obey a submarine's order. Instead they will ram any submarines that challenge them. We're installing guns on their fantails. Concealed, of course. The U-boats will have to inspect the ships to be sure they're British. And if they are British, the submarine is going to find itself under attack."

Fisher's dark expression began to brighten. It wasn't just a matter of flags. It was a counterattack that would blunt the submarine threat. "Which flags are you planning to use?" he asked.

"Principally the U.S. flag," Hall responded. "The Germans are particularly determined to keep the Americans neutral."

"And Washington will go along with this?" the admiral asked.

"We're not planning on asking them," Churchill responded through clenched teeth. "We'll change flags at sea and switch back to the British flag when we enter port."

"But surely they'll find out," Fisher protested.

"The only ones who could possibly see the flag would be German submarine captains," Hall said. "But suppose one of them knows the ship. Suppose he is able to positively identify it as one of ours flying a foreign flag. What can the German government do other than raise a protest? We will simply deny the charge."

Fisher nodded slowly. "Well," he gasped as he lifted himself out of the chair, "I suppose I'm in favor of anything that could make life more difficult for Admiral von Pohl."

The mischievous twinkle returned to Winston Churchill's eyes. "Wonderful," he said. "I do hope you understand how grateful I am for your counsel on this matter." He jumped up to assist the admiral.

Fisher brushed the helping hand aside. He retrieved his hat and walking stick from the rack next to the door and let himself out.

"Tell me, Captain," Churchill said, "which of our codes are the Germans reading?"

Hall looked shocked. "Absolutely none that I'm aware of."

"That's comforting news," Churchill allowed. "But I'm afraid I can't buy it. If they haven't got through one of our ciphers yet, it's only a matter of time before they do."

"You want them changed more frequently?" Hall asked.

Churchill shook his head, a conspiratorial smile slowly spreading across his face. "To the contrary. I want to find one code they are

Rules of Encounter

reading, and then I want to make sure that we never change it."

Hall's eyes narrowed. "You want to get information to the Germans. Information they'll assume is classified. About ships."

"Not ships. A particular ship." Churchill could see that his intelligence officer was baffled. "When our ships begin turning on the submarines, what do you think the Germans will do?"

"Begin firing without warning. They'll have no choice." Then Hall's eyes glowed in recognition. "And you have a particular ship you'd like them to fire at." Churchill nodded. "You'll use the compromised radio code to direct them toward the ship you want them to attack," Hall went on. "May I ask which ship you have in mind?"

"Of course," Churchill answered. "A ship that will bring the Americans into the war. On our side."

New York. The city stopped and turned to face the Hudson River as *Lusitania* appeared around the tip of Manhattan. In downtown offices, clerks and brokers slipped away from their desks and pressed against the windows. On the docks, longshoremen left crates they were loading, and wandered to the water's edge. On the streets of the West Side, pedestrians ran toward the waterfront to get a better look.

New Yorkers called her the Greyhound, which seemed a more fitting name for the fastest ship afloat. She was not the largest ship in the world. *Olympic,* sister ship of *Titanic,* was both longer and beamier. But the Greyhound seemed to be the tallest. The rapier-shaped black hull climbed five stories from the waterline. Three more decks, painted glistening white, were built above that. And then there were the four enormous funnels rising another seven stories. As she slipped past lower Manhattan, she was one of the tallest buildings in the city.

William Day heard the Greyhound's mournful whistle signal to the tugboats that came alongside to assist her. Slowly they began swinging her bow in toward the Cunard piers. She would spend the next two days loading her cargo and filling her coal bunkers. Then the passengers would come aboard, and she would head back to the cold, hostile waste of the North Atlantic.

Day watched as the black hull slid along the dock, blocking out the sun and casting the Cunard offices into shadow. High above his head, on the bridge, he could make out the ship's master as he kissed *Lusitania* cautiously against the pilings. Caution was Captain "Fairweather" Dow's trademark, and it was his caution that had summoned Day to Cunard's New York offices.

Charles Sumner, the Cunard line's American representative, looked up from behind a cluttered desk as Day was shown into his office. "Ah, Commander!" He began digging through stacks of correspondence until he found the typed copy of the wireless message that had preceded *Lusitania* into port. "What am I supposed to do with this?" He pushed the message toward Day.

> Upon arrival, demand briefing on all structural changes made to *Lusitania*. Demand full access to all areas of ship closed off by Admiralty order. Have no intention of sailing until I am fully satisfied as to safety of ship and cargo. Captain Daniel Dow, Master.

"It's not as if *Lusitania* weren't causing me enough problems," Sumner chattered while Day read. "Alfred Booth is constantly haranguing me about costs. Everything from coal to oysters."

"What does this mean?" Day asked, giving the message back.

"Just what it says," Sumner answered. "The man is responsible for everything on the ship. He can't accept that responsibility unless he's fully informed."

"What kind of man is he?" William Day asked.

Sumner began to snicker. "He's a little old lady—that's what he is. He got the name Fairweather because he'll take a ship a hundred miles off course to avoid a rainsquall."

"Can he be trusted?" Day asked.

"Trusted? You mean—"

His secretary interrupted him. "Captain Dow is here."

Fairweather Dow marched into the office. He was a slight man, seemingly too small to command a ship. Even before he was seated, his eyes darted apprehensively between Sumner and Day.

"Commander William Day, from the Admiralty," Sumner said.

Day offered his hand and took care not to crush the thin, manicured fingers that he grasped. "I've seen your wireless, Captain," he said. "Is there something wrong with *Lusitania*?"

"Something?" Fairweather Dow said sarcastically. "Everything is wrong. Since you put her in the yard, she's a different ship."

"Ridiculous," Sumner snapped, dismissing the charge.

Dow directed his comments to Day, a fellow sailor. "*Lusitania* was always a roller. But when the sea put her over, she snapped back into trim. Now she's unsteady, unsure. I'm steaming with coal bunkers only half full. That makes her top-heavy. Even worse is the yawing of the bow. She doesn't track in a straight line."

"Are the problems just westbound, when you're traveling empty?" Day asked.

"It's certainly worse when she's light," Dow said. "The cargo we take back to England helps keep her tighter. But that's another problem—these last-minute cargoes that are sealed into the holds before I can inspect them. How can I assure the safety of my ship when I don't even know what I'm carrying?" He turned to Sumner. "Well, I won't have it. I demand to be shown the holds."

"Captain Dow, may I remind you that we are at war," Sumner began to scold. "Those cargoes—"

"I agree with Captain Dow," Day interrupted. He turned to the ship's master. "I have the keys for all of the areas that the Admiralty has secured. Would you like to inspect them now?"

Dow was stunned by the Admiralty's acquiescence. Sumner was flabbergasted. Even he was forbidden from venturing beyond the new hatchways that the Admiralty had installed.

Day and the captain boarded the ship and walked forward, around the great rotunda that rose like the dome of a statehouse above the first-class dining room. They passed the two caged elevators that waited to carry passengers down two levels to their staterooms or up two levels to the lounges, libraries, and music rooms. Farther forward, Captain Dow led Commander Day down a stairwell into the lower decks of the ship, descending two levels, past the third-level saloon, until their passage was blocked by a heavy steel door secured by a padlock. A small metal sign warned SECURED BY ORDER OF THE ADMIRALTY. Day took out a ring of keys, selected one, and opened the padlock. He pulled the door open. Dow stepped through the hatch and turned into a passageway that he assumed would lead him to the third-class cabins on the main deck. He stopped so abruptly that Day charged into him.

There were no cabins. Before him stretched nearly a hundred feet of open cargo deck. Sixty cabins, with accommodations for nearly two hundred passengers, had vanished.

"The deck below is exactly the same," Day told him.

"What about the athwartship coal bunker?" Dow asked.

"Removed," Day answered. "It was valuable cargo space."

Dow looked around, mentally measuring depths and dimensions. "All the bulkheads," he calculated, "and portions of six decks have been removed. There's nothing left but a hollow shell."

Day nodded. "That's the yawing motion you're noticing when she's empty. We use these holds to carry war materials."

"What kind of war materials?" the master persisted.

"Artillery shells. Rifle cartridges. Range finders—"

"Artillery shells?" Dow's thin face was turning ashen.

"They're not particularly dangerous by themselves," Day assured. "We store the explosive materials well above the waterline. It would be impossible for a torpedo to score a direct hit. And nothing short of a direct hit would pose any significant danger."

Dow shook his head in disbelief. "If it's all so safe, then why all this damn secrecy?" he demanded.

"Because it's completely illegal. American law doesn't allow us to ship any war materials on passenger ships."

"I've seen enough," Dow said, and he started back.

They were at the companionway leading to the pier when Dow announced his conclusion. "I'll take her out." He stopped and turned. "I appreciate the truth. I've heard nothing but lies from the Admiralty and from the owners of my company."

"They were simply trying to protect you," Day answered. "What I've told you is a top Admiralty secret. If you should ever breathe a word of what you now know to anyone, you can count on spending the rest of the war in a naval prison."

It was midafternoon when Beecham's motorcar picked up Day from the Long Island railroad station. By the time they reached the house, the winter sky had already darkened.

The two men ate their supper off trays in the library while they worked before the fire. Beecham had delivery schedules for hundreds of orders he had placed with American manufacturers, and Day had lists of ships on which cargo space had been requisitioned. They had to match delivery dates with scheduled sailings.

Jennifer paced the hallway outside the closed library door. Each time she passed it, she stopped and listened for an indication that the meeting might be adjourning. All she heard was the mumble of dull business.

Rules of Encounter

"Jennifer!" Anne had come downstairs to make tea, and caught her daughter with her ear pressed against the library door.

Jennifer rolled her eyes in exasperation. "William has come all this way to see me, and Father has him locked up in the library for the whole evening." She followed her mother to the kitchen.

"Commander Day didn't come to see you," Anne said. "He came to see your father. They have important business to discuss."

"What's so important that it can't wait until tomorrow?"

"That's not your affair," Anne scolded.

"William *is* my affair," Jennifer yelled, stopping her mother in her tracks. They stared at each other, Anne stunned by her daughter's rude outburst and Jennifer choking back tears. Then Jennifer turned and rushed off to the music room. Seconds later there was the sound of a lullaby being banged out on the piano.

Anne brought a silver tray with a teapot and cups into the library and tried to be unobtrusive as she set it on the desk. When her husband took his tea, she always served it herself. It was a gesture of caring that she couldn't leave to the servants.

"We've just about finished," Sir Peter said. Anne had left the door open. "What is that infernal banging?"

"That's your daughter enjoying a cultural moment," Anne said. "She was anxious to see you, Commander," she said to Day. "Perhaps she thinks the ruckus will drive you out of your meeting."

Day looked from Anne to Beecham. "Will you excuse me, Sir Peter?" Beecham nodded as he closed his briefcase.

Anne brought Peter his tea. "I don't suppose the commander will want any."

"Probably not. Pour for yourself, and join me."

They sat quietly with their tea while Anne tried to think of the best way to introduce the subject that was bothering her. Finally she decided to plunge right in. "I suppose you've noticed that Jennifer is very much taken by your naval officer."

Peter chuckled. "I think infatuated is a better word. After all, she's just a girl."

"She's eighteen," Anne answered. "I was nineteen when I became infatuated with you."

"A different situation," Peter said. "We were from the same stock. Good heavens, it was our parents who introduced us."

"And you think your daughter is concerned over Commander

Day's stock? I hope you're not underestimating what may be happening between them."

"Believe me," Sir Peter said lightheartedly. "I work very closely with Commander Day. If he were in love with my daughter, I would certainly know it."

DAY followed the furious tempo of the lullaby to the music room and walked to the piano, where he stood beside Jennifer.

For a few moments she played on. Then she jumped up and threw her arms around him. "Oh, William, I've missed you."

"I've missed you, too," he admitted. He tried to wring a smile from her tearstained face. "In fact, the whole city has missed you. Delmonico's is thinking of shutting for the season."

"I don't care about the whole city. I care about you. I thought surely you would come out to see me."

"I couldn't. I have work to do," he reminded her.

"I know you don't have much time. That's why I should be in the city, so that I'm there when you're free."

To make sure they were alone, Jennifer took his hand and led him toward the French doors that opened out onto the terrace. "Come outside," she said.

He felt the cold draft as soon as she opened the door. "Jennifer, you'll catch pneumonia out there."

They walked to the stone wall that marked the edge of the lawn. Day took off his jacket and slipped it over her shoulders.

"I have a friend who lives in Manhattan," she whispered. "She'd take me in. Then we could be together when you weren't busy."

"You can't wait weeks on end for me to have a few hours off. There are so many wonderful things you should be doing."

"Nothing is wonderful without you," she argued, her voice rising.

He tried for a change of subject. "Does your father approve of your going back to Manhattan and staying with a friend?"

"He doesn't know yet," she admitted. She looked up at him anxiously, waiting for his approval.

"Do you always get exactly what you want?" he asked.

Her eyes widened in surprise. "I thought that was what you wanted, too," she said softly.

He leaned on the wall and looked out over the water. "I want so many things. I want a ship. I want to get back into the war. And . . .

I want very much to be with you." He looked back at her. "All those things are beyond my reach. I don't suppose I'll ever have them."

"You think I'm selfish," Jennifer concluded.

"No. I think you're impatient. I think you want your whole lifetime right now."

"I don't need everything right now," she decided. "Tell me that I should wait for you, and I will, no matter how long it takes."

She was looking up at him, waiting for his answer. He took her in his arms and kissed her gently.

PETER Beecham raked the coals with the poker until he was sure that the fire would die. When he looked up, he saw Jennifer and William Day outside. They were at the edge of the terrace, outlined in the light that came through the French doors from the music room. His daughter was in the officer's arms.

He should have been furious. But instead, something about the way that Day was holding Jennifer filled him with a great sadness. She looked pathetically small in the oversized jacket with gold braid and buttons. And Day, despite his brutal strength, was holding her carefully, as if she were a precious crystal. Their kiss was soft—a shared breath of life rather than an urge of passion. Beecham suddenly understood what his wife had seen so clearly. It was not that Jennifer was in love with her prince. It was that Commander Day was hopelessly in love with his daughter. He felt heavy with grief, because it was all so futile.

Later Beecham and Jennifer walked Day out to the car, which was waiting to bring him back to the station. He had to catch the train back to the city. Jennifer leaned against her father as the car disappeared. He suddenly took her hand and held it as if they both were sharing some great loss.

In the middle of the night he climbed out of bed and walked to the library. There, he sat at his desk and in the dim light of a shaded lamp penned a letter to the First Lord of the Admiralty.

> My dear Winston,
>
> May I ask, as a personal favor, that you recall Commander William Day, naval aide to our delegation here in New York.
>
> Commander Day has been an invaluable asset to our activities and is to be highly commended for his intelligence, energy, and

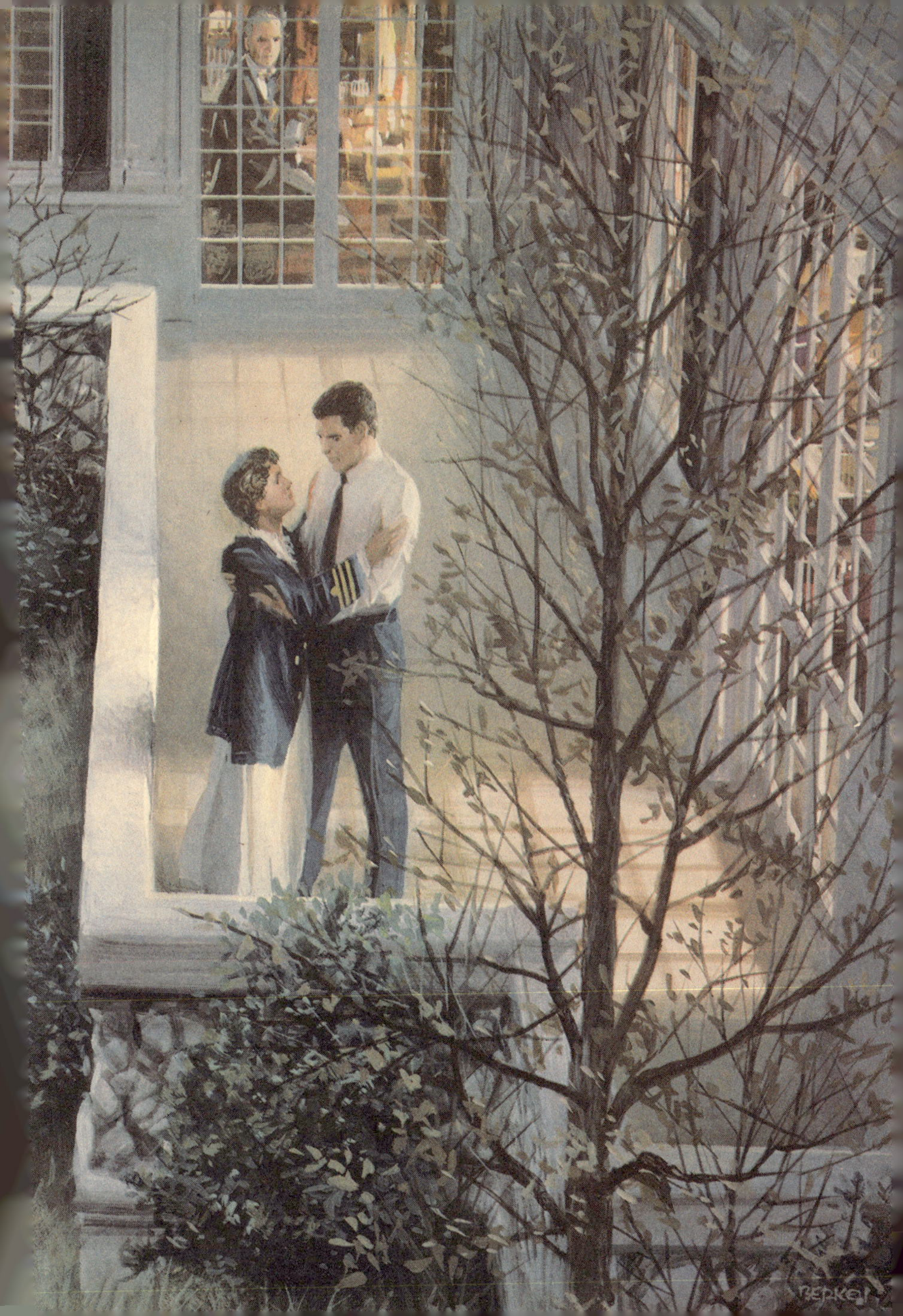

Rules of Encounter

professionalism. My request is made for reasons of harmony within my household and should in no way affect his career adversely. I hope that he can be assigned to an important, yet *safe*, duty station. I would regard his loss as the loss of my own son.

Sir Peter folded his letter into an envelope, sealed it, and addressed it to Churchill. The next day it would be included in the diplomatic pouch headed for London, and put aboard *Lusitania* just before sailing.

CHAPTER 4

Washington. "Ambassador von Bernstorff and Captain von Papen," Robert Lansing's secretary announced.

Lansing could abide von Bernstorff. The man was a bore, but he was well meaning. It was his military attaché who was unbearable. A youthful miniature clone of Kaiser Wilhelm, Franz von Papen was convinced that the German officer was the final evolution of the human species and that he himself was its perfect specimen. He was never seen without his full uniform—a dark blue jacket with a three-inch-high collar of gold brocade, fringed shoulder boards, and an array of medals across the chest. A scabbarded sword invariably hung at his side. And squared on his head he wore a spiked brass-encrusted helmet, its point adding a full four inches to his height.

Captain von Papen was always on duty. Rarely did he engage in genuine conversation. Instead, he spoke orders. On any issue there was only one correct position, which was, of course, his own.

"Count von Bernstorff, how good to see you," Lansing oozed, stepping around his broad mahogany desk.

The count responded with a trace of a smile.

"And Captain von Papen. A pleasure."

The captain's response was a window-rattling click of his heels. His body snapped downward from the waist in a formal bow that aimed his spike at Lansing. Then he ratcheted back up.

Lansing pirouetted back around his desk, gesturing to the two armchairs across from him. "Please be seated, gentlemen."

The ambassador settled into a chair. It was more difficult for von Papen, who had to fit his sword under the arm of his chair before he could lower himself to its edge in perfect attention.

"To what do I owe this honor?" Lansing began.

"Most distressing information concerning the maritime policy of the British government," von Bernstorff began. He turned to his aide. Von Papen opened a leather briefcase, withdrew a gray folder, and snapped it down on Lansing's desk.

"These are Admiralty orders just found on a British steamer stopped by a German military vessel," von Papen said.

Lansing, frowning earnestly, opened the folder, and began to read. Simultaneously von Bernstorff delivered an analysis. "The first order instructs British merchant captains to fly the flags of neutral nations, which is a flagrant violation of international law. Note the preferred neutral flag is that of the United States."

He waited until Lansing had turned to the next page.

"The second document forbids British merchant captains from obeying the lawful search orders of German submarines. When confronted with a submarine, they are to attack her."

"Most disturbing," Lansing agreed. He turned to the third paper, which required each merchant ship reaching certain ports to be held over for several days so that a naval gun could be installed on its fantail. He closed the folder, already organizing his defense. "I will bring this to the attention of His Majesty's ambassador. If such an order had been issued, I'm certain my government would protest the use of the flag."

"The order was issued," von Papen corrected. "Obviously, the British government is abandoning the rules of encounter."

Lansing pursed his lips. "I'm not quite sure I would come to that conclusion."

"There is no other conclusion," von Papen pressed. "If British passenger ships and merchantmen ignore a submarine's warning shot, then the submarine is left with no alternative but to attack."

Lansing's eyes flashed with anger. "Captain von Papen, these few papers, even if genuine, in no way constitute an excuse for German submarines to attack ships without making provision for civilian passengers."

"England is attempting to embroil our submarines with neutral nations," von Papen said. "We must insist that you warn the English that you will hold them strictly accountable for any loss of American lives."

It took all of Robert Lansing's decorum to stay in his chair.

"Captain," he said slowly, "we cannot hold England accountable for events that have not occurred."

The attaché leaned across Lansing's desk and pressed a white-gloved fingertip against the gray folder. "These orders have already occurred, Herr Lansing. If the neutral nations cannot convince the British to retract these orders, then Germany must follow England's lead and abandon the rules of encounter."

Lansing looked at von Bernstorff. "Your aide, sir, is threatening citizens with submarine attack."

The count looked in confusion from one man to the other.

Von Papen snapped to his feet. "The threat, Herr Lansing, comes from England, not from Germany. Will you be so kind as to convey our views to your Secretary of State."

He placed the briefcase under his arm. The ambassador, realizing that his aide was adjourning the meeting, stood up from the chair. Lansing rose as well, his eyes burning at the miniature Prussian warlord. Von Papen's heels clicked like a rifle shot. He marched out of the office, with the ambassador stumbling at his heels.

"Damn," Lansing cursed as soon as the door closed. He picked up the gray folder and slammed it down on his desk. What could have ever prompted the British to put such blatantly illegal decisions into writing? Of course the documents were genuine. If William Jennings Bryan took this folder to the President, then Wilson would have no choice. He would have to prohibit Americans from traveling on British passenger ships and deny the use of American ports to England's armed merchantmen. He would have to demand that England give up the use of American flags. It would mean the end of all material support that America was providing to the side it unofficially favored. It would also mean the end of Lansing's usefulness to the industrialists and bankers who were profiting from filling the British arsenals and whose support was important to his heady political ambitions.

Lansing slipped the documents into his bottom drawer. At his next meeting with Secretary Bryan he would casually mention the "forged British orders" that had gotten von Papen into an uproar.

London. When Captain Reginald Hall entered Churchill's office, Winston was at his desk poring over estimates of the navy's reserves of critical war materials. The information had sunk his generally optimistic outlook into a sea of despair. All mining in the English Channel and along the North Sea coast would have to be suspended in three months because the supplies of guncotton had been exhausted. Everywhere he looked, scarcities of supplies were proving to be a more lethal enemy than the Germans.

"I hope you have some good news for me," he mumbled without looking up to greet his guest.

"I think so," Hall said as he settled into a chair. "I think we've found that mailbox in Germany that you were looking for."

"A communications channel?" the First Lord of the Admiralty asked. "Where?"

"Ireland," the intelligence officer said. "The Germans seem to be reading our traffic through the radio station at Crookhaven."

Churchill's face showed its mischievous smile. "I might have known. The damned Fenians. How did you find it?"

Hall smiled broadly. "We invented a ship and then broadcast messages to it using different radio channels and different ciphers. Of course, we continued listening in on the German submarine frequencies. The first time we used the Crookhaven transmitter, we picked up a German broadcast referencing our fictional ship. Then we invented other ships and radioed to them through Crookhaven, using different ciphers. No matter which code we used, the Germans learned about it."

"Then it's not our codes that have been broken. The Germans seem to have found a spy in Ireland."

"Precisely."

"Any ideas?" Churchill asked.

"That's a bit sticky," Captain Hall confessed. "We deliver our Irish traffic to Admiral Coke, in Queenstown. We use telephone lines between Queenstown and our communications center at Crookhaven. There are two possibilities: the Irishers have a tap on our phone lines"—Hall grimaced—"or it's one of our own people."

Churchill lit a cigar carefully, then puffed it like a steam engine. "For the time being," he concluded, "let's leave things alone. I'd like to find out who the spy is, but I want to leave him in place."

Hall nodded. "And feed him bogus information."

"No. I think the information should be valid," the First Lord answered. "I'd rather not give the Germans any reason to suspect that we're on to the Crookhaven leak."

"Then I won't look too hard for the spy. But still, for appearances, I should send someone out there to look into the matter."

Churchill brightened. "Perhaps an officer with impeccable credentials." He opened his desk drawer, fumbled about briefly, then withdrew a letter and slipped it across to Hall. "I was asked to find a position for this man. Something that wouldn't get him killed."

"William Day," Hall said as he read Sir Peter's letter. "Isn't he the chap who rescued half a dozen shipmates from *Aboukir?*"

Churchill nodded. "A fine officer. We could assign him to Admiral Coke, in Queenstown, and then have Coke put him in charge of the southern coast."

Hall stood and walked to the door. Then he turned back. "You appreciate that if we use Crookhaven, we risk handing the Germans one of our own ships. It could be disastrous."

Churchill lifted his cigar from the corner of his mouth. "If we pick the right ship, it will be disastrous. For Germany."

New York. "You'll be joining us for Christmas?" Sir Peter asked as he pushed an enormous stack of papers into his briefcase.

Commander Day was standing by the window of the British purchasing board's fourth-floor office, looking out at the snow that was beginning to accumulate in the street below. He turned to Sir Peter. "If you're sure it won't be an intrusion."

"Nonsense. You're one of the family." He suddenly looked up, embarrassed at his choice of words. They both knew it was not true. William Day was most certainly not one of the family.

Day's recall orders had come the day before, and Beecham had launched into a tirade, complaining that the Admiralty had no right to rob him of such a valuable assistant. But William knew his transfer had been requested, and guessed that it was precisely to ensure that he would never become one of the family. "That's very kind of you," he said.

"Not kind at all," Beecham said, trying to recover from his gaffe. "We both could do with a holiday."

They had been working long hours and had had only modest success. They had gotten a respectable buy on twenty thousand time-delay shell fuses. But the order for eight thousand bags of black powder had slipped through their fingers when German purchasing agents topped their final price. And then there was the guncotton. Twice they thought they had a contract for Du Pont's entire production of the highly explosive material, only to have the company quote a new and higher price.

"You should have better luck in the new year," Day consoled the older man. "The Germans will run out of credit before we do."

Beecham had slipped into his topcoat. "I'm sure you're right. Things have to get better. But that guncotton would have made a great Christmas present for Winston."

Day stayed by the window until he saw Sir Peter cross the street below. He went to Beecham's desk and found the unsigned agreement for the guncotton. Then he took his cap and greatcoat, and locked the office door behind him.

The snow, which had begun falling at midday, was turning into a blizzard. Day set his head into the wind and walked up Broadway. He could only hope that Harry Sinclair was still in his office.

He reached the Nassau Building and rode the elevator to the Du Pont offices, on the fifth floor. He entered the reception area, where a matronly secretary led him back to the executive offices.

"Commander Day. Did we have an appointment?" Harry Sinclair was a bullet-headed man, with a mournful expression.

"No, we didn't," Day answered, crossing to the uncomfortable leather chair that faced across Sinclair's oak desk. "I just dropped in on the chance that you might spare me a minute."

"That's about all I have. Sir Peter isn't with you?"

"As a matter of fact, he's not. But I thought you and I might be able to wrap this up without him."

"The pyroxylin?" Sinclair said, using the technical name for guncotton. "Are you entering a new bid?"

Day pulled out the unsigned contract. "No. I was simply hoping that we might come to an agreement on the outstanding bid. I've been called back to sea duty, and I'd feel a good deal better if I knew we had the pyroxylin instead of the Germans."

"Commander Day, we are a neutral country, and this is simply a business transaction," Sinclair said. "I don't care who gets the pyroxylin. I do care about getting the best price."

Day opened the contract. "I thought our offer was very generous. It's sixty percent higher than your list price."

Sinclair rose from his chair, signaling the end of the meeting. "I can see you don't know a great deal about business."

Rules of Encounter

Day remained in his chair. "I'm sure you're right. On the other hand, I don't think you know a great deal about war. You're talking about your associates' getting rich. I'm talking about my associates' getting killed." He set the contract on the desk. "Sir Peter has already signed. All we need is your signature."

Sinclair looked down at the document, then looked back up in disbelief at Day. "I have no intention of signing anything."

"That's very brave of you, Mr. Sinclair." Day rose slowly from the chair, walked back to the door, and turned the key in the lock. Then he walked across the room and threw open the window.

Sinclair recoiled from the icy blast that rushed into the room. "Are you crazy? What the hell are you doing?" he demanded.

Day responded with two strong hands that grabbed the astonished businessman under the arms, snapped him off his feet, and lifted him steadily toward the open window. "Diplomatic immunity," the commander explained patiently as he tilted Sinclair's head into the opening. "All they can do is send me back to England. And without that guncotton I'll be safer in jail."

"You can't do this," Sinclair screamed.

Day dropped the man's back down on the windowsill, grabbed his knees, and began pushing him out over the edge. Sinclair let out a bloodcurdling scream, but it was hardly a whisper into the snowy wind that was rushing along the side of the building. Sinclair's hands were flailing in space. Day's grip slipped down to his ankles.

"I'll sign. For heaven's sake, I'll sign!"

Day hesitated for a moment of exaggerated indecision. Then he dragged Sinclair back through the window and set him carefully into his chair. The man sat wide-eyed. Melting snow dripped from his bald head down over his face.

"Close the window," Sinclair panted.

Day nodded toward the contract, scattered on the desk. Sinclair opened his desk drawer and found a pen. He scribbled a shaky signature across the bottom of the agreement.

Day lowered the window. "You've made a wise decision," he commented as he gathered up the contract. "You can tell your people that the Germans never met the price. And I'll tell mine that you wanted us to have it."

"You're crazy," Sinclair blurted, his eyes still wide with terror.

"Desperate," Day answered after a thoughtful pause. "I think desperate is a better word." He unlocked the door. "We'll have our check to you right after the holiday."

"You would have done it—dropped me out the window."

"What kind of a way is that to conduct business?"

PETER Beecham was the Christmas elf, determined to bring magic to the holiday. At home he had supervised everything. The sprigs of holly that were affixed to every door. The candles, one carefully placed in each of the house's windows. The stockings that hung above the fireplace. And of course, the Christmas tree.

"Not another like it in all the world," he had said. It was a thick blue spruce, reaching to the fifteen-foot ceiling in the music room and decorated with the traditional ribboned fruit and candy canes. Delicate candles were set at the tips of the branches and filled the room with a warming glow on Christmas Eve.

He rubbed his hands in anticipation as Anne found her gift under the tree, a small package containing an antique silver ring, which she slipped on her finger and modeled with great joy. Then it was his turn to unwrap the box Anne had given him. It was a gold tiepin, which he pronounced the most beautiful he had ever seen.

"Well now, what have we here?" Sir Peter handed a box to Day. "Saint Nick seems to have left a gift for you, William."

Day carefully removed the paper despite Jennifer's urging him to tear it. He found a small ebony chest, fastened with a gold clasp. He opened it and from its soft felt interior lifted a snowy white meerschaum pipe.

"Peter says that sea captains need a good pipe to smoke on the bridge," Anne explained. "And we all know that you'll soon have your own command."

Day held the pipe as though it were a relic. "It will take a fine ship to deserve such a pipe on its bridge," he told her.

He found under the tree a small flat box, which he gave to Anne. She opened it, lifted out an embroidered handkerchief, and thanked him as though it were the one thing she had wanted since childhood. Then he took an envelope from his jacket pocket. "Merry Christmas, Sir Peter."

Beecham's eyes widened. He ran his finger under the flap and drew out an official-looking document.

"You said it would be a fine Christmas present for Mr.

Churchill," Day reminded him. "I thought you deserved it more."

Peter glanced at the familiar guncotton contract, then flipped to the last page, where he found Harry Sinclair's signature.

"We have it all," Day said. "Delivery by the first of May."

"But how—"

"I appealed to his best instincts," Day said.

Beecham could see that his wife and daughter were bewildered. "A very important contract that I thought I had lost," he told them. "William has saved it for me." He turned back to Day. "William— " Sir Peter tried to begin. But the best he could do was shake his head. "I think there are many men who would want to thank you," he finally managed.

William saved his gift for Jennifer until they were alone, walking on the packed-snow path that led to the carriage house. He had stripped his bank account to find a gift that would tell her how much she meant to him. And yet that was exactly the wrong message he should be delivering to someone whom he would probably never see again.

She opened the package eagerly and gasped when she saw the string of pearls. "Put them on me," she said, handing him the pearls and turning her back to him. "I don't think I'll ever take them off."

He laughed when she turned back to him, the pearls hanging outside her coat.

Jennifer reached into her pocket and produced a small, square package trimmed with lace. "And this is for you, William."

He examined it curiously and took out a heavy gold signet ring, his initials cut into it. "Now this is something *I'll* never want to take off. It's beautiful." He began slipping it onto his ring finger.

"Read it. It's inscribed." She turned it in his palm and pointed with her fingertip: I'LL ALWAYS LOVE YOU. JENNIFER.

Slowly he closed his fist around the ring. His muscles tightened, as if he were fighting against an intense physical pain. She took his strong hand in hers, and slowly his grip on the ring relaxed.

"It's true. I'll always love you. You do love me?" she asked.

Day looked down at the ring in his hand. "If I were half the man your father wants for you, I'd be able to tell you, No, I don't love you. That would be the right thing for me to say."

"Then you do love me," she answered joyfully. "We're in love, and love changes everything, doesn't it?"

He looked at her, then shook his head. "No. Not everything."

She launched into a speech that she had been rehearsing for days. "I know you'll be away and that I won't see you for months on end. But thousands of women are waiting alone. Something could happen to you. And then we would never be together. That's why we should be together now. While we can."

Carefully he took the ring and slipped it onto his finger. He took her hand, and they began walking toward the carriage house.

"A year or so ago," he began, "all the officers in the navy were from important families. I became an officer because with the war they needed people to command their ships. The war will end," he went on softly, "and we'll all go back to where we belong. There are rules among people. Rules that none of us can change. Jennifer, my father is a longshoreman. He carries heavy cases up the sides of ships on his back. The house that I'll go back to after the war is smaller than that carriage house."

"I'd be happy with you in a carriage house," she insisted.

"And when would you wear your pearls?" he asked.

She pulled her hand away angrily. "You're making fun of me!"

He reached for her, but Jennifer backed away, tears showing on her cheeks. "I'm not making fun of you," Day insisted.

"Then trust me. Trust that I can make everything work."

He answered the only way he could. "No, I can't do that."

Her eyes filled with rage. She turned away, lifted the hem of her coat, and began running back toward the house.

"Jennifer!" He tried to call her, but the sound died on his lips. He had ended it. And whether now or later, he knew it had to end.

When he finally returned, the music room was empty, the Christmas tree pretending to a joy that seemed to have fled the house.

Winter 1915

CHAPTER 5

Schull. Emmett Hayes narrowed his eyes behind his wire-framed glasses and bounced the ruler in the palm of his hand. He stared down at the red-haired boy, whose face was rapidly draining of color. "Terrance, is this the best you can do?"

"Yes, sir," the alto voice answered in a whisper.

Hayes looked down at the penciled page that rested on his desk.

He studied it for a moment, then pushed it aside in disgust. "Well, your best isn't good enough. And what does that mean?"

The boy shuffled his heavy shoes. "That I have to do better."

Hayes picked up the paper, jamming it into the small hand. "So do it again. Tonight. Without a single mistake. Is that clear?"

"Yes, sir," Terrance whispered. The boy turned, and tiptoed a few steps before he broke into a run. As he flashed through the doorway he nearly collided with Father Brendan Connors.

The priest sauntered into the room, his biretta square on top of his close-cut white hair, the buttons of his cassock turning in a detour around his ample paunch. "I thought it was a murder he was seeing, Emmett."

The schoolteacher slipped on his topcoat and took his umbrella from the clothes tree. "The boy is lazy."

"You're too hard on them," the priest advised. "They're just tenants. In Ireland it's enough if we can teach them their prayers."

Emmett gathered up his books. "We've been using prayers for five hundred years, Father. It's time we started using our heads."

Connors laughed. "You're on your way to sainthood. You've got no faith and not a drop of charity. But I've never met a man so blessed with hope." He waited as Hayes locked the schoolhouse door, then started down the narrow street.

"Father," Hayes called after him, smiling. "I don't have hope. I have plans."

Emmett was an oddity in Schull, always dressed in a jacket and tie in a population of rough shirts and shapeless sweaters. He was small and delicate, while most of the men were brawny. He was always armed with books, which were a curiosity to neighbors who could neither read nor write. Only forty years old, he carried himself like the village patriarch. And yet they loved him. Hayes represented intelligence to people buried in ignorance.

"Nasty weather, Mr. Hayes," James Corcoran said from behind the counter as Emmett entered his store.

"Nasty indeed, Mr. Corcoran," Hayes echoed.

"Terrible for the rheumatism," Corcoran said.

"Just a bit of cheese today." Emmett hung his umbrella on the counter while he dug for his wallet. "And a pint of milk."

Corcoran lifted a cheese wheel onto the counter, positioned his knife to outline a wedge, and cut down.

Hayes counted out the coins while Corcoran wrapped the cheese in paper and stuffed the package and the milk bottle into a paper bag. Hayes pushed his books into the bag and retrieved the umbrella. "I hope your rheumatism is better, Mr. Corcoran." He swung the door closed behind him.

He walked to the end of the main street, then turned down a row of small stone houses that led up the hill, away from the water. His house was at the end of the row. There were two steps up to the door that opened into a parlor, with the kitchen behind.

Hayes set the paper bag on the kitchen table, unwrapped the cheese, and carried it with the milk to the icebox. He then took the cheese wrapper with him upstairs to his bedroom.

Emmett lifted the small brass key that hung from his watch chain and unlocked the armoire. He took a starched white shirt from a stack on one of the shelves, unfolded it, and removed the shirt cardboard. With the cardboard in one hand and the cheese wrapper in the other, he sat down at a desk beneath the front window.

Carefully he copied the words written on the wrapper.

> Steamer *Edmund Hampton*. Dep. Philadelphia 8 January. Arr. Liverpool 19 January. Escort rendezvous 180 Fastnet 10 miles, 2300 GMT 18 January. HMS *Juno* assigned.

He opened the fold in the shirt cardboard and removed a code table that substituted random letters for each letter of the alphabet. Over the next two hours he calculated the proper substitutions until he had translated the message into gibberish.

When he finished, he folded the shirt around the cardboard, replaced it with the other shirts, and locked the armoire. He crumpled up the cheese wrapper into an ashtray and struck a match to it. Then he carried the coded message down to the cellar.

The radio was built into a sewing-machine cabinet. Hayes lifted the top and swung the radio up into position. As he sat rocking his feet on the metal treadle, the sewing-machine belt turned the armature of a generator. The needle climbed into the required power range. Then he tapped out a call sign on the telegrapher's key. Immediately the signal was repeated, telling Hayes that a German operator was ready to receive.

He keyed his coded message, and then he signed it with his identification name, Leprechaun.

Crookhaven. "Attention on deck!"

Chief Radioman Richard Gore rolled off the dilapidated sofa and sprang to his feet, buttoning his uniform jacket. Radioman Tommy Halliday, who had shouted the order, stood at ramrod attention, still holding the teapot he had been pouring from when Commander Day pushed open the door.

"Stand down," Day responded. He shook the mist from his cap.

"Welcome to Crookhaven radio station," Gore said. "We wasn't expectin' you till tonight. We would've tidied up a bit."

"I got an early start," Day explained, offering his hand. "Commander William Day. It's good to be here."

"Radio Chief Richard Gore," the petty officer responded, shaking Day's hand. "This is Radioman Halliday. Get the commander a cup," he ordered the radioman.

"Not yet," Day said. "I'd like to have a look around first."

Crookhaven station stood atop a rocky mountain that rose two hundred feet out of the sea at the southwestern tip of Ireland. On its western end was Mizen Head Light, the first point of warning for ships coming in from the Atlantic. The gate to the station was just outside the tiny village of Crookhaven, where the road from Skibbereen ended. The station's two buildings were identical to any of the stone cottages that dotted the coastline. It might have been a farm except for the two towers that stabbed a hundred feet into the sky, above the land line.

The cottage Gore stepped out of with Day served as the communications office. It housed the transmitter and receiver—giant boxes filled with glowing vacuum tubes—and two desks, with telegraph keys and telephones. One bedroom served as the coding room.

The other cottage served as the crew's quarters. The loft was fitted out with a row of narrow beds and footlockers. The sink, stove, and kitchen table functioned as the mess hall.

"We've got six men out here," the chief explained as they walked through the deep, wet grass. "Myself, two radio ratings, and three able bodies who stand guard watches."

"Only three guards? Is that enough?"

"I think so, Commander. For show mostly. The locals aren't fond of us, but they mind their business. Shiela McDevitt, our coding clerk, keeps 'em in line. She's Irish and was raised around here."

"Isn't she on duty?" Day asked.

"Oh, she's always on duty. Only coding clerk we have. But she can't live out here, you know, with six men. She lives near Schull and comes out every morning. She's doing some shopping today. We wanted a nice table in the mess. In honor of your arrival."

They walked to the edge of the station, where a sheer wall of stone dropped down into the crashing sea. They were at the western tip of Europe, looking at the sea-lane that carried the blood England needed to stay alive. The radio tower was essential to keep that blood flowing. Yet all Day had to keep it in operation were a few seamen and a coding clerk doubling as a housekeeper.

Day started back toward the communications office, the chief scurrying to keep up with him. As they turned the corner of the cottage Day saw a woman on a bicycle riding up the path from the guard gate. "Looks like our coding clerk is back from her shopping," he said to Gore.

Shiela McDevitt pedaled hard to move the bicycle, with its basket full of packages, into the face of the wind. She wore a wool hat, and a heavy sweater over a long skirt. She was breathing hard when she stepped down. She pulled off the hat and let long red hair fall down around a fair Celtic face with striking green eyes. "You must be Commander Day."

"Our new area commanding officer," Chief Gore added.

"Well, I hope you like fish, Commander," she said, "because there isn't a piece of beef in any store in Schull."

"Fish will be perfect." Day smiled.

"We'll get it started." The chief reached for the packages.

"In the meantime," Day asked Shiela, "I wonder if we could take a look at your coding operation."

Inside, Shiela took off her sweater, revealing a long-sleeved white blouse tied at the collar with a green bow. She was an athletic-looking woman in her late twenties. She had a businesslike appearance, which she confirmed by asking Day to produce his security authorization before she unlocked the door to the coding room.

The room was bare except for a rolltop desk and an iron safe. Messages, Shiela explained, were delivered in plain language from Queenstown over an Admiralty telephone line. She used the code books, kept in the locked safe, to translate them into the day's cipher and then gave the coded copies to the radioman for transmission. Incoming messages were handled in the same way: the radioman copied a coded transmission, and Shiela translated it into plain language before the message was telephoned to Queenstown.

Day saw immediately that the system was anything but secure. Anyone tapping the phone line would have access to the plain-language text. "Why use a telephone?" he asked. "Couldn't the traffic be handled by a messenger?"

"I suppose you've driven the roads," Shiela answered. "You could spend a whole day getting here by car from Queenstown."

Day nodded grimly. "Then we have to be damn sure of that line. Chief Gore tells me you know this country."

"I lived here as a child. Until I was twelve. Then the family picked up and moved to Liverpool, looking for work. I suppose that's why the Admiralty assigned me here. I've been away for seventeen years, but nothing has changed."

"Maybe I can borrow you for a few hours each day?" he asked. "I'd like to get to know the area. Particularly the coastline."

"You're the commanding officer," Shiela said.

HE WAS wearing a civilian suit when he met Shiela next morning at the station. "What do you want to see first?" she asked.

"The fishing harbors. I'm hoping to put a fleet together to help us with the German submarines." She glanced across at him and smiled, wondering if he had any idea what he would find.

It was a motley group of battered boats, tied to a sinking pier. Wooden dories with pegs for oarlocks. Rusted bumboats with single-cylinder steam engines and woodburning boilers. Ancient gaff riggers with patches on their canvas.

They stood on the main street looking down a grass slope, over the harbor at Schull. Beyond it was Roaringwater Bay, dotted with barren rocky islands, and Cape Clear, set into the distant mist.

"They could do it," he told Shiela.

"Battle submarines?" she asked incredulously.

"They don't have to fight the submarines," he answered. "All they have to do is keep them from surfacing. Submarines have to come up for air every few hours and recharge their batteries."

Day and Shiela had spent most of the day touring the weather-beaten coastal towns stretching along the southern cliffs from Glandore all the way to the western tip of Mizen Head.

"There's some fishing," Shiela had explained. "And some of

them carry small cargoes down from Cork. But it's all coastal traffic. None of these boats would ever venture out into the ocean."

But Day hadn't been thinking of long voyages. He had been thinking of the coastal waters that ships inbound from America passed through on their way to Coningbeg Light and Saint George's Channel.

Shiela pointed down to a twenty-foot sloop that was struggling into the harbor, its rails nearly in the water. "A submarine would be afraid to surface next to that?"

Day nodded. "Yes. A submarine is helpless when it first breaks the surface. It's completely unarmed until its crew can get out on deck and man the guns. Any of these boats with a single machine gun could get the crewmen before they ever cleared the hatches."

"But they don't have guns," she said, dismissing the idea.

"I can get the guns," Day said. "And some sailors to man the guns. What I need are the boats, and the people to sail them. Three or four towns could supply all the boats we'd need."

"These people?" she said. "Irishmen? You expect them to give up their livelihoods to help the British navy? We're the enemy, you know. The Germans are their liberators."

"We'd pay them. There are people making a fortune out of this war. Why shouldn't the Irish get a bit of it?"

Shiela smiled and shook her head. "I don't think you'll have much luck. A man who took money from the English would have a hard time finding a friend in Schull. Or Glandore or Baltimore."

They climbed back into Day's canvas-topped touring car. He drove carefully through a throng of gawking children and started down the town's single main street.

"If we could recruit one town," he said, "and people were making money, the other towns might want their fair share, too."

Shiela turned to him sympathetically. "I don't think you know what you're up against. The Fenians would come down hard on anyone who helped you."

He nodded. "I don't expect to win over the radicals. But what about the rest of the people?"

"I was born here," she answered. "But I became English, and now I've come back working for the English. I have cousins in Schull who won't speak to me."

"Insanity," he said.

They were on the main east–west road that ran along the coast from Skibbereen to Crookhaven.

"Could we go right here?" Shiela asked as they reached a small intersection. "There's something I want you to see."

Day turned inland, driving through treeless country—large mounds of stone, with occasional green pastures between the rocks. There was a stark desolation to the landscape.

Shiela leaned forward as they came to a bend in the road. "You can stop anywhere along here."

"Here?" He braked the car. "There's nothing here."

Shiela got out and started up a slope, into a grassy field.

Day caught up with her. "Where are we going?"

"A cemetery. It's right ahead of us."

He was bewildered. There was no trace of a wall, a gate, a monument, or even a headstone. And then, half buried in the grass, he spotted a small stone marker leaning awkwardly to one side.

As she walked, Shiela pointed at the marker, which bore no inscription. Day hesitated at the stone, then ran a few steps to catch up. There was another headstone. And then another behind that. Now Day could make out uneven rows of stones, stretching out into the distance, their tops hardly visible over the swaying grass.

"The children's cemetery," she told him.

"Children? Only children?"

"Three hundred of them. Most of them never had headstones. They were buried sixty-five years ago, during the famine."

He was angered by the sight. "Why in heaven's name doesn't someone take care of this place?"

"Who?" she challenged. "They have no families. No one even knew their names. See—the stones have no names. Just a year: 1851."

"They all died in the same year?"

"At the worst of the famine. There was no food, so the families gave whatever they could scratch from the ground to their children. The parents ate grass. And when they died, there were hundreds of orphaned children roaming the countryside. The English governor, who visited here once or twice a year, left one of his relatives in charge. A cousin from London, if I remember."

He looked at the tiny stones. "We didn't feed them?"

"Parliament tried," Shiela said. "They allocated money and gave it to the cousin. But he put it in his pocket and never left London. The children died in the fields, trying to graze like cattle."

William dropped to one knee and brushed the dirt from one of the stones. "What happened to the cousin?"

"I understand he made quite a success in finance. They tell me he was knighted."

Day walked slowly down a row of stones. He found one fallen, and bent to straighten it. When he reached the end of the row, he turned and walked down the next one, twisting his cap in his hands. Finally he stopped and looked at Shiela.

"I should be getting back," she told him. "There may be messages waiting to be coded."

"Then I'll wait until you finish, and take you home." Day went to her, took her hand, and led her back to the car.

They drove in silence. When they reached the radio station, they left the car at the gate and walked up to the radio cottage. "It has to be difficult for you," he said, "working for the English in a place where Irish children are buried."

"I have a job to do," Shiela answered.

"So do I," Day said. "And I have to have those boats."

Shiela nodded. "I'll do everything I can, Commander. I just wanted you to know what you're up against."

CHAPTER 6

The Irish Coast. Lieutenant Walter Schwieger raised his binoculars and scanned the crystal night air, tracing a horizon illuminated into a silver line by thousands of stars. Still no sign of the British steamer *Hampton,* due from Philadelphia, with a cargo of smokeless powder and electrical apparatus. But he had to be patient.

He had been vectored to his position southwest of Mizen Head by Flotilla Commander Bauer. An Irish agent named Leprechaun had relayed orders intended for the cruiser *Juno,* assigning her to meet *Hampton* ten miles south of Fastnet Light. Bauer had ordered U-20 to take up station thirty miles farther west. To meet up with her escort, *Hampton* would have to steam across U-20.

The temperature was below zero. Schwieger ran his hand over his face, scattering the ice crystals that his breath had formed in his beard. Then once again he began the slow scan with his binoculars.

He saw her—so clearly that he wondered how he could have missed her on his last search. *Hampton* seemed to have jumped up from the horizon—a black hull, with her funnel and masts etched clearly in the light sky. He bent down toward the open hatch behind him. "Haupert, she's here," he called to his executive officer in the control room below. "Let's dive." He dropped through the hatch and spun the locking wheel to secure it.

The clatter of the diesel engines stopped, replaced by the hum of the electric motors. Seawater gurgled into the ballast tanks. Water closed over U-20's deck, and then everything was silent.

"Come to two eight zero," Schwieger told the helmsman, turning his boat toward the target. He guessed that *Hampton* was five miles away; he should wait fifteen minutes before raising the scope.

"You want the boarding party ready?" Haupert asked.

Schwieger shook his head. "She's British, Willi. We just tell the crew to get off, and then sink the thing."

"I hope they have warm coats," Haupert commented idly.

They waited in silence. Schwieger checked his watch, then pointed to the periscope. He bent over to catch it as it came up from its tube. As soon as it broke the surface, he saw *Hampton* dead-on framed against the sky, no more than two miles away. Then he juggled the range finder to bracket the ship from the waterline to the top of its mast. "Three thousand yards."

He stepped back from the scope as it lowered. "Come left to one eight zero." The helmsman spun the wheel. They would run five minutes to the south of *Hampton*'s course line and then come about. That would bring the freighter about five hundred yards across his bow. Schwieger watched the time tick past on the chronometer. "Full left rudder. Come about to north." When the compass settled at north, he signaled Haupert to raise the scope.

Hampton was to port, running in a straight line. Schwieger pushed the scope down. "Right on schedule."

"This is almost too easy," Haupert said.

They heard the propeller, a faint throbbing.

"Stand by for surface attack," Haupert shouted down into the hull. Two seamen charged up into the conning tower, one carrying a machine gun, the other a battery-powered carbon lamp. They took positions under the hatch.

Schwieger exchanged a glance with Haupert. "Surface!"

There was a whistle as valves were opened to release compressed air into the ballast tanks. The lightened boat began to rise immediately, and then there was a crashing sound as the conning tower broke through the surface. Schwieger waited until the gunner had thrown open the hatch cover.

"Surface running! All ahead one third!" Schwieger scampered up the ladder, with Haupert at his heels.

Hampton was still to port, steaming directly across his bow. "Right standard rudder," Schwieger ordered, bringing U-20 to a parallel course. He looked aft. His gun crew was already on deck, swinging the machine gun out toward the target. The first round of ammunition was being passed up toward the breech.

A searchlight switched on aboard *Hampton*. Its beam swung abruptly down the gray hull of the U-boat. Schwieger ordered his own light turned on and aimed directly at *Hampton*'s bridge. He lifted his megaphone. "Heave to! This is the German submarine U-20. I order you to heave to immediately."

The beam of *Hampton*'s light found the submarine's conning tower and lifted until it hit Schwieger in the eyes.

"Turn off that light," he ordered.

The beam painted the tower, then dropped down to illuminate the gunners, who raised their hands to shield their eyes.

"Get the light," Schwieger ordered the machine gunner.

The chatter of the gun exploded through the still night. There was a puff of flame, and then the light went black.

"Heave to!" Schwieger ordered again. The freighter was pulling ahead of him. "All ahead full!" he shouted down into the hatch.

"She has a deck gun!" The frightened scream came from Weiser, his gunnery officer. "On the fantail."

U-20's light snapped to the freighter's transom to reveal a five-inch deck gun, its muzzle swinging toward the U-boat. At the same instant, Weiser's crew was bringing U-20's gun to bear.

"Fire!" Schwieger ordered. Then into the hatch, "Hard right rudder!" He was turning his boat to present the smallest possible target to the freighter.

U-20's gun flashed. There was no explosion aboard *Hampton*. The shell had sailed over the steamer's stern. Endless seconds passed. *Hampton*'s deck gun was now aimed over Schwieger's head, its barrel slowly depressing toward his face.

The steamer's gun roared—a sound twice as deafening as the crack of U-20's deck weapon. The sea just beyond the submarine's hull leaped up into a frothy geyser. The round had passed just inches over U-20's deck.

Haupert cursed as the submarine's gun fired again. *Hampton*'s afterdeck house flashed into flame.

"She's turning on us," the machine gunner screamed.

The freighter's prow was quickly swinging toward them.

"She's going to ram us," Haupert gasped.

"Clear the deck," Schwieger screamed at his gun crew. "Hard right rudder," he yelled into the opening. "Dive! Emergency dive!"

The gun crew had disappeared down the hatch and Haupert was jumping into the hole when *Hampton*'s deck gun roared again. U-20 lurched with a metallic ringing. Schwieger dropped through the hatch and pulled it down on top of him.

"We're hit!" The scream came from the control room below.

Schwieger looked down and saw jets of water flying across his control room. He pushed Haupert toward the lower hatch. "Get me a damage report." Haupert disappeared down the ladder.

Schwieger was suddenly aware of a new sound. *Hampton*'s bow was cutting through the sea almost directly over his head. He cringed from the roar of the charging steamer.

There was a terrifying howl of metal as *Hampton*'s hull grazed across the conning tower. U-20 lurched suddenly onto its right side. The impact smashed Schwieger against the tower wall. Screams echoed through the hull. The entire crew had been tossed from their stations and had fallen against the bulkheads. The deafening pound of the propeller cut through the water inches above the hull.

Schwieger opened his eyes, to find his world totally disoriented. He was lying on one of the walls of the tower, looking up at the other wall. The ladder to the overhead hatch ran from side to side instead of vertically. U-20 was spiraling into a deadly dive even though it was lying on its side. The rudder, locked in a hard right turn, was increasing the angle of dive.

"Amidships," he screamed, crawling up the inclined deck until he could see down through the hatch. "Rudder amidships." But the wheel was unmanned. Streams of water were still firing into the control room.

Schwieger pushed his legs through the hatch opening and scrambled along the ladder. He grabbed the helm and began cranking the wheel to the left. A seaman was fighting his way up the nearly vertical deck toward the bow-plane control. "Neutral," Schwieger yelled to him. "Neutralize the bow."

Haupert had dragged himself forward to the ballast-control levers. "Lighten the starboard tank. Carefully," the commanding officer ordered. Haupert tapped the lever to a slightly open position. Instantly the boat began bringing itself to an upright attitude. The bow was slowly lifting out of its dive, but water was still pouring in through the port bulkhead. Schwieger had to get the boat back up to the surface to relieve the pressure on the hull.

The control-room crewmen were back at their posts. Schwieger checked the depth gauge. The boat had dived a hundred and sixty feet—nearly to its safety limits—but now was rising slowly.

"Take us up to thirty feet," he told Haupert. He couldn't break the surface until he was sure of his distance from *Hampton*. If he came up under its deck gun, he wouldn't be up for long.

Schwieger scrambled up the ladder to get to the periscope. There was an inch of water on the conning-tower deck, fed by a jet from the periscope packing. He pulled down on the counterweight cable. The periscope started to slide upward, then suddenly stopped. It had been bent at the point where it passed through the packing and out through the top of the tower. It was useless.

He cursed and went back down into the control room, where Haupert had ordered the torpedo crew to shore up the leaking bulkhead. It was then that Schwieger heard the distant throbbing of a propeller growing louder—*Hampton* was hoping to finish off the submarine she had crippled.

"Level. Come left to zero nine zero," Schwieger ordered his helmsman. Haupert's eyes widened. Schwieger was turning the U-20 toward *Hampton*.

The propellers pounded directly overhead, but Schwieger ignored them. He was still too far below *Hampton*'s keel to be in any danger, and he had more pressing matters to deal with.

"Steady on zero nine zero," the helmsman called.

"Take her up to twenty feet," Schwieger ordered. The bow struggled upward. Water that had spilled into the forward torpedo room poured back through the hatch into the control room. As the bow lightened, it began to swing into a climb.

Rules of Encounter

"We're going to make it," Haupert said with a smile of relief. "We should get out of here, surface, and pump her out."

"Not while that s.o.b. is still afloat," Schwieger whispered. Haupert's eyes narrowed. U-20 was crippled and, without its periscope, blinded. Schwieger was noted for his caution. It was frightening that he was even considering an attack.

"She'll make one more pass looking for us," Schwieger said softly, as if he were talking to himself. "Then she'll get back on course and head for Fastnet. And that's when we'll take her."

"How will you aim?" Haupert asked cautiously.

"From the surface," Schwieger answered.

"You're going to *surface?*" Haupert asked. Despite his best effort, his disbelief was obvious to everyone in the control room. Schwieger's eyes darted in his direction. Haupert turned away.

"Leveling at twenty feet," a seaman intoned. Schwieger listened carefully. There was no sound from *Hampton*'s propellers. *Hampton*'s captain, Schwieger figured, would have turned in a circle and recrossed the point where he had seen the submarine dive. He'd run another minute or so and then give up the hunt and turn back to his original easterly course.

In the intervening time, U-20 would have moved perhaps fifteen hundred yards down *Hampton*'s course. If U-20 turned back toward her, he could surface dead ahead of her as she ran to the east. Then *Hampton*'s captain would have two choices: he could keep coming, hoping to ram the submarine, or he could turn away, opening up the distance and bringing his deck gun to bear.

"He'll turn," Schwieger said aloud. "The bastard will turn."

It was eight minutes since *Hampton* had thundered past above his head. If he was right, she would be charging back now.

"Steady at twenty feet," the seaman said.

"Very well," Schwieger answered. "Steady as she goes."

Haupert stepped away from a voice tube. "The gun crew is ready," he reported.

"Very well," Schwieger acknowledged. But he wouldn't need his deck gun. When the boat came up, only he would go topside. This was a matter between himself and *Hampton*'s captain. The man had broken the rules. Schwieger could envision the steamer's crew searching for debris to confirm their kill. Would they lower the lifeboat that he had been prepared to afford to *Hampton*'s crew?

He doubted it. They were the ones who had turned the gentleman's game into cold-blooded murder. And he would make them pay.

"Prepare to surface," he ordered. Silently the control-room crewmen eyed one another. "Haupert, open the outer doors and get on the firing board. I want to be ready to fire torpedoes."

"Aye, aye," Haupert answered softly. Schwieger climbed the ladder and opened the hatch into the tower, ignoring the water that poured in on top of him. He closed the hatch and moved up the next ladder. When he felt the tower break the surface, he popped the hatch to the deck and rushed up into the cold night air.

The tower had buckled, the periscope fixtures had been cut away, and the life rails were cut and twisted. Schwieger had to squeeze himself through a tangle of steel. He saw *Hampton* no more than five hundred yards away, headed across U-20's port bow.

"Surprise," he whispered. "Now what are you going to do?"

Hampton did nothing, and continued in a straight line.

"Full ahead," Schwieger called down through the hatch.

He heard *Hampton*'s emergency whistle sound. Then he saw a white spray kick up from the steamer's bow. *Hampton* began turning to starboard, trying to bring its deck gun around.

"Left ten degrees rudder," Schwieger screamed into the hatch. "Stand by to fire one and two." His bow began to swing, until it pointed to the open sea ahead of his target.

"Fire one." He heard the hiss of air and saw the explosion of bubbles at his own bow as the torpedo was blown out of the tube.

"Right ten degrees rudder." The swing of the boat was immediately checked. At the same time, *Hampton* was turning, presenting its port beam. Behind its damaged afterdeck house Schwieger could see the five-inch gun coming into view.

"Fire two," he ordered. He could see the trace bubbles of his first torpedo, pointing ahead of the British ship, in case she broke off her turn. The second trace was aiming directly at her hull.

"Dive," he screamed. He was starting down the hatch when he heard the roar of *Hampton*'s big deck gun, and the sea exploded twenty yards off his starboard beam. As he pulled the hatch cover shut, the ocean washed over the top of the tower.

He lifted the next hatch and dropped into the control room. Anxious faces looked up at him. "Hard right rudder. Take her to fifty feet." He was aiming to get below the impact of the next shell.

Rules of Encounter

They listened in silence. The seconds ticked by like hammer blows on an anvil.

And then there was the muffled sound of a distant explosion. Haupert's face broke into a broad grin. Schwieger responded with the thumbs-up signal. One of the torpedoes had found its mark.

"Come to zero nine zero," Schwieger ordered. "Surface." He nodded to Haupert. "Come with me. You'll want to see this."

They rushed up to the deck as soon as the conning tower broke the surface. The horizon to the south was glowing brightly. At its center *Hampton* was ablaze, spewing jets of white fire.

The torpedo had hit either in the boiler room or the engine room. Secondary explosions were racking the ship.

"Should we get closer?" Haupert asked. If a target didn't sink immediately, they would finish it off with their deck gun.

"Not this one," Schwieger answered. "She's carrying black powder. We don't want to get too close."

As if on cue, *Hampton* exploded in a blinding flash of light, causing the officers to cover their eyes. The thunderclap was nearly deafening. When they looked back, the steamer had vanished, leaving a scattering of burning debris across the surface.

Washington. "Barbaric," President Woodrow Wilson said sadly. "Simply barbaric." He shook his head slowly in despair. "I can only hope we never become involved."

"Let's be sure that we don't," Secretary of State William Jennings Bryan advised. "It's an English ship sunk by a German ship. The United States has nothing to do with it. I don't see any reason why we should file a formal protest."

Wilson bent over the document that had been delivered by His Majesty's embassy only a few hours earlier.

> The steamer *Hampton* was torpedoed without warning. No challenge was given, nor was there any attempt to inspect her cargo. Constant cannon fire from the attacking submarine prevented *Hampton* from launching her boats. No assistance was offered to her crewmen, who were left helpless in the water.

"The point here," said State Department counselor Robert Lansing, "is one of international law. As the Secretary advises, there would generally be no reason for our government to become involved in actions between foreign belligerents. But when confronted with such a flagrant violation of international law, we have a duty to protest in the strongest terms. We must remember that the rules of encounter protect American ships from being accidentally attacked. We can't simply ignore the wanton murder of an unarmed commercial vessel's crew."

"Robert has a point," the President said to his Secretary of State.

Bryan was pinching an enormous handkerchief against his nose. He blew furiously, then stuffed the handkerchief into his trouser pocket. "Are you sure it was unarmed, Robert?" he challenged. "There were two English ships in New York last week that had gun mountings on their fantails, and von Papen is telling anyone who will listen that the Admiralty is arming merchant ships. He mentioned some documents that he had left with you."

"Crude forgeries," Lansing fired back. "Who told you there were gun mountings on English freighters?"

The President knocked gently on his desk. "Gentlemen, please. The issue is how to keep our country out of this madness."

"I think, Mr. President," Lansing offered, "that whatever we do must be solidly grounded in international law. You have spoken eloquently on the rule of law as our only hope for peace. Perhaps I should prepare a brief on the legal precedents involved."

Bryan's eyes rolled. The legal precedents would be as crooked as the people who had written them. Why couldn't this fool President understand that we had no business trying to play the world's peacemaker or—what was that idiotic phrase of Wilson's?—making the world "safe for democracy."

"Robert, how long will it take you to pull something together?" Woodrow Wilson asked.

"A few days. Certainly no more than a week."

"Good," Wilson said, jumping up from his desk. "We'll review Robert's brief. Then we'll decide on the proper course of action."

Lansing flashed his most enthusiastic smile. He'd write a legal brief tracing the righteousness of the rules of encounter all the way back to Henry VIII. He would prove that there was no more honorable principle among men than respect for the right of an unarmed merchant ship passing through hostile waters. When he was finished, the President would have no choice but to call the Germans to task.

Wilhelmshaven. *Friedrich der Grosse*, the flagship of the Imperial Fleet, rose like a castle in the great northern German naval harbor. Topped with colorful flags and bristling with twelve-inch guns, she was a floating military pageant. But the heavy links of iron that chained her to the bottom of the harbor belied the impression of a fearsome naval warrior. Like the rest of the great German High Seas Fleet, *Friedrich der Grosse* was going nowhere.

Submarine Flotilla Commander Bauer hated his visits to the flagship. As he stepped onto the companion ladder he heard the ceremonial boatswain's pipe announce his arrival. Why did his every coming and going require that hundreds of sailors stop work and render a ceremonial salute? He had forbidden the ridiculous piping aboard his beloved submarines. If it had been up to him, Bauer would never have left the submarine docks at Emden, where his little gray boats came and went. But this visit to Wilhelmshaven was different. Bauer was on a mission.

When he entered the conference room, Admiral von Pohl was already holding court, surrounded by his staff of admirals and captains. Bauer took his place at one of the tables, nodding an apology to von Pohl for his tardiness. As he listened to the bland recital of facts and figures he fidgeted with the report he had brought with him. "Captain Bauer," he heard von Pohl's adjutant say.

He was on his feet instantly. "I regret that I must ask permission for my command to depart from the international rules of encounter." Nodding heads snapped to attention. "British merchantmen are now attacking our submarines instead of obeying their challenges."

There was a gasp, followed by a rumble of murmuring. Admiral von Pohl slapped his hand on the table to restore order. "You know this for a fact?" he demanded.

Bauer held up the report from Lieutenant Schwieger, commanding officer of U-20. "The British steamer *Hampton* was challenged by U-20 three nights ago. *Hampton* responded with cannon fire from a five-inch gun mounted on her fantail. Then she turned toward the submarine and rammed her."

"Our boat was lost?"

"Fortunately, no, sir. U-20 can't submerge without taking on water, but I'm pleased to add that she carried out her mission. *Hampton* and her cargo of war materials were sunk."

"I can't believe the English would depart from their cruiser rules," a supply officer said.

"We can't fire without warning," a staff admiral shouted. "It would bring the whole civilized world down on us."

"And I can't ask my crews to expose themselves to five-inch cannons and to ramming," Bauer fired back.

Shouts rang from every corner of the room. If Bauer's boats could fire without warning from beneath the surface, there was little need for the Imperial Fleet's dreadnoughts. Without the rules of encounter, submarines were the most lethal weapon afloat.

Von Pohl's hand exploded on the table, followed by a deadly silence. "The business of this meeting is concluded," he whispered as he rose. The room snapped to attention. And then, almost as an afterthought, he told Bauer, "May I see you in my quarters."

The fleet commander was undoing the top button of his tunic when Bauer was saluted into his stateroom. Von Pohl settled into a chair and gestured Bauer toward a sofa. "One ramming could mean nothing," he said. "It could be a merchant captain panicking at the sight of a submarine. But the deck gun—that's a different story. If they are arming their merchant ships, then they are abandoning the rules of encounter."

"Exactly," Bauer agreed. "Which is why we should no longer be bound by them. It's suicide for a submarine."

The fleet commander wagged his head. "I have no problem when it comes to English freighters. But what about passenger ships carrying Americans? Or English ships flying American flags?"

"The Americans are no better than the English," Bauer answered. He handed von Pohl a page from the report he had prepared. "This is an intercept from our Irish agent. He has direct access to British radio traffic from Queenstown. It orders an escort for an American ship inbound from New York. Why would they be escorting it if it weren't carrying contraband?"

Von Pohl read the message. "My dear Bauer," he said, "you are getting into issues of national policy. The Emperor has personally forbidden me to risk attack on an American ship. You want permission to fire without warning. And you may not always be able to determine whether the target is an English ship flying the American flag, which I would love to sink, or an American ship, which I am forbidden to sink. You see the position you are putting me in."

Rules of Encounter

Bauer nodded. "I believe it is exactly the position that the Admiralty wants to put you in."

"Do you have any suggestions that I can bring to the Emperor?"

"I would declare the waters around Ireland and England a war zone," Bauer said. "I would warn all neutrals that all ships entering the zone do so at their own risk."

"A war zone," von Pohl considered. "I wonder how President Wilson would respond to a war zone."

"It's fair warning. It should certainly encourage him to make certain that English ships aren't flying the American flag."

Von Pohl lifted himself from his chair and paced his stateroom. "For the time being," he concluded, "I will allow underwater attack on merchant ships you can positively identify as English."

Bauer tapped the page of his report. "And here, where an intercept tells us a neutral ship is carrying contraband?"

"Not until I have the Emperor's permission," von Pohl said.

"War materials will get through," Bauer warned.

Von Pohl nodded. "I know that. And I will make exactly that point to the Emperor. Perhaps together with the idea of a war zone . . . Who knows what his Imperial Majesty will decide."

Bauer didn't have much hope. But as far as the British merchant fleet was concerned, the rules of encounter had been repealed.

CHAPTER 7

Schull. The lifeboat staggered into Roaringwater Bay just after daybreak, carrying a cargo of battered, frightened men, with white eyes staring from behind coal-blackened faces. Their hands shook on the cups of hot tea that the people of Schull rushed down to the landing.

They were survivors of the British steamship *Ikeria*, which had been torpedoed and then riddled by gunfire during a night of unspeakable terror. The ship, on course for Liverpool, was carrying artillery shells. She had cleared Mizen Head Light when the U-boat surfaced no more than a hundred yards off her port beam. It attacked without warning, causing explosions that echoed like thunderclaps, bouncing people out of bed all along the Irish shore. From Crookhaven to Baltimore, people with coats pulled over their nightshirts hurried to the beach. They could make out the shape of a ship at the base of the towering column of flame. Then there was a white flash, so brilliant that for an instant the flames were invisible. The impact hit them with the roar of a whirlwind. A moment later the flames were gone.

"Poor lads," the women allowed, even though the survivors were English. Even the men, raised on a venom of hatred for their English oppressors, nodded in sympathy. "Hun bastards," they agreed when they heard of the Germans who had fired without warning and then disappeared without any concern for the survivors.

The bodies began washing ashore the next afternoon. They were scorched black, and bloated with seawater. Some had lost limbs.

"BARBARIC," Father Connors said. He reached for the tea that his housekeeper was serving, then turned to William Day and Shiela McDevitt, who were sitting across from him. "I'll do everything I can to encourage the people to cooperate with you, Commander. Now, I can't promise anything. There's no great sympathy here for the English. But we're all outraged by what the Germans did."

"There are dangers," Day repeated. "I wouldn't want your people to underestimate them."

Father Connors nodded. "I understand. And I wouldn't underestimate the attractiveness of the wage you'll be paying. That kind of money can do a great deal for these poor people."

There was a tap on the door, and a small bespectacled man in an ill-fitting suit peeked into the parlor.

"Ah, Emmett," Father Connors announced. And then, turning to Day, "This is our schoolteacher, Emmett Hayes. And this is Commander Day. You already know Shiela." Day rose and shook hands. Hayes bowed toward Shiela.

"Emmett enjoys great respect in our community," Father Connors told Day. "I think he could be a great help in your efforts."

Day explained his plan for using the town's boats in his submarine patrols. Hayes seemed enthusiastic. "But I wonder," the teacher asked, "how you'll fix the positions of the boats. It would take a great deal of organization. These are not highly educated people."

"A grid based on lines of bearing from the shore," Day said. "Something that any seagoing man with a compass would know."

Emmett Hayes smiled. "Well, I could help you there. I'd be happy to rehearse each group on the bearings you assigned."

Day nodded his appreciation.

"Then you'll help persuade the community to take part in the commander's efforts?" Father Connors concluded.

"Certainly," Emmett Hayes volunteered.

The priest adjourned the meeting with a reassuring smile.

Day was buoyant as he and Shiela walked back to his car.

"Easier than I expected," he told her.

"Much easier," she agreed. "I think the Germans did our work for us when they sank that ship."

His flagship was *Hugh O'Neill,* a thirty-two-foot yacht with a white lapstrake hull, gleaming brightwork, and a woodburning steam engine. His fleet was an assortment of peeling work barges and gut-stained fishing boats, some with engines, some with sails; his crew, a gathering of withered old men and cherub-faced boys.

Shiela and Emmett had done Day's recruiting, with Father Connors standing in the background to nod his approval. They organized into three fleets, so that all in all, they were denying the U-boats fifty miles of hunting grounds, from Fastnet Rock all the way to the Old Head of Kinsale.

In Schull, where one fleet was based, they used Hayes' schoolhouse for meetings. Day had drawn a grid on a chart of the coastline, with one boat positioned at each intersection. All the captains had to do was hold a position at the intersection of the two bearings.

While Day laid out the battle plan, British sailors from Queenstown armed the boats. Machine guns were installed on the bows of boats that had enough good wood on their decks to hold screws and bolts. Rifles were put aboard the others. Day had been able to get only enough sailors to man a few of the guns. On the others they trained Irishmen as the gunners.

And now they were putting to sea for the first time. Thomas McCabe, owner of the long-idled *Hugh O'Neill,* cast off and stood behind the polished teak wheel. His nephew opened the throttle, and the yacht moved away from the pier. Then there was the choking of oil engines, which sent clouds of smoke into the air, and the screeching of wooden blocks as drab sails were hoisted up dozens of masts. The Schull fleet fell into line in the wake of Day's flagship.

They charged out into Roaringwater Bay, heading toward their stations. Captains leaned out over the prows, breathing in the adventure that had suddenly turned the routine of daily voyages into the excitement of the hunt for dark shapes and probing periscopes.

Day watched from the bow of *Hugh O'Neill,* amazed at what he saw. The tattered sails on the sailboats that hung like dead skin at their moorings flexed with muscle when they reached the open sea. Engines that were coughing and sputtering in the safe harbor of Schull began pounding with energy. Voices called from boat to boat with a new camaraderie.

There were mistakes, just as Day had anticipated. Three of the boats rushed up to the same station, nearly colliding as none of them would give ground.

"Do you have any idea where you are, Peter Farley?" an angry Tim Sheehy called.

"I'd be on my mark if you'd get that washtub out of my way."

Hugh O'Neill steamed from station to station, arbitrating disputes and checking on the bearings. But boredom came with the sun. Once they reached their stations, the crews had nothing to do.

Then just before noon the masts of a freighter appeared on the horizon. They sent up a cheer as the ship slipped safely through their formation. And then the endless waiting began again.

One of the sailboats dropped a fishing net over the side, and then a powerboat took to the idea and wandered off its bearings to set its nets in a more promising quarter. Other boats did the same. Day went after them, urging them back to their stations. But by midafternoon there was no trace of the pattern he had on his chart.

A flare suddenly exploded in the sky to the west. Day snapped his binoculars to his face. One of the distant sailboats was coming about smartly, its crew waving wildly at a nearby powerboat. Then another flare shot up from the powerboat as it suddenly kicked up a wake and began rushing toward the sailboat.

"Submarine!" Day heard from a workboat that was drifting off his starboard quarter. The boat roared off to the rescue.

McCabe's nephew began tossing armloads of wood at the base of the boiler. The captain of *Hugh O'Neill* swung the wheel to give chase. "We've got one," he screamed at Day.

In an instant every boat in the formation was charging toward the flares. Throttles were pushed to the stops. The crews leaned into the wind, urging more speed out of their boats.

Through his glasses Day could see that the fleet was beginning to crowd together around the same spot. It was all wrong. A U-boat would have no trouble slipping away in just the few minutes that it would take the fleet to gather. And then if she surfaced, she would have all the boats in one place—a perfect target for her deck gun.

Their safety, he had explained, depended on keeping their stations, giving the submarine no safe place to surface. But there was action at hand, and no one wanted to be left as a bystander.

Day heard a blast of machine-gun fire. On one workboat a crewman was aiming a deck-mounted gun into the gap between the two boats that had launched the flares. His second burst of fire sent the boats scattering in fear of their lives.

Within a fifty-yard radius Day suddenly had ten boats turning in all directions, cutting dangerously across one another. A rifleman was squeezing off round after round into the churning water at the center of the chaos.

"Cease fire!" Day screamed through his megaphone, punctuating his order with blasts on *Hugh O'Neill*'s steam whistle. As suddenly as it had begun, the attack on the submarine ended. The whistle caught the attention of the boat crews, and every head turned toward *Hugh O'Neill*.

"It *was* a submarine," the captain who had fired the first flare announced sheepishly to his neighbors.

"Let's go home," Day said. And *Hugh O'Neill* led its sullen squadron back toward the tilting pier of Schull.

In Emmett Hayes' schoolhouse, Day handed out the assignments for the next day's grid and spent a moment with each of his captains to argue the importance of holding his station. Later he drove in the darkness to Ballydehob, where he met with the officers who commanded the other two fishing-boat fleets—one at Baltimore and one farther east, at Courtmacsherry, near Kinsale. Their reports were similar to his own: a morning burst of enthusiasm, followed by a deterioration in station keeping as boredom set in.

"It's falling apart after one day," one of the officers said. "What's it going to be like after a week?"

Day shrugged his shoulders. "Keep after them," he said. "As long as they're out there, the U-boats have a problem."

He dismissed his officers and motored back to Crookhaven, and spent an hour with Shiela McDevitt and Chief Gore reviewing the day's radio traffic. Messages had gone out to six incoming ships—two British and four neutral. Only three could be assigned escorts.

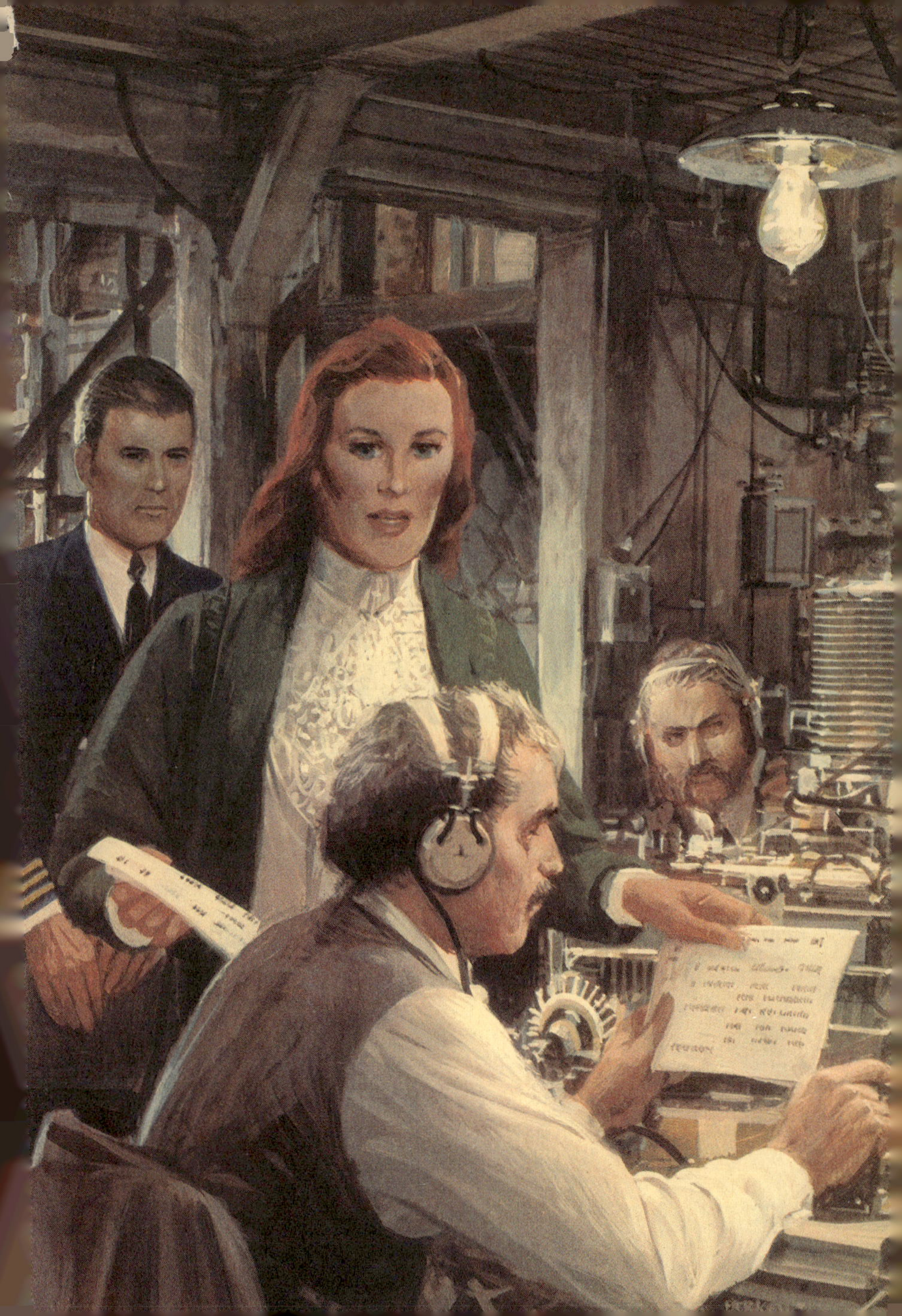

The others were advised that a fleet of fishing boats would be on station to discourage submarine operations. Day allowed himself a smile of satisfaction—Queenstown was already counting on his Irish navy.

He drove Shiela back down the dark road to Schull, telling her about the day's adventure.

"Was it really a submarine?" she asked in disbelief.

"Probably not." He laughed. "Maybe the shadow of a cloud."

He pulled up to her house, a small old stone cottage on a long-abandoned farm.

"Let me make you a cup of tea," Shiela offered.

Day followed her into a small brightly painted parlor, with a freshly covered sofa and soft chairs. He dropped wearily onto the sofa while Shiela raked the coals in the cast-iron stove and set a kettle of water over the embers. She spooned tea into a porcelain pot and put cream into a small pitcher. Then she set a tray with two cups and carried it back into the parlor.

Day was fast asleep. Shiela set the tray down and whispered his name. When there was no response, she brought in a blanket and spread it over him, then lifted his feet onto the cushions.

At the edge of the town, Emmett Hayes tapped out the coded details of Day's patrol plan for the next morning on his radio. He signed off, "Leprechaun."

"STOP here for a moment," Shiela said. There was a smile playing across her lips.

Day pulled the car to the siding. "What are you up to?"

Shiela jumped out and lifted the basket she had placed on the back seat. "Lunchtime," she answered.

"Lunch?" he asked, as if it were an unknown word. "We haven't time."

"You never have time," Shiela answered. "But today you're going to have lunch. In the most beautiful dining room in all of Europe. And you can watch your fleet while you eat." She started up the rocky hill that led to a bluff beyond the harbor. Day hung back for a moment, thinking of all the places he had to be. Then he shrugged in resignation and started after her.

They walked out onto a point of land that held Roaringwater Bay to the west and the sea to the south and east. The warm spring sun sparkled off the waves. Shiela opened her basket, handed Day a tablecloth to spread, and began unpacking the basket.

They had been together for the past two weeks, touring the coastline during the days and working at the radio station at night. Their days began in the darkness, when William turned his car up the path to Shiela's cottage. They drove first to one of the harbors, arriving before the boats set out, so that Day could talk to the officer, deliver new instructions, and review the day's sailing plan.

They stopped at the towns and paid calls on the local leaders. Sometimes they met in the drawing room of an English landowner, who acted as Day's paymaster, handing over the wages when the crews docked at night. In other towns the leader was the parish priest. Wherever they went, Shiela took care of the social necessities, her Irish conversation winning friends and making Day seem more the ally than the area commander for an occupying force.

At night at the radio station, Day checked the afternoon traffic while Shiela translated any coded messages. Then he would drive her to her cottage and continue on to his quarters at a boardinghouse to catch a few hours' sleep.

They took their meals wherever they happened to be. Sometimes it was as the car bounced along the roads, or in a pub or a rectory. Often it was at the mess in the radio station.

Now Shiela spread the picnic fare on the tablecloth. She had sandwiches made with thick cuts of cheese and thin slices of lamb, a salad of pickled vegetables, a dessert of raisin cakes, and two bottles of dark beer. Day's eyes widened when he saw the food.

"You must have been working all night," he said.

She smiled at the compliment. "It's the first quiet meal we've had in a month. I wanted it to be special."

"Special it is. I've worked you very hard," he told her, "and I've never said thank you. Do you understand that I'm very grateful for all the help you've given me? I wouldn't be anywhere without you."

She broke a sandwich and shared it with him. "I understand that you've thrown yourself into this with your whole heart. You're doing a wonderful job, but I'm terribly afraid that you're letting yourself in for a disappointment."

"There are still ships being sunk," he said. "Fourteen freighters last month. And as many more this month."

"You can't stop it. The ocean is too big for you to make it safe."

Day shook his head in despair. He tasted the beer and began devouring the sandwich, but he noticed Shiela wasn't eating.

"You need a ship," she told him. "They owe it to you."

He smiled. "Sounds as if you'd be happy to be rid of me."

"No," she said, looking away from him. "But I'd be happy to see you out of Ireland. This country is a bog that swallows up good men. The jealousy and the hatred are in the air. We take it in with every breath. Sooner or later it destroys everything that's good."

"The Irish are helping me," he argued.

"You're paying their wages," she said. "But heaven help you if a few of them should get killed by one of the U-boats. Then they'd turn on you in a minute because you're English."

"You're English," he reminded her.

"Yes," Shiela said bitterly. "The worst kind. I was one of them, and I left. So I'm not just their enemy. I'm a traitor. But I'm also Irish. I have no place to go."

He reached out to her. "I'll be careful," he promised.

"Careful isn't enough." She pushed his hand away. "There are things happening all around you that you can't understand."

"What things? Tell me."

Shiela looked at him and then jumped up and ran to the edge of the bluff. He went after her, but she turned her back to him. He realized that she was crying.

"Please, tell me what's wrong," Day begged her.

He could hardly hear her answer. "I'm afraid."

"Afraid of what?"

"Afraid for you," Shiela said. She turned to face him, her eyes red. "Make them give you a ship. Get away from here while you can."

He took her in his arms and held her. He could feel her trembling.

"I'm sorry," Shiela finally managed. "I wanted this to be a happy afternoon for you. And now I've spoiled it." She ran back to the tablecloth and began gathering up the remains of the picnic.

They drove back to Crookhaven, where Shiela disappeared into the coding room. While she worked, Day reviewed the day's traffic with Chief Gore. There were eight ships approaching the Irish coast within twenty-four hours. Coded messages had to be prepared for each. It was already dark when she handed her last message to the radioman for transmission.

Day navigated carefully back down the dark road to Schull, with

Shiela sitting silently by his side. They had always filled their journeys with chatter about their work. But now their relationship was changed. *"Afraid for you,"* she had said. And he understood that because of him, she was frightened for herself. He suddenly understood how alone and helpless she was, caught in the no-man's-land of hatred that separated England and Ireland. In her tears, she had shown him how deeply she cared for him. Now he knew how deeply he cared for her.

He swung the automobile to a stop in front of her doorway. On other nights they had continued talking for a few moments before she jumped down from the car. But tonight Shiela said a simple "Thank you" as she reached for her basket. She was stepping out onto the running board when he caught her hand.

"Thank you for the picnic," Day said.

She started to pull away, but he held on to her hand.

"Don't worry about me," he told her.

"I can't help it," Shiela admitted. "Please ask them for a ship. Something that will take you away from here."

Day shook his head slowly. "I can't leave you here alone." He was still holding her hand, leaning across the empty seat as she stood outside the car.

"We shouldn't be holding on to each other," Shiela warned.

"We have no one else to hold on to," Day said.

Shiela leaned across him and raised the magneto lever behind the steering wheel. The engine stuttered and then was silent.

They lay together in her small bed, her head resting on his shoulder, her long hair flowing across his chest. In the faint lamplight he could see the white curve of her shoulder. And the sparkle of the signet ring on his hand, which rested softly on her arm.

Day tried not to think of the inscription that it bore.

New York. Jennifer read the newspapers every day, searching out the most optimistic reports of the war. If she came upon a more pessimistic report, she tried to dismiss it. Surely William had meant that their marriage was impossible only because of his military duty. He was simply trying to protect her from the war.

But even she couldn't ignore the grim reports from the windswept waters off the Irish coast. Reports of British ship losses were appearing every day. She assumed that William had his own com-

Rules of Encounter

mand, probably one of the destroyers that were frequently reported to be hunting the submarines.

"I shouldn't be surprised if he were commanding one of those," her father told her, although he insisted he had no way of knowing where Commander Day had actually been stationed.

During the week, when her father was away in the city, Jennifer wrote letters constantly, beginning them early in the week and then hurrying to finish them by the weekend so that her father could take them back to the city and include them in the diplomatic pouch for London. She addressed them just as Sir Peter had advised—to Commander William Day, in care of the Admiralty. "The navy will see that he gets them," he assured her.

But there were no return letters. Not that Jennifer expected William to match her output of trivial news, coupled with expressions of concern. But still, she longed for an acknowledgment that he was getting her letters and that they were important to him.

As Anne watched her daughter's inexhaustible devotion, her hopes that Jennifer would outgrow her attachment to Commander Day faded. She tried to offer new interests, involving Jennifer in her charitable work, encouraging her to join other young people in their social circle. Jennifer complied, but always with half a heart.

"We're going to have to tell her," Anne finally confronted her husband in the late night quiet of their bedroom.

"Tell her what?" he answered in despair. "That I've been lying to her all along? How will that make things any better?"

"They can only get worse. She's in love with him."

But they didn't tell her. There was never the perfect moment. Sir Peter began to think of writing a frank letter to his former aide requesting that he write Jennifer and put an end to her misunderstandings. He knew where Day was stationed. But each time he was about to take up his pen, he remembered the night when he had seen them together on the terrace and realized that the man was in love with his daughter.

"Do you think that it might work out between them?" he suggested one evening to Anne. "I mean, the world is changing. The old rules—I wonder if they're still so important?"

"I've been asking myself the same question. I wonder if Jennifer will ever meet a more honorable man."

Sir Peter pounded his fist against his stuffed chair. "We carry these blasted class distinctions too far, I tell you. There are young men dying for England who wouldn't be welcome at my table. What is the matter with me?"

Anne placed her hand over his. "I think we should forward her letters. It's their future. They'll have to make their own rules."

Beecham's eyes brightened. "I'll take them on Monday."

He was away from the house when Jennifer recalled an article on British naval operations that she had cut from the *Herald* and given her father. She entered the library. Beecham's huge rolltop desk was open. She glanced across the mail slots, looking for the collection of clippings that she knew he kept. When she didn't see them, she slid open the top drawer. The clippings were there. She lifted them out carefully. It was completely by accident that she noticed the pale yellow envelopes that were her private stationery.

William Day's name was written on the top envelope in her own hand. Beneath it was another, again addressed with William's name. She tossed through the entire stack. When she finally understood, she felt a flash of rage. And then she began to feel sick. She closed the drawer and rushed out of the room.

Jennifer didn't come down for dinner that evening. Early the next morning she walked into the library, where Sir Peter was already hard at work. She carefully placed the letters on top of a document that he was reading. "You sent him away," she said.

Sir Peter looked up helplessly at her. He couldn't bring himself to admit his crime. He could only nod, and then he noticed with horror that her eyes were worn from crying. "Please," he begged. "Let me try to—"

"I'll be going to join him," Jennifer answered.

He knew that she would, and he could scarcely breathe as he watched her walk out of the room. Like all fathers who have ever lied to a child, he realized that he had forfeited his special place in her life and that he would never be welcomed back.

CHAPTER 8

Coningbeg Light. "Lightship two points off the port bow" came the message from the crow's nest.

Captain Daniel Dow smiled and raised his binoculars. He could feel the coiled muscles in his back begin to unwind.

Rules of Encounter

To save coal, Cunard had shut down one of *Lusitania*'s four boiler rooms, reducing her flank speed from twenty-six knots to a hair over twenty knots. It was still fast enough to outrun any submarine, but not nearly fast enough for Fairweather Dow. He had been frozen in terror during his passage along the Irish coast.

He had welcomed the sight of his escort *Juno* when she had appeared, but had begun to worry again when he was forced to shave two knots off his speed so that *Juno* could keep up. The sight of Day's fishing fleet had eased his anxiety, but then *Juno* turned off to her anchorage at Queenstown. For the past three hours he had been running alone.

His passengers were completely unconcerned since sighting land. Now the women were in their staterooms, compressing their wardrobes into steamer trunks, while the men were in the lounges, ordering their last drinks before the bars shut down.

The Coningbeg lightship was now clearly visible, no more than fifteen minutes ahead. Dow would swing around her and send the Greyhound charging into Saint George's Channel. The dangerous part of his crossing was behind him, he thought.

He left the wheelhouse and walked out to the bridge, where he stood beside the lookout and looked straight down at the bubbling wash five stories below. Every bit of space forward of where he stood, from three stories above the waterline down to the keel, was given over to the Admiralty's secret cargo. During the entire crossing Dow had worried about what it might be. Now he didn't particularly care. He turned back toward the wheelhouse.

"Submarine! Submarine! Periscope to port!" The scream came from behind him, from the lookout he had just left.

"Hard right rudder," Captain Dow screamed into the wheelhouse. Then he rushed back out to the bridge. The periscope was only five hundred yards on his port beam.

Immediately *Lusitania* began turning to starboard, away from the U-boat, her slender hull leaning into a sharp list. In the cabins below, steamer trunks crashed into bulkheads. In the lounges, glasses slid onto the Oriental carpets.

Dow saw the periscope swinging toward his stern as *Lusitania* turned away. He watched until the periscope disappeared under his fantail. "Rudder amidships," he ordered. The giant ship began to right itself as it straightened into a southerly course, away from

Coningbeg lightship. He shut his eyes and began to count the seconds it would take a torpedo to overtake his Greyhound.

There was no explosion—only a cacophony of voices as the enraged passengers rushed out onto the weather deck. They had picked themselves up from the force of the sharp turn, realized that something was wrong, and came to see for themselves.

"Submarine!" voices shouted. Hands pointed toward the stern, where the periscope had matched *Lusitania*'s turn.

Dow looked over his stern. The periscope was still there, but it was falling behind. Another minute, and he would be out of range.

The lookout was searching beyond the wake with his binoculars. "She's gone now, Captain." But Dow was anything but relieved. How could he come about and head into the channel if the submarine might be lying there, waiting for him?

He dashed to the chart room. If he ran to the east for an hour, he could open up fifteen miles between *Lusitania* and the submarine. Then if he turned to the north, he could probably beat the U-boat back to Coningbeg. "Left fifteen degrees rudder," he ordered. "Course zero nine zero."

Dow quickly dictated to his wireless operator a report of the submarine sighting to relay to the naval station at Milford Haven, on the western tip of Wales. The naval station, he reasoned, would forward the report to the patrol ships. They would come out and search the area, preventing the submarine from running on the surface. All he had to do was wait until they were at the lightship.

But the high tide at the Liverpool bar wouldn't wait for him. If he missed the tide, he would be forced to circle outside the port until the next day, exposing himself to daylight attack. He had to move north soon enough to catch the tide.

His first mate was standing beside him. "Captain, there's a delegation of passengers. They insist on speaking with you."

A panic among the passengers was the last thing Dow needed. He ordered the mate to plot the point at which he had to turn north in order to reach the Liverpool bar at high tide. Then he stepped back to the officers smoking room, where five men in formal dinner dress had assembled.

"Thomas Astin," their spokesman said. "Apparently, we're in some danger."

"No danger at all," Dow reassured. "All is quite in order."

Rules of Encounter

"That submarine was close enough to touch us."

"We're well away from her," Dow answered with a forced smile. "And now if you gentlemen will excuse me . . ."

He started for the door, but Astin stopped him. "But don't we have to go back toward her to get to the channel?"

"We're taking a different approach to the channel," Fairweather said. "And there are Royal Navy ships coming to escort us. So there's really nothing to worry about."

But there was, the first mate informed him back in the chart room. They had to turn north within the hour, in full daylight, to catch the tide. And there was no response from Milford Haven.

"Have wireless resend our message," Dow ordered the mate. "Tell Milford Haven that we need an escort ten miles east of Coningbeg by 1630." He paced the bridge as he waited.

Half his allotted time had elapsed before the wireless operator rushed onto the bridge with the message from Milford Haven: CONFIRM RENDEZVOUS, 090 CONINGBEG, 10 MILES, 1630.

Dow stepped back into the wheelhouse and ordered a turn to the north. He doubled his lookouts and ordered all his off-duty deck officers to lookout stations. Fifteen pairs of binoculars searched the sea, already beginning to redden from the western sun.

"I'll tell the lookouts to keep a sharp eye for the escorts," the first mate suggested.

"To hell with the escorts," Captain Dow snapped. "We'll see the escorts. Look for the periscope!"

But they didn't see the escorts. The telltale traces of smoke didn't appear on the western horizon. The first thing Dow was able to make out was the distant blinking of Coningbeg Light.

"Where in heaven's name are they?" he shouted.

"We could circle a bit," the first mate said. "They may be running a bit off schedule."

Dow nodded grimly. That was one of his alternatives. He had two other choices: turn back out to sea and add another costly day to his voyage, or rush through the gap between the lightship and the submarine he had imagined in his panic to be lurking ahead. There was no submarine in sight.

"We're going through," he finally concluded. "Break out the zigzag instructions."

The zigzag was a series of turns designed to prevent a submarine from plotting a ship's heading. Without knowing a target's exact heading, the submarine couldn't aim its torpedoes. *Lusitania* headed for the channel, and its bow began carving quick turns.

In the first-class dining room, Thomas Astin noticed his lobster bisque rolling to one side of his soup bowl. The ice in his water glass began to rattle. He glanced at one of the gentlemen from his passengers' committee. The man's expression was as white as his tie.

"Submarine!" the lookout on the port wing sang out. Dow ran to his side and focused the glasses. The periscope was high out of the water, a thousand yards off.

He was past the U-boat but still well within her firing range. Now speed was his best hope of escape, and the zigzag turns were costing him speed. He made his decision instantly. "Steady on course zero two zero."

If the U-boat captain realized that *Lusitania* had settled on a straight course, and fired immediately, the torpedo could overtake the liner. But if he hesitated, then the Greyhound's speed would carry her safely out of range.

"Captain Dow."

Fairweather followed the voice down to the boat deck, where Thomas Astin was standing with one of his associates.

"Where are our escorts?" Astin shouted.

Dow ignored the question, refocusing his glasses on the periscope.

"Escorts ahead," the first mate called. Dow wheeled around. He made out the masts of two ships steaming south toward him. When he turned back, the periscope had disappeared. He stepped to the rail. "Dead ahead, Mr. Astin."

For one horrifying hour it had all come together—the innocent passengers, the deadly cargo, and the submarine. Dow had no intention of presiding over the slaughter that such a deadly mixture was sooner or later bound to cause. The next morning he walked into the offices of Alfred Booth and resigned his command.

"I'll make sure that you never get another command," Booth screamed at his captain. "Nothing. Not even a rowboat."

But even as he was blustering, the Cunard chairman knew Dow didn't want another command. He wanted out of the war. Booth regained his composure. "Who can replace you?" he asked frankly.

"Bill Turner," Dow answered without a second's pause.

"Bowler Bill," Alfred Booth gasped in horror, thinking of

Turner's habit of wearing a bowler hat on top of his uniform jacket. "The man's a savage. He puts ketchup in his consommé!"

"Find someone else to dine with the passengers," Dow advised. "Put Bill Turner on the bridge. He's the best seaman you've got."

Schull. Day's makeshift fleet was doing its job, much to the surprise of Admiral Coke, who commanded the Irish coast from his flagship at Queenstown. The workboats and fishing vessels, armed with nothing more than rifles and light machine guns, were accomplishing off Ireland what His Majesty's mighty armada was failing to achieve in the other waters surrounding the British Isles. Since Germany's proclamation of a war zone, twenty-five British merchantmen had been sent to the bottom—in the North Sea, the North Channel, Saint George's Channel, and the Western Approaches—with nearly half a million tons of war materials. Only one had been sunk in the stretch of coast that Commander Day patrolled, and that at night, when the Irish boats weren't operating.

But Day didn't need to see the figures on ship losses. He could see the results in the faces of his crews. They had perfected their simple formations. They were in the war, doing honorable work, and that seemed more important to them than the fact that they were shoulder to shoulder with their centuries-old enemy.

Often in the mornings he sailed out with one of his fleets, racing back and forth through the formations, shouting encouragement to his captains. Mostly he was just showing a military presence, reminding the crews of the importance of their mission.

And then there was the time he spent working with Shiela McDevitt. Shiela and Day were careful, but it wasn't easy living under watchful eyes only too eager to see their failures. Her isolation, if anything, was worse than his. The women of the villages were outspoken in their scorn for her. And it was they who first sensed the personal interest the two had in each other. "He's living in her cottage," one of them told a parish priest after Day's car had been seen early one morning parked beside Shiela's house.

One day Shiela was vulgarly insulted by a woman in the docks at Baltimore. She and William went straight to her cottage, without checking back at the Crookhaven station. Day held her throughout the night and then faced Chief Gore's suspicious glances with her in the morning.

It was while driving to Shiela's house at the end of an exhausting day that Day first raised a problem that had been troubling him. "Do you think the Germans are reading our coded traffic?"

"The coded traffic? How?" she asked with an expression of fright. "It's a daily cipher. It changes every day."

"Lots of ways. A tap on the line from Queenstown. Or a leak somewhere—at Queenstown or even our people at Crookhaven."

Shiela went white at the suggestion. "I can't believe it," she said. "Do *you* think we're being compromised?"

"I'm not sure," he said. "But there are too many coincidences. Every U-boat attack over the past weeks has been on an unescorted ship. And they've also hit the most important cargoes. I just can't believe that the Germans are that lucky."

They were silent, Shiela seeming to weigh his conclusions.

"The Germans also seem to know where our fishing boats are operating," he continued. "For example, when we move to the western end of our area, they attack to the east."

Shiela was shaking her head. "But we never broadcast our fleet instructions. We hand the assignments right to the crews."

Day smiled grimly. She was correct, and he knew it wouldn't take her long to realize the implications—there was a spy in their midst. Probably the same spy who was tapping into the radio traffic.

"What about the Fenians?" he asked. "This wouldn't be one of our fishermen. Tapping phone lines and running a radio." It would take a bit of sophistication and the kind of organization that the Irish nationalists could provide. "Do you think any of the brothers might be close to us?"

Shiela shrugged. "They're everywhere. I don't know of anyone, though, who does more than talk."

When they reached the cottage, Day raised a fire in the stove for their tea. "What are you going to do?" Shiela asked.

"Inform the Admiralty." He set the kettle on the fire. "Recommend that they stop sending traffic through Crookhaven."

"And our local problem? You can't just abandon the fleets."

"We won't give out the day's patrol areas until just before the boats leave the dock. That will give the submarines less time to act."

Shiela fixed the tea and carried it into the parlor. "If they close down Crookhaven, they'll have no need for me here."

"I thought of that, too," he admitted.

Rules of Encounter

"I won't leave you here alone," she said. "It's dangerous. You should be asking for a transfer."

He reached out to take her into his arms. "You're the only danger," he teased. But she pushed his hands away.

"Don't be making fun of me," she said, a sudden hurt showing in her eyes.

"I'm sorry," he told her. "Why is it dangerous?"

"Because you're asking questions," Shiela said. "They won't want you to have the answers."

London. Captain Reginald Hall rose from behind his desk as Lieutenant Peter Grace was shown into his office. Lieutenant Grace was no ordinary officer. He wore civilian clothes, had never been aboard a ship, and had no intention of ever accepting a naval command. His services to the crown were in other capacities.

"Everything tidy on the India docks?" Hall asked as soon as he had guided his guest to a chair.

"I think so," Grace answered. "Loughton's friends have been arrested. And Mr. Loughton himself is no longer operative."

Loughton, a stevedore who had been selling cargo information to a German, had been crushed under a six-ton pallet that inexplicably broke free from a cargo hoist.

Accidents seemed to follow close behind Lieutenant Grace wherever his work in counterintelligence took him. His efficiency and discretion had earned him the respect of the Admiralty.

"What do you know about southwestern Ireland?" Hall asked as a way of getting into Grace's next assignment.

"Admiral Coke's area," Grace responded. "We have a radio station there, don't we? Traffic in and out of Queenstown?"

Hall nodded. "Crookhaven. Important traffic. Arrival messages for all ships coming across the south coast." He picked up a folder from his desk. "It's run by Commander William Day, one of our best young officers. He sent this to us. Quite an accurate analysis."

Hall sat quietly while Grace flipped through the pages. "Looks as if he's on to something."

"He is," Hall answered. "We've known we had a leak at Crookhaven for quite some time, but after reading this, it looks as if there's a fair-sized operation down there."

"So you want me to check it out," the lieutenant concluded.

"As soon as possible," Hall answered. "You won't need a cover. Simply go out to Crookhaven and report to Commander Day. While he's watching the coast, you'll be watching for spies."

Grace nodded. "Seems simple enough. In fact, too simple."

"There is one complication: we'd like to know who's causing the leaks. But we don't want him to become . . . inoperative."

Grace was clearly confused.

"We need an open channel to Germany. We want them to read certain traffic that they assume we are trying to keep secure. We would like certain ships brought to their attention."

Grace's lips spread into an understanding smile. "Commander Day's discoveries aren't in the national interest."

"They could prove inopportune," Hall corrected. "With you there to follow up on his suspicions, he'll probably focus his attention on his other duties."

Grace handed the folder back to his commanding officer and stood. "You'll cover my assignment with Admiral Coke."

"Of course," Hall promised.

CHAPTER 9

Schull. Thomas McCabe's nephew tossed more logs into the firebox and watched the steam-pressure gauge inch up. He opened the throttle valve, and steam hissed into the cylinder heads. "Ready to go, Commander," he said to William Day. Day's flagship, McCabe's *Hugh O'Neill*, fell in line with the small flotilla heading out into Roaringwater Bay.

Since he had begun holding the patrol assignments until minutes before sailing, Day had gone to sea with his boats every morning. By denying the submarines that information, he was making the entire coast a high-risk area. He knew the submarines wouldn't abandon their hunting grounds. Sooner or later they would have to come to grips with his civilian navy. He wanted to be there when the danger struck.

He had done all that he could to prepare for the eventuality. A heavy machine gun was mounted on top of *Hugh O'Neill*'s wheelhouse and manned by an experienced gunner. He had also scrounged a simple foot soldier's mortar and placed it on the bow.

The boats quickly took up stations on the western edge of the patrol area, where steamers from America would first appear. The flagship began making its rounds, steaming past each of the boats.

"Not a lot of air out here, Commander," old Mike O'Sullivan said, pointing to the ripples in his sail as *Hugh O'Neill* came alongside. "Hope you won't be expecting me to go anywhere in a hurry!"

"Let's hope not, Mr. O'Sullivan," Day answered.

Three miles southwest of Mizen Head he suddenly saw a trace of soot on the horizon. "This first one through is a Yank," he said to Captain McCabe. They began the wide easterly swing beyond the seaward edge of the formation, Day keeping an eye on the American freighter until it had moved into the safe protection of his fleet. Then he searched ahead, hoping to pick up the Baltimore fleet.

They had been moving eastward for over an hour when McCabe pointed south, where a dark shape was kicking up a wake on the horizon. Day raised his glasses. "Come about," he yelled. "That's not ours."

As the yacht was turning, Day could make out the crashing spray of a bow. "Good heavens," he whispered. "It's a submarine."

"Get me all the pressure that this thing will hold," he yelled at McCabe's nephew. He screamed up to the machine gunner, "Load, and stand by to fire."

The mortar crew, on the bow, had heard the commotion, and were already prying the cover off the container of mortar shells.

"Stand by to fire!" Day ordered.

The gunner turned the crank, tipping the mortar to a thirty-five-degree angle. Day raised his hand.

"Fire!"

With a muffled *pop* the first shot he fired in the war exploded into the water ahead. It was only a fraction of the distance between *Hugh O'Neill* and its target.

"Fire!" Day ordered again.

A second explosion shattered the sea halfway to the submarine.

The U-boat commander couldn't ignore mortar fire moving closer to his boat. He would have to dive or turn his attention toward the onrushing *Hugh O'Neill*. Either way, he would be distracted from the murderous attack he was aiming toward the helpless boats in Day's flotilla. But the U-boat wasn't responding. Instead, it continued at top speed toward the boats.

A puff of smoke appeared above the submarine, followed in

seconds by the crack of its deck gun. A tall geyser of water exploded next to a small engine-powered fishing boat.

"Keep firing," Day screamed to the mortar crew. He saw the submarine's deck gun flash again. The geyser lifted the fishing boat out of the water, and the crewmen spilled out into the sea.

Hugh O'Neill's young engineer had the firebox nearly glowing. But the yacht wasn't moving nearly fast enough.

The submarine had the first row of boats at point-blank range. Its machine gun was now chattering, kicking up spray just short of its targets. The next crack of its deck gun splintered a wooden sailboat and tossed it like pieces of kindling into the air.

As soon as Day's first mortar round had exploded, the boat captains had turned to close in on the submarine, not realizing that she had approached on the surface with her gun crews ready. At the first cannon shot, they had turned in panic, nearly colliding with one another in their rush to escape. But they didn't have a chance. Running on the surface with its powerful engines, the U-boat was quickly overtaking them. They looked over their sterns, caught in a deadly lottery as the German gun crew randomly selected its victims. Within a minute, four of the Irish boats were gone, leaving frantic figures struggling in the water. Day could only watch helplessly, the action still beyond the range of his pathetic guns.

The submarine turned and took aim at the second line of the patrol, where O'Sullivan's sailboat was. O'Sullivan appeared on his transom. Defiantly he raised his English rifle toward the oncoming U-boat.

"Nooo!" Day screamed uselessly as the old man tried to steady the rifle against the sway of his own boat. O'Sullivan fired, the recoil lifting the muzzle into the air. The U-boat's gun crew dropped to the deck for cover. Suddenly the submarine commander was jabbing his finger toward the sailboat, where O'Sullivan was trying to strip a new round into the rifle chamber.

Day watched in horror as the U-boat's machine gun swung toward the old man. A hail of bullets ripped into the sailboat's transom. Suddenly O'Sullivan flew backward, tossing the gun into the air as he disappeared over the side.

Hugh O'Neill's mortar popped again, launching another shell. This time the explosion was less than fifty yards from the target. Immediately the U-boat broke off its attack and turned toward the yacht.

"The engine's overheating," McCabe's nephew yelled.

"Full speed," Day screamed back. It didn't matter whether the engine could destroy itself in another minute. The yacht's fate would be decided in the next twenty seconds.

The submarine's deck gun fired, and the sea exploded just off the starboard bow. The yacht pitched off its course, sending Thomas McCabe spinning across the wheelhouse. Day grabbed the wheel and twisted the bow back toward the U-boat. Whoever got off the next shot would probably be the survivor.

Above his head Day heard his machine gun begin to chatter. Bullets began ringing off the U-boat's hull, up toward the gun crew. His crew on the bow dropped another round into the mortar. The instant the round exploded out toward its target, Day spun the wheel to the right. At the same instant the U-boat's deck gun fired.

The three-inch shell ripped into the water where the yacht would have been had she continued on a straight course. A waterspout blasted into the air, pitching *Hugh O'Neill* over on her starboard side. As she struggled to right herself, rounds from the submarine's machine gun began tearing into her wheelhouse. There was a scream from overhead as the bullets raked Day's gunner, blowing him over the side. The last rounds from his machine gun had knocked down two of the German gun crew.

The mortar round was falling toward its target. Warned by its whistle, the U-boat commander ducked behind the conning-tower shield just as the shell exploded a few feet from his hull.

Day turned the yacht back toward the submarine, hoping to get off one more mortar round before the U-boat's machine gunner cut him to pieces. But there was no machine-gun fire. The submarine commander was clearing his decks, preparing to dive.

McCabe, who had been knocked down and dazed by the first shot of the submarine's deck gun, staggered to his feet. "Hold this course," Day told him, pushing him against the wheel. Day climbed up to the machine-gun position.

Through the gunsight he saw crewmen scampering down the submarine's hatches. He threw the bolt and squeezed the trigger. Instantly bullets clanged across the hull. One German dropped before he could reach the deck hatch. Another, halfway into the hatch, threw up his arms and fell into the opening.

In a cascade of bubbling water the U-boat's decks disappeared.

Day fired at the periscope. Bullets ricocheted off the steel weather shield. But with them came pieces of tubing that protected the delicate lens of the periscope. He was still pouring rounds into the U-boat's eye when she disappeared under the sea.

It was then that he realized *Hugh O'Neill* was doomed. The heat from the engine had set the afterdeck on fire; seawater was pouring in through the bullet holes that had raked the hull.

Many of the fleeing Irish boats turned back toward him and toward the crews of the sunken boats, who were struggling in the water. *Hugh O'Neill* was down to her rails when a small workboat came alongside and lifted the crew to safety. There was no satisfaction in the faces of the seamen, even though the first submarine to challenge them had been driven off. Some of their neighbors were not to be found among the survivors.

Day waited on the Schull pier as the day's toll became a reality. Five men were unaccounted for, their wives and families wandering in a daze among the survivors, crying out when their worst fears were confirmed. Two of the men were given last rites by Father Connors, then rolled carefully in sailcloth and carried by their friends toward the church.

William stood aside, the outsider to the town's grief. He saw O'Sullivan's wife, old and frail, standing on the slip where the sailboat had tied up each night. He went to her, touching her hand. When she looked up and recognized him, she screamed, her bony hands flailing out and striking at his face. "Damn you," she cursed in a shrill voice. "What good will your devil's money do him now!"

The people watched while she sagged under the effort of striking him. She fell to her knees, shaking in muffled sobs. Emmett Hayes stepped out of the crowd and helped her to her feet. He led her back to her people, and they all walked slowly toward the village, leaving Day alone on the dock.

SHIELA was waiting in the cottage doorway. She had been at the radio station when she heard of the U-boat's attack, and had begged a ride on a truck that was leaving Crookhaven.

"A bad one?" she asked as Day stepped out of the car.

He slowly nodded. "Jeremy Duke," he began, "the English sailor, shot by the submarine gunner. Pat O'Donnell and the Farley kid, lost over the side. And old Mike O'Sullivan—"

Shiela's hands shot to her face. "Oh, no," she groaned.

"The s.o.b. came right at us. He wasn't after a ship. He was after the boats. We drove him off. But it was a slaughter."

Shiela wasn't listening. She had collapsed sobbing onto the sofa. Day tried to take her into his arms, but she pushed him away and rushed into her bedroom. He had lost good men to the cruelty of war. But she had lost neighbors who had been part of her childhood. She needed her moment of mourning.

Pouring a heavy measure of whiskey into a glass, Day ran the dead men through his mind, forcing himself to see their faces. Had he betrayed their trust? They had died fighting his war. But no matter whose war it was, his Irish volunteers had stopped the submarines. Old Mike O'Sullivan, standing there on the transom of his sailboat, facing off against a machine gun, wasn't a fool. He was a brave man, doing what he had to do.

"It's not your fault." Shiela was standing in the doorway, her dress wrinkled, her eyes red. "It's the damned senseless war."

"I know," Day answered. "But I'm sorry for them." He turned toward her. "I'm sorry for you."

Shiela walked to him and took his hand. "We shouldn't be alone," she said. "Not tonight."

They lay together quietly. The first sounds of morning found them still in an embrace.

WHEN William Day pulled to a stop at the foot of the pier, only a few men were waiting by the boats. Day took a deep breath and tried to look confident as he walked toward them. Then he saw Emmett Hayes start down the pier to meet him.

"I don't think you'll be patrolling today," Hayes said. "Mike O'Sullivan's body came in with the tide. We're waiting on the others."

Day nodded that he understood. "I'll wait with them. I'd like to help bring them to the church."

"We'd appreciate that," the schoolteacher agreed. "But then give us a day by ourselves. We'll decide what to do next."

"NEW officer's aboard," the sentry told Day as he was being saluted through the security gate at the radio station.

"New officer?" Day stopped short.

"Yes, sir. A Lieutenant Grace. Replacement for Miss McDevitt."

Day's confusion was obvious. He turned and started up the hill. Chief Gore was waiting for him in front of the cottage.

"Did you know Shiela was leaving?" Gore asked.

"I had no idea, Chief," Day answered.

Gore threw up his hands in disgust. "Why would they move her? Don't they know how important she is to us?"

"Maybe the new lieutenant can tell us. Where is he?"

The chief pointed to the quarters cottage. "Having his lunch. Looks like he's fresh out of school. Brand-new uniform."

The boyish-looking officer sprang to attention as soon as Day stepped through the doorway. "Lieutenant Peter Grace, reporting for duty, sir," he chanted. He had a plate of kidney stew and a pot of tea set in front of him. He looked uneasily at the food and then back at the commander.

"Finish your lunch," Day offered as he dropped his cap on the table and sat opposite the officer.

Grace talked between bites. "Heard you had a bad day yesterday. This probably isn't a good time for me to be starting."

The commander nodded. "A very bad day. But a good time to have you aboard. We need help." He waited while Grace swallowed some tea. "But a bad time to be losing Miss McDevitt. Do you know when she's scheduled to leave?"

"No rush," Grace said. He glanced around, confirming that there was no one else in the cottage. "Fact is, my assignment is just a cover. I'm with naval intelligence." He pushed another kidney onto his fork, ignoring the shock in Day's face. "Nice coincidence, actually. You tell the Admiralty you suspect your radio traffic is being compromised. The Admiralty tells intelligence. So intelligence has to find a way of getting me in here without kicking up a fuss. Then Miss McDevitt asks for a transfer back to England. What's more logical than for me to arrive as her replacement?"

"She requested a transfer?" Day's surprise was obvious.

Grace shrugged. "That's what they told me." He nibbled the kidney off his fork. "Best if you can keep her awhile. Changes tend to make spies suspicious. Wouldn't help our investigation."

"Who are you investigating?"

"Everyone," Grace said. "In this business the last person you'd suspect generally turns out to be the one you're after."

Day didn't enjoy being lectured by a junior officer. "You're an old hand in intelligence, I suppose."

"I've had a few assignments," Grace said. He carried his dishes to the sink, walked back to the table, and leaned down on two strong hands. "Commander, you're the only one who knows why I'm here. And as long as I'm just a snotty brat out of officer training, we'll be able to keep it that way. Believe me, I'm very good at what I do. Every bit as good as you are in your work. I won't get in your way. Don't you get in mine."

Day looked long and hard into eyes that were suddenly cold. Then he nodded in respect. "You'll keep me informed?"

"You'll know everything I know," Grace answered.

Day stood up quickly and picked up his cap. "Let's get you introduced," he said as he started for the door.

"Aye, aye, sir." Grace stepped along behind.

He had no intention of keeping Day informed. If he had, he could have told him that he had already established that no one was tapping the telephone lines. He could have told him that the teacher who distributed his sailing orders, Emmett Hayes, had spent two years writing inflammatory editorials for a Fenian newspaper. Or he might even have warned him that the coding clerk who shared his bed was the daughter of a Free Irish labor agitator.

Lieutenant Grace was already convinced that the Crookhaven station was surrounded by Irish conspirators. He knew he could get the names anytime he wanted them. But he was in no hurry. His assignment was to keep the station operating until it delivered its critical message to the Germans. Then he would shut it down. And when he did, there would be no witnesses.

New York. Sir Peter Beecham had come to dread his weekends. From Monday to Friday he was caught up in the market for war materials. He now owned most of Du Pont's black powder and a whole production line of General Electric's motor generators. He was a bigger customer for heavy shoes than the Sears, Roebuck catalogue. True, not all his supplies were getting through. But he had passed the crisis in keeping his country outfitted.

On Saturday mornings, however, as his car drove through the gates of his home, his spirit blackened. His well-meaning lies to his daughter had destroyed the joy that once sounded through the estate like strings playing in the music room. He and Anne were sick with guilt.

A servant opened the door and took his hat and briefcase.

"Missus Beecham?" Sir Peter inquired.

"In her room, sir. I'll tell her you've arrived."

"And Jennifer?"

"Out for a walk, I believe."

"Ah, yes. Lovely morning for a walk," he said as he started into the library, which had become his own silent prison.

He went to the French doors that opened out onto the terrace. The trees, which only last week had been yellow with new buds, were now green with young leaves.

Anne entered and set down a tray with tea. "Welcome home," she said. He embraced and kissed her. He listened as she catalogued the week's events while she poured the tea and settled into a chair. Then he told her the news that had been weighing on him.

"Jennifer has booked passage to England."

Her teacup sagged against her lap. "Good heavens."

"Second class on *Atlantic,* one of the small Cunarders. Sumner just happened to come across her name on the booking register. He thought it was a mistake and called me for clarification."

"What did you tell him?"

Peter sighed. "Well, oddly enough, they're in the process of transferring the passengers to other ships. *Atlantic* is being held in England for Admiralty alterations. I asked him not to notify Jennifer. Told him that I'd take care of it."

"She was going to leave us without even saying good-bye," Anne guessed. "How she must hate us."

"Nothing of the sort," Sir Peter lied, even though he had thought exactly the same thing. "Just a show of independence."

"You'd let her go?" Anne challenged.

He held out his arms, gesturing to the silent household. "Hasn't she already gone?"

"At least talk to her," Anne begged, near tears.

His opportunity came within the hour, when Jennifer stepped through the front door and crossed toward the stairs.

"Jennifer," he called from the library doorway. She stopped abruptly, hesitating while she decided whether to acknowledge her father. "May I have a word with you? It's important."

She walked slowly into the library, never glancing in his direction, and sat down as he closed the door behind her.

"I understand you've decided to go back to England."

Her eyes widened in shock.

"I wasn't prying," Beecham hastened to reassure her. "I just happened to learn that you've booked passage."

"Even Cunard does your bidding," she said coldly.

"Nothing of the sort. It's just that the ship you booked is being pulled out of service," he said, walking to his chair.

She smiled at the irony. "The one ship I was able to get aboard is being removed from service?"

Peter reddened in embarrassment. "Now really! I don't have the power to order ocean liners about."

"No. Only people," Jennifer answered.

For an instant he thought he might explode with rage at her effrontery. But he realized that her wound was even greater than his. "I suppose I deserve that," he admitted. "I doubt I'll ever forgive myself, much less expect forgiveness from you. But if you're determined to go, at least let me help get you there safely."

"I think you've helped enough."

"For heaven's sake, Jennifer, there's a war on. Ships are being sunk right and left. At least let me get you aboard a safe ship."

She eyed him suspiciously.

"All your life your mother and I arranged things for you. It was the right thing to do. Then suddenly it was the wrong thing. We hurt you terribly. But that doesn't mean we can stop loving you."

"You'll arrange my passage?" she asked, not sure that she wasn't being led into some sort of trap.

He nodded. "*Lusitania* sails on May first. It's only one day later than you were scheduled. And she's the safest ship afloat."

"Thank you," Jennifer said. She stood and started for the door.

"You'll want to let William know that you're coming," he called after her. "I'll make sure your letter gets into Monday's pouch."

Jennifer turned and looked back at him.

"I will," Sir Peter said. "I swear I will."

Schull. The bodies of the Irish crewmen were carried into the church in plain pine boxes. Widows and mothers, their grief hidden in black veils, were led into the front rows; then the townspeople, with Shiela in their midst, filed in. William Day and his English sailors, in full-dress uniform, came in last and stood in the back.

Father Brendan Connors had decreed a High Mass. His sermon pulled together the myriad mysteries of Irish theology to prove that their fallen comrades were already in the company of the Blessed Virgin. "But these men are more than saints," he concluded. "They are also heroes in God's army. And their earthly commander is here with us today." He looked to the back of the church. "Commander Day, will you say a word?"

Even when he reached the pulpit, Day had no idea what he could say. All he could tell them was what he believed. He began with a litany of all the ships that had passed safely down the Irish coast. When he finished, he had counted more than a thousand people who had sailed under the protection of the Irish boats.

"I believe that we are all brothers," he said. "When we find ourselves caught up in a war, I believe the best of us do what we can to save one another from the slaughter. These men offered safety to a thousand of their brothers. They are the best of us."

The English sailors formed an honor guard on the steps as the bodies were carried out. After the coffins had been secured on a wagon and the procession had disappeared toward the cemetery, Emmett Hayes came out of the church and walked up to Day.

"Thank you," Hayes said. "We all appreciated your words."

"Will the men go back on patrol?" Day asked.

"I'm not sure," Hayes said. "Father Connors will know when it's time to raise the subject. Perhaps in a few weeks."

The English contingent returned to Crookhaven, where Shiela disappeared into the code room, while Day began reviewing the day's traffic. But after a short while he walked out to the edge of the cliff. He looked at the empty ocean and realized that his work in Ireland was nearly over. He had demonstrated conclusively that a fleet of small boats could keep the submarines out of the sea-lanes. But Day doubted that the Irish fleet would ever sail again. Even if the men could erase the image of the U-boat, the women would never forget the line of coffins down the center of the church.

Perhaps the Admiralty would organize a new fleet, operating from English ports. But that wasn't his affair.

Even his personal attachment to Ireland would soon be broken. Shiela's request for transfer back to England had been genuine.

Rules of Encounter

She believed that Peter Grace was her replacement and that in all probability she would be gone before summer.

"I think I'm finished here," he told Shiela as they drove together back to her cottage. "I want to get back into the real navy."

"I'm glad," she said as they turned into her road. "You're better off out of here." As they opened the door to her cottage she added, "They won't forget the men they buried today. You've overstayed your welcome, if you were ever all that welcome."

They worked in silence preparing a simple supper, the question of their future hanging over them. They had come together in a moment of need, when their loneliness had driven them into each other's arms. But now the truth was upon them. Could they simply walk out of each other's lives?

Day mulled the question until they were getting ready for bed. He puffed his pillow and sat up under the comforter while she changed into her nightgown. "Can I ask you something?" he tried cautiously.

Shiela glanced at him, looking suddenly defensive.

"You never mentioned your transfer. We could have talked about it. What you're thinking, what you decide—it's important to me."

Shiela slipped under the comforter. "You would have asked why."

"And you couldn't have told me?"

"All I could have told you was that I loved you."

"And that's why you want to leave me?" Day asked.

"That's why I have to." She touched his face with her fingers. "Sooner or later these people will hurt you. I don't want to be here when it happens."

"I don't understand what you mean," Day told her.

"I know," she responded. "And I can't make you understand."

Day slipped down in the bed beside her. "Maybe we should get transferred together. I think I need to be close to you."

She kissed him gently. "You're close to me now."

"But when you leave?"

"What will happen, will happen," Shiela said. "If we're meant to be together, then we'll find each other."

"Then this is only for now?" Day asked.

Shiela looked up at him, and in the soft light of the lamp he could see that she was crying. "Now is all we have," she told him. She pulled him toward her with all her strength.

Spring 1915

CHAPTER 10

London. Reginald Hall was splendid in his full-dress uniform, his traditional fore-and-aft hat pinned under his left arm. He had just left a party at the Italian embassy, where he had talked with one of his agents. Hall had been given information that he was sure would interest Winston Churchill.

He took a cab to Whitehall, where the light was still burning in the window of the First Lord of the Admiralty.

"You smell of mothballs," Winston Churchill said when he saw Hall's full-dress uniform. "On the diplomatic circuit, I see."

"Visiting one of our sources, actually," Hall answered. "I think the Germans are about to go after our passenger ships."

"All of them?" Churchill asked, his gaze suddenly sharpening.

"Anything that comes into the war zone."

Churchill closed the folder of papers that he had been scanning. "Captain, you know what's at stake here? One insignificant American, lost in a sinking, isn't going to change their national policy."

Hall nodded. It was going to take a truly barbarous provocation to tip the United States out of its official neutrality and bring it into the war. "What we need is a prize valuable enough so that the Germans will try for a ship carrying a number of prominent Americans. Something that will make the risk acceptable."

Churchill opened the folder, took out one of the papers, and pushed it across his desk. "Something like this?" he asked.

It was a wire from Sir Peter Beecham, in New York.

HAVE SIXTY TONS OF PYROXYLIN AVAILABLE FOR SHIPMENT, BUT UNABLE TO SECURE WATERTIGHT CONTAINERS AT ANY PRICE. DU PONT ADVISES IT IS HIGHLY DANGEROUS TO LOAD PYROXYLIN WITHOUT CONTAINERS. I RECOMMEND THAT SHIPMENT BE DELAYED UNTIL CONTAINERS CAN BE FOUND.

"The Germans are absolutely determined to keep us from getting the guncotton," Hall said. "They had their agents planning to bomb the train when it reached the New Jersey piers."

"Then they'd find it an irresistible target no matter what kind of ship it was aboard," Churchill concluded.

"Why don't I respond to this," Hall offered.

Churchill turned back to his papers. "I hoped you might."

Crookhaven. Commander Day looked at the plain-language copy of the message that Chief Gore had just received by phone line from Queenstown. It was addressed to WMPB in New York.

> Embark cargo of pyroxylin on *Lusitania,* departing New York, May 1. Assure material in dry holds above waterline. Greatest secrecy imperative.

Day knew the WMPB call letters belonged to Sir Peter Beecham's War Materials Purchasing Board. And he knew the cargo. It was the guncotton he had given Sir Peter as his Christmas present.

"Call Queenstown and request a confirmation," he said to Gore. "I don't believe they want this broadcast from Crookhaven."

He had told the Admiralty of his suspicions that the station was being compromised. Now they were telling Crookhaven to send a message linking a critical cargo with a specific ship. If the message was genuine, they would be putting their guncotton—not to mention the passengers of *Lusitania*—at enormous risk.

Day stuffed the message into his pocket and walked to the quarters cottage. Peter Grace, as he suspected, was inside, stirring his breakfast in a skillet.

"How's your investigation progressing?" Day asked.

"A few leads, but nothing definite," Grace said. He slid his eggs from the skillet onto a plate and sat down in front of it.

"Then traffic through Crookhaven is still being compromised?"

"Yes, as far as I know."

Day took out the message and unfolded it. "Then why would they send us this to forward to New York?"

Grace glanced at the message. "Looks routine to me."

"Do you know what pyroxylin is?"

Grace swallowed his bite. "Haven't the foggiest."

"It's guncotton. The stuff we use in our mines. We're out of it, and this is the only supply we'll get for the next six months."

"An important cargo, I take it. I suppose that's why they're putting it aboard *Lusitania.* Safest ship afloat, from what I hear."

"But why broadcast it over a station that the Germans are probably listening to?" Day asked.

"Does sound silly. Why not query the Admiralty on it?"

"That's what I've done," Day said. "I just wanted to be sure that this wasn't part of your investigation."

Grace shook his head. "Nothing to do with me. All I'm doing here is poking around, asking questions. Routine investigation."

Day smiled sarcastically. "Is that how you hurt your hands?"

Grace looked down. The knuckles of both hands were swollen. "Oh, these. Thought I'd try getting about on a bicycle. Went right over the handlebars. Lucky I didn't break my neck."

When Day got back to the radio cottage, Chief Gore was hanging up the telephone. "No mistake, sir. I ended up talkin' to an officer in naval intelligence. He wasn't exactly pleased that I was questioning his instructions. 'Code the damn thing, and send it,' he tells me."

"Naval intelligence?" Day couldn't figure it out. It made sense that they would put the pyroxylin aboard *Lusitania*. It was their most valuable cargo and their safest ship. But why was naval intelligence involved?

"What do you want me to do?" Gore asked.

"Send it, I suppose," Day said. "Is Shiela here to code it?"

"She should be back any minute. Trouble down in Schull. Some poor bloke she knows tied on a snootful and fell into his well."

New York. *"Lusitania?"* Sir Peter could scarcely believe what he was reading. He held the decoded Admiralty message that answered his query concerning the guncotton. It instructed him to load the lethal cargo without the protective watertight cases into the ammunition hold of *Lusitania*. "Is that safe?"

Captain Guy Gaunt, naval attaché to His Majesty's embassy, raised his eyebrows as he read the cable. "Really no way to ship guncotton that's perfectly safe. But I suppose they're right. *Lusitania* is the safest ship we have."

"There could be fifteen hundred passengers aboard."

"Which is exactly why the U-boats won't dare go after her," Gaunt countered. He stood and retrieved his cap from the coat rack. "Safest place in the whole war, if you ask me."

Well, I'm not going to put Jennifer at risk, Peter decided. Send her off on top of a cargo of guncotton? Out of the question.

He rehearsed his words as he rode out to his Long Island estate. A temporary delay. Just long enough until he could book another ship. Why? Well, we're loading a rather dangerous cargo aboard *Lusitania*. . . . Except Jennifer would raise the logical question of why he was allowing *any* passengers aboard a ship carrying a deadly cargo. How could he explain that he was using civilians to shield contraband? Or why she was an exception?

But it had to be the truth. His family had scarcely survived his lies. He couldn't risk that again. The first glimpse of civility had returned to his home since he had agreed to let her join William Day. Jennifer was allowing Anne to help her pack. There were even bursts of laughter as the two women worked together.

When the car dropped him at his door, Anne was waiting. "Jennifer's new dresses have arrived. She wants to model them for you."

"For me?" Beecham couldn't conceal his delight.

He sat in the library applauding the outfits that Jennifer modeled. And when she spun around in an evening dress well off her shoulders, he said, "My goodness! Would you wear that in public?"

"Really, Father." Jennifer laughed. "You're falling hopelessly behind the times. Everyone is showing their shoulders."

Anne watched with delight as her family came back together before her eyes. "What a wonderful evening," she said to Peter after Jennifer had rushed out of the room in her final outfit.

"Wonderful, indeed," he agreed. But there was a distracted vagueness to his enthusiasm.

"Is something wrong?"

"Oh, no." But then after a pause, "It's just the danger, I suppose. Traveling through the war zone. There have been several incidents."

"Sinkings?" Anne was suddenly frightened.

"I was thinking of suggesting a slight delay. Just until the navy gets control of things." He saw Anne's eyes narrow with concern. "Or perhaps a different ship."

"Not *Lusitania?* But you've said she's the safest ship afloat."

"She is. It's just that now, with all the submarine activity . . ."

"Peter, is there something you're not telling me?"

What could he tell her? That he had been using passengers to protect his military cargoes for the past six months? That he was about to use their daughter as a screen for sixty tons of explosives? That he was weighing the risk of her losing her life against the risk of their losing her affections?

"Peter, if we're going to disappoint her, I have to know why."

"Oh, needless worry, I suppose," he finally answered, squeezing her hand. "In a war nothing is perfectly safe. But *Lusitania*—she's the fastest ship afloat. No submarine would dare try for her."

Emden. *"Lusitania?"* Captain Bauer looked up from his plotting table at submarine flotilla headquarters. "Where did we get this?" he asked his communications officer, who had just brought the message.

"Crookhaven," the officer replied.

"Genuine?"

"Most certainly, Captain. It was signed by Leprechaun."

Just yesterday Bauer had received a report from his New York harbor watchers. The Admiralty's guncotton, they said, was sitting on a railroad siding in New Jersey. Now, if his Irish agent was correct, the Admiralty was ordering it loaded aboard *Lusitania*.

"Contact Admiral von Pohl: 'Imperative I meet with you this evening.' Then get me a car and driver for Wilhelmshaven." The officer saluted, and Bauer returned to his plotting table.

The table was a twenty-foot-square chart, with the western coast of Europe projecting from one edge and the Atlantic approaches to the British Isles disappearing off the opposite edge. Lines of latitude and longitude were drawn in blue. Superimposed was a red grid that marked off the operating sectors for his submarines.

Each U-boat was represented by a miniature wooden model painted white. Ships were represented by other models, colored according to nationality. They were placed on the table as soon as they entered the war zone, and were moved along their course at their best projected speed. By glancing at the table, Bauer had a complete picture of the battlefield and all the information he needed to vector a specific U-boat toward its target.

Lusitania would normally pass about twenty miles off Mizen Head and then about fifteen miles south of Fastnet. Bound for Liverpool, she would move up the Irish coast toward Coningbeg Light, then turn and run up Saint George's Channel.

If he were going to set a trap for *Lusitania,* Bauer thought, he should try for the three most logical points of interception. One boat would cover her most likely course of approach from the Atlantic. Another would wait off Fastnet in the hope that she slowed to fix her position before her escorts from Queenstown arrived. The third boat would cruise completely around Ireland—to avoid the mines in the English Channel—and move directly to Coningbeg, by which time the escorts would have fallen behind and *Lusitania* would not have reached the escorts from Milford Haven.

Rules of Encounter

One of the U-boats should get a clear shot at the Greyhound.

But should he tie down three submarines just to get a shot at a single difficult target? There was no certainty that *Lusitania* could be sunk. Her speed would turn the slightest miscalculation into a clear miss. And should he be attacking *Lusitania* at all—the world's most beloved ship, carrying the cream of the upper class of a half-dozen neutral nations? But he had proof that she would also be carrying the most important munitions cargo that had crossed the Atlantic since the beginning of the war.

To Bauer's logical mind it was the British who were tossing their prize ship, with all its innocent passengers, onto his plotting table. But war was anything but logical. The answers, Bauer knew, would have to come from someone more adept at politics than he was. He would show von Pohl the Irish message to prove that *Lusitania* was carrying the guncotton. Then he would show how his boats could be moved into intercept positions. But as they talked, von Pohl would know they weren't discussing the important question: whether *Lusitania* was a legitimate target. And to get the answer, von Pohl would probably look all the way up to the Kaiser.

Schull. Father Connors led the procession out of the church, then stood aside as the pallbearers struggled to carry James Corcoran down the steps. Across from the priest William Day stood at attention with a small contingent from the radio station.

"A sad day, Commander," Connors said as the coffin was pushed up on a wagon. "Corcoran was a fine man. Bitter, I suppose, since he lost his dear wife. But always a kind word for anyone who went into his store. Will you be walking with us to the cemetery?"

"I have to get back to the radio station," Day explained. "Miss McDevitt will be there for us."

The priest nodded. He led his parishioners and the wagon up the hill toward the grave site.

Day said to Grace, "You come with me." The lieutenant followed Day to the car, and they drove away.

"What happened to him?" the commander asked as soon as the car reached the edge of the village.

"I'm told he was drunk," the lieutenant answered.

Day nodded. "That's what the doctor said. But he also told me that he took one hell of a battering in his fall. Broke all the fingers on both hands, and ribs on both sides of his body. How do you suppose that happened? The well's only fifteen feet deep."

"I suggest you accept the official verdict, Commander. Mr. Corcoran fell into his well. That's all there is to it."

"The same night you fell off your bicycle, as I recall. Isn't that how you bruised your hands? Now, what happened?"

Grace sighed. "He was a Fenian. Someone was dropping off your radio traffic at his store, someone else picking it up."

"So you killed him?"

"I interrogated him."

"And he died under questioning?"

"Apparently."

Day slammed his foot on the brake, and the car screeched to a stop and stalled. "Damn you. He was a decent man."

"He was the same decent man, Commander, who called a submarine in to attack your boats."

Day was stunned into silence. He looked openmouthed at the junior officer, then restarted the car and continued toward the radio station. After a long silence he asked, "What did he tell you?"

"Nothing much," Grace said. "If he had, he'd still be alive."

"You still don't know who's broadcasting to the Germans?"

"Nothing positive. It takes a bit of time, Commander."

Day nodded. "I'm sure it does. But while you're 'interrogating,' Captain Bauer is reading our coded messages. I think the best thing for me to do is to take Crookhaven off the air. Shut it down."

"I wouldn't recommend that," Grace said.

Day looked startled. "I wasn't asking for a recommendation."

"Then without your permission, sir, I'm going to give you a bit of advice." Grace's tone was polite but with an edge of anger to it. "You don't know a thing about intelligence work. That's my specialty. Just follow the Admiralty's orders. You may not like it, but there are more important issues involved than just a few coded messages."

Day started to respond but stopped himself. The little blighter was right. It was an intelligence matter, and that wasn't his field.

When they reached the radio cottage, Day went to his desk and thumbed through the messages. There was nothing that couldn't wait for Shiela. Then he opened the weekly pouch of correspondence from Queenstown. His eyes went to a pale yellow envelope addressed in a flowing hand.

My dearest William,

I have thought of nothing but you since you left, and have written to you constantly. But my parents thought we might not be suited for one another, and have tried to keep us apart. Father never forwarded the letters that I wrote to you.

But now all that is in the past. I am free to live, and for me there is no life except my life with you. I am coming to be with you because, as my parents now understand, we belong together.

I have passage on *Lusitania*, sailing from New York on May 1st, and arriving in Liverpool on May 8th. Please write me, care of Cunard in Liverpool, with arrangements for my coming to you. I shall wait in Liverpool until I hear from you, even if it is forever.

I love you,
Jennifer

Berlin. America's ambassador to Germany, J. W. Gerard, and the German Foreign Minister, Alfred Zimmermann, didn't care much for each other. Zimmermann, despite his diplomatic training, was quick-tempered, given to issuing orders. Gerard was emotional and took the rough edge of Zimmermann's personality as an affront to the United States.

But today's request from Zimmermann had been cordial to a fault. "Would Mr. Gerard be so kind as to stop by at his convenience to discuss a matter of some urgency?" Gerard's curiosity had been piqued, and he had rushed straight to the meeting.

"Mr. Ambassador," Zimmermann said, rising from behind his massive desk. "How good of you to come."

"Nice to be asked." Gerard dropped into a chair with a nonchalance that he knew would infuriate his host.

"I regret to say," Zimmermann began, "that we have information that the British are loading contraband aboard their passenger vessels. Specifically, that they are loading high explosives aboard *Lusitania*."

"*Lusitania?* You can't be serious." Gerard was stunned.

"This message," Zimmermann said, handing him a paper, "was intercepted by the Imperial Navy. I believe it speaks for itself."

Gerard read the paper quickly. "There has to be some mistake. We require a complete cargo manifest of every departing ship."

"Manifests can be falsified," Zimmermann countered. "I'm sure the English have no intention of registering this particular cargo as 'sixty tons of high explosives.' "

"You'll appreciate," Gerard said lamely, "that we can't inspect every package loaded in a port as busy as New York."

"Naturally," Zimmermann agreed. "Just as you will appreciate that we must regard English passenger ships as legitimate targets of war. Perhaps your government will want to advise your citizens against traveling aboard them."

Gerard stood awkwardly, fumbling for his hat, and left.

His dispatch was already composed by the time he reached his office.

> Germany in possession of Admiralty message indicating cargo of high explosives to be carried aboard *Lusitania*'s May 1 sailing. Germany considers *Lusitania* legitimate war target and suggests Americans be prohibited from booking passage. Please advise.

He scribbled out the message and handed it to his coding officer for transmission. He knew that Great Britain and the United States were involved in a conspiracy of lies, and he was their spokesman. But now Zimmermann had thrown the lies back in his face. The German Foreign Minister had presented Washington with two choices: either enforce its own laws preventing military cargoes from being loaded on passenger ships or warn American citizens that their own government had placed their lives in danger. Gerard never suspected his government would concoct an even more deadly lie.

But that was precisely what he learned the next evening, when Washington's response was decoded.

> The United States government appreciates the concern of the Imperial German government for the safety of United States citizens who travel aboard British ships. But the Imperial German government has been misinformed as to the loading of contraband cargoes in the Port of New York. Cargo manifests of all departing ships are carefully scrutinized. We feel that any documents to the contrary in the possession of the Imperial German government are questionable and do not constitute a sufficient reason for denying United States citizens their right to sail aboard any ship of their choosing.

It was signed by Robert Lansing, counselor to the Department of State.

Gerard was infuriated. Cargo manifests are scrutinized, Lansing had written. But that wasn't the issue. It was the cargo that should be scrutinized, and Lansing was offering no indication that the United States would search *Lusitania*'s cargo with extra care.

Gerard remained silent as he placed his government's answer on Alfred Zimmermann's desk and watched him read it.

Zimmermann looked up. "This is not responsive."

"My government feels that it is," Gerard whispered.

"You know, of course, that we intend to attack *Lusitania*."

Gerard nodded. "I think it's apparent that my government will regard such an attack as unwarranted and barbarous."

"*Barbarous?*" Zimmermann hissed the word as if it were a profanity. "And what would you call the actions of a government that loads women and children on top of a cargo of guncotton?"

"Officially, there's no guncotton aboard *Lusitania*."

"If your wife and children were boarding the ship, would you tell them that 'officially' they were safe?"

"I'm not here as a husband and father," Gerard answered. "I'm here as a representative of the United States government."

After a long and heavy silence Zimmermann asked, "Then you will not warn your countrymen?"

Gerard indicated the note on the desk. "I think not."

Emden. Lieutenant Walter Schwieger boarded U-20, which was tied to the pier, and began his inspection. He started at the bow, between the two torpedo tubes. He noted that each tube was loaded and that the two replacement torpedoes, hanging in overhead racks, were tightly secured.

He moved aft, squeezing between the compressor and the tanks of air, and passed the water pumps and the crew's compartment. He lifted the deck boards and looked down at the storage batteries—steel containers of lead plates, filled to the top with acid. They were his only source of power once the boat dived. He inspected the officers quarters, then the control room and, farther aft, the engine room and the after torpedo room.

Schwieger returned to the control room. "Let's take her out," he said, starting up the ladder into the conning tower. The tower was his command post. He climbed one more ladder to the conning-tower bridge, an open deck behind a steel windscreen. It was from here that the watch officer maneuvered the boat while it was on the surface, shouting his commands through a voice tube to the control room two levels below.

"Take in all lines," Schwieger called into the voice tube. He heard the rattle of the idling engines turn into a throaty growl. Seamen on the pier lifted the docking lines from their cleats and tossed them across the widening space of water to the U-20's crewmen. The boat was under way, heading out to the North Sea.

U-27 had left just hours before, the first boat in the series of traps that Captain Bauer was setting for *Lusitania*. U-27 was to head north and take a station twenty miles west of Mizen Head. U-30, already on patrol off the southwestern tip of England, would pause at Fastnet during her return journey. U-20's orders sent it around Ireland to a position southwest of Coningbeg.

Bauer's instructions to his captains had been incomplete. During the night of May 6 and the day of May 7, a large British cruiser, operating as a troop carrier and ammunition ship, would be making her way toward Liverpool. But the U-boats were not yet authorized to attack, pending decisions of national policy. Authorization would be sent by later broadcast.

It hadn't taken Schwieger a second to fill in the missing details. The ship had to be *Lusitania*. Her sailing schedule could be read in every major newspaper. She was the only ship listed in official publications as a cruiser sailing the Atlantic. He could guess at the "reasons of national policy." Along with stores of ammunition, *Lusitania* also carried many passengers of neutral countries.

But Schwieger had no compunctions about the legitimacy of *Lusitania* as a target. Nor did he have any intention of surfacing and putting a gentlemanly shot across her bow. He had done that with *Hampton*, and it had almost cost him the lives of his crew.

It was a two-hour run to the North Sea. Schwieger dropped down into the tower and checked the course that his executive officer, Willi Haupert, had laid out. They would go north, then north-northwest, to a point midway between the heavily patrolled Orkneys and the Shetlands. They would pass between the two British strongholds in the middle of the next night.

Schwieger tested his radio, sending a message of random words that identified his boat to the radio station at Emden. The response "Good hunting" meant that his signal had been received. When his charts indicated that he had fifty feet of water under his keel, he began the routine diving test.

When the boat leveled at thirty feet, Schwieger ordered the periscope raised. Quickly he scanned the horizons to check that he had clear lenses and full mobility.

He felt a drop of water splatter against the peak of his cap. "Dammit!" he cursed. There was a slow drip of seawater from the packing around the scope. The housing, crushed by the *Hampton*, had been repaired twice, but the repairs had obviously been faulty.

"What's wrong?" Haupert asked, climbing up through the hatch.

Schwieger pointed up to the packing, and Haupert illuminated the wet rubber gasket with his flashlight.

"This is the last thing we need," Schwieger snapped. The periscope was his most important weapon. The leak wasn't a good beginning to his hunt for the fastest ship afloat.

Schull. Their separation was approaching. Shiela was expecting her recall to England at any moment. There was no commitment between her and William. Shiela still hadn't explained why she had asked for a new assignment without telling him. Nor had she suggested that they leave together.

And yet William Day was living a lie. He was taking Shiela into his arms, with the words of Jennifer's letter fixed in his mind. Jennifer's words had cut through his despair and filled him with hope. He couldn't deny that she was part of his life.

He had to tell Shiela. But tell her what? That once, in a different world, he had fallen in love? William Day wasn't sure why he had left Jennifer behind. Most likely it had been his blind adherence to the social rules of encounter: they defined which relationships were proper and which were entirely unacceptable. And yet all the canons of behavior were being shattered by the cannons in France and by the deadly gray wolves that roamed the Atlantic.

"There's something I have to show you," Day said to Shiela when they reached her cottage at the end of the day. He led her to the sofa and took the small envelope from his jacket pocket. Then he went into the bedroom, leaving her alone while she read.

"I had to tell you about this," he said when he returned.

Shiela handed the letter back to him. "What will you tell her?"

"What I told her when I left—that it's just not possible." Day sank slowly into the chair opposite her. "We're in two different worlds. I knew it. Her father knew it. Jennifer was the only one who didn't understand."

Shiela stood up. "I'll get dinner started."

But Day caught her hand as she passed. "I thought of not showing you the letter. But that didn't seem honest."

"I don't think we're talking about a letter," Shiela answered. She pulled away and went into the kitchen. He followed at her heels.

"At the time, I loved her very much."

"And now?"

"Now I don't know. I thought it was over."

She answered softly, busying herself with the food. "If it were over, there would have been nothing to tell me."

He nodded. "I'm sorry."

"For telling me the truth?"

"Yes."

Shiela set down the food she was preparing. "It's good that I'm going away," she said. "I don't think I can live with the truth." She walked into the bedroom, closing the door.

Day waited the rest of the evening without disturbing her. Then he fixed a tray with a cup of tea and brought it to her.

"I think I should leave," he said.

"Is that what you want?" Shiela asked.

He couldn't answer her.

"Because I'll be alone soon enough," she continued. "And I'll be alone for a long time."

He put the tray aside and held her in his arms.

May 1915

CHAPTER 11

New York. Thirty feet below the Hudson River, *Lusitania*'s stokers began pumping life into the great ship. An army of men, stripped to the waist, were shoveling huge piles of coal into the furnaces that fired the ship's nineteen operating boilers.

Sixty feet above on her shelter deck, in a gold-encrusted blue uniform, Staff Captain John Anderson greeted the arriving first-class passengers. Each received a salute and a broad ivory smile.

Sir Peter Beecham flashed Jennifer's ticket to the porters. Anne and Jennifer walked ahead as he completed the arrangements for Jennifer's trunks.

"Sir Peter!" It was a reporter from the New York *Sun*. "Are you planning to sail?"

"My daughter is boarding. A visit home," Beecham explained.

"And you're letting her sail aboard *Lusitania*?"

Beecham's expression reflected his confusion. "Of course."

"Have you seen the German advertisement?" The reporter was already unfolding the New York *Sun*, pushing it under Sir Peter's nose. "Do you think it's safe?"

Beecham read the advertisement placed adjacent to *Lusitania*'s sailing notice.

> Travellers intending to embark on the Atlantic voyage are reminded that a state of war exists between Germany and Great Britain; that the zone of war includes the waters adjacent to the British Isles; that vessels flying the flag of Great Britain, or of any of her allies, are liable to destruction in those waters and that travellers sailing in the war zone on ships of Great Britain or her allies do so at their own risk.

Sir Peter handed the paper back without comment. He pushed past the reporter and headed directly for Charles Sumner's office, on the upper level of the pier building.

The area was packed with passengers and newspaper reporters, pressing against the entrance of Sumner's private office. Beecham elbowed his way through the crowd to where Sumner's secretary was barring the entrance to his office. He glowered at the man, stepped around him, and walked through the door.

Captain Bowler Bill Turner was standing next to Sumner's desk. "Of course the manifest is complete," the Cunard official was screaming into the telephone. "*Lusitania* will sail exactly on schedule." He listened impatiently to the comments from the other end of the line. Then he yelled, "She's been cleared by customs in New York. If the State Department wants to inspect her cargo, they can talk to the port officials." He slammed the phone down.

"Well?" Captain Turner asked.

"You heard," Sumner answered. "We're cleared to sail."

"And what do I tell the passengers?" Turner persisted. "They're all asking about the advertisement."

"Tell them that it's nothing more than German propaganda. *Lusitania* is the safest ship in the world."

"I've already told them that," Turner said. "That wasn't enough. Alfred Vanderbilt is still sitting in the first-class entryway, with his steamer trunks stacked beside him."

"Captain Turner, *Lusitania* sails exactly at noon! With or without Mr. Vanderbilt."

Turner lifted his bowler, which he had placed on Sumner's desk. "Any special sailing orders?" he asked.

"There is nothing special about this crossing," Sumner fired back. "It is absolutely routine. And Captain, please leave by the side door. I'd rather if you didn't give any interviews to reporters."

He watched while Turner exited quietly. Then he turned his attention to Peter Beecham. "A madhouse," Sumner complained. "Out of nowhere I'm told that the Department of State is sending an envoy to inspect *Lusitania*'s cargo."

"Have you notified Lansing?" Beecham asked.

"I have," Sumner answered. "He says we're to get the damn ship out of port. Under no circumstances are we to await any inspection party from the State Department."

Beecham nodded. "Is the advertisement authentic?"

Sumner waved his hands helplessly. "The German embassy claims to know nothing about it, although they agree the warning is timely. The *Sun* says the ad came from a group of concerned German American citizens here in New York."

"So maybe it is just propaganda," Beecham thought aloud. "But why now? Why on this trip?"

Sumner snatched the cargo manifest from his desk. "How would I know? I don't even know what the ship is carrying." He looked down the list of items. "Maybe it's this sixty tons of cheese. Do you suppose the Germans are suddenly in need of cheese?"

Beecham lowered himself into a chair. "Charles, my daughter is sailing on *Lusitania*." He looked imploringly at Sumner.

"And you want to know whether you should take her off," Sumner said. He walked to the window and saw passengers filing up the companionway. "You're the only one who can answer that question, Sir Peter. If it's really cheese, there's no reason the Ger-

Rules of Encounter

mans should single out *Lusitania*. But if it's something else . . ."

Beecham rose slowly. "I'll use your private exit, if you don't mind." He shuffled toward the door.

As he climbed the companionway he made up his mind. The "cheese" was the most important cargo he had ever sent across the ocean. The German warning was too timely to be a coincidence. Somehow they knew. They were going after the guncotton, and they didn't want any American passengers standing in their way.

"Ah, Sir Peter!" It was Captain Anderson. "Miss Beecham has already gone to her cabin. Our chief steward will lead you there."

Damn, Beecham thought. He followed the steward inside to the elevators on the main deck and rode up one level to the promenade deck, then walked forward to one of the parlor suites on the starboard side. When he stepped in, Jennifer and her mother were already unpacking.

He waited until his daughter had disappeared into the bedroom. Then he turned to Anne. "You've seen the German ad?"

She seemed surprised that he should mention it. "Yes, of course. Captain Anderson told us that it was just propaganda."

"I'm very concerned," Peter whispered. "Perhaps a different ship. It would only take a few extra days."

"Not *Lusitania*?" Anne questioned. "Is anything safer?"

"Of course not," he snapped. "It's just the damned timing."

Anne's expression sank. And then Jennifer's voice called cheerfully from the bedroom. "Did you hear about the German advertisement, Father? Isn't it the most ridiculous thing?"

He looked around the cabin, already littered with Jennifer's belongings. He glanced back at Anne, whose expression was pleading with him not to upset her parting moments with her daughter. "Ridiculous, indeed," he called into Jennifer's bedroom. He felt Anne touch his hand, and he flashed her a reassuring smile, even though his thoughts were locked on the awful cargo below them.

Jennifer walked with them to the companionway. The deck was alive with feigned gaiety. Sir Peter watched as his wife and daughter fell into each other's arms, Anne rocking Jennifer gently, as if she were a child. Then Jennifer turned to him. "I love you, Father," she whispered in his ear as she embraced him. "Even when I hated you, I loved you." He squeezed her until his arms ached.

They stood on the dock looking up at the tiny figure that waved down at them. Then *Lusitania*'s massive whistle shook the sky, and the black wall of steel began easing away from the pilings as she backed out into the river, her bow finally clearing the end of the dock. An instant later she began to ease forward.

She passed the tip of Manhattan, out into the broad harbor, heading toward the open sea. All along her rails the passengers stood in silence watching the land disappear behind them.

Emden. "Damn," cursed Captain Bauer. He crumpled up the message from U-27 and hurled it at the wall chart in the flotilla headquarters' operations room. U-27 had radioed that she was turning back to port.

"Bow planes," he whispered. He turned to his operations officer. "Klaus, how many boats have had failures to their bow planes?"

Captain Klaus Schopfner searched through his memory. "None that I recall, sir."

"Not one," Bauer agreed. "Until now." He shook his head in despair. The boat's captain had no choice. With the bow planes inoperative he couldn't dive, and his only option was to return on the surface, running far north, around the Shetlands, to avoid the British fleet.

"God be with them," Bauer said. He walked slowly to the plotting table and pointed the miniature of U-27 back toward Emden.

The loss of the boat punched a gaping hole in the snare he had stretched across *Lusitania*'s line of approach. It left him without a boat on the western approaches to Mizen Head. That meant that U-30, on her way to a station near Fastnet, would be the first boat to get close to the Greyhound. But U-30 couldn't stay on station very long. She was already at the limit of her fuel, and he had to leave her enough to get home.

"It won't work," Bauer said.

"Marginal at best," Schopfner agreed.

The flotilla commander walked around the table. He lifted the model of U-30 and moved it up to Fastnet. Then he picked up U-20. "What do you think, Klaus?"

Schopfner tapped the table just below Fastnet. "Perhaps both boats here, with five miles between them."

Bauer nodded. "But there could be an escort waiting." He set the U-20 model where Schopfner had indicated. "Besides, U-30

Rules of Encounter

can't hold station very long. If *Lusitania*'s arrival changed by even a few hours, we'd have only one boat left for the trap."

Schopfner shrugged. "I suppose Coningbeg Light would be my next choice. But U-30 would be too far from home, unless you let her come right up Saint George's Channel and through the Irish Sea instead of going all the way around Ireland."

Bauer pointed to the narrow North Channel, at the top of the Irish Sea. "Would you send a boat through there?"

"Ordinarily, no. Too dangerous. But this is no ordinary prize."

Bauer knew Schopfner was right. One submarine for the Greyhound was an exchange even a novice chess player would make. Hold U-30 at Coningbeg, take his best shot at the incoming *Lusitania*, and take his chances on U-30's making it through the North Channel past the British patrols. But still he might be able to set the trap at Fastnet. Then U-30's chances of returning to Emden would improve dramatically.

"We need more information, Klaus," he decided. "There must be some instructions to *Lusitania* on rendezvous times and locations. Nothing from our Irish friend?"

"Nothing for several days," Schopfner said.

"Can we reach him?"

"I think so. He's supposed to be listening for us 2300 to 2315, their time." Schopfner went to the communications room and returned with a radio officer.

"This is for Leprechaun," Bauer began. He dictated, " 'Imperative we have all traffic directed to *Lusitania*. Forward as soon as copied. We will stay up on your frequency all hours.' "

Schull. Emmett Hayes took a stack of school papers with him into the basement, lit the oil lamp, and turned its flame low. He had picked the late hours of the evening to guard his radio frequency because no one would come knocking at his door.

He waited for the vacuum tubes to get warm, and peaked his gauges at his assigned frequency. Then he spread the pencil-written essays out on the sewing machine's workbench and started to correct them.

The radio came to life, sounding out a group of letters that he knew as well as his own name. Hayes threw open the sewing-machine door and began pumping the treadle furiously, trying to generate enough power to respond. The needle reached the green band, and he keyed his call sign.

As the message began coming through, he turned over one of the essays and began frantically writing down the clusters of letters sounding from his radio. As soon as he had them all, Hayes rushed up the steps in the dark. In his bedroom he fumbled the key into the lock of the armoire and felt through his shirts. With the laundry cardboard in hand, he rushed back to the basement and began breaking the message. When he finished, he had Bauer's request printed out across the back of a little girl's essay.

LIEUTENANT Grace recognized the sound of Tom Duffy's truck long before it crested the hill behind him. Even in idle, the engine sounded consumptive. Now, climbing the hill that led south, toward Colla, it was blasting out a series of random explosions.

Grace had been following Duffy, one of the two names he had been able to beat out of James Corcoran. But he had been following at a distance. Despite his broad smile and explosive laugh, Tom Duffy was a frightening man. He was enormous in stature, barrel-chested, with a great belly that rolled over his belt buckle. His arms and hands were massive. Tufts of thick white hair protruded around his ears. His nose bore the scars of several shattering breaks.

Duffy's strength was legendary. He and his truck earned their livelihood by moving things that were too heavy to move, like the boulders that were dumped into the harbor to serve as moorings for the boats. But even more legendary was his viciousness. He had earned his way into the Fenian brotherhood as a leg breaker, sent to coax the uncooperative and punish the disloyal.

Corcoran had mentioned Duffy's name as a threat. As his battered body was being tipped into the well he had gurgled through a bloody mouth, "Tom Duffy will get you for this." Grace had made it a point to find Duffy, and when he did, he returned to the radio station and strapped a large-caliber pistol to his belt. He wanted to be armed if he and the giant man should cross paths.

Grace froze in the tall grass as the truck rattled by him. He lifted his head only when the engine sound had faded in the distance. Then he jumped up and lifted his bicycle over the stone wall. He pedaled out onto the road and began following at a safe distance.

Something was up. He had been watching Emmett Hayes—the

other name that Corcoran had delivered—and observed several whispered meetings between the teacher and Duffy. It figured—the Fenians were an unlikely combination of intellectuals and dockworkers, and the two men represented both wings of the brotherhood. When Grace had reached the schoolhouse to take up his daily vigil over Hayes, he'd found the school closed. "He was called away," one of the children had said. "To Colla." Grace had taken up his post on the Colla road, and only minutes later Duffy appeared.

At the Colla dock, the truck turned away from the harbor and headed toward the poor inland farms. When Grace reached the turn, he could see the truck's smoky trail leading up to a nearly toppled barn. He left his bicycle in a hedgerow. Then he moved on foot toward the back of the barn and looked in through the space between two weathered boards.

There were four of them. Emmett Hayes was facing him, looking down at someone who was sitting in a chair. Tom Duffy's broad back was blocking his view of the person. Another of the townsmen was standing beside Duffy. Grace could hear Hayes' voice clearly.

"I haven't seen you since poor Jimmy Corcoran's funeral," Hayes was saying. "I've missed you." Grace couldn't hear the reply, but then the schoolteacher continued. "I told you that you could leave things with Father Connors' housekeeper."

Duffy walked away from the interrogation, and Grace got a look at the spy who was compromising the Crookhaven radio traffic.

Shiela was sitting in the chair, wilting under Hayes' eyes.

"I just can't do it anymore," she answered. "When we buried Mr. O'Sullivan . . . the others . . . The information I was bringing you was killing people."

"That wasn't your doing," Hayes reminded her. "Commander Day handed me the patrol schedules. We didn't need you for that."

"But the others," she protested. "The bodies from the ships. I was telling you what ships were coming."

"English ships," Hayes snapped. "Have you forgotten who the enemy is? The Englishman in your bed may be decent enough. But you're not whoring for the whole country, are you?"

Shiela jumped up. "You've no right to talk to me that way. I've worked for the cause. But it's over. I'm leaving all this behind me."

"It will be over when we own our own country," Hayes said calmly. "Until then, the only way you leave the movement is in your best dress, with your rosary wrapped around your fingers." He walked away from her, then turned abruptly. "There's something we need right now. Something only you can bring us. Just once more, and then you can take yourself back to England."

She looked at him suspiciously. "What do you need?"

"*Lusitania,*" he answered. "She'll be arriving in three days. I need to know every message that is sent out to her."

"You can't be serious," Shiela answered.

"Dead serious, lass. Everything since the last message you gave us—the one about loading the cargo aboard her."

"I don't think there's been anything since," Shiela said.

"There will be. And I need it the instant you have it."

Shiela shook her head slowly. "I can't."

Hayes glanced from her toward Tom Duffy, who was leaning against the barn door. "There's two places he can take you," he told Shiela. "I was hoping it would be back to your radio station."

Shiela knew the other place. It was a root cellar behind a deserted farmhouse. They used it as a holding cell while a tribunal was convened. The brotherhood didn't hang women. They turned them over to the ladies, who stripped them, doused them in tar and feathers, and paraded them through the villages. It was worse than hanging. At least the dead men didn't have to live with their shame.

She pushed back her growing terror and tried to think carefully. "Just this once?" she asked. "And then I'm out?"

"Out of the country, yes. We won't try to stop you. And we won't turn you in to your English masters, either."

She stood looking at him, weighing her choices. "All right," she concluded. "And I'm to bring it to the rectory housekeeper?"

He nodded. "Mr. Duffy, would you be so good as to bring Miss McDevitt back to Crookhaven?"

The Atlantic. "I think perhaps the pheasant," Alfred Vanderbilt told the waiter who hovered near his elbow. "Miss Beecham will have the filet of sole amandine."

Vanderbilt turned his attention back to Staff Captain John Anderson, who was explaining the importance of fixing the ship's position immediately when they raised their first sight of land.

"How can you be certain of your exact position?" asked a plump woman encased in lace.

"Ah." Anderson, arranging the salt and pepper shakers as props, began an explanation of a two-point fix.

"Does this interest you?" Alfred Vanderbilt whispered to Jennifer. He rolled his eyes in boredom, bringing a smile to her face.

"I don't care how he gets us there," she admitted.

"You seem distracted," he said. "I hope you're not worrying about the German warnings."

"Not at all," she answered. "It's just that I was expecting to be met. But now perhaps the arrangements . . ."

Vanderbilt understood immediately. This was something that even Sir Peter Beecham couldn't arrange. "A young man?"

Her skin flushed red. "A naval officer," she answered. "I have no idea where he might be stationed."

Vanderbilt leaned close to Jennifer and said, "I wouldn't give it a moment's thought. If I were your naval officer, I would take my ship right up onto the beach in order to be waiting for you."

She smiled at his kindness. But it didn't really help. It had all seemed so simple when she had written William Day about her arrival in Liverpool. Now, with each mile closer that *Lusitania* carried her, her doubts grew stronger. He was fighting a war. Was there any room left to shelter a memory of a love that he had left behind? How ridiculous to expect that he would be waiting.

Anderson droned on, explaining every aspect of the crossing, until the fruit compote had been finished. Then he rose to indicate to the first-class dining room that dinner was over. Jennifer rode the elevator with her dinner companions to the boat deck. But as the women headed forward to the library and the men moved aft to the smoking room, she stepped out into the open night and found a space where she could see the Atlantic sliding past.

Jennifer wondered what was waiting for her. The image she took to bed each night was of William looking up from the pier and then waving wildly when he caught sight of her looking down from the railing. But it vanished each morning, with the light of day. Most likely there would be a letter with places and names of people who would make her welcome until they could meet.

Her thoughts turned darker in the afternoon. A letter courteous to a fault but restating why their lives could never fit together.

Her worst fears, however, came in the evening. What if he had found someone else? What if there was no letter at all? Oh, William, she thought. Don't leave me hoping for things that will never be.

"You'll catch a death of cold." Jennifer was startled by Alfred Vanderbilt's voice as he stepped up beside her. He placed his topcoat over her shoulders. "You shouldn't be outdoors on the Atlantic until at least the middle of July. Let me walk you inside."

Jennifer took his arm and started across the deck.

"Still worried about your young man, I imagine."

She smiled. "The one you're so certain will be waiting."

"And you're not? Why?"

"We quarreled," she admitted.

"Then he'll certainly be waiting. To apologize for what he said."

"What he said was that he wasn't from an important family."

"And that concerns you?"

Jennifer laughed. "No. But it concerns him. He thinks that after the war we'll all have to go back to where we belong."

Vanderbilt stopped as they reached the door. "I don't think so," he told her. "This damned war may finally teach us that we all belong together. It has broken all the rules. I think the old ways are finished, and good riddance."

Jennifer looked pleasantly surprised.

He opened the door. "Take my word for it. He'll be waiting."

CHAPTER 12

Crookhaven. "There's coded traffic," Chief Gore told Shiela when she stepped out of Day's car in front of the radio station.

She felt the fear tighten in her throat. "Who's it for?"

"Two ships," he answered. "Don't remember their names."

She breathed easier. The chief would certainly remember the name *Lusitania*. Shiela had been given another reprieve.

Since the previous morning, when Tom Duffy had dropped her at the station, she had thought of nothing but the next message that would go out to *Lusitania*. The Germans knew the Greyhound's call letters. They would spot the message and then ask Emmett Hayes for its contents. She would have to deliver it to him first.

But Shiela knew that she couldn't. She had reached the decision to break from the Fenians when she finally admitted to herself that William Day was the center of her life. That was when she had requested her transfer, hoping the Admiralty would end her deceit by taking her out of Ireland even though it would mean leaving William.

The fact that it was *Lusitania* reinforced her decision. Left with no alternative, Shiela might well have pointed her finger at one more insignificant steamer. But she knew about the special cargo, and this ship was also alive with passengers. Shiela couldn't betray them to the madness that was gripping the world.

And then William had shown her the letter. The thought of another woman's coming to him had crashed the fragile hopes she had been protecting. It was obvious that Jennifer was very important to him. Yet while Shiela wished she had never learned about her, she knew that placing Jennifer in danger would be a betrayal of the decency she was trying to reclaim.

The chief's words had bought her perhaps another day.

Day had taken his coffee and stepped outside the cottage, walking to the edge of the cliff near the radio tower. His eyes searched the horizon where the Greyhound would appear, but his mind was locked on the letter that he had mailed to Liverpool.

He had written twenty pages, tearing them to shreds as he read them. His meaning was simple. She had to go back to America. But the explanation baffled him.

Because he couldn't take care of her. He was a soldier at war. That was true enough. But it was entirely beside the point. A million women were waiting without knowing.

Because there was someone else. True again. But the someone else was leaving. He knew Shiela was telling him that it could never be. And Shiela wasn't the reason he was telling Jennifer to go home.

Because he didn't love her. These were certainly words that would leave her with no reason to stay. But the lie was so transparent that he knew she would see through it. How could he make her understand that there were barriers dividing people into different worlds?

He had finally realized that a letter couldn't tell her what he felt. So it had been short. His delight that she was visiting England. His excuses that he couldn't be there to meet her. His advice that she go to stay with family friends. His promise that as soon as he was able, he would come to England to see her. It said nothing that would answer her question. That was an answer that he had to deliver to her face.

He walked back to the radio cottage.

It was the chief who picked up the Queenstown telephone when it buzzed. "One for *Lusitania*," he said absently when he set down the telephone. He was still filling in the message form. Day walked around him and read over his shoulder.

> Rendezvous elements Cruiser Squadron E, 7 May, 0600 hours, 260 Fastnet, 40 miles, then elements Destroyer Squadron A, 1800 hours, 120 Coningbeg, 7 miles.

"Good grief," Day whispered. He reread the message. Squadron E was the patrol ships out of Queenstown that met incoming vessels at Fastnet and escorted them up the coast. It was normal to send arriving ships the time and coordinates for the rendezvous. But the details of the second rendezvous—with the Squadron A ships, from Milford Haven—were never broadcast. That information was signaled over to the ship by the Squadron E vessels.

"Get me a confirmation," Day ordered.

The chief sighed and lifted the telephone.

"Where's Lieutenant Grace?" Day asked.

"In his quarters, I think," Gore answered.

Day took the message pad and pulled out the carbon copy.

Grace was at his washstand, hunched over a shaving mirror. His chin was hidden in a thick lather. "Good morning, Commander," he said to the image that suddenly appeared behind him.

"Do you know anything about this?" Day responded, thrusting the copy of the message into his line of sight.

Peter Grace set his razor down, took the message, and read it. "The Queenstown lads meet *Lusitania* at Fastnet, and then they turn her over to the Milford Haven fleet at Coningbeg." He gave the paper back to Day. "Makes sense to me."

"That's the problem," Day countered. "It will make sense to the Germans, too. With these two points I can plot her course all the way up the coast. We never send anything this specific."

Grace went back to his shaving. "I have no idea," he concluded. "Escorting ships is really not my cup of tea."

"No, but security is. This message will be coded and on the air in less than an hour. Can I be sure that the Germans won't read it?"

"Sure?" Grace chuckled. "Commander, in my line of work we're never sure of anything. Even that you're not working for von Pohl. But I doubt that you have to worry."

"There are civilians aboard that ship."

Grace toweled off the lather. "The Admiralty knows that."

Day stormed out of the cottage, back to the radio building. "Who sent it?" he demanded of Chief Gore.

"Dammit, Commander, I got routed to naval intelligence again. 'Send it,' he tells me. 'And be quick about it.'"

"Where is it?" Day asked.

"Miss McDevitt is translating it right now."

Day still had time to think. Why was intelligence involving itself in routine traffic? And why had Queenstown broadcast the coordinates of the second rendezvous? There were no answers that made sense. Except the one answer that had been drilled home during officer training—you don't question orders; you carry them out.

"Message is ready." It was Gore calling from the open doorway of the coding room. Shiela was standing beside him.

"Send it, Chief," Day said.

London. Reginald Hall, head of naval intelligence, sat alone in his conference room staring up at a map of the war zone and sipping slowly from a glass of deep red port. It was nearly midnight, and the windows throughout Whitehall were darkened.

It was all quite simple, really. Like a chess game. You watched the enemy move and tried to deduce his plan. He and Flotilla Commander Bauer were at the opposite ends of Europe. But they might as well have been sitting across a chessboard from each other. Hall had made his move, pushing *Lusitania* out into the center of the board. Bauer had then countered by moving his submarines toward the sacrificial queen. Now Hall was studying Bauer's response.

What were Bauer's options? He had every reason to take *Lusitania*. But he was making no effort to hide the presence of his U-boats. The boats already on station weren't lying low. Four ships had been sunk off Lands End in the past two days. He might be making us think he's going after the cargo of guncotton so that he can have a field day sinking everything else. Not a bad plan, Hall thought.

Hall might counter by moving the escorts away from *Lusitania*. But Bauer was no fool. If *Lusitania* were suddenly left open, he would certainly wonder why. So what move should Hall make? He had to make *Lusitania* appear to be an impossibly well-protected target. But would Bauer attack in the face of an escort of warships? Probably not, unless he could find a gap in the coverage. And if Hall were going to open a gap, he needed a convincing reason. Like the one on the map in front of him: the sinkings off Lands End. Bauer was raising hell there, off the southwest tip of England. Maybe, Hall thought, the logical response, the one Bauer might be hoping for, was to pull the Milford Haven fleet out of Saint George's Channel and send it south. And that would create an opening for the U-boats.

"All right, Herr Bauer," Hall whispered to the map. "I think I know what you're up to."

STAFF Admiral Oliver stood next to the wall chart, a pointer held under his right arm. He stared blankly at the First Sea Lord, Admiral John Fisher, who had just asked an embarrassing question.

"Why in heaven's name is the Milford Haven fleet rushing down to Lands End? What are they supposed to do down there?"

Oliver stammered as he aimed his pointer toward the area off the southwest tip of England. "Well sir, the submarine activity. Four ships sunk in two days. Our thinking—"

"Whose thinking?" Fisher demanded. He glanced around the room at the other officers of his staff. To his mind none of them had ever had a useful thought in his life. Then his squinting eyes found Winston Churchill and Captain Reginald Hall.

"Sir John," the First Lord of the Admiralty answered, "we can't just sit back while German U-boats run unchallenged ten miles off our coast. We have to do something."

Fisher shook his head. Gestures, he thought. He turned his attention back to Oliver, who was delivering the daily briefing.

"The day after tomorrow we have *Lusitania*, due off Fastnet at dawn," Oliver continued. "Squadron E will provide the escort to Coningbeg. From there . . ." His voice trailed off. With the Milford Haven ships out of position, there would be no further escort.

"She'll be escorted part of the way," Winston Churchill added. "And if there seem to be unusual dangers, we can pull her into Queenstown. But I think we can protect her."

"I'm sure," Fisher agreed. "Escorts don't do much for *Lusitania* anyway. She has to slow down so that they can keep up."

Hall smiled. "An excellent point, Admiral. We don't want to slow her down. The U-boats can't hit what they can't catch."

Fisher rose, signaling the end of the briefing. He turned to Churchill. "You'll be on call during the weekend?"

"No," Winston said. "There's a meeting in Paris. General French asked me to attend. Captain Hall will be here."

The First Sea Lord left, his staff following like a family of ducklings. Churchill and Hall stayed behind, along with Admiral Oliver.

"I suppose the First Sea Lord is right," Churchill pondered aloud. "Who would Squadron E send as an escort? Probably *Juno*—smoky old bucket. All she'll do is give away *Lusitania*'s position and slow her down in the process."

Hall nodded. "She's certainly no match for a submarine."

"Then perhaps we should cancel the rendezvous," Oliver suggested. "I mean, if she adds nothing to *Lusitania*'s safety."

"An excellent observation," Winston Churchill said. He looked toward Captain Hall.

"I certainly agree with Admiral Oliver," Hall responded.

Churchill looked back to Oliver. "Then you'll see to it, Admiral."

Oliver was pleased to have made a contribution. "I'll draft a message to all parties right away."

"I don't think I'd broadcast it," Hall offered. "*Lusitania* will be in radio silence and won't be able to confirm. I think if you would just advise Admiral Coke to recall the escorts."

"Of course." Oliver gathered his papers and left the room.

"Should raise one hell of a row," Churchill said to Hall. "And if the Germans manage to kill an American or two, then Mr. Wilson will fall right into our lap."

The Irish Coast. "Fastnet," Walter Schwieger told Willi Haupert. He glanced down at his watch. "And right on schedule."

"I didn't think we'd make it," Haupert answered.

U-20 was finally making a good cruising speed, making up the ten hours they had lost turning the northern tip of Scotland. Twice they had been forced to dive at the approach of a British patrol. They had been three hours late reaching the Orkneys, and this had cut down the length of darkness available for passing through the British stronghold. When the sun rose, once again Schwieger had taken U-20 under in order to avoid being seen. He had been tempted to raise the periscope to search around him, but the leak in the packing worried him, so he had decided to make minimum use of it.

But for the past day and a half they had been lucky. There had been a blanket of fog for cover, and they had been able to stay on the surface, covering the five hundred miles from the Hebrides in thirty-five hours. That left them a day and a half to reach Coningbeg, only a hundred and seventy miles away. It would be an easy passage.

Bauer had promised to confirm his order to attack the large troop transport and to give the precise position of the intercept. But so far, the flotilla commander had said nothing. Schwieger couldn't send a message asking for instructions—the U-boats went into radio silence as soon as they entered British coastal waters. All he could do was wait until he was on station, then send his call sign. That would tell Bauer that he was in position.

Schull. Father Connors was pacing in his garden, mouthing the words of the breviary he held. He looked up as Day approached, but finished the verse. Then he closed the book. "Good evening, Commander." The priest settled onto a stone bench, leaving a place for Day to sit beside him.

"I'm sorry to interrupt you, Father," Day said. "But I need the fleet out on their stations by dawn tomorrow."

Connors' eyes widened. "Tomorrow? That's difficult."

"There's a ship coming in tomorrow—a passenger ship. I think it may be in danger."

"Passenger ship?" The priest was startled. They had never been concerned with passenger ships before. He climbed to his feet and began walking the path. Day fell in next to him.

"Have you spoken with Emmett Hayes?" the priest asked.

"I can't find him. I thought you might know where he is."

"No," Connors said. "I haven't seen him, either. But it would be good if we could find him. The people respect Emmett."

"They respect you, too, Father. They listened to you before."

"That they did," Connors agreed. "But I was telling them that it was all right to help themselves to English money. Then their neighbors began washing up on the beach. And now I'd be telling them that they should risk their lives again for the English."

"But there are women and children on the ship."

"Ah, yes. Women and children." He nodded his sympathy and turned to face the British naval officer. "You're a fine man, Commander Day. I remember your words at the funeral: *'The best of us do what we can to save one another from the slaughter.'* That's what you're doing now, and that's why I'll try to help you."

It was growing dark when Day headed back toward the Mizen Head road. As he passed Shiela's cottage he was surprised to see a dull lamp glowing in the window. He braked, and turned through the gate. Shiela was startled when he opened the front door. She stood in the middle of her parlor unable even to mouth a greeting.

"I thought you were still at the station," Day said. He looked into the bedroom. Her suitcase was open on the bed, with her clothes stacked beside it. Shiela followed his eyes. "I'm leaving," she said.

Day looked bewildered. He knew that no orders had come in for her. "You can't," he said. "Not yet."

She rushed into the bedroom, where she began pushing the clothes into the suitcase. "I have to. I can't stay here any longer."

"Why? Another few days. Your orders will come through."

"I don't have another few days," Shiela answered.

He watched her as she tried to close the suitcase. Then he bolted into the room and pulled her hands away from the valise. "What are you talking about? What's wrong?"

She tore away from his grasp and backed into a shadowy corner. "Leave me alone," she shouted. Then her hands came up to her face, and the fight drained out of her. Sobbing, she slid down the wall until she was sitting with her knees drawn up in front of her.

"Shiela, what's happened? Is it me? Did I do this?"

Her face lifted slowly. Through the racking sobs she said, "It's me. I did it to myself." Her eyes glistened in the lamplight.

He watched as Shiela struggled to her feet. "Please let me help you," Day whispered.

"You can't." She was speaking more to herself than to him.

"Why?"

He could hardly hear her when she said, "I'm Grace's spy."

For a second he didn't understand. Then it was all perfectly clear. Every word he had spoken to her, every thought he had shared in the night, had been heard in a German officers mess. She had used him.

His eyes fired, and his fists clenched. He took one murderous step toward her. But then he stopped. Shiela was standing helplessly, not even bothering to raise her hands to defend herself. Nothing he could do could hurt her anymore. His rage subsided as quickly as it had flashed. He backed away and sat on the bed. "Everything?" he asked. "Did you tell them everything?"

"Oh, no!" Shiela rushed to him, dropping on her knees. "Not what you said to me. Just the radio messages. I couldn't have told them anything about you. I love you."

"And I—" he started.

She pressed a finger to his lips. "Don't. You love her, and you always will. It would be worse if I believed you loved me."

He stood and took her hand. "I won't leave you like this. We'll go to Queenstown together. We'll make them understand."

"It's not the English I'm running from," Shiela said. "It's the Irish. They want something, and I'm not giving it to them. I can't let them find me. You don't know what they do to their traitors."

"What is it they want?" he asked.

"*Lusitania,*" Shiela told him.

Instantly he remembered the message—the coordinates that gave away *Lusitania*'s position mile by mile along the coast. He had handed the information to Shiela.

"But I didn't give it to them," she continued. "I couldn't."

Day tried to think, but it was all happening too fast. "You've got to come with me," he decided. "We have to get this to Peter Grace. He's with naval intelligence. He'll be able to help."

"Peter Grace knows," Shiela said. "He's been watching me."

Day was stunned. "He can't know," he insisted. "He was the one who told me to send the message. He knew I would give it to you. If he knew about you—"

His words stopped. The station was compromised. Peter Grace knew it, and he knew that Shiela was the agent. Yet he had given her the information that would sink *Lusitania*. Which meant . . .

"They want her sunk," he whispered.

She read the horror in his eyes. "The English?" she asked.

"The English want the Germans to sink *Lusitania*. It's the Americans they want killed." He focused on her. "You've been used. Not just you, all of us, to set up a shipload of Americans."

Now the shock was in Shiela's eyes. She understood.

311

Rules of Encounter

"You've got to tell me everything. Who gets your messages? Who talks with the Germans?" Day asked.

"Emmett Hayes," Shiela said.

"Come on," he ordered. "They're not going to kill the people on *Lusitania*. We're not going to let that happen."

She ran with him toward the car.

The Irish Coast. U-20 ran slowly, hiding under the cover of darkness. Schwieger had moved twenty miles south of the shipping lanes that converged at the entrance of Saint George's Channel.

He had a pressing matter to deal with: the periscope had to be repacked. In the few times he had brought the periscope up, gallons of water had poured into the boat. If he was going to stalk *Lusitania*, he might well need to use the scope over and over again.

His engineers had fashioned a new rubber gasket. To install it meant he had to stay on the surface for two, perhaps three hours. He didn't want any ships stumbling on him while his men were working and he was unable to dive.

And then there was the radio. To mount the jack that would force the packing into position, the men would have to disconnect the boat's low-frequency antenna. He would be without communications until the repair was completed. Schwieger had sent his call letters the minute he was on station. Seconds later the call letters had been returned, acknowledging that Emden knew where he was. But there had been no order to strike at the large troop carrier. He had waited as long as he could before starting the repair, but the work had to be finished before daylight, even if it meant that he couldn't receive Bauer's message.

"They'll keep resending," Haupert encouraged him.

It was true. Emden wouldn't consider the message delivered until they received an acknowledgment. But at some point if U-20 didn't respond, Bauer would have to discount her as part of his trap.

"Let's get moving," Schwieger snapped at the engineers, who had brought their tools to the tower. "I want this finished in one hour."

Their glances told him he was demanding the impossible.

CAPTAIN Bowler Bill Turner stood at the window of *Lusitania*'s wheelhouse, in one hand a cheese sandwich, in the other a mug of tea. He hadn't been able to get an evening fix on their approach to

Fastnet because of the fog. And even when the fog lifted, the horizon had remained an indistinct blur, and the haze had obscured the first stars. Now he was in the clear, with a hundred stars overhead to choose from. But without a horizon they were useless.

He walked to his speed indicator: twenty-one knots, the best speed he could make with the number four boiler room shut down to save coal. "Fastest ship afloat," the passengers told one another whenever the subject of the German warning was raised. But Bill Turner knew that with one boiler room shut down, *Lusitania* was just another passenger ship. The accountants at Cunard had taken away her best weapon.

If he made his rendezvous with Squadron E, then things would be relatively simple. But the weather conditions promised more fog in the morning. If he couldn't find Squadron E, he would have to turn north in hope of sighting land and then head toward Coningbeg on his own. He felt safer with escorts. But without them he could at least run at his best speed.

"Home tomorrow," the first mate said as he stepped up beside the captain.

Turner grunted. "I certainly hope so."

CHAPTER 13

Schull. Day parked the car at the edge of town, and he and Shiela turned toward Emmett Hayes' house. They found a dark doorway across from Hayes' front door. Then they waited.

During the short drive into Schull, Shiela had spilled out her involvement with the Fenians. In the first days of the war the Irish patriots had gone over to the Germans, hoping that the defeat of England would bring freedom to their country. German submarines had smuggled them guns, and a radio the Irish could use to organize coast watches, keeping track of the English ships that patrolled the Atlantic approaches. With this information the U-boats could operate safely off the coast of Ireland.

Shiela's arrival had been a godsend. An Irish woman working inside the English radio station! Now they could know the ships' movements days in advance. All they had to do was get the woman working for the movement. After all, her parents had been forced into exile on the docks of Liverpool by English landlords.

Shiela had resisted Emmett Hayes' first overtures. The Germans, she told him, weren't liberators. She was sympathetic to the centuries of Irish poverty and slavery, and wished the Irish patriots well. But she was English now. Then Emmett made it impossible for her to be English. He had taken her to the children's cemetery. He described the little girls and boys who had died lying on the ground with their mouths full of grass. She looked about sadly, but then the sadness was pushed aside by rage. She had never hated anything as much as the people who could do this to children. And right there she had joined the movement.

Then the fresh bodies floated ashore. At first the bodies of English sailors, then Irish bodies—those of her townsmen. She understood that past murders couldn't be undone by new murders, and she decided to break away.

Now Day understood why Shiela had warned him that Ireland would destroy him. It was destroying her. But if she could help save *Lusitania*, she could undo the treachery in her past.

They saw Hayes as he passed under the light of a house window. He vanished in the darkness, only to reappear on his front steps. Day darted across the street as Emmett turned the lock in his door. He grabbed the teacher by his coat collar and threw him into his parlor. Shiela followed, and closed the door behind them.

Hayes' shock gave way to indignation. "What in hell do you think you're doing?" he demanded of the naval officer.

"Stay back," Day ordered. He pulled the shades in the window, then touched a match to the wick of a lamp.

He took Hayes by the shoulders and placed him firmly in a soft chair. Then he set a straight-back chair directly in front of him and sat down. Shiela remained standing near the window.

"I know who you are and what you've been doing," Day said.

Emmett's eyes widened. He looked at Shiela, then at Day. "I don't know what you're talking about. What have I been doing?"

"Sending information to Germany. You're a German agent."

Hayes started to get up. "That's ridiculous."

Day shoved him back into the chair. "Right now I don't give a damn what you've been doing. I need your help. Whoever your contact is, I need to get him on your radio."

Emmett blinked in bewilderment. He turned to Shiela. "For heaven's sake, what's he talking about?"

"We've been used, Emmett," she answered.

"Listen carefully, Emmett," Day began, "because we don't have much time. Right now there's a flotilla of submarines waiting for *Lusitania*. And she's steaming right into their trap. The Germans asked you for information about *Lusitania* because they know she's carrying a valuable cargo. And the English provided the information because she's also carrying nearly a thousand American passengers. The English want the Germans to attack the Americans. Can you understand that?"

Hayes' pretended confusion began to disappear.

"England wants America to come into the war," Day went on. "Don't you see? The English know all about your little nest of spies. They're using it to bring America into the war."

Hayes turned to Shiela for confirmation. She nodded.

Day took a copy of the *Lusitania* rendezvous message from his pocket and handed it to Hayes. "There's an English intelligence officer at Crookhaven. He knows that Miss McDevitt has been giving you messages. Yet he gave her this to code, knowing that you would send it to Germany."

Hayes fumbled for his glasses and read the message. "Sweet Mother Mary," he whispered.

"That's why we have to raise Germany," Day concluded. "To convince them they're walking into a trap. *Lusitania* arrives off Fastnet in about five hours."

Emmett handed the message back to Day. "There's just one thing wrong with all this, Commander. You're English. If this is a trap for the Germans, then it's your trap."

"We all have to draw the line somewhere, Emmett," Day said. "I draw it short of women and children."

Hayes turned to Shiela. "There's paper and pencils on the kitchen table. Write what you want to send to the Germans."

They huddled together in the kitchen as Day wrote.

> Cargo not repeat not aboard *Lusitania*. England wants Germany to kill American passengers. High-placed Americans ready to declare war. Sources are within Royal Navy. Most reliable.

They rushed upstairs, and Emmett pulled out the shirt cardboard and began translating the message. He worked for nearly half an hour, retranslating each coded phrase back into plain text to make sure of its accuracy. Then he locked the code back in the armoire. They ran downstairs, and were halfway across the parlor when they stopped short.

Peter Grace was lounging casually in the kitchen doorway. His large-caliber revolver was dangling from his fingers. "Well now, this is a surprise," he said. "You two, I expected." He gestured with the pistol toward Shiela and Emmett. "But you, Commander?"

"Peter, we're setting up *Lusitania* for sinking," Day tried.

Grace shook his head. "That's not our affair, Commander. Higher-ups, you know." He reached for the papers that Hayes was holding. "May I?" Reluctantly Hayes handed them to him. Grace let the page of code drop to the floor and read the plain-language version. "No, this will never do. I think we should send the original version. You have a copy, don't you, Commander?"

"No," William Day lied.

Grace pointed the revolver into Shiela's face. "You have a copy, don't you, Commander?" he repeated. Day remembered James Corcoran's broken body. He took the message out of his pocket.

"Give it to our unassuming German agent," Grace said.

Emmett took the message.

Grace smiled. "Now Emmett, why don't you run upstairs and put that into code. I'll give you exactly twenty minutes."

Hayes looked at Day, who nodded. He started for the stairs.

"And Emmett," Grace called, "bring the code down with you. I'll want to be sure you haven't made any mistakes."

Upstairs, Hayes unlocked the armoire and carried the code to his desk. But before he began working, he lifted the lamp from his desk and placed it carefully in his window, making sure that it was far to the left. Then he raised the shade.

Emden. Captain Bauer was up from the dayroom bed at flotilla headquarters the instant he heard the tapping at his door. He stepped into the operations center. "Message from Leprechaun," his communications officer told him.

It was the information he had been waiting for: the coordinates of *Lusitania*'s two rendezvous with her escorts—one off Fastnet, the other near Coningbeg Light. He took the message to his operations officer. "Plot these, Klaus," he ordered.

The officer leaned over the plotting table and marked small circles at each coordinate. He stretched a tape measure between the two circles and laid out *Lusitania*'s course into Liverpool.

Bauer looked down at the Irish coast. He moved the models of the Squadron E ships out of Queenstown and aimed them toward the Fastnet rendezvous. He twisted the model of *Lusitania* until it was headed for the same point. Then he took the marker for U-30, under Lieutenant Rosenberg's command, and moved it from Lands End toward Fastnet.

"How long will it take Rosenberg to reach here?" He touched the table at a point to the west of the Fastnet rendezvous, where *Lusitania* would still be traveling without her escorts.

The operations officer did a quick calculation. "Too long," he answered. He drew another circle on *Lusitania*'s course line, due south of Cape Clear. "This is the best intercept U-30 can make. Half an hour after *Lusitania* meets her escorts."

"Just so!" Bauer said. He stepped toward Coningbeg. The small U-20 marker was alone, surrounded by open water. "Then this is where we will have to attack."

He turned to his communications officer and began dictating messages. One was for Lieutenant Rosenberg, on U-30. It gave his intercept point and authorized the attack. But it cautioned that *Lusitania* could be heavily escorted. Rosenberg was not to risk his boat if enemy warships were close at hand. The other went to Lieutenant Schwieger, on U-20, giving him an intercept point southeast of Coningbeg Light. It advised that when *Lusitania* reached that point, she should be steaming unescorted. Each of the boats had been given the best opportunity for attack.

Schull. Peter Grace smiled. "Nicely done, Emmett. You should have taken a position with naval communications."

They were in the cellar, Hayes seated at the sewing machine. He had just received acknowledgment of the message he had sent to Germany. Day and Shiela were standing against the back wall.

"We won't be needing the radio any longer," Grace told Hayes. "Just pull it free, and set it down on the floor."

Hayes pulled the antenna wire and the power cord from the sheet-metal box and placed it carefully on the hard dirt floor.

"Now smash it," Grace ordered.

Hayes looked horrified at the suggestion, but he did as he was told, kicking at the instrument until the hollow back panel collapsed and the glass vacuum tubes burst.

"Come to think of it, we won't be needing you any longer, either, Emmett," Grace said.

Hayes had barely understood the meaning of the words when he felt a hot flash burn into the center of his back. As he fell forward over the ruins of his radio, Day and Shiela saw the handle of a knife sticking out of his coat.

Shiela screamed. Day started toward the dying man, but stopped as Grace cocked his pistol. He saw the satisfaction in the young lieutenant's face—another assignment completed with the usual efficiency. Day backed up to the wall, next to Shiela.

"We'll be leaving together," Grace announced. "I'm going to back up the stairs, and you two are going to follow me. Miss McDevitt first." He backed onto the first step. Shiela fell into line in front of him, and Day followed behind Shiela. "We're going to walk to your car, and then we'll drive to the radio station. The code room should hold you nicely until the military police come for you."

Grace was halfway up the stairs, with Shiela and Day following. "Not much I'll be able to do for you," he said to Shiela. "Fenian. German agent." He backed up another few steps. "But in your case, Commander, I think we may be able to buy a bit of leniency. Taken in by the wiles of a seductive woman. Not really a traitor. Of course, I wouldn't count on getting your own ship. . . ."

He was still taunting when a massive fist fired across the doorway. Grace's head flew sideways, and he staggered and then fell across the parlor floor. Tom Duffy's giant form moved in front of Shiela, across the doorway, in pursuit.

Grace skidded on his back. He raised his head, and his clouded vision caught the enormous shape lumbering across the room toward him. He lifted the gun, firing wildly. He got off three shots before Duffy's hands closed around his neck. He felt himself being lifted into the air. The revolver dropped to the carpet.

"Let him down," Day screamed as they rushed up into the parlor. He dove for the gun. But Duffy wasn't taking orders. He had come in response to Emmett's signal, only to find his leader murdered. Now the murderer had to be executed.

Duffy held Grace high in the air. Then with a quick shake of his arms he snapped the head like a whip, breaking the English officer's neck. Duffy turned, walked to the cellar door, and tossed the limp body down the steps. He took a deep, discouraged breath. Then he started downstairs to retrieve his fallen field commander.

Shiela was on her knees, bending over the discarded warning message that Hayes had been going to send to Germany.

"Are you all right?" Day asked as he got up.

"I can send this from the radio station," Shiela answered. "The call letters are here. And Emmett's identification letters. We can still warn them."

"Can you drive my car?" He helped her to her feet.

"I think so." Then she added, "But Mr. Duffy can drive me."

"Then go!" Day said. "I'll get down to the dock. Father Connors is trying to get the fleet together." He saw that Shiela was not steady on her feet. "Are you all right?"

She nodded at him. "I'll be fine. Get to the dock."

Day rushed out through the front door. When he was gone, Shiela reached around to her back and touched the point of pain that had nearly made her faint. When she brought her hand back, it was stained with blood.

The Irish Coast. Schwieger looked at the message that the radioman had brought to the top of the conning tower. He smiled and passed the clipboard to Haupert. "She's ours," he said.

Haupert read the orders from Captain Bauer. "Unless Rosenberg gets to her first."

"Not likely," Schwieger told his executive. "With the escorts, he'll never get close enough. We're the ones who are going to get her if this damned periscope is working." He glanced to the east, where the morning horizon was brightening. "Let's try her out!"

His engineers had finished their work less than an hour earlier. The fabricated gasket had been sealed against the periscope casing, and the deck plate had been refitted and the low-frequency antenna restrung. And now they had the message. Everything was falling into place. Schwieger shouted the order to dive to forty feet.

He stood inside the tower and listened to the sea close over his head. He looked up at the packing. It stayed dry. He followed the boat's gradual descent, letting the pressure build on the new gasket. Even at forty feet no water was leaking in. So far, so good. The real test would come when he tried to raise the periscope.

Rules of Encounter

They took the boat back up, to fifteen feet. "Let's try it," he told Haupert, and the executive officer reached for the counterweight cable. Nothing happened. The periscope didn't budge.

"It's jammed," Haupert said in horror. "The deck plate must have squeezed it too tight."

"Of all the luck!" Schwieger ripped off his cap and fired it at the deck. "Surface," he screamed into the control room, and scampered up into the tower.

The sun was rising, and there was light in the sky. Schwieger spun quickly in the tower, checking the sea around him. He was still alone. "Repair crew topside," he shouted down to Haupert.

How long would it take? An hour at most. The problem was that in a few minutes he would be in open daylight and, while the repair was in progress, unable to dive.

The two machinists squeezed through the hatch and dragged their tools up behind them. Schwieger stepped to the edge of the deck to give them room, reaching for the radio mast to steady himself. He nearly toppled over the edge—the radio mast was gone.

The stub of the low-frequency antenna was flapping from the insulator near the end of the deck. The mast had not been fully secured. It had torn away in the dive and trailed the antenna out behind the boat, and when it reached its full length, it had snapped.

U-20 had no communication with Germany.

Crookhaven. Chief Gore jumped up as the radio-station door blasted open. Shiela came in with a giant man, squeezing through next to her so that he could keep his arm around her waist.

"Miss McDevitt," Gore said. But his eyes locked on the man's round red face. He thought of the pistol resting in his desk drawer.

"I've got a message to send," Shiela said. She pulled away from Duffy and came toward Gore, unfolding a paper. "It's priority."

Gore looked from Duffy to Shiela and, finally, to the paper she was holding. He took it and read it. "Whose call sign is this?"

"It's German," Shiela said. "Please, Chief. Just send it. Commander Day wants it on the air immediately."

Gore reached behind him and began easing the desk drawer open. "Where is Commander Day?" he demanded.

"In Schull. At the dock." Shiela's voice was fading. "He's sending the boats out to escort *Lusitania*. Please send the message. That's what it's about—saving *Lusitania*."

Gore's hand found the pistol. He eased it slowly out of the drawer and then snapped it in the direction of Tom Duffy. "All right, both of you, back up," he ordered. "I'm not sending any messages to the Germans. Not until Commander Day gets here."

"There isn't time," Shiela begged. Instead of backing away, she began walking toward the chief. But her step faltered. She staggered, then fell against his desk.

Gore saw with horror the dark, wet stain down the side of Shiela's dress. He put down the pistol and rushed to help her. But Duffy was already there. He lifted Shiela in his arms as if she were a doll.

"What happened to her?" the chief asked.

"Your Lieutenant Grace shot her," Duffy said. Then he screamed at Gore, "Send the damn message. She's been bleedin' to death just to get it here."

"She needs a doctor," Gore said to Duffy.

"I'll get her to a doctor," he yelled. "You send her message."

Gore nodded, and Duffy ran out the door with Shiela in his arms. The chief's hand trembled as he dialed in the frequency. He peaked his power gauge, and then he tapped in the strange call letters. A response came back immediately, loud and clear.

Carefully he began sending the coded letters. He was soaked in sweat when he finished the message. He signed off the coded characters that spelled Leprechaun.

It was the first time Gore had received a coded acknowledgment from a German operator. But when he saw the bloodstain on his desk, he knew he had done the right thing.

Emden. "It wasn't sent by our agent," the communications officer was telling Bauer. "It didn't come from Leprechaun."

"But it's his code," Bauer argued. "And those are his call letters."

"But it didn't sound the same. It wasn't his hand, sir. We know the way Leprechaun keys his letters. And it was a different radio. Much more powerful."

Bauer was angry. It was a vital message, and he had barely an hour to act on it. By now *Lusitania* should be past Fastnet, headed up the coast. U-30 should be racing to intercept her. But his communications officer was telling him that the message might not be genuine.

As soon as they realized it was a complete reversal of Leprechaun's earlier message, they tried for a confirmation. They sent out Leprechaun's call letters and waited for a response. Nothing happened.

"What do you think, Klaus?" Bauer asked his operations officer.

"I think it's a trick," Schopfner answered. "It says that the guncotton isn't aboard *Lusitania*. But our agents in New York saw it put aboard. Why would the British—"

"To make us do exactly what we're doing," Bauer said. "To make us attack American passengers."

He walked away to a corner of the room, where he stood alone. Then he turned abruptly. "It can't be the English. Don't you see? If they sent this message to trick us, they would be standing by to confirm. To send this, the English would have had to capture Leprechaun. How else would they have his call sign and his code? If they've gotten to this man," he continued, "and sent us a hoax, then why don't they answer to confirm their message?" Bauer frowned. "Who's more likely to be away from his radio? A single agent? Or a British communications station?"

He dashed over to his communications officer, snatched the message pad, and began writing. "Something happened in Ireland," he said. "Between the first and second messages something changed. I don't know what, but I think this warning is genuine."

He tore off a message addressed to U-20 and U-30: "Do not repeat not attack large troop carrier. British trap. Stand clear."

"Get that off immediately."

He paced back and forth, rerunning the decision he had just made. Did the British know that he was reading their traffic? Did they know that he would get the message that gave *Lusitania*'s rendezvous points? They were either very stupid or very cunning. And if they were cunning, then he had been played for a fool.

His communications officer rushed back into the room. "We can't raise either boat," he announced, panic in his voice.

Bauer went to the plotting table. U-30 was close to the escorts. More than likely she was submerged. But U-20 was still hours away. She should be on the surface. She should be answering.

"Keep sending," he told the communications officer. "Just keep trying to raise them."

CHAPTER 14

The Irish Coast. *Lusitania*'s great horn bleated out into dense fog. She was moving slowly, feeling her way across what Captain Turner hoped was the rendezvous point. But there was no answering call from Squadron E. He had already lingered too long. Without a fix he could be as much as fifteen miles away from *Juno* and her destroyers, and they would never hear him.

"Full ahead," he decided. "Steer course zero six zero." His plan was simple. Turner knew he was at least twenty miles off Fastnet. Later on in the morning the fog would burn away, and he would get a positive fix. In the meantime, he would be closing in on his second rendezvous, near Coningbeg Light.

And maybe the escorts would realize he had missed the rendezvous, and would start up the coast in the direction they knew *Lusitania* would have to take. There was a chance, Turner thought, that they would see one another when the fog lifted.

But *Juno* had already broken out of the fog. Admiral Oliver's order, recalling *Lusitania*'s escorts, had been received two hours earlier. *Juno* had no intention of meeting up with the Greyhound. She was thirty miles to the east, heading back into Queenstown for an easy weekend tied up to the pier.

ABOARD U-30, Lieutenant Rosenberg saw *Juno* through his periscope. Something was terribly wrong. She was still supposed to be well to the west of her rendezvous with *Lusitania*. But *Juno* was five miles inside her course line, and much closer to the beach. Perhaps there had been some new information from Emden, information he couldn't know, because he had been running under the surface.

"Down scope," he snapped to his executive officer. *Lusitania* was probably coming in right behind *Juno*, he thought. His best chance was to move in toward the beach. Ideally, he would have preferred to keep his periscope up so that he would see *Lusitania* the instant she appeared. But that damned Irish fleet had reappeared.

"All ahead full," he ordered. "Take her down to thirty feet."

His batteries were low. He had just one chance: get to *Juno*'s course line, and then take one quick look through the periscope. If *Lusitania* was there, he would take her. If not, he would get out before the Irish boats spotted him.

WALTER SCHWIEGER SCREAMED in frustration. It was another freighter, the second in the past hour—this one no more than three miles off his port quarter. But he couldn't dive to avoid being spotted. His machinists were just now tightening the bolts on the deck plate that protected his periscope.

"The s.o.b. is probably on his radio right now," he told Haupert. "The whole English navy will know we're out here."

In running out of the shipping lanes while he made the repairs, Schwieger could not have guessed that he was moving into the path of two meandering tramp steamers. Now there was no way he could head back to his intercept point. The whole Milford Haven squadron would probably be waiting for him.

"Finished," the machinist announced proudly.

Schwieger nodded. "Let's hope it works this time." He looked at the sea around them—clear and bright, marked by small patches of hazy fog. "We might not be finished yet," he said. "*Lusitania*'s still coming toward us. Somewhere in the next few hours our paths could cross." There was a chance that by midday his target would appear on the horizon directly on his bow.

"Bring her to three zero zero," he told Haupert. "Flank speed. We'll give it one more try."

London. It was all coming apart, Reginald Hall admitted to himself. Two freighters had reported sighting one of Bauer's submarines thirty miles southwest of Coningbeg Light, well off the route that *Lusitania* would be taking into Saint George's Channel. What was she doing so far out of position? And there had been the panicky phone call from Admiral Coke, in Queenstown: the Irish fishing boats, operating out near Fastnet, had spotted a periscope only ten miles from shore. That was well inside *Lusitania*'s course, and with the boats all around her, Bauer's second submarine probably couldn't do anything even if she sighted the Greyhound. Why in hell were the Irish out there anyway? He had counted on Grace's keeping that situation under control. But Grace was obviously having difficulties. He hadn't even reported in.

Worse, the sighting reports had brought the Milford Haven fleet back up from Lands End. That was exactly what they should have done when they learned that there was a submarine operating near the Irish coast. He certainly couldn't order them to stay away. Now

Admiral Coke had figured out that *Lusitania* was in great danger. He had wired Admiral Fisher requesting permission to divert the Greyhound into the safety of Queenstown's harbor. Fisher would undoubtedly agree and order *Lusitania* to turn inland, out of harm's way.

So the chess game with Bauer was a stalemate, Hall supposed. He had failed to draw the United States into the war. Bauer had failed to stop the guncotton from reaching England. It was time to reset the board. There would be other matches, Hall consoled himself. But this one had been so perfect.

The Irish Coast. Suddenly William Day was caught up in the hunt. The image of the brutality in Emmett Hayes' cellar had quickly faded at the sight of a periscope that sneaked up only a hundred yards from Tim Sheehy's boat.

"There," Day had screamed, pointing to the glass lens. He had launched a flare, and immediately the closest boats converged on the periscope.

The U-boat's captain had seen them coming, and dived to safety. Day could see the huge dark shape fall away below him. He pointed in the direction that the submarine was headed. Sheehy followed, keeping the boat directly over the fleeing submarine.

Day looked up to the west, where a low wall of fog still obscured the horizon. *Lusitania* would be coming out of that fog at any moment. But where? He wanted to maneuver his fleet between the submarine and her target.

"Spread out," he screamed over the water. The dark form below him was no longer visible. The U-boat had gone down deep and could now turn in any direction.

Where would she go? If she had come for *Lusitania*, then she would probably try to break out into the open sea, where she had the most room to maneuver into an intercept position. Day pointed south, and Sheehy turned the boat seaward. "There's *Lusitania*," Sheehy shouted. There was no doubt it was *Lusitania* in the distant haze, riding high above the water, with four funnels towering above her decks.

Day calculated that she would pass well out to sea of them. To have a chance for attack, the submarine would have to run to the south, the direction in which they were already heading.

"Slow her down a bit, Mr. Sheehy," Day advised. "We don't want to get too far ahead of our friend down there." The Irishman tapped his throttle back, and his old boat slowed to a leisurely speed, to match the probable speed of the U-boat.

Day thought of Jennifer, probably standing on an open deck looking at the coast. Then for an instant Shiela's frightened eyes reappeared. And he felt a pain of guilt.

ROSENBERG glanced at the clock. Ten minutes had passed. If he had guessed right, he had escaped a mile or so out into open water, and the Irish boats were all far behind him. "Let's take a look," Rosenberg decided. "Take her up to fifteen feet." U-30 began rising up from the depths.

The instant the scope broke the surface, he swung it to the south and gasped as the lens filled with the image of *Lusitania*.

"We've got her!" he said. He began twisting the range finder to calculate his firing commands when a small boat cut across his field of vision. It was one of the Irish boats that were waiting for him to show his periscope.

"Damn!" Rosenberg screamed. He dropped the scope down into the hull. "Dive," he yelled into the control room. "Dive!"

As his boat started back down, he turned to his executive officer. "That devil. He read my mind. He was waiting for me. We had her. We had *Lusitania* right in our sights." He pounded his fist against the bulkhead. "To lose her! To a rowboat!" By the time he could get free to come up for another look, all he would see was her stern as she raced away from him. "Let's go home," he said.

CAPTAIN Turner read the message that his wireless operator had rushed to the bridge: SUBMARINE ACTIVITY SOUTH OF CONINGBEG LIGHT. DIVERT TO QUEENSTOWN TO AWAIT FURTHER INSTRUCTIONS.

Bowler Bill bounded out onto the port wing and raised his binoculars. The coastline was still hazy, but he had no trouble finding the Old Head of Kinsale. It stood like a mountain on the end of a finger of land. He could run in toward the beach and put the lighthouse atop the Old Head off his port beam, at perhaps fifteen miles. From there he could plot a direct line to Queenstown, less than an hour's steaming ahead. With a bit of luck *Lusitania* would be tied up in Queenstown in less than three hours.

"Keep a sharp eye," Schwieger screamed down to the lookout on his foredeck. They had raised land directly off the starboard bow, ten miles to the east of the harbor entrance to Queenstown. He was entering the home waters of the British fleet that guarded the Irish coast, a very dangerous place for him to be running on the surface. He guessed that he was fifteen miles offshore.

Haupert climbed up through the hatch. "Are we there?"

"On her course line and turning toward her," Schwieger answered. "If we're going to find her, it will be someplace between here and the Old Head of Kinsale."

After a while Haupert pointed to a shape of land coming into sight off the starboard beam. "Old Head of Kinsale."

Schwieger nodded in agreement. He swung his glasses slowly toward the bow and saw a haze of smoke on the horizon. "There they are! Squadron E!" he told Haupert. Then he asked, "What do you make out? Two ships? Or is it three?"

"Looks like two. Two big ships. Probably both cruisers."

"In a tight formation," Schwieger said. "Or— Look, Haupert, it's one ship with four stacks. It's *Lusitania!*"

"Headed into Kinsale?" Haupert asked.

"Not if we can get there first," Schwieger said. He called into the voice tube, "Right standard rudder. All ahead full." The diesels growled, and the bow began swinging toward the landmark as the boat quickly added speed. "Steady on new course three one zero."

"Do we have a chance of catching her?" Haupert wondered.

Schwieger could see that his relative bearing to *Lusitania* was slowly changing. The damned Greyhound was too fast. "We can try," he answered. "Maybe something will happen. We're overdue for a bit of luck."

Jennifer Beecham stood on the portside boat deck, a scarf wrapped over her head against the twenty-knot wind that *Lusitania*'s speed was generating. The shoreline was coming into focus. She could see gray rocks, and patches of deep green where farm fields bent over the cliff tops. Ahead was the jagged edge of a mountain, and if she squinted, she could make out a lighthouse on its crown.

"Beautiful, isn't it?" Alfred Vanderbilt stepped up behind her.

"What is it?"

"Ireland. The Old Head of Kinsale. There's a harbor behind it that used to be a refuge for Spanish pirates."

"It looks so peaceful. Like paradise!"

"Hardly that." Vanderbilt laughed. "I was just taking a stroll. Would you care to join me?"

Jennifer took his arm, and they started toward the fantail, along the first-class promenade.

"SHE'S getting away from us," Schwieger snapped at Haupert. He had to stay up, hoping that her lookouts were concentrating on the shoreline. Then when he got into range, he would fire his torpedoes. The odds of one of them finding its mark were slim. But it was better than doing nothing.

He studied the towering bow and the blasts of white spray it threw as it cut through the sea. "She's turning," Schwieger shouted. "She's turning toward us." Apparently she was headed farther up the coast.

"Queenstown." He nearly laughed. "She's going into Queenstown. We've got her, Willi." Then he scampered down the right hatch behind his executive officer. "Dive! Dive!" he screamed.

Schwieger leveled off at twenty feet. "Bring the periscope up," he ordered. Haupert reached for the cable, hesitated for just an instant, and then tugged it down. The periscope rose through the repaired packing. The two officers smiled at each other.

"Our luck is changing, Willi." Schwieger dove to the eyepiece. As soon as he saw daylight, he saw *Lusitania* racing toward him. He was on her starboard bow.

"Set the torpedoes for eight feet," he said. That would put them a full deck below *Lusitania*'s waterline. If she held course, she would pass less than seven hundred yards across his bow.

He knew a torpedo hit couldn't finish her off. But if the first one slowed her down, then maybe he could put a second one into her propellers and rudder.

Haupert cranked his firing orders into the calculator. "Twenty seconds," he announced. Schwieger lowered the periscope.

JENNIFER and Alfred Vanderbilt had passed beneath the soaring second stack and were walking up the starboard side, toward the ladder that led up to the bridge.

They were startled by a sharp crash from up ahead. The deck lurched beneath them, and Vanderbilt heard Jennifer scream as she slipped and fell against the bulkhead. An instant later he lost his footing, staggering across the sloping deck until he landed beside her. A torrent of water began pouring down on top of them. The sea had exploded into the air, and the giant waterspout was washing down the side of the ship.

Suddenly the deck was pitching in the opposite direction, and they were both sliding toward the rail. Vanderbilt grabbed Jennifer's jacket and reached out frantically for the base of the davit that held the first lifeboat. He caught it with one arm, but Jennifer broke free and crashed against a collapsible lifeboat fastened to the deck. Then Vanderbilt lost his grip and rolled on top of her.

"What's happened? What's wrong?" Jennifer cried.

He struggled to his feet, lifting her up with him. "An explosion, I think. But we're all right." He tried to lead her up the angle of the deck. The ship had first lurched to port, but now it was listing too far to starboard.

"Are we going to sink?"

Vanderbilt could see that she was close to hysteria. "Of course not. They'll be able to right her. It will only take a few moments." He clutched at a handrail fastened to the bulkhead and began leading her toward the doors. "Everything will be all right," he kept repeating. But he was battling his own fears. *Lusitania* still seemed to be falling to starboard. Whatever it was—a mine or possibly a torpedo—it had obviously opened that side to the sea.

"A HIT!" Schwieger told Haupert, his eyes fixed to the periscope. "Forward of the number one funnel. There's a hole in her side. I can see flames inside. She's listing ten, maybe twenty degrees to starboard. She looks as if she might roll. Only one torpedo!"

Below the waterline the torpedo had blown its way into the front end of the nearly empty starboard coal bunker, instantly drowning the buoyancy along *Lusitania*'s starboard side. Seawater rushed in. But the heat of the explosion had ignited the coal-dust fumes that filled the bunker, and as the gas was compressed by the rising seawater, it burst into flames. The fire roared through the bunker and climbed past the torpedo hole, licking against the giant cases of guncotton that were stacked in the cargo hold two decks above.

VANDERBILT HAD REACHED THE door and was trying to push Jennifer inside. But he couldn't get any footing against the slope of the water-slick deck. He was suddenly aware of a distant rumbling, a sound like a freight train running through the hull of the ship below. It quickly grew louder. Then there was a flash of light, blue-white, like lightning on a dark summer's night. The deck lurched violently, tossing him off his feet. He caught the edge of the door and held on for dear life. Jennifer spun through the doorway and was tossed into the passageway inside.

SCHWIEGER watched in horror as an enormous explosion tore through *Lusitania*'s bow. A white flash lifted her foredeck right off the hull, and the graceful schooner mast shot into the air and disappeared over the far side. "Brace yourself, Willi," he screamed.

The shock wave slammed against U-20 like an enormous fist, stopping her dead in the water and driving her bow to port. There were screams from the control room below. Haupert spun against the bulkhead and grabbed a cable rack to keep from falling. "What the hell happened?" he demanded.

Schwieger turned from the periscope, wide-eyed with fright. "The whole front of the ship," he said. "It just . . . blew off."

CAPTAIN Turner had heard his starboard lookout scream, "Torpedo! Torpedo wake!" He had barely looked up from the chart table when he felt the ship shake. First he was slammed against the table. A moment later he had to hold on to the table to keep from tumbling across the listing wheelhouse.

He knew immediately what had to be done. The starboard bunker was flooding, and the ship was in mortal danger unless he could stop its roll. "Call the engine room," he bellowed to his watch officer. "Order them to flood the port coal bunker."

Two of the small red lamps on the damage-control board were blinking furiously. He had a fire in the transverse coal bunker, but he knew there was no longer a coal bunker—it had been ripped out to make room for cargo. He threw the toggle switch that would close the enormous watertight doors, separating the bow from the boiler rooms. Then he turned on the fire extinguishers that would pump smothering steam into the forward cargo spaces.

Turner started out to the starboard wing, moving carefully from one handhold to another. The ship was already over by about fifteen degrees, and he knew that if it rolled past twenty-five degrees, it could never right itself. "Call out the list. Every degree," he ordered the quartermaster. "Tell wireless to send out a plain-language signal. All stations. 'SOS *Lusitania.* Come quickly.'"

He was nearly to the bridge when his whole world exploded. There was a deafening blast, which knocked him down as if he had been hit with an axe. He felt ice-cold hail pouring down on top of him. It was a moment before he realized that it was the shattered glass from the wheelhouse windows. Lying on his back, he could see the control board blinking crazily. The forward-boiler-room bulkhead had been incinerated, and the whole front of the ship had been opened to the sea. Turner climbed to his feet. "Sound abandon ship," he said.

The ship was still rolling, and he doubted that anything could check its list. But there was a more immediate danger. *Lusitania* had no bow, no foredeck. Yet she was still racing ahead, the full force of the sea pounding into her forward boiler room. When the next bulkhead gave way, the ship would sink instantly.

Turner needed to keep her afloat long enough to launch her lifeboats. But he had to stop the ship. He staggered back to the wheelhouse, took the handles of the telegraphs, and threw them to full astern.

"HER engines are exploding," Schwieger announced, his face still pressed in morbid fascination against the periscope. Angry clouds of steam were suddenly blasting from *Lusitania*'s funnels. "The whole ship is coming apart, Willi. She's twisting herself into the ocean. Like a screw!"

VANDERBILT knew from the staggering explosion that *Lusitania* was doomed. Already the bow was beginning to dive. He stumbled into the passageway and found Jennifer crumpled on the floor. He reached under her arms and lifted her to her feet.

"Come with me," he told her, the gentleness gone from his voice. "We have to get you to a lifeboat. This damn thing is sinking!"

"It can't," Jennifer protested feebly.

"It can, and it is," he said, pulling her after him through the door and back out onto the boat deck.

The ship's officers and groups of seamen were already rushing toward the boats. Overhead, there was the repeated blasting of the ship's whistle.

The starboard lifeboats were directly ahead of them, and Vanderbilt led Jennifer toward them. Crewmen were lifting the boats from their chocks. But *Lusitania* was now listing twenty degrees to starboard. The instant the boats were free, they swung out almost ten feet from the side of the ship—too far for the passengers to reach. Each boat weighed several tons, and with the list of the ship, no number of men could pull them back.

"Stay here," Vanderbilt ordered Jennifer. He pushed through the crowd of passengers assembled next to the first boat and scampered up the sloping deck. He picked up a deck lounge and carried it back to the boat. He and an officer turned the lounge chair over and stretched it like a gangplank from the ship's rail to the gunwale of the boat. A crewman began handing life jackets to the women.

Vanderbilt helped Jennifer into her jacket. "Get aboard," he said. She stepped to the rail, then looked down at the angry wash of white water that raced past almost fifty feet below. She jumped back into Vanderbilt's arms. "I can't," she screamed.

"Get on that chair, and get into the boat," he ordered. "If you go, the other women will follow. If you don't, they'll all drown."

The ship lurched another degree to starboard. The boat jumped inches farther away, and the crude gangplank shook for an instant. "Go!" Vanderbilt told her. "Go before it's too late."

Jennifer stepped up to the rail. A seaman took her arm to steady her as she reached out and grabbed the edges of the lounge chair. Then she pulled her dress up above her knees and knelt on the back of the chair. Don't look down, Jennifer reminded herself. Slowly but steadily she began to crawl out into the gaping space between the ship and the lifeboat. In a few seconds she was able to catch the gunwale of the boat. Then she threw herself aboard.

A seaman stretched another lounge chair over the abyss, and within seconds other women were following Jennifer's lead. Within two minutes the boat was filled with women and children.

One crewman went to the stern of the boat to tend the rope falls.

Another went to the bow. "Lower away," the officer ordered. The lifeboat began to sink toward the rushing sea below.

Vanderbilt touched a finger to his forehead in a salute to Jennifer. "He'll be waiting," he called. Then he turned away to tend to others. Vanderbilt had no intention of trying to save himself. This, he thought, was as good a place to die as any.

High above them, Turner climbed to the signal bridge on top of the wheelhouse. Having backed his engines, he could do nothing more to slow the ship. He guessed she might have a minute left, two at the most.

He turned aft to look after his passengers and screamed in rage at the slaughter he saw. Unlike the boats on the starboard side, the portside boats had swung inward, crushing the crewmen tending their falls. Then the boats had dropped onto the deck and slid forward, cutting like a scythe through the waiting passengers.

Seeing there was no escape from the port rail, passengers had rushed across to the starboard side, pushing into those who were waiting to cross out onto the deck chairs and into the boats. In the confusion two chairs had been jostled off the rail and fallen into the sea, carrying passengers with them. *Lusitania* was down to her last moments, yet only one lifeboat had been lowered.

The first boat had almost reached the water. After the swaying journey down, the sea seemed like a safe haven. The terrified passengers felt themselves breathing again. Then the bow dropped and hit the water while the stern was still suspended on the ropes. It swung wildly with the flow of the sea until the boat broached.

Jennifer felt herself being tossed through the air, with bodies flying all around her. She slammed into the water, and was buried in darkness as the huge lifeboat came down on top of her.

"THERE she goes," Schwieger said. His voice had become a monotone, as if he were commenting on a lawn-bowling match. "Her stern is high in the air, swinging back and forth. Now she's settling, rolling over on her starboard side." Haupert endured a long, tense silence. Then Schwieger continued. "She's slipping under rapidly. She's gone."

He remained crouched against the periscope for another minute, watching a sea that was clotted with bodies, some thrashing about wildly, others staring openmouthed at the afternoon sun. He panned from side to side, finding nothing but an ocean of human devastation. There wasn't a single lifeboat anywhere.

"Down scope." Schwieger stood silently a moment and then dropped slowly down the ladder into the control room. "Take her down to thirty feet," he whispered to his silent crewmen. "Set course for Fastnet. All ahead two thirds. We'll stay under until sunset." He stepped forward through the men and went to his cabin, unable to look any of them in the eye.

CHAPTER 15

Schull. With U-30's disappearance and *Lusitania*'s crossing safely behind them, Day took his fleet home. He saw his car waiting before Sheehy's boat reached the dock. He jumped over with the first line and ran to Tom Duffy.

"The message is sent," Duffy told him. "But Miss McDevitt was hit in the shooting at Emmett's place. I took her to Dr. Tierney. She's in a bad way, I think."

Then Day saw the awful stain on Tom Duffy's sleeves and the smear across the belly of his shirt. "Take me there. Please!"

As they sped off, Duffy explained, "She sort of fell as we were gettin' into the car on the way to the radio station. Then I saw the blood. I wanted to take her straight to the doc's, but she wouldn't hear of it. She said they'd never be sendin' the message if a stranger brought it to them. She had to take it to them herself."

Finally Duffy skidded the car to a stop in front of a row house with a fresh coat of whitewash. The lamps in the windows were still bright, left burning from their all-night vigil. Dr. Tierney had thrown his trousers and a collarless white shirt over his nightshirt. He smiled, but there was no joy in his eyes.

"I'm sorry, Commander," he said. He turned to lead Day into one of the bedrooms. "It was such a terrible wound. I couldn't close it. All I could do was take away the pain."

When the door opened, Father Connors turned away from the bedside. "I gave her the last rites," he told Day as he folded his purple stole. Then he stepped out of the room.

Shiela's white face was staring at the ceiling. She heard Day enter, and her eyes flashed with fear. "Don't let them take me," she begged in the little voice that was left to her. "Please."

He rushed to her side and reached for her hand. It was icy cold. Day knew who "they" were. The English. The Irish. Everyone in her life. She thought she had betrayed them all.

He fell to his knees beside her bed. "You saved them," he told her. "The message got through. You saved them."

Her eyes brightened. "Oh, thank God. Then there'll be no more children for the cemetery," she whispered.

"No," Day told her. "No more children. You saved them all."

There was a moment of peace in her smile. And then her breathing stopped.

If heaven was a land of peace, Day thought, then Shiela was surely there. The razor-edged loyalties that were cutting her to pieces no longer mattered. In death she had found a place she could call home.

Father Connors was waiting in the parlor. "Will you tell them?" Day asked him. "I want her neighbors to know that she died trying to save people. No matter whose side they think she was on."

The priest sighed. "Maybe you'd like to tell them yourself."

"I won't be here," Day answered.

Father Connors looked stunned.

"I'm a traitor, Father. It *was* a message to the Germans. The British sent a man to stop me. They'll be sending another."

"But where will you go?"

Day shrugged. "Someplace where Shiela would have gone. I'm a man without a country." Then he said, "Father Connors, could you bury her in the children's cemetery?"

"The deserted place, where the little orphans are?"

"It was important to her."

"Yes, we could do that."

Day walked out to his car, started the engine, and drove the short distance to Shiela's cottage. He found her suitcase still on the bed, where she had left it. It was open, with her few things flowing out. He packed them carefully and set the suitcase next to the closet. Then he began throwing his own things into a bag.

There was a pounding on the front door. "Commander Day! Commander Day!" It was Chief Gore.

Day bolted to the door and snapped it open.

"It's *Lusitania*," Gore screamed. "She's been sunk. We got the SOS at the station."

"Where?" Day demanded. "Where did she sink?"

"Off the Old Head of Kinsale. There are no lifeboats. Everyone's in the water."

Kinsale. Small boats from all along the coast converged on the Old Head of Kinsale. The first arrived at twilight and began sorting through the floating debris in search of survivors. It was after dark when the boats from Schull reached the scene. They could see nothing beyond the small circles of light that fell from their lamps.

Day was on the bow of Sheehy's boat. They motored into a drift of debris—the random artifacts of a world that had disappeared. There were upholstered chairs, a broad-brimmed lady's hat. Wine bottles bobbed like buoys, and deck chairs, still folded to a comfortable angle, lay inches beneath the surface. Life jackets were everywhere, floating empty.

Day asked Sheehy to shut down the engine. "Hello!" he called, waving the lamp. But the only response was the sea slapping against the boat. The motor coughed, and they chugged on.

They saw a man's body, face down and spread-eagled, the tails of the jacket pointing in opposite directions. They dragged it up over the side and laid it gently in the bilge. As they searched the dark water, they saw a colorless face staring back up at them. It was a matronly woman with a jeweled necklace resting on her shoulders. The top of her body was formally attired, but someone had torn her skirt off at the waist to make it possible for her to swim.

"They're all dead!" Sheehy said, looking around at the desolate waters. "The earlier boats must have gotten the survivors."

"Let's keep searching," Day said.

He was thinking of Jennifer, as he had every moment since Chief Gore had pounded on the door of the cottage. He had sailed from Schull with the thought of her trembling in a lifeboat. He had to get to her. But now he was afraid of finding her. He fought against the image in his mind of her still face staring up at him from the water.

They stopped the engine again, and Day was about to call out when he heard a gasping voice from the darkness off his starboard bow. Using an oar as a paddle, he moved the boat toward the sound.

It was a cork raft with two men clinging to its edge. Across the rope netting that served as its deck, two women were sprawled.

Day and Sheehy pulled the raft alongside. One of the women was alive, weak with shock. The other was dead. They hauled them aboard, then the two men.

All through the night they cruised back and forth. At first light they headed for the dark shape of the Old Head. They carried five living passengers from *Lusitania* and six dead bodies.

The sun was up when they turned into Kinsale Harbour. The docks were a confusion of seamen, some with old blankets wrapped around their wet clothes. There were faces animated with tales of rescue and expressionless faces stunned by images of sudden death. A British naval officer rushed to the dock as Sheehy tied up his boat. He gathered the survivors and hurried them up to the shore.

Day worked his way up the pier, questioning the seamen who were able to talk. "Were there many survivors?"

There were. Most of them had been brought in early and taken into family homes. The British were rounding up all they could find and bringing them to a church and a schoolhouse.

"And the dead?"

There was a morgue in a warehouse by the harbor head. One of the seamen pointed out the building.

Day started at the church. A British sailor with a rifle guarded the door. No one was being admitted, and Day was referred to the officer in charge.

"Name?" the lieutenant demanded.

"Her name is Beecham. Jennifer Beecham."

"No. Your name. I need the name of anyone who inquires."

Were they already hunting for him? he wondered. The Royal Navy had a disaster on its hands. He was a witness who knew that England had played a role in the atrocity.

"Day. Mr. William Day. I'm a personal friend of Sir Peter Beecham's. It's his daughter I'm looking for."

"Oh, excuse me, Mr. Day." The officer was suddenly solicitous. "There are reporters, you know. We don't want them talking to passengers." He was flipping through a list of survivors. "Jennifer Beecham doesn't seem to be here. Or at the school." His expression turned solemn. "Have you tried the warehouse?"

The navy, Day understood, had already begun its cover-up. They were frantic to find the passengers before they could speak with the press. They didn't want any witnesses to the absence of escorts. And they wouldn't want witnesses to the messages sent through the compromised Crookhaven radio station. He guessed there were navy people looking for him.

He used another name when he reached the warehouse. A naval officer led him inside, where a medical officer escorted him up and down the rows of bodies laid out on the floor.

He walked quickly, embarrassed to stare at people who had been reduced to carnival displays. There had been no time to compose the bodies. Mouths were gaping open, hair was tossed wildly, and limbs were scattered at awkward angles.

He slowed only once, when there was a slim young woman in an ivory-colored gown. The hands seemed familiar. Still secure around the neck was a string of pearls. He raised his glance. Long dark hair was matted over the face.

"You recognize her?" the doctor asked.

Day couldn't speak, but his stare said that he did.

The doctor bent over the body and gently parted the hair.

Day's breath escaped. It wasn't Jennifer.

"There's still hope," the doctor said as they finished their search. "Hundreds are unaccounted for. Many of them are being cared for in homes all along the coast."

"Thank you," Day answered, and he went outside. There was certainly reason to hope. But he knew that many would float in with the next tide. And many more would forever be locked in the steel coffin that rested at the bottom, fifteen miles from the beach.

"William! William!" He turned and saw Father Connors—the dark stole of the death rites flapping from his neck—coming toward him. Connors wrapped an arm around his shoulders and led him forcefully away. "They're looking for you," he whispered. "There are naval officers in Schull asking for you."

"I was expecting them," Day said, showing little concern.

Connors was frightened. "They've taken over the radio station. There are two armed guards standing in front of Emmett's house. They found him this morning. Him and your young officer friend. You can't go back, William. You've got to get out of here."

"I'm looking for someone, Father," he answered angrily. "I have to find her. Her name's Jennifer Beecham."

Connors shook his head furiously. "Don't be daft, man. We'll find her for you. We've got to get you off the streets."

He ushered Day into one of the narrow streets that climbed

the hill. "I have friends here in Kinsale. They'll take you in. And they can find anyone you're looking for. Believe me, lad, we'll find her." He pushed on the picket gate of a small whitewashed house.

Day stopped at the doorstep. "Your friends could get in trouble, Father. I'm a fugitive."

"My friends have been in trouble for three hundred years." He tapped on the door. "Now get inside. I'll be coming back for you."

Washington. President Woodrow Wilson wore his bathrobe into the Oval Office, where the Secretary of State and his counselor were waiting. He had been relaxing in his bed, reading the afternoon papers, when news of the attack on *Lusitania* had reached Washington. Now he was about to hear the grim details.

"Mr. President," Lansing said, rising as Wilson entered. William Jennings Bryan tried to clear his lap of papers, but Wilson was already seated before he could get up.

"Americans have been killed?" the President asked, referring to the note that had been brought upstairs to his bedroom.

"That seems to be the case," Bryan reported. He had a cable from the ambassador to the Court of Saint James's. "There are over a thousand passengers dead or unaccounted for. At least a hundred of them are U.S. citizens."

"Dear Lord. How could so many— Weren't there lifeboats?" Wilson was stunned by the count.

"Apparently she sank very quickly," Bryan said.

"There seems to have been several submarines," Lansing explained. "If they were all firing torpedoes—"

Bryan interrupted. "Our ambassador is simply relaying what he was told by the British. He hasn't had time to verify any of this. I don't think we'll have all the details for several days."

"But I'll have to say something," Wilson reminded them. "The American press will be calling for a statement."

"Perhaps you should simply lament the loss of life and tell them we are trying to ascertain the facts," Bryan offered.

The President looked toward Lansing. "Do you agree, Robert?"

"With all due respect," Lansing began, "I think something much stronger is required. The Germans have knowingly attacked American citizens. To my mind that constitutes an act of war."

Bryan's round face swelled with outrage. "Rubbish," he snapped.

"The Germans have sunk an English ship known to be carrying ammunition."

"Ammunition?" Wilson's eyes widened beyond the wire frames of his glasses. "*Lusitania* was carrying ammunition?"

"Ridiculous," Lansing said. "I can assure you, Mr. President, that there is no ammunition listed in *Lusitania*'s cargo manifest."

"If there were ammunition aboard *Lusitania*, we certainly should have known about it," Wilson mused. "If we didn't, then we're terribly stupid. And if we did, then we certainly should have prohibited Americans from boarding her. Either way, we stand indicted." A tight smile appeared. "So our position has to be that there was no ammunition aboard *Lusitania*. Isn't that so?"

"I agree completely," Lansing said.

Bryan was shaking his head in protest. "The Americans were sailing into a war zone aboard a belligerent ship. It isn't as if the Germans had shot them down in the streets of Berlin."

Wilson stood and paced behind his desk, his chin high, his hands behind his back. "As I see it, we have two choices: either deny the German right to attack ships carrying Americans and call them severely to task, or grant their right and prohibit Americans from sailing on English ships."

"We can't force the Germans to assure that there are no Americans aboard, before attacking an enemy ship," Bryan said.

"We can't prohibit Americans from their constitutional rights," Lansing countered.

But Wilson wasn't weighing legalities. He was guessing at public reaction. He turned to his advisers. "I think we have to condemn this barbarous assault on U.S. citizens," he decided. "I think we have to hold Germany strictly accountable."

Bryan folded the papers in his lap. "If that is your decision, Mr. President, then I must respectfully ask you to accept my resignation. I simply can't support such a one-sided policy."

Robert Lansing tried to look humble. He was the obvious choice to be the new Secretary of State. His political star was rising.

Paris. Winston Churchill folded the cable he had just been given and turned to General John French. "I'm afraid, General, that I have to get back to London immediately. *Lusitania* has been sunk."

"*Lusitania?*" The general went white. "How? Where?"

"Off the Irish coast. I don't have the details. Just that it was submarines and that there is a considerable loss of life."

"The audacity," the general said, rising to console his friend. "The damned audacity." He placed a hand on Churchill's shoulder. "I'm just thankful that you were here, not back at the Admiralty, at the helm. There will be hell to pay for this."

Churchill shrugged. "I can't say that it much matters where I happen to be. I bear full responsibility. An old navy tradition."

"You're not going to resign?"

"I suppose I'll have to."

Churchill went to his bedroom to pack his things while General French summoned a staff car. The general was waiting in the foyer of the mansion when Churchill came down the curved stairs, ahead of the corporal who was carrying his luggage.

"You should reconsider, Winston. The King will need your services now more than ever."

"I have considered," he answered, holding out an arm so that a private could help him on with his topcoat. "But there's a bright side, General. The stalemate in the trenches? I think you'll soon have Americans to tip the balance in your favor. I think that at this very moment, for the first time, you can count on winning the war."

"Americans?" French questioned.

"*Lusitania*," Winston Churchill reminded his host. "She's a favorite with American society. It wouldn't surprise me if some of Woodrow Wilson's closest friends were aboard."

He winked at General French, whose expression showed that he was beginning to understand.

"So try not to take this too hard," Churchill recommended. "I'll be back!"

Kinsale. Day jumped up from the parlor chair as soon as he heard the squeak of the front gate, and rushed to hide behind the door to the basement. The soft tap on the front door told him that the caller was a friend.

"Father Connors sent me," a man's voice whispered.

Day heard the door close quietly, and then the landlady stepped toward the cellar and called his name. He came cautiously out of hiding and found a tall young man, scarcely through his teens, standing in the center of the room.

"Tom Downey." They shook hands. "Father Connors has a boat waiting for you in Courtmacsherry. He said that he'll be meetin' you there." He held the front door open for Day.

It was long after midnight now. Downey led the way up the narrow street, to a flat horse-drawn wagon. Day stopped short when he saw the six newly made wooden coffins that were stacked on the back.

They lifted one of the coffins aside, and then Downey pulled the lid off one in the bottom row. Day climbed up onto the wagon and then squeezed himself into the coffin.

"You should be able to push up the lid a bit to change the air," the young man guessed as he fitted the top of the coffin over Day's face. Then he replaced the box that had been on top.

Day felt the wagon jerk, and they began moving in time with the slow, steady metronomic pace of the horse's hoofbeats. Crushed into the dark tomb, Day had no image of the new world he was moving toward. He could think only of death. Of Shiela, her shrouded body now waiting alone in the church for burial. Of Jennifer, the horror frozen on her blinded eyes as she was lifted out of the sea. He tried to think of them as martyrs to some cause, to find a purpose more important than the first glimpse of the new day's sunrise that had been taken from them. But they weren't martyrs—only victims. Victims of the holy causes of great men determined to reshape the world in their own likenesses. In their global strategies *Lusitania* was just a small, expendable piece. The people who would die aboard her or die trying to save her had no significance at all. No more than the soldiers in the trenches, whose names weren't as important as the names of the battles that tortured them and killed them. But from the darkness of his coffin Day couldn't see anything more important than life.

They had been traveling for hours when he heard hushed voices, then felt the wagon stop. There was a shuffling of the board over his face and then a crack of pale morning light.

"Good as new," Tom Downey said as he lifted the lid away from the coffin. He helped pull Day free, then steadied him while he tried to find his balance. Day was standing on a rotted pier, next to a small decrepit schooner. The crewmen were leaning along her gunwales—dark figures who stared at him curiously.

"She's Portuguese," Downey said. "You're her new deckhand."

The schooner's captain swung himself over the rail, onto the dock. "This him?"

Downey nodded.

The captain took Day's measure. "Then get him aboard. I'm missing the tide."

"Where's Father Connors?" Day asked Downey. "He was going to find someone for me—one of the *Lusitania* passengers."

Downey looked around, then lifted his hands helplessly. "He'd be the one to try. But there's so many of them."

Day turned toward the schooner and saw that the captain was climbing aboard. He heard him bark an order in a strange tongue. The crewmen began taking in the schooner's lines.

Day took a step, then stopped. "I can't," he said to Downey. "Not without knowing."

The young man looked shocked. "There's no goin' back, Commander." The mooring lines were slipping across the pier toward the boat.

The grind of an automobile engine broke the morning stillness. A black car bounced around the curve of the harbor, heading toward the pier. "It's him," Downey said. "Wait here." He ran up the pier. Day waited for only a second and then ran after Downey. He saw Jennifer as soon as she stepped from the car.

She rushed toward him, bursting into tears before he could get his arms around her. She said his name over and over again as he rocked her in his strong embrace.

"You're safe. Thank God, you're safe," Day kept repeating. He looked over her shoulder at Father Connors, who was beaming like an angel.

"In the hospital," Connors explained. "Right there where you'd expect her to be. Asking everyone did they know Commander William Day. And still the Brits couldn't find her."

Day stepped back and held her at arm's length. She looked ridiculous in a borrowed oversized dress and big work shoes. "You're beautiful," he told her, and then he took her back into his arms.

"The tide," the captain shouted from the fantail of the schooner. He waved his arms in frustration. "The tide!"

"He has to get aboard," Downey told the priest.

"I need a minute," Day begged. "Just a minute."

Connors nodded. He looked at Downey. "Run and tell that savage I'll excommunicate him if he sails without Commander Day."

"A minute?" Jennifer was suddenly frightened. She looked at the boat and at Day. "Where are you going? Why?"

He pulled her close to him and walked her slowly down the pier. "I have to go away," he began.

"Why?" She broke his grasp and turned to confront him.

"Because I know things—things that England has to keep secret. I betrayed them, Jennifer. They're hunting for me."

"Betrayed them? What are you talking about? What things?"

He pulled her close to him. "I can't explain. There isn't time. And it would be dangerous for you to know. Just believe that there's no other way. I have to go into hiding."

She pushed him away and looked at him with sudden determination. "Then I'm going with you."

"No," he said with a hard edge to the word. "No. You're going back to your home. To your parents. That's where your life is."

"But my life is with you." She threw her arms around his neck. "I won't let you go."

"Commander"—Father Connors was standing beside them—"he has to cast off. He can't miss the tide." Day saw that the sails were already hoisted, luffing in a breeze that came over the schooner's bow. He reached behind his neck and broke Jennifer's grip. Then he placed her hands in Father Connors'.

"Go home, Jennifer," William told her. "You have a life to live."

"I'll take care of her," Connors promised.

Day turned away and jumped aboard the boat. The captain took in the last line, the crew hauled the sails across, and the schooner began sliding forward.

"I love him," Jennifer whispered helplessly.

"And he loves you," Connors said. "That's why he's doing what's best for you."

She looked at the priest, her eyes suddenly flashing in anger. She broke away from him and rushed down the pier, stumbling on the hem of the borrowed dress. When she caught up with the boat, she saw Day standing at the gunwale, slowly drifting away from her as the schooner moved off the pilings.

"William," she screamed, "do you love me?" She was running to keep up with the boat.

He knew he should lie to her. Only by denying what was true

would he be able to send her away. But it was as impossible now as it had been when he'd left her once before.

"I love you," he called back, his face dark with despair.

Jennifer ran to the edge and leaped out over the water, just reaching the boat. Day's face exploded in laughter as he caught her hand and pulled her aboard.

The schooner heeled as her tired canvas locked onto the breeze. She gathered speed and headed out into the ocean, passing due south of the Old Head of Kinsale.

※ ※ ※

July 21, 1915

Dearest Mother and Father,

I am so sorry for not having written to you immediately to tell you that I am well and blissfully happy. But that was not possible. As Father may explain, there were circumstances involved in the sinking of *Lusitania* which must forever remain secret. William knows the details of England's involvement and has been made a fugitive from his own country.

Because I love him, I am going with him into exile. I won't tell you where, nor shall I be able to write you. Knowing where he can be found would pose great difficulties for you and great dangers for him. But please believe that at every moment I will love you both and regret the sorrow that I have caused you.

I don't know what our future will hold. I can only hope that some day our world will find the peace and joy that I have found, and that William and I will be able to come home to you again.

With all my love,
Jennifer Day

ABOUT THE AUTHOR

William P. Kennedy has always been intrigued by cases in which an individual is caught between political necessity and personal morality—very much the position young William Day finds himself in in *Rules of Encounter*. In fact, the author's next book will pursue a variation on this theme. It will be set on an American army base where young people are taught methods of torture and resistance—necessary to combat enemy counterinsurgency but which conflict with their inherent sense of decency.

The idea for Kennedy's current novel came to him during a visit to Ireland, when he found himself in a small churchyard looking down upon the graves of an "unknown girl" and an "unknown boy." According to the markers, both children were "victims of the *Lusitania* outrage." He knew right away this could be the basis of an intriguing tale.

Years of experience as an economist and business journalist have made Kennedy an expert at teasing the real story from masses of deceptive statements. "Time often blurs the distinction between fact and fiction," he says, "and that is certainly true of the *Lusitania*." Passengers did dine and dance in luxury unaware that tons of contraband were stashed below. But whether or not Winston Churchill truly played any part in the sinking of the ill-fated liner remains a moot point at best.

Creating exciting fiction competes for time with the author's career as president of a Connecticut advertising and public relations firm specializing in high technology. The devoted father of five children, Kennedy may at times find his life hectic, but he manages. *Rules of Encounter* is his fifth novel and the third to appear in Condensed Books. Previous selections were *Toy Soldiers*, which has been made into a motion picture, and *The Himmler Equation*.

William P. Kennedy

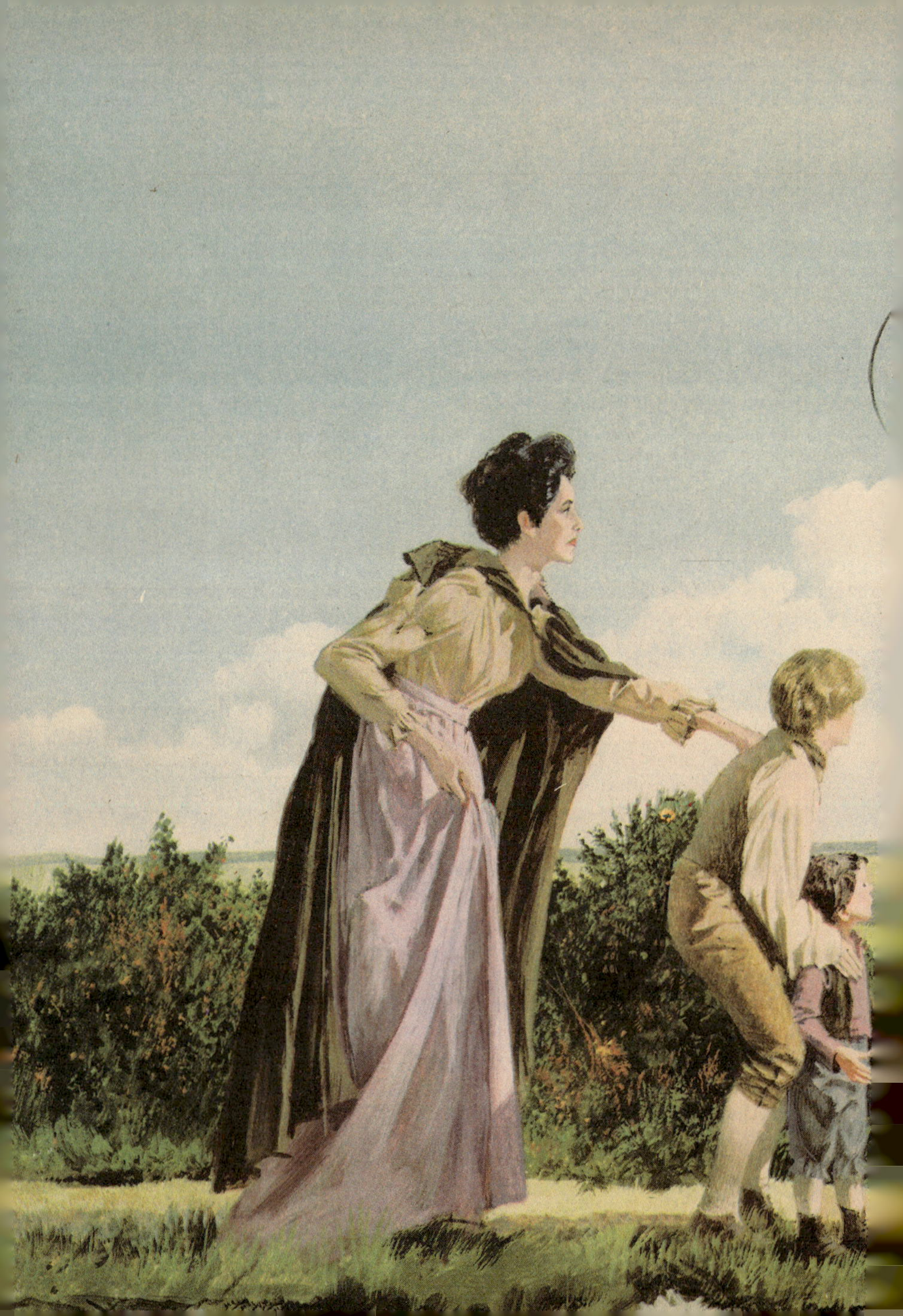

Catherine Cookson
The Love Child

Their parents paid dearly for a love that defied convention. Now for those sins, their illegitimate children are scorned and shunned, branded by the villagers as wicked.

Beautiful young Anna Dagshaw vowed she wouldn't make the same mistake as her mother. But temptation comes in the person of two very different men—one, proud and bold though already married; the other, kindly and sensitive but afraid to marry.

PART ONE
The Family

"I TELL you, Dada, that's what I mean."
 Her face bright with merriment, the young girl read again from the magazine: " 'Ladies and farmers' wives will benefit equally from the scented sachets on their pillows. The fragrance is derived from rose petals, sweetbrier blossom—' " At this point the dark, bright eyes lifted from the page and swept over her family before she went on, gurgling now. " 'Cow pats, well ground, as in farmer Cox's boxings, sold by the pound and dampened, for poultices on the chin, and boils where boils have never bin. . . .' "

Her voice trailed off and joined the peals of laughter as she turned and clung to her sister, while her two older brothers made guttural sounds and their younger brother Jimmy lay on his back on the mat before the open fire, his legs in the air treadling as if he were on a mill; the youngest of them all, a nine-year-old boy, leaned against his mother's side, and they shook together.

The father, rising from his seat at the fireplace, slapped his older daughter playfully on her bent head, saying, "One of these days, Miss Anna Clever Clops, that tongue of yours will get you into mischief. Now come on, all of you. It's half past eight, and bed is calling."

Slowly the laughter subsided as one after the other of the family rose to their feet and wished their mother good night. First, there were Oswald and Olan, the eighteen-year-old twins, both dark like her. Oswald, almost half a head taller than his brother, and broad with it, kissed his mother on the cheek. "Now, I've told you, Ma, you're not to get up to see us out." When, however, Olan bent

The Love Child

towards her, she gripped his arm, saying, "D'you think you'll be able to stick to that driving and the winter coming on?"

"Don't worry; I would drive the devil to hell rather than go down in the mine again. And the smell of the bread keeps me awake. A wonderful idea, isn't it, Ma? To send bread out to the houses?"

"Well, they do it with tea; why not bread?" said Nathaniel.

"You're right, Dada," Oswald said. "And Mr. Green said there'll be other commodities on the carts before long."

Nathaniel smiled with pride on his sons. "Good night," he said. And they both answered, "Good night, Dada."

Nathaniel now turned to his daughters. "You two scalawags, get along with you into your bed before trouble hits you."

"Oh, you wouldn't whip us, Dada, would you?"

"Stop your antics, Cherry, else you'll see whether I will or not. And you, Anna, stop your jabbering in bed."

The two girls kissed their mother and ran down the long room.

When the door had closed behind them, Nathaniel turned an unsmiling face towards his wife, saying, "Those two are so full of the joy of life it frightens me at times."

As Maria said, "Oh, don't say that," fifteen-year-old Jimmy asked, "Why, Dada? Because they laugh and sing, and Anna can make up funny rhymes? What is there in that to frighten you?"

Nathaniel walked towards the fair-haired boy, who was a replica of himself when young. "I'm always afraid they'll be hurt eventually," he said. "And you know why, don't you?"

"Yes, Dada. I know why. But as you said, the boys have weathered it; the girls are weathering it in their own way, and I in mine. I have learned to fight like Ossie. I can use my fists to match any two—"

"Jimmy! Jimmy, quiet. You've heard me say the pen is mightier than the sword, and the tongue is mightier than the fist."

"Not when you're dealing with Arthur Lennon or Dirk Melton."

"You should keep away from them."

"How can I, when I have to pass the village to get to the farm?"

"Well, being the son of a blacksmith, Arthur Lennon's tough. But still, if you can use your tongue, it's better in the long run." His father smiled now. "Off you go, and take Ben with you if you can drag him from his mother's arms." He bent down and ruffled the brown-haired boy, and a strange pang went through his chest as he asked himself how he had come to breed this child, Ben, who had the look of an angel in a church window.

Ben kissed his mother and drew himself from her hold, then put his arms about his father. Then Nathaniel led Jimmy and Ben up the room to the ladder against the end wall. "Don't let the boys get you talking," Nathaniel said. "They've got to get up in the morning."

"Yes, Dada. Good night, Dada."

He watched them climb through the trapdoor into the long roof space that held four beds.

He went back down the room to the fire, and with the liveliness of a man half his forty-four years, he twisted his body into a sitting position at Maria's feet, and laying his head on her knee, he remained silent for quite some time before he asked quietly, "How long d'you think it can last from now on? The twins are near men, the girls near women."

"Oh, Nat. You mean our way of life?"

"Yes, that, Maria. Our way of life and this present happiness."

"It'll last as long as we're together, and nothing can part us except death. And if you were to go, I wouldn't be long after."

He put up his hand and placed it on hers. "It's been a strange life."

"And it'll go on being strange. It's the way we've made it."

"Yes. And, consequently, they'll all have to fight their way through it. Yet they know where they stand, even down to Ben. He knows he's one of a family that lives apart. . . . You know what tomorrow is?"

"Yes, dear. It's the seventh of September, 1880, and the anniversary of the day we first met. As if I could ever forget it."

"I can see you now," he said, "standing at the schoolhouse door. You were holding a lantern up high, and it showed me your face as you said, " 'Can I come in? I want to learn to write. . . .' "

There was another silence, and Maria saw herself walking into that bare schoolroom. She had looked at the books and papers as if they were bread and water and she were starving.

He had told her to take a seat; and when he asked her, "Haven't you attended this school?" she had shaken her head and said with bitterness, "No, no. I would be breakin' into a fourteen-hour day's work for me father. I am from Dagshaw's farm, down the valley. Some prefer the mines to workin' for him."

"Couldn't you talk to him or stand up to him?"

The Love Child

"You can't talk to him; he's an ignorant man. But I have stood up to him with a shovel afore now; it can't go on, though. Me mother put it to me to come to you. She said if I could write me name and read, perhaps then I would get a position in a house. If my father knew I was here now, he'd come and lather me all the way back."

"But it's dangerous for you to come this way at night, and if it was found out that you were visiting me so late. . . . You understand?"

"Aye, yes, I understand. I'd be careful. You're afraid an' all. An' you're a respectable man."

He had smiled and said, "Not all that respectable," which caused her to peer at him through the lantern light and say, "Oh, aye. You must be the schoolteacher with the drunken wife?"

It was some seconds before he answered, "Yes, I am."

"Oh, I'm sorry. I'm sorry. I won't trouble you anymore, cos you've got enough on your plate," to which he replied quickly, "Let's risk it. Twice a week, Tuesdays and Thursdays. Should there be anyone here, I shall open the curtains, and you'll see the lamp-wick up high."

At the door she had turned and said, "I'll never forget this night."

Nathaniel turned his head now to gaze up into her warm, dark eyes. "It's a long time since we have spoken of that night. What followed was so painful." He looked towards the fire as he envisaged all that had followed the night she first came to his door.

Within a month she could write her own name and read complete sentences. And during that month Nathaniel's wife had visited him again from her mother's house, in South Shields, with the intention of staying. But he had warned her that if she stayed, then he would pack up and go, and she would have no support from him. She left, cursing him.

That visit had brought him before the board of school managers in Fellburn. They informed him that his wife had again disturbed the peace, and should another such disgraceful incident happen, he would be relieved of his post.

With this, he had written a letter to his wife. He told her that if she once again showed her face in the town, he would lose his position, and consequently she would lose her support.

Apparently the question of his conduct and dismissal had been put to a vote, and it was only Miss Netherton's vote that had saved him. Miss Netherton was a power in the surrounding countryside.

Her people had owned quite a large area of the town, though her father had been a gambler and had had to let the manor go. But even now, although she lived in Brindle House, which was no size in comparison, she still owned a number of properties in the village as well as in Fellburn. Moreover, she was connected with big names in Newcastle and farther afield still.

He had been tutoring Maria for three months when one night their hands accidentally met, but only slowly did the fingers withdraw from one another while their eyes clung in the knowledge of what had been happening to them. Even so, no word was said.

Then on a December night something happened that changed their lives. He had been to a long meeting with the church elders, and it was almost ten o'clock when he entered his house. Then there was a knock on the door, and when he opened it, there she was, standing shivering.

He had pulled her swiftly into the room, saying, "You're like ice. What is the matter?"

"I . . . I had to see you. My . . . my mother wants your advice."

He had pushed her down into a chair, taken the bellows, and blown up the fire. Then he had brought the bedcover from the other room, and when he had put it round her, his arms remained there as he said, "How long have you been waiting?"

"An . . . an hour. It doesn't matter."

"But why have you come?"

She put her hand inside her coat and brought out a stiff, yellowish leather bag about nine inches long and four wide, and her voice trembling now with excitement, she said, "We were cuttin' down wood, Mother an' me. There was a tree leaning over—the wind had got it—so we pulled it down, and . . . and as me mother went to hack off the root, she saw this bag sticking up at the bottom of the hole. It was stiff, brittle. Feel it."

He felt it. Then she said, "Guess what we found in it?" He shook his head and said teasingly, "A fortune?" only for her to reply, "It could be. I don't know." And she withdrew from the bag a cross studded with precious stones.

After gazing at it he had pulled the lamp towards them and bowed his head over it. And then he had said, "My heavens!"

"If he knew . . . Father. That's the last we would see of it."

"This could be classed as treasure trove, you know, belonging to the crown. A priest must have buried this years ago, likely during the Reformation. Once you bring it to the authorities, it will pass through so many hands that your prize money would be worth nothing when you got it, and it might take years." Then after a pause he added, "Look, will you leave it with me? I'll try and get advice. The best person to ask is Miss Netherton. She has helped me. But I won't say who you are; just that you have something to sell, and could she advise you. Will that do?"

"Oh, aye. Aye, I know you'll do your best. Oh!" She had put out her hands and touched his cheeks; then the next minute her arms were about him, and his free arm was holding her, while his other was gripping the precious find. And thus they stood for some time before, slowly, he laid the cross on the table and then held her body so close to his that they could scarcely breathe. When they looked into each other's eyes, their lips came together, and long they remained so.

And so it was. . . .

HE BROUGHT his gaze from the fire, and again looking up into her face, he said, "There are fiends in this world, but thank God there are friends. And if ever there was a friend, Miss Netherton has been one to us all these years."

"How old is she now?"

"Oh, I should think in her early sixties. She must have been in her early forties when I first saw her as one of the school managers. But I'll never forget the night I went to her with the cross. . . ."

Again he turned and looked towards the fire, and he saw himself standing in Miss Netherton's drawing room. Ethel Mead, the housekeeper, had shown him in, and Miss Netherton had greeted him warmly. Then laying his overcoat on the arm of a chair, she had sat opposite him by the fire, saying, "I hope you're not in trouble again."

"No, not this time, I can say. Thank goodness." They had both laughed; and looking at her, he had thought what a marvelous woman she was and wondered why she hadn't married.

The coffee came, and a cupful was drunk before he said, "This is very private business. I think, in a way, it could be illegal."

"My! My! My! Let's hear it, then. It will be a change to deal with something really illegal and not the piffling things that come my way."

"A friend of mine is in dire poverty; in fact, both she and her mother lead a life of hard work and restraint. They found something that I'm sure you will think is very precious." He now put his hand into his inner pocket and drew out the stiff leather bag and, handing it to her, said, "See what's inside."

A minute later she was staring down at the cross on her palm. "How very very beautiful," she said. "Where did she find it?"

"In the woodland attached to a farm. The husband owns the farm. Unfortunately, the mother and the daughter are treated like serfs."

"Oh. Oh. I could put my finger on that farm. Is it Dagshaw's?"

After he moved his head slightly in acknowledgement, she said, "Oh, yes. He's an awful man. But what do you want me to do?"

"I thought you might be able to advise them what should be done. If it is treasure trove, it will go to the crown, won't it?"

"Yes, I should think so. And then that's likely the last anybody will see of it until it appears in some museum or a private collection. But if they were to get money for it, what would they do with it?"

"Escape, I think. I know the daughter will, and I should think the mother, too. The mother has relatives in Cornwall."

"But what will the daughter do?"

It was a long moment before he answered. "She will come to me. We have discovered that we love each other."

The small body in the chair seemed to bristle slightly. "But you are married. . . . Well, will your wife allow this to go unheeded?"

"All she cares about, ma'am, is that she gets enough money for her drink. My stipend from the school hardly supplies that, yet it keeps her at bay. I had two years of literal hell living with her. When we married, I did not know that she was addicted to drink."

"Do you know what will happen to you if you take this girl into your house—because she is a young girl, isn't she?"

"We will likely have to take to the road until I find other work."

"Oh." She got to her feet, really bristling now. "Don't let me hear you talk such nonsense! You with your brain and capacity for teaching. And let me tell you, you shouldn't be teaching in that little school. You should be in the university taking a higher course. I have listened to you. You don't just Jack and Jill your pupils, do you? You drop in bits of Shakespeare and Pope. But now, back to this gem."

Her fingers stroked the stem of the cross. "Rubies, sapphires, diamonds. Oh, my! There's a great fortune here. But who might

The Love Child

pay its worth? Look, there's a plan forming in my mind. Could you leave this in my care until tomorrow?"

"Yes, Miss Netherton."

They had shaken hands like old friends.

He saw Miss Netherton again before he could tell Maria his news. And Miss Netherton suggested that she would, in a way, buy the cross from them over a period of time. If she were to take a large sum out of the bank, her agent who saw to the estate would wonder why; but it would be quite in order, owing to her generous nature, to pass over Heap Hollow Cottage and an acre and a half of land as a gift. Also, she would be able to afford two pounds a week out of her income, which could be divided between mother and daughter. And an immediate payment of twenty pounds would enable the mother to travel to her relatives in Cornwall. This arrangement was to last until the whole totaled five hundred pounds, which would cover practically five years. Did he think Mrs. Dagshaw and her daughter would agree?

When, that night, he told Maria of the arrangement, she burst into tears and became almost hysterical. What he did not tell her was what Miss Netherton had said concerning the reaction in the village should they take up their abode in the cottage.

It was Maria herself who said, "What will they do to us should we live there together?" He had answered, "We'll find out, won't we?"

And they were to find out. . . .

HE GOT to his feet now, and taking her hands, he pulled her up, saying, "Come to bed. You've got a lot of cooking to do tomorrow for our anniversary tea, and I've the two Fowler boys from Fellburn, both as thick as fog in the morning. They'll have to work some, and so will I if they want to get into that fancy school. But it's that pit lad, Bobby Crane, I'm interested in. I hope he can cut across without being noticed after his shift tomorrow."

"It's risky for the boy, don't you think?"

"Yes. But he wants to carry on, and he wants to get out of the pit, but heaven help him. He'll be out soon enough if they know he's learning to read and write. Praggett and the owners, they think that once a man can read and write, he'll never go down a shaft again."

Together they walked down the deep shadows of the room to the door of their bedroom, opposite the girls' room.

They lay in bed, their hands joined as usual; and he said, "Go to sleep. I can tell when you're thinking. There's been enough thinking for one night. Good night, my love"—he kissed her—"go to sleep."

But she was far from sleep. Her eyes wide, she stared into the blackness, and she was back to the day when she first saw this house. It was now twice the size it had been on that day.

She could see the grass where it grew up to the windowsills of the long, low, one-storied building, and when they had pushed the door open, the smell of staleness and damp assailed them. Nat had taken her hand and run her through the two long rooms into a scullery-cum-kitchen. Then they were out through a door. And there stood a large barn and a stable. The barn was an old structure, but the timbers were sound.

She could hear him saying, "It's wonderful, wonderful." She was speechless with the promise of joy to come. "Wouldn't it be wonderful if this could be one big room. Could you break the wall down?"

"Why not, my love?" he had said. "Why not? We'll take the wall down and we'll make a fine kitchen of that scullery. And you'll have a fancy stove with an oven and a hob and a flue." And they had kissed, and he had waltzed her round the uneven floor.

How splendid that day had been, but how they'd had to pay for it—how terrifyingly they'd had to pay for it.

Three days later her mother had left the farm, leaving a letter for her husband, penned by Nathaniel; and the irony of it was that Mr. Dagshaw had rushed to the schoolmaster's house in a rage and asked him to read it. And it was with obvious pleasure that Nathaniel had read his own writing. Her father was puzzled by that, and it was a full two weeks before the puzzle was solved for him when he went to the market, and some toady commiserated with him about his daughter disgracing herself and going to live with the schoolmaster in Heap Hollow Cottage. And didn't he know the village was up in arms, and the schoolmaster had been dismissed, and the vicar had practically put a curse on them both?

The day her father confronted her at the cottage, spittle running down his chin, he screamed, "I'll see you crawling in the gutter. D'you hear? And I'll have the village about your ears. They'll stone you out. And not a penny of mine will ever come your way. And you'll rot, d'you hear? You'll rot inside. You filthy hussy, you!"

And she had cried back at him, "Well, as a filthy hussy, I've worked for you since I could toddle, and never a penny piece for it. Even the food was begrudged us; we only got what you couldn't sell." And then she laughed inside. If he'd had even an inkling of the cross they had found, he would have gone really mad.

After he disappeared round the foot of the hill, her knees began to tremble. She had pushed the bolt in the door and crouched shivering near the fire, waiting for Nathaniel's return. And when he came, she flung herself into his arms and cried while she related her father's words. And Nathaniel said, "Well, it's what we expected, and we've got to weather it. . . ."

The onslaught began a week later, when the barn was set on fire. She could see herself, even now, springing up in bed to see the rose glow and hear the crackling sound of burning wood. They had rushed out to the well but stopped when Nathaniel said, "It would take a river to put that out. A bucket is no use."

In the flickering light they saw shapes seeming to emerge from the shadows, and a voice cried through the night high and loud, "It'll be your house next, the whorehouse." And from different areas voices began to hoot and yell.

The following week they had brought home the first goat. She was already in milk, and they thankfully drank their fill from her—at least before she was found with her front legs broken.

Maria remembered holding the poor animal and crying over it as if it were a child. Because Nathaniel had never handled a gun, Miss Netherton's coachman, Rob Stoddart, had come, and shot the animal and put it out of its misery.

The matter of the goat had incensed Miss Netherton, and she had her coachman drive her into the village. And she had told the vicar that if he didn't stop incensing his parishioners against these two tenants, as she had called them, he would in future be doing without her patronage. Following this, she had walked boldly into the bar of The Swan, which caused comment, because no woman ever went into the main bar of a public inn. There she addressed not only Reg Morgan, the innkeeper, but also Robert Lennon, the blacksmith, and his elder son, Jack, as well as Willie Melton and his son, Dirk, who were painters, and she reminded them that of the thirty-two cottages scattered round, she owned seventeen. Next she had gone to the King's Head and addressed Morris Bergen and John Fenton, the grocer, and two pitmen from the nearby pit, pointedly reminding the latter two that the mine owner was her friend.

For the next four weeks Nathaniel and Maria were left in peace. However, Miss Netherton had warned them to keep clear of the village, even if this meant going across the fields and over the quarry top to reach Fellburn to do their shopping. Then the climax came. It happened when they were walking just inside the copse that adjoined the hill called the Heap, and from which the cottage had derived its name. Maria let out a fear-filled yell as she cried at Nathaniel, "Don't move!" Then she pointed to a distance not two feet away and hissed, "A trap. A man trap!"

"No." He had stood stock-still. "Not that. I'll have the law on them. Traps are forbidden now, even for animals. I'll stay here near it. You run to Miss Netherton's, and tell her to come and see for herself. Then I'll have a constable here."

The outcome of this was a visit from the law to Reg Morgan, the innkeeper of The Swan, the consequences being that he had to appear before the justices to answer the charge of unlawfully setting a man trap to the danger of human life and limb. Moreover, every tenant of Miss Netherton's in the village received a legal letter indicating that were Miss Netherton's tenants in Heap Hollow Cottage troubled in the future, the recipients of the letter would be given immediate notice.

So they were left alone, and they spoke to no one except Miss Netherton or Roland Watts, the village carpenter, and the dressmaker, Miss Penelope Smythe.

When the twins were born, the vicar had a field day in the pulpit on the Sunday. A kindly parson in Fellburn, Parson Mason, christened the children. The record went as follows: "September 24, 1862. Oswald and Olan, baseborn sons of Maria Dagshaw, begotten by Nathaniel Martell. Baptized October 20, 1862."

From the birth of her sons began the spitting. Maria would be walking through the town, and two out of every three times she would hear the hiss and spring aside only too late, for her skirt would be running with mucus, and she'd see the back of a woman walking away.

And the sight of Dagshaw's gillyvors, as they were called, brought folks running to the cottage doors and out of the inns.

The Love Child

It was Anna who had followed the boys. She had been born beautiful, but she was of a strange nature that seemed to stretch to opposite poles within her—one to a depth of quietness and serious thinking, the other to laughter, mimicking, and quick temper. What was sad, however, was that Maria's daughter, so clever in so many ways, was still a sort of maid to Miss Netherton, though this included being a companion to the older woman, who took her into Newcastle visiting the museums and twice to a theater show.

And then Cherry came, and she was as fair as her father, with merry blue eyes and a tripping tongue. The daughters each caused gaiety and laughter in the house, where there would have been none, for the twins were sober young men, and Jimmy, at fifteen, was a questioning boy. And then there was Ben. The name didn't suit him, but it was the name of Miss Netherton's father.

Miss Netherton had constantly been a guardian angel to them all. The payment of money for the cross had ended a year after Jimmy was born. But they had managed because by that time they were on their feet, so to speak. The barn had been rebuilt, a bedroom built for the girls at one side of the house, and their own at the other. The vegetable garden and fruit trees yielded all that they needed for most of the year. Four goats supplied them with milk and cheese, and twenty hens with eggs, and a fowl for the table every now and again.

What would they have done without Miss Netherton? But oh, Maria wished she would get Anna, now near eighteen, a position of some kind. Miss Netherton had hinted at it more than once.

But she must get to sleep; it would soon be four in the morning.

PART TWO
Anna
1

MARIA had cooked all day for the big tea; the table was laden with her efforts. There was a currant loaf and a rice loaf, and caraway seed cakes, and pastries decorated with pieces of ripe cherry; there was a large earthenware platter containing two chickens, a bowl of pig's-head sausage, and molds of soft goat-cheese. It was a fare that would have done credit to a banquet hall.

Maria turned from the table as two voices hailed her from the kitchen, one saying, "We are home, Ma," the other, "What can I smell?"

She went quickly down the room, saying, "What I can smell are muddy boots. Leave them outside."

She was met at the kitchen door by her two sons, both in their stocking feet, and Oswald, laughing, said, "Oh, Ma, let's get near the fire. It was freezing coming over the fields." Both young men sat down opposite the open hearth.

"You're a bit early, aren't you?"

"Yes, Ma. We've been good boys, and Mr. Green let us off. And we've got some news for you, too, both of us."

"Oh, good. Will it keep till the others get in?"

"Yes, Ma. It'll keep. Where's Dada?"

"He's in the barn with Bobby Crane, the pit lad."

"Oh, the pit lad. That poor beggar. We heard in the town there's trouble at the Beulah mine. They've been routing out some of the men from the cottages because they've been agitating. The men have only got to mention union, I understand, and they're for it."

"Heaven help them if they've got to live out on the moor this winter," Maria said. "D'you remember three years ago? Four children died out there." Her tone lightened. "Come and look at the table."

"I could smell it down the road, Ma."

Oswald punched his slender brother, saying, "Olan, you can smell food from Land's End to John O'Groat's. But look at that. My, you have been busy, Ma."

The far door opened, and Nathaniel came up the room with his youngest son and said quietly, "You have put some spreads on that table, but that's the best yet."

Maria's eyes shone with pleasure. "How was your pupil?"

"Doing nicely. Oh, he just gollops up knowledge."

"I golloped up your knowledge, Dada."

Nathaniel put back his head and laughed. "All you golloped up, Olan, was food. And you're still as lanky as a bean pole." And he slapped his son on the back, then turned to Maria again, saying, "We're going to wait until they all come, aren't we?"

"Of course, of course," she said, nodding emphatically. "But let's hope Mrs. Praggett doesn't keep Cherry late tonight."

"She should stand out for her time. She's paid for eight till six," said Oswald; then on a laugh, "Eh, she was funny, wasn't she, that last time she described the row when Mr. Praggett's wife tipped the dinner over him?"

They were laughing again when the kitchen door opened and Anna, home from Miss Netherton's, came into the room. "Dada, I have news for you, and for you, Ma."

"We have, too, Olan and me here," Oswald said, "but we're keeping ours for the tea."

"Oh. Oh, I'm glad. Well, I'll keep mine an' all for tea. And, Dada, when the postman brought Miss Netherton's mail, he said he had a letter for you. Here it is." She handed him an envelope.

After looking at it Nathaniel glanced at Maria. Then he went to the small desk in the corner, and picking up a paper knife, he slit open the envelope and read the letter. Maria, who was watching him, saw one hand go down to the desk as if for support. "What is it?" Then he walked across into their bedroom, and she followed.

Slowly he handed her the letter, and she read it; and it was a long moment before, in a pained murmur, she said, "Five years. Oh, Nat. Shall we tell them?"

After a moment he said, "After the meal I'll tell them."

THE meal was over, they were all replete, and they had congratulated their mother on the wonderful feast.

"Now who goes first?" said Nathaniel. "I think ladies should have the choice."

Anna said, "Mine can wait. Let Oswald and Olan tell their news."

"Well, go ahead, Oswald."

All eyes were on the bright-faced, bulky form of the eldest of the family as he said, "Mr. Green has asked if I would like to manage his other shop, in Gateshead Fell."

"Oh! Wonderful!"

"Managing a shop! All by yourself?"

"Will you get more money? Double pay?"

"Be quiet." Nathaniel waved them down. "Go on, Oswald."

Oswald took a deep breath before he said, "Of course, it isn't as big as the Fellburn one, and it's in rather a poor quarter near the river, but it's got prospects. I am to do part of the baking to begin with—nothing fancy, you know, just plain bread and tea cakes."

"How much money are you getting? Twice as much?"

"No. No, Mr. Moneybags." Oswald laughed at Jimmy. "But I'm

going up to seven shillings a week." He nudged Olan, saying, "Tell them your piece."

"Well," Olan said, "I am to take the cart with trays of fancies, and approach private houses and inns and ask if they would place an order with George Green, high-quality confectioner, established 1850. And for every order over a pound I get one penny commission."

"A *penny?* What's that to brag about?" Jimmy butted in again.

"If the weather keeps fine, I could make a shilling in a week, bighead," replied Olan. "And Mr. Green is supplying me with an oilskin cape and covers for the trays; he's thought about the weather."

Jimmy was laughing now. "But what about the poor horse?" And when Anna's hand came out and slapped him across the ear, he laughed louder, and at this they all joined in.

"Well now, that's us settled." Oswald was looking towards his sister. "Out with it."

All eyes were on Anna now, and she said, "I'm to be a teacher." They all rose at once and crowded round her.

When the hubbub had died down, Anna began. "Miss Netherton took me to the school this afternoon. Apparently it's been under discussion for some time. I am to take up my position at Miss Benfield's Academy For Young Ladies next week."

"The Academy For Young Ladies. Oh, Anna!" Cherry's arms were about her, and the sisters were hugging.

"Miss Netherton never let on to you?"

Anna looked at Maria, saying, "No, Ma. Not a word. The only thing is, she has been pushing all kinds of books towards me over the past week—not only English and history but philosophy and such. I won't need this with the little ones, but it may help me later on."

"What was the house like, the classrooms?"

"Oh, Dada, grim. The one room I saw upstairs was partitioned off, and there were eight desks. What was the drawing room is the main classroom. And part of the dining room is the music room."

"How many teachers are there?"

"I think just two. Miss Benfield—she's big. And another one."

"It doesn't sound like a very high-class establishment."

Anna now looked at Olan, saying, "Nor did it to me, and I'm sure it didn't to Miss Netherton. But, as she said, I have to begin somewhere. I'm . . . I'm sure, Dada, it's the best she could do for me."

The Love Child

Her expression was serious and so was Nathaniel's, for they both knew why: a bastard and one of a family of bastards would not be classed as a fit person to instruct young ladies.

"Well now, what more news have we? Anyone else got a surprise?" Anna looked round the family.

"Well," Jimmy said, "today Daisy kicked a bucket of milk over. And farmer Billings raged about, cursing. Mrs. Billings chastised him, shouting, 'Be grateful you have milk to spill; you won't find any in hell.' And you know what he shouted back at her?" Jimmy chuckled so much that he almost choked. " 'Go boil your head, woman!' "

This aroused laughter. Looking at Cherry, Maria said, "Have there been any high jinks in your establishment?"

"You wouldn't believe it, but it's been 'My dear Florence' and 'My dear Mr. Praggett.' They've been cooing like two doves. And I wanted to say to her, Look, woman, don't be hoodwinked. He's a dreadful man, really. He gets so mad at times that he actually jumps. Like the day I'd just hung out a lineful of washing, and he came rushing out straight into it and brought the whole line down."

The room was filled with laughter, which trailed away as one after another they turned their attention to the young boy who was saying quietly, "I'm going to be a doctor when I grow up."

"Why this decision to be a doctor, Ben?" his father asked gently.

"Because I want to mend things . . . like sores on legs, Dada."

"Sores on legs? Who has sores on legs?"

"The children that came into the wood this morning."

"What were they doing in the wood?"

"Gathering blackberries, Dada. They were very small, not as big as me. They had no shoes on, and they had sores on their legs."

Nathaniel rose from his chair and picked up his son and held him, saying, "You will be a doctor someday, son, God willing."

"What if he's not, Dada?"

"What if who's not?"

"God. God willing. You said the other day you were willing to help the pit lad to read and write, but what if God isn't willing?"

A shiver ran through Nathaniel's body, and he repeated to himself, Yes, what if God isn't willing? This last child of his—this small, strange, and continuously happy child—filled him with foreboding.

Maria was standing close to Nathaniel, saying, "Tell them our news. It's time."

"Oh, yes. Yes, we have some special news for you." And he took Maria by the shoulders and pressed her down into his chair; then dropping onto one knee, he said, "Maria Dagshaw, I love you. Will you marry me?"

"Oh, Nat. Nat." Maria covered her face with her hands, and now they were surrounded by their children. "Oh, Ma. Oh, Dada."

"Dry your eyes, my love." Nathaniel picked up the corner of her white apron and gently drew it over her wet cheeks. Then he addressed his family, saying, "I have never kept anything back from you. You have all been brought up to face the situation that we brought upon you by our love for each other. Yet, in spite of the so-called shame, I doubt if there is a happier family in the whole of the county. So now I will tell you the news I received tonight, a letter that should have been delivered five years ago. My wife, as you know, was addicted to drink. In order to keep her from plaguing me, I had to send her a ten-shilling note once a fortnight, care of the penny letterwriter. Well, his letter tells me it was only by accident that he found out my wife had died five years ago. After her old mother had missed two visits to collect the money, he thought he'd better take it to the address he had been given. It was kind of a lodging house, and through the landlady he learnt my wife was already dead. So five years ago I could have said the words I said a moment ago to your mother. But still"—he moved his head slowly—"we would have been no happier than we are now, and, unfortunately, our marriage cannot erase the stain we have put upon you all."

"Oh, Dada. Dada." The girls were kneeling by his side, and it was Olan who said, "Ma and Dada, I'll always thank God that I was born of you, and Oswald says the same, don't you, Oswald?"

"Oh, yes. Yes, Ma . . . Dada. Then where will you be married, Ma?"

Maria glanced at Nathaniel and said, "Parson Mason will do it—gladly, I'm sure. He christened all of you."

"Yes." Nathaniel rose and pulled Maria to her feet. "Now your mother and I are going to take a walk because there's a moon out tonight, and after proposing marriage one should always walk in the moonlight with the beloved." He hugged Maria to him.

As Nathaniel and Maria went out into the moonlight, the family set about their separate duties: Oswald lifted up the large black

The Love Child

kettle from the fire and took it into the scullery and poured the water into the tin bowl that Anna had half filled with cold water.

"Well," she said to him, "what do you think about their news?"

"It's not going to make much difference to us, is it?"

She looked up sharply at Oswald and asked softly, "Have . . . have you minded?"

"I wouldn't have been human if I hadn't. And what about you?"

"Oh." She looked at her hand sluicing the water; then she said quietly, "Just now and again when I heard the word."

"The word. Aye, it twists your guts up, doesn't it? If it were only the one word used—bastards—you'd get used to it. But somebody comes up with a new one—gillyvors, baseborns."

She brought her hand out of the water, then dried it on a rough towel. "But they couldn't have done anything else the way they felt. And they're wonderful people. You *do* understand?"

"Oh, yes." He put out his hand and patted her cheek. "Of course they are wonderful people. It's all the others that are not."

With the rest of the children now crowding into the kitchen with dirty plates and crocks, the happy façade was resumed.

2

"I CAN'T believe you'll not be popping in the door tomorrow morning. I'm going to miss you, my dear."

"And I'll miss you, too, Miss Netherton. Yet"—Anna smiled—"I'm just going into Fellburn and to . . . Miss Benfield's Academy For Young Ladies."

They laughed together now, and Miss Netherton surveyed her up and down in her gray woolen dress, saying, "You look very smart." She turned now to Ethel Mead and called, "Doesn't she look beautiful, Ethel?"

"Well, 'andsome is as 'andsome does," the housekeeper said. "So I hope it's a good start for you. I wish you well."

In the yard Robert Stoddart assisted them into the brake, saying, "Up with you then, miss, and let's get you to that school an' knock sense into those bairns. What d'you say, ma'am?"

"I say the same: let's get her there. But we'll never arrive on time if you stand arranging rugs. Get up, man!"

As they reached the village Anna told herself to sit straight and

368

hold her head high, for they could do nothing to her when she was with Miss Netherton. Only once before had she ventured to pass through the village on her own, and she had ended up crying in the wood, beating her fists against a tree trunk, imagining it was the face of Arthur Lennon, the blacksmith's younger son, who had made a gesture to her that she would never forget.

Miss Netherton now leaned towards her, and in a raised voice over the noise of the wheels, she said, "You will soon get into the routine. Two miles will be nothing to walk in the summer, but the nights are cutting in quickly now."

"A carrier cart leaves the market at ten past five. I shall get that."

"Oh, well, that won't be bad, but you'll have the fields to cross."

"Father or the boys will meet me; at least, someone will."

"Ah." And Miss Netherton sat back against the padded rail of the carriage. "We are about to enter the underworld. Sit up straight. But don't look at me; look from side to side. Keep talking; look amiable because, you know, they'll be at their doors before we reach the end of the village."

Miss Netherton went on chatting and looking round, and Anna, taking up her mood, said in a light tone, "Mr. Cole is unloading a carcass from his handcart. There's a young man with him; I suppose it's his son." Then she muttered, "Mrs. Fawcett, the vicar's wife, has just emerged from the vicarage lane."

"Oh, I must bow to her."

The vicar's wife stopped at the village pump, and Miss Netherton inclined her head to her and smiled while saying under her breath, "By the look on her face, I think she's going to have a seizure, and they will have to send for Dr. Snell."

At the end of the straggling street the road began to narrow, and it was here that they met up with an approaching gig, and Miss Netherton said, "Pull into the side a moment, Rob, and pull up."

The open carriage had been approaching at a pace, but now the horses were brought to a stop by the brake. Two men were sitting in the front, and the one holding the reins touched his cap. "Good day, Miss Netherton. You're out early."

"Apparently, I'm not the only one, Simon . . . or you, Raymond." She had turned her head slightly to address the other man, and he said, "I've had a gallop already, Miss Netherton."

"Oh, my. You have almost done a day's work." There was sarcasm in the tone. Then looking back at Simon, she said, "Oh, may I introduce my companion. Miss Dagshaw, Mr. Brodrick."

The man's eyes had widened, and there might have been a slight hesitation before his hand went to his cap again. "Pleased to make your acquaintance, Miss Dagshaw."

Anna inclined her head in acknowledgment. The other man was looking at her, but did not acknowledge the introduction.

Quick to notice this, Miss Netherton said, "Well, we must be away, or we'll be late for an appointment. Good-bye, Simon. Good-bye, Raymond." And they went bowling down the lane.

It was some minutes before Miss Netherton spoke. "Do you know who those gentlemen were?"

"Yes. I've seen them in the distance when the hunt was on. I . . . I didn't know they were from The Manor until Dada pointed them out to me."

"Well, there are very few saints in the world, Anna; we're all a mixture of good and bad. Those two brothers have got their share, with more good than bad in Simon, but more bad than good in Raymond; at least, that's how I see them. Simon is the younger by a year, so Raymond is in charge of the estate, the farms, and such business deals as the Beulah mine. The family have a good share of it, and by all accounts he is a hard enough taskmaster. Poor old Simon has tied himself well and truly to that house, with his mother, wife, and child."

Anna said, "The mother is an invalid, I understand."

"Yes. She broke her back while holidaying in Switzerland some years ago. When she's not in bed, she is wheeled about on a spinal carriage, and Simon has that job most of the time."

"The father? Isn't he there?"

"No. Arnold Brodrick travels. It's to get away from responsibility, a sick wife, and a vixen of a daughter-in-law. Now you could get your teeth into that family for a story. By the way, have you written anything lately, besides those little rhymes of yours?"

"I started, but the only thing I could write about with any strength of feeling was our family, because, I've got to face it, I've had no experience of the world. Nor have any of us, have we?"

"Well, I won't say that. I think you've all had some experience of the world, and forcibly. And you know, Anna"—she now leaned forward and gripped Anna's knee—"it isn't ended. Your mother and father, as you know, have defied convention—they have spat in its eye. But they picked the wrong place to do it, for if one desires to be burnt alive, then I would say go and live in a village and do something that half of them would like to do, but haven't the courage. Oh, it's amazing how frustrated desire can appear under the heading of righteousness. But I've said it to you before— Aha! Here we go into the street of learning, my dear."

Anna put out her hand and gripped the older woman's, saying, "Now don't get up. I shall slip across tonight and tell you all my news and how I have implanted wisdom and knowledge into the five- and six-year-olds in Miss Benfield's academy."

"My wishes go with you. You know that." And as Rob helped her down, he said, "Best of luck, miss."

Anna walked to the door and pulled on the iron-handled bell.

The brake disappeared down the street before a small disheveled maid of no more than twelve pulled the door open and let her enter. Then the maid showed her down stone steps and through a rough basement kitchen. Anna walked into a part of the room that had been partitioned off as the dining room.

Miss Benfield, a large woman, was sitting at a table on which were the remains of a cooked breakfast: there was a greasy plate in front of her, which showed the traces of egg yolk. Another person stood behind a chair.

Miss Benfield looked steadily at Anna for a full minute before she drew in a breath; then turning to the other woman, she said, "This is Miss Kate Benfield, a cousin, and my first assistant."

Anna looked at the woman behind the chair and smiled, but she received no answering smile, merely a slight movement of the head. The woman looked miserable and emaciated, the antithesis of her relative.

"You are not suitably dressed," the large Miss Benfield said.

"What? Why?"

"When you speak to me, you will address me as Miss Benfield."

"Why do you consider me not suitably dressed, Miss Benfield?" Anna turned her glance quickly from the big woman to the slight one because she thought she had heard her gasp.

"You wish to be a pupil teacher; then you should have some idea of how such a one should appear before a class of children. The uniform is as Miss Kate's here: a white blouse and a black skirt, that

The Love Child

to reach the top of your shoes." Her employer leaned her head sideways, observing Anna's gray skirt, which was showing an inch of stocking.

"I'm afraid, Miss Benfield, that I do not possess a black skirt and white blouse; but I have a dark blue dress, and I will come attired in it until I can acquire a uniform."

Miss Benfield was on her feet, her huge chest heaving as if being assisted by a pump. "You are getting off to a bad start, young woman. Now, if you wish to rise in this establishment, you will be wise to adopt a deferential tone. Have I made myself plain?"

"Very plain, Miss Benfield."

The indignant lady turned to her first assistant and said, "You will introduce Miss Dagshaw to her duties."

Anna turned and followed the first assistant through the kitchen, past the little maid, up the dark stone stairway, and down a passage, to a room with two long, narrow tables, each with its bench facing the blackboard.

Miss Kate Benfield opened a cupboard, and taking down two boxes from the top shelf, she pointed to the pieces of cardboard inside, saying briefly, "The alphabet." She picked up a piece of cardboard. "You ask them what that is; then you make them all repeat it ten times. Then you do cat, dog, rat, mat, sat, fat."

The woman put the boxes back, saying, "That occupies the first hour." Then pointing to a shelf on which were a number of tattered books, she said, "Nursery rhymes. They'll know some of these already, having learnt them at home." Pointing to a third shelf, of trays and tin boxes, she said, "You won't need the clay until the afternoon. They are getting tired by then. But these"—she was lifting some picture books—"are for the last hour in the morning if they are getting restless. You can ask them to tell stories about the pictures. Think you can do that?"

"I should think so." Anna's tone was cold, and the woman said, "Well, you knew what you were in for, and you're starting at the bottom."

There was something in the voice that didn't match the countenance and caused Anna to say, "Thank you for your help. You're right. I'm starting at the bottom."

Then the clock struck nine, and the woman said, "The horde will be arriving at any second now," and she left the room.

"Good morning, children."

"Good morning, miss." There followed a silence in which Anna wondered what she should say; then she was saying it. "I am your new teacher, and so I hope you will help me to get over my first day. Will you?" There was silence for a moment; then, "Yes, teacher." She looked at the eight bright-faced little children sitting upright and said, "Now tell me your names." And one after the other they said their names, some in a whisper, some loudly.

"Now, shall we start with the alphabet? You usually start with the alphabet, don't you?"

"No, miss. You call the register."

She looked helplessly towards the open cupboard. She had no register. She hadn't been told about the register.

"Oh. Well, we'll see about that later. . . ."

There was no actual break until twelve o'clock, and at twenty minutes past eleven there were one or two yawns, so she decided to brighten things up in the rhyme section by getting the children to demonstrate the words by the use of their hands. Looking through the book, she said, "Now children, let's be Jack and Jill, shall we? What did they do first?"

"They went up the hill, miss."

"All right, we'll all go up the hill."

Eight pairs of arms clawed their way up the hill.

There were only six rhymes in the ragged cloth books, and when they had demonstrated the last, one child called out, "Tell us another, miss," and this was echoed by the others, "Yes. Do, miss."

She thought of all the nursery rhymes her father had taught them. Which one would be good for demonstrating? She said aloud, "I know a nursery rhyme you can all act to. It is called, 'There Was a Little Man.'"

And so she began. *"There was a little man,/And he had a little gun"*—she stretched out both arms as if she were holding a gun to her shoulder—*"And his bullets were made/of lead, lead, lead . . ."*

"And his bullets were made/of lead, lead, lead," they repeated. Then there was a chorus of "Bang, bang," followed by high laughter and "Do it again, teacher. Do it again." So she did it again, and the responses grew louder, and the laughter became higher.

Then suddenly the door burst open, and the first assistant appeared, her face expressing amazement. "What on earth!"

"We are just demonstrating a nursery rhyme."

"I heard. I'm in the next room. Come outside a moment."

In the dark corridor the woman whispered, "She just needs to hear that, and you'll be out the door. Bullets through the head; I've never heard such a thing."

"It's a nursery rhyme: *There was a little man,/he shot a . . .*"

"Well, look, if you want to remain here, stick to the rules. I'll say this much: I think you'll work out all right, for you're the best teacher we've had for a long time."

Anna wanted to thank this miserable-looking woman, put on her hat and cloak, and go home. And admit defeat?

She drew in a long breath and returned to the classroom.

AT FIVE o'clock Miss Benfield called Anna downstairs and reminded her of her dissatisfaction with her apparel. She also said that from what she had overheard, her discipline needed a great deal of improvement.

To Miss Benfield's surprise Anna made no reply. She was feeling weary. Moreover, the house was cold. And she was hungry. . . .

When she reached the market square, the carrier cart had already left, and she had never been so near to tears. She would have to walk; and if she didn't hurry, it would be dark before she reached the shortcut home. That path passed close to the edge of the quarry, and although the quarry wasn't all that deep, she wouldn't like to fall into it in the dark. If her father saw that she wasn't on the carrier cart, most likely he'd go back and get their own cart.

She had been standing on her feet for most of the day, and so by the time she left town and took to the country road, her step had slowed. And when she reached the cut, no one was waiting. The cut ran between open fields, then uphill onto the edge of the quarry, and once again between fields until it merged into the moor. At the edge of the moor another path led to their own patch of woodland, which, in turn, gave way to the hill and home.

As she rounded the bottom of the hill she saw in the distance the lights on the cart picking out Neddy's rump, and she went into a stumbling run, shouting, "Dada! I'm here!"

In the yard they were all about her, and her father's voice demanded harshly, "Where've you been, girl?"

"Oh, Dada, let me get in and sit down. I'm worn out."

In the kitchen, eager hands were at her feet, and they took her shoes off and lifted her cold soles towards the fire.

"May I have something hot, Ma?"

"Yes, my love, yes. It's all ready—some mutton broth."

She was eating the soup and two large slices of bread when Nathaniel came in and stood in front of her, saying, "Well, what kept you?"

So she told them all exactly what had happened: from the meeting in the so-called dining room, what she was expected to teach, and, lastly, what had prevented her from catching the cart, which was the lecture from Miss Benfield.

"She can't go back there again, can she?" Maria appealed to Nathaniel; and he looked at his daughter and said, "Well, it's up to you. Why not leave it until after I go across to Miss Netherton and give her a report, because I can see you're all in."

"Dada." She looked up at him, and she said, "It's your fault, you know; you've made it too easy for me all these years."

3

ANNA continued to teach at Miss Benfield's academy through October and November, and she had experience with all the children, from the five-year-olds right up to young ladies of fourteen.

Miss Kate Benfield, the first assistant, who usually supervised the nine-to-eleven and the twelve-to-fourteen children's classes, was subject to severe bouts of head colds, during which Miss Benfield the elder would allow her to go to her room. When this happened, Anna would take one or other of these classes. She liked taking those of the older girls, although twice she had been pulled over the coals by Miss Benfield for taking liberties with Shakespeare. Miss Benfield had insisted that she herself choose passages that the girls must learn by rote.

Anna also had to deal with religious instruction. Miss Benfield would mark a particular psalm or proverb that Anna must read to her class, after which they were to write a short essay on the subject. Today she had marked the Thirty-sixth Psalm, "Wickedness confronts God's love," consisting of twelve verses.

So here she was, facing nine young ladies, and their faces were full of interest. She was aware that they liked her, and with the

The Love Child

exception of one girl, she liked them. Miss Lilian Burrows, Anna considered, was too advanced for her age, and she was sure that the girl's knowledge hadn't all come from Miss Benfield's academy.

So Anna began. "Well now, you are all aware what day this is, and you know what lesson we have on a Friday."

"Oh, yes, teacher, yes." They had to address her as teacher. Earlier she had pointed out they could call her Miss Dagshaw. This had caused another storm in Miss Benfield's bosom. The only one to be addressed as miss was herself. There were many nights Anna caused her brothers and sisters to roll on the floor when, with a pillow pushed down a bibbed apron, her dark, thick shining hair dragged up to the top of her head, and her feet turned outwards, she performed a remarkable imitation of the mistress.

"Now we are having Psalms, and listen carefully. This is the Thirty-sixth Psalm, and it is headed 'To the chief Musician, A Psalm of David, the servant of the Lord.' Just write, 'A Psalm of David.' " She waited a moment; then she read the psalm.

When she finished, she said, "As you know, you will have to write a short essay dealing with the wickedness that confronts God's love. Shall I read it again?"

"No, miss, no. Miss Pinkerton read it on her last day here."

It was then that the bright spark, Miss Lilian Burrows, put up her hand, and in a superior tone said, "Read us from the Songs of Solomon, teacher, please."

Anna's eyes widened. She looked at Lilian and said quietly, "How many of the songs have you read?"

"Oh"—the girl shrugged her shoulders—"I know bits and pieces here and there. Do you know them, teacher?"

"Yes. Yes, I know them. My father taught me; he's a teacher. They are difficult to understand at first, but they are beautiful."

Lilian slowly stood up. Her quiet demeanor vanished, and the bright bragging spark took over. In a voice belying that it was from a fourteen-year-old girl, she began: *"The voice of my beloved! behold, he cometh leaping upon the mountains, skipping upon the hills. My beloved is like a roe or a young hart."*

Anna stood amazed; her lips were following each word. Then she heard her own voice joining in: *"Behold, he standeth behind our wall, he looketh forth at the windows, showing himself through the lattice."*

She herself paused, but the young girl was oblivious, her voice getting louder as she went on, until Anna finally said, "That's enough! That's enough!"

Lilian slowly sat down. The rest of the girls were staring at Anna, waiting for her words of chastisement; but she couldn't chastise the girl, even though she knew what the girl had put into those lines had nothing to do with religion.

"Now," Anna said, "we shall all write our essays. . . ."

Nothing seemed to go right for the rest of the day, and later when she saw her father's lantern in the distance, she wanted to jump off the cart and run to the comfort of his arms. But when the cart stopped, Nathaniel had actually to help her down, so stiff was she with the cold.

"You're shivering like a leaf. Here, put my scarf round you. Anyway, what kind of a day have you had?"

"Awful. I'll tell you about it later."

"By the way, we've got visitors."

"Visitors? Who are they?"

"Two pit families. They had been on the moor; I hadn't seen them. Apparently they had been coming into our wood at night to get shelter from the wind and had erected a kind of tent against the woodpile. It was Ben who brought the five bairns to the door."

"Five?"

"Yes, five. Rags on their feet, the same on their backs. Your ma brought them in and gave them broth. The father of two of them said they would have to make for the poorhouse—he couldn't see his wife and bairns freeze to death out there. So we told them to bring their bits and pieces down—they hadn't much. Anyway, there's plenty of dry hay in the barn, and I lit the boiler in the tack room. The men rigged up a stove, so they can eat there and be warm."

"Life's very unfair, Dada, isn't it?"

"In some cases it is, dear, but I must admit that many get more than their share of unfairness."

"You did."

"Me? Oh, no. I've been very lucky, my dear. There's many a man who'd envy the six children such as I have." He put his arm round her shoulder and pressed her to him.

"Dada, do you think there's anything bad about the Songs of Solomon?"

377

The Love Child

"Bad, about the Songs of Solomon? They have some of the most beautiful lines in the Bible. What makes you ask such a question?"

"Oh, something that happened today. I'll tell you about it later; all I want at this moment is my feet in front of the fire, a bowl of hot soup in my hands, and Ma's fingers gently rubbing the back of my neck. You know, Dada, I look forward to that every day from one o'clock onwards. I wouldn't exchange it for Solomon's temple."

4

ON THE Monday morning as soon as Anna arrived at Miss Benfield's front door, the little maid said, "She wants to see you in the big room."

Anna went to draw the pins from her hat, but stopped. If Miss Benfield was calling her to the main room, something was afoot.

"Good morning, Miss Benfield. It's a very cold—"

"Be quiet! Don't give me any of your pleasantries. I wonder that you dare show your face in my house."

Anna stared at the woman a few seconds before saying, "Would you mind telling me, please, what you mean by that remark?"

"Corruption. *Corruption.*" The last word was almost yelled.

"I don't understand you."

"You have corrupted my girls." The chest heaved. "Lilian Burrows and the Songs of Solomon. Now do you understand?"

She didn't, really, until Miss Benfield said, "Lilian had some friends with her on Friday evening, and when they returned home, they told their mother that Lilian had recited pieces to them from the Bible, funny pieces that they hadn't heard before." The bosom rose, and on the deep deflation, she said, "Just imagine it."

"Yes, I can imagine it. She's a very bright girl. Miss Benfield, are you acquainted with the Songs of Solomon?"

"I . . . I may be. I am an adult—I understand the real meaning of the words of Solomon. But a young mind would put a wrong construction on them. And you have imbued this child—"

"I have done nothing of the sort. Lilian must have been well acquainted with that part of the Bible. She can rhyme it off."

"Yes, under your tuition, as she said."

"What?"

"Don't pretend innocence, young woman. That child would have not been aware such things were in the Bible, but your corrupt mind introduced her—"

"Shut up!"

Miss Benfield actually took a staggering step backwards, and her mouth opened and shut, but she hadn't time to bring a word out before Anna cried, "I have never read anything to my pupils except that which you dictated. Lilian Burrows is well acquainted with the Songs of Solomon. She stood and recited line after line of the second verse. . . ." She stopped.

Miss Benfield just stared at this daring, beautiful creature whom she had disliked on sight, this bastard child of wicked parents, whom she had taken in out of pity and whose knowledge could only be promoted by the devil's pride.

Miss Benfield opened her tight lips while pointing towards the door. "Get out! Leave my house! You've sullied the name of my school, and I will see that you find no engagement in this town for your corrupting talents in the future."

Anna stared silently at the woman for some seconds before she said, "This is not a school, Miss Benfield, because you have no knowledge to impart. You are an ignorant woman. The little teaching that is done here is supplied by your cousin, that poor downtrodden woman. If the school board were to examine you, you wouldn't even be allowed to teach in a village school, because the standard there would be so far above you. So when you are blackening my name and my ability to teach, I shall not restrain myself from giving my opinion of your establishment."

As she turned away, she thought that the woman was about to have a seizure, and when she opened the door, it was to see the children and Miss Kate Benfield coming in.

For the first time she could see a smile on the thin, worn face of the first assistant, and she did not lower her voice when she said, "Stand on your feet, Miss Benfield. Face up to her, because without you there would be no 'Academy For Young Ladies.' Make your own terms." She took a step backwards, then said, "Good-bye."

The children were surprised to see their nice teacher making for the front door and the first assistant scampering after her.

Anna was on the pavement when the thin, weary woman spoke, gasping as if she had been running. "Thank you," she said. "I'm glad you came." And again she said, "Thank you."

The Love Child

Anna said nothing. She could only raise her hand in farewell, and she walked away from the academy.

It was only nine in the morning. The farther she walked into the town, the farther her anger rose. That dreadful woman. How dare she say her teaching would corrupt?

There would be no carrier cart going her way until twelve o'clock. She crossed the empty marketplace to walk down Victoria Road and past the park at the foot of Brampton Hill. Here the shops on one side of Victoria Road petered out, but did so grandly, with an imposing structure that held the post office.

She was actually walking blindly when a voice said, "Oh, I'm sorry. I beg your pardon."

The man, who had turned from unfastening his horse's reins at the horse post, put out his hand and gripped her arm as she almost overbalanced. "I do beg your pardon. I didn't see you . . . Miss . . . Miss . . . You are Miss Dagshaw, aren't you?"

She blinked at the man. He was the one who had acknowledged the introduction that first day, when Miss Netherton had driven her to the school, and here on her last she was meeting him again.

"Are you all right?" He was looking into her face, and she closed her eyes for a moment before she said, "Yes, thank you, sir. It was not your fault. I . . . I wasn't looking where I was going, because"—she now forced herself to smile—"I was in a temper, which could even be translated into the saying, Blind with rage. So you see, it is my fault. But I am all right, thank you."

His concern had changed to merriment, and he went on to say, "I understood from Miss Netherton that you were in a teaching post?"

"I was, sir. Up till about twenty minutes ago."

His shoulders began to shake, and she herself laughed. Then, remembering who she was and who he was, she adopted a more sober air and said primly, "Good day to you."

As she went to move past him he said, "Since what you say suggests that you are no longer a teacher, at least for today, may I inquire if you are on your way home?"

"Yes. Yes, I am."

"And you mean to walk?"

"Well, sir, having no other means of propulsion but my legs . . ."

"Would you allow me to give you a lift home? It would take the weight off"—he paused—"your means of propulsion."

As she looked from him to the high, two-wheeled gig with but two seats, she asked herself if it was right to accept his offer. What would Miss Netherton have done? Oh, she would have said, Let's get away. "Thank you. That's very kind of you."

Touching her elbow, he helped her up onto the step of the gig, then onto the leather seat. Taking his seat beside her, he shook the reins as he cried to the horse, "Gee up, there," and off they went.

They had passed through the outskirts of the town before Simon Brodrick spoke. "Will you be looking for another situation?"

"Not yet. Well, not until after the holidays. In any case, I think I'll have difficulty in finding one."

"How's that?"

"Well, firstly I don't think Miss Benfield will give me a reference, judging by our last conversation."

"Oh, a battle of words, was it?"

"Yes. You could say that—biblical words."

He turned to her in surprise. "You were arguing about the Bible?"

She told herself that he appeared to be a nice man. So she heard herself saying, "I was accused of corrupting the young ladies by allowing one of them to read a passage from the Bible."

"May I ask which?"

She looked ahead as she said, "The Songs of Solomon."

Once again his shoulders were shaking. "You were teaching your pupils the Songs of Solomon?"

"No." The word was emphatic. "One of them was out to teach me. She had rendered part of the second song to the entire class before I had the wit to stop her. Then it appears that she entertained some friends at home with her repertoire. And I was accused of corrupting young minds. You find it funny? Amusing?"

"Yes. Yes, I do. And you do, too; I can tell by your tone, at least now. But you were in a fury, weren't you?"

"Yes. But I don't mind being laughed at. Dada—my father—often laughs at me and my ideas. I'm quite used to it."

She was surprised when he made no reference at all to her last words, and she thought, Oh, now he's recalling the gillyvor bit, and Dada is the cause of it. And when he remarked, "You would like to be put down at the quarry end, wouldn't you?" she felt she had surmised correctly.

About five minutes later he pulled the gig to a halt. Quickly now

The Love Child

he alighted from his seat and went round to assist her to the ground. And when they were standing facing each other, he said, "I must tell you something. I'm not laughing at you. But I haven't laughed as much as I've done this morning for a long, long time, and I can't look back to a time when I felt more interested in what a human being had to say. Good-bye, Miss Dagshaw, and thank you."

His hand was held out to her. She placed hers in it, and as their palms touched, they looked steadily at each other.

She moved away, walking with a straight back down the narrow path towards the quarry. She knew that the gig was still there, and she wondered why she wanted to burst into tears when just a short while ago she, too, had been laughing.

"Miss Netherton will be upset."

"No, she won't, my dear." Nathaniel put his hand on Maria's shoulder. "She'll understand."

"You know, Nat, I become afraid for Anna at times. Her tongue is too ready: she comes out with things she should keep in her head—the things that you've put into her head."

"Yes, I know, and I'm glad I've done that one good thing: I've made her think and be honest in her opinions, as well as fearless."

"It'll get her into trouble someday. That's what I'm afraid of."

"Well, if she gets into trouble, it will be for a righteous cause."

"You know, Nat, underneath all her cleverness she has still got to learn about life and men."

"It was Simon Brodrick she was driving with, dear. If it had been the other one, Raymond, then I would have been anxious. But Simon is a married man with a three-year-old son."

"Yes. And you can add to that, his wife is a vixen. And there is hell let loose in that house at times between him and his wife. And another thing. The two brothers don't seem to get on. The Raymond one acts all high and mighty, and he's hated at his pit."

"Well, it isn't exactly his pit; it's his father's—at least the share that he holds. The other two owners keep out of the way. Anyway, I shouldn't be surprised if I have a visit from our Mr. Praggett, the pit official, to tell me what'll happen to us for harboring agitators. One thing, they can't turn us out of our house. But let's talk about us, dear. Tomorrow I'm going to see Parson Mason. You know, all those weeks ago, when I went to him, I think he would have been willing to marry us then if it had been left with him. But the dear bishop got to know about it. And through whom? None other than our vicar, the Holy Reverend Roland Albert Fawcett. I'm really of a mild nature, Maria, you know that, but I could see myself flailing those so-called men of God, all except our dear Reverend Mason. Anyway, his letter says the matter is settled, and I go in tomorrow to propose a date." He was smiling as he added, "Do you think they'll arrange the service for midnight?"

She looked up at him. "Could be, if they want the devil there."

"Oh, my dear." He pulled her up towards him, saying, "There is a God. I know there is, although I feel at times he is furious at what goes on down here among his so-called Christian community."

She turned her head to the side and smiled. "Odd that I'll become Maria Martell. Sounds nice. Yes"—she nodded—"I could grow to like it."

He slapped her playfully on the cheek, then went out.

When Nathaniel was crossing the yard from the barn, one of the pit wives cried, "See who's coming, mister!"

Nathaniel looked towards the man fast approaching him. He did not go forward to meet the man, but walked towards the house, and was standing by his front door when Howard Praggett came to a puffing standstill about a yard from him.

"Mr. Praggett. Would you care to come in?"

"You can drop your politeness, mister. I'm going to put it to you plainly; you're breaking the law, you know, in housing that scum." He jerked his head towards the barn.

"Mr. Praggett. I object to the word scum. I am housing two miners and their families because you have turned them out. Now, what is the name of this law I am breaking?"

"They are criminals, agitators, rioters. Wait until Mr. Raymond Brodrick gets back from London. He'll have them into the house of correction for inciting workmen to riot. Aye, you can sneer, but the men are eatin', and they're housed."

Nathaniel's tone now became bitter. "I'd insult a pig by placing it in one of those mud-floored, stinking hovels you call houses. And you can tell your master, when he returns, that my barn will be open to any other of his men you decide to victimize."

The man stepped back and cried, "And your daughter will be out of a job. She'll be one less for you to live on."

The Love Child

As Nathaniel raised his arm, fists clenched, Maria's voice cried out from the open doorway, "No, Nat. No! Don't!"

Praggett shouted, "You'll get the worst of it. I could knock you flat because you've never done a decent day's work in your life."

Maria, gripping Nathaniel's arm, whispered, "Let him go."

The scurrying figure disappeared round the foot of the hill.

Nathaniel muttered, "He'll make trouble."

"Well, we're used to that. As for sacking Cherry, his wife will have something to say on that point, and she'll likely emphasize her words with the frying pan."

"That's what they must all be thinking, that I'm living on the children's wages."

"That's ridiculous. They know you do coaching for the best families in the town. Come on inside. You're cold."

IN THE meantime Anna was down by the woodpile taking out her feelings with the chopper and the saw. They had previously felled a tree, and during the last hours under the weak winter sun she had cut its branches on the saw block.

She had added the last logs to the woodpile by the railings that skirted their land when her attention was caught by the sight of a riderless horse in the rough land beyond. The reins were trailing on the ground, and the horse was trotting gently towards her. Then from round the hedge that bordered the field to the right came another strange sight: a man was running erratically after the horse. Suddenly he stopped, and Anna watched his arms go up in the air, as if to ward off a swarm of wasps. Then she saw the figure fall forward. She climbed onto the pile of logs, jumped down to the field beyond, and ran towards the prostrate figure.

As she neared the man she stopped, for he was writhing on the ground. There was foam round his lips, and his teeth were clenched. She knew instinctively that this man was suffering a seizure. And now she forced herself to kneel down by his side, and taking hold of one of his arms, which he was still attempting to flail, she said, "It's all right. It's all right." The spasm was subsiding now; his body was rocking from side to side but slowly, as if he were spent.

She groped in the pocket of her coat. There was a clean handkerchief in it, and tentatively she went to wipe the man's lips, but her hand stayed when his lids suddenly lifted and his eyes gazed upwards. They were blue eyes, as deep a blue as you could find in the sky on a summer's day. She saw now that he wasn't, as she had thought at first—elderly—but a man of perhaps forty.

Slowly he turned his head towards her, and his lips moved, but no sound came; then, after a moment, she thought he said, "Sleep." And he closed his eyes and turned his head to the side.

She turned about when she thought she heard her mother calling. The horse was standing near the woodpile now. Shaking the man gently by the shoulder, she said, "Wake up. Wake up."

The eyelids flickered; then she heard him sigh, and he turned his head, as if on a pillow. She must get her father, she thought.

Rising quickly, she picked up her skirts and began to run, and she was halfway across the field when she saw her father. He was standing within the railing, by the woodpile, patting the horse, and she called to him, "Dada. Dada. Come here."

His voice came back to her, asking, "Where is this horse from?"

"The man who was riding it had a seizure. He's lying back there in the field. Come, please. . . ."

NATHANIEL stood looking down at the figure, who was now apparently fast asleep. "Dear, dear! Yes, he must have had an epileptic fit. There was a boy at school; after a bad one he always slept straightaway. Look, run tell your mother, and bring that piece of canvas that covers the straw. And tell the pit wives from the barn to come; we won't be able to manage him on our own."

Nathaniel knelt down by the man and loosened the fine cravat at his neck. He was obviously of the gentry, but from where? He couldn't recall having seen this man before.

Anna, Maria, and the two pit wives arrived, and Maria asked, "Who is it?" One of the pit women said, " 'Tis Mr. Timothy, the old mistress's half brother. I used to work years ago at The Manor. But however has he got this far? He hardly goes out. He was all right once, but the fits started when he came back from foreign parts. After the mistress was hurt with the snow coming down on her."

They lifted him onto the canvas sheet and walked him along the edge of the wood until they came to the cottage gate. In the meantime Anna had caught the wandering horse at the bridle, saying gently, "Come on with you. Come on."

The Love Child

After stabling the horse she hurried into the house. They had laid the man before the fire, and she asked, "Has he come round?"

"No sign of it yet," said Nathaniel. "We've got to get word to The Manor. They'll likely be worried and out looking for him by now."

One of the pit wives said, "Well, we'll do anything for you, mister. But that's one thing we couldn't do, go up to The Manor, cos we wouldn't be able to keep our mouths shut."

"That's all right. Thanks again. Are you all right over there?"

"Oh, aye, sir. And that boiler next door is God's blessin'."

Maria waited till they had gone, before exclaiming, "Well, we can't go, can we? So what's to be done?"

"The best thing, probably," said Nathaniel, "is to get word to Miss Netherton. She will let Rob drive to The Manor." He had turned to Anna. "Would you go, dear, and ask her?"

Anna, looking down at the man, said, "Yes, I'll go. I think he'd be more comfortable with a pillow under his head."

"Well, leave that to me, will you?" And Maria pushed her aside. "You get about your business, and I'll see to mine."

Outside, Anna again picked up her skirts and ran. Ten minutes later, out of breath, she was knocking on Miss Netherton's front door. Ethel Mead opened it, and then Miss Netherton, looking out at her, cried out, "What on earth!"

"I'll explain it later, Miss Netherton, but at the moment, will you allow Rob to go to The Manor and tell them Mr. . . . Mr. Timothy has been hurt and that we have him in the house."

"Good heavens! Tim. What was he doing near your place?"

"I think he was riding, but he . . . he had a sort of seizure."

"Oh. He had one of his fits. Look, Rob"—Miss Netherton put out her hand—"get yourself over there, and tell them what's happened. You'll hear all about it when you get back."

The old man said something that could have been in the nature of a grumble, but he left. Then Miss Netherton pointed to Anna's old coat. "Why are you dressed like that?"

"Because I've been sawing wood."

"Sawing wood? What do you mean, sawing wood?"

"Just what I say. I came back this morning. I'm finished."

"Oh, dear. Oh, dear. Let me sit down." Then Miss Netherton said to Ethel Mead, "We'll have two cups of strong tea. And bring the brandy in; I've had the most trying day. Now, young woman, come along and tell me the reason why you got the sack or you left, whichever it is."

As briefly as possible Anna described what had happened. When she finished, Miss Netherton gazed at her and said, "Well, you've done it this time. Of course it wasn't your fault, I know, but the Songs of Solomon! Let me tell you, and I could bet on it"—there was a grin on her face—"those songs are Miss Benfield's bedtime reading. But having said that, she's going to make hay out of this. There isn't much chance now of my getting you set on, at least in Fellburn. Anyway, you may come and talk to me again. That'll make you mind your p's and q's and stop you corrupting young girls." She laughed aloud now, and Anna with her.

When Ethel Mead brought in the tea tray, there was no decanter, and Miss Netherton said, "And where's the brandy?"

"I didn't bring it. Remember what you said: you told me not to bring it in before seven o'clock cos you just go to sleep after."

"Bring that brandy in, woman, or you can pack your box tonight."

"I won't bother; I'll only have to unpack it in the morning."

When the door closed, there was glee on Miss Netherton's small face. "It's so nice when your servants are subservient."

Their laughter mingled softly; then watching Anna pour out the tea, she said, "Take that coat off. You look dreadful."

"I can't, because I'm going immediately after I drink this cup of tea. I want to know what's happening to that man."

"Oh, he'll survive. But I wonder why on earth he got on a horse; he couldn't have been on one for years. He spends most of his time in his room or in the conservatory. He grows the most beautiful orchids, you know, and he writes. And he's a very nice fellow at heart, different from the rest. Simon and Raymond's mother, she's an invalid, and I'm sorry for her; but more so for Simon, being married to that upstart of a vixen who never bothers about anything but her painting and horse riding. And I'm sorry for the little boy, too—that's Simon's son. What! You're going now? Oh, well, I suppose you must. You're dying to go. But come in the afternoon, and stay to dinner. Don't answer me back. Go on."

Anna went out, smiling, and as she ran home she felt a sense of well-being. Perhaps it was because she was free and tomorrow she'd be able to enjoy the company of that little woman.

The man was awake, but only just. Even so, Maria took Anna to

The Love Child

one side before she whispered, "He seems a little . . ." She tapped her head. "He asked where the angel was."

"The angel? Miss Netherton seemed to know all about him and said he was a very nice man, but, unfortunately, had these fits."

"Is he touched? I mean . . ."

"She didn't seem to think so. Anyway, there'll be somebody here soon from The Manor. Don't worry."

She went down the room to where her father was sitting in his chair by the man, and she exchanged a glance with Nathaniel before kneeling down and gently putting her hand on the man's brow. She quickly withdrew it as the eyes opened wide and stared at her; and the face went into a smile as he said, "The angel."

She turned her head quickly and looked to her mother, and Maria nodded at her, as much to say, There, what did I tell you?

The man now sighed and said in quite an ordinary tone, but slowly, "I thought I had died at last. You are not an angel."

"No, sir." She laughed softly. "In no way am I an angel."

He continued to look at her, then asked quietly, "Where am I?"

"You are in my home. This is my mother and my father."

He looked up at Nathaniel and Maria. "I am sorry. I am sorry for troubling you. My illness is no respecter of time . . . or place."

He made an effort to sit up, and Nathaniel put his arm round the man's shoulder. "But are you fit enough, sir?" he said.

"I will lie back for a while if it will not . . . inconvenience you."

"Not at all. Not at all. You are welcome to stay as long as you like. We have sent word to The Manor. Would you like a cup of tea, sir?"

The man's gaze rested on Maria for some time before he said, "Tea? Oh, yes. I would be grateful for a cup of tea."

A few minutes later their guest had taken a sip of tea from the cup placed at his side.

"Well, it is a long, long time since I lolled on a rug before a fire," he said. "It is very pleasant, indeed, yes."

What he would have said further was interrupted by a voice crying, "Ma! Ma! It's me; I've got the push. Mr. Praggett gave me the push, but the missus says I've got to turn up in the morning." Cherry's voice trailed away as she entered the room.

Nathaniel half grumbled at her, "This gentleman has had a slight accident." Then looking down at the man, he said, "This is my daughter, Mr. . . ."

"Oh. How do you do. My name is Barrington. Timothy Barrington." And to this Nathaniel answered, "And ours is Martell."

There came a knock on the door. Anna, being nearest to it, opened it, and standing there was the man who earlier she had laughed with and who, for no reason she could understand, had made her want to cry. "Oh, do come in."

He stepped into the lamplit room, then turned and stared at her; but then, becoming aware of others in the room, he said, "I am sorry for the inconvenience."

"There has been no inconvenience to us, sir." Nathaniel was coming towards him.

Simon Brodrick followed Nathaniel up the room towards the fire, then stood in amazement, looking down onto the mat to where Mr. Barrington was lying, and said with concern, "Oh, Tim."

And Mr. Barrington answered, "Now, Simon, don't you start. I just had to get out, else I would have exploded."

"Well, you did explode, didn't you?"

"Yes. Yes, I suppose I did."

For the moment it was as if the two men were alone, such was the way they spoke, for Simon said, "If you wanted to ride so badly, why couldn't you have told me? I would have come with you."

"Yes, I knew you would, but, my dear fellow, I'm sick of people; I'm sick of close proximity, even of you." And as Simon looked at Maria and began, "I'm sorry we've had to inconvenience—" Timothy Barrington interrupted, saying, "I'm not, Simon. No, I'm not sorry this has happened, because these dear people have been so kind to me, and they have let me lie on the rug by the fire. How long is it since you lolled on a rug by a fire, Simon?"

Simon looked at him and said, "As usual, you are well enough to talk and prompt an argument, but are you well enough to get onto your feet?"

"Yes. Yes. Perhaps. Give me your hand."

Between them, Nathaniel and Simon drew him to his feet, then sat him in a wooden chair. Once seated, he looked about him, taking in first Maria, then Nathaniel, then the two girls, who were standing together, one very dark and one very fair, and both beautiful. Then he sighed and said, "You must think it's a very strange fellow who is partaking of your hospitality. Perhaps on further acquaintance I can prove that I am just odd and not all that strange."

This brought a laugh from Nathaniel, and he answered, "Odd or strange, sir, it would be my pleasure were you to partake of our hospitality whenever you feel so inclined."

"Well, sir, I shall certainly take you up on your invitation. But now I really must go, for I have outstayed my welcome."

With the support of Simon he walked to the door, where he said a single good-bye, which included them all. But Simon Brodrick said nothing until, with the help of the coachman, he had placed his errant relative in the coach and then hurried back to Nathaniel, saying, "I'm indebted to you. But about the horse?"

"Oh, yes," Nathaniel said. "He'll be all right until morning."

"I'll send for him first thing. Thank you again. Good night."

They all answered, "Good night." And when the door closed, Anna experienced the same feeling she had when, withdrawing her hand from Mr. Simon Brodrick's, she had then turned from him and walked along the quarry path.

5

THE news seemed to set the village on fire: those two from the hollow had the nerve to go and get married after breeding that lot. And what d'you think? Miss Netherton was there at the church, so it was said, and at the do they had afterward. And that wasn't all. Oh, no. It was unbelievable, but true—flowers and fruit had been sent from The Manor. To that lot of scum! And why? Oh, you needn't go very far to see the reason for it. Tommy Taylor, the postman, could tell you; he saw Mr. Simon Brodrick with that young piece. She was outside the post office, bold as brass in the gig. *He saw it.* Now there was the reason for the flowers and all sent to the hollow. But the nerve of that young hussy. Like mother, like daughter.

Some said they were surprised that it was Mr. Simon she had caught, and him married, with a three-year-old son. Now had it been Mr. Raymond, they could have understood it. Yet who could understand any decent man going within spitting distance of one of that litter. And that particular one was supposed to have been a teacher in Fellburn. Well, that surely was another cover-up. They would like to bet that young gillyvor had a house there, and what she taught wasn't the a.b.c.

This was the talk in the village before the end of the year 1880, but by the beginning of March, 1881, the villagers were dumbfounded by the news that that particular one was being taken on at The Manor to instruct the young son in his letters and such. What next? To think the hussy had the nerve to push herself into the house, and under her mistress's very nose. But there was one thing sure—she wouldn't reign there long, for didn't the young Mrs. Brodrick have a temper like a fiend? Well, there was going to be sparks flying. Just you wait.

But there were those in the village, as well as a farmer or two round about, who dared to voice their doubts about this opinion of the young gillyvor. Nobody had seen her out riding with Simon Brodrick since that day Tommy Taylor saw her. And why keep on about them down in the hollow? They'd had the ceremony performed as soon as it had become possible.

Yes, they knew that, but it didn't make any difference; the bairns were still bastards.

The Love Child

Still, said the moderate ones, they were all well spoken and in decent jobs and kept themselves to themselves.

As Miss Netherton said, after listening to Ethel, who related the gossip of Rosie Boyle, the housemaid who came daily from the village, there were now two camps of thought there. But she'd be sorry if the day ever came when all the inhabitants turned into kindly sensible people, because then she would realize they had all died, including herself.

PART THREE
The Child
1

"Must you go to this house, Anna?"

"It isn't that I must go, Ben; I want to go. I want to teach, and it's an amazing opportunity that's been offered to me."

The boy took her hand as they walked across the frost-spangled ground towards the wood, and in an affectionate gesture he leaned his head against her arm. "I shall miss you."

She stopped and looked down at him. "I don't have to be there until nine, and I leave at four, and they will take me back and forth in the gig. You'll see much more of me than you did last year."

His eyes were showing a sad expression, and she stooped down, taking his face between her hands. "What's wrong, Ben?"

"I don't know. It's just that I don't want you to go."

"Oh, Ben." She looked at him, troubled. Ben was the happy one, yet there was something in this small brother of hers she couldn't name. Was he fey? No, no. There was nothing pixyish about Ben. He was a boy, a highly intelligent boy. At times he seemed to know the answer before half the question was put to him.

THE coachman helped her down from the gig and led her across the flagged yard to the back door. It was opened by a young girl whose uniform termed her a menial but whose features expressed disdain.

At first the girl didn't speak, but walked ahead of Anna through a long, narrow boot room, then across a large scullery, before thrusting open a door and exclaiming, "She's here!"

Anna stepped into the kitchen, to be confronted by three pairs of eyes. The hostility was almost visible, and she met it as she meant to meet all such. Addressing the big woman in the white-bibbed apron and large starched cap, she said, "Will you kindly inform Mrs. Hewitt that I am come and wish to be shown to the schoolroom?"

As the cook said later, you could have knocked her down with a feather. The cheek of that one. If the housekeeper, Mrs. Hewitt, hadn't come in at that moment, she would surely have let her have it.

Mrs. Hewitt looked at Anna in silence before she said, "Will you come this way?" Her tone was civil but her mien stiff. Anna followed her out of the kitchen and up two flights of stairs, onto a wide landing with a number of doors leading off. Unceremoniously opening one door, the housekeeper said, "She's arrived, Eva."

"Oh, come away in. Come away in, and sit down, lass." The nurse flapped her hands towards Anna.

Mrs. Hewitt turned to Anna and said, "Today you'll be sent for at half past ten; the mistress wishes to see you. Is there anything you would like to know?"

"Not at present, thank you."

The housekeeper abruptly left the room. And nurse Eva Stanmore, looking at Anna, chuckled as she said, "It would be advisable, lass, if you altered your tone when speaking to them above you."

When Anna made no answer, the old woman chuckled again and said, "You likely don't consider them in that way, eh? It wouldn't be any use, would it, to tell you to keep your tongue still, no matter what's said to you. You're of that type, and being brought up as you have been, you're at a disadvantage, fallin' atween two stools, as it were."

Anna took no offense at the old woman's talk, for she felt that the nurse was wishing her well.

"Anyway, the child's sitting in there, waiting, as good as gold. Not that he's always as good as gold, but he's got quite a bit up top for his age, and he's interested in somebody new coming to look after him. That's your room." She pointed across to what was evidently her sitting room. "There's a cupboard in there for your clothes, and the master's put in slates and pencils and things you'll need. And, of course, the child's got his own bricks and toys."

Anna had risen to her feet, and as she made her way to the door indicated, the nurse said, "You're a funny lass."

The Love Child

At this Anna stopped, and looking at the wrinkled face, she said, "And you're a funny woman, but in a nice way," and they smiled at each other before the old woman said, "Go on, you." And she went.

The schoolroom was well lit by two long windows, and standing gazing out of one was her charge. At her approach he turned quickly, and she held out her hand and said, "Good morning, Andrew."

"Hello. Good morning. Did you see the horses going out? Look." He grabbed her hand and drew her to the window, and she saw three horses being led from the yard. "I have a pony," he said.

"You have? That's splendid. You like riding?"

"Yes. When I don't fall off." His mouth went into a wide grin.

She took off her hat and coat and hung them in the cupboard, then looked round the room. It was quite comfortable. There was a wooden table on which there were books and slates, pencils and paper, already laid. An abacus was standing to the side, and on another table were colored blocks with letters on them. At the far end of the long room a fire was burning brightly in a small grate.

When she stood by the table examining the plain exercise books and those for copying scripts, the child said, "Papa bought them, but I have a lot more—and my coloring books."

"Show me."

He ran to a row of cupboards and pulled out an assortment of books, saying brightly, "I like making pictures, not learning letters."

Anna looked at the splash of color on a page and said, "You're very clever at making pictures. But I'm sure you'll be just as clever learning your letters. And we'll paint the letters, too."

"I can count up to ten."

"Oh, that's good. Come on, let me hear you."

As she caught his hand he tugged her to a stop, saying, "Will you take me for a walk this afternoon, please?"

"Yes, my dear, if you would like that." She had the desire to sweep him into her arms and hug him. As she looked down into his face and he looked up into hers, she knew she would love this child.

BETTY Carter, the upper housemaid, came for her at twenty past ten. She didn't greet her in any way; she just stared at her. The maid, walking quickly a step ahead of her, led her down to a broad corridor with four deep bay windows. From this they passed into an open gallery, where a grand staircase led down to the ground floor.

Off the gallery a shorter corridor ended in three steps to a door on which Betty Carter knocked twice.

There was a long pause before the order came to enter. Anna walked into a large room, bare except for a long wooden table on which there was an array of brushes, palettes, and paints. Lying against the wall were a number of canvases. And standing facing an easel was the lady to whom she had been bidden to present herself.

There was also another person in the room, and she recognized him as the second man in the gig. Unlike his present companion, he turned and looked at Anna with a hard penetrating stare; then without speaking, he strode past her and the maid and left the room.

When Betty Carter dipped her knee and said, "I brought her, ma'am," her mistress said, "Very well. You may go."

When the door had closed, Anna watched the woman put her head to one side while staring at the canvas on the easel, then stroke some paint onto it. Only then did she turn and look at Anna, saying, "You know you are on probation?"

Anna answered, "If you say so, madam."

"I do say so." It was a bawl. The woman was glaring at her now, her face suffused with temper. And Anna returned her stare until the woman returned to the easel and once more applied paint to the canvas. There was no sound in the room, and Anna was about to say, May I take my leave, madam? when the woman said in a surprisingly quiet tone, "How long have you known my husband?"

The question perplexed Anna. "What did you say, madam?"

"You heard what I said, girl." The eyes were still directed towards the canvas, but the voice had changed. It was deep and seemed to have a threat in it. And, in answer, her own tone changed. "I don't understand you, madam. I first saw Mr. Brodrick when out riding with Miss Netherton."

"You are lying, girl."

"I am not lying, madam. I don't lie. I have no need to lie. I have seen your husband twice since that time: the first after I left my post in Fellburn and had to walk home, when your husband kindly offered me a lift part of the way. The other time was when Mr. Timothy had a seizure, and your husband came to collect him. Then I had a letter asking if I would take the post and—"

The woman turned to her now, crying, "Enough! Enough!" Then with an imperious movement of her hand she said, "You may go."

Anna did not immediately turn about, but when she did, she was halted again by the voice, saying, "Girl!" She did not this time turn round, and the voice went on. "You will be wise if you forget our conversation. You'll also be wise if you speak only when spoken to. I hope you understand me."

Still Anna did not turn round, but walked towards the door.

The woman's scream almost lifted her from her feet. "Girl!"

Slowly Anna forced her body round. The words were flung at her like darts. "Don't you dare—ever dare—stand with your back to me when I'm speaking to you. Do you hear me? Answer me!"

"Yes, madam. I hear you."

"Well, hear this. You will stand until I give you leave to go."

Before the last word hit her, the door was abruptly opened, and a voice said, "Oh, I'm sorry. Oh, good morning. You arrived, then."

She looked at the kindly face of Timothy Barrington, and she had the desire to burst into tears at his warm greeting. When he held the door open for her, she did not wait for the order of dismissal from her mistress, but walked past him without a word. And she almost fell off the second step into the corridor.

When she reached the top landing, Peggy Maybright, the nursery maid, was coming out the schoolroom door. "Eh! What's the matter, teacher?" she exclaimed.

Anna didn't answer the girl, but went into the schoolroom and closed the door none too gently.

The child was sitting at the table. She sat down opposite him, and when she rested her head on her hand, he inquired, "Have you a headache, teacher?"

As she was about to say, Yes, dear, the door leading into nurse Stanmore's room opened, and the old woman called to her. "I'd like a word with you if you have a minute. And you, Master Andrew, keep on with what you're doing. That's a good lad." Reluctantly Anna rose from the chair and went slowly towards the nurse, who closed the door behind them, asking, "She go for you?"

Anna swallowed deeply. "Yes. You could say she went for me."

"What about?"

"Nothing I can give any reasonable answer to. Whatever I said—"

"Did you cheek her?"

"No, certainly not. I just spoke and answered her questions. I must tell you I don't intend to stay."

"Ah, now, come on. Come on. If it's any comfort to you, we've all gone through the mill with her. She's got a temper like a fiend. The house has never been the same since the day she stepped into it. Sometimes I think she's not right in the head. Why Master Simon took her on and didn't let the other one manage her, God alone knows; it's put years on him. Anyway, it's about time for her trip to London, and she sometimes stays a couple of months. So be a good lass, and I'll bet you a shilling when Mr. Simon gets word of this, she'll leave you alone. And he's concerned that the boy should be learning his letters and such. I'm glad he's taking an interest in him. He didn't seem to bother much afore." She went to a cabinet, took out a bottle, and filled a wineglass. "Drink that."

"What is it?"

" 'Tis herbs. I have it made up specially. It'll pull you together."

The potion tasted very nice, like honey but with a tang to it. "It's very pleasant tasting," Anna said. "You're very kind, and . . . and your kindness contrasts with the feelings against me in this house."

"Oh, take no notice. We're not all alike. But some can't help being ignorant. Now, go in to the boy, and give him of your best."

Anna looked at this old woman, and again kind words were about to be her downfall, so she swiftly went into the schoolroom.

It was about an hour afterwards when a tap came on the outer door, and after calling, "Come in," she rose to her feet at the sight of Mr. Timothy Barrington entering the room.

"Am I disturbing you?"

As she said, "No, not at all," the boy jumped from his chair, saying, "Oh, Uncle Tim, have you come to take lessons?"

"Well, I need them, Andrew, but I don't think Miss Dagshaw will have time for me, because you have such a lot to learn. What are you doing now? Oh, you have drawn a dog."

"No, no"—the boy laughed now—"silly; it's a cat."

"But where are its whiskers?"

"I haven't put them on yet, Uncle."

"Oh. Well, I think you had better, and put some legs on it, too."

As the child scrambled back onto his seat Timothy walked to the window, saying, "You have a lovely view from up here, Miss Dagshaw." He leaned towards the window, and in a lower voice he said, "You've had a taste of Mistress Brodrick junior's temper. One wall of my sitting room also happens to be the wall of her studio. I . . .

I just want to say, don't let it disturb you. I am so sorry you have been subjected to this on your first day here. My half sister, Mrs. Brodrick senior, would never have allowed such a thing to take place. By the way, as soon as she feels able, she would like to have a word with you."

"Thank you for your concern, but I shan't be able to stay on."

He turned quickly towards her, and said, "Oh. Oh, give it a chance. Do, please, reconsider. Mistress Brodrick junior is leaving for London shortly. She spends a lot of her time there, and"—now he smiled—"when that happens, the house returns to normal."

She was forced to return his smile; then he asked brightly, "How is your family? I have meant to visit, but I've been rather taken up with my own doings. You see, I write. . . . Well, I'm interested in history, but now and then I write silly stuff, like . . . poetry."

He had whispered the word, and she actually laughed as she said, "You do? How interesting! I, too, attempt to write silly stuff. It's merely rhyme, not real poetry."

"Look, Uncle . . . there."

They turned towards the table to see the boy holding out a sheet of paper. Timothy took it and looked at the drawing and exclaimed in admiration, "Oh, yes! Yes, *that* is a cat."

"Uncle, I changed it to a dog. Don't you know the difference?"

Timothy looked at Anna. "I am the most stupid fellow on this earth," he said. "I must go look up books and learn the difference between a dog and a cat." Then turning to the boy again, he said, "You can laugh. Everyone isn't able to draw like you can. But I must be away now. I'll pop in tomorrow, if I may?" He glanced towards Anna, then said, "Good-bye, Miss Dagshaw."

"Good-bye, Mr. Barrington."

She was sitting at the table again, guiding the child's hand to make the capital D, while saying to herself, What a nice man. And to be stricken like he is. It isn't fair. Oh, yes, it was true, as the nurse had said. There were kind people in the house.

And those same words she repeated later on that evening while sitting round the fire telling the family her experiences. However, she omitted that part of the interview with the mistress when she was asked, "How long have you known my husband?" There was a meaning in those words, she knew, which would have upset her parents.

2

Anna had hardly begun the lesson the next morning when the door was opened unceremoniously and Simon entered. And the child ran to him, crying, "Oh, Papa! Papa! Have you come to take me for a ride?"

He patted the boy's head, saying, "No. Not this morning." He drew the child towards the door to the old nurse's sitting room, and opening it, he called, "Are you there, nanny? Keep the boy with you for a few moments, will you, please?"

"Yes. Yes. Come here, my dear, come here."

Simon pressed the boy towards her, then closed the door, and now, turning to Anna, he said, "Good morning."

She was standing by the table. "Good morning," she answered.

He began to explain why he had interrupted the lesson. "I was informed that you were subjected to some annoyance yesterday."

He dropped down onto the child's stool, pointing to her chair and saying, "Sit down. Sit down. If you are to remain here, then I'm afraid that sooner or later you will be subjected, I am sorry to say, to my wife's temper. I am embarrassed—"

"Please, please, don't continue. I understand the situation. In the future I will endeavor not to arouse your wife's ire in any way. I have never been in service. I . . . I have the unfortunate knack of speaking my mind, and I have not as yet learned to be subservient."

She watched his face now break into a smile and his head wag. "Oh, Miss Dagshaw, you will, I think, in your life achieve many things, but subservience, never. You are your father's daughter if not your mother's, and they certainly have always been anything but subservient. And from what I gather, there's another mine strike impending, and your father is likely to arouse the wrath of the coal gods by sheltering some of the outcasts."

She stared at him. This family owned shares in the Beulah mine—his brother ran it—and yet here he was, speaking disparagingly of it. This was a strange family, all at odds. And she was finding it hard to understand, for she had been brought up among eight people who thought as one.

He was saying, "How are you getting on with the boy?"

"Oh, it's early yet, but I find him most receptive and bright, and he's a"—she paused—"warm, loving character."

The Love Child

Slowly he repeated, "A warm, loving character. Strange, that."

It seemed that the next instant he was standing on his feet, so promptly had he risen from the table. "My mother would like to see you later today. I assure you your interview will be different from your experience of yesterday. I'm glad you're here . . . to see to my son."

She made no reply as she now watched him walk towards the far door, open it, and say in quite a loud voice to his son, "Well, you, sir. Back to the grindstone!"

She smiled at Simon, then held out her hand to the boy, and as they went up the room she heard the door close and the father's voice, subdued now, talking to his old nurse.

It was two o'clock when Betty Carter again entered the schoolroom unceremoniously. Anna was sitting alone at the table going through some books, and the girl said, "Madam wants to see ya."

"Thank you," Anna said. "If you will lead the way."

On the landing, she gently pushed open a door and looked at her charge taking his afternoon nap; then she walked towards where the girl was standing impatiently at the top of the stairs. Once down the stairs, Betty Carter's hurrying step became almost a trot, and when Anna did not follow likewise, the maid stopped abruptly in the gallery, muttering, "Anything the matter with your legs?"

Anna did not answer, but with a gesture of her hand told her to go on. The girl glared at her, then rushed down the main staircase.

They carried on through a maze of corridors before stopping at an embossed, gray-painted door. Having rung the bell, the girl stood facing the door until it was opened by an elderly maid. "Madam wants to see her," Betty said under her breath.

The maid looked at the slim young person standing erect; then turning her attention to Betty again, she said, "We'll call you." The girl walked quickly away, and the older woman said, "Will you come in, please?"

The smile was pleasant; it was as if Anna had entered a different house. And this was confirmed when the maid escorted her across a hall, this, too, a pretty gray, into a small sitting room where a woman in a nurse's uniform said with a smile, "Will you come this way, please? Madam will see you now."

As she entered the large room it was the bed in the middle that drew her attention. Lying on it was a figure, with the head resting on a single pillow.

The nurse led her to the foot of this bed, and she looked at the pale face topped by a mass of white hair and was immediately struck by the brightness of the eyes. They were large, intelligent eyes. And then the person spoke, and the voice was as alive as the eyes when it said, "Bring Miss Dagshaw a chair, please, nurse."

A chair was brought, and Anna thanked the nurse and sat down. When the lady said, "Nurse, I shall need you in five minutes," Anna was aware that they now had the room to themselves.

"How are you finding my grandson?" The eyes riveted on her.

"An apt pupil, madam, and of a very pleasing disposition."

"How do you intend to instruct him?"

Anna paused before she answered. "Well, madam," she said, "I think he should become acquainted with the whole of the alphabet and that he should be able to count up, but gradually, to a hundred, during which time he will be doing little sums and putting his letters into one-syllable words."

"That seems practical and will lead to when he is due to have a tutor. . . . I understand you have been educated by your father?"

"Yes, madam."

"How did he instruct you?"

"Mainly through reading. He is a great reader."

"What did he advise you to read?"

"History, geography, and literature."

"Have you many books?"

"Not as many as we would like, madam."

"We have a good library here; you have my permission to take the loan of whatever you need."

"Oh, thank you, madam."

There was a long pause now while Anna had to bear the scrutiny of the bright eyes; and then the lady said, "I am sure you will instruct my grandchild well. One last thing—should at anytime anything be troubling you in this house, I would wish you to speak to the child's father or to Mr. Barrington, and they will convey the matter to me. Thank you, Miss Dagshaw."

As if a bell had rung on the lady's last words, the door opened and the nurse entered. Anna rose and said, "Thank you, madam." She did not dip her knee, but inclined her head gravely forward.

The Love Child

The nurse smiled at her, and she was handed over to the maid. When the door was opened for her, Anna said, "Thank you," and the maid said, "You're welcome." And this exchange brought the waiting upper housemaid's mouth agape.

As Anna followed Betty Carter back to the nursery she realized that having left madam's quarters, she had entered a hostile world.

WHILE the family was sitting round the fire that evening Nathaniel said, "Well, Oswald, tell Anna your piece of news."

Oswald now stuck his thumbs inside the straps of his braces. "I've been offered a position. Manager, with Olan under me."

"With Mr. Green?" Anna said.

"No. With Mrs. Simpson. You see, Anna, we go to this shop now and again near the riverfront for a pie-and-pea dinner. There used to be a man serving, elderly. Well, he was the boss, and he died. The mother and the daughter did the baking and such, and they had a lass in to help them. But there's some ruffians on that riverfront, you know. Well, 'twas last Wednesday I had told Olan here that he should try servicing the pies-and-peas place, so we brought the tray in. The place was a bit full, and it should happen that a drunken fella started to take liberties with the lass behind the counter, and so I went to stop him. . . ."

Olan laughed. "That's how he got his black-and-blue jaw. It was supposed to be from a bread tray falling on him."

"Never," cried Maria now. "You didn't tell me that."

"There was no need, Ma," Oswald said. "Anyway, the mother thanked me, and then she asked me what my job was. And the top and the bottom of it is, she's asked me if I'd manage the shop. And I can have Olan here as an assistant."

There was a nudge from Olan. "Tell her what she offered us."

"Well, me, twelve and six a week to begin with, and Olan, ten shillings; a rise every year and our cart fare paid."

Anna shook her head slowly as she said, "That's wonderful, marvelous. Are you going to take it?"

"I don't know." Oswald thumbed towards his brother now, saying, "We thought we should put it to Ma and Dada."

"How old is the woman?" It was Maria asking now. Olan said, "In her fifties, about fifty. And the daughter is twenty something, I would say."

Maria exchanged a twinkling glance with Nathaniel, then said, "Well, your dada should go have a look at the place."

Looking at Cherry, Anna said, "You've been quiet in all this."

Cherry didn't answer, but her father put in quietly, "Cherry witnessed something disturbing coming back tonight from the Praggetts'. You know the pit lad Bobby Crane? Well, he was attacked by two other pitmen, and they threatened what would happen to him if he didn't stop coming here. Apparently, he lettered a large notice for one of the men pushing the union, and our dear Mr. Praggett's henchmen set about the lad. And my brave daughter here"—he put his arm round Cherry's shoulder—"did some screaming, then took up a staff, and actually hit one with it. I think they were so astounded that they just went off."

"Oh, I am sorry. And oh, Cherry, you were brave to stand up to them. . . . Poor Bobby. What will he do now?"

"Well, he's not going back to the pit," Cherry said. "He's asked if he can stay in the barn tonight; but he's going into Gateshead tomorrow, and he says he'll take anything."

"Wait and see," her father said, then added, "Now then, to bed."

Anna did not rise with the others, but sat gazing into the fire for a moment, seeing there the child who needed love so much.

She started as her father's hand came on her shoulder and he said, "Where were you? What were you thinking?"

She looked up at him and said, "I was thinking how lucky we all are." And he said simply, "Thank you, daughter."

3

ANNA had two more encounters with the mistress before she left for London. The first one was in the schoolroom. It was about half past ten in the morning when Peggy Maybright, the nursery maid, scurried into the room, saying, "She's on her way."

"Who's on her way?"

"The mistress, so look out." She plonked down a tray of hot milk and biscuits, then went out as quickly as she had come.

Anna felt a tightness in her stomach. She made herself go about her duties: she put a bib on the boy, then poured out his hot milk. And he said, "Why don't you have milk, Missanna?"

"Because I prefer tea." Even while saying this, Anna half turned her head towards the door to the nurse's room, from where a voice was now coming. When the door opened to reveal the figure dressed in a riding habit, Anna told herself she must keep calm and keep her tongue quiet.

The child got down from his seat slowly and greeted his mother in a most polite manner. "Good morning, Mama," he said.

"Good morning, Andrew. What are you doing?"

"I am going to have my milk, Mama."

She looked down to the tray, then turned her cold gaze on Anna. "He should not be eating off a tray; a table should be set apart."

"I shall see to it, mistress."

"Yes. Yes, you will see to it." She now looked round the room, and when her gaze halted as she saw an easel, the child cried excitedly, "Papa bought that for Missanna to write on. It is called a black . . . board."

His mother walked towards the easel that supported the blackboard, and the child in his excitement ran to it and said, "This is a weasel."

"Easel. Say, easel."

"Yes, Mama, weasel. It . . . it is difficult, Mama, to say weasel."

The eyes were turned on Anna now. "Why haven't you done something about this?"

"It is an impediment of a sort, mistress. I'm aiming to cure it, but it will take time."

It was as if the child sensed the hostility and aimed to soothe it by saying, "I know my two-times table, Mama, and I can count on the ab . . . a . . . cus. And Missanna says I am—"

"Who is this Missanna?"

"Why"—the child put out his hand—"teacher is Missanna."

Now the voice was so loud that the child shrank back as his mother yelled at him, "She is the teacher, and you will call her teacher. You understand?" And it was a moment before the child answered, "Yes, Mama."

Slowly the woman turned towards Anna, saying, "In future you will report his progress to me every week. You understand?"

Anna couldn't force Yes, mistress through her lips.

"I am speaking to you, girl!"

Now she was answering, her words coming fast. "I am aware of that, mistress. Well, I am speaking, too, and let me tell you, I have no need to put up with your treatment. I was engaged by Andrew's father and take my orders from him. Is that plain?"

She watched the high collar of the riding habit move in and out as if the woman were choking, and she was prepared for the onslaught. The words were fired like bullets from a gun. "You slut, you! You lowborn slut! Get out of my sight before I take my whip to you!"

"Mama! Mama! Don't! Don't smack Missanna."

The sight of her son throwing his arms protectingly round Anna's waist was too much. Her hands grabbed the child's collar, and she actually flung him across the room. His screaming died away as his head hit the skirtboard and he became still.

There followed a deep momentary silence until the door from the sitting room flew open and the nurse hurried in.

Penella Brodrick was now leaning against the table, her hands gripping the edge. She didn't acknowledge the nurse or even turn her head when she heard the child begin to cry, but dragging herself up straight, she went from the room.

"Missanna. Missanna."

"I am here, dear. Don't cry, don't cry." Anna felt the back of the child's head where a bump was slowly rising, and she picked him up from the floor. "It's not cut, only a lump."

"She could have killed him," the nurse said. "But you, lass, your tongue'll get you hung. She's never been spoken to like that in her life. . . . Bring him in, and lay him on the couch."

A few minutes later, when the child was tucked up on the couch, the nurse stood beside the fire and looked down on Anna, who was now actually shivering. "Lass, you've got to learn to still that tongue."

"How could I? The things she said, the way she went for me."

"Aye, I heard it all. I've sharp ears. She takes some standing, she does. Of course it was her upbringing; she was spoilt from the day she was born. Rotten with money, on her mother's side anyway; French she was, so they tell me, but she had relations in Newcastle, and the mistress came to a dance here with them. She had all the men round her, like a queen bee, but from the beginning she had her eye on Mr. Simon, and he on her. An' then Mr. Raymond came into the picture. The three of them were always riding together. And then started the tug-of-war as to who was going to get

The Love Child

her. But who did she really want? Anyway, she marries Mr. Simon, and mind, she could give him three years, although she doesn't look her age."

The old woman walked towards the couch and looked down on the child, who was now asleep; and almost under her breath she said, "From the minute they came back from the honeymoon there was a change. Nobody knows to this day what happened."

"I can't stay here, nurse. I love the child, but it's impossible. . . ."

"And the child loves you, me dear. He's been a different boy since you came. Look, me dear." She now pulled a chair up and sat in front of Anna. "She'll be gone in a day or two. So stick it out. Mr. Simon's for you, and Mr. Timothy an' all. Just give it a day or two more, and you won't know you're in the same house."

"She doesn't seem sane. There's no reason for her attacks."

"Oh, that's what you think. Why, that woman is as jealous as hell of anyone Mr. Simon has a good word for. She dismissed her other maid, a good-looking lass with a fine figure, and her present one is as plain as a pikestaff. Come on, lass, cheer up. An' look"—she thumbed towards the couch—"there's somebody sitting up and taking notice."

The child came forward, saying, "Are you hurt, Missanna?"

"No. No, dear, I'm not hurt."

He climbed up on her knee and put his arms round her neck. "You won't go away and leave me, Missanna, will you?"

She looked into the innocent countenance, and she paused before she answered. "No, dear. I won't go and leave you."

That evening, sitting round the fire, she did not relate the event to the family. In any case, the interest was focused on the affairs of Bobby Crane, who had been offered a job of sorts in Gateshead Fell.

There was a small boatbuilder on the riverbank who wanted an apprentice. But the wage was very poor—only seven shillings a week—so would Nathaniel allow him to sleep in the barn until something better came along? He could offer two shillings.

"Heaven help him," Nathaniel had said. "I have already told him there would be no rent charged here. What I'm really pleased about is, he's so determined to keep up his learning, he'll go round the markets and pick up some cheap books. He's got the bug all right."

It was Cherry who put in, "He's even speaking differently. And he looked quite nice today. Ma had given him one of Olan's coats."

Leaning back against the head of the bench, Anna looked round at the fire-illuminated faces, and for the countless time she told herself there couldn't be another family on earth like this one.

THE mistress was leaving for London; and the bustle made itself felt on the nursery floor when Betty Carter rushed into the schoolroom and said, "Give him here! Peggy Maybright has to get him ready; the mistress wants to see him."

"Leave him alone!" Anna almost snapped the girl's hand from the child's arm. "He doesn't need to be got ready except that his hands need to be washed, and I will see to that. Kindly wait outside."

The girl drew herself up to full height. "One of these days . . ."

"Yes? One of these days, you were saying?"

Betty Carter flounced out of the room, and Anna said to the child, "Come along, dear," and went over to the table on which stood a basin and a ewer of water, and as she poured out the water the child said, "Why don't you take me down, Missanna?"

She paused for a moment before she said, "Your mama hasn't asked for me. Anyway"—she was drying his hands now—"it is you your mama wants to see. Now, be very polite, won't you? And tell her you hope that she has a nice holiday."

She took the boy to the door, where Betty Carter was standing with the light of battle in her eyes. And when Anna saw her thrust her hand out towards the child, she said quietly, "He is quite used to walking alone. Go along, Andrew."

IT WAS during the child's rest hour that Anna decided to take advantage of Mrs. Brodrick's offer of the use of the library. She knocked on the nurse's sitting-room door, and when the voice said, "Come in. Come in, my dear," she went in and said, "If you don't mind, nurse, I'm going to slip down to the library. I told you I had permission."

"Aye, yes, you did. Go to the foot of the stairs here, and a door opposite leads down to the west wing, and in the corridor there is a black oak door with a rounded top. Well, that's the library."

"Thank you, nurse." She went out and, following instructions, came to the black oak door with the arched top. When she opened

The Love Child

it and looked down the long room, she could only gasp at the magnificence of it. It had a painted, domed ceiling, and at the far end were two long windows looking onto the garden.

She turned her head first one way and then the other, and finally her gaze came to rest on a wide stone fireplace. At each side of the fireplace enormous glass bookcases filled the walls, but it was the long wall opposite the fireplace that held her interest. Apart from two small alcoves, the entire wall was made up of bookshelves holding what must be, she told herself, thousands of books.

She walked to one of the alcoves. About two and a half feet deep and four feet wide, the little place suggested study. She moved on, running her hand along a row of books. She must find her book and get back before the child woke. Along the shelves she noticed brass slots holding cards. One read SEVENTEENTH CENTURY, and the books here were in alphabetical order. And so she moved along to the next section, EIGHTEENTH CENTURY. There was Pope's *Essay on Man*. She took it from the shelf and looked farther along and was not disappointed: she took down Pope's translations of the *Iliad* and the *Odyssey* in one volume. Her dada had told her the story in the form of mythology; it was almost, to her, a fairy tale.

Anna wasn't sure when she actually became aware of someone talking. She looked up and down the room. Perhaps it was someone in the garden. She walked towards the windows and passed another door in the room. She noticed that it was slightly ajar, and she was startled as she recognized the mistress's voice coming from the room beyond.

She was about to turn and tiptoe up the room when the words that came to her halted her movement. "You'll come over to France, won't you, darling. Promise me?"

The master had been gone these last two days, and now the mistress was using endearments with someone.

"I promise you, my love. I promise you."

"But what about next week?"

"I'll be up there like a shot if those damn savages behave themselves. But if they come out on strike, well, I'll have to be here."

"Why can't the other two owners take their share?"

"I've told you, my dear one, I'm single minded in everything I do, what I own, what I manage, and . . . and whom I love."

As her mind opened to the situation presented by the words she had overheard, Anna turned, and at a tiptoeing run reached the alcove. There she made to snatch at the two leather-bound volumes, but they slipped from her fingers, landing flat on the floor with a loud plop.

She was in a panic as she stooped to pick them up, for she heard the door being pulled fully open, and trembling, she stood up to face the infuriated stare of Penella Brodrick.

Raymond Brodrick was at her side. His voice light and over-hearty, he said, "Ah, Miss Dagshaw, you are sampling the library?"

Before she could answer, the woman moved swiftly towards her, demanding, "What are you doing here?"

"I am choosing some books, mistress."

"Choosing some books? Who gave you permission?"

"Madam did."

The woman said to her brother-in-law, "Did you hear that?"

"Yes. Yes, I heard." And he looked at Anna and asked quite politely, "Did my mother give you permission?"

"I would not have said so, sir, nor would I have dared to take the liberty of entering this room if I—"

"I've told you," Penella Brodrick cried at Raymond. "The insolence of her! She wouldn't dare talk like that if he—"

"Be quiet! Be quiet!"

"I won't be quiet." She swung round to Anna again, ordering her, "Put those books down."

Slowly Anna put the books on the table, and immediately Penella Brodrick grabbed them up, and reading the titles aloud, she cried, "Pope's *Essay on Man!* The *Iliad* and the *Odyssey!* Don't have the effrontery, girl, to tell me that you can read these books!"

"Yes. I could read them and—"

"Penella!" Raymond had his hand on her upraised arm.

The books were now flung to the floor; the woman cried, "You insolent bastard! And you are a bastard, every inch of you, and from a litter of bastards birthed by a whore. . . ."

Anna watched Raymond Brodrick almost drag the infuriated woman down the library and through the door. Anna felt she was going to faint. She had dropped into the alcove seat and laid her head on her arms on the table when Raymond Brodrick's voice came quite plainly through the paneling, saying, "Why do you hate her so?"

The Love Child

"Because he's flaunting her at me."

"You don't mean—"

"Yes, I do mean. He's never away from the nursery now, and he hardly ever went there before, and you know the reason why."

"Penella, look at me. You say you love me. Why are you so concerned about who he may be taking to bed? You still care for him, don't you?"

"No, I *don't*. What I feel for him is hate. He tortured me for years with his silence. He ignores me except on occasions such as when he told me to leave her alone. Yes, do you know that? He warned me what will happen if I go up there again."

"But you never did frequent the nursery very much, did you? The child was always brought down. You've got to stop this, Penella; it'll burn you out."

"Oh, Raymond, Raymond, take me away. I have enough money for both of us, darling."

"You have enough money for yourself, my dear one, and your extravagant tastes, but not for us both. Anyway, I like the life I lead. I like to work, and I like to play. Now, come on; the carriage is waiting. I will see you next weekend, in London, then within a fortnight in Paris. Away you go now. Let me kiss you once more."

In the silence that followed, Anna raised her head, then pressed her hand tightly across her mouth as if to still the emotion that tumbled from it. The knowledge of the situation that had been revealed to her and the fact that she was implicated in it made her feel sick. She couldn't stay in this place; she would have to go.

As she attempted to rise, she felt dizzy—as if she had suffered a physical attack. Had she done so, it couldn't have hurt her more than had the verbal one. *Bastard!* It had a dreadful sound. The word implied something bad, dirty. And the woman had called her mother a whore.

She actually sprang up as the hand touched her shoulder. She thought for a moment that the woman had returned; then she was gaping up at Timothy, and he was saying, "Oh, my dear, I'm sorry I startled you. I . . . Oh, my dear, tell me what happened to upset you so."

"I can't explain, except to tell you that I must leave here."

"But why? She's gone, and all the tension has gone with her." He paused. "Did you see her before she left? I mean—"

"She was going to strike me. If it hadn't been for Mr.—"

She stopped as abruptly as she had started. And when he said quietly, "Go on," she said, "No, no."

"Raymond was with her?" When she remained silent, he turned his head slowly towards the paneling. "You overheard them talking in the next room? That's it, isn't it? And what you heard must have amazed you, and when she knew that you had overheard—"

"No, no," she put in. "No, I don't think she knew I had overheard. I dropped some books, and that must have told her there was someone in here, and unfortunately, the sight of me at any time seems to arouse her anger. She . . . she did not believe that I had been given permission to take the books, and she called me names."

When Anna stopped abruptly, he did not question her further. "She is a very unhappy woman," he said. "And not very intelligent. She's to be pitied, in a way. It is because you are young and learned and—" He smiled now before he said, "Beautiful." Then he added quickly, "Don't shake your head. I'm sure your mirror doesn't lie to you. Moreover, your straightforward manner must infuriate her, for you do not act like the servant class. You are an unusual girl, you know, and come from an unusual family. . . ."

"*Oh, yes, yes*"—she nodded now—"I come from an unusual family, and I'm never allowed to forget it."

"Please. I meant that as a compliment, believe me, for I admire your father and mother for the stand they took and the way they have brought up you and your brothers and sister."

She wanted to smile at him. He was so kind. He treated her like an equal, as did Mr. Simon. And for that woman to think that she and her husband— She would never be able to face him now.

"That boy up there loves you."

"What? Oh, yes, yes, the child. I'm very fond of him, too."

"Well then, how can you talk about leaving? Penella will not return before Christmas, and if she goes to France, where she still has relatives, it could be three months before she comes back. Come." He took her hand. "What will happen to me if you go? I will only have to trudge across that moor to see you."

As she rose to her feet she did smile at him, saying, "You should have been a diplomat; in fact, I think you are one. By the way, may I inquire how you have been feeling lately?"

"You mean the epileptic seizures? Oh, I have ceased to worry about them. But, strangely, I have not had a seizure since that day you came to my rescue. Well anyway, not a serious one. They first started after a shock, you know. We were in Switzerland, my half sister and I, and I saw the avalanche coming. I remember screaming a warning to her, and then it enveloped us both. But now my doctor thinks it may not be epilepsy. He has another name for it. You see, it all happens up here." He tapped his head. "One of the main cells decides it's not getting enough attention, so it hits out, and down I go fighting. And that's odd, because I'm a coward."

"Oh, Mr. Timothy, I think . . ."

"What do you think?"

"I think you're the nicest man I've ever met."

The color of his face changed; it was as if he were blushing. "Don't say that. Don't be too kind to me, or I may take advantage of it."

"I'm sorry. I didn't mean to up—"

"You didn't upset me, my dear. Anyway, now that the coast is clear, I would like to bring Andrew to visit your family sometime."

"Oh, you'd be welcome, Mr. Timothy."

"Ah, well, then there's going to be no more talk of leaving?"

She sighed before she said, "Well, not for the present."

"Good news. Now we can look forward to a happy Christmas, eh?"

4

IN THE weeks leading up to Christmas, 1881, Timothy had three times brought the child to visit them, and the boy had been enchanted with the long, cozy room, but more so with the family, and they with him. So it was proposed by Maria that Mr. Timothy and the child should be invited to their usual Boxing Day party.

Oswald and Olan had worked at the pies-and-peas shop up till one o'clock on Boxing Day, as did Cherry at the Praggetts', and Jimmy at farmer Billings'. But by three o'clock they were all ready to meet their guests: besides Timothy and the child, Miss Netherton was coming, and also Bobby Crane.

The lad had spent Christmas Day with them and surprised them with his ability to play the penny whistle almost as well as Oswald could play the flute. In consequence, the get-together round the fire after Christmas dinner had been a jolly affair.

Now it was Boxing Day and party day, and the room was packed.

The tea had been merry and noisy, the center of attraction being Andrew. Everybody seemed intent on making him happy, and if his squeals of delight were anything to go by, they had succeeded.

When the meal was over, the family cleared the table, which was then pushed to the end of the room to give space for some games. As Anna and Cherry removed the two lamps to the mantelpiece, and the candelabra to the windowsill, the child looked about him with open mouth, then turned to Anna and said, "It's like the story you tell me about Cinderella's palace."

This brought a great hooting laugh from Nathaniel, and gauging the moment to be right to start, he cried, "What game are we going to play first? Here we go round the mulberry bush, eh?" And nodding towards Oswald and Bobby, he said, "You know the tune."

And so, to the faint, sweet music of the two pipes, they joined hands and danced and sang until Miss Netherton stopped and, panting, sat down in a chair.

"Another game! Another game!" Andrew cried. "Let us play a dancing game, Missanna, like the one in the book."

"Oh, that was a polka."

Nathaniel, turning to Oswald, cried, "Play us a polka." And holding out his hand, he said, "Come on, Maria. Jimmy, you take Ben; Anna has already got her partner." He laughed to where the child was clinging to Anna's hands. And before he had time to appoint a partner for Bobby, Cherry went over and held out her hand. And while Oswald played a brisk tune Miss Netherton and Mr. Timothy clapped in time with the music.

After one and another had dropped out exhausted and laughing, Nathaniel said, "Well now, it's time for a little rest," and Jimmy put in, "Tell us a story, Dada. One of your ghosty ones."

"Blindman's buff!"

They all looked at Andrew and laughed, and Nathaniel said, "Well, I waive my right; the guest of honor's wishes must come first. Blindman's buff, it is."

"Missanna. Missanna, be blind man, and catch me."

Laughing now, she said, "Oh, all right."

The sound of a horse's neighing turned the attention of the party towards the door, and Mr. Timothy exclaimed, "That'll be the carriage! I said six o'clock, but it's only half past five."

"Oh, Uncle Timothy, we can't go home yet. Please, please."

When the door was opened, Timothy was the first to exclaim, "Oh, Simon. What a nice surprise!"

Nathaniel said, "Come in, sir! You're welcome."

"Oh, Papa, Papa, we are having a lovely party. We have danced and sung, and there are nice things to eat and—"

"All right. I'll hear all about it later." He patted his son's head. "Let me say how do you do to Mr. and Mrs. Martell." He turned to Maria and Nathaniel, saying, "Thank you not only for the kindness you have shown today but mostly for allowing your daughter to impart her knowledge to my son."

The words were very formal and seemed to dampen the atmosphere until Miss Netherton said, "Well, don't stand there, Simon;

come over and sit down. They are about to play blindman's buff."

"As you wish. As you wish." Simon was smiling now, and he went and stood near Miss Netherton's chair, while Oswald, taking a scarf, said to his sister, "Turn round, and no peeping, mind." After tying the scarf at the back, he swung her about three times, crying, "Ready! Set! Go!"

With hands stretched out before her Anna groped towards the giggles and the whisperings. "Where is that fellow who won't learn his lessons?" she called. "Where is he?"

Now she turned about and made her way towards the heat of fire. Once her feet touched the mat, she swung swiftly left, and from behind the armchair came giggling and scampering. And when

Cherry took up the chant in which the boys joined, "Name the one you want to catch;/name the one you want to hold," she answered, "I name the one I want to hold./It's Master Andrew, I make so bold."

When she heard the child's giggle, she made a little run in his direction and knew that someone had lifted him out of reach.

"Move round, move round./the blind man can't see./Be quick! Be quick!/Or he'll catch thee."

She could hear them all changing places. She moved towards the big armchair again, and she knew the child was there by the suppressed little squeak he made, and so, thrusting her hands quickly out, she made a dive for him. But she had misjudged the distance, and she realized her hands were gripping the lapels of a coat. She heard a child's voice shouting with glee, "You've caught Papa. You've caught Papa."

In the next second Anna pulled off the scarf, and there she was, looking into the unsmiling face of Simon. Withdrawing her other hand sharply from his coat, she picked up the boy from the chair and said lightly, "Why didn't you give me a better signal?"

"I did! I did, Missanna."

"Well, you didn't squeak loud enough."

"Can we have another game? Then you can catch me and—"

"No, no." His father was smiling now, speaking. "You've had enough for one day, and the horses are getting very cold, as is Grafton. And you know, when Grafton gets cold, what he does."

"He shouts."

Miss Netherton said to Simon, "I've ordered my trap for half past six, but I'd be more comfortable in your carriage if you would care to drop me."

"It would be a pleasure indeed."

There was bustle and chatting, and then they were all crowded round the door, and Timothy was saying, "I have no words with which to express my thanks. May I come again soon?"

Nathaniel and Maria's assurance of welcome was drowned by laughter as Miss Netherton said to Timothy, "You would make a wonderful professional beggar." Then, turning to the family, she said, "Thank you for a most happy time."

The child was saying his good-byes, shaking each hand, and saying, "Thank you. Thank you." Then as his father lifted him the child, of a sudden, reached forward and tugged Anna towards him, and with his lips pouted out, he kissed her—an audible kiss on the mouth. For a second her eyes were again looking into Simon's, and she gave a slight gasp and tried to loosen the child's grip. But he held on and said, "I love you, Missanna."

There were laughing murmurs all round her, and Simon was saying, "You must forgive my son for expressing his feelings so publicly." Then he said, "Good night. Good night, all," and made his way towards the carriage.

They watched until the lights of the carriage had disappeared through the gate; then they made for the warmth of the fire, and a quietness seemed to descend on them. Presently Oswald said, "It's one of the nicest Christmases I can remember, and we've had some nice ones, haven't we, Dada?"

"Yes, Oswald. But I think this is the nicest because we've made a child happy, and he needed to be made happy."

"Oh, I know what you mean, Mr. Martell," said Bobby. "An' I've watched the bairn the day; it's just as if he had been let loose." And then with a look at Maria he said, "You'll never know really what you've all done for me this Christmas. To me dying day I'll remember it."

Cherry laughed, her mouth wide, saying, "I can see how they wanted to throw you out of the pit; you talk too much."

Their reactions to something funny were back, and again there was general laughter, for the whole family had noted how the young fellow hardly ever opened his mouth.

IT WAS after the two girls had lain silently in bed for some time that Cherry said softly, "I like him."

"Who?"

"Bobby."

Anna turned on her side. "What d'you mean, you like him?"

"I'm not quite sure, Anna. Neither of us have had the chance to meet boys. But to my mind Bobby seems to stand out. He did, even in his pit clothes. But I'm older than him."

"Oh, it's how you feel; it's got nothing to do with age. What is he? Seventeen, and you're eighteen. If you like Bobby, get to know him better. Anyway, you know nothing could happen for years."

"I know that, but I can hope."

"Well, go on hoping, dear; it's better than no hope at all."

After a moment Cherry said softly, "There's someone interested in you, but there's no hope in that quarter, and I feel sorry, I do."

"What d'you mean?" Anna was half sitting up in bed.

"Oh, you know what I mean. You could see the way he looked at you when you were holding his lapels in blindman's buff."

"Cherry Dagshaw! Don't ever bring that subject up again."

"All right, all right. Lie down. If I had my doubts before how you felt, you've dispelled them now."

Anna gripped the edge of the feather mattress. She would have to leave that place; there must be no waiting.

PART FOUR
The Blow
1

THE winter of 1881–82 had been severe. She hadn't kept the promise to herself to give up her post, telling herself that the child needed her. However, she was relieved whenever the heavy falls of snow made her visits impossible.

The severest snowstorm occurred in February. Huge drifts blocked the roads, and when eventually the thaw came, the rivers flooded much of the land; only the moors seemed to escape. And perhaps this was as well, for three pit families had made their home on the moors, as near as possible to Nathaniel's woodland fence in order to get a little shelter from the trees.

The families had been there for three days before Nathaniel and Anna came across them, and they were aghast at the sound of a child coughing its heart out under one of the rough tarpaulin shelters. One man had a fire going in a tin box and a kettle swinging on a tripod over it. Nathaniel spoke to him across the railing, saying, "Dear, dear! This can't go on. You know you could have used the barn; others before you have done so."

The man came towards the fence now and spoke in a quiet voice. "Aye, I know that, mister. You've been very good, and you needn't have been, but we didn't want any more trouble to come on you. The next day or two we'll get something; if not, the workhouse will have us. But that'll be over me dead body. I'm a union man, mister. The three of us are, and there's many more back there. If they'd only stand up for what they think. That's why we're here. We tried to get them out, and that bloody keeper, Praggett, put his oar in again."

"Why is it Praggett always has the last say in the evictions?"

"Oh, well, mister, he just works to orders an' all. And it's been worse since Morgansen, the second owner, come up from London and put his nose in. I suppose cos of his lass goin' to marry Brodrick. An' Brodrick's lordin' it an' all since his old man died."

Looking at the man, Anna wondered, What was this about Mr. Raymond going to marry the other mineowner's daughter? Oh dear, what about his brother's wife? What would she do now? How would she react?

Penella was wintering in the south of France; and except for the two weeks of deep mourning for the loss of the master, Arnold Brodrick, the news of whose death had only reached them a week after he had been buried in some remote area abroad, the house had taken on a peaceful air. And Anna had felt herself to be accepted more and more by the staff, with one exception: Betty Carter, the upper housemaid. Maybe it was because Betty had been bred in the village and was the blacksmith Robert Lennon's niece.

Her father was saying to the pitman, "Why won't you accept the barn? It is weatherproof and warm, and that child needs shelter."

"We would like to, mister, but Praggett tells us that if any more of us are given shelter from you, they can ring off the land, and then you would have no way out for your cart, and the only other way on foot would be through the village. And we know that you've had trouble there as well."

Nathaniel cried, "They cannot enclose us; the moor is common land. And we are bounded by farmer Billings' land."

"Aye, well, you know, sir, Billings only rents the farm from the Brodricks. It's their land, you see. And Brodrick must be out to please Morgansen, seein' as he is goin' to join his family."

"There are public rights of way that even all the Brodricks and Morgansens have no control over. Now get yourselves into the barn. There's plenty of wood to keep the boiler going, so you needn't worry. . . . Fencing us in, indeed!" He turned and said to Anna, "Did you hear that? What will they try to do next?"

"Well, they've said it before, Dada, and they'll likely carry out their intent and leave us to fight it after."

"Just let them try. What a pity Miss Netherton's away! I know nothing about the law."

The Love Child

ANNA HAD HARDLY REACHED THE landing before the nurse's sitting-room door opened and the old woman said, "Oh, lass, 'tis good to see you again. Come in, come in. He's all ready and waitin'. Here, give me your hat and coat, and let me have your news. I hear they've started fencing the land in. How's your da taking that?"

Anna gave the old woman a brief account of her father's worries, but went on to say that, otherwise, the family were all fine.

"Oh, lass, you should have been here yesterday. There was high jinks downstairs. Her Ladyship returned the previous night, and Grayson said he had seen happier faces at a funeral than was round the dining table. Yesterday she had a screaming match in the library with Mr. Raymond. Then he came upstairs and told his man to pack a case, and off he went. And all this, you know, because of his engagement. When Mr. Simon came in later, well, this led to another shindy and then another black dinner." Here the door burst open, and the child darted in, crying, "Oh, Missanna! I knew it was you. Have you come to stay now the snow has gone forever?"

The boy had his arms round her, and she wanted to bend and kiss him. But all she did was stroke his hair back and ask him, "Have you been a good boy and kept reading your books?"

"Oh, yes, Missanna. And I have teached Peggy."

"Taught Peggy."

He gave a gurgle of a laugh and repeated, "Taught Peggy."

Anna thought to herself how she would miss him, because soon the fencing would cut off the road to the gate, and she would have to walk through the village before she could reach the gig. And having to walk through the village would provide her an excuse for leaving.

It was as she was about to take a cup of coffee in with the nurse that Betty Carter appeared in the classroom; no knocking, just an abrupt opening of the door and that broad, thick twang saying, "The mistress wants you downstairs."

"And where does she wish to see me?" Anna asked.

"Where d'you think?" The girl went out, banging the door.

Anna tapped on the nurse's door, and at the "Come away in, lass," Anna said, "The mistress wishes to see me downstairs."

"Oh, dear, dear. Well, all I can hope for is, she's in a better temper. But now, lass"—she put her hand on Anna's shoulder—"just stand there and take it. The others do; so learn a lesson."

"I'll try, nurse. That's all I can tell you. I'll try."

A voice from behind said, "Can I come with you, Missanna?"

"Not now, dear. You come and sit with nurse." She bent to him, and in a stage whisper said, "See if she can recite the alphabet." And she pressed the boy towards the old woman, then went out. But at the top of the stairs she hesitated. That girl hadn't said where she would find the mistress. Perhaps she was in the library. And so she made for the library, only to find no one. Oh, that girl. She should go and find her, but that would mean keeping that woman waiting. The only other place the mistress might be was in the studio. So it was to the studio that Anna made her way.

She tapped on the door, but heard no reply, then knocked again; and when she wasn't bidden to enter, she gently pushed the door open, and in one sweeping glance she took in the chaotic scene. Canvases were strewn over half the floor, some with holes in them, others ripped across. On the easel was a full-length picture of a naked man. Dripping paint almost obliterated his face and had run down his chest onto his loins; but although the face was hardly recognizable, she knew the picture to be that of Mr. Raymond.

Looking about her at the chaos, she came to the frightening realization that she must get out of here, and quickly, before—

But she was too late, for through the open door now strode the enraged figure of the mistress. "You. You. How dare you! You were sent for to my office."

"I . . . I didn't get any directions, mistress, so—"

"Shut up. Shut that yapping, slimy mouth of yours!" She was advancing now, and Anna steeled herself for a blow. "Legal separation and . . . and then divorce so your bastards would be recognized. That's it, isn't it? But I'll see you in hell first! You brazen black-haired bastard, you."

The hand wasn't extended towards Anna but to a palette thick with still wet paints, and though Anna knew what was about to happen, she wasn't quick enough in jumping aside. The palette came flat against her shoulder. Then as she screamed, a heavy object hit her on the side of the head, and she felt liquid flowing over her face. She knew that the woman was screaming, too, but Anna was sliding down into somewhere, and she mustn't let herself faint, because that woman might kill her. As she felt her body hit the floor she knew that now there were more people screaming.

Unaware that she'd had her eyes shut, she now opened them to see the tall figure of Simon Brodrick pushing his wife against the wall. She couldn't make out what either of them was yelling, but she saw him lift a hand and catch his wife a blow across one side of her face. The woman bounced from the wall, and when Anna saw him grip her by the shoulders and throw her onto the floor, she again closed her eyes.

A voice was crying, "Anna, Anna! Wake up! Are you all right?" She opened her eyes to look into Timothy's face, and then the housekeeper's voice came to her as if from a distance, saying, "The blood's coming from just above her ear, I think, sir."

They helped her up and led her from the room. There were more people in the corridor. There was something spilling over her face. She seemed to be floating; then someone thrust her down into some dark place. . . .

She became aware that she was lying on a bed. There was someone speaking near her. She recognized the voice as Mr. Timothy's. Dear Mr. Timothy. He was saying, "When did you tell her that?" The answer came. "Last night. I'd had enough. To make a show of herself like that with Raymond. It was impossible to bear. So I told her, a legal separation and then divorce."

"What about the child?"

"I said she could have custody of him, but you'll not believe it; she doesn't want him. I told her his father should have him."

"Oh, Simon, Simon, you didn't."

"I did. And it was about time. I've lain under this since she spewed it at me during our honeymoon, because I knew then I hadn't been the first. And she had the nerve to tell me who had."

Timothy's voice came again. "Have you flaunted the girl to her?"

"No. No, definitely not."

Then Mr. Timothy's voice. "I am not blind. I know of your feelings towards her. You think, or you have the impression, that she cares for you?"

Anna, awake now, waited for the answer; and then it came. "I don't know, but I mean to find out. The fact that she's put up with Penella's insanely jealous antics gives me hope."

"I . . . I wouldn't bank on it. She's very fond of the child."

"Yes. Yes, I know. Still, we'll see what transpires in the future. Now I must go to Mother. She'll have heard about this already."

There was the sound of a door closing. Then she felt Timothy's hand on her brow lifting her hair gently to the side, and she heard a whispering voice, saying, "Oh, my dear. My dear."

There was such feeling in the words that she wanted to cry and to put her hand up and stroke the cheek of this kind, thoughtful man.

Slowly she opened her eyes, and he said, "How are you feeling?"

"Tired."

"Yes, my dear. Just rest. The housekeeper is going to prepare a bath for you so you can wash your hair. It was linseed oil."

She put a hand up to her hair. "I shall never come back into this house again. . . . She is mad."

"No"—he shook his head—"not mad. She is very unhappy. Spoilt women are often unhappy, I have found."

"I would rather go home and wash there."

"No, my dear. You're in no condition to go home yet. Do this to please me because, may I say it, we are friends, aren't we?"

"If you say we're friends, Mr. Timothy, then we are friends."

"Do you think you could say Tim?" He smiled.

She made no answer, but found that her lids were closing. She did feel sleepy, and as he said, she couldn't go home like this. Perhaps later.

IT WAS three o'clock in the afternoon. Mrs. Hewitt had helped her wash her hair and then supplied her with a dress and put a bandage round her head to cover the cut behind her ear. She was now sitting in a room off the hall, her coat and hat on, and Simon was standing in front of her. He was saying, "The child is going to miss you desperately." Then he added softly, "And I, more than he." She looked up into his face, but didn't answer. And he said, "If you feel strong enough, my mother would like to have a word with you. Do you think you could see her? I will take you along."

"There won't be any need; I . . . I would rather go on my own."

"We must talk, Anna. You know that, don't you?"

She stepped back, saying in a tone as harsh as she could make it at that moment, "No! No, I don't!"

"Anna, look, I will come see you. You must know; you must have guessed."

"Please, please, don't say any more."

He bowed his head, then went to open the door, and walked

The Love Child

slightly ahead of her until they reached his mother's bedroom; then tapping on the door, he entered, saying, "Miss Dagshaw, Mother."

Again she walked across the large room to the foot of the bed and looked into the bright eyes, which were so like Mr. Timothy's.

"I am deeply sorry you have had to be subjected to such awful treatment in this house, Miss Dagshaw," Mrs. Brodrick said.

Anna could not think of a reply, so she remained still.

"You require an apology at least, and . . . and I'm sorry it must come from me alone, as my daughter-in-law stresses the fact that you were asked to see her in her office, but you went into her studio."

"Madam, I am sorry to interrupt you, but I was just told to come down and see the mistress. There was no explanation of where I must see her. I had never been to her office. She had spoken to me once in the library and once in her studio. When she wasn't in the library, I naturally went to the studio."

"I understand that the message was given to the upper housemaid and that she passed it on to you."

"I'm sorry, madam, but you have been misinformed. Had I known I had to see your daughter-in-law in the office, I should not have gone to the library."

"No, of course you wouldn't. . . . Nurse, tell them to send the upper housemaid to me. And place a chair for Miss Dagshaw."

The chair was brought, and Anna was thankful to sit. And then Mrs. Brodrick said, "What will you do now? Perhaps you will marry?"

The blue gaze held hers until she said, "I have no intention of doing so yet, madam."

The door opened, and the nurse brought in Betty Carter. The girl was definitely nervous, and she dipped her knee. And then Mrs. Brodrick said, "Tell me exactly, girl, what order your mistress gave you when she wished to speak to Miss Dagshaw."

The girl wetted her lips, her head moved slightly. " 'Go and tell the teacher to come to my office. I wish to speak to her.' "

"And what did you say to Miss Dagshaw?"

"I . . . I told her that, madam."

Anna turned her head. "You did not mention the office."

"I did so. But your nose was too high in the—"

"Look at me, girl!" Mrs. Brodrick's head was raised. "I am saying that you are lying, that you merely told Miss Dagshaw that your mistress wanted to see her. Isn't that so?"

"No, madam. She's lying. I said, 'Go to the office.' I did."

"Then why did she first go to the library, then to the studio? You are lying, aren't you?"

The girl was looking into the cold blue eyes now, and her own lids were blinking rapidly. Then she burst out, "Well, madam, she's so hoity-toity. She never listens. She acts like—"

"Be quiet, girl. Nurse, send for Mrs. Hewitt immediately."

"Yes, madam."

Mrs. Brodrick turned to the girl again, and now she said, "You were aware that your mistress didn't want anyone to go near her studio this morning, weren't you? Lift your head and look at me."

The girl lifted her head slowly. "I . . . I knew she was in a temper, that's all."

The door opened again, and Mrs. Hewitt scurried in and dipped her knee to the old lady, saying as she did so, "Madam?"

"Hewitt," Mrs. Brodrick said, "you will take this girl and dismiss her. Give her a week's wage, but no reference, for she has been the means of causing a disturbance in my house."

Anna wished to protest, Oh, don't do that. It'll only make things worse for us in the village. But looking into those blue eyes, she knew she would not be believed. And so she remained silent.

Mrs. Hewitt went to take Betty Carter's arm, but rounding on Anna, the housemaid cried, "You watch out; our lads will have you for this."

"Get her out of here." The voice was small now; the blue eyes were closed.

The nurse, holding a glass to her mistress's lips, beckoned to Anna. She rose to her feet, and the nurse whispered, "Madam gets easily tired. You understand?"

She nodded, then went out through the corridors until she entered the main hall, where Simon was standing.

Moving towards her, he said, "Are you all right? You are so white." And she answered, "I'm all right; but I think it has been a trying time for madam. I think she may need you."

"I'll see you to the carriage first."

He helped her into the covered carriage, then placed a rug over her knees before saying, "I will call tomorrow and see you."

The Love Child

"Please don't. I beg you."

"Someone must deliver your dress when it is laundered, and if they cannot get it clean, you must be compensated for it."

She turned her head away; he closed the door, then gave a signal to the coachman, and the horses walked sedately forward.

Anna leaned back against the padded seat. She felt ill and tired. Her head was aching, as was the cut behind her ear. Fortunately, the bowl had only grazed the skin. If the aim had been true, it could have killed her.

Well, she was free. . . . But was she? He would come tomorrow, and the scene would be painful. But now she asked herself, Would it have been so painful this time last week? Behind her closed lids was the picture of a man taking his hand and bringing it with force against one side of his wife's face, then knocking her to the floor. Yet, had he not suffered at that woman's hands by deceit . . . and worse? But then, had not her dada suffered at *his wife's* hands, too. Moreover, he'd had to scrape for years to keep her at bay.

She looked down the years stretching ahead and knew that her life would indeed be barren if she waited until she found a man whom she could compare with her dada.

2

THE following morning Anna was sitting in the big chair by the fire, with a rug over her knees.

She looked from her mother to her father and said, "I'm half expecting a visitor, and, please, Ma and Dada, I'd be grateful if you didn't leave me alone during the time he is here."

They both looked hard at her, and Nathaniel answered for them both, "As you wish, my dear, as you wish. . . ."

It was half past eleven when Simon arrived. After politely greeting Maria and Nathaniel, he said to Anna, "I'm very sorry, but they can't get your dress clean, and I'm afraid I must replace it." After a pause he asked quietly, "How are you feeling?"

"Almost quite well, thank you. Will you take a seat, sir?"

"Thank you. I'm on my way to town, but I thought I might call and"—he glanced at Anna—"express my regrets for what happened yesterday."

When neither of her parents spoke, he turned to Anna again and said, "We have a very unruly boy on our hands this morning. I think I must see about a tutor for him straightaway."

"You told him that . . . that I wouldn't be coming back?"

"Yes, I did. I thought it would be better to do so, but regretted it at once because we had tears and stamping of feet."

"Children soon adjust," said Maria. "With love and kindness they soon forget."

"Well, in his case, I hope so." Simon got to his feet, and looking from Anna to Maria, he said, "Would it be in order if, when I'm in the city, I make arrangements for a dress to be sent—"

"No, sir." It was Nathaniel speaking. "My daughter is not short of dresses, as my wife is very clever with her needle."

After a moment's pause Simon again looked at Anna, saying, "I will call soon, if I may, to see how you are faring." She simply inclined her head, and he turned and went out, followed by Nathaniel. But immediately outside the door he said, "I'm sorry if you took my suggestion in the wrong way, sir . . ."

"I knew how your suggestion was meant, Mr. Brodrick, but you are a man of the world, and my daughter is a young and vulnerable girl. So I ask you to imagine the tale that would be woven if it became known that Mr. Brodrick from The Manor is buying clothes for one of Nathaniel Martell's daughters."

Simon nodded. "Yes. You are quite right, sir, quite right. However, I hope you will have no objections to my calling again?"

"It will all depend upon the purpose of your visit, sir."

"Well, Mr. Martell, I hope to make that plain within a short while, or at least when I am lawfully free to do so."

Nathaniel stared at this very presentable man who seemed determined to court his daughter while still married. And if he won her heart, would he bother to get his freedom? And then would his dear, dear Anna do what her mother had done? No, that must not happen.

Simon bowed towards him and said, "Good day to you, sir."

Nathaniel didn't wait to see him ride away. Instead, he returned indoors and went straight to Anna. "Do you like that man?"

Her gaze was unflinching. "Yes, Dada, I like him."

"But do you love him?"

Now she looked towards the fire. "A few days ago I would have said yes. Now I am far from sure." She couldn't bring herself to say, Because I saw him knocking his wife to the floor.

The Love Child

THE SECOND VISITOR FROM THE house was given a different welcome. Timothy came in carrying four beautiful orchids in a wrapped box. "Aal grown be me own 'and, ma'am," he said in broad dialect.

"Oh, Mr. Timothy."

"Ah, ah, ah! What did we say about prefixes? I want the mister knocked off."

"Well, that is easily done . . . sir. But let me first say what extremely beautiful blooms. And you grew these?"

"Yes. It's my only talent," he replied.

"Tim"—Anna stressed his name now—"will you please sit down; and my mother here, I am sure, is dying to ask you if you would like a drink."

He turned to Maria. "Well, Mrs. Martell, I would indeed. You make tea better than anyone else I know."

When Maria left the room to go to the kitchen, Anna asked, "Did you come in the gig?"

"Yes, I did. I came on my own."

"Well, in that case," Nathaniel remarked, "I'll get Ben to help me put your horse into the barn; it's spitting on to rain."

The room to themselves, Anna looked at Timothy and said, "Was that wise to drive the gig yourself?" And he, all merriment now gone from his face, replied, "I had a slight turn after yesterday's do and seeing you in that state. You know, you're the only one to whom I can speak of it."

She took hold of his hand and said, "Thank you for your trust, Tim. It . . . means a lot to me."

He stared into her face for a while, then turned his head away, towards the fire. "You've had a visit from Simon already. Are you aware of his intentions?"

"Yes. Yes, I'm aware of them."

His head jerked round towards her, and he said, "Well, are you—Well, he intends to divorce her. But that'll take time because he has to have proof, and the only proof he could offer at the moment is his intention of marrying someone else, and exposure might then wreck other lives. You understand that?"

"Yes, Tim, I understand." Then very quietly she said, "I am not going to do what my mother did. Even should my feelings direct me, I am not strong enough. We always have been a happy family, but there has been a shadow over us from our birth. We have all suffered from it, and I wouldn't ever bring that on anyone else."

He was holding both her hands. "I understand, my dear."

There was the sound of voices coming from the kitchen, and so, releasing his hold of her, he said in a clear voice, "I have news for you now. I am setting up my own establishment."

"No! Really? Where? Far away?"

"No, not at all far. It's at this end of Fellburn. Briar Close. It's a nice house but very small, so it will only need a small staff. I would love you to see it and perhaps advise me on decorating. I'll be able to work there in peace. And there's a small conservatory."

"Is this a new idea?" she asked quietly.

"No, not really. But one gets tired of being a buffer. There's going to be changes in The Manor, whether Penella goes or stays. I've always been fond of Simon—and Raymond, too—but the brothers never cared much for each other. So there was always buffering needed. I am their uncle, but I never felt old enough for the position—my half sister is quite a few years older than I. Anyway, now that Raymond is top man in the family, things have changed. It's amazing what a little power will do."

Maria entered the room with a tray on which were two cups of tea, and when Anna said, "Aren't you having one, Ma?" Maria replied, "Yes. But I'll wait until your father and Ben come back from the barn." She went out smiling, and Anna, taking a cup of tea and saucer, handed them to Tim, saying, "Drink this while it's hot."

After sipping the tea Tim remarked quietly, "I suppose you know that Simon is not the father of the child?"

"Yes. I gathered that some time ago. So may I ask you why she married one brother while she loved the other?"

"Oh, she married the one she loved; that was after she had made him jealous enough. Yet I shouldn't say that, because he loved her, too. She's continued to love him while flaunting her association with Raymond, hoping, I suppose, that jealousy once again would stir him to prove his love for her. But it hasn't worked. And she sees Andrew as the cause of all her misery. Raymond, I'm sorry to say, couldn't care less about parenthood. And until recently, too, Simon had resented the child. Naturally. But, in law, the child is Simon's responsibility, and he must see to his future."

He took another sip from his cup, then smiled wryly as he said,

"Life is a strange affair, isn't it, Anna? Of late I have come to think there is a pattern in it, a certain plan. You know"—his face brightened now—"if I had never had the seizure in that field and you hadn't been sawing wood at that particular time, we would never have met and I wouldn't be sitting here with you now. Instead, I should have gone on being aware of the emptiness in my life. But since you've come into it, my dear, the whole aspect has changed."

"Oh, my dear Tim." She smiled at him now, and there was a little quirk to her lips. "You talk just like my father."

"Well, I could have been. I am thirty-six, thirty-seven . . . just about." And he laughed. "You, I think I am right in saying, are nineteen. So I am in a position to have been your father."

She looked into his kind, attractive face and asked herself, Why had he been afflicted like this?

He was saying now, "You will marry someday, and likely soon, but I would like to think, Anna, that whoever he is, he will accept—" His voice was cut off by Nathaniel coming in, followed by Ben, who cried, "It's a beautiful horse, sir. He let me stroke him."

"Did he?" said Tim. "Well, you are indeed favored because he's very particular as to whom he allows to take liberties."

With Maria's entry into the room, the conversation became general, and after a short while Timothy rose to his feet. "I always outstay my welcome here. It is unpardonable, yet you are all to blame. But I must away now." Good-byes were said, and he went out, accompanied by Nathaniel.

Maria went to the window and said, "There he goes. What an affliction to have! A life ruined, and no prospect."

"Oh, Ma, I don't think he needs to be so pitied. He writes, and he grows orchids, and he reads a great deal."

"What's that for a man of his standing"—she turned—"when he'll never have a woman in his life?"

As Anna watched her pick up the tray her mind confirmed her mother's words: *He would never have a woman in his life.*

Two days later the sun was shining, the air was warm, and Maria said, "Why don't you take Ben and go for a little stroll. You look peaky. See how far they've got with their railing us in. Oh, I do wish Miss Netherton was here. They expected her home last week."

Anna made no protest. She put on an old coat and went out. Her mother, she knew, was uneasy about the fencing. She wondered why Simon, knowing how it would curtail their liberty, had not spoken of it. But it was his brother who was in charge.

"Ben, Ben," she called. "Are you coming for a walk?"

The boy stopped digging in his patch and looked up. "Where?"

"Oh, as far as we can go along the quarry top." She walked over to him, adding, "They can't take that away from us."

The boy stuck his spade into the ground. "Must you go for a walk?"

"No. But go on with your digging if you don't want to come."

"Oh, I want to be with you, Anna. I'll come."

They walked side by side along the quarry top, to where the quarry itself petered out with only a four-foot drop from the path, which merged into the moor.

"They've stopped the fencing by the side of the beet field," said Ben. Then suddenly he cried out, "Look, Anna," and when she followed his pointing finger, she couldn't believe what she was seeing. "Can't be!" she said. Then she shouted, "Andrew! Andrew!"

The little figure in the far distance stopped for a moment, then came scrambling towards her, and she ran to meet him, her mind exclaiming, Oh, my God! How has he got this far?

"Oh, Missanna." He was clinging to her, his face awash with tears. "I've been looking for you. Please come back."

"Oh, my dear." She lifted the child up in her arms and stumbled back across the uneven ground to the path. There she put him down and said to Ben, "We'll have to get word to the house. They'll be looking for him."

"No. I don't want the house, Missanna. I want to stay with you."

Ben turned round. "Look," he said.

Galloping across the moor came two riders. "It is Mama, Missanna. 'Tis Mama. I don't want to go back."

"Be quiet, Andrew. Be quiet."

As the two horses drew almost to a skidding stop within a few feet of them, Anna had to grab the two children and jump back. She glared up at the woman, who now glared down at her. "How dare you! You steal my husband, and now you have taken my child."

"I have only this moment found the boy; he was wandering!"

"You told him when to come and how to come." Jerking her head to the side, she cried, "Pick the boy up, McBride."

The Love Child

The man jumped from his horse, and when he put his hands on the boy's shoulders, the child kicked out at him, crying, "No, No! I want to stay with Missanna." As the child broke free and made to run under the horse's head, Ben pulled him away.

Whether it was the woman cracking her whip or pulling on the horse, or the two children together startling the horse, it reared, and instinctively Anna pulled the child clear. But Ben remained where he was, and the hoof came down on the side of his head and lifted him in the air over into the shallow dip of the quarry. Anna sprang at the woman, aiming to tear her from the saddle, and the whip came down across the side of Anna's face, blinding her for a moment. Then she was screaming and struggling to get away from the man's hold. She saw the woman ride to the edge of the dip and say, "He's moving. He's only stunned." Then the man let go of her and lifted the crying, thrashing child into his mother's arms.

When Anna looked over the edge of the quarry to see the still form of her brother lying crumpled among the stones, she cried, "Oh, my God!" The man halted his horse and looked back at her, as if he were going to dismount again; then he changed his mind and rode after his mistress.

She scrambled down the bank now and lifted Ben's head onto her arm, crying, "Ben, Ben! Come on. Wake up!" She patted his cheek. But when his head fell limply to the side, she cried aloud, "No! No!" Then she lifted the boy, and staggering like someone drunk, she carried him back along the path and through the cottage gate. There she started yelling, "Ma! Ma!"

Maria met her halfway. "What's happened! What's happened?"

"She did it! She did it! With her horse. She did it!"

Maria lifted her son into her arms and ran back into the house and laid him on the mat. And she felt all over him; then, in a low agonized voice, she said, "My lad is dead. He's dead, Anna. Ben is dead." And when Anna screamed and continued doing so, Maria shook her by the shoulders while yelling at her, "Stop it! Stop it, girl. Go and get help," only to say in further distress, "Oh, no! No!" for the red weal on Anna's face was oozing blood. But she pushed her towards the door. "Go to Miss Netherton's. Tell Rob Stoddart to get the doctor."

"But he's dead, Ma."

"Go on! Go on!" Maria, half crazy now, screamed, "Run! Run!"

Anna didn't remember running to Miss Netherton's house. She didn't remember the doctor's coming; nor did she remember Simon and Timothy standing before her father with bowed heads.

It wasn't until the fourth day, when she rose from her drugged sleep and saw the coffin lying on the trestle table and looked down on Ben's face, that she finally realized he was dead.

But she remembered the following day, when she stood by his grave and Parson Mason said kind words over him. The family had come in two cabs; the carriage from The Manor, holding Simon and Timothy, followed, and beyond that another carriage, in which sat Miss Netherton. There were also half a dozen people from the village, only that same night to be censured by the clients in The Swan.

The bar was packed, the counter aflood with spilled beer. Willie Melton, the painter, stood at the end of the counter and looked across to where Robert Lennon, the blacksmith, was seated by the fireplace, and he said, "Well, I can understand old Miss Smythe following them, and Roland Watts, but for John Fenton and his Gladys to go to the cemetery . . . Well, that beats me."

A voice shouted from the other end of the barroom, "It should have been no surprise to you or anybody else, Willie." It was Dan Wallace, the shoemaker. "I've always said they've kept themselves to themselves. Asked us for nowt and weathered some bad times. An' we could name names who helped with those bad times. I think it beholds everybody to live and let live."

Robert Lennon took a long draft from his mug, then looked at Dan. "You should talk like that to Parson Fawcett."

"I could an' all."

"Aye, well, I'd like to be there an' hear you. An' does your opinion cover the mischief that that one's done? All right, all right, the bairn was killed, but accidentally. But what happened up at The Manor when Mr. Simon found out that the bairn was dead? He goes back and nearly tries to do his wife in. It took two men to get him off her. Now why did all that happen, eh? It happened cos that hussy, not satisfied with tempting the husband, had tempted the bairn. It was a natural thing for the mother to go after it and to raise the whip. I would have done it meself."

"Oh, aye, you would. There's no doubt about that," said the shoemaker. "Strikes me you've wanted to do it for years."

The Love Child

"Now, now, gentlemen. Now, now!" Reg Morgan intervened from behind the counter. "We all know who's right and who's wrong in this business. Don't forget what Betty Carter said happened to her. Thrown out on her face she was, and blamed for that hoity-toity miss being covered in paint. And as Michael Carter and his lad said when Betty came back cryin', if it was left to them, they would have tarred and feathered her, not just covered her with paint."

During all the talk the blacksmith's younger son, Arthur, had said nothing, but looked from one to the other as if studying some deep point. When he muttered something, his father said, "What's that you say?" and he replied, "Nowt. I was just thinkin'."

3

THEY were sitting close together round the fire as they had done each night since the day they buried Ben. When they talked, it was in low tones; and after the day of the funeral Ben's name was never mentioned among them. Sometimes they cried together, but generally they cried in private. That was, until this particular night—the evening of the day of the inquest that looked into Ben's death.

Nathaniel had not allowed Anna to go to the court. He had told the justice that she was still very unwell, and that was no lie. Oswald and Olan had accompanied him, while Maria stayed home with Anna, together with Cherry and Jimmy, for they both refused to go to work this morning. Now here he was, sitting before the fire, and the others were gathered round him waiting for him to speak, and it was Anna, bending towards him, who said, "Tell us, Dada, what happened, or let the boys."

It was Oswald who, looking at the others, said, "She got off."

A quiet stunned period followed. Then Oswald went on. "The court was packed, and there she stood, that woman, and her voice was so low, I couldn't hear half of what she said. But when one of the solicitor men had the stable man, McBride, in the box to explain what he saw, well, the man seemed hesitant, but then he said, 'The young master was about to run under the horse's head, and the boy pulled him out of harm's way. Then the horse reared, and the front hoof caught him on the head and sent him flying.'"

434

Oswald looked at his father, but Nathaniel remained silent, and so he continued. "The solicitor man then asked him what happened next. And he again seemed hesitant to speak; but then he said, from what he could see, the young lady went to grab the mistress, and the mistress brought her riding crop down on her. And when the solicitor asked, 'Did you not hear your mistress accuse the teacher of something?' I could see the man was upset, and he said, 'There was a lot of confusion and yelling. She said something, but I couldn't make out what it was.' And no matter how the solicitor man kept on, the stable lad wouldn't say any more. Then it was the doctor's turn, and he said . . ." Oswald paused here and wetted his lips before going on. "He said Ben was dead when he examined him, and Anna—Miss Dagshaw, he said—her face was bleeding from a whiplash. What was more, she was hysterical and had to be put to sleep. After that, the justice told the jury that it would seem there had been no intent to harm the boy, whose action in trying to save the younger child must have startled the horse.

"The jury wasn't out very long, and when they came back, they said it was . . . accidental death." Oswald now turned and looked at his father. Nathaniel was sitting with his head bowed, and Oswald's voice was very soft as he said, "It was then that Dada sprang up and cried, 'She killed my child! She killed my child!' And there was an uproar in the court, and the justice said if Dada couldn't be quiet he would have to leave the courtroom. But he wouldn't. He shouted at them how that woman had attacked his daughter and split her head open with a bowl. But by this time the policemen were pulling Dada outside."

There followed a long silence until Olan remarked, "There was nobody from The Manor there—none of the men. Anyway they said she's been left The Manor for weeks; in fact, he put her out."

"Oh, Dada." Anna was kneeling in front of her father now, holding his hand, and he, looking down on her, said, "It's all right, my dear. But it was a sorry day when you went to that house."

Then raising his head, he glanced round his family, saying, "We have never spoken of death, but I know now we must because he is still here among us. I also know that he was due to die. Ever since he was a baby, I have felt that. And you know something, my dear family?" He paused here before adding, "I saw him last night. I came down the room to lock the door, and he was sitting on the mat there, in front of the fire, his legs tucked under him, and he turned and looked at me, and his smile was so serene."

His voice now broke, and the tears rolled down his cheeks, and he turned and laid his head on Maria's shoulder. She patted his head, saying, "Enough. Enough. The weeks of mourning have passed. We must go on living. As Dada says, he is still here. We will talk about him as if he hadn't gone from us. Now, none of us has eaten today. Come to the table."

As Anna rose, she thought how her dada had insinuated that it was she who had brought his end about by going to that house. Yes, yes, he had. And she wasn't mistaken when she imagined she had caught a look of censure in his eyes.

It was a full fortnight later, and Anna was at the woodpile when she saw the rider coming across the moor, and she would have turned and hurried towards the house, except that she knew, were he to follow her, her father would order him away.

She went on sawing until he dismounted and came in by the gate, and only then did she look at him when he said, "How are you?"

"I'm quite well, thank you."

"Come here. I want to talk to you."

"I'd rather you didn't. We have nothing to say to each other."

"I don't agree. We have a lot to say to each other."

"What do you want of me?" she said harshly.

He smiled. "You know, Anna. What I've wanted from the first time I saw you. The day you lost your position, through the Songs of Solomon. I knew that something had happened to me. You must have wanted it, too."

"I did not." Her words were emphatic.

"Well, my dear, you are much stronger than I am."

She stepped back. "You are still as you were that morning—a married man with a child, whether he is your son or not."

Dull red color flooded over his face like a blush. It was some seconds before he could speak. "All I'm asking is that you give me some hope and that in the meantime until . . . until I can get a divorce, we can be friends. You have no hesitation in being friends with Timothy; so why not with me?"

"Timothy is not asking for a closer association."

"Oh, isn't he!"

Her eyes widened, and after a moment she said, "How can you suggest such a thing? He is an . . . an invalid, he is . . ."

"He's a man, and he's not an invalid; he is subject to fits, but so was Caesar and many other men in the past, and they had their women. And why do you think he is never off your doorstep? The least excuse, and he is over here. Oh, I know what I know."

"I'm sorry to hear you have such a low opinion of him."

"You take me up wrongly. I've a very high opinion of Tim. I'm only pointing out that he is a man, and he sees you as a beautiful girl."

He had taken a step towards her, and she couldn't move backwards now, because the sawing cradle was in the way. "Oh, Anna, I somehow got the impression some time ago that you didn't dislike me. What made you change towards me, Anna? Tell me."

She stared into his face for a full minute before she said, "When I saw you strike your wife and knock her to the ground."

He stepped back, his face screwed up in disbelief. "You mean to say, because I was outraged at the way she had treated you and perhaps could have killed you—that turned you against me?"

"No. It didn't turn me against you. I still think kindly of you, but if you were free tomorrow, I wouldn't marry you. My father had a wife, whom I am sure you have heard about, who drank and showed him up in public. And I'm sure he had more provocation to strike her than you had your wife, at least as fiercely as you did."

As he shook his head she went on, her voice rising. "You say you did it because you were angry at her treatment of me. That wasn't the reason. You did it because you had wanted to do it for a long time, because she had deceived you, because she had made you father of a child that wasn't yours. That was it, wasn't it? Before, you had just ignored her. And that's what turned her into the fiend that I knew and made her jealous of anyone you looked at."

There was a look of amazement on his face, but he made no effort to halt her, and she went on, her voice sinking. "So now you must see that it would be foolish to go on hoping there could be anything between us. What is more, my father could not bear it."

"Oh, your father!" The words came out in a loud, indignant burst. "It is always *your father.* Have you ever thought what that man has done to you? He has scarred you all for life. He has made you all the butt of the village. He prides himself on educating you all, but if he had left you like the rest of those clodhoppers, they would have accepted you. Oh, don't talk to me about your father."

She sidled along by the wood cradle until she was standing a good arm's length from him, and gasping, she said, "No. I won't talk to you about my father, or anything else. I'll only say this; then I'll never talk to you again. You would have been quite willing to act as my father did and take me as a mistress until you got your divorce, by which time—and not having the strength of my father—you would likely have become tired of me. Good-bye, Mr. Brodrick."

He didn't move away, but just remained staring at her, his jaws tight. Then suddenly swinging about, he strode from her.

She hurried down through the trees and into the house. Maria, meeting her, said, "What's the matter, girl?" Anna merely shook her head and made for her room, threw herself on the bed, and burst into tears.

Back in the living room, Maria turned as Nathaniel entered, and said to him, "She's in a state. She's gone into her room." And he, nodding, said, "He's been. I saw him go, and I saw her cross the yard. And by the look on her face, I don't think we'll see him again."

Maria answered, "Thank goodness," then added, "What did Miss Netherton say about the fencing? Has she heard any news?"

"I didn't go to her, my dear. It doesn't matter anymore. If we have to go through the village, well, we'll have to, dear."

He smiled wanly, went to the fireplace, and sat in his big chair. He had become a lost man. He might think Ben was still here, but because he couldn't touch him, he had become a lost man.

4

ON HER visit during the following week Miss Netherton once more came to the rescue. First, she said their horse fodder and groceries would be brought from town in her trap and put over the fence, and in the meantime she was going into the matter of the law concerning the enclosure of land. And secondly, she raised a more important issue. She was touching the fading scar on Anna's cheek, saying, "It'll disappear gradually," then, turning to Maria, she asked, "Does she know about the cross?" And when Maria said, "No. None of them does," Miss Netherton said, "Well, it's about time they did." Anna saw a glance exchanged between her parents.

When they were all seated at the table, Miss Netherton said, "Remember the contract we made? I bought the cross for five hundred pounds. Now listen. I had recorded in my will what was to become of it; but on thinking further I came to the conclusion that I could go on for years, and it's now that you need more help. So I told a friend in the jewelry business in Newcastle how I had bought the cross, and he was more than interested to see it. Well, I've never seen a man struck dumb in such admiration. I then told him I wanted to sell it, and to the highest bidder. And to this he said there should be no bidding—that would bring it into the open. It must go to one man—someone who bought precious things like this just to possess them, and he said he would take it to London, where he had a friend in the business who was a frequent visitor to Amsterdam, looking for rare jewels. He asked if I would trust him with this precious and ancient thing, and I said yes. He went to London last week, and he told me that he had never seen his friend so excited in his life and that his friend knew of someone who would be very interested in an article like that and that he might get as much as six thousand pounds." She wagged her finger at each of them in turn. "I'm telling you, if my friend said six thousand, being a businessman, I bet the deal would be eight. However, my dears, whatever the mysterious big man gives, we will share. Mind again, my friend in London will take his cut; then my friend in Newcastle. However, we should get at least two thousand each."

Maria and Anna sat back gasping, but Nathaniel did not move. Miss Netherton said, "Nathaniel, aren't you impressed?"

"I am amazed, but more so at your kindness and concern for us."

"Well, I've always been concerned for you because I like you. And whatever I've done for you, this girl"—she waved in Anna's direction—"has repaid me with her company over the years. And I knew that those devils had cut off your entry, and your tutoring has naturally been brought to a halt because you cannot use the cart. So I would like to think that when you get the money, you will consider moving to the town or wherever you like."

Maria's head was already slowly shaking. "I would hate to leave this house, Miss Netherton. We have brought the family up here within these four walls, and we have been happy—up till lately."

"Well, my dear, it will be up to you, of course. I was just thinking of your welfare and that tribe in the village. But you have friends

The Love Child

there, more than you know. . . . Well, I must be off to see Timothy. He hasn't been well these last few days. He had a strong exchange with Raymond over the fencing, and I understand that Raymond pointed out that he isn't entirely in control now. But don't you worry; they'll not beat us." Miss Netherton rose from the chair. "Come, Anna, walk with me to the main road. Stoddart will have the trap. The sun is shining. There are things to look forward to even now." She spread her glance quietly over the three of them, but neither Nathaniel nor Maria made any response.

Anna picked up a shawl and followed Miss Netherton out.

They walked along the path to the steps that led down the bank to the main road. Miss Netherton said, "Ah, here's Stoddart." Anna held on to her until she reached the road.

Anna watched the trap bowl away before turning to walk back to the house. The sun was glinting through clouds, making it appear as if the hillsides were running with rivulets of silver. Of a sudden she longed to be there on those hills and beyond, anywhere but here. She drew her shawl tight about her before hurrying on, telling herself that she must get rid of this feeling. They had lost Ben, so how would they take to letting her try to find a post far away?

During the past weeks she had seen herself going on year after year until she died here after a wasted life: digging in the garden, sawing wood, sitting round the fire at night. As the years went on, the family would assuredly disperse. The boys would marry. And Cherry? Whenever Cherry and Bobby could be together, they were.

And what was her future? What had she to look forward to here? She could have become Simon's mistress, and what would that have mattered? To the surrounding countryside she was a bastard already, and she would just be acting out the part again. At this moment she only knew that she felt lonely and lost.

Her father met her at the gate. "Billy got out. He's taken the carrots. You mustn't have put the latch on. You should be more careful."

She stood and looked after him as he walked away. It was as if she were a little girl again, being told how to see to the animals. But her father would never be the same again, nor would she.

She went into the house. It seemed as if her mother was waiting for her.

"Sit down," Maria said. "I must tell you the beginning of what Miss Netherton was on about. I mean the cross."

After Anna listened to her mother she said, "Will you tell the others as well tonight, Ma?"

"Your dada and me had a talk about that, and we thought it best not to say anything. You never know how a word might slip out."

"But when you get the money, they'll want to know."

"We've thought of that. It'll supposedly have come from my mother's people in yon end of the country. And we trust you not to say anything, either. If anything of this ever did leak out, there'd be a lot of trouble. And we've had enough trouble, haven't we?"

Her mother was staring into her face as if she were saying, Whether you admit it or not, you're to blame. You know it, I know it, and your dada knows it. Oh, yes, your dada knows it.

IT WAS almost three weeks later when Timothy called. After knocking on the door he had shouted, "Anyone in?" And she had opened the door and said, "Oh, hello. Oh, I am pleased to see you." And she was. For during the past fortnight she had often wondered why he hadn't called, and she had missed him. He seemed to be the only one she could smile at or with.

"Let me have a look at you," he said. "How many years is it since I last saw you?"

She said, "I hear you've moved."

"Oh, yes, yes. That's what I've come to see you about. I am stuck about the drapes. They are very drab, and I was wondering if you would come over and give me some advice. Will you come?"

"I should love to and to see your home. Do you feel you're settled in it?"

"Oh, yes, yes. I feel different altogether." A somber look came over his face as he added, "Life became really unbearable up there. My sister tells me there's going to be further changes. Raymond's fiancée's father has taken quite a big place outside Newcastle, and Raymond may end up there. That, of course, would leave Simon in charge of the house." He stopped abruptly. "Did I tell you I've acquired a trap? I've tied it up at yon end of the fence. Would you like to take a jaunt and see my little hut?"

"Oh, yes." She smiled at him, for he appeared like a bright light suddenly illuminating her dull existence.

She donned her black cloak, then stood in the yard while Timothy had a word with her parents. As she and Tim drove away, she lifted her hand in farewell to them, but received no response.

She admired the horse and the trap, and she laughed at him as he said, "Get up there, Daisy."

"You call her Daisy?"

"Well, it is her name instead of Lazy."

On entering the village Anna was immediately aware that there were people standing outside the forge, where a horse was being shod, and she saw the blacksmith drop the horse's hoof, then straighten his back, and stare towards her. Next, a woman about to enter the grocer's shop turned and stared; then two faces seemed to pop up in the window in the King's Head.

After driving some distance farther on, Timothy said, "It'll be all over the village tonight. Will you mind?"

"Why should I?"

"Yes, why should you? Anyway, they consider me harmless. Poor Mr. Timothy. I get angry when I hear that."

She put her hand out and touched his knee, saying, "You shouldn't let that trouble you. They are ignorant. I . . . we have all suffered from their ignorance for years. But they would do you no harm, whereas us, they would like to burn us alive. I'm still afraid of the village, Tim."

"Oh, my dear, you mustn't be; they can do nothing more. You're under the patronage of Miss Netherton and also, may I say so, of me, for what my patronage is worth. Ah, here we are!"

The drive was short, but it opened into a large gravel square, and there stood the house, creeper-covered, with large flower heads of wisteria hanging over the upper windows.

He held out his hand and helped Anna down from the step; then he led her onto the pillared porch, through the front door, and into a large hall. Taking her cloak, he led her into a room at the far end and said, with a theatrical gesture, "The drawing room, ma'am. It's hardly bigger than the housekeeper's room in The Manor. But it's comfortable."

She stood in the middle and looked round. "It's beautiful, Tim. And I don't know why you want to replace the curtains." She went over to one of the bay windows and said, "It's beautiful brocade."

"But it's faded. It should be a deep rose. Look; pull open the pleats, and you will see."

"Yes. Yes, I can see, but it goes with this room. New ones would be untempered and shouting at everything else in here."

He turned slowly and looked about him. "I think you're right. Well, well, I'm so glad you came, Miss Dagshaw. You have saved me quite a bit of money."

They were in the hall again when a thickset middle-aged man approached, saying, "Would you care for some tea now, sir?"

"Yes. Yes, I think we would, Walters. By the way, this is Miss Dagshaw. She's come to help me choose curtains, but she tells me now I would be wrong to change the drawing-room ones."

The man smiled at Anna. "They are magnificent curtains, sir."

"But Walters, they're faded."

"A lot of faded things are magnificent, sir."

"Ah. Ah." Timothy pointed to his butler-cum-valet. "We've got a philosopher here." And at that, he led her into the dining room, saying, "Now don't tell me you like these curtains."

She looked round the room, at the mahogany table, chairs, and sideboard. "Yes, I like them. But this room is not so light, and so I think you could have a less heavy curtain."

"Ah, well, new curtains for the dining room. Now come along and see the study."

The room had shelves from floor to ceiling, filled with books. The table was littered with more books, but in the middle of it was a large writing pad, which he dismissed, saying, "Scribbles, scribbles. I keep scribbling in the hope I may astound myself. You see, the Renaissance interests me, particularly the influence of Florence." He pointed to the French window and said, "That leads out into a little conservatory."

A few minutes later she was standing under a covered glass dome, and she turned to him, saying, "Little? Why did you call this little? It must run the length of the side of the house."

"It does, but I'm comparing the rooms with those in The Manor. I'm not belittling it—oh, no—because this is mine. The conservatory up there was only loaned, and much against the grain of the head gardener. We didn't get on together."

"I couldn't imagine you not getting on with anyone."

His face unsmiling, he said, "Under my be-pleasant-on-any-account façade, if I don't think a thing is right, I'm almost like you; I speak out. I may tell you, I wasn't loved by all the staff in The

Manor. It took quite a time for some people to realize I knew too much about their pilfering, and it was on a big scale, too. I stopped their game. So you see, Anna, everybody doesn't love me. But come. We'll go visit cook and the girls; then we'll have some tea."

The cook, Mrs. Ada Sprigman, dipped her knee at the introduction, as did the kitchen maid, Lena Cassidy, and the housemaid, Mary Bowles. What a difference from her reception at The Manor.

Walters brought tea into the sitting room. There were dainty sandwiches and small cakes, and she ate, feeling suddenly hungry, and she hadn't felt so for weeks, or months, for that matter.

After tea she chose from the samples sent from Newcastle certain materials that might do for the dining-room curtains. When, later, they sat by the window in the drawing room, he took her hand and said, "I cannot tell you when I've enjoyed an afternoon more, Anna. Promise me you'll be kind and come see me often."

"The kindness will be on your part, Tim, because I wouldn't like anything better. You see"—she looked down at their joined hands—"I cannot any longer talk to Dada; something died in him when Ben went. Ma is kind and good, but we never have a discussion together. At one time Dada and I would talk for hours . . . but not anymore."

She now looked quickly towards the window, saying, "The sun's going down; I must get home. You know I would love to read some of your work, some of your poems."

"Oh, my dear, I'll have to be either very very drunk or very very ill before I let you or anyone else read my poems."

"Well, I'll come some evening when you're very very drunk."

They went out laughing.

PART FIVE
The Cross
1

IT WAS a strange summer. Towards the end of May the heat became intense. Then on the seventh of June, there was a heavy snowfall, followed by hot weather again. It was very noticeable that tempers were frayed. But since Ben's death so many things had happened, the latest being that Oswald and Olan hadn't returned home until well after nine o'clock the previous night. They were both very tired; it had been too hot for people to bother cooking,

The Love Child

and the shop had been packed all week. And so Mrs. Simpson had suggested that they both sleep in the rooms above the sitting-down shop, then come home at the weekends. Oswald had looked from his mother to his father, then said, "It's a long trail, Dada, when you've had a day on your feet."

Nathaniel had looked at Maria, and she had looked at the floor before she conceded, "Well, if you want it that way, Oswald, so be it. You're both men now and have to live your own lives."

So it was settled that the boys were to leave home, and for most of the week only Anna, Cherry, and Jimmy were at home during the evenings. And then there was a lot for Cherry to do outside, especially where Bobby Crane was concerned.

Anna now often found herself walking with Jimmy. Since Ben's going he seemed to have lost his impishness. On this particular night, walking by her side to the woodpile, he proffered the remark, "The house is breaking up, isn't it, Anna?"

"What do you mean, Jimmy? The boys had to go into town."

"Oh, I know that. But the next to leave will be Cherry. She'll marry Bobby. Anyway, if she doesn't get married soon, there'll be trouble."

"Oh, Jimmy." She stopped abruptly, and he did so, too.

This was her young brother, not yet eighteen. Yet Jimmy was a farmer, living with raw nature every day.

Then he said, "I want to get away, Anna."

Dumbfounded for a moment, she whispered, "Why, Jimmy?"

He smiled at her. "Why? Because what is here for me? I'd like to go to sea."

"They'd be upset if you were to leave."

"Well, they'd still have each other, and that's the main thing in their life, isn't it? And, of course, they'll still have you. Oh, Anna, the thought of you ending your days stuck back there with the pair of them. They see nobody else but themselves. The older we've grown, the more they've grown back into their early days. They could lose the lot of us as long as they have each other."

"Jimmy! Dada's been distraught over Ben. Really! I didn't think you looked on them like that."

She turned from him and walked slowly to the chopping block and looked over the railings to the moor, and in her mind she saw riding across it a man who would have taken her for a mistress;

and she also saw a man writhing on the ground in an epileptic fit.

She asked Jimmy quietly, "Do you intend to go soon?"

"Aye, yes, before the winter sets in. But it's strange because the only one I'm going to miss is you; and wherever I go, I'll be thinking of you. You're beautiful, Anna."

"Oh!" She closed her eyes. "Don't, Jimmy. Don't."

"Why shouldn't I say it? Cherry's pretty, but you're beautiful. And where's it going to get you? Wasting away in this square of ground from which you can't even drive out on the cart. Oh, Anna, it makes me sick when I think of it."

She stared at this young boy, who was now a man. She put out her arms towards him, and they clung together for a moment, and then he swung away, leaped the railings, and ran across the open moor, leaving her with her head bowed over the wood block and moaning as if she had lost another brother, which she had.

TWICE of late she had walked to Timothy's house. It was exactly a mile and a half away if she went by the path and dropped down the bank into the road, so avoiding the village. She had enjoyed the walk and had met only one person, a man driving a farm cart.

It was towards the middle of July, about four o'clock in the afternoon, when she said to her mother, "I think I'll walk to Mr. Timothy's, Ma. I've got these books I would like to change. Anyway, I want to stretch my legs."

"Miss Netherton comes back tomorrow; you'll have something to do then. Fancy her going all the way to Holland! She's been gone five weeks now." Then she added, "We haven't seen Mr. Timothy for a week or so. Perhaps he's had another turn."

"Oh, I wouldn't think so. He goes to Newcastle quite a bit. I know he's researching some old books in the literary library."

Anna left the house wondering why her mother always alluded to Timothy's infirmity. Negotiating the bank, she put down her two books and turned her back to the roadway, feeling carefully for a foothold. Then she let out a scream when a hand gripped her calf and a voice said, "Want a helpin' 'and, miss?"

When the hand pulled her to the ground, she swung round and fell against the bank and looked into the grinning face of Arthur Lennon, the blacksmith's younger son. He was a man of twenty. His hair grew long over his brow and down his cheeks.

For a moment she couldn't speak, but looked beyond him to where another man had stepped through a gap in the hedge across the road. He was holding a large tin by its handle, and a brush in the other hand, and to his side stood a young boy.

"Get out of my way!"

But the grinning face was hanging over her now and said, "Ask civilly." And when next his hand came onto her breast, she screamed, "Take your filthy hands off me, you lout!"

"Who you callin' a lout, you whorin' bastard? Not satisfied with breakin' up one family, you have to go for the fitty one." His arms came about her, and he dragged her screaming through the opening and into the field. When his hand came across her mouth and her teeth bit into it, he pulled it back, bawling; then he brought her a blow on the face that sent her head spinning. Then she was on her back, and he had one knee across her legs and was tearing at the front of her dress while he shouted to the man, "Drop the can here, an' fetch your Betty. Tell her to bring a pilla."

"A pilla? You don't mean the tar—"

"Aye, I do. Me da said it should have been done a long time ago. An' look! Stop that boy from scootin'. "

The man, Betty's brother Davey, put down the tar, saying, "Arthur, they'll have you up." But he was laughing, and Arthur said, "Just let them try. Lucky you had the job of doin' the railings. Get after him. Quick!"

Davey Carter caught up with the boy and hauled him back, and Arthur grabbed him by his shirt and threatened, "You open your mouth about this, and I'll cut your tongue out. D'you hear me?"

The boy made no sound, but trembled visibly as he watched Arthur Lennon pin Anna's clawing hands to her side.

"Untie the york on me legs," Lennon growled at the boy, "an' put it across her mouth. Go on! Untie it."

With shaking hands the boy untied the rope from beneath the man's knee, where it held up the trouser leg, and when he leaned over her, his eyes seemed to say, I can't help it. Then he put the rope across her gaping mouth.

The man stood up; then bending over, he turned her onto her face, as if she were a sheared sheep. He tied her wrists with the piece of rope from his other leg, and her ankles with his necktie. This done, he turned her on her side, and with one pull he split her dress from top to bottom, then her underskirt, then her thin camisole. She was now naked to the waist.

It was when Anna felt his hands on her drawers that her whole body writhed. She was screaming inside her head, praying to die now. But after the first brush of tar was slapped on her breasts and dragged over her stomach, she knew no more.

He had finished tarring her when the other man returned, accompanied by his sister, Betty Carter. She was carrying a pillow, and stood looking down at the black-streaked body, and she said, "You did it, then. Uncle Rob said you would one day. She's only gettin' what she deserves."

"Split that pilla!"

Betty Carter split the pillow down the middle. But she didn't hand it to Lennon; instead, she said, "Let me do it." And so she shook the feathers down onto the wet tar.

"Turn her onto the other side," she said, and both men, using their feet, turned the unrecognizable form. And as Betty Carter emptied the pillowcase she cried, "You didn't put any on her hair!" She drew the brush a number of times over the shining dark hair; then, gathering up some loose feathers, she finished her job. And now they all turned and looked at the boy, who was vomiting.

"He'll talk," Davey Carter said.

Lennon pulled the boy up by his hair and hit him. "One squeak out of you an' I'll cut out your tongue. Understand?"

The boy gasped and made a motion with his head.

"Who's gonna find her?" Betty Carter said.

"Oh, they'll find her right enough. She was likely goin' on a jaunt to the fitty one, an' he was likely expectin' her. I wonder how much he pays her? Somethin's keepin' that lot in clover up there. Oh, they'll find her all right. Afore the night's out there'll be a hue and cry, but by that time we'll be off. I was due for the sack the morrow, anyhow, cos old Peterson will have found out that he's a pig short. An' Davey here, he's fed up, so we had made our plans. It was just honest luck that we came across her. I've been wantin' to do that for years. She'll not stick her nose in the air now."

"What about me? He knows it was me." She pointed to the boy.

"Don't worry about that." And Lennon pulled the boy towards Betty Carter, as he said, "Look, you've never seen her in your life afore, except in the village. Understand? Cos if you don't, we'll get you. We're not goin' far; we're just goin' to lie low for a times. And if you squeak, one of these nights I'll pick you up. Oh, yes! You get me?"

The boy was so sick he couldn't say anything, but Lennon said, "He understands all right, Betty. Don't you worry. But let's get some of this tar off our boots. Anyway, that's what we've been workin' at, tarrin'; expect to get dabbed up a bit at this job. Oh, an' bring her books off the bank; she may want to have a read." He laughed, throwing the books into the hedge. Then saying, "Goodbye, Miss Gillyvor," he turned to the others, and they followed him out of the field, towards the village.

The sun still shone, and birds in the thicket still sang.

2

Mrs. Bella Lennon stood at the window and looked out on the unusually busy village street. There was something up.

Hurrying out her front door, she went into the smithy, where her husband was standing talking to their elder son, Jack.

"What's up?" she said. "What's all the bustle?"

Her son turned to her and said on a laugh, "The gillyvor's lost— the whorin' one. It seems that Mr. Tim called in at her dear papa's around six o'clock. They've been runnin' like scalded cats ever since. Damn fools, them. I bet she's laid up with somebody else."

"It wouldn't be our Arthur," said the blacksmith on a deep guffaw, then added, "By the way, where is he?"

"He's gone into Fellburn with Davey," his wife answered. "He wanted a night out. He had been down with Davey, who was tarring the new railin's for Dobson."

About two hours later the village street was still abuzz, with small groups here and there gossiping, when Dan Wallace came to the forge and asked, "Seen anything of our Art, Rob?"

"Young Art? No. Is he lost an' all?" the blacksmith asked.

"Well, he was helpin' Davey Carter the day, and he hasn't come in for his tea. His mother's goin' up the pole. I wonder where the young kite has got to. . . ."

The young kite was now sneaking in the back door of his home. And when his mother saw him, she said, "Where d'you think you've been?" then stopped and said, "Art! What's the matter?"

"Get Dad, Mam! Get Dad."

The woman pushed the boy into a chair; then she ran out of the house and up the village street. "Dan! Dan! He's in. Come on. Something's wrong, he can hardly speak."

When they entered the house, the boy straightaway got up and gripped his father's hand. "Dad, he said what he would do, Arthur Lennon, but . . . but you won't let them, will you?"

"What are you talkin' about? What'd he say he'd do?"

"Cut out my tongue. You've got to go and get her."

"Get who, lad?"

"The young lass, the young lass. She's lyin' in the field. Tarred . . . tarred and feathered her, he did. Tied her up."

"He *did?* He'll swing if I get my hands on him. Come on, lad, show me where she is. Come on. Come on. Be a brave lad."

Dan Wallace now led his son out into the street, but he had to keep pressing him forward. Then his wife, at the other side of him, said, "Here's Mr. Timothy's carriage comin'!"

Dan Wallace waved his hand, and when the coachman, Edward, pulled up the carriage, Timothy put his head out the window and Dan said to him, "My boy here, sir, knows where the girl is." Seated beside Timothy, Nathaniel cried, "He does? Where?"

"Sir, I think you'd better prepare yourself for somethin'. My boy here seems to know all about it." He took his son's arm, and they ran down the street, the carriage following, and this brought people out of their houses, asking questions.

Beyond the village, when they came to the gap in the hedge, the boy shrank against his father, but his father dragged him into the field. When the boy pointed, Dan Wallace muttered, "Mercy!" And when Nathaniel and Timothy stood looking down on the tarred and feathered body, with its torn clothes spread like broken wings, both had to hold on to each other for support. Then Nathaniel was kneeling on one side of her and Timothy on the other; and Timothy took her smeared face between his hands and said not a word, for his mind was screaming against the obscene cruelty that had been inflicted on this innocent girl, on his beloved Anna.

Nathaniel looked at him and whispered, "She's breathing." They both stood up and looked about them. It seemed that a crowd of people had gathered from nowhere and were standing awestruck.

Timothy said to his coachman, "Get into Fellburn at top speed.

The Love Child

Bring the doctor, and the police." And Edward raced off in the carriage.

"We must loosen her arms and legs," said Nathaniel.

Timothy muttered, "A knife? Has anyone got a knife?"

At least three knives were handed towards him; then as Tim cut the rope round Anna's wrist Dan Wallace said, "I wouldn't move her arms, sir, not for a bit. She'll be in cramp."

The crowd had grown now, but it was silent; it was definitely a group of frightened people, for they could surely see the outcome of this dreadful deed. The boy was clinging to his mother and crying openly, and when a voice near them said, "Did he do it?" Mrs. Wallace startled everybody by screaming, "No, he didn't! Your bosom drinking mates did it. Arthur Lennon and Davey Carter. And aye, his sister, dear little Betty."

Here and there a person moved out of the crowd and went quietly away, and one of these was the blacksmith. . . .

It was exactly twenty-five minutes later when the doctor and the policeman pressed through the crowd and looked down with horror at the tarred and feathered girl.

The doctor knelt on the ground. Putting his ear to the discolored mouth and then roughly rubbing the sticking feathers to one side, he felt the flesh below the breast. Standing up, he said, "We must get her to hospital." He now looked at the policeman and said grimly, "She should be laid out on something flat."

A voice from the crowd shouted, "Me flat cart an' horse is here in the road, sir, and you're welcome."

The people moved, and the cart was backed up, and Anna was lifted onto it. Nathaniel sat beside her, and Timothy went to the carriage with the doctor and the policeman, and the carriage followed the cart in the long twilight to the Fellburn hospital, leaving a subdued and not a little fearful village behind them.

THE following day the police arrested Arthur Lennon and Davey Carter as they were about to board a boat at South Shields, and an inspector arrived in the village to arrest one Betty Carter for her most atrocious attack on a young girl.

The village was quiet; people spoke in undertones. The King's Head was full that night, but The Swan was practically empty. The blacksmith and his son, the painter Willie Melton and his son, and a number of others were all conspicuous by their absence.

In the King's Head it was said that all the lass's family had remained at the hospital most of the night; Mr. Timothy had been at the hospital, too, and Mr. Simon from The Manor. And it was touch and go for the lass. If she didn't come round, it would be a hanging job for two, that was sure. As for Betty Carter, well, she only put the feathers on, so it could be just a long stretch. But whichever way it went, this village would never be the same again. Why couldn't they have left them in the hollow, alone? They had done nobody any harm; in fact, in some ways they had done good. Look how they had taken those families off the moor. And did anybody really believe the lass had broken up the couple in The Manor? Those two had been at each other's throats ever since their honeymoon. As for the lass being free an' all with Mr. Timothy, was it likely, seeing he had those fits? But young Lennon had always been a vicious type.

And so it went on from day to day while everyone waited.

When, a week later, the news spread through the village that the lass had woken up and it was thought she might live, the majority drew in long breaths and said, "Well, thank goodness for that! There'll be no swingin' job, no matter what else." It only took a swingin' job to get a village a very bad name.

TIMOTHY's carriage drew up outside his house, with Simon following on horseback. After alighting they went inside together, and the first words the butler said were, "How is she, sir?"

"She's still very low, but she's holding her own."

"That's good news, sir."

A little while later the two men were settled in the sitting room with brandy. After no words had passed between them for some minutes, Simon walked to the window, saying, "I know how you are going to respond, but I must say it: She's suffered this terror for things she hasn't done; so she wouldn't have suffered any worse if she had done them. In fact, it wouldn't have happened."

"You mean if she had become your mistress?"

Simon swung round. "Yes, that's exactly what I mean."

"Well, she refused you, didn't she? She'll always refuse you."

"We'll see about that. Who's to stop me? You?"

"Yes, if I can."

The Love Child

"You would ask her to marry you?"

Timothy's mouth went into a hard line. "No," he said. "Because I wouldn't ask anyone to marry me. But she trusts me. I am her friend. And if it's the last thing I do, I'll prevent her from following the pattern of her mother. However, there will be no need. She won't have you. Something happened to kill her feelings for you. Perhaps you know what, apart from your having a wife."

Slowly Simon turned away and looked out the window again, and Timothy asked, "Have you heard from Penella?"

"No. Only that she's living in Newcastle as near Raymond as possible. Not that that's going to do her much good."

"I've always thought you were wrong in that direction, Simon. If she had thought so much of Raymond, she would have married him when he gave her the child. It was you she wanted and has always wanted. And I must say this: if you had been of a more forgiving nature, your life together would have been quite different."

"Oh, shut up!" Simon threw off the rest of his brandy and said, "I must be on my way. Thank you, dear Uncle, for your advice."

"You are very welcome, nephew. You can see yourself out."

Timothy walked to the window to see Simon emerge from the house and mount his horse, and the sight of the smart, lithe figure riding down the drive swept away the assurance he had assumed just a few minutes ago. Will she? he thought; and he answered himself, Yes, she might now. She might think, What does anything matter anymore? Life would never be the same for her again.

ANNA was in hospital for three weeks. On the day they brought her home it was into a house full of flowers and with the long table covered with gifts and pretty cards. There were even presents from some of the villagers: ginger cake, jam preserves, a box of home-made toffees; then the large boxes all tied up with ribbon from Mr. Simon and Mr. Timothy and Miss Netherton.

Anna expressed her thanks quietly and in just a few words.

This was what was troubling the family: she didn't talk anymore. And the doctor said it could be months before she would really be herself again; she was a lucky girl to be alive at all.

She listened to the buzz of conversation round her, but didn't appear to hear anything that was being said. Her mind wandered back into the past, when she was a girl sitting in the barn learning her lessons or spreading the books out on the long table and looking across at her dada's bright face. . . .

"What are you smiling at, dear?"

She looked up at Maria. "Was I smiling, Ma?" she said.

"Yes. You must have been thinking something nice."

"Oh, I don't know. . . . Ma, I would like to go to bed."

"Then you shall go to bed. It's been a very trying day." So Maria and Cherry helped to undress her and tuck her up in bed. And then Nathaniel came in and took hold of her limp hand. "You are home, my dear, and I hope never to leave it."

And at this Anna closed her eyes, and her mind left her childhood dreaming and leaped ahead into the everlasting future, during which time she would never again leave this house.

3

IT WAS the end of August when Arthur Lennon and David Carter, together with Beatrice Carter, were brought before the justice in Newcastle. His Lordship sentenced Arthur Lennon to five years' hard labor and David Carter to four years' hard labor and Beatrice Carter to three years in the house of correction.

Ten days later Miss Netherton visited the cottage in the afternoon. When she entered the room, Anna was sitting in the big chair, and she took her hand. "How are you feeling, my dear?"

"All right, thank you, much better."

"That's good. That's good." Then turning to Nathaniel and Maria, she said, "Please sit down, and I'll tell you my news. At last it is settled." She sat next to Anna, opened her beaded bag, and took out a check, which she passed to Maria, saying, "Read that."

"Seven thousand, two hundred and fifty pounds. Oh!"

"Well—" Miss Netherton took the check from her fingers, saying, "This is the amount after all their bits and pieces have been taken off. The cross was sold, so I'm told, for ten thousand pounds. You can guess what it's really worth."

"I can't believe it. I just can't believe it."

"Well, my dear, you can, you can. Now the agreement was, we would share this. Five hundred pounds deducted from your share leaves you with three thousand, one hundred and twenty-five pounds, isn't that right? Maria, don't cry. This is a happy event."

"I can't believe it. And you are so good to go to all this trouble."

"It was no trouble. You have no idea how I've enjoyed myself over this transaction. Nathaniel, smile, please. Come on, let us rejoice in this good fortune. And here I am, bearing gifts, and not a drop of tea am I offered." And when Maria rose hastily to her feet, saying, "Oh, Miss Netherton," and then quickly kissed her on the cheek, the older woman swallowed for a moment before she said, "Go on with you! I want a strong cup of tea. And Nathaniel, it's raining. Bring Stoddart into the kitchen, will you?"

When they had the room to themselves, Miss Netherton, taking Anna's hands, said, "I wish my news could have altered the look in your eyes, my dear. But no money in the world will do that. The only person who can do that is yourself. Now I want you to think about your future."

Anna shook her head slowly. "I don't seem able to think at all."

"Oh, my dear, that feeling will pass. But Timothy was saying that you might like to study in some ladies' college?"

The faintest of smiles came on Anna's face. "He said that?"

"Yes, and much more. Oh, he is indeed worried about you. You are so dear to him. Anna—" She looked into Anna's face and said, "Tim is a very special person. Have you yet found that out?"

After a pause Anna said, "Yes. Yes, I have. I've never met anyone as kind as him in my life, except yourself."

The answer seemed to make Miss Netherton impatient for a moment, for she dropped Anna's hands, sat back, and said, "I'll talk about it later when you're feeling stronger. He's gone to London."

"London? He didn't say."

"Well, you see, his book's been accepted."

"*His book?*" Anna pulled herself up in the chair. "I didn't know he had written a book; he said he just scribbled."

"Oh, yes. He's going to publish a book on the Renaissance period. He's too humble for his own good is Tim. . . . He deprecates himself just because of the one little handicap he's got. Unfortunately, he doesn't know when it's going to hit him. But to my mind, otherwise it is of no great importance. So, my dear, yes. The book's in the publisher's hands, and they seem to think highly of it."

Half dreamily now Anna said, "Strange that he never mentioned it to me. We talked such a lot about books."

"Here's that cup of tea." Miss Netherton turned towards Maria, who put the tray down, and then she said, "Ah, there you are, Nathaniel," as he entered the room. "I know what I wanted to say to both of you. I don't know what you intend to do with the money, but I would suggest you get yourselves a horse and trap now that the fences are down. Both Raymond Brodrick and his father-in-law have been pulled over the coals for that piece of lawbreaking; there are old land-enclosure laws, and those two didn't do their homework. Anyway what about the horse and trap?"

Nathaniel looked at Maria and she at him, and they both smiled, and Nathaniel said, "That is a marvelous suggestion. Oh, Miss Netherton, neither of us will live long enough to thank you for all you have done for us."

Miss Netherton looked to the side as she said, "I must away now." She rose to her feet; then turning to Anna, she said, "Get out and walk. Yes, that's a good idea. Walk over to my place every day."

"I will. I will in a short while."

Anna watched her parents escort her dear friend out of the house. Then closing her eyes, she said to herself, Get out and walk. Get out and walk. She didn't care if she never walked again. She was dead inside. She had died when that tar brush swept down the front of her body.

IT HAD rained for days; then had come a muggy period with a hazy sun, followed by damp cold nights. Anna spent quite a bit of her time now in the barn or in the new stable that had been erected to house the horse they had acquired.

Twice Timothy had brought the carriage over and taken her back to the house, telling her about London and making light of his book. On the last occasion he had taken her hand and said, "Oh, Anna, Anna, come back." She didn't need to ask, Come back from where? She knew what he meant.

Today she was sitting in the tack room rubbing a wax mixture into the harness when the door opened and Jimmy appeared, which made her say, "You're back early. Anything wrong?"

"I asked if I could come away. I've had the runs since the day afore yesterday, and I'm not feeling too good."

He sat down on an upturned box, then said quietly, "I must tell you, Anna, I'm leaving for sure."

"Oh, Jimmy. Please."

The Love Child

"I've got to, Anna. There's something inside of me raging to be away. Anyway, I've shot me bolt: I gave farmer Billings me notice. A month, I said. He doesn't believe I've got the bellyache; he thinks I'm gettin' uppish because I asked to come off early."

"They're going to be upset." She motioned towards the door.

"Oh, as long as they've got themselves, that's all they need. You could have died, any of us could have, and they would have mourned us; but if one of them were to go, the other would go an' all."

"Why do you think this, Jimmy? You're bitter about something."

"Aye, perhaps I am. But I can see nothing ahead here. I want to get away, escape. And there's another one that'll be escaping shortly, and that's Oswald. He's sweet on the daughter." He laughed, but then put his hand to his stomach, saying, "Here I go again," and he went out.

Jimmy couldn't go to work the next day. He had bad diarrhea and headache, and Anna said to Maria, "You should call the doctor, Ma. Jimmy's bad."

"All right, dear. I'll get your dada to go."

Nathaniel luckily caught the doctor coming out of a house in the village, and when he told him his boy had diarrhea, the doctor looked at him hard and said immediately, "Well, let's get away."

He was now standing in the kitchen, saying, "I'm sorry to tell you the lad's got cholera. There's one case in the village and a number more in Gateshead Fell. It's the water. Now, you get your water from the pump, don't you?"

No one answered him.

"Well, boil every drop of it, every drop. And let's hope the lad's a light case. Who have you got coming home?"

After a short intake of breath Nathaniel said, "My daughter. She works for the Praggetts. And tomorrow my two eldest sons come in from Gateshead. And there's a young man sleeps in the barn."

"Oh, you must put a stop to that. Get word to them to stay away." He bit on his lip, saying, "Well, you'd better all stay put. I will call at Praggett's on my way home. Where do your sons work? And the young man?"

When Nathaniel told him, he said, "I'll tell them. Now, do what I tell you. Boil the water; then wash everything that comes in contact with him. There's no need to worry; he's a strong fellow. Best of luck with the lad."

They all looked stunned. "Cholera, that's all we need now," Anna said. "Another affliction. Why?"

Both Anna and Maria looked at Nathaniel, and he, looking at Anna, said, "Fate never lets up, does it?"

FOUR days later it looked as if Jimmy might take a turn for the better: his diarrhea had eased; he hadn't been sick once during the day. And now it was one o'clock in the morning.

Anna sat by his bed. For the last three nights she had sat there, sleeping part of the day, during which time Nathaniel and Maria took over. But the strain was showing on them, for Jimmy had to be changed every two hours, and his nightshirt and sheets washed.

The only one they had been in contact with was Timothy. He brought food, medical supplies, and linen, and put them over the fence.

When Jimmy stirred, Anna picked up a wet cloth from a plate and placed it across his sweating brow. When his lids lifted and he looked at her, she said, "Try to sleep, dear. It'll soon be over."

"Yes, Anna, 'twill soon be over. I . . . I'm going to be free."

She stared down into his face. "Now, now, Jimmy, be quiet."

He gasped before he said, "No time, Anna . . . Anna."

"Yes? Yes, my dear?"

"Escape. You escape soon, or else they'll not let . . . you go. They'll . . . want someone to . . . to look after them. Selfish, yes . . . yes, selfish. Get away . . . Anna."

"Jimmy, please! You don't know what you're saying, dear."

"Love you, Anna. Love you."

"Yes, and I love you, too, Jimmy. You'll be better in the morning. Doctor said you're on the turn."

He closed his eyes and made a sound like a sigh, and she said, "That's it. Go to sleep."

She sat gently stroking his square hand. For how long she sat like this she couldn't remember, but something caused her to look at her brother's face. It seemed unchanged, just as if he was sleeping. Yet, no, his eyes were half open. She gave a gasp, then let out a low moan. "Oh, Jimmy. Jimmy. No! No!" She took his face between her hands, and when she released it, the head lolled to the side. She dropped forward over the slim, depleted body, murmuring all the time, "Oh, Jimmy. Jimmy."

The Love Child

When finally she stood up, she was amazed at her calmness, and she said, "You did what you wanted to do; you escaped. Oh, my dear."

Turning now, she lifted up a candlestick and went to her parents' door. But she didn't knock. Walking straight into the room, she held the light above her head and looked down on them. They were lying face to face in bed, and her father's hand was resting on her mother's shoulder. She said quietly, "Dada."

She had to say his name three times before he turned on his back, looked at her, then pulled himself upwards. "What is it?"

"Jimmy has gone," she said simply.

She saw them spring up and rush from the room. Slowly she went out and down the long room, and blew the embers into a blaze.

Her father came staggering down the room. She watched him drop into a chair and rest his head on his hands, and then she heard him say, *"The sins of the father indeed shall be visited on the children, and the children's children, even to the third and fourth generations."* He turned his head slowly towards her. "I always knew we should have to pay. Which one will He take next?"

4

THERE was no formal funeral for Jimmy. They came in a black hearse and took him away, as they also did the butcher's son.

Two days later Maria went down with cholera, and Nathaniel seemed to enter a period of madness. For four nights and days he hardly left her side. And Anna seemed to spend her whole life running with the pail between the bedroom and the cesspool. The doctor's voice was harsh when he spoke to Nathaniel, saying, "There's other things to be done besides sitting beside the bed. Your daughter will be next if she doesn't get help." And Nathaniel said, "I'm sorry, but I can't lose Maria. I can't."

It was the evening of the fourth night that he came into the long room and sat at the little desk and began to write. As Anna passed him for the countless time with the emptied pail, he stopped her and said, "I've written a will here. If we should go"—he didn't say your mother or I, but we—"the house and the money will go to Oswald and Olan. They'll look after you; Bobby will take care of Cherry."

She put the pail down and stared at him, and he said, "What is it?"

She couldn't tell him, You're leaving me in care of the boys; you're not saying to me, there is fifty pounds, or a hundred pounds. I am to grow old here in this house . . . in care of the boys. With a quick jerk she lifted the pail and hurried from him, and he said, "I could not live without your mother. Don't you understand?"

Yes. Yes, she understood. She understood that a caring father could have quite another side to him—caring because he wanted his children all around him as protection from the outer world and its condemnation. As he had bred each one he hadn't thought of their future, only of his needs of the moment. She had thought him advanced in his thinking, but now, females still had their place, and it was subordinate to men's.

The next morning, as Anna sat by her mother, Maria turned her head to look at her and said, "Look after your father. Promise me you'll look after your father. He'll need you. Stay with him."

When Anna made no reply, Maria said, "Promise me?"

Still she made no answer; and then Maria, her hand groping for Anna's, said between gasps, "Don't . . . marry that man. Don't . . . saddle yourself. Far better . . . take what . . . the other one offers."

Anna couldn't believe her ears. She withdrew her hand and stood up. Her mother was saying, Do what I did. Don't marry a good man, because he has fits. Anna had the most awful desire to shout, I'd marry him tomorrow if he asked me, but he never will. And I'll tell you something else. I love him, and if he asked me to live with him, I'd do it. But the other one? Never!

Nathaniel came into the room now and, looking at her, said, "What's wrong? Is she worse?"

Anna stepped aside, but said nothing, and Maria put her hand out to Nathaniel, and he gripped it and sat down by her side. Anna went outside into the fresh morning air. The mugginess was gone, and there had been a frost in the night, and she took in great gulps of air while telling herself not to let go, for she knew there was something in her head on the point of snapping.

MARIA did not die. From that night on, she slowly recovered. Perhaps, Anna thought later, it was because she had refused to conform to her mother's wishes, and Maria couldn't bear the thought of her beloved husband's being left without someone to take care of him.

The Love Child

The first day it was considered safe for the others to return to the house was one Anna tried to forget, for they all cried over Jimmy's going. But *she* didn't cry, for all the while she could hear Jimmy's voice saying, "Get away. Escape." Odd, Jimmy knew the other side of his parents, the selfish side she had never guessed at.

At the family reunion her father cried, "Why had my second son to be taken when that woman who killed my last born is spared?"

"What, Dada?" Oswald said. "She got it, too?"

"Yes. And so bad she landed up in Gateshead hospital. Yet she is spared and brought back to live in comfort. There's no justice."

This was news to Anna, which brought home the fact that there had hardly been any exchange of words between her and her father since the night he had written his will. It was as if he knew by her reactions that he had failed her in some way.

The next visitor was Miss Netherton. She commiserated with Nathaniel and Maria over Jimmy's loss; then when she was leaving, she said to Anna, "Come, walk with me to the trap," and once outside, she said, "What on earth has happened to you, girl? A ghost could have more substance. Tim said he was worried to death by the look of you. He's in London again, you know."

"Yes. Yes, I know."

"He's been not only keeping you going, but seeing to Penella."

"Penella? Mrs. Brodrick?"

"Yes. She had written him from Newcastle; she wanted to see him. And when he got there, she had already been taken to the Gateshead Cholera hospital. Well, he went there, and as he himself said, there was nothing of the grand, imperious lady left. She was a very ill and frightened woman. So he tells Simon. I don't know what passed between them, but it was something pretty strong; the doctor didn't think there was much chance of her surviving. So Simon went, and the result was, she didn't die. However, Tim says she must have got the fright of her life, because she's a very changed individual. Oh, by the way, I must tell you, the child's got a tutor, and he seems to have taken to him. As Simon said, the first words the child always utters to him are, 'When are you going to bring Missanna back?' Anyway, my dear, we've got to forget about other people and concentrate on you. Now, what I suggest is that you come over to me and stay for a week or so, and Ethel will fatten you up."

Anna smiled softly on the elderly woman. "You're always so kind to me . . . but on this occasion would you mind if I left your invitation open? There is something I'd like to get straight."

"Such as?"

"I can't explain it yet. I want to be sure that I can do this."

"Let me guess. Your father is going to provide you with enough money to start a school of your own. That's it, isn't it?"

The smile disappeared from Anna's face. "No, Miss Netherton. My father has never even thought along those lines."

"What do you mean? Has he not settled something on you?"

"No. No. Not a penny. In fact, I can speak to you about it because you are my friend. But when he thought my mother was dying, he knew he would go, too. And I'm sure he would have, even if it meant taking his own life because he couldn't live without her. He made out a rough will"—she turned her head away—"and he turned to me and said, 'I am leaving the house and what money there is to the boys. They will look after you. Cherry will be all right; Bobby will see to her.'"

There was silence between them now. Anna watched the older woman pull her collar tighter under her chin before she said, "I am very disappointed in Nathaniel and in Maria, too, I must say. The boys are in good positions, by all accounts. That house should be yours and enough money with which to keep it up. That cross was originally Maria's. The money that I first gave them was originally Maria's." She put out her hands now and gripped Anna's wrists, saying, "Don't worry, my dear. I'll see you won't be left in care of the boys, you know that."

"Thank you. That is comforting."

"Now I will away, but I won't rest until I find out what is in that top story of yours. You know me." They parted smiling.

Anna didn't return immediately to the house, but walked through the wood as far as the sawing block, and there she stood and looked over the moor as she often did. But today she muttered aloud, "Wait and see what happens when Oswald breaks the news, which he will do shortly. Jimmy wasn't wrong. Propriety will go to the wind now. There'll be no waiting a year in honor of the dead. He's as ready as Cherry is for marriage." Then she bowed her head as if in shame at her thoughts. Yet, more and more, they were facing her with facts.

The Love Child

SHE HAD EXPECTED TIMOTHY TO return at the end of the week, but a letter arrived instead, saying that he had a little more business to do in London. He hoped to see her soon, and he signed himself, "Ever your friend, Tim."

They were in winter now, and the long evenings became a time of excruciating tension for Anna. After supper, which was often passed in silence, the depleted family would sit round the fire: Nathaniel, Maria, Cherry, and herself. Often Bobby would be there, too.

As Anna sat looking from one to the other she tried to thrust her mind back to the times when most of the family were rolling on the mat with laughter. And the quiet times, when her father would be reading aloud. Where had they gone? What had happened? This house was now weighed down with misery. Tonight she felt she couldn't stand any more, and so, rising, she said good night and went to bed.

It was a good hour later when Cherry came into the bed, saying, "Isn't it awful down there at nights? I dread coming home."

"I'm home all day, Cherry."

"Oh, yes, I know, Anna. And you've had a rough time of it."

Anna said nothing. They lay in silence until Cherry said, "You don't talk like you used to, Anna. You're miles away, and"—her voice broke—"and I need to talk to you, Anna."

When Anna turned round in the bed, Cherry put her arms about her and muttered something, which Anna could not make out.

"What did you say?" she said.

Then when Cherry repeated it, Anna felt herself stiffen. And so, all she said was, "When did this happen?" and Cherry said, "One Sunday when I went down to see him. It was a room above the—"

Anna pulled herself away from her sister's hold, hissing, "I don't want to know details. I mean, how long have you gone?"

"Nearly three months."

"Oh, no! And they don't know? I mean, Ma."

"No, no. I've wanted to tell you, but, well, we didn't seem like we used to be. But . . . but I love Bobby, and he'll get on. And I can always work."

"Having a baby? Who's going to look after the baby?"

Anna closed her eyes tightly and saw herself nursing Cherry's baby, for Cherry would have to work because they'd never be able

464

to live on what Bobby earned. And there again came Jimmy's voice, urging, "Escape. Escape."

"What am I to do, Anna?"

"You've got to tell them, and soon. Now stop crying. Dada is very fond of Bobby, and Ma is too."

"Oh, Anna, I'm frightened. I'm . . . I'm the only one that . . . well, has gone wrong, and they'll be ashamed."

"They can't be ashamed of you for doing what they did."

"The people in the village."

"Damn the people in the village. I've paid the people in the village for all of us. It wasn't for me alone; it was against Ma and Dada, for their daring to flaunt society. Dada used to be always bragging we were the happiest family in the county; he had us all in this little nest, and he knew we would never be able to fly far."

"Oh, Anna, fancy you thinking that. They did what they did because they were in love, and I understand exactly how they felt."

"Shut up! Shut up! They only knew one kind of love. The same kind as you do. There are other kinds: sacrificing love, love that is shriveled up through convention and the dirty tricks of fate, and—" She stopped suddenly and muttered, "I'm sorry." Then she turned on her side, only to turn quickly back when Cherry said, "It's a shame. I know you wanted to go with Mr. Simon, and you should have."

"Cherry"—it was a deep whisper—"if you don't shut up, I'll slap you across the face. I had no intention of ever being Simon Brodrick's mistress. Never! Never! Do you hear me? Even if I'd loved him desperately, I still wouldn't have become his mistress."

"All right, you wouldn't, but I don't see why you are blaming Ma and Dada for doing what they did. People are saying the same thing about you and Mr. Timothy. And whether you are or not—"

Anna sprang from the bed and yelled at the top of her voice, "I am not sleeping with Mr. Timothy! Do you hear me?"

In the deep silence that followed, she heard the quick steps on the floorboards. The door burst open, and her father, holding the lamp high behind their mother, said, "What is it? What is it?"

Cherry was sitting up in bed, rocking backwards and forward.

"What were you yelling at? What was the matter?"

It was her mother whom Anna now addressed. "I am not sleeping with Mr. Timothy. Do you hear, Ma? I am not his mistress."

"No one said you were, daughter." Maria's voice was quiet.

The Love Child

But Nathaniel seemed to ignore Anna's outburst, for he put his arm round Cherry's shoulder, saying, "What is it, dear?"

Cherry shook her head, and Anna cried, "Tell them!"

When Cherry still continued to shake her head, Maria came to Anna's side and said, "What has she to tell us?"

"Only that she's going to have a baby, Ma."

Maria said, "Is this true, girl?"

Cherry fell back onto the pillow. "Yes, Ma. Yes, it's true."

"Well, well." Nathaniel looked at Maria, and she at him. And Maria put her hand out. "Come on. Get up and tell us about it."

Their reception of the news seemed to deflate Anna completely.

Now Cherry's head was resting on her father's shoulder, and he was saying, "Don't worry, dear. The first thing we must do is get you married. He's a good boy, and I like him. But you can't go live above that boathouse. You must come home."

And Maria agreed. "Yes, dear, yes," she said, then added, "It'll be good to have a child about the house again."

Anna closed her eyes, and there she was, nursing the baby. Of a sudden she was so tired that she couldn't even hear, "Escape. Escape."

But she heard Jimmy's voice loud and clear on Saturday when the boys came home. They were excited, and when Oswald began with, "Ma and Dada, it's not so long ago since we lost Jimmy, but I'm engaged to Carrie—you know, Mrs. Simpson's daughter. And you'll never guess what. Mrs. Simpson's taken me into partnership, and Olan an' all. What d'you think?"

It was his father who answered. "I think it's excellent news, Oswald. And from what I saw of that place, it should prosper."

"It is, Dada. It is already prospering, but it will do more so. We can open up another place; we've got it all planned."

Nathaniel now looked from one to the other. "The saying is, Never one door closes but another opens. And it's true in this case. The house will know a family again, and children."

"Yes, Nat," Maria said. " 'Tis something to look forward to."

"Well, let's drink to it. Go and bring out the elderberry, Anna."

Anna went into the kitchen and picked up a bottle of elderberry wine. And she stared at it for a long while before she spoke, saying, "I hear you, Jimmy, my dear. I hear you. I'll wait till Monday."

5

SHE had milked the goats, then brushed the horses and swept down the yard.

At twelve o'clock she joined her parents for the midday bite when her father said, "I shouldn't be a bit surprised to see it snow. I think there'd better be some more logs cut. Eh?"

She returned his look and said, "I'm sorry, Dada, but I'm going visiting this afternoon."

Maria was all attention. Nathaniel asked, "Is he back, then?"

"Yes. He was due back yesterday."

"Wouldn't it be better if you waited for him to call?" Maria said.

"Not in this case, Ma. I have a question to ask him."

"Well, I've always answered your questions up to now," Nathaniel said. "Can't you ask me?"

"No." She smiled a tight smile. "Not in this case, Dada." As she rose from the bench, he said, "The log pile's going down fast."

"Yes, it is." She nodded at him and only just stopped herself from adding, So you should spend more time down on the block instead of reading.

It was a full twenty minutes later when she emerged from her room to be greeted by a gasp from Maria. "Oh, no! Anna, you're not flaunting convention to that extent, not wearing black."

"My cloak is dark, Ma."

"Your cloak reaches only just below your knees, girl."

"Ma." She walked up to her mother and looked straight into her face. "I ceased to be a girl some time ago."

"You are twenty, not twenty-one."

"One is considered to have left girlhood at twenty, Ma. I would have thought you, above all people, would be aware of that."

"What's come over you? You used to be so pleasant. Let's hope that when the baby comes, you'll feel different."

Anna's face actually stretched, and then she laughed before she said, "I certainly shall," and went out.

Avoiding the old way, she crossed the edge of the moor, then followed a bridle path that led onto the coach road. When she finally turned into the drive, she saw the carriage standing in front of the house. And Walters answered the door, exclaiming, "Why, miss! You're just in time; the master was for visiting you."

"Oh, Anna. Anna."

She turned quickly to look up the stairs and see Timothy descending, his hands outstretched. "Come in. Come in." He helped her off with her cloak, then turned to the maid. "Oh, Mary, go and ask cook if she would please let us have some tea and a cake or two."

Timothy led Anna into the sitting room, saying, "Oh, I have so much to tell you." He pressed her into the upholstered chair by the fire and pulled up a footstool. "Oh, dear me; you . . . you still look pale. But is it any wonder? It was a miracle that you survived—in that weak condition and having to cope with that dreadful plague. I've wondered at the bravery of many people during that time, but mostly of yourself. Did . . . did you ever think you would catch it?"

"Yes. Every day. But there was no bravery to my efforts, Tim, just necessity."

She let out a long, slow breath and looked at him. "Tell me what you did in London."

"With regard to books, my business could have been seen to in two days . . . but Walters took me to a theater, and afterwards another and another. We did the galleries, and time and again I thought of how I'd have loved you to be there. You must go to London sometime. I will take you to London. Yes, yes, I will."

She laughed at him and said, "All right, all right. Yes, I will go to London with you, sir, anytime, anytime. I . . . I have missed you."

He stared into her face before he said, "You really have?"

"Yes. Yes, very much. Oh, very much of late. Have you ever thought, Tim, how changeable human nature is? Do you think a character can change, really change?"

His voice was slow and thoughtful as he gave his opinion. "Not fundamentally," he said. "If life went smoothly, I think our characters would remain the same except when we are hit by circumstance. To give an example. Penella, as you heard, caught the cholera. Everyone in the hospital thought she was dying. This prompted me to go and tell Simon it was his duty to see her. I don't know what transpired between them, but when I next saw her, she was a different creature. She had undoubtedly been terrified by what had befallen her, but the experience must have acted like a cleansing balm, because she said to me, 'Do you think he will ever forgive me?' You know, Anna, she was still in love with him. And I know at bottom, while being deeply hurt, he was still in love with her.

Anyway, I wasn't surprised that when she was able to be moved, he took her home. Cholera, my dear, is a potent drug."

Quietly Anna asked, "Will they remain together?"

"Yes. Yes, I think so. . . . Ah, here's Mary and Walters with the tea. And a cream sponge cake! Oh, Mary, tell cook I love her."

"Yes, sir. I'll do that." The girl grinned widely, and Walters wheeled the trolley up to the end of the couch.

"Would you kindly pour out, madam?" Timothy said.

Anna poured out the tea, then cut into the sponge cake, and he, leaning towards her in order to take it, said, "You know, I think the essence of a happy household starts in the kitchen."

"Yes, I think so, too."

She sat at one end of the couch, and when he sat down next to her, he took her hand and just stared into the fire. "It's odd the dreams one conjures up by looking into the flames. I see pictures there, but the print, so to speak, is in my mind." And after a pause he added, "You always have nice fires up at the cottage."

"Fires are only nice when the prints are nice, and the prints are only nice when people are in accord; otherwise, flames can arouse anger."

"*Anna.*" He twisted round. "What is it? You're unhappy. What's happened?"

"The simple answer, Tim, would be to say I've been left out in the cold, and I don't like it. But it's more than that. It's a great unrest, and it's been in me for a long time."

When her head drooped and she couldn't go on, he said, "Tell me. We're friends, close friends; you can tell me anything."

She began, hesitantly, to tell him how she had felt over the last two years. She even mentioned that she had thought she might be in love with Simon, but found she wasn't. Then her voice broke when she came to Jimmy and how he had almost begged her to get away. Then she talked of how her father seemed to hold her responsible for Ben's death because of her association with The Manor.

She next told him that her mother had been left a considerable sum of money, but they had never offered her a farthing. She then related her mother's words when she thought she was going to die, of the promise, which would have tied her to the house and her father. But then she came to Cherry's predicament, and she could

The Love Child

not keep the hurt from her voice as she said, "They welcomed it, Tim. They welcomed it because it would mean starting another family. And only today my mother said that I would feel better when the baby came. You see, I am to be the handmaid, the baby-minder, relegated to one of the boys' beds in the roof. And my father is welcoming Oswald's engagement, too, because he is hoping for more children. He can see the house coming alive again, and him instructing, teaching . . . teaching. Oh, I know what's in his mind. Well, Tim, I'm escaping. I have decided to leave."

"Oh, my dear. Have you talked this over with Miss Netherton?"

"Miss Netherton wants me to stay with her. I have other ideas."

He turned from her and leaned forward with his elbows on his knees, joining his hands together. He seemed to be in a reverie.

"Don't you want to know what I'm going to do?" she said.

"Oh, yes, of course." He turned to her again.

She drew herself up, walked to the tea trolley, and arranged the dirty cups and saucers, while he sat watching her. But then he got to his feet and walked over and said, "What is it, Anna?"

At this, she gave the trolley a push that would have sent it halfway across the room had he not grabbed it; then taking her hand, he drew her to stand on the rug in front of the fire, and she said, "I've . . . I've got a proposition to put to you."

"Yes? Yes, well, go ahead and put it."

"Well—" She hesitated, then said, "First of all, I must tell you one thing, and I'm very very sure of this and have been for a long time, whether you have known it or not. . . . I love you."

She watched the color seep from his cheeks. Then she went on. "The proposition is this. You can either marry me, or I can become your mistress."

When he dropped back onto the couch and covered his face with his hands, she thought she had embarrassed him. She was about to say, I'm sorry, when his arms shot out and round her, and the next minute he had swung her onto the couch, and they were lying on their sides looking at each other. "Oh, Anna, my love. What have you said? Only what I've longed to hear for years and years. I've longed to hear those words—I love you—because I couldn't say them to you, not in the state I am in. To offer to be my mistress . . . Oh, Anna, that in a way is a great compliment, but I don't want a mistress—I want a wife. I've always wanted you as my wife. . . .

Don't cry, my love. Don't cry." And now he laid his lips on hers, and the kiss was long and tender. When their lips parted, they looked at each other in silence until he said, "Oh, Anna, I think Byron's words *Let joy be unconfined* fit how I feel. How soon can we be married?"

"As soon as you like, my dear."

"So be it, as soon as I like." And when she whispered, "Well, let it be that soon or sooner," they fell together and laughed and rocked each other.

"Oh, Tim. My dear, dear Tim, I do love you, and I have for a long, long time. Looking back, I think the seed was sown the day you looked at me from the mat and spoke one word—angel."

"Well, my love, that's how I've thought of you ever since. But now"—he lifted her hand—"we will go into town tomorrow, and you'll have a ring." He kissed her gently, saying, "I want to shout this out to someone. Shall we tell the staff? Would it upset you?"

"Upset me? Oh, no, Tim. You do me an honor, and I am well aware you know my history. It isn't everyone who would—"

He clapped his hand over her mouth, saying, "You are worth the love of any man, and *I am honored.* Honored and so very very grateful. Oh, Anna, you said you had felt rejected. Well, I have felt rejected ever since this cursed thing struck me. People were even afraid to be in my company in case I had . . . one of those. Many a time I have left a company to prevent myself crying in front of them, because I knew they couldn't differentiate between someone who had fits and a mental defective." He nodded his head now. "Yes, my dear, till the day I die, I will be indebted to you. But I shall tell you this. When I was in London, I saw the specialist, and he has come up with a pill that although it cannot prevent the attacks, it can decrease their severity. Well, so far, so good. Now let's go and tell them."

He led her out of the drawing room, and seeing Walters, he called, "Would you be kind enough, Walters, to bring in Edward and Fletcher. I have some news I would like you all to share."

"Yes. Yes, of course, sir." He smiled widely before hurrying out.

And now Tim led her into the kitchen. "Where is that woman who stuffs me with cream sponge cake? Oh, there you are, cook!"

Mrs. Ada Sprigman turned from the table, her face beaming. And the kitchen maid, Lena Cassidy, bobbed from one to the other. And Mary Bowles said, "Is there anything you want, sir?"

The Love Child

"Yes, I want all your attention; Walters has gone for Edwards and Fletcher. I have some news for you."

And at this, Walters entered with the coachman and the gardener just as Timothy, looking round his small staff, said, "It is with the greatest pleasure I tell you that Miss Dagshaw has consented to be my wife."

There was a slight gasp or two, then a chorus of "Oh, sir. Oh, miss. Oh, congratulations!"

"When is it to be, sir?" said Edward, and Timothy answered, "Well, it would be tonight if I had my way, but it will be by special license sometime within the next week or so."

"Oh, I'll make you a spread like you've never seen afore, sir—that's if you're having it in the house."

Timothy turned to Anna, and Anna, looking at the cook, said, "That would be lovely, Mrs. Sprigman, to have it in this house." And Timothy, nodding, said, "I think a drink would be in order. Have we any Champagne, Walters?"

"No, sir. But there's a very good claret and a port and, if the ladies would prefer it, a sherry."

"Well, bring the three choices into the sitting room, and we'll drink there. So, come along. . . ."

His hold on Anna's hand was only released when they all held a glass and the staff drank to their health. And when Tim's glass of claret touched Anna's glass and he said, "May you know nothing but happiness, my dear, from now on," there was a concerted chorus of, "Hear! Hear, sir. Hear! Hear!"

Just before the staff left the room, the cook, looking at Timothy, said, "Would you like me to knock you up a nice dinner, sir? I had two pheasants come in this mornin'."

Timothy said to Anna, "You'll stay to dinner, won't you?" And she, without hesitation, said, "Yes, I'd be delighted to."

It was turned seven o'clock when they finished their dinner in the dining room. Anna had never sat down to such a table, nor had she ever eaten such a meal or drunk so much wine. And so, when Walters said to Timothy, "It's snowing heavily, sir," Timothy said, "Oh, dear. The carriage is going to have a job. Is it sticking?"

"It's a good inch, sir, and the wind's blowing. There'll be drifts already."

"Go see what Edward thinks. We'll go by that, eh?"

With the room to themselves, Timothy murmured, "Well, now, milady, what's to happen if you can't get home?"

She smiled back at him across the table as she answered, "I'll take great pleasure in staying the night here, sir."

"Oh, Anna, Anna. Seriously, would you stay the night?"

"Why not."

"Why not, indeed! I shall get Mary to put a warming pan into the spare-room bed. But I do feel your people should be told. I'll ask Edward to go over on horseback. If it's only an inch or so, the horse will get through, whereas the carriage . . . well, that's a different thing. Excuse me, my dear."

After he had gone from the room, she sat back and closed her eyes and said to herself, Oh, Jimmy, Jimmy, what a beautiful escape! And they'll say, Why him? Look what she's saddled herself with—a man who has fits . . . a wonderful man, a thinking man, a kind and generous man.

Timothy came back into the room, saying, "It's all been taken care of. Come, my dear, we'll have coffee in the drawing room."

They were crossing the hall when he suddenly stopped and exclaimed, "Christmas! We'll have a big tree in the corner there, aglow with candles, and holly and mistletoe everywhere."

"How old did you say you were?" she said. And he replied, "You've put me into my second childhood, dear." A moment later he placed his hands on her shoulders and asked quietly, "Would you like children?" and as quietly she answered, "I'd love children, Tim. How many would you like?" And he said, "Let me think. Well, ten's a round number. I like round numbers, but I'll be satisfied with five."

"Oh, Tim." She put her arms about him, and when they now kissed, it wasn't gentle, but hungry. And when at last they stood apart, he said, "It must be soon, mustn't it?" And she answered, "Yes."

IT WAS nine days later when they were married by Parson Mason in the little church at Fellburn. All her family were present, as, of course, was Miss Netherton and also Timothy's own staff, but his two nephews were conspicuous by their absence. There were also present Dan Wallace and his wife and son, Art; Miss Penelope Smythe, the dressmaker; and Roland Watts, the carpenter, and his wife.

It would seem that with this representation from the village the inhabitants were wishing her well. But still, in the King's Head there were those who reminded others that it was through her that two men and a girl languished in jail. Anyway, she had always lived up to her name; in fact, both lasses had, for there was one with her belly full and not married yet. And this one had stayed the night with him, hadn't she? Oh, once a gillyvor, always a gillyvor. Just wait and see when she sprouted the next little gillyvor, for that would give the game away. Wait till August or September; we'll see.

And there's another thing: Where did the old uns in the hollow get the money for a new horse and trap? Also buying that pit lad a share in the boatyard, and his not being apprenticed a year yet. Who said the wicked didn't prosper, especially when the devil took a hand in molding them, like the new Mrs. Barrington, driving here and there in her carriage and pair. Aye, the trouble that one had caused in high and low quarters alike.

It was certainly true what Parson Fawcett said: The evil that men do lives after them, but the evil that women do goes on for countless generations through their breeding.

Epilogue

THERE was an announcement in the BIRTHS column of *The Times* and also in the local papers, which read as follows:

> On the 1st December, 1884, a daughter to Mr. and Mrs. Timothy Barrington of Briar Close, Maple Road, Fellburn. Joy unconfined.

ABOUT THE AUTHOR

The lively give-and-take of family life was a major ingredient in Catherine Cookson's last Condensed Books selection, *The Bailey Chronicles*. Now it reappears in *The Love Child*. Such an interest in the affections and strains of large family groups should come as no surprise. Cookson's own family was both large and diverse: together with her mother, she lived with her grandparents, her uncle, and as many as three lodgers in a three-room flat. Needless to say, their kitchen, in East Jarrow, like the long room in Heap Hollow, was a very busy place.

However, in Catherine Cookson's home there was far more strain than sensitivity. Born illegitimate and in dire poverty to an alcoholic mother, she had to struggle hard to overcome difficult circumstances. After going to work as a domestic at age fourteen, she saved for years to buy her own business, then married her true love, math teacher Tom Cookson. Writing more than eighty works of fiction, she went on to become Britain's best-loved storyteller. Now, despite advancing age, she's still hard at work, making the very best of her world.

Catherine Cookson

She and Tom have simplified their life by moving from their large house in the Northumberland countryside to a bungalow in Newcastle upon Tyne. With failing eyesight, Cookson must now dictate her novels. It's a painstaking process, but nothing stops her from writing. "She tells a story hot into the tape," Tom says. "When it comes back from the typist, I read it to her slowly. She sees it in her mind and edits it." Each morning they devote two hours to opening the author's fan mail and determining which letters need her personal response. "She's a very strong person with this tremendously strong personality," says her proud husband. "She's really magnificent."

$100,00
THE MU
Of our late beloved Presiden
IS STILL AT
$50,000 R
$25,000 RE
$25,000 REV
EDWIN M. STANTON, Secret

AMERICAN GOTHIC

The Story of the Booth Tragedy
GENE SMITH

There was a streak of madness in the family. In some, it took the form of an uncanny gift for the stage that made the theatrical Booths the toast of Europe and America. But it had a dark side as well: alcoholism, violence, melancholia—and in John Wilkes Booth, the capacity to turn his frightening obsessions into terrifying reality.

By 1881 THE house on the sandy country lane two and a half miles out of Port Royal, on the way to Bowling Green, was streaked from need of painting, and looked badly weather-beaten to the Massachusetts reporter. But then, he had found all of the Virginia of after the war desolate and run down. The house's cattle shed was crumbling, the wooden mill for crushing sugarcane was idle, the servant quarters almost tenantless, and the hands of the women who received him were roughened by labors performed by no southern lady before.

There were no men. The oldest of the women remembered perfectly the visitor to what had been her parents' home sixteen years earlier. "I thought he was the handsomest man I had ever seen," she said. The reporter was shown a charred-post remainder of the vanished tobacco barn. The previous summer, he was told, a piece taken from it and tipped with gold was offered for sale in a Baltimore store. "Think of it—five dollars for a piece not as big as your little finger!"

By the 1920s the house was abandoned. The walls sagged, the broken windows gaped, and the roof appeared ready to collapse. Before the beginning of World War II it had done so. In 1965 the sandy country lane, which had become U.S. Route 301, was widened and made into a divided highway. There is a thickly wooded little hillock in the median strip; that is where the house once stood. Down the road a few yards is a historical marker.

Far away to the north the statue of John Parker Hale, Congressman, United States Senator, and minister to Spain, stands before the capitol of the state of New Hampshire. Not one in ten thousand people passing by knows who his daughter was and what it meant to her that once along a farm lane in Virginia a tobacco barn burned, and on the porch of a house now vanished beneath a highway median strip a man died looking at his paralyzed hands and murmuring, "Useless, useless."

Still farther away, in Hanover, Germany, a cemetery became the last resting place of the daughter and son-in-law of one of John Parker Hale's Senate colleagues. She was dead by her husband's gun, and he, horribly wounded by his own knife, was entirely insane and destined to live out his days in a German mental institution. A son of that fatal marriage grew up to be an Illinois Congressman, successfully proposing in 1930 that the government establish a museum in a former Washington, D.C., theater to commemorate what his mother and father had seen and undergone there and what the father had so frightfully duplicated long after. Madness. His father had never recovered from that night in the theater—the feeling that he should have, could have, averted all.

The museum is visited by no less than eight hundred thousand persons annually, six to eight thousand people a day in the spring, when tourists flood Washington. Most of the visitors know something beforehand of the exhibits they study, but so many years have passed that old legends have faded from public consciousness. Each April by the Hudson River a black crepe–hung train, which once had gone through vast crowds of weeping people, was said to come again, now as a spectral pilot engine pulling an open car with a band of unattended instruments playing silent dirges. And behind the funeral train itself were skeletons sitting by a coffin and vast numbers of blue-coated men, the ghosts of the Union army, bearing more coffins. Spots on the brick pavement before the former theater were said to glow a brilliant, terrible red; in the dark building, a woman screamed and suddenly all was lit up; and the alley behind filled with black cats and howling dogs through which came a galloping horse bearing a rider frantically lashing his mount as voices cried, "Get him! Get him!" Then, in a twinkle, all would go dark and silent again.

Time has run its course, and the legends have faded; and the Victorian era's marble-topped tables, wax flowers under bell glass, and heavy lace curtains have given way to other things. Once the New York theater area was in Park Row, below the Five Points. Then it moved to Union Square, then up to Madison Square, and in the end located at Times Square, Broadway. Across the country a multitude of old theaters have burned or become storage houses or factory lofts. It is natural. Everything changes.

But not quite everything. On the third floor of number 16 Gramercy Park South, in New York, an elaborate clock with a bronze bull beneath and a bronze woman above is set at the moment of the death of the only person ever to occupy this room. At one seventeen on a June morning in 1893, the lights went out momentarily as a woman screamed, "Don't let Father die in the dark!" When the electricity came back on, he was gone. His pens are in the room, pictures of his father, the book he was reading when his last stroke took him, opened at the last page he ever saw.

In a corner is Macbeth's sword. Outside in the halls are Lear's robes and Shylock's and those of Richard III. Down below, on the ground floor, are his crowns of kings, and helmets of warriors, and his portrait done by John Singer Sargent. Even now, a century later, he is annually toasted before this portrait as the greatest actor and the finest gentleman the American stage ever produced. Outside, in the center of Gramercy Park, stands his statue in bronze.

Above the sleeping alcove of his suite is carved in wood, NOW BLESSINGS ON HIM THAT FIRST INVENTED THIS SAME SLEEP. Facing the bed is the largest picture in the room, the wife of his youth he never ceased to love and for more than three decades longed to join in death. It is so placed that it would have been the last thing he saw at night before closing his eyes and the first thing in the morning.

In the room is a picture of one whose name could never be mentioned in his presence. He himself would not speak that name, not for nearly thirty years. Yet by the bed is a photograph of a superlatively handsome face. Johnny.

I

HE WAS, of course, quite mad, and well known for being so. THE MAD TRAGEDIAN HAS COME TO OUR CITY, newspaper headlines said. His father had tried to make of him an artist, a printer. He had put him in his office to learn the law. His son became an actor. Who can say why? In later years it was said of Junius Brutus Booth that if the stage had not existed, he would have created it. That he *necessitated* the stage. That his nature lay in Shakespeare's mind, and that when, centuries after Shakespeare's death, this interpreter of his words appeared, it was as the destined representative of the playwright's grandest creations. Booth was sublime, supernatural, the purveyor of a dynamic, tortured power that left audiences deeply shaken. He filled up the stage with his personality. His blue eyes shone with a terrible light. The tones of his voice were immense.

It was quite amazing. An undersized youth who rehearsed in the most desultory fashion, whose physical presence offstage was—when he was sober—mild, modest, unpretentious, and shy, whose bowed legs made him, people said, a poor prospect to stop a runaway pig, seized the theater and made it his.

Those who saw him never forgot. "I can see again," the aged Walt Whitman wrote, "Booth's quiet entrance from the side, as with head bent he slowly walks down the stage to the footlights with peculiar and abstracted gesture. Though fifty years have passed since then, I can still feel the perfect hush of perhaps three thousand people waiting."

The father, Richard Booth, had been born in London, the son of a silversmith said to be descended from a Spanish Jew named Botha who had been expelled from his homeland in the seventeenth century for speaking against the royalist government. Richard Booth continued in the family tradition, and when the American Colonists revolted against George III, he and a cousin decided to join their cause. On October 28, 1777, the two young men wrote the leading parliamentary opponent of the war, to ask aid for a journey to America. A stormy libertine, the author of pornographic works that at one time brought him banishment from England, but withal a genuine devotee of liberty, John Wilkes was a distant relative of the Booths. He turned the letter over to Richard's father, who had his son arrested and then arranged such restrictions as would make it improbable that Richard would be able to attempt the journey again.

With a silver presentation sent to John Wilkes by way of thanks for not encouraging the wayward son, the father convinced Richard to become a lawyer. In time he became a mildly prosperous one. Whatever his thoughts about what the hoped-for sponsor of his trip had done, they did not prevent him from marrying John Wilkes's niece. He never lost his regard for the Colonies that had become the United States, and kept a portrait of George Washington in his parlor, requesting all who came before it to offer a bow.

Mr. and Mrs. Richard Booth had three children, the wife dying in childbirth when the last one, a girl, arrived. The would-be revolutionist kept his antimonarchical principles. He named his first son Algernon Sidney, in honor of the antiroyalist sent to the scaffold for opposing the rule of Charles II, and the second, born on May 1, 1796, for Junius Brutus, the remote ancestor of Caesar's assassin, who had opposed the Roman monarchy and was a founder of the republic. The girl was unideologically named Jane.

Junius Brutus Booth

Junius Brutus Booth began his career on December 13, 1813, as Campillo in *The Honeymoon*, and trouped the provinces playing in tents on market day, and from booths in fields where fairs were held. He competed with trained dogs, jugglers, stilt walkers, prizefighters. The footlights were tallow candles set on plates floating in a trough of water. The crudely painted backdrops scarcely differentiated between Bosworth Field and a drawing room. He was indifferent to his costumes, as he always would be.

He joined a troupe going to Belgium, where the British were massing men to meet Napoléon at Waterloo, and at a Brussels lodging house he took up with the landlady's daughter. Adelaide Delannoy was four years older than he. She left home to troupe about with him. On May 8, 1815, they were married. Then they went to London, where his playing was such as to make Edmund Kean, of whom Samuel Taylor Coleridge had said that to see him play was "as to read Shakespeare by lightning," fear for his laurels.

Mary Ann Booth

The couple seemed happy enough. They went out in London society a great deal, or at least that part of society that would socially accept an actor. In 1819 Adelaide Booth presented her husband with a son, who was named Richard, after his grandfather.

483

American Gothic

One day in a flower shop near Covent Garden, Booth took note of a girl selling blooms. Mary Ann Holmes was six years younger than the twenty-four-year-old actor, who had been married for more than half a decade. She was beautiful—one need only study the pictures of the children she would have to see that it was so. Booth took up with her. As had his wife before their marriage, Mary Ann trouped about with him. In 1821 he managed a trip with her to Madeira, taking with him his piebald pony, Peacock. It was on Madeira that she learned she was pregnant.

His wife, his father, and his child awaited him in London. But he loved Mary Ann and, indeed, in the decades of life remaining never looked at another woman. Flight with her seemed the answer to his problem. America beckoned. And the clipper *Two Brothers* had put in at Madeira. Its next port of call was Norfolk, Virginia. They loaded Peacock on board and set sail.

The voyage lasted forty-four days. They landed in June of 1821. He wrote to Adelaide that he had run into some trouble with British stage people and so would play in America for a time; he would faithfully send money for her and Richard. The last was true.

Within a year he was the most prominent actor on the American continent. "He was followed as a marvel," said the critic William Winter. "Mention of his name stirred an enthusiasm no other could awaken."

Yet very shortly it was seen that he was difficult. More than difficult. He was the wildest drinker anyone had ever seen. Nothing was beyond him when he was drinking. He could desert Ophelia to dash up a ladder where, perched among the overhead backdrops, he crowed like a rooster. Carried to his lodgings, he could escape and be found walking entirely naked down a road. Managers all over the country learned to lock him up before a performance. He was adept at getting liquor despite all efforts aimed at prevention. He bribed hotel bellhops to bring a bottle and the stem of a long tobacco pipe to the keyhole of a locked door so that he could use the latter to sip the former dry. Then, at the theater, it would be a great question of what might happen. Once he fell on stage, and the audience booed. Another actor got him up, and he staggered to the footlights to shake his fist at the people and shout, "Wait! Wait! I'll be back in five minutes and give you the damnedest performance of King Lear you've ever seen!" He probably did.

Mary Ann Holmes—Mrs. Booth to everyone in America—gave birth to a son, Junius Brutus, Jr. There followed a daughter, Rosalie. The family lived in Exeter Street, Baltimore. He rented a cabin and some hundred and fifty acres for summer use in Bel Air, Harford County, Maryland, about twenty-five miles from Baltimore, and then purchased it. He called his place The Farm. All life on his property must be sacred, he said, for it came from the Almighty. He absolutely forbade the killing of anything found on The Farm. He would not permit the branding of his cattle and hogs, for it might pain them. They were never consumed on his grounds, nor were his chickens, and his children were brought up as the strictest vegetarians. No one was permitted the use of firearms on vermin. Lizards, turtles, and mosquitoes he regarded as deserving of life no less than himself. He refused to own slaves, but leased them from neighbors, housing and nursing and burying them. He forbade the cutting of flowers, and only already fallen trees were used for the fireplaces.

He farmed seriously, subscribing to journals on the subject. Often he drove a wagon filled with goods to Marsh Market in Baltimore. There he would stand surrounded by his produce, wearing a blue coat with brass buttons, and a broad-brimmed hat. To the neighbors he was Farmer Booth.

No greater contrast to the hustle and lights and glare and travel of an actor's life could be imagined than the remote and forest-bound farm in Bel Air. Some wondered how he endured it. Yet he seemed happy there with Mary Ann and a growing family of children, ten in number, of whom four died young. But wreathed in glory, he suddenly applied for the full-time job of keeper of the lighthouse on North Carolina's Cape Hatteras. The pay for the

Booth's Bel Air home

position was three hundred dollars a year. He could make that and more any week he appeared in a theater. Actors and managers finally talked him out of the idea, and it was well that they did so, said one friend, for it would be wiser to douse the light completely and let the ships take their chances than to leave its running to Junius Brutus Booth.

It could not have been said that he was drunk when he undertook to secure the lighthouse job, for he pursued the matter for many weeks. Something deeper was involved, and it was soon said of him that he was the premier example of Plato's rule that for an artist of the very highest rank a dash of insanity is indispensable. He was a kindly man, generous, loving, sincere, almost childlike in his faith in the essential goodness of human nature; and usually his seizures harmed nobody except possibly himself. That he sometimes painted his face and dressed as an Indian chief, that he howled "Murder!" in a restaurant each time a friend swallowed an oyster—whom did it hurt?

Well read and intellectual—his library contained works by Shelley, Keats, Coleridge, Racine, Dante, Plutarch, Milton, and Locke—he was a linguist capable of performing in French and conversing in German. He knew Greek and Latin and Spanish, and worked on Arabic and Italian. But there was always that madness, which sometimes, not often, could turn potentially lethal. There was a distinct danger to the well-being of Mary Ann Holmes when, upon the pony Peacock's death, he forced her to wrap herself in a sheet and sit on the body while he walked about with a shotgun in his hand reading a funeral service. The death of anything or anyone close to him always had more than a normal effect upon him. Told at a theater in Baltimore that a daughter had died, he flung himself on a horse and, with his Richard III cloak streaming behind him, galloped home. He broke into the vault, got out the child's body, and lay in bed with it, crying and laughing. Mary Ann Holmes did not interfere nor argue with him. She seemed to understand that when at times he was not himself, he could not help it. She loved him, and he was very sweet when he was himself.

The couple's last child was born in 1840, nearly twenty years after they had left Madeira with Peacock, the pony. During all that time several letters a year and sufficient money for her to live on had regularly been dispatched to the real Mrs. Junius Brutus

Booth, who had gone to live with her mother in Brussels. Twice, the husband had gone back to call upon the wife, taking with him, but carefully hiding, Mary Ann and a growing number of children. Adelaide Delannoy Booth's marriage was of a quarter century's duration, and she appeared to have accepted its long-distance nature. Then she found out everything.

WHAT happened was that Mrs. Booth's son, reaching his middle twenties, decided to visit his father in far-off Maryland. He soon discovered that Junius Brutus Booth was a wild drinker. Then he discovered something infinitely more startling. Theater people told him that his name could not legitimately be Booth. To them, the real Booths were the half-dozen children of Baltimore's Exeter Street and The Farm. Richard wrote his mother. Her reaction may well be imagined. She took a ship to America. The ship was wrecked. She survived, went back to Europe, and booked passage on another. She arrived in New York and made for Baltimore. It was October of 1846.

Her husband was away. He was beginning a winter tour, she wrote her sister Thérèse, back in Brussels. "I don't want to do anything to prevent him from making money, so I shall wait until he comes to Baltimore, and as soon as he arrives my lawyer will fall on his back like a bomb."

It was not only the lawyer who exploded upon the actor when he returned. His wife's detonation was even more violent. When he came to Marsh Market to sell his vegetables, he was likely to find her there offering her opinion of him in tones audible to all who cared to hear. Sometimes she paraded in front of the Exeter Street house, shouting. In an age when to be illegitimate was to be a social leper, she defined, loudly, what she called the Holmes set as exactly what they were, each and every one: bastards.

It was quite horrible. Mary Ann endured the insults silently and with what the neighbors felt was considerable dignity. It can only be guessed how she and Junius Brutus Booth explained the situation to their children—the oldest in his twenties and the youngest six years of age. Booth appealed to his wife to return to Brussels; she would not. She took a flat to wait out the period of Maryland residency necessary before filing for divorce. So for five years the parents and children had to live through a state of matters with which all Baltimore was conversant. Booth had always looked upon his home as a resting place from the rigors of the theater and the road. Now trouping seemed almost a vacation.

Yet when he was away, he drank more than when he was at home, and when he drank, his madness intensified. For a time Mary Ann prevailed upon the oldest son, Junius Brutus, Jr., to accompany him, but it did not work out well. June, as the family called him, was not suited to be his father's guardian. So the job was given to the second son, Edwin. He was barely into his teenage years, born November 13, 1833, on a night of spectacular celestial display that saw star-shower rains of meteors shoot through the skies in such fashion that people thought the heavens were falling. He came into the world with a caul, which was carefully preserved. Such a child, the black workers on The Farm said, would be gifted to see ghosts and guided by a lucky star.

Edwin grew into a frail-looking, withdrawn youth, notably different from his active older brother. He took up no sports, and appeared gloomily mute and ill at ease in most situations. He was slim and no taller than five feet seven. He had great dark luminous eyes.

School was in session when it was decided that Edwin would replace his brother June as their father's guardian. He was taken out of class, never to return save for haphazardly spaced periods when his father was between engagements. They set out, the strange pair, a brilliant actor who was also a madman, and a somber boy. Edwin entered a world of endless travel by springless stagecoach jolting over muddy roads, indifferently heated trains, dismal hotels and hostelries. Up and down and across the country the quiet, frail son attended a father whose frenzies on stage could lead him so to attack Desdemona that when he pushed the pillow down on her face, it became apparent that she might actually perish at his hands. She was saved only when cast members rushed out and pulled Othello away.

After a performance in Boston the father declared that the hotel room, situated just over the stables, was too odiferous to endure. "I won't stay here," he told Edwin. "I'm suffocating."

"You're not going out, Father." To go out meant he would find drink. They stared at each other. The older man turned and stepped into a closet and bolted the door. Edwin waited. The amount of air available in the closet was limited. He banged on the door. There was no response. He kicked and smashed and rattled the handle. He was about to run into the hall to scream for help when his father opened the door, came out, and got into bed.

Sometimes he could not be restricted to the indoors, and when that happened, Edwin simply stuck to him. In Louisville, after a performance, Junius felt he must walk the streets. He ended in a long, covered market, walking its length back and forth all night, Edwin behind him every step. At daylight he concluded his pacing and headed back to the hotel, Edwin alongside. In the course of the endless marching neither had spoken a single word.

In September of 1849, in the theater called the Boston Museum—in deference to Boston's Puritan traditions—the stage manager complained to Edwin about being slated to play Tressel to the Richard III of Edwin's father in addition to his regular duties. "This is too much work for one man. *You* ought to play Tressel."

The elder Booth had never wanted to have any of his blood play. He did not wish any of his offspring to know of his profession, much less follow him into it. But Edwin knew the few lines. That night the father sat with his feet on the table of his dressing room, wearing his costume, a long and belted purple velvet shirt ornamented with jewels. "Who was Tressel?" he asked his son.

"A messenger from the field of Tewkesbury."

"What was his mission?"

"To bear the news of the defeat of the king's party."

"How did he make the journey?"

"On horseback."

"Where are your spurs? Here, take mine."

Edwin unbuckled them from his father's heels and went out and played his brief part. When he finished, he returned to his father's dressing room to find him exactly as he had left him, with his feet still up on the table.

"Have you done well?"

"I think so."

"Give me my spurs."

Edwin was not yet sixteen. For the rest of his life he believed that his father had watched his debut from the wings before running to his dressing room to put his feet back on the table.

But the elder Booth could not hold forever to his policy of forbidding the stage to Edwin. Following that night, he capitulated.

Edwin began playing small parts opposite his father. But when he was not on stage, his father forbade him to watch from the wings. He could listen, but not see, for the elder Booth wanted his son's ear educated first. He offered no other suggestions, Edwin remembered, no "instructions, professional advice, or encouragement." This seeming indifference was very painful, he told his intimates decades later. But it made him think for himself. That was what his father must have wanted.

They were playing New York's National Theater in February of 1851 when one night at the hotel, for no apparent reason, the father announced he would not appear as scheduled. "Who can they substitute at the last moment?" Edwin asked.

"Go act it yourself." The father refused to leave the room.

Edwin had himself driven to the theater and announced that he would be playing that night. In his father's robes, which hung loose upon him, he went on. The audience had come expecting the great Junius Brutus Booth and got instead a seventeen-year-old impersonating King Richard III. At first there was some grumbling. Then there was intent silence. Something was happening on stage. Edwin Booth was playing the first lead role of his life.

Two months later the uncontested divorce suit of Adelaide Delannoy Booth was granted. Junius Brutus Booth and Mary Ann Holmes were wed on May 10, 1851, the thirteenth birthday of one of their children, the one named for the slight relative who had blocked old Richard Booth's plans to join the American revolutionists, the English statesman John Wilkes.

II

JOHNNY Booth and his sister Asia were best friends. Their brother June, older by fifteen years, was out in the world. Rosalie, older by more than a decade, was neurotically withdrawn. Edwin was perpetually on the road with Father. The youngest, Joseph, was almost another Rosalie—strange. In later years Joseph said he had first begun suffering from what he called melancholy insanity at the age of ten or twelve.

But Johnny and Asia had each other. She was two and a half years the elder, but never played the role of big sister. That Johnny was the favored child of both parents did not bother Asia. Johnny was her best-loved brother, the perfect playmate and confidant.

Theirs was a happy home. They were very healthy—"dyspepsia and heartburn were strangers to our abode," Asia wrote—which they attributed to getting up early, eating simple meals, and relying for illnesses upon home remedies of licorice and green figs, or chamomile, or sassafras. There was a cider press on The Farm, a swimming pond, great cherry trees to be climbed, sheep whose wool was spun into blankets, and many horses and dogs. Once a week the postboy rode down the rough coach road by The Farm to toss letters and newspapers and Father's agricultural magazines over the gate. There were no locks or bolts on any of the doors.

Asia was named for that continent upon which, her father said, man first walked with God. When she grew older, she sometimes fell into dark moods of what she called hours of self-inflicted torment, and what one of their rented servants termed Missy's long sulks.

Johnny wasn't that way. He was cheerful, joyful, full of fun, kinder, Asia said, than she, much more gentle. Both of them loved botany and geology, but he was tender of insects and butterflies and lightning bugs. Once she caught a katydid and said she wanted it for her collection, but he said, "No, you don't, you bloodthirsty female. Katy shall be free and shall sing tonight out in the sycamores." He kissed the little thing and put it on a tree leaf.

He taught her to ride, with and without a saddle. With his help she became what she called a reckless, if not accomplished, horsewoman. Johnny himself had a horse of pure black, with a mane and tail Asia braided in tiny plaits. He broke the colt and named it Cola di Rienzi, for the great Roman tribune. He taught him to stamp for no and bow and neigh for yes. Once Cola bit him. He burst into tears. "I could have stood anything but that, I love the creature so. For a pet horse to turn and bite is *vicious*."

But he could not stay depressed for long, whatever the cause. Unlike the somber Edwin, John was exuberant. Edwin rarely smiled and never laughed aloud; John always had a bright smile for people, and his laugh was charming and full. "How glorious it is to live!" he said to Asia. "To breathe this breath of life with a clear mind and healthy lungs!" They read aloud from Byron's poems as they sat together in a swing under the gum trees and hickories. When she was eighteen, Asia wrote a poem of her own. It told of a vision her mother had had when Johnny was born. She had looked into a fire, wondering what the future held for the infant in her arms, and the flames formed a single word: country.

THEY went to separate girls' and boys' boarding schools and at various times he was known as Jack Booth and as Billy Bowlegs, for he had inherited his father's limbs. At the end of one school year he gave Asia a paper upon which he had written what a Gypsy fortune-teller had told him. Asia kept the paper always. "Ah, you've a bad hand," the Gypsy had said. "You're born under an unlucky star. You've got in your hand a thundering crowd of enemies—not one friend—you'll make a bad end, and have plenty to love you afterwards. You'll have a fast life—short, but a grand one.

"Now, young sir, I've never seen a worse hand, and I wish I hadn't seen it, but every word I've told is true by the signs. You'd best turn a missionary or priest and try to escape it."

She was finished. "For this evil dose do you expect me to cross your palm?" Johnny asked. The answer was yes. She took his money, he told Asia, and said that she was glad she wasn't a young girl "or she'd follow me through the world for my handsome face."

He laughed with his sister. If his destiny was in the stars or written on his hand, how could he escape? It was his fate. He laughed, but often in future days referred to the Gypsy's words.

IN 1848 GOLD was discovered in California. An enormous migration of fortune-seekers headed west to dig into the colossal lode. Among the new arrivals was Junius Brutus Booth, Jr., just under thirty years of age. He had married and had a child by his wife and then taken up with Harriet Mace, whose brother Jem was the famed bare-knuckled prizefighter. Matters in the East were not pleasant for June and his paramour. Precisely as his father had aroused the wrath of his wife, so did June's activities enrage *his* wife. As his father before him, June took his lover and headed west.

June had picked up the rudiments of acting, but he knew he had no inspiration on the stage. What interested him was theater management. Gold-rush California was the proper place for him, for the miners were starving for entertainment of any type. The amount of compensation that could be realized was unprecedented in the history of the performing arts. Miners were capable of tossing chunks of gold on the stage to display their approval of a production. June set up theaters in Sacramento and San Francisco. Often his jerry-built constructions burned to the ground. June built new ones. His productions were primitive and the actors hardly of the first rank. It came to June that if he could induce a really first-class actor to come out to California, he could be rich. The really first-class actor whose name suggested itself to June was, of course, his father.

In early 1852 June and Harriet Mace made the tortuous trip to Maryland and found the head of the family engaged in remodeling The Farm's main residence into a pseudo-Elizabethan construction of leaded windows and what was called the Romeo and Juliet balcony. He had already picked out a new title for the Booth country residence: Tudor Hall. It was going to cost a lot of money. There was money to be made out on the Coast. In the spring of 1852 June and Harriet, accompanied by Father and Edwin, set out.

They sailed down the East Coast to Aspinwall (now Colón, Panama), a hellishly steamy and falling-apart place filled with rum shops selling quinine to ward off or cure malaria. The travelers jolted to the railroad terminus on the Chagres River, then went through terrifying green jungle. Their fellow journeyers were soldiers, escaped convicts, bail jumpers, and prostitutes, all flowing towards the western gold fields. The travelers slept with pistols in their hands.

They made Panama City and sailed north to San Francisco to find people living in board shanties, and boats abandoned in the harbor because their crews had run off to seek gold. There were lice and bugs everywhere, mud and rats. The town was known as the wickedest place on the continent, and it was said there was not a country in the world not represented there by at least one prostitute. There were seven hundred and forty-three bartenders listed in the city directory and a total of twenty-one clergymen.

They opened in June's Jenny Lind Theatre in San Francisco in July 1852, with Father playing Sir Edward Mortimer in *The Iron Chest* and Edwin supporting him as young Wilford. The shaggy miners and courtesans did not accord the great actor the reception to which he was accustomed. He went with Edwin to Sacramento, played for a time, returned to San Francisco, and appeared half a dozen times more. Then he was finished. He said he was going home, but Edwin should remain. Junius Brutus Booth told his son that if he was going to act, it was time he got out from under his father's shadow. After four months on the Coast the elder Booth booked sea passage to New Orleans.

Edwin's entire career had consisted of being his father's son. Now he was on his own. He was nineteen. He joined a troupe of strolling players and began the life he lived for years: playing the so-called theaters of the mining camps, Cock-Tail Cañon, Shirt-Tail Bend, Haytown, and Jackass Gulch. The stage was sometimes a few billiard tables pushed together with a dozen candles for the footlights. He blacked his face to thrum away in minstrel shows, while the "bones" rattled instruments. He played Richard III, Othello, and Iago. Years before, the French traveler Alexis de Tocqueville noted that even the rudest cabins of the American frontier contained two books—the Bible and the works of Shakespeare—and an astonishing number of wild men knew the King's lines and the Moor's, and showed their irritation by discharging their revolvers if a player confused his part.

Edwin drank like his father and perhaps more. No one not subject to that urge could understand its pull, he said. There were times when he would have sold his place in heaven for just one drink. Once, entirely done in, helpless, he fell into a river. A passerby pulled him out. Otherwise he would have drowned.

In the winter of 1852–53 Edwin's troupe became stranded in Nevada City. Snowdrifts had completely isolated the town. The theater was closed. The actors were hungry. Through the snow Edwin saw a courier he knew coming with a lantern. "What news is there?" Edwin asked. "Not good news for you, my boy." At once Edwin understood. He felt himself half-crazed with guilt for letting his father go somewhere by himself, without his son for the first time in more than half a decade.

Junius Brutus Booth had made New Orleans, played Sir Edward Mortimer in *The Iron Chest*, and then taken a Mississippi River steamboat for Cincinnati. On board, he grew feverish and drank of the river water. He grew worse. As he lay alone, a ship's steward asked if there were any help he could offer. "Pray, pray, pray," Booth said. Those were his last words. He was fifty-six. "There are no more actors!" cried the statesman and orator Rufus Choate.

He lay in state in his Baltimore home for three days, the walls draped with white and all ornaments removed, save for a bust of Shakespeare. People connected with the stage from Boston to New Orleans wore black crepe on their left arms for thirty days.

Edwin went back to San Francisco. June had built a third Jenny Lind Theatre in place of two burned ones, and was able to offer work in blackface productions, comedies, musical extravaganzas, burlesques, and Shakespeare.

In late 1854 Edwin and some others journeyed out to Australia, where the pickings were said to be immense. For nine months they labored back and forth across the Pacific, playing Hawaii, the Samoa Islands, Tahiti. When they made their way back to California, Edwin played Shylock and Lear. Then he went north on tour again, competing with dog and monkey shows and temperance lectures.

The fall of 1856 came. He had been away from home since the spring of 1852 and possessed five hundred dollars, enough to afford passage east. He had played every conceivable kind of theatrical role in front of audiences whose patience was limited and demeanor difficult. He had learned that for some, acting was a trade or a craft, but for others it was something higher that could not be taught or defined, but was a gift whose bestowal was only within the power of God.

When her husband died, in November of 1852, Mary Ann Booth's instinct was to continue farming. The oldest son at home would supervise the work. "John is trying to farm," Asia laconically wrote to a lifelong Baltimore friend.

But try as he might, Johnny's heart wasn't in it. He didn't see how he'd ever get anywhere trying, as he put it, to scratch a living from the soil. Asia understood. Her brother wanted to shine in the world. He was ambitious. Perhaps, she reflected, it came from reading dramatic plays.

Perhaps he never actually decided to be an actor; more likely he never thought of anything else. It seemed natural that when he saddled Cola and took a saber given Father by someone back from the Mexican War, he would spout Shakespearean lines as he galloped about flailing the weapon.

One day in August of 1855, with Father dead and Edwin and June away in the West, John rode up to where Asia was gathering apples and berries and said to her, "Well, Mother Bunch, guess what I've done! I've made my first appearance on any stage." It had been in Richmond at the St. Charles Theatre, under the management of British-born actress Laura Keene. The event had been a benefit for the actor John Sleeper Clarke—born John Clarke Sleeper—a boyhood chum of Edwin's who was on his way to becoming a noted comedian and who in time would marry Asia. John had played Richmond, athletically dueling with Richard III. His face shone with enthusiasm when he described it, but in fact he had forgotten his lines at one point and the audience had hissed. His mother was not happy at his debut. They had put him on, she said, for his name. He was seventeen years old and completely without performing experience. This was premature, Mrs. Booth said. He had been used by others.

He took to heart his mother's opinion, and it must have come to him what he had done, for that night, sitting in a swing with Asia, he said he knew he could never be as great as Father and did not think to try to rival Edwin, but that he wanted to be a southern actor and be loved by the southern people. He had always identified with the South, aped southern mannerisms, been offended when told to eat at the same table with hired white laborers. He certainly never got that from his father, who detested snobbery, but it was in him.

He had stuttered and stammered on the stage. He had assumed too much, been given too much. It was because his name was Booth. So he said he would renounce that name. He would seek acting assignments as J. B. Wilkes. When he made a success on his own, he said, he would take back his name. For three years he was Mr. J. B. Wilkes.

In late 1856 Edwin came home.

He had gone to California nearly five years earlier as the son of Junius Booth. Within a few months of his return to the East he was seen as the heir to his father's position on the American stage. But unlike his father, Edwin was the least extravagant actor imaginable. He seemed most to stir audiences not by the violence of his feelings, but the repression of them. He never exaggerated or overstepped, but was the picture of quietude on stage—reflective, restrained, seemingly natural.

He seemed to court rapturous silence rather than clamorous applause. He studied stagecraft and the work of other actors, but was unable to define how he achieved what he did. Asked to compare himself with his father, all he could offer was, "I think I am a little quieter."

In May of 1857 he opened in New York at Burton's Theatre, on Broadway opposite Bond Street. Among the people who came to see him was a thin, pale little man who wore glasses and had poor posture. Adam Badeau was an intellectual newspaper essayist of ambiguous sexual orientation. He believed the stage was the only art truly representative of American life, and soon he came to believe that Edwin Booth was the finest flower the American stage had yet produced. Badeau could not keep away from Burton's Theatre. He arranged an introduction to the young actor.

All his life Edwin lamented his lack of education. He was shy with everyone, but particularly with those who had been to college and knew Latin, knew books and art. Now, here was someone who belonged to The Century Association, membership in which was reserved for men of culture and letters. And Adam Badeau was hardly a threatening persona. Edwin took him as the closest friend he would ever know. He went with him to the literary salons Adam frequented, thrilled to be in such company. The two visited museums to see clothing of the times Shakespeare chronicled. Together they studied interpretations of Edwin's roles and argued the meaning of words and lines. Adam became his first confidant. Then things changed suddenly, as classically and dramatically as in any play. Enter Mary Devlin.

THE actor Joseph Jefferson, whose relation to comedy was for forty years what Edwin Booth's was to tragedy, had been, like Edwin, born to the stage. Once, a troupe he was in arrived at an Illinois town to find that due to the efforts of church fathers who had preached against the stage, a new law had been passed requiring an extraordinary licensing charge to perform so unholy a calling. A young lawyer turned up to tell the actors he would lodge an appeal without a fee. Perhaps the lawyer's wife put him up to it, for long before they met she had told a schoolmate that as far as her needs in a future husband went, "her choice should be willing and able to let her see as much of the theater as she wanted, and beyond that she did not expect to be too particular." When the schoolmate heard that she "had chosen a struggling young lawyer, the plainest

American Gothic

looking man in Springfield," the issue of the theatergoing immediately came to mind. In any event, the volunteer took up the exorbitant licensing fee before the city government and saved the day for Joseph Jefferson's troupe by getting the tax rescinded. The lawyer was Abraham Lincoln.

In the late 1850s Jefferson was managing a theater in Richmond, Virginia. His players included a young woman born in Troy, New York, in 1840. Her family was not well off, and Jefferson and his wife had taken her into their home when she was fifteen. Mary Devlin was thin, her face more sensitive than beautiful. Her eyes were her best feature, very large and exuding keen intellectualism. She was an accomplished but not brilliant actress.

In Richmond, Jefferson said to her, "Tomorrow you are to rehearse Juliet to the Romeo of our new and rising tragedian." At the end of the rehearsal Mary Devlin said, "He is the greatest actor I have ever known." For his part, Edwin wrote his mother, "I have seen and acted with a young woman who has so impressed me that I could almost forget my vow never to marry an actress."

When they had known one another for a week, Edwin presented Mary Devlin with a beautiful turquoise bracelet. She would, he wrote a friend, make "my heart a happy one, if aught on earth could make it so." He was correct.

John Booth had been acquainted with Mary as long as Edwin had, for he had achieved his aim of becoming, at least at the start, a southern actor. He was happy. "I would have written you before this, but I have been so busily engaged, and am such a slow writer that I could not find time," read a September 10, 1858, letter to Edwin from Richmond. "I have played several good parts since I have been here. I believe I am getting along very well."

There were two aspects to his theatrical performances that combined to secure for John a greater success than Edwin had at the same period of his career. One was his appearance.

"He was the idol of women," said the actor and British baronet Charles Wyndham. "His conquest embraced the sex, and with no effort. They would rave of him, his

John Wilkes Booth

voice, his eyes." "Lovely," said actress Anne Hartley Gilbert.

Beyond those looks, there was something else. Edwin's acting in no way resembled his father's, for while Edwin was contained, delineated, precise, Junius Brutus Booth on stage was explosive, fiery, dangerous, liable at any moment to lose all restraint. That was John, too. He played his roles with the utmost emotional impact and married to it his physical capabilities, for he was very strong and athletic. "A veritable sensation," said the New York *Herald*. He could be "*the* actor of the country," said the Boston *Daily Advertiser*. "An actor with the suddenness of a meteor now illuminates the dramatic horizon," said the Baltimore *Sun*. In Louisville the *Democrat* said of his Macbeth's battle with Macduff that "in all our recollection of the stage we have never seen anything to surpass it. The hackneyed word talent cannot be used in speaking of this young actor with such wonderful promise. It is genius."

It sometimes seemed to Asia, Mrs. John Sleeper Clarke now, that perhaps her brother John had gotten everything too easily. He was not like Edwin, who had a far rougher schooling, a fiercer struggle with himself, and had learned through the drudgery of art.

Edwin and Mary were married in July of 1860 in New York City. The bridegroom had been offered appearances in London, and a few months after the wedding decided to accept and to make the trip a belated honeymoon.

In Fulham, England, Mary gave birth to a baby girl, Edwina. It was a matter of great concern to him that his child would come into the world on foreign soil, and he hung an American flag over Mary's bed so that it could be said that Edwina was born under the Stars and Stripes. The Civil War had begun by then.

THERE was an Ohio tanner's son who grew up to believe that the Almighty had destined him to free the black people of America. Half soldier and half man of God, John Brown carried his crusade into the heart of the enemy's country. Armed with rifles purchased by northern supporters and followed by seventeen men, he swept down on Harpers Ferry, Virginia, to raise a rebellion that would spread, he said, into the southern coastal states. When he was finished, slavery would be dead.

John Brown was captured and condemned to hang. The execution would take place in Charles Town, Virginia, on December 2,

1859. No one knew if masses of his supporters might try to save him from the gallows, and so thousands of troops were ordered to Charles Town to hold themselves ready for any eventuality.

ON THE morning of November 24, John Booth took a break from rehearsals in a Richmond theater and stepped outside for a breath of air. In the street he saw lined-up members of two city militia units. They were off for duty at Charles Town. He asked if he could join them. A uniform was found, and in a matter of moments he was a private of the Richmond Grays. He had always wanted to see what it would be like to be a soldier, Asia knew. It was a dashing role to play. Someone asked who would take his part in the play that night, and he replied that he didn't know and didn't care.

On December 2 the troops lined up around the scaffold. Booth was less than fifty feet from it. The man about to die handed a note to a jailer:

> I John Brown am now quite certain that the crimes of this guilty land will never be purged away but with Blood. I had as I now think vainly flattered myself that without much bloodshed it might be done.

A moment later he swung at the end of a rope.

Philip Witlock of the Grays saw how pale one of his fellow soldiers had become. It was John, who asked Witlock if he had a flask with him, for he needed a drink. "A brave old man," John said of Brown when he talked to Asia about the hanging. "His heart must have broken when he felt himself deserted."

John went on with his career. "The genius of the Booth family has been bequeathed to this third son," said the Detroit *Advertiser*. "Without having Edwin's culture and grace and without that glittering eye, Mr. Booth has far more natural genius," said the Philadelphia *Press*. The Boston *Post* summed up: "Edwin has more poetry, John Wilkes more passion; Edwin is more Shakespearean, John Wilkes is more melodramatic; and in a word, Edwin is a better Hamlet, John Wilkes a better Richard III."

By then he had ceased to bill himself as J. B. Wilkes. He had taken back his name, and on his posters he arranged to have printed a quote from *Richard III:* I HAVE NO BROTHER, I AM NO BROTHER . . . I AM MYSELF ALONE.

III

In November of 1860 the Illinois lawyer who had gotten an excessive tax rescinded for Joe Jefferson's troupe of players became President-elect of the United States. Lincoln was then as he would remain: tall, plain, bony, gawky, sallow, scruffy in his dress, careless in his manners, and often ungraceful in his movements. He was not a cultured person and, indeed, apart from lawbooks and newspapers, never read anything but the Bible and his shabby old set of the complete works of Shakespeare. He had no hobbies beyond going to theatrical performances of all types. His wife Mary's desire to marry a man who would take her to the theater as often as she wished was fulfilled.

Their shared love of performances was one of the few traits the couple had in common. Save for occasional moods of deep depression, he was entirely unexcitable, calm, easygoing. She was an abnormally tense woman who became terrified if a child vanished for a moment. "Bobbie's lost! Bobbie's lost!" she would shriek if little Robert Todd Lincoln wandered away. Thunderstorms paralyzed her, and at the first sign of one, her husband would hurry home from his Springfield office to calm her. He spent nothing on himself; she was a ferocious spendthrift who wasted enormous sums. She was ashamed of his social origins, which were far beneath her own, and deeply concerned about the fact that both he and his mother were possibly born out of wedlock. The matter did not arouse his interest. He was quite content with his own company, while she hated to be alone and hired people to stay with her when he was off riding the law circuit.

On the evening of the day he was elected President, he went home and lay down to rest. Opposite the chaise longue stood a swinging mirror. He looked up and saw himself reflected full length but with two faces: "I was a little bothered, perhaps startled, and got up and looked in the glass, but the illusion vanished." He lay down again, and again saw his face doubly reflected, but with one image five shades paler than the other. That night he told Mary. It was a sign, she said. It meant he would be elected twice, but "that the paleness of one of the faces was an omen that I should not see life through the last term." This omen, Mary Lincoln told their journalist friend Noah Brooks, was a warning.

American Gothic

Within a few days her fears were given a focus. Abraham Lincoln was entirely a sectional candidate of the North and West. No one in the South wanted him. (In Maryland, the most northerly of the border states—"We are of the North," Asia maintained, her brother John violently disagreeing—ninety-two thousand votes were cast in the 1860 election, of which only twenty-three hundred were for Lincoln.) To the southern states his election meant the imposition upon them of an impossible President, an abolitionist who was, their papers said, ape and buffoon, a poor, white-trash, illiterate, ill-bred rail-splitter. Letters threatening his life poured into Springfield. "The first one or two made me a little uncomfortable," Lincoln said. "But I came to look for a regular installment of this kind of correspondence in every mail. There is nothing like getting *used* to things!"

It was different with his wife. She was seized with a terror that would never leave her. For all the qualities that would soon make the President's two principal secretaries term her the Hell Cat and Her Satanic Majesty, Mary Lincoln deeply loved her husband. From childhood on, she had predicted she would one day be First Lady of the country. When he was an obscure small-town lawyer, she said of him that he looked like a President. When the brilliant Stephen A. Douglas pressed his suit with her, remarking that if she married him, she might be a President's wife, she replied that indeed she would be a President's wife, but not Stephen Douglas'. Now her dream was near fulfillment—if he lived until his inauguration. There were predictions Lincoln would never take the oath of office. The chief of the army, General Winfield Scott, took serious alarm. It was suggested to Mary that she and the children not go on the four-car special leaving Springfield for Washington, because of the danger that it might be blown up in transit. She received in the mail threatening letters and pictures of her husband with a noose around his neck, and was beside herself with hysterical fear; but she said they would go with her husband—"danger or no danger."

To the welcome relief of President James Buchanan, who for weeks had paced an executive mansion porch weeping as he prayed war would not come while he still held office, the Lincolns arrived safely in Washington. But the threat of danger seemed ever present, and General Scott took every precaution.

The Inauguration Day trip to the Capitol—of unfinished construction, with bare ribs against the sky—was conducted like a military movement, with Lincoln and Buchanan surrounded by double files of District of Columbia cavalrymen. Artillery batteries were strategically placed.

In his inaugural address Lincoln asked the South for peace. "We must not be enemies. Though passion may have strained, it must not break, our bonds of affection. The mystic chords of memory, stretching from every battlefield and patriot grave to every living heart and hearthstone all over this broad land, will yet swell the chorus of the Union, when again touched, as surely they will be, by the better angels of our nature." But soon Washington was filled with the noise of cavalry bugles and troops, and when the guns began to sound and the soldiers to march, ambulances zigzagged their way through the rutted streets as the drivers sought to avoid jolting mutilated and bloody occupants. There would be other wagons, whose occupants no jolting would disturb. On those wagons' sides would be written U.S. HEARSE.

IN ENGLAND, Mary—Molly to Edwin—worried for a time that the baby would come between her and her husband, but it did not happen, and she wrote home that little Edwina made even more precious the hours husband and wife spent with one another. The hearts of both were entirely with the North in the great conflict at home. Edwin wrote Adam Badeau that he had given up reading the pro-South London *Times* because it was "so very rabid against us." Adam had joined the Union army. His career as a soldier was one of the world's wonders. The sexually ambiguous little intellectual found himself on the staff of Ulysses S. Grant. As Grant rose, promotion after promotion was handed out to his people, and so Adam ended up wearing a general's star on each of his slumped shoulders.

When the three Booths came back to the United States, they took rooms at the Fifth Avenue Hotel, in New York, but because Mary was delicate, subject to headaches and a perpetually exhausted feeling, they took a house in Dorchester, Massachusetts, as well so that she could be placed under the care of an eminent Boston physician who specialized in cases like hers. Their place was comparatively modest, not so grand as the Philadelphia residence of John Sleeper Clarke and his wife, Asia. Clarke was managing theaters in several cities while acting on the side, and making a great success of it. Asia seemed happy in her marriage, writing her friend Jean Anderson of her two babies and of how when her brother John visited he "lays on the floor and rolls over with them, like a child."

In early 1863 John went to Boston for an extended stay. Edwin and Mary were in the audience to see him in *The Apostate*. After that, Edwin was off for a series of New York appearances. "I have not dared to think of parting with him," Mary wrote her friend Mrs. Richard Henry Stoddard—Elizabeth. "You know well enough how I will suffer." Edwin would be low-spirited without her, she wrote Elizabeth; would she and Richard not try to comfort him? The Stoddards understood her meaning. Mary had almost completely quenched the evil that possessed his soul. But not even Mary could utterly cleanse him. Drink still drew him. It was, he said, a spark covered but still smoldering.

Now in New York, away from his Molly, the spark burst into flame. "What is Edwin thinking about?" a friend asked Elizabeth Stoddard. "Why does he give himself up in this way when he has everything to live for?" Richard Henry Stoddard and another friend, poet-journalist-writer Thomas Bailey Aldrich, appointed themselves to keep liquor out of his grasp. But a drunkard can always find what he desires.

From the Dorchester house Mary took a trolley into Boston to fetch a friend. It was snowing. The trolley was delayed. When she got home, she was freezing. "Take me upstairs and put me to bed," she told a servant. "I feel as if I should never be warm again."

Her doctor, Erasmus Miller, stopped by and felt it was just a cold. It got worse. But there was no cause for concern, Dr. Miller wrote Edwin on February 18. Should the patient's condition worsen, "which I do not expect," Edwin would be instantly informed. The next day the doctor wrote that if all did not progress satisfactorily, Edwin would be told at once.

That night Edwin awoke from a drunken sleep, feeling a puff of cold air touch his cheek. He wondered where it came from, he later wrote Adam, and turned in bed and felt it again, and then heard, "as plainly as I hear this pen scratching over the paper," Mary's voice: "Come to me, Darling. I'm almost frozen."

But the doctor's messages were encouraging—a total of six of them over a period of two days, February 18 and 19. Mary wrote and said that she was bothered by pain at night, but that she would be all right.

His drinking was out of control, and finally Elizabeth Stoddard took the bull by the horns. "Sick or well, you must come," she wrote Mary. "Mr. Booth has lost all restraint and hold on himself. Last night there was the grave question of ringing down the curtain before the performance was half over. Lose no time. Come."

From Dorchester, Mary replied, "I cannot come. I cannot stand." That evening she suffered a turn for the worse. She asked Miller to speak plainly, and he told her the illness was a fatal one. The cold had turned into pneumonia. She begged him to keep her alive long enough to see Edwin one more time. The doctor sent a telegram to his dressing room, telling him to come at once. He was too drunk to open it. The doctor sent another. It joined its predecessor on the dressing-room table. The doctor sent a third.

The play ended. Richard Stoddard was with him when the theater manager came into the dressing room with a telegram Dr. Miller had sent to him:

> THIS IS THE FOURTH TELEGRAM. WHY DOES NOT MR. BOOTH ANSWER? HE MUST COME AT ONCE.

At last Edwin opened the three previous telegrams and realized what was happening in Dorchester. The midnight train for Boston had gone. He must wait for the seven o'clock. He went to the Stoddards' and drank coffee till gray dawn came. Stoddard went with him, and they took the train.

He gazed out at the winter landscape as they headed for Boston. It was February 21, 1863. "I saw every time I looked from the window Mary dead, with a white cloth tied round her neck and chin," he wrote Adam. "I saw her distinctly, a dozen times at least."

At the depot, a friend waited with a carriage. When he approached, Edwin raised a hand and said, "Do not tell me. I know." He got in with Stoddard, and the three drove to the Dorchester house in absolute silence. Not yet twenty-three years old, Mary lay in her room with a white cloth tied around her neck and chin. She wore a gold chain with a miniature of her husband. He went in alone and sat with her silently for hours. He never touched liquor again.

HE GAVE UP THE DORCHESTER house, took one at 107 East Seventeenth Street in New York, lived there with his mother and sister Rosalie, and went to spiritualists in an attempt to contact his dead wife. He canceled all his engagements for the season, saying he would devote himself to making a life for Edwina. But nothing had changed from the moment on the train when it came to him that she was gone, and nothing ever really would. Two and a half little years of happiness, he said. Now? "Poor Molly is lying out at Mount Auburn, cold and lonely. Would to God I was there with her."

JOHN was about to turn twenty-five and of a theatrical stature to set himself up as a resident star in a leading city. He chose Washington. The wartime capital was bursting out of its seams with people, and entertainments of any type drew capacity crowds. He opened as Richard III at Grover's Theatre on April 11, 1863. President Lincoln attended. The *National Republican* said he scored a "complete triumph" and took "the hearts of the people by storm."

The war dragged on—Shiloh, the Seven Days, Fredericksburg. In Washington the President turned ever more gaunt and haggard and careworn. His only relief, noted his old friend Noah Brooks, was the theater. He had seen Edwin in *The Merchant of Venice, The Fool's Revenge,* and *Ruy Blas*. Once Lincoln "rapturously" applauded John's playing, said the reporter George Alfred Townsend; when told, John said he would rather have the applause of a black. Lincoln wanted to meet him, and told the actor Frank Mordaunt he had sent him an invitation to call. Booth had not responded. Mordaunt said he knew John Booth well and would arrange a meeting. He failed to do so.

For to John, as to the vast majority of Marylanders, Abraham Lincoln was an odious tyrant oppressing a southern state. The capital's communications with the North flowed through Maryland, so the state had to be kept tamped down. The Constitution was suspended, free speech was forbidden, arrests were made without warrant, and people were imprisoned without trial. As Caesar had said, in times of war the law was silent.

And who was this Caesar, emperor, king? "This man's appearance, his pedigree, his coarse low jokes and anecdotes, his vulgar smiles and frivolity are a disgrace to the seat he holds," John told

Asia. Lincoln did his evil work with foreigners. There were entire regiments of the Union army where not a single soldier was American-born. Like a Bonaparte, John said, Lincoln saw himself with a future crown on his head, put there by these foreigners. He was a false President. "If the North conquers us—"

"If the North conquers us!" Asia interrupted. "We are of the North."

"Not I, not I!" he replied. "So help me holy God! My soul, life, and possessions are for the South."

Then why, she asked, did he not join the Confederate army?

"I have only an arm to give," he answered. "My brains are worth twenty men, my money worth a hundred." She began to understand. Once a man had come to her Philadelphia residence asking for Dr. Booth. "I am he," John told her, "if to be a doctor means a dealer in quinine." He sent it through the Yankee lines in horse-collars and he got through other things the South needed in other ways. With a thousand others he was a smuggler, piercing the North's blockade of the South.

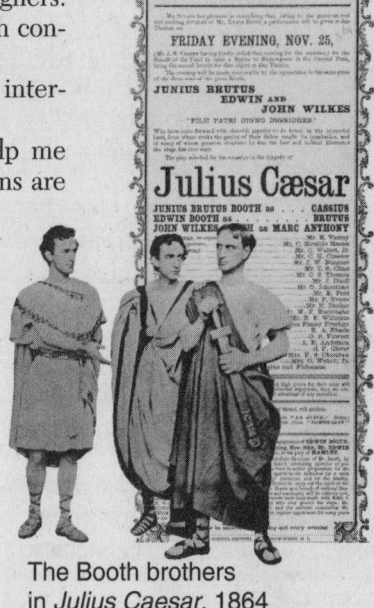

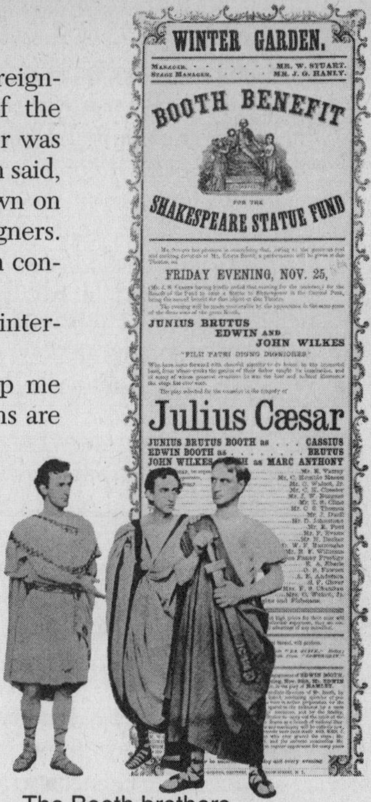

The Booth brothers in *Julius Caesar,* 1864

To Edwin his brother's views were entirely mistaken. They argued, but there was no great passion from Edwin's side. He supported Lincoln and the Union. That was all there was to it. He had other, more involving, concerns. After many months of stage inactivity he returned to his profession. He had a daughter to support. With John Sleeper Clarke he purchased Philadelphia's Walnut Street Theater, and together they took on the management of the Winter Garden in New York. In order not to be too far from his mother and daughter, in New York, Edwin largely confined his acting to no farther away than Philadelphia or Boston.

John went touring now and then out of Washington, garnering

507

splendid reviews. But it was all beginning to pall for him. Did acting, he asked, really mean anything at all? Often it seemed to John that the whole business was silly and ridiculous. Was it not unworthy, even humiliating, to play at war and combat when a couple of hours from the Washington theaters, real soldiers were really dying? He began to talk of getting out.

In November of 1864 Lincoln was reelected. He won with little help from a Maryland where there were counties in which less than half a dozen voters from a roll of thousands put down his name. Edwin was among the few, voting for the first and only time in his life. Back from California, June tried to smooth over family political arguments by telling John that the war was simply a family quarrel on an immense scale. Later in November theatrical placards in New York announced a great event. June, Edwin, and John would appear together in *Julius Caesar*. Proceeds would go for the erection of a statue of Shakespeare in New York's Central Park.

Two thousand people crowded the Winter Garden. Seats went for up to five dollars. At the end, the three brothers came on stage and together bowed to the box where their mother sat, June as Cassius, Edwin as Brutus, and John as Mark Antony. Applause rolled over them, "the eldest powerfully built and handsome as an antique Roman, Edwin with his magnetic fire and graceful dignity, and John Wilkes in the perfection of youthful beauty," as one reviewer put it.

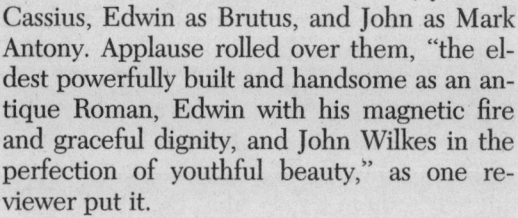

The following night, November 26, 1864, Edwin Booth began a run that gained him the position by which, for half a century and more, all other actors were judged. Prior to that night few actors appeared in the same play for a week's time. Edwin that night began a run of one hundred nights as Hamlet. History would remember him for what he had been in that performance; statues would be erected of him as Hamlet, the Prince of Players.

In other roles, Adam Badeau thought, Edwin's nature was cloaked in the character he played. He was no Richard III, nor Iago, but

Edwin Booth as Hamlet

Hamlet—moody, dreamy, melancholy, tender, at odds with himself and his world. The character was Edwin. When, wearing a miniature of Junius Brutus Booth on a chain, he called the Ghost "Father," there was an inescapable pathos in his voice. When he wandered between thoughts of action and revulsion for action, when he mourned Ophelia, when he showed the prince's inner feelings, sadly distant from all about him, fearful of a terrible future, he was Hamlet no less than he was Edwin Booth.

Once the actress Clara Morris heard some people praise John Booth's Hamlet. "No!" John said. "No, no! There's but one Hamlet to my mind, that of my brother Edwin. You see, between ourselves, he *is* Hamlet."

IV

IN LATE 1864, as night after night Edwin Booth transfixed New York, his brother John went about lower Maryland, just south of Washington. He told people he wanted to buy land there. He did not wish to buy land.

The Civil War was three and a half years old. The Confederacy was still in the field, its army a gathering of heroes, to John Booth's thinking. And what had he done while men died and epic battles were contested? He had been arrested in St. Louis for making known his hope that "the whole damned government would go to hell." He had slung his brother-in-law, John Sleeper Clarke, around in a railroad car for speaking ill of Jefferson Davis. On a window of a hotel in which he frequently stayed, the proprietor found inscribed in the glass, ABE LINCOLN DEPARTED THIS LIFE AUGUST 13TH, 1864, BY THE EFFECTS OF POISON. Who knew what that meant? The President was perfectly well on that date.

John developed a fibroid tumor on his neck. Washington doctor John Frederick May removed it, but told him that the area must not be disturbed. John told Dr. May he would be careful, but shortly he was back: the actress Charlotte Cushman, he explained, had embraced him on stage with such force that the wound had opened. So Dr. May had to tell what he remembered as this "remarkably handsome young man" that there would always be a scar. John asked the doctor to say, if questioned by anyone, that the scar came from removal of a bullet.

Embarrassing. He was stage king and hero, warrior and chieftain, but asked to be described as a wounded battler in some wholly imagined affair. He aspired to greater things than this. So he went about saying he was interested in land. To some people he told the truth. One such was John Surratt, a twenty-year-old Confederate spy. "I have a proposition to submit to you," John told Surratt. His listener had found life as a spy "fascinating." His older brother was in the Confederate army, serving in the West. "Well, sir, what is your proposition?" he asked.

John got up, looked under the bed of the room in which they were, into the wardrobe, through the doorway, and into the passageway. "We will have to be careful," he said. "Walls have ears." He drew his chair close to that of Surratt. He spoke in a whisper. "Kidnap President Lincoln and carry him off to Richmond."

"Kidnap President Lincoln!"

The idea, Surratt remembered, struck him as foolhardy; he was "amazed, thunderstruck." But John was saying a captured Lincoln could be exchanged for who knew how many captured Confederates languishing in northern prisons. To John his plan was eminently reasonable. That neither Edwin nor June nor their brother Joe would dream of partaking was beside the point; what was happening in America was, after all, called the war of brothers.

He needed time to consider, Surratt said, and for two days he turned the idea over in his mind. Kidnap the President. Was it impossible? Often Lincoln rode out alone to his summer residence on the grounds of the Soldiers' Home—a heavily wooded, remote area three miles from the executive mansion—using whatever army horse happened to be available. Once, mounted on a horse named Old Abe, he had his hat shot off. Perhaps it was a hunter, Lincoln told his former law partner made marshal of the District of Columbia, Ward Hill Lamon. Whoever it was, "he unceremoniously separated me from my eight-dollar plug hat." At the sound of the shot, the horse bolted for home. "I tell you," Lincoln said, "there is no time on record equal to that made by the two Old Abes." Lamon was not amused.

When Secretary of War Edwin Stanton assigned a cavalry detachment to accompany the President and Mrs. Lincoln on carriage rides, Lincoln got rid of the soldiers, saying the clatter of hoofs made it almost impossible for him to conduct a conversation with

Lewis Thornton Powell

his wife. When late at night he walked over to the War Department through the White House grounds to see the latest army reports, his wife often told him to be careful. The trees shadowed out the thin gaslights, and anyone could hide in those shadows. "All imagination," Lincoln told his wife. "What does anyone want to harm me for? Don't worry about me, Mother, as if I were a little child."

"But, Father, you should not go out alone. You know you are surrounded with danger." But he went alone.

So capturing him, Surratt reasoned, would not be impossible. And to do so could conceivably mean independence for the South. The plan was rash, surely, Surratt thought, but honorable. He told John he would go in with him.

George Atzerodt

Around the chief conspirator gathered others, attracted by John's money, his charm, his inspiring presence, and the possibility of doing something for the southern cause. Lewis Thornton Powell was a hulking, bull-like twenty-year-old born in Alabama, whose family had moved to the rural area of Live Oak Station, Florida. He joined the Second Florida Infantry at sixteen, when the war began, and fought in the Peninsula campaign, at Chancellorsville and Antietam. Powell saw John's plan as a military operation and addressed the plan's originator as Captain and Cap. He took new names wherever he went: Payne, Pain, Wood. He would do whatever his new captain told him to do.

David Herold was a twenty-three-year-old sometime druggist's clerk who looked seventeen and acted no older. A frivolous boy whose late father had specified in his will that his son must have no part in any supervision of the father's estate, his main interest in life was hunting. From countless expeditions he knew the areas south of Washington very well.

Samuel Arnold was a former schoolmate of John Booth's who had not seen him in ten years, until in Baltimore he got word his old friend wanted to renew their acquaintance. Arnold became "perfectly infatuated" with the "social man-

David Herold

ners and bearing" of his former schoolmate. The money he was given also attracted him to the plan. He was a former Confederate soldier, as was Michael O'Laughlen, another schoolmate who joined in. Edman Spangler, a stage carpenter at Ford's Theatre, who years earlier had worked for Junius Brutus Booth in the remodeling of The Farm, was recruited. George Atzerodt, a Prussian-born carriage maker who doubled as boatman getting blockade runners and spies across the Potomac, would be the ferryman.

The usual meeting place for the conspirators was the H Street, N.W., home of John Surratt's mother. Mary E. Jenkins Surratt, forty-one, widowed two and a half years, had moved to Washington from Surrattsville, Maryland—named for the late head of the family—some thirteen miles south of Washington. She was not well off, so she leased out the tavern–post office in Surrattsville as well as rooms at her Washington place to make ends meet.

Mary Surratt

That winter—January and February and March of 1865—as Edwin, in New York, finished up the one hundred nights as Hamlet, John, in Washington, was acclaimed by the *National Intelligencer* as a flawless Romeo. "What perfect acting! We have never seen a Romeo bearing any near comparison with the acting of Booth." But he performed only rarely, turning down parts in favor of riding through lower Maryland along an underground route for Confederate smugglers. Union patrols moved about the trails and rivers, but the area was so thinly settled and so filled with swamps and woods that it was an easy matter to avoid the North's soldiers and sailors. Here was the path along which Abraham Lincoln would be taken as prisoner.

Often the explorer came back to Washington exhausted and dirty. The actor Charles Warwick received a visit from him one day and found him splashed with mud. The weather outside was wet and chilly. Warwick told him to take off his boots and dry his feet

Mrs. Surratt's boardinghouse

by the fire, and John did so and also accepted his friend's loan of a pipe filled with tobacco. Warwick's room was in a Tenth Street boardinghouse just across from Ford's Theatre. A reproduction of Rosa Bonheur's *The Horse Fair* hung on a wall, along with J. F. Herring's *The Village Blacksmith, The Stable,* and *The Barnyard.* Apparently the owner of the boardinghouse, William Petersen, liked horses. John seemed done in, Warwick saw. He fell asleep on the bed, smoking his host's pipe.

In New York, in another house—Edwin's house—strange visions troubled the sleep of another Booth, the family's mother. She wrote John that the visions were about him. Her dreams were "fearful." She wanted him in New York, and sent June down to Washington to urge him to come to her. Mrs. Booth had always been strangely aware of John's doings even when far from him, remembered the actress Anne Hartley Gilbert. "No matter how far apart they were she seemed to know when anything was wrong with him. If he were ill, or unfit to play, he would often receive a letter of sympathy, counsel, and warning, written when she could not possibly have received any news of him."

When June arrived in Washington, the brothers walked down a street and John looked south across the Potomac to where Grant's forces waited for warm weather so they could seek Lee's battered and starving scarecrows. Little was left of the once grand Confederacy save a long half circle before Petersburg and Richmond, and a little slice of North Carolina. "Virginia, Virginia," John said brokenly. He had many things on his mind that February. He sat up with June until three thirty on the fourteenth day of the month, writing an acrostic Valentine's Day greeting. It was for the young lady to whom he was engaged to be married.

JOHN P. HALE of New Hampshire represented his state in the U.S. Senate. An abolitionist twenty years before there was an Emancipation Proclamation, he was before the war twice presidential candidate of the Free-Soil Party, which opposed the extension of slavery into the western areas of the country. In early 1865 Hale was serving out his last days in the Senate, for he had been defeated in the November elections. He desired to go abroad and asked for a foreign ministership. Secretary of State Seward told him he could have Spain. He would take up his new post in the spring.

Senator and Mrs. Hale had two daughters. The younger of the two, Lucy, was twenty-four. By no means was she a beauty. Pressed for a description of her, while once testifying under oath, the Ford's Theatre proprietor, John T. Ford, came up with one word: "Stout." But she had something far beyond mere physical allure. The Harvard undergraduate and future Supreme Court Justice Oliver Wendell Holmes met her on a Maine vacation and in April of 1858 wrote that after parting from her he was "so cross" for three days that no one could come within "a mile" of him. Then there was Robert Todd Lincoln, who had the White House conservatory send her flowers. And there was John Booth.

They met at their mutual residence, the National Hotel, at Sixth Street and Pennsylvania Avenue, where she lived with her family. It would be impossible for her not to take notice of him, for he was a familiar figure at the National's weekly hops, was frequently prevailed upon to give recitations in one of the hotel's parlors, and was, after all, John Booth. John told his brother June that he found in Lucy something worth more than all the money he could ever hope to make on the stage. She gave him a ring, which he repeatedly kissed when he spoke of her to friends. Asia learned that she had said she would go to Spain with her family when her father took up his duties as minister there but would return to marry John in a year, "with or without her father."

ON THE evening of March 15, 1865, John Surratt, Lewis Powell, and two young ladies from the Surratt boardinghouse attended a production of *Jane Shore* at Ford's Theatre. After the play the young ladies returned to the boardinghouse, while the men went on to dinner and a meeting with John Booth at Gautier's Restaurant on Pennsylvania Avenue. Davy Herold was there, along with George Atzerodt, Sam Arnold, and Michael O'Laughlen.

Their host ordered cold meats, cheeses, oysters, Champagne, and cigars for the group. He outlined a definitive plan to kidnap the President. Time was short. Spring had arrived, and soon the Virginia roads would be dry and hard. Then the Yankee guns and wagons would be able to move, and the Confederate lines would be in danger. This would lead to the surrender of Richmond.

The capture of the President, he said, would be accomplished in Ford's Theatre. They would seize him in the box from which

Surratt and Powell had viewed *Jane Shore* that evening, lower him to the stage, and get him out the back door. They would handcuff him, chloroform him if necessary. Stagehand Edman Spangler would douse the houselights so that they could work in the darkness.

The conspirators heard out their leader in silence; then John's ex-schoolmate Sam Arnold offered an opinion. The plan was utter madness, he said. Get the President down on the stage in front of an audience likely to contain a few hundred soldiers of the Union army? Spirit him out the back, past the actors? Then expect to pass through the city filled with troops and police to a Potomac bridge? "The height of madness," Arnold said.

It wasn't what John wanted to hear. Anyone who disagreed with the plan ought to be shot, he declared. "Two can play at that game," Arnold replied. The others got them calmed down, and the next day John apologized to Sam, saying it was the Champagne speaking. They agreed to go ahead, but not at the theater.

Two days later, March 17, their opportunity appeared to have arrived. They learned that the President was going to join an audience of wounded soldiers in viewing a matinee performance of *Still Waters Run Deep* at Campbell Hospital. Located in a heavily wooded and thinly settled area, the hospital was reached by the Seventh Street Road, which led to the President's Soldiers' Home. The road presented itself to the conspirators in the past as a possible place to seize him. Now theater and place merged.

They rendezvoused in a tavern along the road at around two in the afternoon, all mounted. A carriage appeared carrying a single occupant. They surrounded it and looked in. It was not the President. The carriage went on. They waited, but Lincoln's plans had changed, and the wait was in vain. That night Arnold and O'Laughlen left to get jobs in Baltimore, and soon Surratt also would be gone. Powell, Herold, and Atzerodt stayed in Washington, eating on John's money. The next night, March 18, he appeared as the villain Pescara in *The Apostate* at Ford's Theatre. Louis Weichmann, one of Mrs. Surratt's boarders, never saw a man play with such intensity and passion. John's face as he put a woman to torture on the wheel was hideous, malevolent, distorted. Four days later President Lincoln departed Washington to visit General Grant at his Virginia headquarters. John went to New York.

American Gothic

EDWIN'S GREAT HUNDRED-performance run of *Hamlet* ended on the day Lincoln left for Grant's headquarters. It seemed to him in those days that his dead Mary was with him yet in spirit, and when he began a romance with Blanche Hauel, the only child of a prominent Philadelphia jeweler, and reached an understanding about marriage with her, he said it was Mary who had sent Blanche to him. Their wedding would be in September.

Edwin Booth was glad that the war seemed about to conclude, but he did not wish to discuss the matter with John, did not want to hear his arguments about how the South was right nor the bitter song he sang, whose verses predicted that soon Lincoln would be King of America. John went back to Washington to drink wine with the Ford brothers, whose theater bore their name. In two weeks, he told them, something would happen that would astonish the world. "What are you going to do?" Harry Ford asked. "Kill Jeff Davis, take Richmond, or play Hamlet a hundred nights?"

John visited Asia in Philadelphia. She was pregnant, expecting her third child in August. If it was a boy, she had told him, it would be named for him—John Wilkes Booth Clarke.

Her marriage was not happy. Not for the first time her brother suggested divorce. When they parted, he knelt by where she sat on a sofa, and she stroked his black hair. "Oh, my boy, I shall never be happy till I see your face again," she said. Over her children's bed he had put a picture of himself, saying, "Remember me, babies, in your prayers."

On Saturday, April 1, the forty miles of Lee's line north of Richmond and south of Petersburg began to crack. The next morning, in Richmond, Jefferson Davis was handed a telegram from Lee. Richmond must be evacuated at once. The population began to run for it, wagons loaded with valuables bouncing through the streets. In the evening darkness the Confederate army poured through. Ammunition magazines were exploded to save them from the Yankees; gunboats were loaded with kegs of powder to be burned and sunk in the James; the railroad trestle and bridge were readied for destruction. In the early morning hours of April 3 the fuses in the gunboats ignited the powder kegs, and the boats vanished in a roar of spray and noise that shattered windows two miles distant. The immense tobacco warehouses, fired by Confederate government order, sent flames hundreds of feet into the air, and cinders from those fires came down to light new ones, which would destroy a third of Richmond. The rebel army and government went on its way, and behind it the capital of the Confederacy endured a fate no other American city ever knew.

V

WASHINGTON exploded. Bands played, parades wound their way through the streets; earthshaking roars of artillery shattered the windows around Lafayette Square. In the evening all government buildings were illuminated; rockets and fireworks shot off into the sky. There were gorgeous transparencies everywhere showing words of praise and thanks—U.S. ARMY, U.S. NAVY, U.S. GRANT—GLORY TO GOD WHO TO US GRANTED THE VICTORY. The Confederate army was in North Carolina, under General Joseph E. Johnston, preparing to surrender to William T. Sherman. Lee's men had stacked arms at Appomattox. Go home, obey the law, put in a crop, their ex-leader had told them. Farewell.

JOHN walked through the city with Lewis Powell and Davy Herold, saw the crowds of triumphant Yankeedom, and heard the cheers. "We are all slaves now," he told Harry Ford. How could Lee have surrendered? When he had accepted the sword put in his hands, he swore he would never surrender it.

He went on Tuesday night with Powell and Herold to the White House grounds to hear Lincoln speak. Across the Potomac at what had been the Arlington estate of Mrs. Robert E. Lee, thousands of ex-slaves gathered to sing "The Year of Jubilee." The house was brilliantly illuminated, and colored lights blazed on the lawn.

The President stood on a balcony reading his speech by the light of a candle held by Noah Brooks. Beneath him sat Tad Lincoln, catching the pages the President dropped as he finished with them. The theme of the speech was clemency for the South. Let the erring brethren come back into the Union with all privileges, Lincoln said. As for the freed slaves and the possibility of giving them the vote, Lincoln said he thought it should be conferred upon those who could read and those who had served in the Union army.

In the darkness John hissed, "That means nigger citizenship!" The word did not possess quite the pejorative connotation it would gain at a later time. He had grown up with blacks, felt their transport to the New World was a blessing for them, had said he would do anything to elevate the race. Citizenship and voting—that was different. He began urging Lewis Powell to shoot the President as he stood on the balcony. John Brown had been hanged. Now Lincoln was doing Brown's work. One had been a criminal. What was the other? His voice was attracting attention, and Powell and Herold urged that they leave.

"That is the last speech he will ever make," John Booth muttered as they got him away.

TWENTY-SIX years old, intelligent, well paid, engaged to a much-sought-after girl of the highest social standing and with a plenitude of other women on the string, the son of a great actor, charming, well beloved by his fellows. How many men would have declined to change places with him?

Yet in those days after the fall of Richmond and the surrender at Appomattox, he took liquor as never before. In the early morning hours of Friday he wrote a letter:

Dearest Mother,

I know you expect a letter from me. But indeed I have had nothing to write about. Everything is dull; that is, has been until last night. Everything was bright and splendid. More so in my eyes if it had been displayed in a nobler cause. But so goes the world. Might makes right. I only drop you these few lines to let you know I am well. With best love to you all I am your affectionate son ever.

John

HE SLEPT, though not at the National Hotel. When the maid came in, she found his bed made up. Perhaps he had been with Ella Turner, a nineteen-year-old good-looking blonde who lived in a Washington bordello run by her sister. Despite his engagement to Lucy Hale, John continued to amuse himself with other women, and Ella Turner was a favorite. He returned to the hotel, the last person entering the dining room for breakfast. Afterwards he sat in a parlor and talked with Lucy, was shaved in a barbershop, and walked over to Ford's Theatre to pick up any mail they had for him.

It was around noon, Good Friday, April 14, 1865. He was in a dark suit and light drab overcoat, with a black silk hat, slightly tipped, on his head. The theater manager, John T. Ford, was off to occupied Richmond to be with an uncle, but his brother Harry was standing in front of the building with some friends. "Here comes the handsomest man in Washington," Harry Ford remarked.

At that hour the President of the United States was at a White House gathering he had convened through Frederick Seward, acting Secretary of State. Frederick Seward, normally his father's assistant, held his temporary position because Secretary William H. Seward had been injured nine days earlier in a carriage accident. His right arm had been broken, his jaw fractured, his face terribly bruised. His son, acting in his stead, sat in at the meeting and heard Postmaster General Dennison ask if the President would pursue the rebel leaders fled from Richmond. Lincoln replied he had no urge to take them prisoners and would wish them gone. "Enough lives have been sacrificed," he said. "No one need expect me to take any part in killing these men, even the worst of them."

The meeting ended. Everyone left, save for the lieutenant general commanding the armies of the United States. It was an awkward moment for Grant. That morning Mrs. Lincoln had sent an invitation for the general and Mrs. Grant to join the presidential couple in a visit to the theater. But Julia Grant had had some unpleasant experiences with Mrs. Lincoln, who had once accused her of being disrespectful by seating herself while the wife of the President was standing. She had also indicated that she expected Mrs. Grant to back out of her presence in the fashion of someone leaving European royalty and had nastily asked if it was Mrs. Grant's plan to succeed to her executive mansion position. Julia Grant told her husband to tell the President they were leaving to visit their children at school in New Jersey. To stiffen his resolve, she sent him a note reiterating her desire. He showed it to Lincoln, who excused him from the theater expedition.

But that was not known at Ford's Theatre, and so an advertisement announcing the forthcoming attendance of the President and general and their wives was written up and sent off for insertion in Washington's afternoon papers, the *Republican* and the *Star*.

The box reserved for the presidential party, top stage left, was the one occupied by Lewis Powell and John Surratt and the two boarders from Mrs. Surratt's on the night the conspirators met at

Gautier's Restaurant. To accommodate the Lincolns and Grants, it was enlarged and specially decorated. The enlargement was achieved by removing a partition separating it from the adjoining box, thus combining the two boxes into one. For decorations Harry Ford had two United States flags put across the box balustrade and hung other flags at both sides. At the center pillar were the regimental colors of the Treasury Guard, white spread eagle and stars on a blue ground. Attached to the colors was a framed portrait of George Washington. Harry Ford placed a rocking chair of black walnut with seat, arms, and back upholstered in red damask in the box. There were side chairs and a small sofa.

At the White House, the President informed his wife that the Grants would not be joining them that evening. Originally Mrs. Lincoln had invited Speaker of the House Schuyler Colfax and then, believing the Grants would come, rescinded the offer. Now she reinvited him. But he had meanwhile decided to leave for a western trip and so could not accept.

Robert Todd Lincoln arrived that morning from a brief stint as an officer on Grant's staff—he had spent the war years at Harvard—and was invited to come along. He replied that he had not slept in a decent bed for weeks and was exhausted and wanted to go to bed early. He gave his father the most recent photograph of Lee, which he had picked up in Virginia. Lincoln looked at the picture and said, "It is a good face; it is the face of a noble, noble, brave man. I am glad the war is over at last." Lincoln's appearance and manner were remarkably changed from the sad picture he had presented all through the long years of war. Secretary of the Treasury Hugh McCulloch noted at the Cabinet meeting that his face was "bright and cheerful." Secretary of War Stanton said to Attorney General Speed as they went down the White House steps together after the meeting, "Didn't our chief look *grand* today?"

John Booth went to the livery stable of James Pumphrey on C Street, behind the National Hotel, and said he wished to rent a particular little bay mare. He would pick her up later in the afternoon. He went down Pennsylvania Avenue and stepped into the dining room at the Williard Hotel. He sat down and stared at Julia Grant as she dined. She did not care for the manner in which he regarded her. He went to Mrs. Surratt's boardinghouse and spoke with the proprietor, and shortly she left for her Maryland place in a rented buggy carrying two parcels to her tenant there, John Lloyd, an alcoholic former Washington policeman. General Grant got back from the executive mansion, and his wife said, "When I went in to my lunch today, a man with a wild look followed me into the dining room, took a seat nearly opposite me at the table, stared at me continually, and seemed to be listening to my conversation."

"Oh, I suppose he did so merely from curiosity," the general replied.

After lunch at the White House the President met briefly with Vice President Andrew Johnson, one of at least a dozen people with whom he spoke privately on that day. He had planned a carriage ride with Mrs. Lincoln, but first he walked over to the War Department to see if the telegraph had brought any news of a Johnston surrender to Sherman. White House guard William H. Crook went along. "Do you know," Lincoln said, "I believe there are men who want to take my life. And I have no doubt they will do it."

"I hope you are mistaken, Mr. President," Crook said.

"If it is to be done, it is impossible to prevent it."

He had said that before, many times. When on Inauguration Day, six weeks earlier, the Secretary of War spoke of keeping a better watch on the President's life, Lincoln told him, "Stanton, it is useless. If it is the will of Providence that I should die by the hand of an assassin, it must be so." He recently had an odd dream. "It is strange," he had said to Mrs. Lincoln and Marshal of the District of Columbia, Ward Hill Lamon, a couple of weeks earlier, "how much there is in the Bible about dreams." He had always believed that in each dream there was meaning. He also believed that he was what the world calls a man of destiny, and as such was interested in visions and strange and wonderful things, far boundaries to what was seen by human eyes.

Yes, strange, the President had said, how the Bible so often spoke of dreams. "I had one the other night which has haunted me ever since," he told his wife and Lamon:

> About ten days ago, I retired very late. I had been up waiting for important dispatches from the front. I could have not been long in bed when I fell into a slumber, for I was weary. I soon began to dream. There seemed to be a death-like stillness about me. Then I heard subdued sobs, as if a number of people were weeping. I

thought I left my bed and wandered downstairs. There the silence was broken by the same pitiful sobbing, but the mourners were invisible. I went from room to room. It was light in all the rooms; every object was familiar to me; but where were all the people who were grieving as if their hearts would break? I was puzzled and alarmed. What could be the meaning of all this? I kept on until I arrived in the East Room, which I entered. There I met with a sickening surprise. Before me was a catafalque, on which rested a corpse wrapped in funeral vestments. Around it were stationed soldiers; and there was a throng of people, some gazing mournfully upon the corpse, whose face was covered, others weeping pitifully. "Who is dead in the White House?" I demanded of one of the soldiers. "The President," was his answer, "he was killed by an assassin!" Then came a loud burst of grief from the crowd, which awoke me from my dream. I slept no more that night, and although it was only a dream, I have been strangely annoyed by it ever since.

He could not forget the dream, just as he had never forgotten the double vision in the mirror he had seen back in Springfield the night he was elected President: one image clear, the other wan and faded. It meant, Mary Lincoln had said, that he would be elected to two terms and serve but one. But he believed, Lamon knew, that the inevitable was right. "With that firm conviction," Lamon wrote, "Mr. Lincoln moved through a maze of mighty events, calmly waiting the inevitable hour of his fall by a murderous hand."

With the guard Crook he entered the War Department, learned there was no news yet of a Johnston surrender to Sherman, asked Secretary Stanton if a certain one of his aides might accompany him to the theater that night, was told the officer had work to do, and headed back for the White House. Crook would be going off duty, and the President said, "Good-bye, Crook."

Always before, the President had said "good night" and not "good-bye." Crook was quite certain of that. "I remember distinctly the shock of surprise and the impression, at the time, that he had never said it before."

In the carriage with his wife he said, "I have never felt so happy in my life," and a certain unease took her. She remembered that they had been happy just before their son William Wallace Lincoln—very bright, far more promising than Tad, a scholarly little fellow—

died at the age of twelve. She reminded her husband of this.

"We must be more cheerful in the future, Mary," he answered. "Between the war and the loss of our darling Willie we have been very miserable." Now things would be different. They would go back to Illinois, and he would open a law office and do enough to give them a livelihood. And they would travel out to the West Coast or perhaps abroad—Europe, the Holy Land. Of all places on earth he longed most to see Jerusalem.

JOHN Booth picked up his rented mare, went over to Grover's Theatre, and went into the manager's office, where he wrote a long letter. He rode up Pennsylvania Avenue and on the north side of Thirteenth Street saw the actor John Mathews on the sidewalk. He had once tried unsuccessfully to recruit Mathews for the kidnapping scheme. Mathews would be appearing that night at Ford's Theatre. "John," Mathews asked, "have you seen the prisoners?" A long line of stragglers from Lee's army was being marched through the street under guard, an increasingly common Washington sight.

"Yes," John said, "I have." He put his hand to his forehead. "Great God!" he cried. "I no longer have a country!" He seemed extremely agitated and nervous to Mathews, who decided that he must have been drinking. He leaned over the horse's neck and took Mathews' hand and gripped it so tightly that his fingernails dug in. "I wish to ask you a favor; will you do it for me?"

"Of course." Mathews had always liked him, found him "a most winning, captivating man." John was still holding his hand.

"I have a letter which I wish you to deliver to the publishers of the *National Intelligencer* tomorrow morning, unless I see you in the meantime." It was important, he said. He hesitated to trust it to the mails. Mathews agreed to do as asked. An open carriage passed up Pennsylvania Avenue. "John," Mathews said, "there goes General Grant. I understood he was coming to the theater tonight with the President." His listener turned in the saddle with an anxious look, squeezed his hand, said, "Good-bye; perhaps I will see you again," and galloped after the carriage.

John went up past it, reversed the mare to go back, and stared directly into the faces of the occupants. "That is the man who looked at me during luncheon," Julia Grant told her husband. The carriage went on its way to the depot from which the Grants would begin the trip to New Jersey. The horseman put his mount into the stable he had rented in the alley behind Ford's Theatre and had Ed Spangler feed and water her.

Inside the theater, the propman, James Maddox, asked John if he'd like to get a drink at the Star Saloon, next door. Maddox had always been fond of him. "He had such a very winning way that it made every person like him."

"No, thanks," John said. "I've a touch of pleurisy, and I don't think I'll drink anything." But he said he'd walk with Maddox; "Peanut" John Burrough, a chore boy whose nickname came from his sales of that commodity to theatergoers; Spangler; and young W. J. Ferguson, a callboy whose duty it was to alert players that their cue to go on stage was coming up. Young Ferguson, who was hoping to be an actor, had always worshipped John, thinking him high-spirited, dashing, buoyant, amusing, and full of fun.

In the saloon, Maddox had a beer and Ferguson a sarsaparilla, and John said, "I think I'll reconsider and have a glass of ale." He paid the bill, and the group left, they to take an early dinner before the play, and he to spend some time in the theater by himself.

He went to the National Hotel and was seen by a woman guest who had noticed that since Lee's surrender he seemed more silent than usual, even cold. The woman had considered going to Ford's Theatre that evening with Lucy Hale's mother, but John Booth had advised the two not to do so, "that it was Good Friday, and that few people would be present, and the play would drag on that account." They decided to postpone attendance until the following night. He sat with Lucy in a parlor brilliantly lit in front but dark to the rear, where they were.

They dined—the woman, Mr. and Mrs. Hale, an English lady visiting Washington, Lucy and her fiancé. He took out his watch when they finished, and said, "I must go." He bowed, walked to the door, came back, and took Lucy's hand. *"Nymph, in thy orisons/Be all my sins remembered."* He smiled and was gone.

At a little past eight o'clock the President went with his wife to his carriage. Coachman Francis Burns and valet and

Ford's Theatre, April 1865

messenger Charles Forbes were on the box. There were two cavalry outriders. The White House guard John F. Parker walked off to Ford's Theatre, a few minutes' stroll. Parker had held his job for eleven days, appointed from the Metropolitan Police to replace guard Thomas Pendel, who had been promoted to doorkeeper, in place of the former holder of that post, fired by Mrs. Lincoln for lingering about after she had directed him to take notices of a forthcoming reception to the newspapers.

The carriage headed toward the home of Senator and Mrs. Ira Harris to pick up Henry Rathbone and his fiancée, the Senator's daughter, Clara Harris. Henry was twenty-eight and a major in the army. Clara was twenty-three and a friend of Mrs. Lincoln's.

The two couples entered Ford's Theatre. The theater program boy, Joseph Hazelton, standing in the lobby, handed out four programs. Both Lincolns smiled at him. He had once been presented to the President at the White House through an army officer relative. "Joseph, I am glad to form your acquaintance," the President had said, and twice thereafter greeted him by name at Ford's.

Earlier in the day young Hazelton had talked about his ambition to go on the stage with John Booth, whom he believed to be the best actor in the Booth family. "We have been good friends, Joseph, eh?" John had said when they finished their chat. "Try to think well of me. And this will buy a stick of candy." He handed over a ten-cent shinplaster—paper money.

The play attended by the four members of the presidential party, *Our American Cousin,* by Tom Taylor, was, despite long-lived popularity, regarded as a silly farce. It had to do with a New England Yankee who becomes heir to an English fortune and the people he deals with when he goes to claim his prize: the harridan seeking to marry off her daughter, the imbecilic British lord who mangles language and concepts, the grasping sharpster attempting to get hold of the money, and, of course, the sweet heroine, who captures the Yankee's heart.

The Lincolns, Miss Harris, and Major Rathbone mounted the staircase leading to the rear of the balcony, which curved around to the door of their box overlooking stage left. Ford's had been a Baptist church whose cornerstone was laid in 1833. At about the time the war began, it was converted to a theater by John T. Ford, who presented musicals in it. In early 1862 Ford halted productions to convert the building for theatrical showings of all types. He reopened it in March of 1862, but before the year ended, a fire destroyed the building. Ford had a splendid new theater constructed on the site, the last word in modernity. There were seats for twenty-four hundred people, selling for from twenty-five cents to a dollar, and boxes going for up to ten dollars. Police were stationed at the door to bar prostitutes from the premises.

The four people entered the box, not noticing that a small peephole had been drilled in the inner door by an awl or that a rough cavity about three inches across had been cut into the plaster of the wall near the outside door opening on a short passage. Laura Keene was on stage as Mrs. Trenchard, the matriarch of an English family, trying to explain to the dim-witted Lord Dundreary the point of a joke. He kept saying he couldn't see it. "Well, anyone can see that!" she ad-libbed, gesturing toward the President and dropping a curtsy. The audience of some seventeen hundred broke into applause as the band played "Hail to the Chief." With his hands on the box's rail, Lincoln bowed. He sat down in the rocking chair just in front of the box's door, with Mrs. Lincoln in a chair to his right, Miss Harris beside her, and Major Rathbone on the small sofa at the far end of the box. It was eight thirty or a few minutes after.

John Booth was in the Herndon House at Ninth and F Streets, in the room he had been renting for Lewis Powell, meeting with Powell, Davy Herold, and George Atzerodt. He wore a black suit, hip boots, and a dark slouch hat. The spurs on his heels he had inherited from his father. They were the ones Junius Brutus Booth had lent to Edwin for Edwin's first stage appearance, as Tressel in *Richard III*. He left the Herndon House for the alley behind Ford's Theatre, asked an actor to get Ed Spangler to hold his horse for him, was told Spangler was on scene-shifting duty, and got Peanut John Burrough to do it.

John entered the theater through the rear door, asked if he could cross the stage, and was

Playbill for *Our American Cousin*

told he could not. He went through an underground passage and reached the street. He went into the Star Saloon and ordered whiskey. Farther down the bar the President's coachman, Francis Burns, and his valet-messenger, Charles Forbes, were having a drink with guard John Parker.

Booth went up to the theater door, where ticket taker John Buckingham was standing with his back turned but his arm blocking the entrance. He took hold of two fingers of Buckingham's hand and asked if Buckingham wanted a ticket from him. They had known one another for years, and Buckingham passed him through the door. In the course of the next half hour he came and went several times. At a few minutes past ten Buckingham stepped next door to the Star to get a quick drink and saw Booth having one. Buckingham went back to the door, and a little later John came past him and went up the stairs to the balcony. He was humming a tune, Buckingham remembered.

He walked behind the dress-circle seats, his all-black attire, almost like that of a stage villain, accenting the extreme paleness of his face. He continued his traverse to the rear of the theater. His mother was in New York, Asia in Philadelphia, June playing in Cincinnati, and Edwin in Boston.

The play went on, the President remarking to his wife, as he had earlier, that he longed to see Jerusalem. She leaned against him, then whispered, "What will Miss Harris think of my hanging on to you so?" and he said, "She won't think anything about it."

John walked to the door opening onto a short passageway leading to the presidential box. Guard John Parker had taken a seat and was watching the play. Valet-messenger Charles Forbes was sitting near the passageway door. There was a brief conversation, the delivery of an important message was spoken of, and the cards of some government officials were displayed. John Booth opened the door inward, closed it, and jammed the end of a length of wood into the cavity gouged in the wall, with the other end braced against the door so that it could not be opened from the outside.

The door at the end of the short passageway leading to the box, with its recently drilled finger-size peephole, was ajar. On stage, the harridan with the marriageable daughter learned that the Yankee did not possess four hundred thousand dollars, as previously believed. He had given it to the sweet heroine.

"No heir to the fortune, Mr. Trenchard?"
"No."
"What!" shrieked the daughter. "No fortune!"
"Augusta," said the mother, "to your room!"
"Yes, ma. The nasty beast!"
"I am aware, Mr. Trenchard," said the mother, "that you are not used to the manners of good society, and that alone will excuse the impertinence of which you have been guilty."

She swept indignantly offstage. The actor Harry Hawk, as the

Lithograph of Booth's assassination of Lincoln

Yankee Trenchard, was alone on stage in the brilliant footlights.
"Don't know the manners of good society, eh?" he drawled. "Wal, I guess I know enough to turn you inside out, you sockdologizing old mantrap."

The laugh he got partially drowned the sound of the detonation that sent forward a bullet of nearly half an inch diameter. It was fired from a distance of about two and a half feet, entered below the left ear, went diagonally through the cerebrum for more than five inches, and shattered, by shock waves, the orbital plates of both eye sockets before halting in the anterior lobe of the left hemisphere of Abraham Lincoln's brain.

others, knocking them down and trampling them. "Order, order!" Laura Keene cried. But it was hopeless.

In the dress circle, some forty feet from the entrance to the passageway to the presidential box, Charles Leale had seen a man raising a dagger. Then he heard shouts that the President had been shot, followed by cries for a surgeon. Leale had been a doctor six weeks, since his graduation from Bellevue Hospital Medical College, in New York. He was twenty-three years old and stationed at the Army General Hospital at Armory Square. He stood up, started vaulting over chairs, and reached the door of the passageway. People were banging on it, trying to force it open. Inside, the heavily bleeding Major Rathbone was trying to pry loose the piece of wood jammed into the wall cavity. From the stage and balconies rose wild yells: "Kill him!" "Shoot him!" "Burn the theater!"

Leale forced his way through the people outside the passageway. Rathbone got the wood removed. The door opened. Leale stepped inside. Rathbone was holding his severely wounded arm and asking for help. Leale looked into his eyes, saw he was in no immediate danger, and went forward. Mary Lincoln and Clara Harris were standing by the rocking chair in which the President sat silently, eyes closed. Leale identified himself as a United States Army surgeon. "Oh, Doctor!" Mary Lincoln cried. "Is he dead? Can he recover? Will you take charge of him? Do what you can for him. Oh, my dear husband!"

The young doctor said soothingly that all that could possibly be done would be done. He put his fingers on the right radial pulse and felt no movement of the artery. Having seen that Rathbone had been slashed, Leale began looking for a blade wound. It was difficult with the President in a seated position, so he got some men to help him lay the President on the floor. He told a man to get the coat and shirt open to stomach level. He saw no wound. He reached forward and lifted the eyelids and at once saw evidence of brain injury. He ran his fingers through hair matted with blood and found an opening terrible in its size. From it he removed a clot of blood. From all over the theater came screams: "Kill the actors!" "Kill the goddamned rebels." "Kill the traitors!"

Laura Keene came into the box. She had raced out of the theater to an alley on the building's south side, up the stairs of an adjoining building connected to it, and through a door into the dress circle near the passageway. She was a social acquaintance of the presidential couple—Mary Lincoln had several times had her to the White House. She got down on her knees by the President's head. Mary Lincoln had sunk into the box's sofa with her arms outstretched. Miss Harris sat by her, speechless. Major Rathbone stood, blood steadily flowing from his deep elbow-to-shoulder wound.

It seemed to Leale that the President had stopped breathing. He straddled him, opened the mouth, and put two extended fingers as far back as possible, pressing the base of the paralyzed tongue down and outward to open the larynx. The President breathed shallowly. Leale had two men manipulate the arms to expand the thorax, pressed the diaphragm up to force air in and out, and slid his right hand beneath the ribs to stimulate the apex of the heart. A feeble beat resulted, and irregular breathing. He leaned forward chest to chest and forcibly expelled air into the mouth and nostrils. He saw that for the moment the President could continue independent breathing. Still straddling the President, Leale straightened up.

In the dimly lit box the face was pale and in repose, the eyes closed, countenance calm. "His wound is mortal; it is impossible for him to recover," he said.

What the President had related earlier came into his wife's mind: "I fell into a slumber. I wandered downstairs. Before me was a catafalque. 'Who is dead in the White House?' I demanded."

"His dream was prophetic," Mrs. Lincoln gasped.

They must get him out of here to some nearby place, Leale said. Dr. Charles Taft and Dr. Albert King stood by. Despite Leale's youth and inexperience, medical protocol dictated that as the first to attend the patient, he was the physician in charge. He asked King and Taft to take hold of the President's shoulders. Some other men would support the torso, legs, and arms. They bent down. Laura Keene sat holding the President's head. Leale replaced her as they lifted the limp form. "Guards, clear the passage!" Leale shouted. Soldiers lined up to keep people back.

The awkward procession went down the stairs with its burden and out into the street. Several times Leale had the bearers halt so that he could remove a clot of blood from the opening of the wound. Each time he did it, the President's almost halted breathing seemed to improve. Across Tenth Street, a man stood in front of a house, holding a lighted candle and beckoning. They headed toward him slowly, while all around them people shouted, some running away from the scene, horrified, terrified.

The man with the candle led them through his boardinghouse into a small rear bedroom. On the wall were reproductions of Rosa Bonheur's *The Horse Fair* and J. F. Herring's *The Village Blacksmith, The Stable,* and *The Barnyard.* They put the President into the bed where John Booth had fallen asleep smoking Charles Warwick's pipe.

AT A home in Lafayette Square some half dozen blocks away, whose owner had that morning for the first time since his carriage accident nine days earlier taken solid food, a servant admitted a strongly built young man, who said he brought a message for the Secretary of State from his physician. He must deliver it personally. The servant said that was impossible, for Mr. Seward was asleep. The young man clumped noisily up the stairs. From his room, the Secretary's son Frederick heard the noise and opened the door. The young man told Frederick he must deliver a message to Mr. Seward. Frederick told him the Secretary could not be disturbed. "I am his son," he told him, "and the assistant Secretary of State. Go back and tell the doctor that I refused to let you go into the sickroom because Mr. Seward was sleeping."

"Very well, sir. I will go." The young man turned, took two or three steps, whirled, and pointed a navy revolver at Frederick's chest. He pulled the trigger. It misfired. He raised it and smashed it down on Frederick's head. Inside the Secretary's room, his daughter, Fanny, heard a disturbance in the hall and opened the door slightly. She got a glimpse of Frederick covered with blood as a man came in with a gun in one hand and a knife in the other and flung himself upon her father. The knife came down, seeking Secretary Seward's throat, and caught his cheek, almost severing it from his face and instantly covering the brace and bandages protecting his fractured jaw completely in red. The knife was coming down again. Fanny began screaming.

There was a soldier-nurse assigned to Secretary Seward for the period of his recuperation. He leaped on Lewis Powell's back, took two backward stab wounds, and hung on. Brought from his bed by his sister's screams, a second Seward son, Augustus, ran in. In the half-light he saw two struggling men and thought his father had become delirious and that the nurse was trying to subdue him. Augustus leaped forward, and Powell stabbed him. The Secretary rolled off the end of the bed. Powell broke loose and ran down the stairs. A State Department messenger was coming in. Powell sank his knife into the man. Some impulse caused him to yell, "I'm mad! I'm mad!" Behind him were five bleeding people, Secretary Seward horribly disfigured, Acting Secretary Frederick Seward in an unconscious state that would last for days.

Powell reached the street. His horse was there—but not Davy Herold, assigned to lead him out of Washington when Powell had proved unable to memorize the route. At the screams of the servant, now running out of the house, Herold had put his spurs into his horse and run for it. Powell mounted. At a walk he went off. The servant ran behind him, shouting for help. After a time Powell whipped up the horse and vanished.

When Secretary of War Stanton learned what had happened to Lincoln and Seward, he was convinced that the war was on again in a new and terrible form. He sent orders to the dozens of forts and military posts in and around Washington to turn out every man. Soon bugles and the long roll of drums sounded from every direction, and cavalry patrols plunged through the streets. There was something terrifying about the hoofs clattering on the cobblestones, the clanking sabers, the shouted orders. Few people went to bed that night, and many sat gathered together like frightened children. In the rear bedroom of the Petersen boardinghouse, the doctors had not a hope of doing anything. The tiny bedroom, almost of a size with the log cabin in which Abraham Lincoln had been born fifty-six years earlier, was silent. Outside, it was raining heavily. The enormous derringer bullet had driven a disc of bone almost an inch in diameter three inches into the brain. Then the bullet had split, and a fragment of it had gone on to a depth of seven and a half inches from the point of entrance.

In the front parlor, Mrs. Lincoln sat on a horsehair sofa with Miss Harris. Major Rathbone crumbled over in a faint before them. Miss Harris took out her handkerchief and stuffed it into his wound, and he was seen to and taken home. Mrs. Lincoln's almost continual screams could be heard throughout the house: "Oh, why didn't he kill me? Kill me! Kill me too!" She went in to where her husband lay diagonally on the bed; he was too tall for it. "Do live!" Mary Lincoln cried to her husband. "Do speak to me!"

Young Dr. Leale, who had not been off his feet since the moment he rose to leap over chairs to the door of the theater box, gripped the dying man's hand in his so that should for a moment reason return, just at the last, his patient would know that he was not alone, "that he was in touch with humanity and had a friend."

Deathbed vigil at 453 Tenth Street,
across from the theater

At seven twenty-two a.m. the heart ceased to beat. Coins were put over the eyes and a white bed sheet drawn up over the face. Across the country, in every city or town reached by telegraph service, the news came in with the morning papers: the President had been shot and could not recover. It was the greatest shock the American people had ever received. For those who knew the man who shot Lincoln, the shock was beyond description. In Philadelphia, John Sleeper Clarke was shaving when he heard a scream from his wife, Asia. He ran to her. Five months pregnant, she was in bed with a newspaper in front of her. She pointed to the headline. He could not halt her cries. Even as he tried, the bell rang and a United States marshal came to arrest him. She screamed again and again. She thought of her father, who held all life sacred, who would kill nothing, and who, were he alive, would cry, "The name we would have enwreathed with laurels is dishonored by a son."

Her husband was not the only person arrested by Secretary of War Stanton's orders. Many were taken into custody, including the actors and employees at Ford's Theatre, and George Atzerodt, Mrs. Surratt, and Lewis Powell, who wandered about after attacking Seward and eventually found his way to the Surratt boardinghouse.

Junius Brutus Booth, Jr., was appearing at Pike's Opera House in Cincinnati. When he came down in the morning, Emil Benlier, the hotel clerk of the Burnet House, saw he was about to take a walk and told him it would be best for him not to go out into the streets. June did not understand. "Haven't you heard the news?" the clerk asked. June had heard nothing. Benlier told him. He suggested that June return to his room, and it was well that he did so, for moments later a mob of five hundred came into the hotel. "They would have hanged him in a minute if they could have laid their hands on him." Smuggled out of the hotel, he was arrested and imprisoned.

In New York, newsboys were shouting the headlines of their papers, including the assassin's name. "O God," Mary Ann Booth moaned, "if this be true, let him shoot himself, let him not live to be hung! Spare him, spare us, spare the name that dreadful disgrace!" The postman rang the bell and handed in a letter written hardly more than twenty-four hours before, at two a.m. on Friday morning:

Dearest Mother:
Everything is dull. I only drop you these few lines to let you know I am well. With best love to you all I am your affectionate son ever.

John

When Edwin Booth heard the news and read of the dagger flourished in the bright stage lights and the cry *"Sic semper tyrannis!"* he knew it was true. Others had said, "Impossible." But not Edwin. "My mind accepted the fact at once," he told Joseph Jefferson. "It was just as if I had been struck on the head by a hammer."

VII

JOHN Booth lay in agony with his face turned to the wall in an upstairs bedroom of the home of Dr. Samuel A. Mudd, near Bryantown in lower Maryland, twenty-five miles southeast of Washington. His leg was broken—a straight fracture of the tibia near the ankle. It had snapped when he landed on the stage of Ford's Theatre, his balance undone by the spur caught in the Treasury Guard flag adorning the presidential box.

He had come running out of the theater's rear entrance to where Peanut John Burrough sat on a stone bench holding the reins of the livery stable mare. Peanut John stood up, to be knocked down by the butt of the knife that had slashed Major Rathbone's arm and cut orchestra leader William Withers, Jr.'s clothes. The mare danced about, but he got a foot into a stirrup and was aboard. He pointed her up the alley, dug in the spurs, clattered over the cobblestones to Ninth Street and from there to the Capitol and the ungraded hill leading down to the navy yard and the bridge spanning the Potomac. Throughout the war all bridges leading south had been closed at nightfall. The previous day the President had ordered the end of restrictions on travel between Washington and the former Confederacy. Sergeant Silas T. Cobb of the 3rd Massachusetts Heavy Artillery let him pass, as he would also Davy Herold, fleeing Lewis Powell's carnage at the Seward house. The two riders had met at Soper's Hill, some eight miles down from Washington, and rode through the remote countryside to the house owned by Mrs. Surratt in the tiny settlement named for her late husband. That afternoon she had delivered a package there to her tenant, John Lloyd, to be held for picking up.

It was midnight then. Drinking by himself and intoxicated, as he often was, Lloyd was awake. Davy Herold dismounted and went inside. "Make haste and get those things!" he told Lloyd. Herold took a carbine, but Booth did not. To carry it would have been almost impossible for him. He had difficulty even sitting his horse for the pain of the fractured leg. Herold handed up a bottle. That helped, but not enough. He needed the services of a physician. They headed for the home of Dr. Mudd.

It was sixteen miles over primitive rough roads from Surrattsville, every jolt agonizing. Once, the mare fell. At four in the morning Herold dismounted and knocked on Mudd's door. The doctor was an 1856 graduate of a Baltimore medical school and violently anti-North. Herold told the doctor that his companion had taken a fall from his horse and injured his leg.

Doctor and patient had met before. Five months earlier the actor J. Wilkes Booth, saying he was interested in buying land, spent a night in Mudd's house. In December they had spent an evening drinking wine and smoking cigars with several of the kidnap conspirators in the National Hotel, in Washington. It was Mudd who had introduced the conspiracy leader to John Surratt. But, Mudd said later, he did not recognize his patient as J. Wilkes Booth. His wife backed up the story.

Mudd examined the patient, cutting off his boot to do so. He wrapped the injury in cotton and splinted it with pieces of a bandbox pasted together. The patient was put to bed upstairs. Herold dozed in a chair. At around seven breakfast was served to the doctor and his wife and Davy Herold, who talked cheerfully of his hunting experiences in the neighborhood. By the time they rose from the table, Abraham Lincoln was dead.

Herold told the doctor and his wife that he and his companion must be on their way. Where might a carriage be hired? Mudd said he was going to Bryantown, four miles away, to pick up his mail and see some patients; let the visitor accompany him and perhaps a vehicle might be found. Herold was unable to find a carriage, but he learned in Bryantown that the entire area was swarming with Union cavalry seeking the man who killed Lincoln.

They would go their way on horseback, Herold said. With two crude crutches put together out of a piece of planking, the patient descended the stairs. He had shaved his mustache, but wore a false beard. It became dislodged, Mrs. Mudd said, as he hobbled down.

After they left, soldiers came and found the boot Mudd had cut off and saw that inside was inscribed the name of its New York maker and that of the customer: J. WILKES. Then it was clear exactly who the assassin was, for in the excitement it had been said that it was Edwin Booth who had killed Lincoln and then leaped down onto the Ford's Theatre stage.

In Boston, Edwin wired his mother that he would take the midnight train to New York. When he arrived, a small group of friends, all weeping, had gathered to receive him. He was stonelike, the only one not to cry. To William Bisham he seemed a man stricken and in actual danger of losing his mind: "Nothing but the love poured out for him by his friends saved him from madness. His sanity hung in the balance."

All agreed he must not be left alone for a minute, and when he went to sleep that night, it was in a room on whose wall hung a life-size portrait of John. They had neither the heart nor the courage to have it removed.

The subject of the painting had left Dr. Mudd's to enter the vast fifteen-mile-long Zekiah Swamp, an uninhabited damp wasteland of bogs, stagnant ponds, snakes, decaying vegetation, and dense growths of dogwood, gum, and beech. He and Davy Herold lost their way in the darkness and came upon a native of the region to whom they offered ten dollars if he would lead them to the residence of Samuel Cox, a well-known local Confederate sympathizer.

It was past midnight when their guide brought them to Cox's house, some five miles from the Potomac. The moon was out, and in its light Cox was shown the india ink initials JWB, on the back of one of his caller's hands. He was told he stood in the presence of the man who hardly twenty-four hours earlier fired the shot that killed Abraham Lincoln. Cox was flabbergasted. He had heard of the President's death, and now the man who caused it was asking, in the name of his mother, that he be given help.

Cox thought of his family, of the danger in which he would place them if he took the fugitives into his house, where black servants would at once know of their presence. He temporized. Let them spend the night outside, and he would see what could be done. They went off to huddle in a ditch, where at dawn Cox found them. He directed them to a little pine forest a mile from his home and said he would send help soon. His emissary would whistle in a

Booth escaping Ford's Theatre

American Gothic

particular fashion so that they would know him as a friend.

In the morning, Easter morning, women all over the country forewent seasonal finery for mourning black, and church choirs sang no hymns of life, but offered instead dirges. Black Easter, it was called. Samuel Cox's emissary came to the pine forest. He was the farmer-fisherman Thomas A. Jones, Cox's foster brother, who had spent the war ducking Yankee gunboats and land patrols to put men and supplies across the Potomac. He whistled the notes Cox had demonstrated for him. Davy Herold came out of the clearing with his carbine cocked. "I come from Cox," Jones said. "He told me I would find you here."

Herold led him thirty yards into the undergrowth to John Wilkes Booth—so he would be remembered in the history books, never as John Booth or Johnny Booth, as he had been known for most of his life—and Jones saw a man lying on the ground with pistols and a knife nearby. There was a blanket partially covering him, a donation from Cox. He was exceedingly pale and looked to be in pain, but, Jones remembered, "I have seldom, if ever, seen a more strikingly handsome man."

He greeted Jones in a pleasant voice and impressed his visitor as courteous and polite. It was clear his leg was intensely painful, swollen, and discolored. His main concern was for newspapers. "Very desirous to know what the world thought of his deed," Jones remembered. Jones told him he would come each day with food and newspapers, but that for the moment the fugitives must stay hidden where they were, to avoid the Yankee searchers. When it was not suicidal to do so, they would attempt the river. It did not occur to Jones to turn the wounded man in. The South was down and out, and Tom Jones with it. "But, thank God, there was something I still possessed—something I still could call my own, and its name was Honor," Jones said.

In Washington, workmen began preparing the East Room for the President's funeral, but the sounds of construction of a wooden platform to hold the coffin utterly unnerved Mary Lincoln as she lay upstairs. Each time a hammer came down on a nail, she was reminded of a pistol shot, and the son of the Secretary of the Navy wrote an urgent request that the work go forth more quietly.

Away from the White House, the world sought the assassin. He was said to have been spotted in three Pennsylvania towns, in Brooklyn, and in Chicago. Rumors spread that he was still in Washington—in secret passages below Ford's or in an abandoned house. The sight of two Confederate officers being escorted through the streets raised a cry of "Booth!" and a mob instantly materialized, ready to tear them to pieces. The two officers were hurried into the office of the provost marshal, and an army general and John P. Hale, the minister-designate to Spain, went out to offer assurances that neither of the men was the President's slayer. It could not have been easy for Hale to speak so in public, for the world was learning whose fiancée his daughter had been. LUCY HALE'S GRIEF, a New York *Tribune* story was headlined:

> The unhappy lady to whom Booth was affianced, is plunged in profoundest grief; but with womanly fidelity is slow to believe him guilty of this appalling crime, and asks, with touching pathos, for evidence of his innocence.

Edwin Booth now sat in his New York home in frozen silence. Word came that he was to be imprisoned, like his brother June and Asia's husband, but friends begged authorities not to do it, and so he was put under a kind of house arrest. As did his mother, he repeated that his only hope was that John would not live to be hanged. As for himself, he wrote Colonel Adam Badeau, "Oh, how little did I dream, my boy, when on Friday night I was as Sir Edward Mortimer exclaiming, 'Where is my honor now? Mountains of shame are piled upon me!' that I was not acting but uttering the fearful truth."

On Wednesday, Abraham Lincoln lay in his coffin in the East Room among weeping people, just as he had dreamed. His catafalque was dressed with black silk, and the domed white-lined canopy was so tall that the room's central chandelier had to be removed. General Grant, in white gloves and sash, was at one end of the coffin, and President Andrew Johnson, with his arms crossed over his breast, at the other. There were flowers, a cross of lilies at the dead man's head, an anchor of roses at his feet. When the services were over, the body was borne on a hearse drawn by six white horses to the Capitol, the bells of Washington and Georgetown and Alexandria tolling as minute guns thudded in the distance.

He lay in state. From inside the dome of the Capitol, his friend

Lincoln funeral procession in Washington

Noah Brooks looked down at the casket far below and saw two endless lines of mourners creeping in dark lines across the pavement of the rotunda, around the raised coffin, and then joining to go to the door and vanish. The lines never stopped. It did not escape people's thinking that as with Jesus Christ, Abraham Lincoln suffered his death wound on Good Friday, and that like Moses it would not be given to him to lead his people into the Promised Land—peace. Those concepts, and that he was so suddenly and shockingly dead, made him at once an almost holy figure.

For his assassin, there was not a single word of anything but universal and bitter condemnation. The slayings of Julius Caesar, William the Silent, and Henry of Navarre had found their defenders. No such ever appeared for that of Abraham Lincoln. From every Sunday pulpit of Black Easter ministers denounced the man who killed him as "an accursed devil," "fiend," "miserable, wretched assassin." Lincoln had died for his country's sin, slavery. Like Christ, he had been a long time dying from his mortal wound, the one on a cross, the other on a bed in the Petersen house, each in the end a dying god. He had died so that his country's new birth might occur; he was, after Washington, the second father of his country. Who had killed him was beyond execration.

It was not only the North that in one voice damned the man who shot Lincoln. It was the South also. In Charlotte, North Carolina, Jefferson Davis told his daughter, "This terrible deed is the bitterest blow that could have been dealt to the Southern cause." Robert E. Lee first refused to hear details of what had happened, but finally said a crime unexampled had been committed.

In the little clearing amidst the pines, where each day Thomas Jones came with food and tidings, the fugitives lay on the wet ground and read the newspapers. They could not light a fire for fear its smoke might invite attention from the searchers, and they had to shoot the horses, whose nickers when a mounted patrol came by could have had troops on them in a moment. Jones, Davy Herold, and his own aching leg and rising fever constituted the assassin's universe. He had seen himself in the family tradition of generations when he did as he did: his grandfather Richard Booth had attempted to join the American Colonists rising against the tyrant George III, his father had been named for that Junius Brutus who fought Rome's despotic Tarquins, and he himself had been named for the John Wilkes whose fame was based on opposition to the crown. He had seen himself dispensing justice to an absolute autocrat. Here was Caesar. Deservedly, Caesar had been slain.

He must write of what he had done. He had with him a little appointment book for the previous year, 1864. At the top of the first page he had written, in another life as a romantic actor, *"Ti Amo,"* which correctly should have been *"Te Amo,"* for "I love you," perhaps meant for one of the women whose photographs were in the little appointment book. In the pine clearing, alone save for Herold, sought by thousands of soldiers, he wrote under the space for April 14:

> Friday the Ides. Until today nothing was ever thought of sacrificing to our country's wrongs. For six months we had worked to capture. But our cause being almost lost, something decisive and great must be done. I struck boldly and not as the papers say. I shouted "Sic semper." In jumping broke my leg. I passed all his pickets. Rode sixty miles that night, with the bone of my leg tearing at every jump.
>
> I can never repent it, though we hated to kill. Our country owed all her troubles to him, and God simply made me the instrument of His punishment. I care not what becomes of me. I have no desire to outlive my country. The night before the deed, I wrote a long article and left it for one of the editors of the *National Intelligencer*, in which I fully set forth our reasons for our proceedings. He or the gov't—

He interrupted his writing. Perhaps the pain of his leg or the fever overcame him. Perhaps Jones came. He could not know that his letter to the *National Intelligencer* would never see light there. "Great God!" the actor John Mathews had cried when it fell out of his coat pocket. "There is the letter John gave me in the afternoon." He opened the letter, and read that its author had devoted his money, time, and energies to arranging the President's "capture," but had been unable to get it done.

"The moment has arrived," Mathews read, "when my plans must be changed. The world may censure me for what I am about to do; but I am sure that posterity will justify me. Men who love their country better than gold or life: J. W. Booth"—and Davy Herold and Lewis Powell and George Atzerodt.

The terrified and bewildered Mathews considered what to do with the letter. "If this paper be found on me," he reasoned, "I will be compromised—no doubt lynched on the spot. If I take it to the newspaper office it will be known and I will be associated with the letter, and be ruined." Mathews threw the letter into his fireplace and burned it to cinders.

John had written in his letter, and in his little appointment book, solely of a political slaying, but to Adam Badeau what he had done had to do with things far more complex and personal. It had to do with John Wilkes Booth the actor, from a family of actors; it had to do with his family and the family troubles that characterized Shakespeare's plays, with what weighed down Romeo, Hamlet, Lear— love, hatred, death, bastardy, murder. And the limelight actors seek. "It was all so theatrical in plan and performance," Adam wrote. "The conspiracy, the dagger, the selection of a theater, the cry *Sic semper tyrannis*—all was exactly what a madman brought up in a theater might have been expected to conceive; a man, stock of this peculiar family, the son of Junius Brutus Booth, used all his life to acting tragedy."

In fact, the whole of his part in history was like a play. As a private in the Richmond Grays, Lincoln's slayer had seen what could be called the first fatality of the Civil War, John Brown swinging at the end of a rope. With his derringer he had killed what might be called the war's final victim. The first act and the last.

"Madman," Adam had said. Madman, others thought. But where was any evidence of madness before the evening of April 14, 1865? John Booth had been rated as kindly and sociable and generous by all who knew him best, and was universally admired and liked by the members of his profession. Where was any sign of madness?

That Edwin was a deeply disturbed personality no one questioned. That their father had been insane seemed apparent. Rosalie was silent and withdrawn. The youngest member of the family, Joseph, had suffered from what he himself termed melancholy insanity from childhood on. He had been in England and then Australia for three years, then had gone from Australia to California to sail to New York. He learned of the assassination when his ship docked at Panama. He was told that a man named Booth had killed the President, but recalled, "I did not think anything of that. I knew there was a hundred Booths." Then he learned who the Booth was: "My own brother." Joe felt his reason leave him. "I was insane in Panama," he told the detectives who arrested him under Secretary Stanton's order. "That news made me insane."

It would not have surprised the eldest brother, June, that the youngest had become mentally ill. In 1862 June wrote Edwin that he felt Joe was "not sound in mind." He did not mean positive madness, "but a crack that way, which Father in his highest had and which I fear runs more or less through the male portion of our family myself included." So June was on record as saying that he felt all men of his family were liable to be unbalanced. But no one had ever said that directly about John.

Yet to Asia, in Philadelphia, her husband in jail, her life shattered forever, it seemed that John must have been mad. She lay in her home filled with police and under perpetual surveillance. The government ordered her to Washington, and when she said an approaching confinement made it impossible for her to travel, she was told to produce a medical assertion that this was so. She was followed by a detective from room to room. All mail was opened before it was handed to her.

Among the letters were ones from Edwin. "Think no more of him as your brother," he wrote. "He is dead to us now, as he soon must be to all the world, but imagine the boy you loved to be in that better part of his spirit in another world."

IN WASHINGTON, plans were made for Abraham Lincoln to go home to Springfield in a black-draped train of eight coaches, six for mourners, one for the guard of honor, and one for his coffin, on a raised pedestal with that of his son Willie resting by. All along the route, guns would pulse and bells toll and the sides of the tracks would be thickly lined with people, entire towns turning out at

American Gothic

midnight, bands playing dirges, draped flags held up, raised signs: WE MOURN OUR LOSS. THE DARKEST HOUR IN HISTORY. HE LIVES IN THE HEART OF HIS PEOPLE. REST IN PEACE NOBLE SOUL. GONE TO GLORY. Of the thirty million people of the North, seven million would see his slow train pass, and one and a half million would file by as he lay in state in a dozen cities.

As the bells tolled and muffled drums rolled, the assassin of the second father of the country waited with Davy Herold in the dense thicket of young pines, the weather always chilly and misty, the swollen and discolored flesh mortifying around his broken leg bone, fever coming and going.

VIII

HE HAD been with Davy Herold for six days and five nights in the clearing in the sighing pines when Thomas Jones came and said the moment had come to cross the Potomac. Jones heard a cavalry officer tell his men the fugitives had been spotted to the south, in St. Marys County. The soldiers saddled up and headed out. That meant, Jones reasoned, that at least for a little time the immediate area would be free of bluecoats.

"Friends," Jones said, "this is your only chance. My boat is close by. I will get you some supper at my house, and send you off if I can." He had planned for this moment, having his ex-slave Henry Woodland go out each morning to fish for the shad running in the river, thus establishing the boat's legitimacy.

Jones and Herold got the assassin up on Jones' gray mare with the greatest difficulty. Booth could not suppress a moan of anguish when he got his swollen and inflamed leg over the saddle. They set out in the darkness for Jones' house, some two and a half miles distant. They came to the grounds of his home and stopped under an old pear tree. The Potomac was another mile on, through uninhabited wooded land. "Now I will go in and get something for you to eat, and you eat it here while I get something for myself," Jones whispered.

From the horseman he heard back, "Oh, can't I go in the house just a moment and get a little of your warm coffee?" The request was so pathetic that Jones felt his throat choke up. "It cut me to the heart that this poor creature, whose head had not been under a roof for nearly a week, there in the dark, wet night, made this piteous request to be allowed to enter a human habitation."

But it would be impossible to comply. "Oh, my friend," Jones said, "it would not be safe. I have Negroes in the house, and if they see you, you are lost and so am I." He went in to his ex-slave Henry Woodland. "Did you bring that boat back to Dent's Meadow where I told you?" he asked. The meadow was a secluded clearing on the high Potomac bluffs. Below it was a tiny valley through which flowed a stream feeding into the river. Woodland told him the boat was there. Jones asked how many shad Woodland had caught that day—about seventy. They chatted some more. Jones managed to get some food out to the men under the pear tree, ate by himself in his kitchen, and went outside.

They slowly made their way through the rough terrain to the Potomac, two walking, one riding. It would have been impossible to get the horse down the high bluff bordering the shore, and so Jones and Herold carried the crippled man, each movement torture for him. It was around ten thirty p.m., Friday, April 21—one week since the derringer bullet entered Abraham Lincoln's head.

Jones got his boat from its berthing place in the stream. It was about twelve feet long, flat bottomed. They got the assassin into the stern, where he would use an oar to steer while Davy Herold rowed. Jones got out an oilcloth coat and shielded a candle and on a compass showed the course the travelers must follow. They must make for Machodoc Creek on the Virginia side of the river, Jones said, and there find Mrs. Elizabeth Quesenberry. Like himself, she had been active during the war in helping Confederate agents.

Jones said good-bye, and started to shove the boat off. From the stern came "Wait a minute, old fellow." Jones was offered money. He said he would take eighteen dollars—the price of the boat. More was proffered. Jones said that what he had done was not for money. The sum he had mentioned was handed over. Then in a choked voice John said, "God bless you, my dear friend, for all you have done for me."

For a moment Jones could hear the oars moving in the water, and then the sound died away. He climbed up the bluff and went home. Shortly he joined the hundreds of others locked up in Washington's Old Capitol prison on suspicion or whim. He revealed nothing to his questioners and eventually was freed. He believed

American Gothic

that the assassination of Lincoln was the worst blow the South had ever been struck. He never regretted what he had done for John Wilkes Booth.

IN THE darkness out on the great river, they quickly lost their bearings. The winds and tides pushed them about. Dawn was coming. They put in to shore—still on the Maryland side of the Potomac, nine miles west of Dent's Meadow instead of eight miles south, at Machodoc Creek.

They went inland on a stream and hid on its shore as best they could. When the skies lightened, Herold recognized their location. He had been there on hunting trips. He left his companion and went to a local landowner who knew him and knew also that he was now the escaping accomplice of John Wilkes Booth. The man offered some food for Herold to bear away, but refused to permit the object of the greatest manhunt in history to be brought into his home. So they spent the day, Saturday, waiting for darkness to come so that they might again attempt the great river. Lincoln's funeral train was on its way west.

After sunset they went out again on the water and this time found their way to an inlet a mile from their destination. When it became light, Herold went to Mrs. Quesenberry, told her he was an escaped Confederate prisoner of war, had a brother with a broken leg, and needed a carriage. She refused him anything, then changed her mind and said she would send some food to where the boat was. Her choice for its deliverer was a Confederate agent who had been in on the abduction scheme. Thomas Harbin passed them off to William Bryant, a local farmer, suggesting that they get Bryant to take them to the home of Dr. Richard Stuart, eight miles away.

Dr. Stuart was accounted the richest man in Virginia's King George County and was a relative of Robert E. Lee. He had spent some unpleasant time in Union custody for assisting rebel spies and agents. Now there appeared at his home two men whom to help would bring more than unpleasantness. He said his house was filled with friends and relatives returning from the war and that there was no room for additional guests. They asked him, as a physician, to attend to the injured man's broken leg; he refused, saying he was not a surgeon. They asked if he could arrange them transportation to Fredericksburg. Impossible. Could they at least have something to eat? He said they might—in the kitchen.

So they took what was offered them there, like tramps, then left with Bryant, who took them to the nearby cabin of William Lucas, a black tenant farmer. Perhaps Lucas would take them in, Stuart had said. It was past midnight. Lucas was asleep when the barking of his dogs awakened him. He found two men, one crippled, on the doorstep of his modest home. He heard, "We want to stay here tonight." "You cannot do it," Lucas said. "I am a colored man and have no right to take care of white people."

"We have been knocking about all night, and don't intend to any longer." The crippled man was pushing his way into the cabin. "Gentlemen, you have treated me very badly," Lucas said. The man on crutches pulled out a knife. "Old man, how do you like that?" he asked. "I do not like that at all," Lucas answered.

"We were sent here, old man, we understand you have good teams," the lame man said. Lucas replied that he needed his horses for planting corn. "Well, Dave," the lame man said to his companion, "we will not go on any further, but stay here, and make this old man get us his horses in the morning." The black man got his wife up, and they spent the night on the porch of their cabin while the visitors, or appropriators, occupied their home for the night. In the morning Lucas' son Charlie drove the fugitives in his father's wagon to Port Conway, some ten miles distant. It was midmorning when he dropped off his passengers on the little ferry wharf where a fisherman named William Rollins was preparing to go out and check his nets for running shad. He told them in an hour or so, by noon, the tide would make the river high enough for the ferry to take them the few hundred yards across to Port Royal. They waited. Three ex–Confederate soldiers heading home rode up, local boys, Private William Jett, eighteen, Private Absalom Bainbridge, also eighteen, and Lieutenant Mortimer Ruggles, twenty-one. Herold engaged Willie Jett in conversation, saying that he and his crippled companion were brothers by the name of Boyd. They were headed south to join in any further fighting against the Yankees that might be going on down there. The story sounded improbable to Jett. Finally Herold told him the truth: "We are the assassinators of the President."

Something in Jett's reaction must have communicated itself to the lame man sitting on a wagon on the ferry slip, for he took his crutch and limped over and said, "I suppose you have been told who I am?" Jett confirmed that he had.

"Yes, I am John Wilkes Booth, that slayer of Abraham Lincoln, and I am worth just one hundred and seventy-five thousand dollars to the man who captures me." That was the sum recent newspapers had been quoting. The ex-soldiers found his coolness impressive.

The ferry came, poled over by the black man who ran it for his owner. He took them across the quarter mile of water, the crippled man sitting on Ruggles' horse. They went up into Port Royal to the home of a man who lived with his two spinster sisters. Jett asked one of the women if she could offer shelter to a soldier wounded in the war. She consented and then changed her mind, suggesting the travelers go on to the farm of Richard Garrett, three miles south on the way to Bowling Green.

He knew the Garrett family, Jett said after they left the women's place. They headed there, arriving at a farmhouse standing in the midst of Caroline County pines, with orchard, yard, and outbuildings. At the long drive leading to it from the road Herold said that he needed new shoes and so would go on to Bowling Green, a few miles south. "I'll be with you soon, John. Keep in good spirits."

"Have no fear about me" was the reply. "I am among friends now." He raised his hat to Bainbridge, who indicated he would remain on the road with Herold and leave the introduction to the Garretts to Jett and Ruggles. "Come and see me again," the fugitive said politely. To Bainbridge such calmness and savoir faire were almost unearthly. The area, after all, was filled with Yankee patrols, and he was the most-sought-after man in history.

The three men—Jett, Ruggles, and the fugitive—went down the driveway. Richard Garrett was on the porch of his home. "Mr. Garrett," Jett said, "I suppose you hardly remember me."

"No, sir, I believe not." Jett identified himself as the son of a longtime friend of Garrett's and then introduced Mr. John W. Boyd, a soldier wounded at the siege of Richmond. "Can you take care of him for a day or two until his wound will permit him to travel?" Garrett said he could, and invited the three men into the house. Ruggles and Jett said they were headed for Bowling Green and must be on their way. They helped their wounded companion onto the house's veranda, then left.

IN WASHINGTON, LIEUTENANT Edward Doherty of the 16th New York Cavalry was ordered to report at once, along with twenty-five men and three days' rations, to Colonel Lafayette C. Baker, the head of the War Department's detective bureau. From telegraph reports, interrogations, and perhaps intuition, Baker had decided that John Wilkes Booth and David Herold were heading for Fredericksburg. He wished Lieutenant Doherty to take his men there. Two civilian detectives, both ex-officers of the District of Columbia Cavalry, former Lieutenant Colonel Everton Conger and former Lieutenant Luther Byron Baker, Colonel Baker's nephew, would go along. The command would travel by water down Aquia Creek to Belle Plain on the government tug *John S. Ide,* a propeller-driven steamer of one hundred and eighty-six tons. It was waiting at the Sixth Street wharf.

One of Doherty's soldiers was Sergeant Boston Corbett, a fearless battler who had survived the notorious Confederate prison camp at Andersonville, Georgia. He was born Thomas P. Corbett, in England in 1832, came to Troy, New York, when he was seven, and grew up to be a hatmaker. He married. His wife died in childbirth, as did the infant girl she delivered. He turned to drink. While working at his trade in Boston he experienced a rush of religious passion, gave up liquor, and renamed himself after the city of his spiritual rebirth. He became a great shouter for street evangelists.

In the summer of 1858, shouting God's glory in the streets, he was approached by two prostitutes suggesting he could do better to avail himself of their offerings. When he went home after the encounter, Boston Corbett decided to make sure that no possible impure thoughts could ever contaminate his mind again. With a scissors he cut open his scrotum and snipped off his testes. Then he went to a prayer meeting. Swollen up and in pain, he was eventually taken to the Massachusetts General Hospital, where he spent a month recovering: the Mad Hatter.

After seven hours on the *John S. Ide* the cavalrymen of the 16th New York and the two detectives went ashore at Belle Plain, sixty miles from Washington, to spend all night and into the dawn knocking on doors to ask whether anybody had seen two men heading south, one lame. No one had. The command drifted southeast and learned that the previous evening the north side of the Rappahannock had been pretty well swept by cavalry. They decided to cross the river and go down the south side. They made for the ferry, and they came to Port Conway. The shad fisherman William Rollins was on the little wharf. Baker showed photographs of the men they sought. Had Mr. Rollins by any chance seen the two men pictured? Yes, he had. They had crossed over the river about twenty-four hours before with three local boys. Heading where? His wife, Mrs. Bettie Rollins, thought she could guess: "Jett has a ladylove over at Bowling Green, and I reckon he went there." The ladylove, Izora Gouldman, sixteen, was a daughter of the Bowling Green family that owned the town hotel.

WHEN young Richard Garrett, Jr., that morning looked at his family's sleeping guest, he saw that two enormous revolvers were hanging on a belt slung across the sleeper's bedpost. With them was a knife, and on the mantel an expensive set of field glasses with several adjustments. How white Mr. Boyd's brow was, Richard thought. And his hand thrown above his head was as white and soft as a child's. Mr. Boyd was different from other soldiers who had stopped with the family, Richard reflected. The others had skin roughened and tanned from exposure.

The guest arose and went downstairs and out onto the lawn, where all morning he lay under an apple tree. The weather had turned warm and sunny. The children of the house grouped around him, and he showed them his compass and laughed at the puzzlement on their faces when he made the magnetized needle move by holding the point of a pocketknife above it.

Around noon, before lunch was served, he asked young Richard to get down a large map that hung on a wall. The boy spread it out on the floor, and leaning heavily on a chair, Mr. Boyd knelt by the map and studied it, marking a route to Norfolk and then to Charleston and Savannah. Richard asked where he was planning to go. To Mexico, he replied. That seemed strange to Richard, for the previous evening he had talked about going south to keep up the fight against the Yankees.

At lunch the subject of the President's assassination came up, Mr. Garrett saying he didn't believe the story. "It is some idle report started by stragglers." But one of the sons, fresh from Appomattox, said he had talked with a neighbor who had seen a Richmond paper. The story was true. And the man who had done

Poster offering a reward for the murderer

it had a one-hundred-thousand-dollar price on his head. He was an actor, Booth. Not Edwin. A brother. "That man had better not come this way, for I would like to make one hundred thousand dollars just now."

"Would you do such a thing? Betray him?" the guest asked.

"He had better not tempt me, for I haven't a dollar in the world."

In the afternoon Bainbridge and Ruggles came up from Bowling Green to drop off Davy Herold, who was introduced as Mr. Boyd's cousin David Harris. Bainbridge and Ruggles headed on toward Port Royal, three miles north, but before they reached it ran into an ex-soldier who had served with Bainbridge in the war. He was coming from Port Royal. "The town is full of Yankees in search of Booth," he told them. Bainbridge and Ruggles wheeled their horses and galloped to Garrett's. The houseguest was back to lying on the ground in the waning sunlight. He arose and hobbled over to them. "Well, boys, what's in the wind now?"

They told him, and Bainbridge pointed to a thick stretch of forest by the house and said, "Get over there at once, and hide yourself. In those wooded ravines you will never be found."

"I'll do as you say, boys, right off. Ride on! Good-bye! It will never do for you to be found in my company." He hurried as best he could to the house, urgently asked one of the Garrett boys to rush upstairs for his pistols, and with Herold made for the woods. Down the road came the Yankee cavalry, pounding past the Garrett drive as they made for Bowling Green. When they were gone, Mr. Boyd and Mr. Harris returned to the house.

Their reception there was chilly. The family found their behavior suspicious: two very heavily armed men, one with two great revolvers and a knife, and the other shouldering a gun—Herold was carrying the carbine picked up at Mrs. Surratt's tavern—who dash madly to hide in the woods? Something was not right. An explanation was demanded, and Herold said, "I will tell you the truth. The other night we got on a spree and had a row with some soldiers and as we ran away we shot at them and I suppose must have hurt somebody." Mr. Boyd's contribution was that he had been afraid the Yankees were going to make him take an enforced oath of loyalty to the Union, as was being done all over the South.

The stories didn't go down. The Federals weren't going to send a couple of dozen cavalrymen galloping in the wake of two fellows who had been on a spree, and still less to force a cripple to take the loyalty oath. The Garretts had women and children in the house. They didn't want trouble. The men would have to leave.

Darkness had come. It was difficult for Jack Garrett simply to throw them out. He compromised, saying they could sleep not in the house, but in the tobacco barn. They bedded down there.

Jack and his brother William and their father were still uneasy. Perhaps these strangers would decide to steal their horses in the middle of the night. Jack and William locked the barn door from the outside and for additional safety decided that they'd bunk for the night in the nearby corncrib. Everyone, then, was settled in, and silence enveloped the Garrett farm as the last hours of the night of April 25 came and passed.

The atmosphere was quite different at the Star Hotel in Bowling Green, where Willie Jett had been asleep, for he was looking up into the hard faces of Detective Baker and Detective Conger.

"What do you want?" Jett asked.

"We want you. We know you took Booth across the river."

"You are mistaken in your man."

"You lie!" Conger put his revolver against Jett's head. "We are going to have Booth. You can tell us where he is or prepare to die."

Soldiers with drawn revolvers crowded in on Jett, who asked if he could speak to Conger privately. It was arranged. The men they sought, Jett told the detective, were at Garrett's farm, to the north. It was past midnight. The command headed back through the dust and sand of the road they had just traversed. There was no moon, and no stars could be seen.

At about two in the morning they got to the Garrett drive. Orders were given in a whisper: the troops were to file in as quietly as possible and take up position in a circle around the house and outbuildings. Baker went up on the porch and thundered on the door. A window opened cautiously. Baker reached in and grabbed the arm of Mr. Garrett. "Open the door. Be quick about it."

The order was complied with. The farmer saw his yard was filled with men carrying swords and revolvers. Soldiers searched the house. "Where are the men who have been staying with you?" Baker demanded. Garrett began to say that after the men had run off to the woods he had no longer wanted them in his house.

"I don't want any long story," Baker interrupted. "I just want to know where those men have gone." Garrett suffered from a slight speech impediment, which intensified when he was agitated. Now his powers of expression degenerated into protracted stuttering. Detective Conger said, "Bring a rope and I'll put him up to the top of those locust trees."

One was brought and knotted around Garrett's throat, and he was dragged into the yard. Awakened in the corncrib by the commotion, Jack Garrett came out. "Don't hurt Father," he begged. The detectives demanded to know where the two men were. Jack said, "We were becoming suspicious of them, and Father told them they could not stay with us—"

"Where are they now?" Baker interrupted.

"In the barn, locked up for fear they would steal the horses." His brother William, still in the corncrib, had the key. Soldiers got him up and out and told him to unlock the door, go into the tobacco barn, and get the fugitives to surrender. He protested, "They are armed to the teeth and they'll shoot me down." Baker stuck a revolver in his face. They went to the tobacco barn, some fifty yards from the house, and soldiers surrounded it. William Garrett unlocked the door and went in.

From outside, Baker shouted for the men to turn over their arms to young Garrett: "If you don't, we shall burn the barn!" At the door Garrett cried, "Let me out! He's going to shoot me."

Baker shouted, "You can't come out unless you bring the arms."

"He won't give them to me. Let me out quick." Baker opened the door, and Garrett bounded out.

From inside, a voice called, "Oh, Captain! There is a man in here who wishes to surrender." The words were delivered in what Baker felt was a "full, clear, ringing voice—a voice that smacked of the stage." At the door, Davy Herold was whimpering, "Let me out." He was told he could emerge if he brought his weapons with him. The voice from inside called, "The arms are mine and I shall keep them and may have to use them on your gentlemen."

Herold could be heard weeping. "Let me see your hands," Lieutenant Doherty said, and the door opened, and two hands were thrust forward. Doherty grabbed them and yanked Herold out. From inside the barn came, "Tell me who you are and what you want of me. It may be that I am being taken by my friends."

"It makes no difference who we are," Baker shouted back. "We know you and we want you. We have fifty men stationed around this barn. You cannot escape." The detective was exaggerating the numbers, but the men had all their weapons on full cock. They knew more than one hundred thousand dollars was awaiting them.

From inside came, "Captain, this is a hard case, I swear." He was balancing himself on a crutch while holding a revolver in one hand and the carbine in another. "I am lame. Give a lame man a chance."

Perhaps he had suspected that it would come to this, for the final lines he had written in his appointment book were:

> I have too great a soul to die like a criminal. Oh! May He spare me that, and let me die bravely. I bless the entire world. I have never hated nor wronged anyone. This last was not a wrong unless God deems it so, and it is with Him to damn or bless me. I do not wish to shed a drop of blood, but I must fight the course. 'Tis all that's left me.

The last words were Macbeth's. Now, like Macbeth, like Lear shouting defiance, like Richard III before his foemen, he stood alone and called, "Draw up your men twenty yards from here, and I will fight your whole command."

Fight the whole command. One actor, crippled, against twenty-five enlisted men, an officer, and two ex-officers of the greatest army in the world. To Baker the concept, the voice, the words themselves, the style seemed to be studied, theatrical. He must want to come out and fight until he dies, Baker thought. "We are not here to fight, we are here to take you," he shouted.

From inside came a request for time to consider. Baker shouted he would hold off any action for two minutes, no more. From inside, one more request echoed out: "Captain, I believe you to be a brave and honorable man. I have had half a dozen chances to shoot you. I have a bead drawn on you now, but I do not wish to kill you. Withdraw your men from the door and I'll go out."

"Your time is up," Baker called. "If you don't come out we shall fire the barn."

"Well, then, my brave boys, you may prepare a stretcher for me." A pause. "One more stain on the glorious old banner." The clear and ringing-toned words carried to the Garretts, huddled on their porch, sung out, Detective Conger thought, in a singular, stagelike voice. Conger came from the back of the barn and asked Baker if he was ready. Baker was. Conger thrust a handful of dry corn fodder through a crack in the barn wall and scratched a match.

At once the fire caught. The interior of the barn started to brighten. Through the wide gaps in the walls, which allowed air to circulate so the tobacco leaves could be cured, soldiers looked in and saw a man on two crutches, with a revolver and carbine. He dropped one crutch and made as if to fling a table on the flames, but saw it would do no good. He stood still as the flames went upwards toward the barn roof, widening as they rose. They rolled across the roof to the opposite side and the floor below.

Baker inched open the door to see drawn up to full height a man with his hat off, with wavy dark hair tossed back, lips compressed. "Booth had been said to have the form of an Apollo," wrote Baker. "Now it was the picture of an Apollo in a frame of fire."

He threw away his remaining crutch, dropped the carbine, and sprang toward the door, holding his revolver. Watching through the side of the barn, Sergeant Boston Corbett heard a voice. It was, he said, that of God Almighty, and it directed him to shoot. He did so. The bullet took his target in the side of the neck, piercing three vertebrae and cutting the spinal cord.

Booth pitched forward, completely and permanently paralyzed

Booth shot dead by Union soldiers at Garrett's farm

American Gothic

below the neck. The detectives and soldiers rushed into the flaming barn. He was lying on his face. They dragged him out to an apple tree. He was conscious but in terrible pain. "Tell Mother— Tell Mother—" he said, and fainted. The heat from the flames was so intense that they carried him to the porch of the house and put him on a straw mattress produced by Mrs. Garrett. A cloth was dampened with brandy and placed against his lips. He opened his eyes. "Oh, kill me, kill me," he said.

"No, Booth," Baker said. "We don't want you to die. You were shot against orders." But they all knew what the result of such a wound must inevitably be.

The unbearable pain dropped him into unconsciousness again, and then he came to, his breast heaving. He wished to say something, and Baker put his ear to his mouth and heard, "Tell Mother I died for my country. I did what I thought was best." In horrible agony he asked to be turned on his face. He asked to be turned back over. Lucinda Holloway, Mrs. Garrett's sister, dampened a cloth with water and wiped his face. The burning barn collapsed upon itself. Dawn was coming, its light replacing that of the dying fire. Booth asked Baker to raise his paralyzed hands so that he could see them. Baker did so. They were utterly limp. Booth gasped, "Useless." He gasped it again. "Useless, useless."

IX

HER husband in jail because of what her brother had done, her home invaded by detectives, Asia was dangerously ill, entering the last stages of a pregnancy whose result if a boy she had expected to name John Wilkes Booth Clarke. Her mother, in New York, decided she must go to her. On the train, surrounded by strangers talking about the news, Mary Ann Booth read of what had happened at the Garrett farm.

Borrowing a darning needle from the Garrett women, Lieutenant Doherty had sewn the body into a saddle blanket and then loaded it on a wagon. The face of the body was clean, for Mrs. Garrett had washed it and then tied on a covering handkerchief. Her sister had cut off a curling lock of hair.

All day long, as the exhausted men and horses of the 16th New York Cavalry rested at the Garretts', and Abraham Lincoln's train moved slowly west, the wagon labored the thirty dusty miles to the Potomac.

The body was placed first on board the *John S. Ide*, the blue blanket surrounding it gray from dust, the big U.S. letters on it dark with blood. A tug pulled up alongside the *John S. Ide* on the morning of April 27, and this same tug soon after dropped an object wrapped in a saddle blanket on board the monitor *Montauk*. It was placed on a carpenter's workbench on the forward deck.

Later that morning three people came aboard the *Montauk*, which, like all navy vessels, had been the province of the head of the Senate Committee on Naval Affairs, John P. Hale, now minister-designate to Spain. Two of the party were naval officers. With them was a heavily veiled young woman.

The officers undid the horse blanket shrouding the body on the carpenter's bench and exposed the head. With a wild outburst of grief Lucy Hale fell across John Booth. One of the officers cut off a lock of hair for her to take away.

Later in the day an official identification of the body was made by people who had known the dead man in life. The surgeon John F. May was shocked at the corpse. Less than two years earlier he had removed a fibroid tumor from the neck of John Booth, but now on the *Montauk*, looking down at the haggard cadaver, he said, "There is no resemblance in that corpse to Booth, nor can I believe it to be that of him." Then he asked that the body be propped up in a sitting position, and when it was, he studied the surgical scar and so identified his former patient.

The assassin satisfactorily identified by May and others, an autopsy was conducted by Surgeon General Joseph K. Barnes. The cause of death was found to be the shot fired by Sergeant Boston Corbett. There would be no penalty imposed for the act, Secretary Stanton decreed; the villain was dead and the patriot lived, and there was not need to go further. Barnes cut out and preserved the three vertebrae pierced by Corbett's bullet.

On another ship, the monitor *Saugus*, lying at anchor in the eastern branch of the Potomac just below the *Montauk*, were Lewis Powell, George Atzerodt, Samuel Arnold, Edman Spangler, and Michael O'Laughlen, who had been in on the original plan to kidnap the President, and Dr. Samuel Mudd. Their hands were manacled by handcuffs, and the left leg of each was attached by chains to seventy-five-pound balls of iron. They wore hoods with small openings for the nose and mouth. Mrs. Mary Surratt was in an annex of the Old Capitol prison. General Robert E. Lee was free, as was General Joseph E. Johnston, who had finally surrendered to Sherman. Jefferson Davis would serve but a brief term before being freed. But anyone associated with John Wilkes Booth, Secretary of War Stanton was saying, was going to be tried, convicted, and hanged before Abraham Lincoln was buried.

Held entirely incommunicado, and soon to be joined by Davy Herold, the prisoners could not know that the body of the man who killed Lincoln, now with the head detached by Barnes' knife, would be taken off the *Montauk* and dropped at the end of a little pier near the Old Penitentiary, at the foot of Four-and-a-Half Street, S.W. At the beginning of the year the building's convict population had been shipped elsewhere, and it became an arsenal. There the body stayed under guard of soldiers told to shoot anyone who approached, as was discovered by Assistant Surgeon George Loring Porter, a medical officer of the arsenal, when he returned from a boating expedition. Only when the officer of the guard was called could he get ashore and go to his quarters. At midnight he was back at the pier, ordered there with the arsenal's military storekeeper and four soldiers, one of whom led two horses pulling a wagon.

The only commissioned officer present, Porter was put on his word of honor never to tell of what he was about to see until the need for secrecy passed. Forty-six years went by before he spoke. The body in its blanket was put in the wagon and taken inside the penitentiary, where Porter saw that a shallow hole had been dug in the unpaved floor. The body was put into a gun case and lowered into the hole by the flickering light of Porter's upheld lantern, dim shadows coming and going on the walls. The excess dirt was shoveled up into the wagon. They left, the room turned dark again, and the key to the lock, the only one in existence, was taken to Secretary of War Stanton. In the silent room the earth settled over the gun case and its occupant. Early Saturday morning had come. In a few hours it would be two weeks since Lincoln died.

Two midnights later, joined together by clanking chains, the prisoners were taken to the Old Penitentiary and individually locked up in cells. Their trial would be held in a large adjoining room. It would begin on May 9. (Secretary Stanton had abandoned his hope to swing them all before Lincoln was buried.) On that day, their fetters rattling and scraping, they came in to sit blinking and dirty-faced when the hoods were taken off. They were as the cast of a play, the always heavily veiled Mrs. Surratt an enigmatic leading woman, the trifling Davy Herold as the small-featured juvenile, crude George Atzerodt with his thick German accent the low comedian, hulking Lewis Powell as the menacing heavy, Dr. Mudd as the educated interloper. No one knew that the star lay moldering just three stories below the courtroom.

That the prisoners would all be found guilty to one degree or another was known by anyone who read the newspapers. The only question was who would hang. For Lewis Powell the issue was hardly debatable. The matter did not seem to concern him, and he maintained an impenetrable silence. Finally, after twenty-two days, he told his court-appointed lawyer, General William Doster, that he was sorry about what happened to Frederick Seward. As for Frederick's father, Powell considered himself as acting under the orders of the man he called Cap and Captain. The Captain told him to do it, and he did.

Along with Powell—or Payne, as they called him—Mrs. Surratt was the defendant people came to see. Here was a motherly-looking boardinghouse keeper, a fervent Catholic found not in church on Good Friday, but instead delivering a package for the assassin. Would she swing? No woman had ever been hanged by the United States government.

The trial went on for seven weeks, the courtroom temperature going up as Washington's brutal summer came. Mary Todd Lincoln rose from the bed upon which she had lain for forty days and nights since leaving her husband at the Petersen house. In the heavy black mourning attire she would wear for every day but one of the seventeen years of life remaining—once, at Tad's insistence, for his birthday she took it off—she went back to Illinois. There she seemed unable to speak of anything but what had occurred at the theater. The madness the President had always dreaded would take her came and fulfilled his fears.

In that spring of 1865 it seemed to Lewis Powell's lawyer, William Doster, that his client was scarcely above animal intelligence, and he conceived the idea of a defense based upon the influence a John Wilkes Booth would have had upon one of so low an intellect.

American Gothic

To this end he subpoenaed Edwin, thinking he could testify to the power of his late brother's personality.

Edwin arrived in Washington perhaps more terrified than he had ever been before. Desperately lying, he told Doster he "knew less of his brother probably than anyone—that he had had nothing to do with him for years." The lawyer could easily have found that John had always stayed with Edwin in New York and had visited him in Boston two weeks before shooting the President, but perhaps Doster took pity or decided such a witness's testimony would do the client no good. He let him go. Edwin never again set foot in the city where his brother shot Abraham Lincoln.

His career as an actor, he was certain, was over. The public would never permit him to appear on a stage. He was happy that his fiancée, Blanche Hauel, was away, and so spared much horror. By September, when they planned to marry, perhaps some of the excitement would have died down. It was the dead Molly in heaven who had sent Blanche to him—"I faithfully believe it," he wrote. She would be a mother to Edwina. That her intended's brother had done what he did was not a matter of concern to her—her "great heart" was "faster bound to me than ever," he wrote.

Asia was happy for him. But for herself, she knew, all happiness was gone. Such as she, Asia wrote, never again learn to trust in human nature. They "never resume their old place in the world," she continued, "and forget only in death." When at last her husband was released from prison, he said things to her that confirmed her feelings and worked to destroy their marriage. The "secretiveness of the whole Booth race," Clarke told her, "stamped them as Iagos." Soon she would leave the United States for England, there to drag out a sad existence. After many long years her body was returned, to lie in Baltimore with that of her family, including the dear brother she never ceased to love.

THE military judges reached a verdict. For the physician Mudd and the supporting players Arnold, Spangler, and O'Laughlen, terms of hard labor. For Powell, Herold, Atzerodt, and Mrs. Surratt, the gallows. Later Mrs. Surratt's son, John, who had been in Elmira, New York, when the fatal shot was fired, was tried and found not guilty. Later still, the man who had been in the theater box with Lincoln on the night of April 14, 1865, went insane.

Hanging the conspirators, July 7, 1865

Henry Rathbone recovered from the knife wound he suffered on Good Friday of 1865, and married Clara Harris. But the assassination preyed on his mind, and he faulted himself for not preventing it. Headaches and stomach upsets plagued him. He resigned the army and with his wife toured European spas seeking relief. His health did not improve, and by 1881 Clara Harris Rathbone was telling relatives that in fits of temper her husband threatened her life. She considered a separation or divorce but ruled it out for the sake of the couple's three children.

In Hanover, Germany, before daylight on Christmas morning of 1883, she awoke to find him wandering about her room. He said he wanted to see the children. She pointed out the earliness of the hour. He produced a revolver and shot her, as once Lincoln had been shot, then took a knife and stabbed himself, as once he had been stabbed. As with Lincoln, she died, and as with his earlier stabbing, he lived—to be, as was Mrs. Lincoln, committed to a mental institution, where he died.

Of the insanity of Mary Lincoln there was no doubt. Compulsively speaking about what had happened to her husband, she alternated between irrational fear of poverty and extravagant spending frenzies. She was capable of publicly putting up for sale

American Gothic

her used clothing while carrying on her person tremendous sums of cash—sometimes more than fifty thousand dollars.

Tad died in 1871, age seventeen. She feared that Robert was dying, decided he was out to kill her, and ran from him half-dressed through a hotel corridor. Weeping as he testified to her condition at a sanity hearing, he had her committed to an institution. The end of her broken life came in the summer of 1882.

Still, John Wilkes Booth lived on. His ghost was seen, people said, furiously lashing his horse as he fled from the theater, and hurriedly limping across the fields of his escape route, using a crutch as he ran. He was, said the New York *World*, reported to have been observed playing rouge et noir at Baden-Baden and visiting St. Peter's in Rome. He was reported to be captain of a pirate vessel that was "the terror of the China seas" and to have played Richard III in Shanghai, glaring "like a tiger."

Mary Lincoln

He became a mythical figure, undead, who had not died on the Garrett porch. A corner of the collective mind of the American people willed that he wander friendless forever, like a vampire, like the *Flying Dutchman,* whose captain for his sins was doomed to sail the seas and make no port until the Day of Judgment. On their deathbeds men averred that they were he, and as late as 1925 five skulls identified as his were on view simultaneously in carnivals and sideshows around the country. For the members of his family it was an agony most horrible to know what, in death, he had become. They dealt with his heritage as best they could, Asia by fleeing to England; Mrs. Booth and Rosalie by living the most secluded of lives;

Tad Lincoln

Joseph by burying himself in long studies aimed at making him a doctor—he finally became one at the age of thirty-nine; June in his practical way by saying that time would set all things right.

They dealt with it, Edwin never. For many months he cooped himself up in his house, never venturing out for a breath of air until darkness came. Physically worn down, he presented a sad, shamed, grief-stricken appearance. His fiancée, Blanche Hauel, broke off their engagement. On his deathbed her father had extracted from her a promise that she would not marry into the family of Lincoln's assassin. With the hope of marriage to Blanche gone, she whom he had counted upon as sent by Molly in heaven, he had nothing in life to cling to but what he had always had. He must return to the stage.

X

"THE blood of our martyred President is not yet dry in the memory of our people, and the very name of the assassin is appalling to the public mind," said James Gordon Bennett's New York *Herald*. "Still a Booth is advertised to appear before a New York audience." There were reports that he would be shot when he came on stage. Police were inside and outside the Winter Garden. But when he was discovered as the second scene of *Hamlet* opened, sitting with bowed head, the audience rose, and cheer after cheer rolled across the footlights, women waving their handkerchiefs, the stage filling up with flung bonnets. When at great length the people quieted and the last shout died down, he found himself unable to begin for long moments.

After that, he toured the country to enormous crowds while wondering always if the people paying unheard-of prices came to see not Edwin Booth, but the brother of the man who shot Lincoln.

For two years he toured the West, and when he had accumulated sufficient funds, he built Booth's Theatre. In a day of great playhouses, with fringed curtains, ornate banisters, and scrollwork cascading down from the balconies, his was the most elaborate of all, with towers reaching a hundred and twenty feet above the sidewalk at New York's Sixth Avenue and Twenty-third Street. He laid out more than a million dollars. It wasn't enough. He took out loans, repaid them with more loans.

Booth's Theatre opened in early 1869, with its owner playing Romeo to the Juliet of Mary McVicker. He had asked her to marry him. She was the daughter of the owner of Chicago's leading theater, McVicker's. She was musical, practical, ambitious, restless, and had a great sense of humor. But underneath the fun and animation there was something else: the germ of a madness that would destroy her. Perhaps it was always destined to grow and overwhelm her, perhaps her solemn and brooding husband unwittingly fed it, or perhaps the death in a few hours of a child born a year after their marriage. Within a few years she was under the care of mental specialists and in and out of institutions. Sometimes she cried for hours as Edwin rocked her in his arms. Sometimes she screamed and raved, the sounds audible outside their New York home or rented summer cottages or the estate he bought her on the Connecticut shore, at Cos Cob.

He put his soul into Booth's Theatre, staging productions the splendor of which had never been seen before. Everything was done with no regard for the enormous bills, and when he needed money, he took out loans at ruinous rates of interest. When the bills for interest payments came due, he went touring to make money, sending the money back to New York and never doing anything but going to the theater and then to the hotel and then to the train. He had always been withdrawn, but now he was ten times more so. Friends such as John Ellsler, who had known the Booth family for years, said that a somber curtain hung before Edwin's eyes, always with the sound behind it of that haunting shot on the stage at Ford's: *Sic semper tyrannis.*

At three o'clock one morning the owner of Booth's Theatre led Garrie Davidson, his personal attendant, to the theater's furnace room, where Davidson saw a large trunk tied with ropes. He was told to get an axe, and with it cut the cords and knock off the top. The odor of camphor rose in the air. The trunk was packed, Davidson saw, with costumes. He realized at once whose they had been. Edwin silently took one out. It was a steel-blue broadcloth Louis XVI coat. Claude Melnotte, Davidson said to himself—*The Lady of Lyon.* His employer held it up at arm's length and turned it, trying, Davidson thought, to remember what it had looked like on its owner, and when last it had been worn. "Put it in there." Davidson opened the furnace door and looked at him. It seemed such a shame to do it. Edwin stood, Davidson thought, like a statue.

The coat settled in the flames with a hiss as a bit of lace at the throat caught. There followed a satin waistcoat, knee breeches, several pairs of tights. Some of the things had "J.W.B." on the linings in marking ink. Silk stockings went in, velvet shoes, a velvet coat, a broad-brimmed hat with ostrich feathers. There was a photograph with the trunk's owner in Indian dress, dated Richmond,

1859–60. It went in, joined by a packet of letters tied with ribbon.

Edwin took out a long, belted, purple velvet shirt ornamented with stage jewels, and an armhole cloak trimmed in fur, both creased and worn in places. Holding them, he sat down on the trunk and began to cry. "My Father's," he sobbed. "Garrie, it was my father's Richard III dress. He wore it in Boston on the first night I went on the stage, as Tressel."

"Don't you think you ought to save that, Mr. Booth?"

"No. Put it with the others."

The fire scorched Davidson's hands and face as he turned the coals with a furnace poker. Edwin took it from him and did the work himself, then gave it back, then took it again as they continued. At the end Davidson was told to the toss the trunk into the furnace.

They stood and watched the snaky metal rims of the trunk in the ashes. "That's all," Edwin said very quietly. "We'll go now." It was nearly six in the morning.

FROM the very first, Mary Ann Booth had wanted to see her son's dead body and to give him a proper burial. Her wound would never heal, but that John lay in an unknown and dishonored grave made it ache. Soon after his death, friends prevailed upon the New York political figure Thurlow Weed to inquire of Secretary Stanton the disposition of the remains. Stanton sent word that when the excitement over Lincoln's death somewhat subsided, the family could have the body. Seven months later Edwin wrote to him about the matter. There was no answer. A year and a half passed, and John T. Ford asked Edwin if he could be of assistance in requesting the body. Ford was still a Washington figure of some prominence, although his former theater was now a government-owned building housing, among other agencies, the Surgeon General's Office of the War Department, which held the three cervical vertebrae of John Wilkes Booth that had been removed from his body in the *Montauk* autopsy. "Do what you can," Edwin wrote Ford. But Ford was unable to accomplish much. In July of 1867 Edwin wrote to the new Secretary of War, General Grant:

> Having once received a promise from Mr. Stanton that the family of John Wilkes Booth could be permitted to receive the body when sufficient time elapsed, I yielded to the entreaties of my

Mother and applied for it I fear too soon, for the letter went unheeded. I now appeal to you, on behalf of my heart-broken Mother, that she may receive the remains of her son.

Grant did not reply. Edwin tried again in February of 1869, writing President Andrew Johnson. Almost four years had passed since Boston Corbett fired what had come to be seen as the last shot of the Civil War. Edwin could not know that his brother no longer lay under the Old Penitentiary. The section of the building under which he had been put had been razed, and on October 1, 1867, his gun-case coffin had been buried in the bottom of a warehouse on the eastern side of the arsenal grounds.

In a month Johnson would be leaving office to go home to Tennessee. One of his last official acts would be to pardon the conspiracy trial defendants who had escaped the scaffold. O'Laughlen, Spangler, Arnold, and Mudd had been condemned to hard labor at the island fortress of Dry Tortugas, in the waters off Key West. O'Laughlen died of yellow fever there, as had much of the garrison and many other prisoners. Dr. Mudd, with the assistance of Spangler and Arnold, helped fight the epidemic. They were ordered freed, and Johnson sent word to Edwin that his brother's body would be given over. Edwin retained the services of the Baltimore undertaker John H. Weaver to bury John in the Booth family plot at Greenmount Cemetery, Baltimore.

In the plot could be seen the names of Junius Brutus Booth and three children who died in infancy. Mrs. Booth, Rosalie, Asia, and Joe would one day join them under stones bearing their names. One grave remained unmarked. Years later the funeral director who took over John Weaver's business asked Edwin if he thought a stone ought to be put up, and Edwin said, "Leave that as it is."

OWNED and run by a monetary simpleton, Booth's Theatre was probably always destined for financial ruin. The Panic of 1873 settled any doubts about the question. Edwin's bankruptcy took from him his books, pictures, furniture. He still owed. So he toured for years to make money he must immediately hand to others. "I have done great things," he ruefully joked, quoting Don Caesar de Bazan in *The Fool's Revenge;* "If you doubt me ask my creditors." Wherever he went, his brother Johnny accompanied him. Every newspaper mentioned that next week would be appearing, or last night had appeared, the brother of the man who killed Lincoln.

For the second Mrs. Booth, Edwin could not feel what he had felt for the first. As her mental condition degenerated, he became her keeper. In 1881 she and her husband and Edwina went to England, where her mind completely collapsed. She turned on her husband, marking him as a monster of cruelty and neglect. They went back to America, where her parents accepted everything she told them, took her under their care, forbade Edwin to see her, and denounced him in newspapers. On his forty-eighth birthday, November 13, 1881, he was told his second wife was dead.

A year later he went to Germany and Austria to play leads in English while supported by actors speaking their own language. The audience wept for his Hamlet. At his first appearance the stage manager–director kissed his hand. "Herr Meister," he said.

Edwin returned to the United States and affiliated himself with the actor-impresario Lawrence Barrett, a scholar of the theater and a brilliant producer-businessman. With Barrett making all the plans and attending to all the details, Edwin's income rose to the level of the country's richest men, amounting to as much as a quarter of a million dollars a year, at a time when the average laborer earned nine dollars a week. He gave away much of it, paying for the funerals of actresses' mothers and buying annuities for aged actors. When he learned that the government refused to pay the Garrett family for the replacement of their barn, he sent money for a new one.

In 1877 a minister, who as a child had gotten down from the wall a map for the gentleman he knew as John W. Boyd, wrote, saying his family still had the lock of hair cut from the head of the man who they had learned was John Wilkes Booth:

> We have never had an opportunity of telling you before that my mother and sisters did everything in their power to make your brother comfortable in his last hours.

If Edwin wanted the lock of hair he could have it.

It had been twelve years. Edwin wrote:

> The painful subject is never referred to by any of us, although everything associated with the unfortunate boy is sacred to his heart-broken mother, and I am sure will be dearly prized by her.

The Reverend Richard Baynham Garrett sent the lock. Edwin wrote:

> I have received and forwarded to our Mother the memento of the misguided boy whose madness wrought so much ill to us. Though his name has never been spoken by us since his untimely end, I desire to express our gratitude to your family for your kindness to him in his last hours.

Years later he was still sending the Reverend Garrett books not affordable on a minister's income.

In 1885 his mother died. His knowledge that one day he too must die, Edwin said, was something for which he daily thanked God.

Two years later, in the summer of 1887, Edwin took a cruise with some friends on the steam yacht of industrialist E. C. Benedict. During the voyage he told his friends that he had it in mind to found a club for actors. Actors did not mingle enough with other people, he said, and so the club would have members from outside the profession. Above all, it must exude respectability, decorum. All he would want from it was that a couple of rooms upstairs be allotted to him so that he could stay there until he died.

At Booths Bay the group put in for supplies, and in a druggist's shop he asked after the origin of the town's name, to be told it had no connection with "that damned scoundrel who shot Lincoln." He went out with his lips tightly set. Even after so many years no scar had formed on the wound. He could not bear to look upon a picture of Abraham Lincoln. When he saw one in the home of sculptor Launt Thompson, he left the house immediately and did not return until he was told the picture was no longer on view.

And of course there was the name he never mentioned. Once he did. It was in Boston, on a Christmas night. The veteran actress Eliza Eldridge and others appearing with him in Boston's Park Theatre gathered in his private sitting room at the Hotel Vendome. The play had ended hours before. It was very late. He spoke of his father, whom Eliza Eldridge had supported as a child performer. He talked of his boyhood life, cheerfully, and said, "Yes, my brother John and—"

The listeners all looked at each other. He looked straight ahead and said slowly, "Yes, my unfortunate brother John." He dropped his head, so that his face was almost hidden. They saw tears run down his cheek. There was dead silence in the room. He seemed to realize suddenly that he was not alone, pulled himself together, stood up, forced a smile, and said, "Come, come, I have displaced the mirth. Let us drink to a merry Christmas." They all stood and drank and then begged to be excused. Years later Eliza Eldridge wrote that those words, "My unfortunate brother John," rang in her ears with the bells of each succeeding Christmas and that she believed they would for so long as she would live.

"SEE *the players well bestowed*," Hamlet told Polonius. Edwin named his club The Players. It faced Gramercy Park in New York, in a mansion he purchased and had remodeled by Stanford White. He asked Mark Twain and General Sherman to be members, and they joined, as would Grover Cleveland, George M. Cohan, Ford Madox Ford, Hamlin Garland, Eugene O'Neill, Thornton Wilder, Ernest Hemingway, Herbert Hoover, and John Barrymore, who, in 1924, sixty years after the one hundred nights of *Hamlet*, would break the record, despite the appeal of a group of aged men who asked him not to do so in honor of the Great Master. Barrymore said he had known the Great Master in his childhood—his parents and grandparents had played opposite him—and that he didn't think he would mind.

Downstairs in the great high rooms of The Players hung portraits Edwin had collected over the years of the actors and actresses of the past, and upstairs in the library were his books, including several Shakespeare folios, and all about were mementos of the theater—old playbills, props, costumes, statues, paintings by Gilbert Stuart, John Collier, John Singer Sargent, including a heroic and larger than life-size Sargent of the club's founder. On the last night of 1888, as whistles and bells sounded outside to welcome 1889, The Players officially opened as Edwin lifted a vessel of ancient silver and, standing beneath his father's portrait, said, "Let us drink from this loving cup, this souvenir of long ago, my father's flagon, let us now, beneath his portrait, and on the anniversary of this occasion, drink: 'To The Players' perpetual prosperity.'" It was passed from lip to lip, as it would be each New Year's Eve for one hundred years into the future, with the same toast with the addition of "And to the memory of the finest actor and the greatest gentleman the American theater has ever known."

Upstairs in his suite of two rooms, Molly's portrait the largest adornment on the wall, he read, smoked, lay awake at night, gazed out at Gramercy Park, where in 1918 his statue would be dedicated, with Edwina's son pulling off the covering.

Rosalie died in Joe's house in New Jersey, and Asia died in England. Both sisters went to lie in Greenmount Cemetery, in Baltimore. Soon, he knew, he would also be gone. Not yet sixty, he was old. When he stood up, he hung on to something to steady himself. Occasionally he made theatrical appearances in his old familiar parts. In March of 1891 he was told, "Mr. Barrett is gone."

"Gone where?" he asked. Then he understood. Larry had taken care of everything for him, all details, had made him rich. Days later he kept a scheduled date to play Hamlet at the Brooklyn Academy of Music. In some mysterious way people sensed that he would never again step on a stage, and so the theater was packed, to see him softly go through his part, saying the lines as if speaking to himself, and there were masses outside in Montague Place to cheer him when he came out the stage door. Across the street a building was being repaired, and the scaffold was filled with people waving their hats and handkerchiefs. He recoiled and pulled back before the police cleared a path to his carriage, and he drove away. The acting dynasty founded by Junius Brutus Booth when he came to America from Madeira on the *Two Brothers* and continued by Edwin and John was concluded.

After that, he largely kept to his two-room suite at The Players, his mind remaining perfectly clear even as his strength ebbed away. He made it a point personally to welcome all new inductees into his club. On the day when that ceremony was scheduled for the famed journalist-author Richard Harding Davis, the new member stepped into a Fourth Avenue bookshop and bought some old playbills, intending to contribute them to The Players' holdings. The playbills were in a packet. Davis did not look through them. At his induction he handed them to the club president, who riffled through them and then staggered into someone's arms and had to be physically half carried from the room. Among the playbills was one for *Our American Cousin* on the evening of April 14, 1865. Even here, members told one another sadly, the founder of their club was pursued by the furies of the past. Then why the picture of Johnny right by his bed? There was no picture of Asia in the room, nor June, nor Rosalie, nor Joe. He never explained.

On April 11, 1893, Edwina and her husband, who lived nearby at 12 West Eighteenth Street, took him to see *The Guardsmen*. Eight days later he failed to ring for his breakfast. When a concerned servant went in, he was found partially paralyzed and voiceless. A stroke. For weeks Edwin lay in bed, his powers of speech returning, but he was obviously destined never to arise. On June 7 Edwina came with her little son, who asked, "How are you, dear Grandpa?"

"How are you yourself, old fellow?" was the reply. He never spoke again. The next night a violent electrical storm raged over New York, thunder booming and lightning flashing. Fifty-nine years and seven months earlier he had been born on a similar night of spectacular celestial display, with star-shower rains of meteors shooting through the skies, and the black workers on The Farm had said he would be guided by a lucky star. And gifted to see ghosts.

In the early morning hours, just after one o'clock, there was a tremendous crash of thunder, and the lights of The Players went out. "Don't let Father die in the dark!" Edwina screamed. When the lights came on after a moment, he was gone.

The services were on the morning of June 9 at what was officially the Church of the Transfiguration, on Twenty-ninth Street near Fifth Avenue, but what was more generally known as the actors' church, and even more so as The Little Church Around the Corner. It had gotten its nickname in 1870, when the actor George Holland had been refused burial from another church because of his profession, the declining minister telling those who would have arranged it that they had better take the matter up with the people at the little church around the corner.

Following the services, one hundred and fifty Players were to march together from the club behind the hearse. The coffin would then be loaded into the hearse for the short trip to Grand Central and a Boston train and interment beside Molly at Mount Auburn Cemetery. Hamlet leaping into Ophelia's grave after three decades.

Yet even as the services went on at the Little Church, in New York, there occurred what was mystical, allegorical, baffling, beyond coincidence—Shakespearean. The man being mourned would have understood, for like Abraham Lincoln he believed in omens, visitations, in a whole world that could neither be defined nor understood. As Edwin's funeral progressed, in Washington, the walls of what had been Ford's Theatre simply caved in. Twenty-three clerks were killed, twice that number injured. It was the worst accident of Washington's history. There was no warning. All of a sudden the top floor came down, taking the second with it. A woman working where Lincoln had been sitting when the building was last used as a theater came falling through twisted girders, broken beams, and flying bricks. In Washington every man in the fire department and every manual laborer employed by the federal government was sent to dig through the rubble for survivors.

The funeral service ended. The coffin was loaded. The Booth hearse headed for Grand Central and the Boston train. All cavalry units in Fort Myer, outside the capital, were ordered to Tenth and F Streets to keep sightseers back. The train arrived in Boston. The broken building would be put back together and then, seventy years into the future, painstakingly reconstituted so that it would exactly duplicate its appearance on the night of April 14, 1865.

Across the street, the Petersen house, where Lincoln died, was opened for viewing. From the alley behind Ford's Theatre, tours run by the Surratt Society, an organization housed in Mrs. Surratt's old tavern–post office, leave to trace the route to the Garrett place, where the man who shot Lincoln met his final destiny. They are filled months in advance. Much has changed along the way, yet Ford's Theatre looks exactly as it did. As in Edwin's suite in The Players, time has stood still.

Twilight had come to Boston when the body was interred. Several hundred people were present. In the silence a bird could be heard twittering. The scent of syringa blossoms came from a slope below the gravesite next to Molly. Thomas Bailey Aldrich thought of Horatio's farewell to his friend in *Hamlet* and repeated it under his breath: *"Good night, sweet prince."* Others thought of the prince's last words: *The rest is silence.*

ABOUT THE AUTHOR

While preparing to write *American Gothic,* author Gene Smith virtually set up shop at the Players Club. With his love of history, it was the perfect place for him—a glimpse into nineteenth-century New York. Etched windows overlook Manhattan's Gramercy Park, and the paneled walls are lined with portraits—Junius Brutus Booth, Sarah Bernhardt, and, painted by John Singer Sargent, a majestic and life-size Edwin Booth, the founder of the club.

While researching his book on the Booths, Smith spent many hours in the Players Club library, gathering inspiration from visits to Edwin's room, upstairs. But the author's real inspiration for the book began when he was a child and first read about the man who shot Lincoln. His fascination has never palled.

According to the author, writing has always been "the only thing I could do." He graduated from the University of Wisconsin in 1952,

Gene Smith

with a major in history, then went on to prepare for the career his family had assumed he would have: head of the family law firm. But six weeks in law school convinced him that the law was not for him. Fortunately, Uncle Sam intervened to solve his dilemma: Smith was drafted into the army, served two years in West Germany, and never returned to law school. Instead, after his discharge, he took a job as a reporter with the Newark *Star-Ledger,* in New Jersey. A few years later he quit to write a biography of Woodrow Wilson's last years called *When the Cheering Stopped*—a Condensed Books selection in 1964. He's been writing ever since.

Gene Smith lives in Poughkeepsie, New York, with his wife and daughter. Though he likes to take plenty of time off between books, he says he enjoys both research and writing. "I was given a gift," he says. "I'm doing what I'd do even if I didn't get paid for it."

PHOTO: © PAULINE AND LIZBETH STUDIO

ILLUSTRATORS

Robert Hunt: *Such Devoted Sisters*
John Burkey: *Rules of Encounter*
Bob McGinnis: *The Love Child*

ACKNOWLEDGMENTS

Page 2: from Reader's Digest *Country Ways*.

Pages 476–477: Edward Vebell.

Pages 483, 485, 508: The Hampden-Booth Theatre Library at The Players.

Pages 498, 542, 564: The Meserve-Kunhardt Collection.

Page 507: Harvard Theatre Collection.

Page 511 (middle, bottom): courtesy of The New-York Historical Society, New York City.

Page 512 (top): National Archives.

Pages 512 (bottom), 524: Ford Theatre National Historic Site.

Page 526: J.M.R. National Park Service.

Page 528: The Lincoln Museum, Fort Wayne, Indiana, a part of Lincoln National Corp.

Page 530: Abbie Rowe—courtesy of National Park Service.

Page 535: from *Harper's Weekly,* May 6, 1865.

Pages 538, 557: from *Leslie's Illustrated Newspaper,* May 13, 1865.

Pages 553, 563: Library of Congress.

Reader's Digest Fund for the Blind is publisher of the Large-Type Edition of *Reader's Digest*. For subscription information about this magazine, please contact Reader's Digest Fund for the Blind, Inc., Dept. 250, Pleasantville, N.Y. 10570.

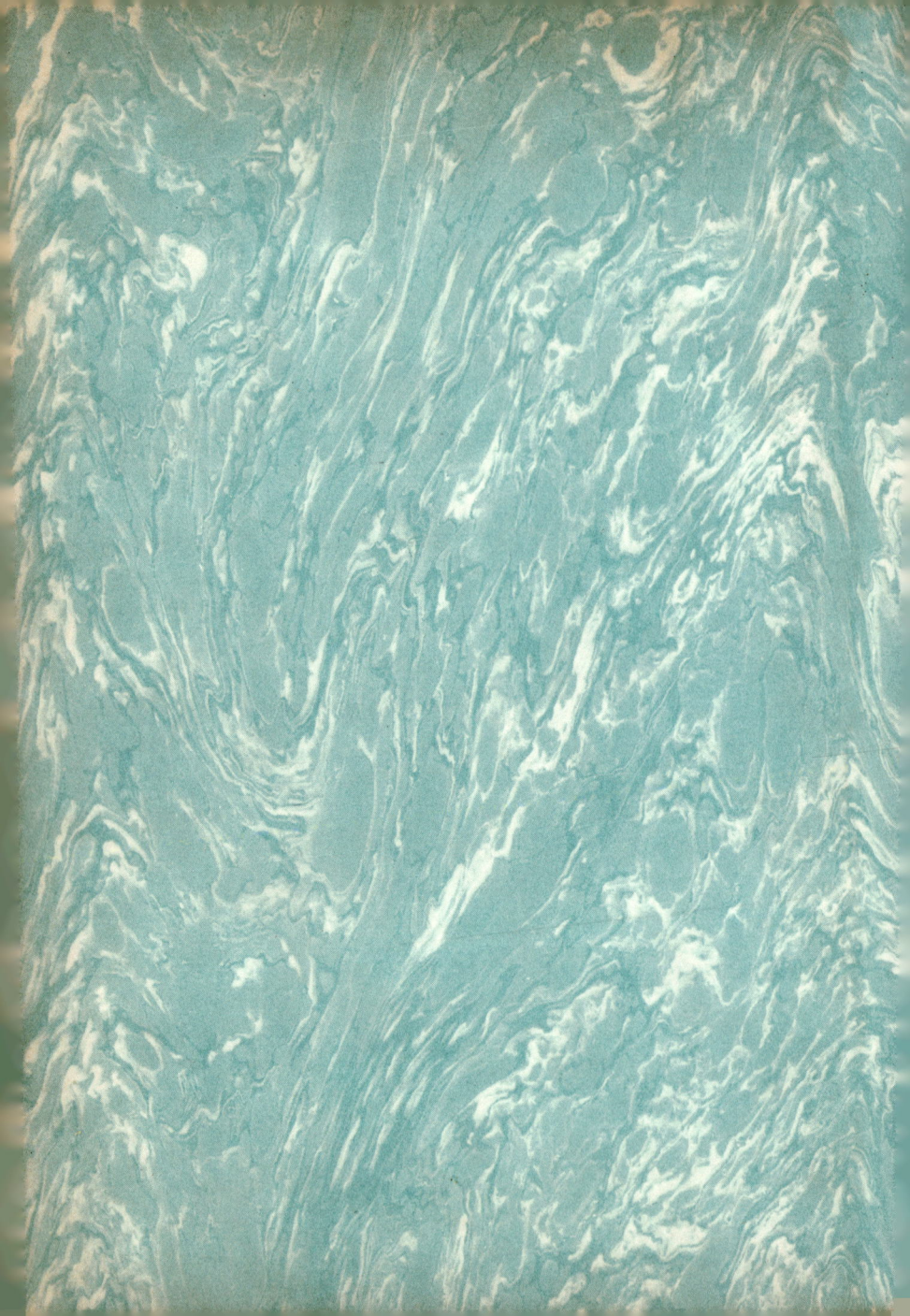